D0935909

The Web

Bad Love

JONATHAN KELLERMAN
OMNIBUS

The Web

Bad Love

LITTLE, BROWN AND COMPANY

A *Little, Brown* Book

This first edition published in Great Britain in 1999 by
Little, Brown and Company.

Copyright © Jonathan Kellerman1999
Bad Love copyright © Jonathan Kellerman 1993
The Web copyright © Jonathan Kellerman 1995

The moral right of the author has been asserted.

*All characters in this publication and any resemblance to real
persons, living or dead, is purely coincidental.*

All rights reserved.
No part of this publication may be reproduced, stored
in a retrieval system, or transmitted, in any form or by
any means, without prior permission in writing of the
publisher, nor be otherwise circulated in any form of
binding or cover than that in which it is published
and without similar condition including this condition
being imposed on the subsequent purchaser.

A CIP catalogue for this book is available from the
British Library.

ISBN 0 316 85366 6

Printed and bound in Great Britain.

Little, Brown and Company (UK)
Brettenham House
Lancaster Place
London WC2E 7EN

The Web

1

The shark on the dock was no monster.

Four feet long, probably a low-lying reef scavenger. But its dead white eyes had retained their menace, and its jaws were jammed with needles that made it a prize for the two men with the bloody hands.

They were bare-chested Anglos baked brown, muscular yet flabby. One held the corpse by the gill slits while the other used the knife. Slime coated the gray wooden planks. Robin had been looking out over the bow as *The Madeleine* pulled in to harbor. She saw the butchery and turned away.

I kept my hand on Spike's leash.

He's a French bulldog, twenty-eight pounds of bat-eared, black-brindled muscle and a flat face that makes him a drowning risk. Trained as a pup to avoid water, he now despises it, and Robin and I had dreaded the six-hour cruise from Saipan. But he'd gotten his sea legs before we had, exploring the old yacht's teak deck, then falling asleep under the friendly Pacific sun.

His welfare during the trip had been our main concern. Six hours in a pet crate in the baggage hold during the flight from L.A. to Honolulu had left him shell-shocked. A pep talk and meatloaf had helped his recovery and he'd taken well to the condo where we'd stopped over for thirty hours. Then back on the plane for nearly eight more hours to Guam, an hour at the airport bumping shoulders with soldiers and sailors and minor government officials in guayaberas, and a forty-minute shuttle to Saipan. There Alwyn Brady had met us at the harbor and taken us, along with the bimonthly provisions, on the final leg of the trip to Aruk.

Brady had maneuvered the seventy-foot vessel through the keyhole and beyond the barrier reef. The yacht's rubber bumpers bounced gently off the pilings. Out at the remote edges, the water was deep blue, thinning to silvery green as it trickled over creamy sand. The green reminded me of something – Cadillac had offered the exact shade during the fifties. From above, the reef's ledges were coal-black, and small, brilliant fish flitted around them like nervous birds. A few coconut palms grew out of the empty beach. Dead husks dotted the silica like suspension points.

Another bump and Brady cut the engines. I looked past the dock at sharp, black peaks in the distance. Volcanic outcroppings that told the story of the island's origins. Closer in, soft brown slopes rose above small whitewashed houses and narrow roads that coiled like limp shoelaces. Off to the north a few clapboard stores and a single-pump filling station made up the island's business district. Tin roofs glinted in the afternoon light. The only sign I could make out read AUNTIE MAE'S TRADING POST. Above it was a rickety satellite dish.

Robin put her head on my shoulder.

One of Brady's deckhands, a thin, black-haired boy, tied the boat. 'This is it,' he said.

Brady came up a few seconds later, pushing his cap back and shouting at the crew to start unloading. Fiftyish, compact, and nearly as blunt faced as Spike, he was proud of his half-Irish,

2

half-islander ancestry and talkative as an all-night disc jockey. Several times during the journey he'd turned the wheel over to one of the crewmen and come up on deck to lecture us on Yeats, Joyce, vitamins, navigation without instrumentation, sportfishing, the true depth of the Mariana Trench, geopolitics and island history. And Dr Moreland.

'A saint. Cleaned up the water supply, vaccinated the kids. Like that German fellow, Schweitzer. Only Dr Bill don't play the organ or no such foolishness. No time for nothing but his good work.'

Now Brady stretched and grinned up at the sun, displaying the few yellow teeth he had left.

'Gorgeous, isn't it? Bit of God's own giftwrap – go easy on that, Orson! *Fray*-gile. And get the doctor-and-missus gear out!'

He glanced at Spike.

'You know, doc, first time I saw that face I thought of a monkfish. But he's been a *sailor*, hasn't he? Starting to look like Errol Flynn.' He laughed. 'Too many hours on water, turn a sea cow into a mermaid – ah, here's your things – lay that *gently*, Orson, pretend it's your honeybunch. Stay there, folks, we'll unload it for you. Someone should be by any minute to pick you up – ah, talk about prophecy.'

He aimed his chin at a black Jeep coming down the center of the hillside. The vehicle stopped at the beach road, waited for a woman to pass, then headed straight for us, parking a few feet away from where the shark was being butchered. What remained of the fish was soft and pitiful.

The man with the knife was inspecting the teeth. In his late twenties, he had small features in a big, soft face, lifeless yellow hair that fell across his forehead, and arms embroidered with tattoos. Running his finger along the shark's gums, he passed the blade to his partner, a shorter man, slightly older, with heavy beard shadow, wild curly brassy hair, and matching coils of body fleece. Impassive, he began working on the dorsal fin.

Brady climbed out of the boat and stood on the dock. The water was flat and *The Madeleine* barely bobbed.

He helped Robin out and I scooped up Spike. Once on solid ground, the dog cocked his head, shook himself off, snorted, and began barking at the Jeep.

A man got out. Something dark and hairy sat on his shoulder. Spike became livid, straining the leash. The hairy thing bared its teeth and pawed the air. Small monkey. The man seemed unperturbed. After shaking Brady's hand, he came over and reached for Robin's, then mine.

'Ben Romero. Welcome to Aruk.' Thirty to thirty-five, five six, one forty, he had a smooth bronze face and short, straight black hair side-parted precisely. Aviator glasses sat atop a delicate nose. His eyes were burnt almonds. He wore pressed blue cotton pants and a spotless white shirt that had somehow evaded the monkey's footprints.

The monkey was jabbering and pointing. 'Calm down, KiKo, it's just a dog.' Romero smiled. 'I think.'

'We're not sure, either,' said Robin.

Romero took the monkey off his shoulder and held it to his cheek, stroking its face. 'You like dogs, KiKo, right? What's his name?'

'Spike.'

'His name is *Spike*, KiKo. Dr Moreland told me he's heat sensitive so we've got a portable air conditioner for your suite. But I doubt you'll need it. January's one of our prettiest months. We get some rain bursts, but it stays about eighty.'

'It's lovely,' said Robin.

'Always is. On the leeward side. Let me get your stuff.'

Brady and his men brought our luggage to the Jeep. Romero and I loaded. When we finished, the monkey was standing on the ground petting Spike's head and chattering happily. Spike accepted the attention with a look of injured dignity.

'Good boy,' said Robin, kneeling beside him.

Laughter made us all turn. The shark butchers were looking our way. They winked and waved. The shorter one had his hands on his hip, the knife in his belt. Rosy-pink hands. He wiped them on his cutoffs and winked. The taller man laughed again.

4

Spike's bat ears stiffened and the monkey hissed. Romero put it back on his shoulder, frowning. 'Better get going. You must be bushed.'

We climbed into the Jeep, and Romero made a wide arc and headed back to the beach road. A wooden sign said Front Street. As we drove up the hill, I looked back. The ocean was all-encompassing and the island seemed very small. *The Madeleine*'s crew stood on the dock, and the men with the bloody hands were heading toward town, wheeling their bounty in a rusty barrow. All that was left of the shark was a stain.

2

'Let me give you a proper welcome,' said Romero. '*Ahuma na ahap* – that's old pidgin for "enjoy our home."'

He started up the same central road. Winding and unmarked, it was barely one vehicle wide and bordered by low walls of piled rock. The grade was steeper than it had appeared from the harbor and he played with the Jeep's gears in order to maintain traction. Each time the vehicle lurched, KiKo nattered and tightened his spidery grip on Romero's shirt. Spike's head was out the window, tilted up at the cloudless sky.

As we climbed, I looked back and caught a frontal view of the business district. Most of the buildings were closed, including the gas station. Romero sped past the small, white houses. Up close, the buildings looked shabbier, the stucco cracked, sometimes peeled to the paper, the tin roofs dented and pocked and mossy. Laundry hung on sagging lines. Naked and half-naked children played in the dirt. A few of the properties were fenced with chicken wire, most were open. Some looked unoccupied.

A couple of skinny dogs scrounged lazily in the dirt, ignoring Spike's bark.

This was U.S. territory but it could have been anywhere in the developing world. Some of the meanness was softened by vegetation – broad-leafed philodendrons, bromeliads, flowering coral trees, palms. Many of the structures were surrounded by greenery – whitewashed eggs in emerald nests.

'So how was your trip?' said Romero.

'Tiring but good,' said Robin. Her fingers were laced in mine and her brown eyes were wide. The air through the Jeep's open windows ruffled her curls, and her linen shirt billowed.

'Dr Bill wanted to greet you personally, but he just got called out. Some kids diving out on North Beach, stung by jellyfish.'

'Hope it's not serious.'

'Nah. But it does smart.'

'Is he the only doctor on the island?' I said.

'We run a clinic at the church. I'm an RN. Emergencies used to get flown over to Guam or Saipan till . . . anyway, the clinic does the trick for most of our problems. I'm on call for whenever I'm needed.'

'Have you lived here long?'

'Whole life except for Coast Guard and nursing school in Hawaii. Met my wife there. She's a Chinese girl. We have four kids.'

As we continued to climb, the shabby houses gave way to empty fields of red clay, and the harbor became tiny. But the volcanic peaks remained as distant, as if avoiding us.

To the right was a small grove of ash-colored trees with deeply corrugated trunks and sinuous, knobby branches that seemed to claw at the sky. Aerial roots dripped like melting wax from several boughs, digging their way back into the earth.

'Banyans?' I said.

'Yup. Strangler trees. They send those shoots up around anything unlucky enough to grow near them and squeeze the life out of it. Little hooks under the shoots – like Velcro, they just dig in. We don't want them but they grow like crazy in the jungle. Those are about ten years old. Some bird must have dropped seeds.'

'Where's the jungle?'

He laughed. 'Well, it's not really that. I mean, there're no wild animals or anything else for that matter except the stranglers.'

He pointed toward the mountaintops. 'Just east of the island's center. Dr Bill's place butts right up against it. On the other side is Stanton – the Navy base.' He shifted into low, got the Jeep over an especially steep rise, then coasted through big open wooden gates.

The road on the other side was freshly blacktopped. Four-story coco palms were set every ten feet. The piled rock was replaced by a hand-hewn, Japanese-style pine fence and rows of flame-orange clivia. Velvet lawns rolled away on all sides and I could make out the tops of the banyan forest, a remote gray fringe.

Then movement. A small herd of black-tailed deer grazing to the left. I pointed them out to Robin and she smiled and kissed my knuckles. A few seabirds hovered above us; otherwise the sky was inert.

A hundred more palms and we pulled into a huge, gravel courtyard shaded by red cedar, Aleppo pine, mango, and avocado. In the center, an algae-streaked limestone fountain spouted into a carved basin teeming with hyacinths. Behind it stood a massive two-story house, light-brown stucco with pine trim and balconies and a pagoda roof of shiny green tiles. Some of the edge tiles wore gargoyle faces.

Romero turned off the engine and KiKo scrambled off his shoulder, ran up wide stone steps, and began knocking on the front door.

Spike jumped out of the Jeep and followed, scratching at the wood with his forepaws.

Robin got out to restrain him.

'Don't worry,' said Romero. 'That's iron pine, hundreds of years old. The whole place is rock solid. The Japanese army built it in 1919, after the League of Nations took the territories away from

Germany and gave them to the emperor. This was their official headquarters.'

KiKo was swinging from the doorknob as Spike barked in encouragement. Romero said, 'Looks like they're already buddies. Don't worry about your stuff, I'll get it for you later.'

He pushed the door open with the monkey still holding on. It had been a long time since I'd left a door unlocked in L.A.

A round whitestone entry led to a big front room with waxed pine floors under Chinese rugs, high plaster walls, a carved teak ceiling, and lots of old, comfortable-looking furniture. Pastel watercolors on the walls. Potted orchids in porcelain jardinieres supplied richer hues. Archways on each side led to long hallways. In front of the right-hand passage was an awkward-looking, red-carpeted staircase with an oiled bannister, all right angles, no curves. It hooked its way up to the second-floor landing and continued out of view.

Straight ahead, a wall of picture windows framed a tourist-brochure vista of terraces and grasslands and the heartbreakingly blue ocean. The barrier reef was a tiny dark comma notched by the keyhole harbor, the western tip of the island a distinct knife point cutting into the lagoon. Most of Aruk Village was now concealed by treetops. The few houses I could see were sprinkled like sugar on the hillside.

'How many acres do you have here?'

'Seven hundred acres, give or take.'

Over a square mile. Big chunk of a seven-by-one-mile island.

'When Dr Bill bought it from the government, it was abandoned,' Romero said. 'He brought it back to life – can I get you something to drink?'

He returned with a tray of Coke cans, lime wedges, glasses, and a water bowl for Spike. Trailing him were two small women in floral housedresses and rubber thongs, one in her sixties, the other half that age. Both had broad, open faces. The older woman's was pitted.

'Dr Alexander Delaware and Ms Robin Castagna,' said Romero,

9

placing the tray on a bamboo end table and the water bowl on the floor.

Spike rushed over and began lapping. KiKo watched analytically, scratching his little head.

'This is Gladys Medina,' said Romero. 'Gourmet chef and executive housekeeper, and Cheryl, first daughter of Gladys and executive vice-housekeeper.'

'Please,' said Gladys, flipping a hand. 'We cook and clean. Nice to meet you.' She bowed and her daughter imitated her.

'False modesty,' said Romero, handing Robin her drink.

'What are you after, Benjamin? A ginger cookie? I didn't bake yet, so it won't do you any good. That's a very . . . cute dog. I ordered some food for him on the last boatload and it stayed dry.' She named the brand Spike was used to.

'Perfect,' said Robin. 'Thank you.'

'When KiKo eats here, it's in the service room. Maybe they want to keep each other company?'

Spike was belly down on the entry floor, jowls spreading on the stone, eyelids drooping.

'Looks like he needs to nap first,' said Romero.

'Whatever,' said Gladys. 'You need anything, you just come to the kitchen and let me know.' Both women left. Cheryl hadn't uttered a word.

'Gladys has been with Dr Bill since he left the Navy,' said Romero. 'She used to work for the base commander at Stanton as a cook, came down with scrub typhus and Dr Bill got her through it. While she recuperated, they fired her. So Dr Bill hired her. Her husband died a few years ago. Cheryl lives with her. She's a little slow.'

He led us upstairs. Our suite was in the center of the second-story landing. Sitting room with a small refrigerator, bedroom, and white-tiled bath. Old brown wool carpeting covered the floors. The walls were teak and plaster. Overstuffed floral-print furniture, more bamboo tables. The bathtub was ancient cast-iron and spotless with a marble shelf holding soaps and lotions and loofah sponges still in plastic wrap. Fly fans churned the air lazily in all three rooms. A faint insecticidal smell hung in the air.

The bed was a turn-of-the-century mahogany four-poster, made up with crisp, white linens and a yellow wilted-silk spread. On one nightstand was a frosted glass vase of cut amaryllis. A folded white card formed a miniature tent on the pillow.

Lots of windows, silk curtains pulled back. Lots of sky.

'Look at that view,' said Robin.

'The Japanese military governor wanted to be king of the mountain,' said Romero. 'The highest point on the island is actually that peak over there.' He pointed to the tallest of the black crags. 'But it's too close to the windward side. You've got your gales all year round and rotten humidity.'

He walked to a window. 'The Japanese figured the mountains gave them a natural barrier from an eastern land assault. The German governor built his house here, too, for the same reason. The Japanese tore it down. They were really into making the place Japanese. Brought in geishas, tea houses, baths, even a movie theater down where the Trading Post is now. The slave barracks were in that field we passed on the way up, where the accidental banyans are. When MacArthur attacked, the slaves came out of the barracks and turned against the Japanese. Between that and the bombing, two thousand Japanese died. Sometimes you still find old bones and skulls up along the hillside.'

He went into the bathroom and tried out the taps.

'You can drink the water. Dr Bill installed activated carbon filters on all the cisterns on the island and we take regular germ counts. Before that, cholera and typhus were big problems. You've still got to be careful about eating the local shellfish – marine toxins and rat lungworm disease. But fruits and vegetables are no problem. Anything here at the *house* is no problem, Dr Bill grows it all himself. In terms of outside stuff, the bar food at Slim's isn't much but the Chop Suey Palace is better than it sounds. At least my Mandarin wife doesn't mind it. Sometimes Jacqui, the owner, cooks up

11

something interesting, like bird's nest soup, depending on what's available.'

'Is that where the shark's fin was headed?' I said.

'Pardon?'

'Those two guys down at the harbor. Was it for the restaurant?'

He pushed his glasses up his nose. 'Oh, them. No, I doubt it.'

A gray-haired, gray-bearded man brought up our bags. Romero introduced him as Carl Sleet and thanked him.

When he left, Romero said, 'Anything else I can do for you?'

'We seem to have everything.'

'Okay, then, here's your key. Dinner's at six. Dress comfortably.'

He exited. Spike had fallen asleep in the sitting room. Robin and I went into the bedroom and I closed the door on canine snores.

'Well,' she said, taking a deep breath and smiling.

I kissed her. She kissed back hard, then yawned in the middle of it and broke away, laughing.

'Me, too,' I said. 'Nap time?'

'After I clean up.' She rubbed her arms. 'I'm crusted with salt.'

'Ah, dill-pickle woman!' I grabbed her and licked her skin. She laughed, pushed me away, and began opening a carry-on.

I picked up the folded card on the bed. Inside was a handwritten note:

> *Home is the sailor, home from sea,*
> *And the hunter home from the hill.*
>
> *R. L. Stevenson*
>
> *Please make my home yours.*
>
> *WWM*

'Robert Louis Stevenson,' said Robin. 'Maybe this will be our Treasure Island.'

'Wanna see my peg?'

As she laughed, I filled the bath. The water was crystalline, the towels brand-new, thick as fur.

When I returned, she was lying on top of the covers, naked, her hands behind her head, auburn hair spread on the pillow, nipples brown and stiff. I watched her belly rise and fall. Her smile. The oversized upper incisors I'd fallen for, years ago.

The windows were still wide open.

'Don't worry,' she said, softly. 'I checked and no one can see in – we're too high up.'

'God, you're beautiful.'

'I love you,' she said. 'This is going to be wonderful.'

3

A rasping noise woke me. Scratching at one of the screens. I sat up fast, saw it.

A small lizard, rubbing its foreclaws against the mesh.

I got out of bed and had a closer look.

It stayed there. Light brown body speckled with black. Skinny head and unmoving eyes.

It stared at me. I waved. Unimpressed, it scraped some more, finally scampered away.

Five p.m. I'd been out for two hours. Robin was still curled under the sheets.

Slipping into my pants, I tiptoed to the sitting room. Spike greeted me by panting and rolling over. I massaged his gut, refilled his water bowl, poured myself a tonic water on ice, and sat by the largest window. The sun was a big, red cherry, the ocean starting to silver.

I felt lucky to be alive, but disconnected – so far from everything familiar.

Rummaging in my briefcase I found Moreland's letter. Heavy white paper with a regal watermark. At the top in embossed black:

Aruk House, Aruk Island.

Dear Dr Delaware,

I am a physician who lives on the island of Aruk in the northern region of Micronesia. Nicknamed 'Knife Island' because of its oblong shape, Aruk is officially part of the Mariana Commonwealth and a self-governing U.S. territory, but relatively obscure and not listed in any guidebooks. I have lived here since 1961 and have found it a wonderful and fascinating place.

I chanced to come across an article you published in *The Journal of Child Development and Clinical Practice* on group trauma. Progressing to all your other published works, I find that you display a fine combination of scholarliness and common-sense thinking.

I say all this by way of making an interesting proposition.

Over the last three decades, in addition to conducting research in natural history and nutrition, I have accumulated an enormous amount of clinical data from my practice, some of it unique. Because the bulk of my time has been spent treating patients, I have not taken the time to properly organize this information.

As I grow older and closer to retirement, I realize that unless these data are brought to publication, a wealth of knowledge may be lost. Initially, my thought was to obtain the help of an anthropologist, but I decided that someone with clinical experience, preferably in a mental health field, would be better suited to the task. Your writing skills and orientation make me feel that you might be a compatible collaborator.

I'm sure, Dr Delaware, that this will seem odd, coming out of the blue, but I have given much thought to my offer. Though the pace of life on Aruk is probably a good deal slower than what you are used to, that in and of itself may have appeal for you. Would you be interested in helping me? By my estimate, the preliminary organization should take two, perhaps three months, at which point we could sit down and figure out if we've got a book, a monograph, or several journal articles. I would concentrate on the biological aspects, and I'd rely upon you for the psychological input. What I envision is a fifty-fifty collaboration with joint authorship.

I'm prepared to offer compensation of six thousand dollars per month, for four months, in addition to business-class transportation from the mainland and full room and board. There are no hotels on Aruk, but my own home is quite commodious and I'm sure you would find it pleasant. If you are married, I could accommodate your wife's transportation, though I could not offer her any paid work. If you have children, they could enroll in the local Catholic school, which is small but good, or I could arrange for private tutoring at a reasonable cost.

If this interests you, please write me or call collect at (670) 555-3334. There is no formal schedule, but I would like to get to work on this as soon as possible.

Thank you for your attention to this matter.

Sincerely,

Woodrow Wilson Moreland, M.D.

Slow pace of life; nothing in the letter indicated professional challenges, and any other time, I might have written back a polite refusal. I hadn't done long-term therapy for years, but forensic consultations kept me busy, and Robin's work as a builder of custom stringed instruments left

16

her little free time for vacations, let alone a four-month idyll.

But we'd been talking, half jokingly, about escaping to a desert island.

A year ago a psychopath had burned down our home and tried to murder us. Eventually, we'd taken on the task of rebuilding, finding temporary lodgings at a beach rental on the far western end of Malibu.

After our general contractor flaked out on us, Robin began overseeing the project. Things went well before bogging down the way construction projects inevitably do. Our new home was still months from completion, and the double load finally proved too much for her. She hired a fellow luthier who'd developed a severe allergy to wood dust to oversee the final stages, and returned to her carving.

Then her right wrist gave out – severe tendinitis. The doctors said nothing would help unless she gave the joint a long hiatus. She grew depressed and did little but sit on the beach all day, insisting she was adjusting just fine.

To my surprise, she soon *was*, hurrying to the sand each morning, even when autumn brought biting winds and iron skies. Taking long, solitary walks to the tide pools, watching the pelicans hunt from a vantage point atop the rocky cove.

'I know, I know,' she finally said. 'I'm surprised, myself. But now I'm thinking I was silly for waiting this long.'

In November, the lease on our beach house expired and the owner informed us he was giving it to his failed-screenwriter son as an incentive to write.

Thirty-day notice to vacate.

Moreland's letter came soon after. I showed it to Robin, expecting her to laugh it off.

She said, 'Call me Robin. Crusoe.'

4

Something human woke her.

People arguing next door. A man and a woman, their words blunted by thick walls, but the tone unmistakable. Going at each other with that grinding relentlessness that said they'd had long practice.

Robin sat up, pushed her hair out of her face, and squinted.

The voices subsided, then resumed.

'What time is it, Alex?'

'Five-forty.'

She took a long breath. I sat down on the bed and held her. Her body was moist.

'Dinner in twenty minutes,' she said. 'The bath must be cold.'

'I'll run another.'

'When did you get up?'

'Five.' I told her about the lizard. 'So don't be alarmed if it happens again.'

'Was he cute?'

'Who says it was a he?'

'Girls don't peep through other people's windows.'

'Now that I think about it, he did seem to be ogling you.' I narrowed my eyes and flicked my tongue. 'Probably a lounge lizard.'

She laughed and got out of bed. Putting on a robe, she walked around, flexing her wrist.

'How does it feel?'

'Better, actually. All the warm air.'

'And doing nothing.'

'Yes,' she said. 'The power of positive nothing.'

She slipped into a sleeveless white dress that showed off her olive skin. As we headed for the stairs, someone said, '*Hello* there.'

A couple had emerged from next door. The woman was locking up. The man repeated his greeting.

Both were tall, in their forties, with short-sleeved, epauletted khaki ensembles. His looked well worn, but hers was right out of the box.

He had a red, peeling nose under thick-rimmed glasses and a long, graying beard that reached his breastbone. The hair on top was darker, thin, combed over. His vest pockets bulged. She was big busted and broad beamed, with brown hair pulled back from a round face.

They lumbered toward us, holding hands. Half an hour ago they'd been assaulting each other with words.

'Dr and Mrs Delaware, I presume?' His voice was low and grainy. Cocktail breath. Up close, his skin was freckled pemmican, the red nose due to shattered vessels, not sunburn.

'Robin Castagna and Alex Delaware,' I said.

'Jo Picker, Lyman Picker. *Dr* Jo Picker and Lyman Picker.'

The woman said, 'Actually, it's *Dr* Lyman Picker, too, but who cares about that nonsense.' She had a sub-alto voice. If the two of them had kids, they probably sounded like tugboat horns.

She gave Robin a wide, appraising smile. Light brown eyes, an even nose, lips just a little too thin. Her tan was as new as her getup, still pink around the edges.

'I've heard you're a craftswoman,' she said. 'Sounds fascinating.'

'We've been looking forward to meeting you,' said Picker. 'Round out the dinner table – make up for the host's absence.'

'Is the host absent often?' I said.

'All work, no play. When the man sleeps, I don't know. Are you vegetarians like him? We're not. My line of work, you eat what you can get or you starve to death.'

Knowing it was expected of me, I said, 'What line is that?'

'Epiphytology. Botany. Tropical spores.'

'Are you doing research with Dr Moreland?'

He gave a wet laugh. 'No, I rarely venture far from the equator. This is a cold weather jaunt for me.' He threw an arm around his wife's shoulder. 'Keeping the distaff side company. Dr Jo here is an esteemed meteorologist. Fluctuations in aerial currents. Uncle Sam's quite enamored, ergo grant money.'

Jo gave an uneasy smile. 'I study the wind. How was your trip?'

'Long but peaceful,' said Robin.

'Come over on the supply boat?' said Picker.

'Yes.'

'Out of Saipan or Rota?'

'Saipan.'

'Us, too. Damned tedious, give me a plane any day. Even the biggest ocean liner's a thumbnail in a swimming pool. Ridiculous, isn't it, big airfield over on Stanton and the Navy won't let anyone use it.'

'Dr Moreland wrote that the airport there was closed,' I said.

'Not when the Navy needs it. Damn boats.'

'Oh, it wasn't so bad, Ly,' said Jo. 'Remember the flying fish? It was lovely, actually.'

The four of us started toward the stairs.

'Typical government stupidity,' said Picker. 'All that land, no one using it – probably the result of some subcommittee. Wouldn't you say, dear? You understand the ways of the government.'

Jo's smile was tense. 'Wish I did.'

'Spend any time in Guam?' asked her husband. 'Read any of those tourist pamphlets they have everywhere? Developing the Pacific, making use of the native talent pool. So what does the military do to a place like this? Blocks off the one link between the base and the rest of the island.'

'What link is that?' I said.

'Southern coastal road. The leeward side is unapproachable from the north, sheer rock walls from the tip of North Beach up to those dead volcanoes, so the only other ways to get through are the southern beach road and through the banyan forest. Navy blockaded the road last year. Meaning no military contact with the village, no commerce. What little local economy there was got choked off.'

'What about through the forest?'

'The Japanese salted it with land mines.'

His wife moved out from under his arm. 'What kinds of things do you craft, Robin?'

'Musical instruments.'

'Ah . . . drums and such?'

'Guitars and mandolins.'

'Lyman plays the guitar.'

Picker scratched his beard. 'Took a guitar into the *hoyos* of central Ecuador – now *that* was a place – ocelots, tapir, kinkajou. Only indigenous thingies around here lack spines, and my bride despises spineless things, don't you?'

'He plays quite well,' said Jo.

'Regular Segovia.' Picker mimed a strum. 'Sitting around the campfire with the Auca Indians, trying to charm them so they'd lead me to a juicy trove of *Cordyceps militaris* – fungal parasite, grows on insect pupae, they eat it like popcorn. Humidity loosened the glue on the thing, woke up the next morning to a stack of soggy boards.' He laughed. 'Used

21

the strings to strangle my supper that night, the rest for toothpicks.'

We reached the bottom of the stairs. Ben Romero was in the front room, KiKo on his shoulder. Picker eyed the animal. 'I've eaten them, too. Gamy. Can't housebreak them, did you know?'

'Evening, Ben,' said Jo. 'Alfresco, as usual?'

Ben nodded. 'Dr Bill will be a little late.'

'Surprise, surprise,' said Picker.

We walked through the right-hand hallway. Raw silk walls were hung with yet more pale watercolors. Nature scenes, well executed. The same signature on all of them: 'B. Moreland.' Another of the doctor's talents?

Ben led us through a big, yellow living room with a limestone fireplace, brocade couches, chinoiserie tables, Imari porcelain lamps with parchment shades. An oil portrait of a black-haired woman took up the space over the mantel. Her haughty beauty evoked Sargent.

The room opened to a wraparound terrace where a banquet table was covered with bright blue cloth. Bone china set for seven. Nascent light from hanging iron lanterns was swallowed by the still-bright evening.

The sun nudged the horizon, spilling crimson onto the skin of the water, a lovely wound. Down in the village tin roofs glinted through the treetops like tiny coins. The road leading up to the estate was a sleeping gray snake, its head resting at the big front gates. I thought of the slaves storming up from the barracks. Some Japanese general watching, helpless, knowing how it would end.

Lyman Picker touched his throat and winked at Ben.

'Bourbon,' Ben said in a tight voice. 'Straight up.'

'Excellent memory, friend.'

'And for you, Mrs Picker?'

'Just a soda, if it's no bother.'

'No bother at all.' Ben's jaws flexed. 'Ms Castagna? Dr Delaware?'

'Nothing, thanks,' I said.

Robin looked at me. 'Me, neither.'

'You're sure?'

'Positive.'

He left.

'Conscientious one, that,' said Picker.

Jo began examining the flatware. Robin and I walked to the pine railing. Picker followed us and leaned against the wood, elbows resting on the cap.

'So you're here to work with the old man. Sun and fun, maybe a publication or two. He's lucky to get you. You wouldn't find a serious scientist here.'

I laughed.

'No offense, man,' he said, as if offended. 'When I say serious, I mean us theoretical and oh-so-irrelevant types. Panhandlers with Ph.D.'s, rattling our beakers and praying stipends will drop in. This part of the globe, you want funding you don't study a place like this, you go for Melanesia, Polynesia. Big, fat, fertile islands, plenty of flora, fauna, agreeably colorful indigenous tribes, serious mythology for the folklore crowd.'

'Aruk doesn't have any of that?'

He coughed without covering his mouth. 'Micronesia, my friend, is two thousand dirt specks in three million square miles of water, most of them uninhabited bumps of coral. *This* bump's one of the most obscure. Did you know there were no people till the Spanish brought them over to grow sugar? The crop failed and the Spanish sailed away, leaving the workers to starve. Then came the Germans, who, for all their authoritarianism, hadn't a clue about colonizing. Sat around reading Goethe all day. Then the Japanese, trying the same damn sugar thing, slave labor.'

He laughed. 'So what was the payoff? MacArthur bombs them to hell and the slaves say payback time. Night of the long knives.' He drew a finger across his beard.

Jo came over. 'Is he regaling you with tales of his wideflung adventures?'

'No,' said Picker, grumpily. 'Reviewing local history.' He coughed again. 'Where's that drink?'

'Soon, Ly. So what led you to become a craftswoman, Robin?'

'I love music and working with my hands. Tell us about *your* research, Jo.'

'Nothing very exciting. I was sent to do a wind survey of several islands in the Mariana complex and Aruk's my last stop. We were renting a teeny place in town till Bill was kind enough to invite us up here. We're leaving in a week.'

'Don't make it sound like the weather service, girl,' said Picker. '*Defense* Department pays her bills. She's an important national asset. Marry an asset, get an all-expense vacation.'

He slapped his wife on the back, none too gently. She stiffened but smiled.

'Do you live in Washington?' said Robin.

'We have a town-house in Georgetown,' said Jo, 'but most of the time we're both gone.'

She recoiled. A lizard, just like the one I'd seen at the window, raced along the top of the railing. Her husband flicked a finger at it, laughing as it disappeared over the side.

'Still jittery?' he reproached her. 'I told you it's harmless. *Hemidactylus frenatus.* House gecko, semidomesticated. People feed them near the house, so they'll stick around and eat all the *buggies.'*

He wiggled his fingers in his wife's face. In grade school, he'd probably been a pigtail yanker.

She tried to smile. 'Well, I just can't get used to them doing pushups on my screen.'

'Squeamish,' Picker told us. 'Meaning I can't bring *my* work home.'

Jo colored beneath her tan.

The young housekeeper, Cheryl, came out with a tray. On it were the drinks the Pickers had ordered and mineral waters with lime for Robin and me.

'Retarded, that,' Picker said when she was gone. Tapping his temple. He raised his glass. 'To spineless things.'

Red light bounced off the ocean and bloodied his beard.

His wife looked the other way and sipped.

Robin drew me away to the opposite corner.

'Charming, huh?' I said.

'Alex, why were you so adamant about not ordering drinks?'

'Because Ben's teeth were clenched when Picker ordered his. He's a nurse, doesn't want to be thought of as a butler. Notice he sent Cheryl with the tray.'

'Oh,' she said. 'My psychologist.' She slipped her hand around my waist and lowered her head to my shoulder.

'Lovers' secrets?' Picker called out. His glass was empty.

'Let them *be*, Ly,' said Jo.

'Looks like they're *being* just fine.'

'Welcome to paradise,' I muttered.

Robin quelled a laugh. It came out sounding like a hiccup.

'Hitting the sauce, girl?' I whispered. 'Tsk, tsk. Damned self-indulgent.'

'Stop,' she said, biting her lip.

I leaned close. 'Great *fun* ahead, wench. Cooked flesh and spirits, and after dinner he'll *regale* us with tales of the giant-penised Matahuaxl tribe. Human tripods, they are. Very virile.'

She licked her lips and whispered back: 'Very, indeed. As they trip their way over the roots of the variegated crotchweed. 'Cause let's face it, when it comes to tribes, bigger *is* better.'

'Ah, love . . .' Picker called from across the terrace. 'Need another drinkie, I do.'

But he made no move to get one and neither did his wife. Welcome silence, then light footsteps sounded from behind. I turned and saw a lovely-looking blond woman walk toward us.

Late twenties or early thirties, she had a nipped waist, boyish hips, small breasts, long legs. She wore an apricot silk blouse and black crepe slacks. Blunt-cut hair ended at her shoulders, held in place by a black band. The honey tint looked real and her sculpted face had a scrubbed-clean look. Her features were fine and perfectly placed: soft, wide mouth, clean jaw, delicate ears. Blue eyes with a downward slant that made them look sad.

Except for her coloring, she could have been the woman in the oil portrait.

'Dr Delaware and Ms Castagna? I'm Pam, Dr Moreland's daughter.' Soft, musical, slightly reticent voice. She had a fetching smile but looked away as she extended her hand. I'd had patients with that tendency to avert; all had been painfully shy as children.

'Doctor *herself*,' Picker corrected. 'All these accomplished *femmes* and everyone's playing the modesty game.'

Pam Moreland gave him a pitying smile. 'Evening, Lyman. Jo. Sorry I'm late. Dad should be here shortly. If not, we'll start without him. Gladys has done a nice Chicken Kiev. Dad's vegetarian, but he tolerates us barbarians.'

She smiled beautifully but the eyes remained sad, and I wondered if physical structure completely explained it.

Picker said, 'Just gave our new chums a history lesson, Dr Daughter. Told them scientists shun this lovely bit of real estate because Margaret Mead showed the key to stardom is witch doctors, puberty rites, and bare-chested, dusky girls.' His eyes dropped to Pam's bodice.

'Interesting theory. Can I get you some coffee?'

'No thanks, my dear. But a refill of this wouldn't hurt.'

'Ly,' said Jo. She hadn't moved from her corner.

Picker kept his back to her. 'Yes, my love?'

'Come here and look at the sunset.'

He nibbled his mustache. 'The old distraction technique? Worried about my *liver*?'

'I just—'

He swiveled and faced her. 'If *Entamoeba histolytica* and *Fasciola hepatica* failed to do the trick, do you really think a little Wild *Turkey* will succeed, Josephine?'

Jo said nothing.

'Lived on metronodizole and bithionol for months,' Picker told Pam. 'Long overdue for a physical. Any referrals?'

'Not unless you're going to Philadelphia.'

'Ah, the city of brotherly love,' said Picker. 'Don't have a brother. Would I love him, if I did?'

Pondering that, he walked away.

'I *will* take that refill, Dr Pam,' he called over his shoulder.

'The man who came to dinner,' Pam said very softly. 'Excuse me.'

She returned with a quarter-full bottle of Wild Turkey, thrust it at the surprised Picker, and returned to us. 'Dad's sorry about not being able to greet you properly.'

'The jellyfish,' I said.

She nodded. Glance at a Lady Rolex. 'I guess we should get started.'

She seated Robin and me with a view of the sunset, the Pickers on the other end, herself in the middle. Two empty chairs remained and moments later Ben Romero came out and took one. He'd put on a tan cotton sportcoat.

'Usually I go home by six,' he said, unrolling his napkin, 'but my wife's having a card party, the baby's sleeping, and the older kids are farmed out.'

'Next time we'll have Claire up,' said Pam. 'She's a marvelous violinist. The kids, too.'

Ben laughed. 'That'll be real relaxing.'

'Your kids are great, Ben.'

The food came. Platters of it.

Watercress salad with avocado dressing, carrot puree, fricassee of wild mushrooms with walnuts and water chestnuts. Then the chicken, sizzling and moist.

A bottle of white burgundy remained untouched. Picker poured

27

himself the rest of the bourbon. His wife looked the other way and ate energetically.

'Gladys didn't learn to cook like this at the base,' said Robin.

'Believe it or not, she did,' Pam said. 'The commander thought himself quite the gourmet. She's very creative, lucky for Dad.'

'Has he always been a vegetarian?'

'Since after the Korean War. The things he saw made him determined never to hurt anything again.'

Picker grunted.

'But he's always been tolerant,' said Pam. 'Had meat shipped over for me when I arrived.'

'You don't live here?' said Robin.

'No, I came last October. It was supposed to be a stopover on the way to a medical convention in Hong Kong.'

'What's your specialty?' I said.

'Internal medicine and public health. I work at the student health center at Temple U.' She paused. 'Actually, it was a combination work trip and breather. I just got divorced.'

She filled her water glass, shrugged.

'Did you grow up here?' asked Robin.

'Not really. Ready for dessert?'

Picker watched her walk away. 'Some fool in Philadelphia's missing out.'

Ben eyed him. 'Another bottle, Dr Picker?'

Picker stared back. 'No thank you, amigo. Better keep my wits. I'm flying tomorrow.'

Jo put down her fork. Picker grinned at her.

'Yes, darling, I've decided to go ahead.'

'Flying in what?' said Ben.

'Vintage craft, but well maintained. Man named Amalfi owns it.'

'Harry Amalfi? One of those crop dusters? They haven't flown in years.'

'They're quite serviceable, friend. I examined them myself. Been buzzing jungles for fifteen years and I'm going to buzz your poor excuse for one tomorrow morning, me and Dr

Missus. Take some aerial photographs, prove to the boys back at the institute that I've been here and that there was nothing to dig up.'

Jo's fingers were gathering tablecloth. 'Ly—'

Ben said, 'It's not a good idea, Dr Picker.'

Picker shot him a fierce smile. 'Your input is duly noted, friend.'

'The forest is Navy territory. You'll need official permission to fly over.'

'Wrong,' said Picker. 'Only the east end is Navy land. The western half is public land, never formally claimed by the Navy. Or so Dr Wife here tells me from her maps.'

'That's true, Ly,' said Jo, 'but it's still—'

'Zoom,' Picker spoke over her. 'Up and away – would you rather I remain bored to the point of brain death?'

'The entire forest is one mile wide,' said Ben. 'Once you're up there it's going to be pretty hard to keep track—'

'*Concerned* about me, amigo?' said Picker, with sudden harshness. He picked up the bourbon bottle, as if ready to break it. Put it down with exquisite care, and got up.

'Everyone so concerned about me. *Touching.*' His beard was littered with crumbs. 'Fonts of human *kindness* to my face, but behind my *back*: drunken *buffoon.*'

He shifted his attention to his wife, glaring and grinning simultaneously. 'Are you coming, *angel*?'

Her lip trembled. 'You know how I feel about small craft, Ly—'

'Not that. *Now*. Are you coming, *now*?'

Without taking his eyes off her, he picked up a piece of chicken and bit in. Chewing with his mouth open, he shot a hard, dark glance at Romero: 'It's a metaphor, friend.'

'What is?' said Ben.

'This place. All the other damn *bumps* in the ocean. Volcanoes ejaculating, then dropping dead. Conquerors arriving with high hopes only to slink away or die, the damned coral parasites taking over, everything sinking. Entropy.'

29

Jo put down her fork. 'Excuse us.'

Picker tossed the chicken onto a plate and took her arm roughly.

'Everything sinks,' he said, pulling her away.

5

Pam came back carrying a huge bowl of fruit and eyed the empty chairs.

'They left,' said Ben. 'They're renting one of Harry's crop dusters and buzzing the jungle tomorrow morning.'

'In one of those wrecks? Are they safe?'

'I tried to talk him out of it. He's a world-class explorer.' He arched his eyebrows.

She put the bowl down and sat. 'I'm afraid sometimes Dr Picker gets a little . . . difficult.'

'Nice of your father to put them up all this time,' I said.

She and Ben exchanged looks.

'They kind of invited themselves,' she said. 'Dad's a soft touch. Apparently, she's quite a prominent researcher.'

'What about him?'

'He works part-time for some wildlife organization with a shoestring budget. Studying some fungus or other. I get the feeling he's having trouble finding grant money. I guess it's difficult . . . Dad should be here any moment.'

She passed the bowl.

'Is it true,' I said. 'About the Navy cutting off contact with the village with a blockade?'

She nodded.

'Why?'

'It's the military,' said Ben. 'They live in their own little world.'

'Dad's working on it,' said Pam. 'Wrote to Senator Hoffman because the two of them go back a ways. And Hoffman knows Aruk from personal experience; he was Stanton's commander during the Korean War.'

'The gourmet?'

She nodded. 'He used to come up here with his wife, sit right on this terrace and play bridge.'

'Sounds like a good contact,' I said. The senator from Oregon had been discussed as a Presidential candidate.

Ben put his napkin down and stood. ''Scuse me, got to pick up the kids. Anything you need for tomorrow, Pam?'

'Just more disposable needles. And vaccine if it's running low.'

'Already there,' said Ben. 'I set up before dinner.'

He shook our hands and left quickly.

'He's terrific,' said Pam. 'Really knows what he's doing. He found KiKo on the docks, dying of infection, and nursed him back to health.' She smiled. 'KiKo's short for King Kong. He sleeps in a cradle in Ben's house.'

'Dr Picker said monkeys can't be housebroken.'

'I'm no primatologist, but sometimes I think animals are a lot more tractable than people.'

The sound of a car engine drew my eyes down toward the road. Darkness had set in, but a pair of headlights shone through.

'. . . one of the most levelheaded people you'll ever meet. Dad wouldn't mind if he went on to med school; the island could use a younger doctor. But the time commitment – he's got a big family to support.'

'In his letter to me,' I said, 'your father mentioned retirement.'

She smiled. 'I don't imagine he'll ever fully retire, but with three thousand people on this island, he could use some help. I've been pitching in, but . . .' She put her spoon down.

'You asked before if I grew up on Aruk and I said not really. I was born here but boarded out very young. Went to Temple for med school and stayed in Philadelphia. I kept thinking I should come back here, but I grew up a city girl, found out I *like* the city.'

'I know what you mean,' said Robin. 'Small towns are great in theory but they can be limiting.'

'Exactly. Aruk is wonderful; you guys will have a great time. But as a permanent place to live, it's – how shall I put this? At the risk of sounding elitist . . . it's just very *small*. And the water all around. You just can't go very far without being reminded of your insignificance.'

'We lived on the beach this last year,' said Robin. There were times the ocean made me feel downright invisible.'

'Precisely. Everywhere you turn, it's *there*. Sometimes I think of it as a big, blue slap in the face.'

She nibbled more fruit. 'And the pace. Cross the international dateline and for some reason everything moves *slow*-ly. I'm not the most patient person in the world.'

Gladys and Cheryl arrived with a rolling tray and coffee, cleared the dishes and poured.

Pam said, 'Everything was delicious, Gladys.'

'Tell your father to show up for dinner. He needs to take better care of himself.'

'I've been telling him that since I got here, Gladys.'

'And I've been ignoring it, mule that I am,' said a voice from the house.

A very tall, very homely man stood in the double doorway. Stooped, gaunt, clean-shaven, bald except for white dandelion puffs over his ears, he had a narrow, lipless mouth, a thick, fleshy nose and a long face bottoming in a misshapen, crinkled chin that made me think of a camel. His cheeks were hollow and limp, his eye sockets deep and pouched. Sad blue eyes – the only physical trait he'd passed on to his daughter.

He wore a cheap-looking white shirt over baggy brown pants, white socks, and sandals. His chest looked caved in, his arms long and ungainly and spotted by the sun, the flesh loose on thin bones. Plastic eyeglasses hung from a chain. His breast pocket drooped with pens, a doctor's penlight, a pair of sunglasses, a small white plastic ruler. He carried an old black leather medical bag.

As I stood, he waved and came forward in an ungainly, headfirst lope.

Not a camel. A flamingo.

Touching his lips to Pam's cheek, he said, 'Evening, kitten.'

'Hi, Dad.'

The narrow mouth widened a millimeter. 'Miss Castagna. A pleasure, dear.' He gave Robin's fingertips a brief, double-hand clasp, then took my hand, sighing, as if he'd been waiting a long time to do it.

'Dr Delaware.'

His hand was dry and limp, exerting feeble pressure, then slipping away like a windblown leaf.

'I'm bringing you dinner,' said Gladys. 'And don't tell me you grabbed a snack in the village.'

'I didn't,' said Moreland, putting his palms together. 'I promise, Gladys.'

He sat down and inspected his napkin before unfolding it. 'I trust you've been well taken care of. Any seasickness coming over?'

We shook our heads.

'Good. *Madeleine*'s a fine craft and Alwyn's the best of the supply captains. She used to belong to a sportsman from Hawaii. Runs fine on sails, but Alwyn upgraded the engines and he really makes good time. He babies that boat.'

'How many boats make the run?' I said.

'Three to six, depending on orders, circulating among the

smaller islands. On the average, we get one or two loads twice a month.'

'Must be expensive.'

'It does inflate the cost of goods.'

Cheryl returned with two plates piled high with everything we'd eaten but the chicken. Beans had been added to the rice. She set the food in front of Moreland and he smiled up at her.

'Thank you, dear. I hope your mother doesn't expect me to finish all this.'

Cheryl giggled and scurried off.

Moreland took a deep breath and raised a fork. 'How's your little bulldog faring?'

'Sleeping off the boat ride,' I said.

Robin said, 'Matter of fact, I'd better go check on him. Excuse me.'

I walked her to the stairway. When I got back, Moreland was looking at his food but hadn't touched it. Pam was sitting in place, not moving.

Moreland's eyes drifted up to the black sky. For a moment they seemed clouded. Then he blinked them clear. Pam was fiddling with her napkin ring.

'I think I'll take a walk,' she said, rising.

'Good night, kitten.'

'Nice to meet you, Dr Delaware.'

'Nice to meet you.'

Another exchange of pecks and she was gone. Moreland took a forkful of rice and chewed slowly, washing it down with water. 'I'm *very* happy to finally meet you.'

'Same here, doctor.'

'Call me Bill. May I call you Alex?'

'Of course.'

'How are your accommodations?'

'Great. Thanks for everything.'

'What did you think of my Stevenson quote?'

The question threw me. 'Nice touch. Great writer.'

35

'Home is the sailor,' he said. 'This is *my* home, and it's my pleasure to have you here. Stevenson never made it to the northern Marianas but he did have a feel for island life. Great thinker as well as a great writer. The great thinkers have much to offer ... I have high hopes for our project, Alex. Who knows what patterns will emerge when we really get into the data.'

He put the fork down.

'As I mentioned, I'm particularly interested in mental health problems because they always pose the greatest puzzles. And I've seen some fascinating cases.'

He aimed the pouchy eyes at me. 'For example, years ago I encountered a case of – I suppose the closest label would be lycanthropy, but it really wasn't classical lycanthropy.'

'A wolf-man?'

'A cat-*woman*. Have you seen that?'

'During my training I saw schizophrenics with transitory animal hallucinations.'

'This was more than transitory. Thirty-year-old woman, attractive, sweet nature. Shortly after her thirty-first birthday, she began withdrawing from her family and wandering around staring at cats. Then she started chasing mice – rather uselessly. Mewing, licking herself, eating raw meat. That's what finally brought her to me: rampant intestinal parasites caused by her diet.'

'Was this a constant delusion?'

'More like a series of fits – acute spells, but they lasted longer and longer as time went on. By the time I saw her the periods between the fits weren't good, either. Appetite loss, poor concentration, bouts of weeping. Tell all that to a psychiatrist and he'd probably diagnose psychotic depression or a bipolar mood disorder. An anthropologist, on the other hand, would pounce on tribal rituals or a plant-induced religious hallucinosis. The problem is, there *are* no native hallucinogenic plants on Aruk nor any pre-Christian shamanic culture.'

36

He ate more rice but didn't seem to taste it. 'Interesting from a diagnostic standpoint, wouldn't you say?'

'Did the woman drink heavily?' I said.

'No. And her vitamin B intake was sufficient, so it wasn't an idiopathic Korsakoff's syndrome.'

'What about the parasites? Had they infiltrated her brain?'

'Good question. I wondered about that, too, but her symptoms made conducting even a gross neurological exam impossible. She'd gotten quite aggressive – snarling and biting and scratching to the point where her husband tied her up in her room. She'd become quite a burden.'

'Sounds brutal.'

He looked pained. 'In any event, the symptoms didn't conform to any parasitical disease I'd ever come across, and I was able to treat her intestinal problems quite easily. After she died, the husband refused an autopsy and I certified cause of death as heart attack.'

'How did she die?'

He put down his fork. 'She screamed out one night – a *cri du chat* – cat's cry. Louder than usual, so the husband went in to check. He found her lying on her bed, open-eyed, dead.'

'No evidence of any kind of poisoning?'

'My lab was rather primitive in those days, but I was able to test her blood for the obvious things and found nothing.'

'What was her relationship with her husband like?'

He stared at me. 'Is there any particular reason you ask that?'

'I'm a psychologist.'

He smiled.

'Also,' I said, 'you said she'd become a burden. And that he only went in because her cat's cry was louder. That implies he usually ignored her. It doesn't sound like marital devotion.'

He looked up and down the table, then past it, into the living room, as if making sure we were alone.

'Shortly after she died,' he said, 'her husband took up with

37

another woman and moved off the island. Years later, I found out he'd been quite a Don Juan.' His eyes dropped to his plate. 'I suppose I'd better get through this or Gladys will have my head.'

Eating a few mouthfuls of vegetables, he said, 'I fibbed. Had some chow mein brought into the clinic. Sudden emergency, influx of jellyfish on North Beach.'

'Pam told me. How are the children?'

'Sore and covered with welts and totally unchastened . . . Any more thoughts on our catwoman?'

'Did she have a history of fainting or any other evidence of syncope?'

'A cardiac arrhythmia to explain the sudden death? None that I picked up. And no family history of heart disease. But the mode – sudden death. Her heart stopped so I called it heart disease.'

'Allergies? Anaphylaxis?'

He shook his head.

'No heavy drinking,' I said. 'What about drug abuse?'

'Her habits were clean, Alex. A lovely lady, really. Until the change.'

'How completely was she bound when she slept?'

'Hands and feet.'

'Pretty severe.'

'She was considered dangerous.'

'And she was tied up the night she died.'

'Yes.'

'Perhaps something frightened or upset her,' I said. 'To the point of heart failure.'

'Such as?'

'An especially severe hallucination. Or a nightmare.'

He didn't respond and I thought he looked angry.

'Or,' I said, 'something real.'

He closed his eyes.

'Maybe,' I continued, 'her Don Juan husband took up with another woman *before* she died.'

Slow nods; the eyes remained shut.

'Tied up at night,' I said. 'But the husband and the girl-friend were in the next room. Did they make love in front of her?'

The eyes opened. 'My, my. You are a remarkable young man.'

'Just guessing.'

Another long pause. 'As I said, it wasn't till years later that I found out about him, and only then because I treated a cousin of his who lived on another island and came to me to be treated for shingles. I gave him acyclovir and it reduced his pain. I suppose he felt he owed me something. So he told me the catwoman's husband had just died and had mentioned me on his deathbed. He'd been married three more times.'

'Any other mysterious deaths?'

'No, three divorces. All because he couldn't stop philandering. But as he lay eaten away by lung cancer, his chest completely ravaged, he confessed to tormenting his first wife. Right from the beginning. The day after the wedding, she saw him kill a cat that had gotten into their yard and eaten a chicken. He choked it to death, chopped its head off and tossed the carcass at her, laughing. She learned of his infidelities soon after. When she complained, he called her a bitch-cat and sent her to clean the chicken coop. It became a regular pattern whenever they'd fight. Years later her symptoms began. The more disturbed she became, the less he cared about hiding his affairs. During her final months, the other woman was actually living with them, ostensibly to clean house. The night she died, the husband and the girl-friend *were* making love noisily. The wife cried out in protest and they laughed at her. This went on for a while, then she entered her cat mode and began mewing. Then hissing. Then screaming.' He touched one cheek and the flesh bobbled. 'They came into her room and continued to . . . in front of her. She strained at her bonds, screaming. I'm sure

39

her blood pressure was skyrocketing. Finally, she gave a last scream.'

He pushed his plate away.

'Deathbed confession,' he said. 'Guilt is a great motivator.'

'Infidelities,' I said. 'Catting around?'

He said nothing for several seconds. Then: 'I like that.' But he sounded anything but happy. 'So what are we talking about, diagnostically? Manic-depression marked by some sort of primitive feline identification? Or a full-blown schizophrenia?'

'Or a severe stress reaction. Was there any psychiatric history in the family at all?'

'Her mother was . . . morose.' He leaned in closer, bald pate shining like an ostrich egg. 'Dying like that. Was it due to fear? Shame? Can a person truly die of *frustration*? Or did she suffer from some physical irregularity that I wasn't clever enough to discover? That's what I mean about puzzles. We'll document the case.'

'Fascinating,' I said, thinking of the catwoman's agony.

'I've got many more, son. Many, many more.' A hand began to reach out. For a moment I thought he'd put it on mine, but it landed on the table and lay there, exhibiting a slight tremor.

'I'm so glad you're here to help me.'

'Glad to be here.'

A bark made us both turn. Robin returned with Spike on his leash.

Moreland brightened. 'Oh, look at *him*.'

He went over and crouched, hand out, palm down.

Spike panted and jumped, then nosed the old man's crotch.

'Oh, my,' said Moreland, laughing and standing. 'You're a *friendly* little fellow . . . Has he had his dinner?'

'He just finished,' said Robin, 'and we took a short walk.'

'Lovely,' Moreland said, absently. 'Do you two have any plans for tomorrow? If you're up to it, you might try snorkeling down on South Beach. The reefs are beautiful and the fish come right into the shallows, so you don't need tanks. I have an extra Jeep for you to use.'

40

Fishing in his pocket, he pulled out some keys and gave them to me.

'Thanks,' I said. 'When do you want to start working?'

He smiled. 'We already have.'

6

We walked back through the silk-papered gallery, Moreland moving stiffly despite long strides, Robin and I slowing down for him.

'I like your paintings,' I said.

He gave a puzzled look. 'Oh, those. They were done by my late wife.'

He made no further comment till we reached the entry hall and a door slammed upstairs from the vicinity of the Pickers' suite.

'I heard about Lyman's behavior at dinner,' he said, stopping. 'I apologize.'

'No big deal.'

'They'll only be here another week or so. She's just about completed whatever it is she came here to do. He has *nothing* to do, which is part of the problem. He's unhappy about the lack of exotic molds and repulsive plants.'

'He may still be hoping to find some,' I said. 'They're flying over the banyan forest tomorrow morning.'

Thin arms folded across his chest. 'Tomorrow?'

'That's what he said.'

'Flying in what?'

'A plane owned by a man named Harry Amalfi.'

'Good lord. Those are junk heaps. Harry bought them from surplus years ago, expecting me to hire him to dust crops. I decided to use only organic pest-control, tried to explain it to him. Even after I compensated him, he convinced himself I ruined him.'

'You paid him, anyway?' said Robin.

'I gave him something because he'd taken initiative. I suggested he use the money to open a car repair business. He and his son know how to do that. Instead, he spent every penny and hasn't taken any initiative since. There's no reason to go up in one of those rattletraps. What do they expect to see?'

'The forest.'

'There's nothing down there. The area is mostly Navy land, the rest public domain that would have been cleared long ago except that it's not safe. Land mines left by the Japanese. And who's going to fly them? Harry hasn't been up in years. *And* he drinks.'

'Picker has a pilot's license.'

He shook his head. 'I must have a talk with them. Those land mines are a real danger if he tries to land. I had barbed wire put up along the eastern wall of my property to make sure no one climbed over. I'd better go up there right now.'

'He may not be receptive,' I said.

'Oh . . . yes, you're probably right. Tomorrow morning, then . . . Now, in terms of your recreation here at the house, we don't get television reception but the radio in your room should be working. There's also a small library on the other side of the dining room.' He gave a little wave. 'Converted silver room. You may not find much of interest there. Mostly condensed books and biographies. There are many more books in your office, and mine. Periodicals come in with the provisions. If there's something specific you're interested in reading, I'll do my best to find it for you.'

He bent slowly and petted Spike. 'Well, I'll let you go now. Is there anything you need?'

Robin said, 'It's so pleasant out I thought we might walk some more.'

Moreland nodded happily. 'Have you noticed the sweetness in the air? I've planted for aroma. Frangipani, night-blooming jasmine, old roses, all sorts of things.'

'Picker said the soil isn't good,' I said.

'He's right about that. Any residues of volcanic ash have drifted into the jungle, and the rest of the island is too high in salt and silica. In some places, the dirt only goes down a couple of feet before you hit coral. With the exception of a few pines planted by the Japanese, this place was scrub when I bought it. I brought in boatloads of topsoil and amendments. It took years. It's turned out fairly well. Would you like to see – no, forgive me, I won't interrupt your walk.'

'We'd love to,' said Robin.

He blinked. 'I believe you're being kind to an old bore. But at my age, one takes what one gets – let's go, little doggy.'

Behind the house was a courtyard planted with privet-hedged rose gardens and precisely cut flower beds. Big conifers, some pruned in the spare, graceful Japanese style. Then, looser plantings of palm and fern and crushed rock walkways lined with low-growing lillies. Artfully placed spotlights allowed just enough illumination for safe passage. The botanic perfumes blended in strange combinations. Sometimes the result was cloying.

'It goes back a ways,' said Moreland, pointing to a wooden arbor at the rear of the lawn. To the side, high-voltage spots exposed a grass tennis court without a net, then more grass. Off to the left stood a group of flat-roofed buildings: one huge hangarlike structure and several smaller sheds. Moreland led us to them, saying, 'It's too dark to see, but I've got all sorts of things behind the arbor. Citrus, plum, peach, table grapes, bananas, vegetables. Feel free to go picking tomorrow. Everything's safe to eat.'

44

'Are you self-sufficient?' I said.

'For the most part. Meat and fish and dairy products, I buy for the staff and guests. I used to keep a goat herd for milk, but we didn't consume enough to justify it. As I wrote you, I conduct nutritional research. Sometimes there's surplus for the village.'

'Do people in the village grow anything?'

'A bit,' he said. 'It's not an agricultural culture.'

As we got closer to the outbuildings, he said, 'Those are my offices and labs and warehouses. Your office is the nearest bungalow, and I've set aside studio space for you, as well, Robin, right next door. A nice room with northern exposure and a skylight. My wife used to paint there. How's your wrist doing?'

'Better.'

He stopped again. 'May I?' Lifting her arm, he flexed the joint very gently. 'No crepitus. Good. Ice for acute inflammation and follow up with warmth for pain. Keep it relaxed and it should knit nicely. The southern lagoon stays very nice all year round. Swimming's a low-resistance exercise that will strengthen the muscles without unduly stressing the joint.'

Releasing her arm, he looked out into the darkness.

'I should, probably dig up some of that lawn. Ridiculously labor intensive and useless, but I grew up on a ranch and the smell of new grass brings me back to my childhood.'

'A ranch where?' I said.

'Sonoma, California. Father grew Santa Rose plums and pinot noir grapes.'

We continued walking.

'Do you see patients here?' I said.

'No, that's done at the clinic in town. The X-ray machine is there and it's a lot more convenient for the villagers.'

'So what kinds of labs do you have here?'

'Research. I have a long-standing interest in *alternative* pesticides – are either of you squeamish?'

'About what?' said Robin.

'Natural predation.' He blinked. 'Spineless creatures.'

'If they're crawling all over me, I am.'

He laughed. 'I certainly hope not, dear. If you're ever interested, I have some very interesting specimens.'

'You keep live specimens here?'

He turned to pat her shoulder. 'Under lock and key in that big building over there. I'm sorry, dear. I should have told you. Sometimes I forget how people get.'

'No, it's all right,' she said. 'When I was a kid I had a tarantula as a pet.'

'I didn't know that,' I said.

She laughed. 'Neither did my parents. A friend gave it to me when *her* mother made her get rid of it. I hid it in a shoebox in my closet for weeks. Then *my* mother discovered it. One of the more memorable episodes of my childhood.'

'I have tarantulas,' said Moreland. Excitement tinged his voice. 'They're really quite wonderful, once you get to know them.'

'Mine wasn't that big, maybe an inch long. I think it was from Italy.'

'Probably an Italian wolf spider. *Lycosa tarantula*. Here's something for *you*, Alex: the bite of the Italian wolf was once thought to cause madness – weeping and stumbling and dancing. That's how the tarantella dance got its name. Nonsense, of course. The little thing's harmless.'

'Wish you could have been there to convince my mother,' said Robin. 'She flushed it.'

Moreland winced. 'If you'd like to see another one, I can oblige.'

'Sure,' she said. 'If it's okay with you, Alex.'

I stared at her. Back home she called upon me to swat mosquitoes and flies.

'Love to see it,' I said. Mr Macho.

'I'm afraid you'd best leave *him* outside, though,' said Moreland, looking at Spike. 'Dogs are still basically wolves, and wolves are predators with all the hormonal secretions that entails. Little scurrying things may set off an aggressive response in him. I don't want to upset him. Or them.'

46

'Humans are predators, too,' I said.

'Most definitely,' said Moreland. 'But we seem to be naturally afraid of them, and they can deal with that.'

We tied Spike to a tree, gave him a cheese-flavored dog cracker, and told him we'd be back soon.

Moreland took us to the hangarlike building. The entrance was a gray metal door.

'The Japanese officers' bath house,' he said, releasing a key lock. 'They had herbal mudpits here, wet and dry steam, fresh and saltwater pools. The saltwater was brought up from the beach in trucks.'

He flipped a switch and light flooded a windowless room. White tile on all surfaces. Empty. Another gray door, closed. No lock.

'Careful, now,' he said. 'I have to keep the light dim. There are thirteen steps down.'

Opening the second door, he flicked one of a series of toggles and a weak, pale-blue haze stuttered to life.

'Thirteen steps,' he reiterated and he counted out loud as we followed him down a stone flight, grasping cold metal handrails.

The interior was much cooler than the main house. At the bottom was a sunken area, maybe sixty feet long. Concrete walls and floors. The floors were marked by several rectangles. Seams, where concrete had been poured to fill the baths.

Narrow windows so high they nearly touched the ceiling let in feeble dots of moonlight. Translucent wire glass. The blue light came from a few fluorescent bulbs mounted vertically on the walls. As my eyes got accustomed to the dimness, I made out another flight of stairs at the far end. A raised work space: desk and chair, storage cabinets, lab tables.

A wide aisle spined through the center of the sunken area. Metal ribs on both sides: ten rows of steel tables bolted to the concrete.

The tables housed dozens of ten-gallon aquariums covered by wire mesh lids. Some tanks were completely dark. Others glowed pink, gray, lavender, more blue.

47

Random spurts of sound from within: flutterings and scratchings, sudden stabs, the ping of something hard against glass.

The panic of attempted escape.

A strange mixture of smells filled my nose. Decayed vegetation, excreta, peat moss. Wet grain, boiled meat. Then something sweet – fruit on the verge of rot.

Robin's hand in mine was as cold as the handrails.

'Welcome,' said Moreland, 'to my little zoo.'

7

He led us past the first two rows and stopped at the third. 'Some sort of classification system would have been clever, but I know where everyone is and I'm the one who feeds them.'

Turning left, he stopped at a dark tank. Inside was a floor of mulch and leaves, above it a tangle of bare branches. Nothing else that I could see.

He pulled something out of his pocket and held it between his fingers. A pellet, not unlike Spike's kibble.

The wire lid was clamped; he loosened it and pushed, exposing a corner. Inserting two fingers, he dangled the pellet.

At first, nothing happened. Then, quicker than I believed possible, the mulch heaved, as if in the grip of a tiny earthquake, and something shot up.

A second later, the food was gone.

Robin pressed herself against me.

Moreland hadn't moved. Whatever had taken the pellet had disappeared.

'Australian garden wolf,' said Moreland, securing the top. 'Cousin of your Italian friend. Like *tarantula*, they burrow and wait.'

'Looks as if you know what it likes,' said Robin. I heard the difference in her voice, but a stranger might not have.

'What *she* likes – this one's quite the lady – is animal protein. Preferably in liquid form. Spiders always liquefy their food. I combine insects, worms, mice, whatever, and create a broth that I freeze and defrost. This is the same stuff, compressed and freeze-dried. I did it to see if they'd adapt to solids. Luckily, many of them did.'

He smiled. 'Strange avocation for a vegetarian, right? But what's the choice? She's my responsibility . . . Come with me, perhaps we can bring back some memories.'

He opened another aquarium at the end of the row, but this time he shoved his arm in, drew out something, and placed it on his forearm. One of the vertical bulbs was close enough to highlight its form on his pale flesh. A spider, dark, hairy, just over an inch long. It crawled slowly up toward his shoulder.

'Does this resemble what your mother found, dear?'

Robin licked her lips. 'Yes.'

'Her name is Gina.' To the spider, now at his collar: 'Good evening, señora.' Then to Robin: 'Would you like to hold her?'

'I guess.'

'A new friend, Gina.' As if understanding, the spider stopped. Moreland lifted it tenderly and placed it in Robin's palm.

It didn't budge, then it lifted its head and seemed to study her. Its mouth moved, an eerie lipsynch.

'You're cute, Gina.'

'We can send one to your mother,' I said. 'For old time's sake.'

She laughed and the spider stopped again. Then, moving with

50

mechanical precision, it walked to the edge of her palm and peered over the edge.

'Nothing down there but floor,' said Robin. 'Guess you'd like to go back to Daddy.'

Moreland removed it, stroked its belly, placed it back in its home, walked on.

Pulling out his doctors' penlight, he pointed out specimens.

Colorless spiders the size of ants. Spiders that *looked* like ants. A delicate green thing with translucent, lime-colored legs. A sticklike Australian *hygropoda*. ('Marvel of energy conservation. The slender build prevents it from overheating.') A huge-fanged arachnid whose brick-red carapace and lemon-yellow abdomen were so vivid they resembled costume jewelry. A Bornean jumper whose big black eyes and hairy face gave it the look of a wise old man.

'Look at this,' he said. 'I'm sure you've never seen a web like this.'

Pointing to a zigzag construction, like crimped paper.

'*Argiope*, an orb spinner. Custom-tailored to attract the bee it loves to eat. That central "X" reflects ultraviolet light in a manner that brings the bees to it. All webs are highly specific, with incredible tensile strength. Many use several types of silk; many are pigmented with an eye toward particular prey. Most are modified daily to adapt to varying circumstances. Some are used as mating beds. All in all, a beautiful deceit.'

His hands flew and his head bobbed. With each sentence, he grew more animated. I knew I was anthropomorphizing, but the creatures seemed excited, too. Emerging from the shadows to show themselves.

Not the panic I'd heard before. Smooth, almost leisurely motions. A dance of mutual interest?

'. . . why I concentrate on predators,' Moreland was saying. 'Why I'm so concerned with keeping them fit.'

A brilliant pink, crablike thing rested atop his bony hand. 'Of course, natural predation is nothing new. Back in nineteen twenty-five *levuana* moths threatened the entire coconut crop on

51

Fiji. Tachinid parasites were brought in and they did the job beautifully. The following year, a particularly voracious destructor scale was done in by the coccinellid beetle. And I'm sure you know gardeners have used ladybugs on aphids for years. I breed them to protect my citrus trees, as a matter of fact.' He pointed to an aquarium that seemed to be red carpeted. A finger against the glass made the carpet move. Thousands of miniature Volkswagens, a ladybug traffic jam. 'So simple, so practical. But the key is keeping them nutritionally robust.'

We moved further up the row and he stopped and breathed deeply. 'If it weren't for public prejudice, *this* beauty and her compatriots could be trained to clear homes of rats.'

Shining the penlight into a dark tank, he revealed something half covered by leaves.

It crawled out slowly and my stomach lurched.

Three inches wide and more than twice that length, legs as thick as pencils, hairs as coarse as boar bristle. It remained inert as the light washed over it. Then it opened its mouth wide – yawning? – and stroked the orifice with clawlike pincers.

As Moreland undid the mesh I found myself stepping back. In went his hand; another pellet dangled.

Unlike the Australian wolf, this one took the food lazily, almost coyly.

'This is Emma and she's spoiled.' One of the spider's legs nudged his finger, rubbing it. '*This* is the tarantula of B-movies, but she's really a *Grammostola*, from the Amazon. In her natural habitat, she eats small birds, lizards, mice, even venomous snakes, which she immobilizes, then crushes. Can you see the advantages for pest control?'

'Why doesn't she use her own venom?' I said.

'Most spider venom can't do harm except to very small prey. You can be sure spoiled Madame Emma wouldn't have the patience to wait for the toxin to take effect. Despite her apparent indolence, she's quite eager when she gets hungry. All wolves are; they got their name because they chase their prey down. I must confess they're my favorite. So bright. They quickly recognize individuals. And they respond to kindness. All tarantulae do. That's why your little *Lycosa* made such a good pet, Robin.'

Robin's eyes remained on the monster.

Moreland said, 'She likes you.'

'I sure hope so.'

'Oh yes, she definitely does. When she doesn't care for someone, she turns her head away – quite the debutante. Not that I bring people in here very often. They need their peace.'

He petted the huge spider, removed his hand, and covered the aquarium. 'Insects and arachnids are magnificent, structurally and functionally. I'm sure you've heard all the clichés about how they're competing with us, will eventually drive us to extinction. Nonsense. Some species become quite successful but many others are fragile and don't survive. For years entomologists have been trying to figure out what leads to success. The popular academic model is *Monomorium pharaonis* – the common ant. Many tenures have been granted on studies of what makes *Monomorium* tick. The conventional wisdom is that there are three important criteria: resistance to dehydration, cooperative colonies with multiple fertile queens, and the ability to relocate the colony quickly and efficiently. But there are insects with those exact traits who fail and others, like the carpenter ant, who've done quite well despite having none of them.'

He shrugged.

'A puzzle.'

He resumed the tour, pointing out walking stick bugs, mantises with serrated jaws, giant Madagascar hissing cockroaches topped with chitinous armor, dung beetles rolling their fetid treasures like giant medicine balls, stout, black carrion beetles ('Imagine what they could do to solve the landfill problems you've got over on the mainland'). Tank after tank of crawling, climbing, darting, crackling, slithering things.

'I stay away from butterflies and moths. Too short-lived and they need flying room to be truly happy. All my guests adapt well to close quarters and many of them achieve amazing longevity – my *Lycosa*'s ten years old, and some spiders live double or triple that amount . . . Am I boring you?'

'No,' said Robin. Her eyes were wide and it didn't seem like fear. 'They're all impressive, but Emma . . . her size.'

'Yes.' He walked quickly to a tank in the last row. Larger than the others, at least twenty gallons. Inside, several rocks formed a cave that shadowed a wood-chip floor.

'My brontosaurus,' he said. 'His ancestors probably *did* coexist with the dinosaurs.'

Pointing to what seemed to be an extension of the rock.

I stayed back, looking, steeling myself for another heart-stopping movement.

Nothing.

Then it was *there*. Without moving. Taking shape before my eyes:

What I'd thought to be a slab of rock was organic. Extending out of the cave.

Flat bodied, segmented. Like a braided brown leather whip.

Seven, eight inches long.

Legs on each segment.

Antennae as thick as cello strings.

Twitching antennae.

I moved further back, waiting for Moreland to play the pellet game.

He put his face up against the glass.

More slithered out of the cave.

At least a foot long. Spikes at the tail end quivered.

Moreland tapped the glass, and several pairs of feet pawed the air.

Then, a lunging motion, a sound like snapping fingers.

'What . . . is it?' said Robin.

'The giant centipede of East Asia. This one stowed away on one of the supply boats last year – Brady's as a matter of fact. I obtain a lot of my specimens that way.'

54

I thought of our ride on *The Madeleine*. Sleeping below deck, wearing only bathing trunks.

'He's significantly more venomous than most spiders,' he said. 'And I haven't named him yet. Haven't quite trained him to love me.'

'How venomous is significant?' I said.

'There's only one recorded fatality. A seven-year-old boy in the Philippines. The most common problem is secondary infection, gangrene. Limb loss can occur.'

'Have you ever been bitten?' I asked.

'Often.' he smiled. 'But only by human children who didn't wish to be vaccinated.'

'Very impressive,' I said, hoping we were through. But another pellet was between Moreland's fingers, and before I knew it another corner of mesh had been drawn back.

No dangling this time. He dropped the food into the centipede's cage from a one-foot height.

The animal ignored it.

Moreland said, 'Have it your way,' and refastened the top.

He headed up the central aisle and we were right behind him.

'That's it. I hope I haven't repulsed you.'

'So your nutritional research is about them,' I said.

'Primarily. They have much to teach us. I also study web patterns, various other things.'

'Fascinating,' said Robin.

I stared at her. She smiled from the corner of her mouth. Her hand had warmed. Her fingers began tickling my palm then dropped. Crawling down my inner wrist.

I tried to pull away but she held me fast. Full smile.

'I'm glad you feel that way, dear,' said Moreland. 'Some people are repelled. No telling.'

Later, in our suite, I tried to extract revenge by coming up behind her as she removed her makeup and lightly scratching her neck.

She squealed and shot to her feet, grabbing for me, and we ended up on the floor.

I got on top and tickled her some more. '*Fascinating?* All of a sudden I'm living with *Spiderwoman*? Shall we begin a new *hobby* when we get back?'

She laughed. 'First thing, let's learn the recipe for those pellets . . . Actually, it *was* fascinating, Alex. Though now that I'm out of there, it's starting to feel creepy again.'

'The *size* of some of them,' I said.

'It wasn't a typical evening, that's for sure.'

'What do you think of our host?'

'Mucho eccentric. But courtly. Sweet.'

'*Dear?*'

'I don't mind that from him. He's from another generation. And despite his age, he's still passionate. I like passion in a man.'

She freed an arm and ran it up mine. 'Coochie-coo!'

I pinioned her. 'Ah, my little *Lycosa, I* am passionate, *too*!'

She reached around. 'So it *seems.*'

I bared my teeth. 'Hold me and crush me, Arachnodella – *liquefy* me!'

'You scoff,' she said, 'but just think what I could do with six more hands.'

8

The next morning swim fins, snorkels, towels, and masks were waiting for us at the breakfast table.

'Jeep's out in front,' said Gladys.

We ate quickly and found the vehicle parked near the fountain. One of those bare-bones, canvas-top models that kids in Beverly Hills and San Marino favor when pretending to be rural. This one was the real thing: clouded plastic windows, rough white paint, no four-figure stereo system.

Just as I started the engine, the Pickers burst out of the house, waving.

'Hitch a ride into town?' Lyman called out. They were in khakis again, with bush hats. Binoculars hung around his neck and a big, yellow smile opened in his beard. 'Seeing as this used to be *our* borrowed vehicle, don't see how you can decently refuse.'

'Wouldn't think of it,' I said.

They climbed in the back.

'Thanks,' said Jo. Her eyes were bloodshot and her mouth looked tight.

From Robin's lap, Spike grumbled.

'Talk about brachycephaly,' said Picker. 'Is he able to breathe?'

'Apparently,' said Robin.

'Where would you like me to drop you?' I said.

'I'll direct you. Terrible shocks on this thing, so watch for potholes.'

I drove through the gates, the Jeep gliding on the fresh blacktop, speeding along the palm-lined road. Soon the ocean came into view, true-blue, unperturbed by breakers. As we neared the harbor, the water swooped toward us; driving toward it was like tumbling into a box of sapphires. I remembered Pam's comment about a big, blue slap in the face.

Picker said, 'Did you notice the rotary phones in the house? Thank God it's not two cans and a string.'

Robin put her hand on my leg and turned back to him, smiling. 'If you don't like it, why stay?'

'We do like it,' said Jo, quickly.

'Excellent question, Ms Craftsperson,' said her husband. 'If it were up to me, we would *not* be staying. If it were up to me we would not be staying within a thouand miles of this *isle*. But Dr Wife's research is urgent. Heard you saw the zoo-ette last night. Rich man's version of firefly in a jar. No systemization. Scientifically, it's a waste of time.'

Spike reared his head and stared. Picker tried to pet him but he backed away and curled up in Robin's lap again.

'Male dogs,' said Picker, 'always go for the *femmes*.'

'That's not true, Ly,' said his wife. 'When I was little we had a miniature schnauzer and he preferred my father.'

'Because, dearest, he'd met your *mother*.'

He didn't mind laughing by himself. 'Hormones. Dogs go after women, men go after bitches.'

He began humming. Spike growled.

'Not a music fan,' said Picker.

58

'On the contrary,' said Robin. 'He likes melody but sour notes drive him wild.'

At Front Street Picker said, 'Go right.'

I drove north, parallel to the waterfront. No boats were in dock and the gas station was still closed, a fuel-rationing schedule posted on the pump. A couple of children rode bikes up and down the waterfront, a woman pushed a baby stroller. Men sat with their feet in the water, and one lay stretched out on the dock, sleeping.

'Where's the airfield?'

'Just keep going.'

We passed the shops. A saltwater tang hung in the air; the temperature was a perfect eighty. The windows of Auntie Mae's Trading Post were filled with faded T-shirts and souvenirs and signs above the entrance advertising postal service and snacks and check-cashing. Next door was the Aruk Market – two open-air stalls of fruit and vegetables. A few women squeezed and bagged the merchandise. As we passed, a couple of them smiled.

The adjoining building was white and shuttered with a Budweiser sign long depleted of neon – SLIM'S ORCHID BAR. Skinny, ragged specimens slouched in front, long-necks in hand. The Chop Suey Palace facade was red with gold lettering, and stone Fu dogs guarded the door. Three outdoor tables were set up in front. A dark-haired man sat at one of them drinking a beer and pushing something around his plate with chopsticks. He looked up but didn't smile.

Next came more stores, all empty, some of the windows boarded, then a freshly whitewashed block structure with several cars parked in front and a sign claiming: MUNICIPAL CENTER. North Beach began as more barrier reef and palms, sand dunes spotted with clumps of white-flowered beach plum. To the right a paved road twisted up the hillside. The stucco houses at the top had been turned to vanilla fudge by the morning sun. I spotted a church steeple and a copper peak below it.

'Is that where the clinic is?'

'Yup,' said Picker. 'Keep going.'

No more outlets appeared as we continued to hug the island's upper shore. No keyhole harbor on the north side, and the water was a little more active. Scattered swimmers stroked lazily and sunbathers offered themselves like bits of cookie batter, but birds outnumbered the human population by far, droves of them searching the water's edge for breakfast.

Front Street ended at a six-slot parking area. To the east was a fifteen-foot wall of untrimmed bamboo. Hand-lettered signs read PRIVATE PROPERTY and < > DEAD END < > NO OUTLET.

Picker leaned forward and pointed over my shoulder at a break in the bamboo. 'In there.'

I turned up a dirt path so narrow that bamboo brushed the sides of the Jeep. A hundred-yard drive brought a house into view.

More Cape Cod than Tahiti, its splintering planks hadn't been white in a long time. The front porch was piled high with junk, and a stovepipe vent spouted from the tar roof.

The property was wide and flat, maybe fifteen acres of red dirt walled by bamboo. The tall plants along the rear border looked puny backed by two hundred feet of sheer black rock.

The western edge of the volcanic range. The mountains hurled shadows so dark and defined they resembled paint splotches.

A smaller house sat fifty feet behind the first. Same construction and condition with a strange-looking doorway – bright white gingerbread molding that didn't fit.

Between the two buildings rested half the fuselage of a propellor plane, its sheet-metal edges sliced cleanly. The rest of the acreage was a grimy sculpture garden peppered with more plane carcasses, heaps of parts, and a few craft left intact.

As I pulled up a man wearing only dirty denim cutoffs came out of the bigger house knuckling his eyes and shoving limp yellow hair out of his face. The younger of the shark butchers we'd seen yesterday.

Picker drew back the Jeep's plastic window flap. 'Where's your father, Skip?'

The man rubbed his eyes again. ''Side.' His voice was thick and hoarse and peevish.

'We're renting a plane from him this morning.'

Skip tried to digest that. Finally he said, 'Yeah.'

'Where's the takeoff strip, Ly?' said Jo.

'Anywhere we please; these aren't jumbo jets. Let's get going.'

The two of them climbed out of the Jeep, and Picker went up to Skip and began talking. Jo hung back, mouth still busy, hands plucking at her vest.

'Poor thing,' said Robin. 'She's scared.'

As I started to turn the Jeep around, another bare-chested man came out of the house. Flowered boxer shorts. The same wide face as Skip but thirty years older. Sloping shoulders and a monumental gut. What was left of his hair was tan-gray. A two-week beard coated a face made for suspicion.

He pointed at us and approached the Jeep.

'You the *doctor's* new guests?' Heavy voice, like his son, but not as sleepy. 'Amalfi.' His tiny blue eyes were bloodshot but alert, his nose so flat it was almost flush. The beard was patchy and ingrown. The skin it didn't cover was a ruin of mounds and puckers.

'What's that you got?'

'French bulldog.'

'Never saw nothing like that in France.'

Robin stroked Spike, and Harry Amalfi drew back his head. 'Having a good time, miss?'

'Very much so.'

'Doctor treating you good?'

She nodded.

'Well, don't count on it.' He licked a finger and held it to the wind. 'Wanna go up in the air, too?'

'No thanks.'

He laughed, started coughing, and spat on the ground. 'Nervous?'

'Maybe some other time.'

'Don't worry, miss, my planes are all greased and tuned. I'm the only way to fly around here.'

61

'Thanks for the offer,' I said, and completed the turn. Amalfi put his hands on his hips and watched us, hitching up his shorts. The Pickers had gone inside the house with Skip.

As I drove away, I looked back and got a closer look at the smaller house. The white molding around the door was a ring of sharks' jaws.

I got on Front Street and drove back toward South Beach. The man with the chopsticks was still in front of the Palace and this time he stood as we approached and waved his arms, as if hailing a cab.

I pulled over and he trotted to the curb. He was around forty, average height and narrow build, with black hair combed down over his forehead and a black mustache too thin to see from a distance. The rest of his face was sallow and smooth, nearly hairless. He wore wide, black Porsche sunglasses, a short-sleeved blue button-down shirt, seersucker pants, and topsiders. Back at his table was a stuffed Filofax next to a platter of noodles-and-something, and three empty Sapporos.

He said 'Tom Creedman' in a tone that said we should recognize the name. When we didn't, he smiled unhappily and clicked his tongue. 'L.A., right?'

'Right.'

'New York,' he said, pointing to his chest. 'Before that, D.C. Used to work in the news business.' He paused, then dropped the names of a TV network and two major news-papers.

'Ah,' I said, as if all was clear. His smile warmed up.

'Care to join me for a beer?'

I looked at Robin. She nodded.

We got out and went over to his table, Spike in tow. He looked at the dog but didn't say anything. Then he stuck his head in the restaurant's open door. 'Jacqui!'

A statuesque woman came out, dishcloth balled in one hand. Her long dark hair was thick and wavy, crowning a full-lipped, golden face. A few lines but young skin. Her age was hard to gauge – anywhere from twenty-five to forty-five.

'The new guests up at Knife Castle,' Creedman told her. 'A round for everyone.'

Jacqui smiled at us. 'Welcome to Aruk.'

'Something to eat?' said Creedman. 'I know it's early but I've found Chinese for breakfast a great pick-me-up. Probably all the soy sauce, gets that blood pressure up.'

'No thanks.'

'Okay,' said Creedman to Jacqui. 'Just beers.'

She left.

'Knife Castle?' said Robin.

'Local nickname for your lodgings. Didn't you know? The Japanese owned this island; Moreland's manse was their head-quarters. They used the locals as slaves to do all the dirty work, imported more. Then MacArthur decided to take over everything from Hawaii to Tokyo and bombed the hell out of them. When the surviving Japanese soldiers were trying to entrench, the slaves grabbed any sharp thing they could find, left their barracks, and finished the job. Knife Island.'

I said, 'Dr Moreland said it was because of the shape.'

Creedman laughed.

'Sounds like you've done some research,' I said.

'Old habits.'

Jacqui brought the beers and he threw a dollar tip at her. She looked irritated and left quickly.

Creedman lifted a bottle but instead of drinking rubbed the top of his hand against the glass.

'What brings you here?' I said.

'Little wind-down from reality. Running with the Beltway movers and shakers too long.'

'You covered politics?'

'In all its sleazy splendor.' He raised his bottle. 'To island torpor.'

The beer was ice-cold and terrific.

Robin took my hand. Creedman stroked the bottle some more,

then the Filofax. 'I'm working on a book. Nonfiction novel –
life-changes, isolation, internal revolution. The island mystique as
it relates to the end-of-the-century zeitgeist.' He smiled. 'Can't
really say more.'

'Sounds interesting,' I said.

'My publisher hopes so. Got them to pay me enough so they'll
break their asses promoting.'

'Is Aruk your only subject or have you been to other islands?'

'Been traveling for over a year. Tahiti, Fiji, Tonga, the Marshalls,
Guam, rest of the Marianas. Came here last year to start writing
because the place is dead, no distractions.'

Taking a long swallow, he gave yet another closed-mouth laugh.
'So how long will you be here?'

'Probably a couple of months,' I said.

'What exactly are you here for?'

'Helping Dr Moreland organize his data.'

'Medical data?'

'Whatever he's got.'

'Any specific diseases you're looking at?'

'No, just a general overview.'

'For a book?'

'If there's a book in it.'

'You're a psychologist, right?'

'Right.'

'So he wants you to analyze his patients psychologically?'

'We're still discussing the specifics.'

He smiled. 'What's that, *your* version of no comment?'

I smiled back. 'My version of we're still discussing the
specifics.'

He turned to Robin. 'And you, Robin? What's your project?'

'I'm on vacation.'

'Good for you.' He faced me again. 'Another beer?'

'No thanks.'

'Good stuff, isn't it? Most of the packaged goods that get over
here are from Japan. Marked up two, three hundred percent –
ultimate revenge.'

He drained his bottle and put it down. 'I'll have you guys over for dinner.'

'Where do you live?' I said.

'Just up there.' He tilted his head toward the hillside. 'Spent a few days up at Moreland's but couldn't take it. Too intense – he is something, isn't he?'

'He seems very dedicated.'

'Easy to be dedicated when you're loaded. Did you know his father was a big San Francisco investment honcho?'

I shook my head.

'*Big* bucks. Mega. Owned a brokerage house, some banks, ranchland all over wine country. Moreland's an only child, inherited the whole kit and k. How else could be keep that place going? Not that it's going to matter. Lost cause.'

'What is?' said Robin.

'Saving this place. I don't want to put a downer on your trip, but Aruk's on the way out. No natural resources, no industry. No industriousness. Talk about your slackers – look at that beach. They don't even have the energy to swim. The smart ones keep leaving. Only a matter of time before it looks like one of those cartoon desert islands, shipwrecked loser under a palm tree.'

'I hope not,' said Robin. 'It's so beautiful.'

Creedman inched closer to her. 'Maybe so, Robin, but let's face it, ebb and flow is part of the life rhythm – that's a theme of my book.'

'How much of the island's decline is due to the Navy's blocking the southern road?' I said.

'Have you been to Stanton?'

'No.'

'If that's a base, I'm a sea anemone. The only incoming flights are to feed and clothe the skeleton crew that runs the place. Letting a few sailors come into town to get drunk and laid doesn't create a viable economy.'

'What happens to Stanton after the island closes down?'

'Who knows? Maybe the Navy will sell the island. Or maybe they'll just let it sit here.'

'The base has no strategic value?'

'Not since the Cold War ended. Main thing is there's no constituency here. Seagulls don't vote.'

'So you don't think the Navy's intentionally shutting the island down?'

'Who told you that?'

'A guest up at the estate suggested it.'

'Dr Picker.' He chuckled. 'Kind of an asshole, isn't he? Couple more weeks in the sun, he'll be spotting Amelia Earhart skinnydipping in the lagoon with Judge Crater. Sure you don't want another?'

I shook my head.

'Actually,' said Robin, petting Spike, 'we were going to do some snorkeling.'

We stood and I tried to put money on the table.

'On me,' said Creedman. 'How often do I get to have an intelligent conversation. And your pooch is okay, too. Didn't pee on me.'

He walked us back to the Jeep.

'I like to cook. Have you up for dinner sometime.'

We got in the car. He leaned into Robin's window and took off his sunglasses. His eyes were small and very dark, scanning slowly.

'There was a good reason for blockading the south road,' he said. 'Public safety.'

'Disease control?' I said.

'If you consider murder a disease. It happened half a year ago. Local girl found on the beach, right where you're headed. Raped and mangled pretty badly. The details never came out. Moreland can give them to you – he did the autopsy. Villagers were sure the murderer was some sailor because that kind of thing just doesn't happen here, right? At least not since they massacred the Japanese.' He chuckled. 'Some of the young bloods worked themselves up and started hiking up to Stanton for a tête-à-tête with Captain Ewing. Navy guards stopped them, a little civil *unrest* resulted. Soon after, the Navy started building that blockade.'

He shrugged. 'Sorry to darken your day, but one thing I've learned: the only real escape is in your head.'

Putting his shades back on, he walked back to his table, scooped up his Filofax, and went inside the restaurant.

I started up the Jeep, shifted into first, and pulled away.

Just as I shifted into second, the sound hit – a giant paper bag being popped. Then a swirling black plume spiraled up from behind the volcano tips, rising high above them, inking the perfect sky.

9

Spike's neck was bow-tight. He growled and sniffed the air and began to bark. The people on the dock pointed up at the explosion.

Robin's hand was clamped around my wrist.

'Navy maneuvers?' I said.

'At a nonfunctional base?'

I reversed the jeep quickly. As I passed the Chop Suey Palace, Jacqui stepped out, still holding her dishtowel. Her curiosity and fear stayed in my head as I sped back to the airfield.

Harry Amalfi stood near his house, looking dazed. Studying the black smoke as if it bore a message.

We drove up right behind him and got out, but he didn't move. Shouts made all three of us pivot.

Skip Amalfi and the other shark carver were running toward us. The older man wore bathing trunks too long for his stocky legs. Harry Amalfi said, 'It's a good craft.'

'Was,' said Skip, Amalfi's companion. His voice was soft, his eyes rainwater gray, very close-set.

Skip said, 'Maybe he fucked up and flooded the engine or something, Dad.'

Amalfi turned back to the sky. The smoke was thinning and curling.

The other man shaded his eyes and looked upward too. 'Looks like it might have gone down right over Stanton.'

'Probably,' said Skip. 'Probably right on the fucking *tarmac.*'

His father started to say something, then shuffled back toward his front porch.

'Want me to call over there?' said Skip. 'See if it went down there?'

Amalfi didn't answer. Pulling a bandana out of his pocket, he wiped his face and kept trudging.

'Shit deal,' said Skip's companion. The gray eyes washed over Robin, then checked to see if I was watching. I was. He nodded.

'Major shit,' said Skip.

'He probably did flood it.'

Skip turned to us. 'Dumb fuck said he knew how to fly. Did he?'

'Just met him yesterday,' I said.

He shook his head disgustedly.

'Probably got it up there and flooded it first thing,' said the gray-eyed man, pushing his hand through wild, curly hair.

'His poor wife,' said Robin. 'She didn't want to go.'

'Asshole said he knew what he was doing,' said Skip. 'You guys come *back* here for something?'

We returned to the Jeep and I drove toward the bamboo thatch. Just as I was about to turn onto the dirt path, Jo Picker came running out, hatless, her big purse flopping against her thigh.

Her mouth was open and her eyes were wide and blank. She kept coming toward us and I jammed the brakes. Slapping her hands on the Jeep's hood, she stared at us through the windshield.

69

Robin jumped out and embraced her. Spike wanted to jump out but I restrained him. He hadn't relaxed since the explosion.

All that remained in the sky were gray wisps.

Jo said, 'No, oh God, no!' She struggled away from Robin and I saw her mouth contort.

Off in the distance, Skip and the gray-eyed man watched.

We finally got her in the Jeep and drove home. She cried softly till we got through the big, open gates and close to the house. Then: 'We had a – I was planning to *go*, but I got scared!'

Ben was already outside, KiKo on his shoulder, along with Gladys and a crew of men in work clothes. This close, I could still see hints of smoke. The noise would have been louder up here.

Jo had stopped crying and looked stunned. Robin helped ease her out of the Jeep, and she and Gladys walked her into the house.

Ben said, 'So it *was* him. I wasn't sure. He couldn't have been up long.'

'Not long at all.'

'Did you see the plane?'

'We saw a bunch of them when we dropped him off.'

'Junk,' he said. 'Whole thing was stupid. No point.'

'Amalfi's son said he might have come down on the base.'

'Or darn close to it. Forget about retrieving the body. 'Course, the alternative's dealing with the Navy. I'm not sure which is worse.'

He turned to the house. 'Why didn't she go up with him? Cold feet?'

I nodded.

'Well, she was the smart one,' he said. 'You try to tell people . . . Dr Bill talked to Picker this morning. Picker just got rude.'

'Does Dr Bill know yet?' said Robin.

He nodded. 'I called him at the clinic. He's on his way up.'

'My first thought was some sort of military maneuver,' I said. 'Does the Navy ever shoot anything in the air?'

'The only things that fly in and out of there are big transports. If one of those went down, you'd think the volcano had erupted.'

A white subcompact came barreling through the gates and stopped short, scattering gravel. POLICE was stenciled in blue on the door. Pam Moreland was in the front passenger seat. A man was driving.

They both got out. Pam looked frightened. The man was good-looking, in his late twenties and huge – six four, two fifty, with nose-tackle shoulders and enormous hands. His skin was bronze with islander features, but his hair was light brown and his eyes pale hazel.

He had on a short-sleeved sky-blue shirt and razor-creased blue pants over military lace-ups. A silver badge was pinned to the breast pocket, but he had no club or gun. Pam matched his stride.

'This is terrible,' she said.

The big man clasped Ben's hand. 'Hey,' he said in a deep voice.

Ben said, 'Hey, Dennis, some mess. Folks, meet Dennis Laurent, our chief of police.'

Laurent shook both our hands, noticed Spike and suppressed a smile. His gaze was intense.

'Anyone know how many people were in the plane?' he said.

'Just Lyman Picker,' I said. 'His wife started to go but changed her mind. She's in the house.'

He shook his head. 'Can't remember anything like this.'

'Never happened,' said Ben. 'Because no one goes up in Harry's heaps. You figure it crashed on Stanton?'

'Either there or right near the eastern border. I called Ewing, got put on hold. Finally his aide says he's busy, will get back to me.'

'Busy,' said Ben with scorn.

Laurent said, 'The wife's probably going to want details.' He put on mirrored sunglasses and looked around some more. 'Guess she's in no shape now.'

71

'She's in shock,' said Robin.

'Yeah,' said Laurent. 'Let me know if she wants to talk to me or if there's anything I can do for her. Weren't they supposed to be leaving soon?'

'In a week or so,' said Pam. 'She's just about finished her work.'

Laurent nodded. 'Weather research. She came into the station a couple of weeks ago with this little laptop computer, wanting to know if we kept storm records. I told her we really never got the big ones so we didn't. Any idea why her husband went up in the first place?'

'To take pictures of the jungle,' said Ben. 'Prove to his colleagues he'd been here.'

'He was a scientist, too, right?'

'Botanist.'

'So what was he looking at, the banyans?'

'He wasn't really working,' said Pam. 'Told us he was bored. Tagging along after her probably made him feel like a third foot. Maybe he just wanted to do some flying.'

Laurent digested that. 'Well, too bad he picked this time and place . . . Harry probably should have been closed down, but like you said, no one used him. I hope the wife doesn't think we're going to be able to do any big FAA-type investigation. If he went down in the jungle, we'll be lucky to get the body.'

He shook his head again. Pam had been standing close to him and she moved nearer. A downward flick of a hazel eye acknowledged her presence. Laurent put his hands in his pockets and stretched the fabric with his fists.

Then he looked at the Jeep, the diving gear still piled on the backseat. 'Someone snorkeling?'

'We were on our way when it happened,' said Robin.

'We were vaccinating,' said Pam.

'How'd the kids at the clinic react?' I said.

'They don't know exactly what happened yet,' she said. 'Some of them looked up when they heard the noise, but their minds

72

were on their shots. We just kept the line going for a while and then broke for a snack.'

'How many shots did you get through?' said Ben.

'About half. We were going to finish this afternoon, but I guess not.'

'Planning to dive at South Beach lagoon?' Laurent asked us.

'Yes,' said Robin.

'It's beautiful there,' he said. 'Give it another go when you're ready. Life generally goes smoothly here.'

Pam walked him back to his car and stayed to talk after he got behind the wheel.

Ben called out KiKo's name, and the monkey and Spike followed us into the house. Cheryl was washing the front room's big windows and didn't turn to acknowledge us. Except for the hiss of the glass-cleaner spray, the interior was silent.

Robin said, 'I think I'll go up and see how Jo's doing.'

She hurried up the stairs.

'Something to drink?' Ben asked me.

'No, thanks. We had a couple of beers in town. A guy named Creedman was buying.'

'Oh?' He stared straight ahead. 'Where'd he snag you, front of the Palace?'

'Does he make a habit of snagging people there?'

'That's his spot. I figured he'd go for you, being outsiders and all that. He used to live here for a while.'

'He mentioned that.'

'Did he also mention he was asked to leave?'

'No. He said it was too intense an environment for him.'

'Intense? I guess you could say that.'

He turned and looked me in the eye. 'The thing you need to understand is that Dr Bill is the most hospitable person you'll ever meet. Anyone visits the island, they get an invite. That's how the Pickers ended up here, and after meeting them, you can see what a patient man Dr Bill is. Creedman was also extended hospitality.

73

He was up here for only three days when we found him snooping around.'

'Snooping where?'

'Dr Bill's office. I caught him red-handed. Not that there's anything to hide, but patient info's confidential. Except, of course, for something scientific like you and Dr Bill are doing. Some thanks for hospitality, huh?'

'Did he have an excuse?'

'Nope.' His jaw bunched the way it had when Picker had asked him to serve drinks, and he pushed his aviators up his nose. 'He tried to laugh it off. Said he was taking a walk and had just wandered in looking for something to read. Except the books were in the back room and he was in the front, so give me a break. I called him on it and he told me to screw myself. Then he complained to Dr Bill that I'd harassed him. Dr Bill might have tolerated the snooping, but he didn't appreciate Creedman badmouthing me. Did he badmouth us some more?'

'Not really,' I said. 'But he did say the reason the southern road was blockaded was because of a murder half a year ago. A local girl killed on the beach, and passions toward the Navy got high.'

'The guy makes like he's an ace reporter – probably told you he was a media hotshot, right? Truth is he was strictly small-time. And keep him away from Ms Castagna. He thinks he's God's gift to women.'

'So I noticed. But she can handle herself.'

'My wife can, too, but he still annoyed her. Right after I kicked him out. Came up to her in the market, making small talk, offering to carry her bags. Real subtle.'

He shoved his glasses harder. 'Did you meet the owner of the Palace, a tall woman named Jacqui?'

I nodded.

'He came on to *her*, too, till he found out she was Chief Laurent's mother.'

'She looks way too young.'

'She's in her forties, had Dennis when she was a teenager. She and Dennis are good people. He was a couple of grades

74

behind me. Jacqui's half islander, half Cauc, originally from Saipan. Dennis's dad was a French sea captain, used to run cargo boats between the bigger islands, died at sea just before Dennis was born. She raised him right. Anyway, do what you want, but in my humble opinion Creedman's someone to avoid. He just hangs out all day, acting superior.'

'He told us he was working on a book.'

'Maybe a book on beer.' His laugh was merciless.

'Speaking of unwanted attention,' I said, 'the guy who was working on the shark with Skip Amalfi seemed to notice Robin too. Any potential problems there?'

'That's Anders Haygood. He's a bit of a lowlife, but no problems with him so far. Came over a year ago, mostly keeps to himself. Lives in back of Harry's place.'

'Working for Harry?'

'Odd jobs now and then. Once in a while someone brings them an appliance to fix or a car to tune. Basically, he and Skip are beach bums and Harry's an old bum.'

He laughed. 'I'm some Chamber of Commerce, huh? By now you probably think Aruk's nothing but lowlife. But between Skip and Harry and Haygood and Creedman, you've just about exhausted the list. Everyone else is great. You'll end up having a great time.'

10

'He wasn't Mr Charm,' said Robin, 'but to go like that . . .'
We were up in the sitting room of our suite. No sounds came through the wall bordering Jo Picker's room.

'How's Jo?' I said.

'Wiped out. She decided to call his family. I left her trying to get a phone connection . . . I know it's trite, but one moment you're talking to someone, the next they're gone.'

She put her head on my chest and I traced her jawline.

'How're you doing?' I said.

'With what?'

'Vacation.'

She laughed. 'Is that what it is? No, I'm fine. Assuming we've used up all the bad vibes, nothing but sunshine and sweetness lies ahead.'

'Ben assures me we've exhausted the island's supply of miscreants.'

I told her about Creedman's snooping, his hitting on Jacqui and Claire Romero.

'I'm not surprised,' she said. 'When we were sitting there he put his hand on my knee.'

'What!'

'It's okay, honey, I handled it.'

'I didn't see a thing!'

'It happened right at the beginning, when Jacqui came out to take our order. You looked up for a second and he made his move. No big deal – I ended it.'

'How?'

'Pinched the top of his hand.' She grinned. 'Hard. With my nails.'

'He didn't react,' I said.

'Nope, just kept on talking and cooled the hand on his beer bottle.'

I remembered that. 'Bastard.'

'Forget it, Alex. I know the type. He won't try it again.'

'Someone else noticed you,' I said. 'At the airfield. Skip Amalfi's buddy, that wild-haired guy. Now that I think about it, both he and Skip were probably ogling you the minute we stepped off the boat.'

'Probably a woman shortage. Don't worry, I'll stick close to home. Work on my pinching.'

'Don't you think Creedman's behavior is pretty risky for a small place like this? You should have seen Ben's face when he talked about Creedman coming on to his wife.'

'Maybe that's his kick,' she said. 'That stupid thrill-of-the-hunt thing. Or maybe Aruk's such a peaceful place the locals are able to laugh him off as a fool.'

'It certainly doesn't seem to be high-crime. The police chief's unarmed.'

'I noticed that. Probably why everyone was so sure the murderer was a sailor.'

'Does the murder bother you?'

'I didn't love hearing about it, but one homicide a year is heaven compared to L.A., right?'

'According to Ben it wasn't the reason for the blockade.'

'What was?'

I thought back. 'He didn't say.'

'He's an interesting fellow,' she said.

'In what way?'

'Nice, but a bit . . . hard, don't you think? Like the way he reacted to the crash. Angry at Picker, no sympathy.'

'Picker gave him a hard time,' I said. 'But you're right, it was cold. Maybe it's his training as a nurse. Struggling to save people and then watching someone take what he thought was a stupid risk. Or maybe he's just one of those perfectionists incapable of suffering fools. He seems awfully meticulous. Proprietary about Moreland and Aruk, too. Now Moreland's getting old and Aruk's having problems, so he could be under stress.'

'Could be,' she said. 'Aruk's definitely having problems. All those businesses boarded up, and did you see the gas ration sign in town? How do you think people make a living?'

'In his letters, Moreland said fishing and some crafts. But I haven't seen much sign of either. Ben's educated, could live anywhere, so perhaps he stays here because of some special commitment.'

'Yes, it must be hard for him.' She snuggled closer. 'It *is* lovely, though. Look at those mountains.'

'Want to try diving tomorrow?'

'Maybe.' She closed her eyes.

'I'd like everything to go smoothly for you,' I said.

'Don't worry. I'll have a great time.'

'How's your wrist?'

She laughed. 'Much better. And I pledge to go to bed on time and drink my milk.'

'I know, I know.'

'It's okay, honey. You like to take care of me.'

'It's not just that. For some reason, after all these years, I still feel I need to court you.'

'I know that, too,' she said softly, and slipped her hand under my shirt.

The phone woke us up.

Moreland said, 'Oh . . . were you sleeping? I'm terribly sorry.'

'No problem,' I said. 'What's up?'

'Picker's accident – I just wanted to make sure you were all right.'

'It was a shock but we're fine.'

'I tried to warn him . . . I want to reassure you that it was a freak event. The last crash we had was in sixty-three, when a military transport went down over the water. *Nothing* since. I just feel terrible that your welcome has been interrupted by something like this.'

'Don't worry about it, Bill.'

'I dropped in on Mrs Picker, gave her some brandy. She's resting peacefully.'

'Good.'

'All right then, Alex. Sorry again for disturbing your rest.' He paused. 'We can start working whenever you're ready. Just give me a call downstairs.'

Robin sat up and yawned. 'Who is it?'

I covered the phone. 'Bill. Do you mind if I work a bit?'

She shook her head. 'I'm going to get up, too.'

'I've got some time right now,' I told Moreland.

'Well then,' he said, 'I could show you your office. Come down when you're ready. I'll be waiting.'

We found him sitting in an overstuffed chair near a picture window, drinking orange juice. His legs looked so thin they seemed to fold rather than cross. He wore the same type of plain white shirt. This time the baggy pants were gray. The chained glasses rested low on his nose. He stood, closed his book and put it down. Leather-bound copy of Flaubert's *L'Éducation sentimentale*.

'Have you read him, son?'

'Just *Madame Bovary*, years ago.'

'A great realistic novel,' he said. 'Flaubert was excoriated for *being* realistic.' Bending slowly, he petted Spike. 'I've set up a little run for this fellow, in a shaded area behind the rose garden. That is, if you feel comfortable leaving him alone.'

'Is there a problem with his coming along?'

'Not at all. No zoo this morning. Come, let me show you the smaller library.'

He led us through the dining room, pale blue with Chippendale furniture.

'We rarely dine here,' he said. 'We go outside whenever we can.'

The former silver room was on the other side of a mahogany door. He opened it halfway. Salmon moiré walls, two dark bookcases, carved moldings, crystal lamps. Dried flowers on the verge of disintegration sprouted from a huge *famille verte* vase.

He closed the door. 'As I said, you'll probably have little use for it.'

We continued through a waxed-pine breakfast room, yellow pantry, industrial kitchen, past wall-freezers and out the rear door, ending on one of the rock paths. The closest bungalow was the same light brown as the main house, the rooftiles replaced with asphalt shingles.

Inside the bungalow was a small, cool room paneled beautifully with red-gold koa and set up with an old but flawless walnut desk topped by a leather blotter, a sterling silver inkwell, and an electric typewriter.

Another ceiling fan, desultory rotations. On the opposite wall was a brown couch and matching armchair, some tables and lamps. A carved Japanese motif ran along the top of the paneling. Seashells and corals rested on high shelves. Below hung more of Mrs Moreland's watercolors.

Two small, open windows let in the breeze and offered a long view of the entry to the estate. The spray from the fountain sparkled like Tivoli lights. Between Spike's heavy breathing, more of that same narcotic silence.

'Very nice,' I said.

Behind the desk was a door that Moreland opened, revealing a much larger room with four walls of ceiling-high bookcases.

The floor was crowded with high stacks of cardboard cartons – brown columns rising nearly to the ceiling.

Hundreds of boxes, nearly filling the space, randomly separated by narrow aisles.

Moreland shrugged apologetically. 'As you can see, I've been waiting for you.'

I laughed, as much at his flamingo awkwardness as at the enormity of the task.

'It's shameful, Alex. I won't insult you by making excuses. I can't tell you how many times I've sat down to figure out some system of classification only to get overwhelmed and give up before I began.'

'Is it alphabetized?'

He rubbed one sandal against his shin, a curiously boyish gesture. 'After my first few years in practice, I tried to alphabetize them. Repeated the process every few years. But somewhat . . . haphazardly. All in all, there are probably a dozen or so independently alphabetized series.' He threw up his hands. 'Why pretend – it's virtually random. But at least my handwriting's not bad for a doctor.'

Robin grinned and I knew she was thinking of my scrawl.

'I don't expect miracles,' said Moreland. 'Skim, peruse, whatever, tell me if anything jumps out at you. I've always tried to include psychological and social data . . . Now permit me to show you your atelier, dear.'

The adjoining bungalow was identical, but the interior walls were painted white. More old but well-maintained furniture, a drafting table and stool, easels, a flat file. Disposable pallets still wrapped in plastic sat atop the file, along with trays of oil-paint tubes, acrylics, and watercolors. Ink bottles, pens, charcoal sticks, brushes in every shape and size. Everything brand-new. The price tag on a brush was from an artists' supply store in Honolulu.

Off to one side was a table full of shiny things.

'Shell,' said Moreland. 'Cowry, abalone, mother of pearl. Some hardwood remnants as well. And carving tools. I bought them from an old man whose specialties were USNC insignia and leaping dolphins. Back when there was a trinket business.'

Robin picked up a small handsaw. 'Good quality.'

'This was Barbara – my wife's special place. I know you're not carving right now, but Alex told me how gifted you were, so I thought you might like to . . .'

He trailed off and rubbed his hands together.

'I'd love to,' said Robin.

'Only when your hand permits, of course. It's too bad you didn't get a chance to swim.'

'We'll try again.'

'Good, good . . . Would you like to stay here and look around, dear? Or do you prefer to be there as Alex discovers how truly disordered I am?'

It was as gracious a way as any to ask for privacy.

'There's plenty here to keep me busy, Bill. Pick me up when you're done, Alex.'

'And you?' Moreland said to Spike.

'Watch,' I said. Walking to the door, I said, 'Come, Spike.' The dog ran immediately to Robin and flopped down at her feet.

Moreland laughed. 'Impeccable taste.'

When we were outside, he said, 'What a lovely girl. You're lucky – but I suppose you hear that all the time. It's nice to have someone in Barbara's studio after all these years.'

We began walking. 'How long has it been?'

'Thirty years this spring.'

A few steps later: 'She drowned. Not here. Hawaii. She'd gone there for a vacation. I was busy with patients. She went out for an early-morning dip on Waikiki Beach. She was a strong swimmer, but got caught up in a riptide.'

He stopped, fished in his pocket, drew out a battered eelskin wallet and extricated a small photo.

The black-haired woman from the mantel portrait, standing alone on a beach, wearing a black one-piece bathing suit. Hair shorter than in the painting, pinned back severely. She looked no older than thirty. Moreland would have been at least forty.

The snapshot was faded: gray sand, the sky an insipid aqua, the woman's flesh nearly dead-white. The ocean that had claimed her was a thin line of foam.

She had a beautiful figure and smiled prettily but her pose – legs together, arms at her side – had a tired, almost resigned quality.

Moreland blinked several times.

I gave him back the snapshot.

'Why don't we work our way downward,' he said, lifting a box from the top of an outer column, carrying it into the office, and placing it on the floor between the couch and the armchair.

The carton was taped shut. He cut the tape with a Swiss Army knife and pulled out several blue folders. Putting on his glasses, he read one.

'Of all things . . .'

Handing me the folder, he said, 'This one isn't from Aruk, but it was a case of mine.'

Inside were stiff, yellowed papers filled with elegant, indigo, fountain-penned writing that I recognized from the card he'd left on the bed. Forty-year-old medical records of a man named 'Samuel H.'

'You don't use full names?' I said.

'Generally, I do but this was . . . different.'

I read. Samuel H. had presented with gastric complaints and thyroid problems that Moreland had treated with synthetic hormones and words of reassurance for eleven months. A month later, several small benign nerve tumors were discovered and Moreland raised the possibility of travel to Guam for evaluation and surgery. Samuel H. was unsure, but before he could decide, his health deteriorated further: fatigue, bruising, hair loss, bleeding lips and gums. Blood tests showed a precipitous drop in red blood cells accompanied by a sharp rise in white cells. Leukemia. The patient 'expired' seven months later, Moreland signing the certificate and directing the remains to a mortuary in a place called Rongelap. I asked where that was.

'The Marshall Islands.'

'Isn't that clear across the Pacific?'

'I was stationed there after Korea. The Navy sent me all over the region.'

I closed the chart.

'Any thoughts?' he said.

'All those symptoms could be due to radiation poisoning. Is Rongelap near Bikini atoll?'

'So you know about Bikini.'

'Just in general terms,' I said. 'The government conducted nuclear tests there after World War II, the winds shifted and polluted some neighboring islands.'

'Twenty-three blasts,' he said. 'Between nineteen forty-six and nineteen fifty-eight. One hundred billion *dollars* worth of tests. The first few were A-bombs – dropped on old fleets captured from the Japanese. Then they got confident and started detonating things underwater. The big one was Bravo in fifty-four. The world's first hydrogen bomb, but your average American has never heard of it. Isn't that amazing?'

I nodded, not amazed at all.

'It broke the dawn with a seventy-five-thousand-foot mushroom cloud, son. The dust blanketed several of the atolls – Kongerik and Utirik and Rongelap. The children thought it was great fun, a new kind of rain. They played with the dust, tasted it.'

He got up, walked to the window and braced himself on the sill.

'Shifting winds,' he said. 'I believed that, too – I was a loyal officer. It wasn't till years later that the truth came out. The winds had been blowing east steadily for days before the test. Steadily and predictably. There *was* no surprise. The Air Force warned its own personnel so they could evacuate, but not the islanders. Human guinea pigs.'

His hands were balled.

'It didn't take long for the problems to emerge. Leukemias, lymphomas, thyroid disorders, autoimmune diseases. And, of

84

course, birth defects: retardation, anencephaly, limbless babies – we called them "jellyfish."'

He sat down and gave a terrible laugh. 'We *compensated* the poor devils. Twenty-five thousand dollars a victim. Some government accountant's appraisal of the value of a life. One hundred and forty-eight checks totaling one million two hundred and thirty-seven thousand dollars. One hundred-thousandth the cost of the blasts.'

He sat back down and placed his hands on bony knees. His high forehead was as white and moist as a freshly boiled egg.

'I took part in the compensation program. Someone upstairs thought it a good use of my training. We did it at night, going from island to island in small motorboats. Pulling up to the shore, calling the people out with bullhorns, then handing them their checks and sailing off.'

He shook his head. 'Twenty-five thousand dollars per life. An actuarial triumph.' Removing his glasses, he rubbed his eyes. 'After I figured out what the blast had done, I put in for extended stay and tried to do what I could for the people. Which wasn't much . . . Samuel was a nice man. A very fine carpenter.'

'How'd the people react to being paid?' I said.

'The more perceptive among them were angry, frightened. But many were grateful. The United States extending a helping hand.'

He put his glasses back on.

'Well, let's crack another box. Hopefully something a bit more routine.'

'At least you tried to help them,' I said.

'Sticking around helped me more than them, son. Till then I thought medicine boiled down to diagnosis, dosage, and incision. Encountering my own impotence taught me it was much more. And less. You worked in pediatric oncology, you understand.'

'By the time I got involved, cancer was no longer a death sentence. I saw enough cures to keep me from feeling like an undertaker.'

'Yes,' he said. 'That's wonderful. Still, you saw the misery, too.

Your articles on pain control – scientific yet compassionate. I read them all. Read between the lines. It's one of the reasons I felt you were someone who would understand.'

'Understand what, Bill?'

'Why a crazy old man suddenly wants to organize his life.'

The other cases *were* routine and he seemed to tire. As I scanned the chart of a woman with diabetes, he said, 'I'll leave you alone. Don't try to do too much, enjoy the rest of the day.'

He stood and headed for the door.

'I wanted to ask you something, Bill.'

'Yes?'

'I met Tom Creedman in the village this morning. He mentioned something about a murder a half year ago and some social unrest that led to the blockade.'

He leaned against the jamb. 'What else did he have to say?'

'That was it. Ben told me he lived here, caused some problems.'

'Oh, indeed.'

I pointed to the rear storage room. 'Was that where Ben caught him snooping?'

'No,' he said. 'That was *my* office. Two bungalows down. Creedman claimed he'd wandered in and was on his way out when Ben found him. I might have let it pass, but he insulted Ben. That kind of thing isn't tolerated around here. I ordered him off the grounds. He delights in accentuating the negative about me and Aruk.'

'He called this place Knife Castle.'

'And probably told you that yarn about the slaves butchering every last Japanese.'

'It never happened?'

'Allied bombs killed the vast majority of the Japanese soldiers. Three days of constant bombardment. On the third night, the Americans radioed victory and some of the forced workers left the barracks and came up here to loot – understandable, after what they'd been put through. They encountered a few survivors

86

and there was some hand-to-hand fighting. The Japanese were outnumbered. Mr Creedman calls himself a journalist, but he seems attracted to fiction – not that there's that much difference, nowadays, I suppose.'

'He also said that you did the autopsy on the murder victim. Do you agree with the theory that it was a sailor?'

He sucked in breath. 'I'm growing a bit concerned, Alex.'

'About what?'

'Picker's accident, and now this. You certainly can't be faulted for seeing Aruk as a terrible place, but it's not. Yes, the murder was terrible, but it was the first we'd had in many years. And the only one of its type I remember in over three decades.'

'What type is that?'

He pressed his hands together, clapped them silently and looked up at the ceiling fan, as if counting rotations.

Suddenly, he opened the door and stepped out. 'I'll be right back.'

11

The folder he returned with was brown with a white paper label.

ARUK POLICE

INVEST: D. LAURENT.

CASE NO. 00345

The first four pages were a typed report composed by the police chief in slightly clearer-than-usual cop prose.

The body of a twenty-four-year-old woman named AnneMarie Valdos had been found at three A.M. on South Beach by two crab fishermen, wedged between rocks overlooking a tide pool. The amount of blood indicated violence at the site.

Other fishermen had been at that exact spot at nine P.M., allowing Laurent to narrow the time the corpse had lain there.

During that period, birds and scavengers had done their work, but Laurent, referring to a conversation with 'Dr W. W. Moreland,

M.D.' had been able to distinguish the 'external shredding and mostly superficial laceration from multiple, deep knife wounds leading to exsanguination and death.'

The victim had lived on Aruk for two years, coming over from Saipan to work as a cocktail waitress at Slim's but losing that job after three months due to chronic intoxication and absenteeism. Her lodgings had been a rented room in the village and she was two months in arrears. She'd been known to socialize with Navy men. The only surviving relative was an alcoholic mother in Guam who had no money to travel or to pay for burial.

Questioning the villagers produced no witnesses or leads but did elicit the repeated claim that the viciousness of the crime proved the perpetrator was a sailor.

Laurent's final paragraph read: *'Investigating officer has repeatedly attempted to communicate with Captain E. Ewing, Commanding Officer of Stanton USN Base, for possible questioning of enlisted men re: this crime, but has been unable to make contact.'*

I started to turn the page.

'You might not want to,' said Moreland. 'Photographs.'

I thought about it and flipped anyway.

The shots weren't any worse than some of the ones Milo had shown me, which is to say they'd be additions to my nightmare file.

I moved past them to Moreland's report.

He'd been thorough, inspecting, dissecting, enumerating each wound.

At least fifty-three wounds, additional ones possibly obscured by scavenger bites.

The killing blow probably a neck slash.

Contrary to what Creedman had said, no sexual penetration.

All the cuts probably inflicted by the same weapon, a very sharp, unserrated blade.

The next page was written out in Moreland's elegant longhand:

Dennis: You may want to keep this private. WWM

Postmortem mutilation

A. The left leg has been severed completely at the patellar joint.

B. The left femur has been broken discretely in three places, with a considerable quantity of bone marrow removed.

C. A deep 26 cm. longitudinal upward slashing wound extends from the pubic region to the sternum.

D. Disembowelment has taken place, with the small and large intestines piled atop the chest region, obscuring both breasts. The breasts are intact. (Extensive crustaceal invasion of these tissues exists, as well.)

E. Both kidneys and the liver have been removed and are not present.

F. Decapitation has occurred between the third and fourth cervical vertebrae with the head left next to the left side of the body at a distance of 11 centimeters.

G. A deep, transverse wound of the neck is visible both above and below the decapitation line. Probable downward stroke from left ear across the neck indicates right-handed person slashing from the back. The trachea and jugular vein have been severed.

H. Significant enlargement of the foramen magnum has been accomplished, possibly with some kind of grasping/crushing instrument. Portions of the occipital skull have been shattered, probably by blunt force.

I. Both cerebral hemispheres have been removed, with the cerebellum and lower brain left intact.

I shut the file and took a slow breath, trying to settle my stomach.

'I'm sorry,' said Moreland, 'but I want you to see that I'm not concealing anything from you.'

'The killer was never caught?'

'Unfortunately not.'

'And the Navy man theory?'

He blinked and fidgeted with his glasses. 'In all the years I've lived here, the islanders have never engaged in serious violence, let alone this. I suppose it could have been one of the cargo boat deckhands, though I've come to know most of them and they're decent chaps. And Dennis did question them. Unlike the sailors.'

Remembering Laurent's remark about not having his call to Stanton returned, I said, 'He never got access to the base?'

'No, he didn't.'

'Why do you still have the file? Is the investigation ongoing?'

'Dennis thought I might come up with something if I studied it for a while. I haven't. Any suggestions?'

'It's not your typical sadistic murder,' I said. 'No rape – though Creedman said there was.'

'You see,' he said. 'The man has no credibility.'

'No positioning of the body, either. Mutilation, but of the head and the back and the legs, not the genitalia or the breasts. Then there's the multiple organ theft – coring out the femur to remove the marrow. It sounds ghoulish – almost ritualistic.'

He smiled sourly. 'The kind of thing some primitive *native* would do?'

'I was thinking more of a satanic rite . . . Were any satanic symbols left behind?'

'None that we found.'

'*Does* the killing bear the mark of some sort of ritual?'

He rubbed his bald head, took a thick, black fountain pen out of his pocket, uncapped it and inspected the nub.

'What do you know about cannibalism, Alex?'

'Mercifully little.'

'Conducting the autopsy brought to mind things I'd heard about when I was stationed in Melanesia back in the fifties.'

He put the pen back, uncrossed his leg, and rubbed a bony knee.

'The sad truth is, from an historical perspective, eating human flesh isn't a cultural aberration. On the contrary, it's culturally entrenched. And I don't mean just the so-called primitive continents. Old Teuton had its *menschenfressers*; there's a grotto in Chavaux in France, on the banks of the Meuse, where archaeologists found heaps of hollowed-out human leg and arm bones – your early Gallic gourmets. The ancient Romans and Greeks and Egyptians consumed each other with glee, and certain Caledonian tribes wandered the Scottish countryside for centuries turning shepherds into two-legged supper.'

He started to sit back, then grimaced violently.

'Are you all right?' I said.

'Fine, fine.' He touched his neck. 'A crick – slept the wrong way . . . Where was I – ah, yes, patterns of anthropophagy. The most common motive, believe it or not, is *nutrition* – the quest for protein in marginal societies. However, when alternative sources are provided, sometimes the preference endures: "tender as dead man" was once high praise among the old tribes of Fiji. Cannibalism can also be a military tactic or part of a spiritual quest: ingesting one's own ancestors in order to incorporate their benevolent spirits. Or a combination of the two: eating the enemy's brain grants wisdom; his heart, courage; and so on. But despite all this diversity, there are fairly consistent procedural *patterns*: – decapitation, removal of vital organs, shattering the long bones for marrow. As the Bible says, "The blood is the soul."'

He tapped the file in his lap. Looked at me expectantly.

'You think this woman was killed to be eaten?' I said.

'What I'm saying is her wounds were consistent with classic cannibalistic practices. But there are also *in*consistencies: her heart, typically considered a delicacy, was left intact. Skulls are frequently taken as trophies and preserved, yet hers was left behind. I suppose both could be explained in terms of time pressure – the killer may have been forced to leave the beach before finishing the job. Or perhaps – and I think this is the best guess – he was just a psychopathic deviant *mimicking* some ancient rite.'

'Or someone who'd watched the wrong movie,' I said.

He nodded. 'The world we live in . . .'

Finishing the job.

I pictured the gentle waves of the lagoon, the arc of a long blade cutting the moonlight. 'What he did to her took quite a bit of time. What's your estimate?'

'At least an hour. The human femur's a sturdy thing. Can you imagine sitting there working at sawing it free?' He shook his head. 'Repulsive.'

'Why'd you suggest to Laurent that he not publicize the details?'

'Both as a means of concealing facts only the killer would know and in order to maintain public safety. Tempers were already running high, rumors spreading. Can you imagine what the notion of a cannibal sailor would have done?'

'So the villagers still don't know.'

'No one knows, other than you, Dennis, and myself.'

'And the murderer.'

He winced. 'I know I can trust you to keep it to yourself. I showed you the file because I value your opinion.'

'Cannibalism's not exactly my area of expertise.'

'But you have some understanding of human motivation – after all these years, I find people more and more perplexing. What could have *led* to this, Alex?'

'God only knows,' I said. 'You said the villagers aren't violent. What *about* the sailors? Any previous incidents of serious violence?'

'Brawls, fistfights, nothing worse.'

'So Creedman's story about locals storming the southern road was true?'

'Another exaggeration. No one *stormed*. A few of the younger men, fortified with beer, tried to reach the base to protest. The sentries turned them back and there was some shouting and shoving. But anyone who thinks the Navy would go to the expense of building that blockade two days later to keep out a handful of kids is naive. I spent enough time in the service to know that nothing moves that quickly in the military. The blockade must have been planned for months.'

'Why?'

He frowned. Hesitated. 'I'm afraid it may very well be the first stage in closing down the base.'

'Because it has no strategic value?'

'That's not the point. Aruk was *created* by colonial powers and the Navy's the current colonizer. To simply pull out is cruel.'

'How do the villagers make a living, now?'

'Small jobs and barter. And federal welfare checks.' He said it sadly, almost apologetic.

'The checks come on the supply boats?'

He nodded. 'I think we both know where that kind of thing leads. I've tried to get the people to develop some independence, but there's very little interest in farming and not enough natural resources for anything commercial. Even before the blockade, basic skills were already dropping, and most of the bright students left the island for high school and never returned. That's why I'm so glad people like Ben and Dennis choose to stay.'

'And now the blockade has sped up the decline.'

'Yes, but things don't need to be hopeless, son. One good trade project – a factory of some kind – would sustain Aruk. I've been trying to get various businesses to invest here, but when they learn of our transport problems they balk.'

'Pam said you've corresponded with Senator Hoffman.'

'Yes, I have.' He placed the murder file on the couch.

'Is there any history of tribal cannibalism on Aruk?' I said.

'No, because there's no pre-Christian culture of any kind. The first islanders were brought over by the Spanish in the fifteen-hundreds already converted to Catholicism.'

'A pre-Christian culture is necessary for cannibalism?'

94

'From my reading it's a virtual constant. Even the most recent documented cases seem to incorporate Christian and pre-Christian ideas. Are you familiar with the term "cargo cult"?'

'Vaguely. A sect that equates material goods with spiritual salvation.'

'A *spontaneous* sect spurred by a self-styled prophet. Cargo cults develop when native people have been converted to a Western religion but have held onto some of their old beliefs. The link between acquiring goods and receiving salvation occurs because basic missionary technique combines gifts with doctrine. The islander believes the missionary holds the key to eternal afterlife and that everything associated with him is sacred: white skin, Caucasian features, Western dress. The wonderful *kahgo*. The cults are rarer and rarer, but as late as the sixties there was a cult that worshiped Lyndon Johnson because someone got the notion *he* was the source of the cargo.'

'Correlation confused with causation,' I said. 'The same way all superstitions are learned. A tribe goes fishing the night of the full moon and brings in a record catch: the moon acquires magical properties. An actor wears a red shirt the night he gets rave reviews: the shirt becomes sacred.'

'Exactly. Groundless rituals provide comfort, but if the belief system is shaken up – the missionary leaves and the cargo stops – the islander may view it as the beginning of the apocalypse. Stick a charismatic prophet into the picture and – years ago I was sent to Pangia, in Southern Highlands Province, to survey infectious diseases. Fifty-five, right after the war. In the course of my research, I learned of a minor government clerk who suddenly quit his job and started reading the Bible aloud twenty hours a day in the village square. Handsome, intelligent young fellow. His association with the ruling class had lent additional status. A small group formed around him, and his delusions grew more florid. And bloody. He ended up slaughtering and eating his own infant son, sharing the meal with his followers in an attempt to bring in plane loads of goods. The morning of the murder he'd been preaching from Genesis. The story of Abraham binding Isaac for sacrifice.'

'Abraham never went through with it.'

'In his view that was because Abraham didn't merit true fulfilment. He, of course, was quite another story.'

Telling the story had turned him pale.

'I can still see his face. Smiling, tranquil.'

'Any similarities to this murder?'

'Several.'

'And some of the factors you've just mentioned are present here, too. Dependence upon the white man, then abandonment.'

'But still,' he said, bending forward, 'it doesn't make sense. Because other factors are absent.'

'No pre-Christian culture.'

'And absolutely no history of cults on Aruk!'

He rapped his knuckle against the file. 'I continue to insist that this hideousness was the work of a single, sick person.'

'Someone who'd read up on cannibalism and was trying to simulate a cult murder?'

'Perhaps. And most important, someone who's moved on.'

'Why do you say that?'

'Because it hasn't happened again.'

He was ashen. I lacked the heart for debate.

'For a while, son, I couldn't stop thinking that he'd simply gone off to do it somewhere else. But Dennis has been checking international reports for similar crimes in the region and none have come up. Now, what say we put aside this ghastly stuff and move on?'

12

For the next hour and a half, we were dispassionate scientists, discussing cases, suggesting different ways to organize the data.

Moreland looked at his watch. 'Feeding time for Emma and her friends. Thank you for a stimulating afternoon. It's not often I get to engage in collegial discussions.'

I thought of his daughter the physician, trained in public health. 'My pleasure, Bill.'

'It'll be dark soon, don't work too hard,' he said. He strode to the door. 'I didn't bring you over here to enslave you.'

Alone, I sat back and looked out the window at the fountain spitting jewels.

My mind's eye kept focusing on the photos of AnneMarie Valdos's murder scene.

White body on dark rock; the details Moreland and Laurent had witheld.

Probably what Creedman had been after when Ben caught him snooping: ace reporter comes to islands to find himself, finds a gore-fest instead, and phones his agent ('What a concept, Mel!').

Then he came up against Moreland and was cut off from the information and resented it.

Moreland had concealed the whole truth from his beloved islanders but offered them to me after a forty-eight-hour acquaintance.

Wanting input from me . . . about *human motivation*.

More worried about recurrence than he'd admitted?

Couching it in *collegiality* – a couple of guys with doctorates having a clubby chat about *two-legged supper*.

A brilliantly colored bird flew past the window. The sky was still a peacock blue I'd seen only on crayons.

I got up and headed for Robin's studio. What would I tell her?

By the time I reached the door, I'd decided on limited honesty: letting her know I'd discussed the murder with Moreland and that he believed it an isolated crime, but leaving out the details.

She wasn't there. Bits of shell were laid out neatly atop the flat file along with a billet of koa and two small chisels.

No dust. Wishful thinking.

I went looking for her, finally spotted her down by the fruit groves, a white butterfly flitting among the citrus trees, Spike a wiggly, dark shadow at her feet.

I jogged to her side, she put her arm in mine, and we walked together.

'So how did work go?' she said.

'Very scholarly. What'd you do?'

'Played around in the studio, but it was a little frustrating not being able to work, so Mr Handsome and I decided to stroll. The estate's wonderful, Alex. Huge. We made it all the way to the edge of the banyan jungle. Bill must have sunk a fortune into landscaping; there are some beautiful plantings along the way – herbs, wildflowers, a greenhouse, orchids growing on tree trunks. Even the walls are pretty. He's got different kinds of vines trailing down them. The only thing that spoils it is the barbed wire.'

She stopped to pick up an orange that had dropped, peeled it surgically as we continued.

'How much of the jungle can you see over the walls?'

'Treetops. And those aerial roots. There's a coolness that seems to make its way over. Not a breeze. Even milder. A subtle current. I'd take you there but Spikey didn't like it, kept pulling away.'

'Our little mine detector.'

'Or some kind of animal on the other side. I couldn't hear anything, but you know him.'

I bent and rubbed behind the dog's bat ears. His flat face looked up at me, comically grave.

'With those radar detectors, it's no wonder,' I said. 'Finally style and substance merge.'

She laughed. 'Umm, smell those orange blossoms? This is great, Alex.'

I kept my mouth shut.

We decided to dive the following morning and got up for an early breakfast. Jo Picker was already on the terrace dressed in a black T-shirt and loose pants, her hair tied back carelessly, sooty shadows under her eyes. She kept both hands on her coffee cup and stared down into it. The food on her plate was untouched.

When Robin touched her shoulder, she smiled weakly. Spike's licking her hand sparked another smile.

As we sat down, she said, 'Ly never liked dogs . . . too much maintenance.'

Her lips tightened, then trembled. She stood abruptly and marched into the house.

We left Spike in the run with KiKo and drove down to South Beach. As I turned off Front Street to park, I looked up the coastal road. The Navy blockade was at the top, a crude wall of grey concrete, at least twenty feet tall. It appeared to be crammed into the hillside. Warning signs applied generously. An extension of chain link and barbed wire snaked up the hill and continued into the brush.

The beach at that point was just a narrow spit and the wall cut across it and continued into the ocean, creating a damming effect. But the water was shallow and still, lapping weakly at the algae-stained base of the sea-barrier. Large chunks of coral were stacked nearby, desiccated and sunbaked: part of the reef had been shattered to accommodate the barrier.

I parked atop the widest section of beach. The sand was as smooth and white as a freshly made bed, the lagoon that same silvery green.

We collected our gear, and as I carried it to the shoreline, I noticed flat, smooth rocks above the tide pools.

The altar where AnneMarie Valdos had been sacrificed.

To what?

We stepped onto the sand. The temperature was holding as mild and steady as Moreland had promised. When I tested the lagoon with my foot, there was no chill, and when I eased in for a swim a soft warmth enveloped me.

'Perfect,' I called out to Robin.

We put on our fins and masks and snorkels, flipper-walked the shallows till the water reached our thighs, then knifed in and floated belly down on the surface of the pool. The reef took a long time to deepen, finally reaching eight feet as we neared the brown-red ring of coral that held back the ocean.

The coral colonies grew in wide, flat beds. Despite the lack of current, the reef's living rock seemed to dance, patches of tiny animals sharing space with bio-condos of sea urchins, chitons, feather duster worms, and gooseneck barnacles. Small, brilliant fish grazed, untroubled by our presence: electric-blue damsels, lemon-yellow tangs, confident gray-black French angels, shocking-pink basslets with the stern little faces of tax auditors.

Orange-and-white clownfish nested in the soft, stinging embrace of fluorescent sea anemones.

The bottom sand was fine, almost downy, spotted with shells and rocks and shreds of coral. The sunlight made its way down easily, dappling the ocean floor. We shattered the light with our shadows, causing some of the shells to move in reflexive panic.

Drifting in opposite directions, we explored separately for a while, then I heard Robin burble through her breathing tube and turned to see her pointing excitedly at the far end of the reef.

Something torpedo shaped was shooting between us, speeding across the lagoon. A small sea turtle, maybe a foot long, head down, legs compressed, skimming the top of the coral as it headed for bluer pastures.

I watched it disappear, then looked back at Robin, making the OK sign. She waved and I paddled to her, extending a hand. We bumped masks in a mock kiss, then swam together, thrilled and weightless, suspended like twins in a warm salty womb.

When we got back on the beach we were no longer alone.

Skip Amalfi and Anders Haygood had spread a horse blanket thirty feet from our clothes. Skip was lying on his back, eyes closed, belly surging and collapsing as he sucked on a cigarette and blew smoke. Haygood crouched nearby, hairy thighs thick as logs, tongue tip sticking out the corner of his mouth. Concentrating as he pulled the limbs off something huge and ugly.

The biggest crab I'd ever seen. Easily thirty inches from claw to claw, with a knobby, blue, spotted carapace and pincers the size of bear traps. My year for monster arthropods.

Haygood looked up at us and snapped a leg free, watched the juice drip out of it, then held it up and waved it.

'Ma'am. Sir.' Again, the gray eyes washed over Robin and I became aware of how she looked in her two-piece, hair dripping over smooth, bare shoulders, hips swelling above the low-cut bottom, the sharp, sweet contrast between bronze skin and white nylon.

She turned her back on them just as Skip sat up. Both men watched her trudge to our blanket. Walking in the sand made her sway more than she intended to.

'Big crab,' I said.

'Stoner,' said Haygood. 'Great eating – can I give you a couple of legs, sir?'

'No, thanks.'

'You're sure?'

'Forget it,' said Skip. 'Old man Moreland don't eat animals.'

'That's right,' said Haygood. 'Too bad. Stoners are great eating. This one liked coconuts – that's why it's blue. When they eat other things, they can be orange. I've seen them even bigger, but he's healthy.'

'Mean though,' said Skip. 'Bite your finger clear off. Best thing is throw 'em in the pot live – how was your swim?'

'Great.'

'See any octopus?'

'No, just a turtle.'

'Little one?'

I nodded.

'Last summer's hatch. They come in, lay at the breaker line, bury the eggs. The natives dig 'em up – makes a helluva omelet. The suckers that make it swim the hell out of here, but most of them get eaten too. Sometimes a real stupid one comes back. Musta been what you saw.'

'Checking out the old 'hood,' said Haygood, laughing. His teeth were widely spaced and white. The sun turned his body hair into dense copper wire.

'Octopus are smart,' said Skip. 'Those big eyes, you swear they're checking you out.' A glance Robin's way.

'Best omelet for my money is tern,' said Haygood. 'Lays pink eggs. First time people see it they freak out, think it's blood. But pink's the true color. Pink omelet.' He licked his lips. 'Salty – like duck.'

'You can have it, man,' said Skip. 'Too fuckin' gamy.'

Haygood smiled. 'Well, I go for the pink.'

Skip snickered.

'Shark's good eating, too,' said Haygood, 'but you have to soak the meat in acid or it tastes like piss – how long are you here for, doc?'

'Couple of months.'

'Like it?'

'It's beautiful.'

They looked at each other. Haygood snapped off another crab leg.

Skip said, 'Rich people would dig this place, right?'

'I guess anyone who likes swimming and relaxing would.'

'What about *you*? What kind of stuff do *you* dig?'

'All kinds of things.'

He dragged on his cigarette and flipped the butt onto the spotless sand. 'Me and my buddy Hay here wanna build a resort. But different. Grass huts, like a Club Med. Pay one price up front, get your food, drinks, the works. No TV or phones or video movies, just swimming and digging the beach, maybe we'll bring some girls over to put on a dance show or something.'

His eyes got hard. 'So what do you think?'

'Sounds good.'

'It does, huh?'

'Sure.'

He spat on the sand. 'I figure rich assholes from the mainland'd go for it in a big way, right? 'Cause otherwise, we'd hafta go for the Japanese tour groups like all the other islands do.' He put both hands in front of his face, hooked his upper teeth over his lower lip and flexed his thumbs.

'Take *pikcha*, crick crick.' He laughed.

Haygood smiled and examined the crab's legless body.

'Full of roe,' he said. 'A girl.'

'We wanna get *Americans*,' said Skip. 'This is America even though no one in America knows shit about this place.'

'Good luck.' I started to walk away.

'Wanna invest?' he called after me.

I was about to laugh, then I saw his face and stopped.

'I'm not really much of an investor.'

'Then maybe you should *start*, man. Get in early. Guys who invested in Hawaii after the war are wiping their asses with hundred dollar bills.'

He held out a palm, as if panhandling.

'Hey, the man came here to mellow out,' said Haygood. 'Give him a break.'

Skip flipped him a middle finger and his weak chin struggled for a jut. 'Shut the fuck up, man. I'm talking business, here.'

Haygood didn't speak but his wrists flexed and the crab's torso shattered wetly.

Skip tried to stare him down, but the older man ignored him.

'Think about it, man,' said Skip, passing some of the anger over to me. 'Talk to your lady; she looks pretty smart.'

Another glance Robin's way. She'd draped her shoulders with a towel and was sitting with her knees drawn up to her chest, looking out at the sea.

A voice to my back said, 'Gentlemen,' and Skip's dull eyes narrowed. Haygood wiped his hands with a T-shirt but his face didn't move.

I turned. Dennis Laurent stood on the sand in full mirrored sunglasses flashing white light. He looked vast. None of us had heard him approach.

He touched an eyebrow. 'Doctor. Got a nice stoner, there, Hay. Must be what, six seven pounds of meat?'

'Eight at least,' said Skip.

'Pull it off a coco?'

'Didn't have to,' said Haygood. 'Lazy one, sleeping over there.' He pointed to the tide pools.

'Nothing like an easy target,' said Laurent. 'I see you finally got in the water, doc. Nice?'

'Perfect.'

'Always is. Have a nice day, gentlemen.' He and I walked to Robin. His shoed feet were steady on the sand. Spotting the butt Skip had discarded, he picked it up and pocketed it.

'Those two give you any trouble?'

'No. Are they troublemakers?'

'Not generally, but they've got too much free time and one IQ between them, most of it Haygood's. Skip hit on you for his resort scheme, right?'

'Just before you arrived.'

'Club Skip. Ready to call your broker?'

'Got a cell phone?'

He laughed. 'Can't you just see Skip greeting a boatload of tourists – "Hey, welcome to fucking Aruk, man."'

'Chamber of commerce should hire him.'

'Yeah,' he said, 'if we had one – hello, Ms Castagna. How was the water?'

'Warm.'

'Always is. Something about the lack of water movement and the insulating properties of the coral. I'm happy to see you two finally enjoying yourselves. Finally got a callback from the Navy: just headed up to the estate to talk to Mrs Picker. They found the wreckage just inside Stanton. Nothing much left; they'll be shipping the remains back to the States, billing her later for the transport.'

'You're kidding.'

'Wish I was. Captain Ewing thinks he's being generous because the plane was trespassing on military property. He says he could have filed a complaint, fined Picker bigtime, and the estate would be financially responsible.'

'That's despicable,' said Robin.

Laurent flicked a speck of sand off his badge. 'Yup. How's Mrs Picker doing?'

'This morning she looked pretty exhausted.'

'I'd better leave out the part about the bill for now. Knowing the military – I'm an ex-Marine – they'll take two years just to finish the paperwork, if they even follow through. Trouble is, I'm not going to be able to get her the body. Even if Ewing was cooperative, there's no real mortuary here, just a couple of guys who dig graves for the cemetery behind the church, and no supply boat for another ten days or so. Without proper embalming it could get pretty ripe—'

He stopped himself. 'Sorry.'

'Why's Ewing so hostile?' I said.

He shrugged. 'Maybe it's his nature, maybe he doesn't like being here. He was involved in Skipjack – that Navy sex scandal in Virginia? Got exiled here because of it. But maybe that's just talk . . . Anyway, I'll just tell Mrs Picker the Navy's doing her a favor by shipping the body. Ewing asked me to get an address. She can have someone claim it in the states.'

He removed his shades and blew sand off the lenses. His light eyes took in the beach, the harbor. Lingering for a split second on the flat rocks above the tide pools. Or had I imagined it?

'Do you know if Dr Bill's up at the house?' he said.

'He wasn't at breakfast.'

'He's usually up way before breakfast. Goes to sleep late, too. Never met a man who needs less sleep, always moving, moving, moving. If you see him, tell him hi. Pam, too.'

13

As we got back in the Jeep, Skip and Haygood were walking along the shore, smoking and flicking ash into the water.

Robin said, 'Let's drive around a bit, explore some of the smaller roads.'

I turned the vehicle around and she looked up at the barricade.

'It's almost as if they wanted it to be ugly.'

'Moreland agrees with Picker that the Navy's shutting the island down gradually. I asked him how people live and he admitted the main source was welfare.'

'End of an era,' she said. 'That may be why he's so eager to document what he's done.'

I headed toward the bowed gray pilings of the dock. The open-air market was closed and the ration sign remained atop the gas pump.

'Did you talk about the murder?'

'A bit.'

'And?'

'Moreland and Dennis are assuming it's a one-shot, that the murderer's gone. Because he hasn't done it again in the region. So it could very well be a sailor who's transferred to another base.'

'Meaning he could be doing it in another region.'

'Dennis has been keeping an eye out for similar crimes and none have come up.'

We were nearing the Chop Suey Palace. Creedman was outside again, with a bottle and a mug. Looking straight ahead, I passed him and hung a sharp right onto the next road, passing more tumbledown houses and empty lots. Then a small, poorly tended patch of grass housing a World War Two cannon and a life-size statue of MacArthur shading his eyes. A wooden sign said VICTORY PARK, EST. 1945. The only obvious triumph was that of birds over bronze.

More shacks and lean-tos and dirt till the crest, where a narrow white church stood. I stopped. Two stories high, with a sharply pitched roof, fish-scale trim, and a badly tarnished copper steeple, the building canted to the right. The balusters of the front stair rail were intricately turned but flaking. The five-pace front yard was thick with high grass edged with leggy white petunias.

'Early Victorian,' said Robin. 'It's sunk a little on the foundation, but the design's nice.'

A display board staked in the lawn said OUR LADY OF THE HARBOR CATHOLIC CHURCH. VISITORS WELCOME. A few feet away a metal flagpole hosted Old Glory. The flag drooped in the motionless air.

Behind the church was more tall grass squared by a low picket fence. Rows of white crosses, stone and wooden grave markers. A few flashes of color. Floral wreaths, some so bright they had to be plastic.

Next door was a large aluminum Quonset hut labeled ARUK COMMUNITY CLINIC. The old black Jeep Ben had used to pick us up was parked near the door next to an even older MG roadster, once red, now faded to salmon. The emergency number on the door was that of Moreland's estate.

Just as I started to drive on, Pam came out, removing her stethoscope. She waved and I stopped again. Taking something out of the MG, she came over. Handful of plastic-wrapped lollipops.

'Hi. Snack?'

'No, thanks,' said Robin.

'Sure? They're sugarless.' Unwrapping a green pop, she put it in her mouth. 'So you guys got to swim. How was it?'

Robin told her about our dive. Through the open door I could see children, their small faces pinched with fright.

'They seemed okay about the crash,' said Pam, 'but still pretty nervous about their shots, so we decided to get it over with. Want to come in?'

We followed her into the hut and breathed in the sharp smell of alcohol. The floor was blue linoleum. Fiberboard partitions sectioned the interior into cubicles. Cartoon posters and nutritional charts nearly covered the walls, but the aluminum fought the attempt to cheer.

Fifteen or so children, all dark haired, none older than eight, were lined up in front of a long, folding table. Two chairs sat behind the table, the one on the right empty, the other occupied by Ben. To his left were steel trays of bandages, cotton swabs, disinfectant pads, disposable syringes, and small glass jars with rubber stoppers. A trash basket near his left foot brimmed with discarded needles and blood-specked pads.

He crooked his finger and a little girl in a pink T-shirt and red-and-white paisley shorts stepped forward. Her hair was waist long; her feet were in beach thongs. She was losing the struggle not to cry.

Ben unwrapped a pad, picked up a bottle, and jabbed the needle through the rubber cap with his left hand. Filling the syringe, he squirted it clear of air, took hold of the girl's arm and drew her closer. Cleaning her bicep swiftly, he tossed the pad in the basket, said something that made her look at him and flicked the needle at her arm, almost teasingly. The girl's mouth opened in pain and insult. The tears flowed. Some of the boys in line laughed, but none with enthusiasm. Then, the needle was out and Ben was bandaging her arm. The whole process had taken less than five seconds and he remained impassive.

The girl kept crying. Ben looked back at us. Pam rushed over and unwrapped a lollipop for the whimpering child. When the tears didn't stop, she cradled the girl.

Ben said, 'Next,' and crooked a finger. A small, chubby boy stepped into position and stared down at his arm. Dimpled fists drummed his thighs. Ben reached for a pad.

'All done, Angie,' said Pam, walking the girl to the door. You did great!' The child sniffed and sucked her lollipop and the white paper stick bobbed. 'These are some visitors from the mainland, honey. This is Angelina. She's seven and a half and very brave.'

'I'll say,' said Robin.

The girl wiped an eye.

'These people came all the way from California,' said Pam. 'Do you know where that is?'

Angelina mumbled around the sucker.

'What's that, sweetie?'

'Disn'land.'

'Right.' Pam tousled her hair and guided her outside, watching as she ran to the church.

By the time she returned, Ben had vaccinated two more children, working rapidly, as rhythmic as a machine. Pam stayed with us, comforting the children and seeing them off.

'School's still in session,' she said. 'They're in class for another hour.'

'Who teaches?' I said. 'The priest?'

'No, there is no priest. Father Marriot was called back last spring and Sister June just left for Guam – breast cancer. Claire – Ben's wife – was our substitute, but now she's the faculty. A couple of other mothers serve as part-time assistants.'

Another weeping child passed through.

'Guess I should do a few,' said Pam, 'but Ben's so good. I hate inflicting pain.'

Cheryl was sweeping the entry to the big house, but when we walked in she stopped.

'Dr Bill said give you this.' She handed me a scrap of yellow, lined paper. Moreland's writing:

Det. Milo Sturgis called 11 A.M., Aruk time.

West Hollywood exchange. Milo's home number.

'That's one in the morning, L.A. time,' said Robin. 'Wonder what it could be.'

'You know what a night owl he is. Probably something to do with the house and he's trying to catch us at a good time.'

Mention of the house tightened her face. She looked at her watch. 'It's two-thirty there, now. Should we wait?'

'If he was up an hour and a half ago, he probably still is.'

Cheryl stood there, as if trying to follow the conversation. When I turned to her, she blushed and began sweeping.

'Is it all right to use the phone for long distance?'

She looked puzzled. 'There's a phone in your room.'

'Is Dr Bill around?'

She thought. 'Yes.'

'Where?'

'In his lab.'

We went back to the run to pick up Spike. He and KiKo stopped their play immediately and he ran to Robin. The monkey shinnied up a low branch, then let go and landed feather light on my shoulder. A small dry hand cupped the back of my neck. He'd been shampooed recently – something with almonds. But his fur also gave off a faint hint of zoo.

We left with both animals. Robin said, 'I'd like to freshen up.'

'I'll go ask Moreland about using the phone.'

She turned back toward the house; KiKo jumped off and joined her and Spike. I walked down to the outbuildings and knocked on Moreland's office door.

He said, 'Come in,' but the door was locked and I had to wait for him to open it.

'Sorry,' he said. 'How was your swim?'

'Terrific.'

He was holding a pencil stub and looked distracted. His office was the same size as the one he'd given me, but with pale green walls and no furniture other than a cheap metal desk and chair. Papers, loose and bound, carpeted half the floor. The desk was blanketed too, though I did notice one high stack that had been squared neatly and placed in the center. Journal reprints. The top one, an article I'd written ten years ago on treating childhood phobias. My name underlined in red.

The door to the lab was open. Tables, beakers, flasks, test tubes in racks, a centrifuge, a balance scale, equipment I couldn't identify. Next to the scale was a tall jar full of the gray-brown pellets he'd used to feed the insects. A smaller container of some sort of brownish liquid sat beside it.

'So,' he said, taking off his glasses. His tone was strained; I'd interrupted something.

'I wanted to check if it was okay to use the phone for long distance.'

He laughed. 'Returning Detective Sturgis's call? Of course. There was no need to ask. Give him my best. He's a pleasant fellow.'

Robin sat there caressing her two hairy pals as I dialed. The phone rang twice and a cranky deep voice grunted, 'Sturgis.'

'Hi, it's me. Still up?'

'Alex.' Milo's voice lightened. I hadn't thought much about his missing us.

'Yeah, wide awake,' he said, reverting to a grumble. 'So how's Bali Hoo?'

'Sunny and clear. Want to hop over and join us?'

'I don't tan, I parboil.'

'Thought you were Black Irish.'

'That's temperament, not complexion. So you pretty much settled in?'

'Very nicely. Just got back from diving in a gorgeous coral reef.'

'Yo, Jacques. There really is a Garden of Eden, huh?'

'My fig leaf says yes. What are you doing up past your bedtime, sonny boy?'

'Working double shifts and building up the overtime. Reason I called is the guy who's handling your house has a couple of questions. Seems the crown and floor moldings Robin told him to order have been discontinued. He can get something similar, a little wider, or go for her exact specifications and have it custom milled. The difference is a couple of thou and he wants authorization. Also, the cost of your alarm is going to be a little higher than estimated. Something about having to connect up with a power line that's outside the basic contractual area. Probably another grand. It's never *below* estimate, is it? Anyway, ask the lovely Ms. C. what she wants to do, get back to me, and I'll forward the message.'

'I'll put her on right now.'

I handed over the receiver. Robin said, 'Hi!' and KiKo's eyes widened. As she began to speak the monkey stuck his head closer to the phone and began talking along in a wordless chittering singsong.

'What? Oh . . . no, it's a monkey, Milo . . . a *monkey*. As in barrel of . . . No, he hasn't replaced Spikey, we still love him . . . No, they're getting along fine, as a matter of fact . . . That's it in terms of mammals . . . What? . . . No, just some bugs . . . *Bugs*. Insects, spiders . . . tarantulas. Dr Moreland does research on them . . . What's up, detective?'

She talked to him about the construction, then ended with more small talk and returned the phone to me. 'I'm putting these

113

guys outside again, then running a bath. Love it if you'd join me when you're through.'

She left.

'Bugs,' said Milo. 'Eden has bugs.'

'God created them, too. What day was it?'

'His bad-joke day. Exactly what kind of research does this guy do?'

'Nutrition. Predatory behavior.'

'He sounded a little spacey when I talked to him.'

'How so?'

'Taking the message, but somewhere else.'

'He thought you were a pleasant fellow.'

'That proves he was somewhere else.'

I laughed. 'What kind of things are you working on?'

'You really want to know?'

'Intensely.'

'Four armed robberies, one with hostages in a meat locker and a near fatality. One drive-by of a drug dealer slash rap artist that we probably won't solve, aw shucks, and the beauty that's been keeping me up late: sixteen-year-old girl out in the Palisades shot her father to death while he sat on the can. She claims long-time molestation, but the mother says no way and she's been divorced from the old man for years, no love lost. The kid has a history of naughty behavior, and Daddy had promised her a brand-new Range Rover for her birthday if she passed all her classes. She flunked, he said no go, and friends say she got mighty pissed.'

'Any evidence of molestation?'

'Nope, and friends say she was a big fan of those two little shits with shotguns from Beverly Hills. She's got dead eyes, Alex, so who knows what was done to her. But that's not my concern, right now. She retained a mouthy lawyer with dead Daddy's dough . . . but enough, Ishmael. You set sail to escape all this barbarism.'

'True,' I said, 'but allow me to raise your cynicism quotient even higher. Even Eden has its problems.'

I told him about AnneMarie Valdos's murder.

He didn't answer.

'You still there?'

'Cracking her bones to eat the marrow?'

'That's Moreland's hypothesis.'

'You go to Paradise and outdo me in the grossness department?'

'According to Moreland, cannibalism's pretty common across cultures. Ever come across it?'

'He an expert on that, too? Tell me, is there some huge guy stomping around the estate with a bad haircut and bolts in his neck? Marrow . . . no, thanks, dear, I'll pass on that breakfast steak and stick with the veggie plate.'

'Funny you should say that. Moreland's a vegetarian. His daughter says he saw things after the Korean War that made him never want to be cruel again.'

'How sensitive. And no, I haven't personally come across any bad guy gourmets. But there are a few years left to retirement, so now I've got something to live for.'

'How's Rick?'

'He says, changing the subject. Doing the workaholic thing as usual, night shift at the ER . . . *Marrow*? Why do I keep hearing jungle drums going *oonka loonka*? Come across any missionaries in a pot?'

'Not yet, and Moreland says not to worry. There's no history of cannibalism here. Both he and the chief of police see it as a sicko killer trying to look exotic. Local opinion pins it on a Navy man who moved on.'

'Moreland's a crime sleuth, too?'

'He's the only doctor on the island, so he handles all the forensics.'

'Cannibalism,' he said. 'Does Robin know about this?'

'She knows there was a homicide, but I haven't given her the details. I don't want to make too big of a deal about it. Other than that, there's been no serious crime here for years.'

'"Other than that, Mrs Lincoln, how was the play." Why a Navy man?'

'Because the locals aren't violent and the killer seems to be transitory.'

'Well,' he said, 'I was Joe Army, so you won't get any big debate from me. Okay, hang loose, don't eat anything you can't identify, and stay away from jokers with bones in their noses.'

'A creed to live by,' I said. 'Thanks for calling, and good luck on your cases.'

'Yeah . . . all bullshit aside, I'm really glad you guys got to do this. I know what last year was like for you.'

A phone rang in the distance and he grunted.

'Other line,' he said. 'More sludge. Sayonara and all that, and if you see a bearded French guy painting ladies in flowery mumus, buy up the canvases.'

14

Robin napped and I took a walk, crossing the rose garden and descending the sloping acres of lawn. Four men in drive-and-mows were working on the turf. The rotting-sugar smell of cut grass brought to mind childhood Sundays.

So had Victory Park, I realized. The war memorial in my Missouri hometown had been only slightly larger. Sunday meant my mother bundling my sister and me off to the park when my father chose to drink at home. Bologna sandwiches and apple juice, climbing the cannon, pretending to fire, Mother's sweet, forced smiles. When she died, Dad's drinking stopped, and so did the rest of his life.

Shaking off melancholy, I continued down to the fruit groves, stepping among fallen oranges and tangerines and a popcorn spray of citrus blossoms. The meadow Moreland had created out of wildflowers was brilliant. A collection of miniature conifers had been trimmed surgically and a boxwood knot garden was as intricate as any maze I'd encountered in graduate school. Then the greenhouses, every pane spotless, and trees full of orchids, the plants tucked into the folds and hollows of branches like hatchlings. I kept going till I spotted patches of granite and the brown, thorny fuzz of rusty barbed wire.

The eastern border. Plumbago and honeysuckle and wisteria covered most of the high stone walls, softening the wire but not hiding it.

On the other side, the banyan tops formed a greener-gray awning, aerial roots shooting through the canopy like the tentacles of a beast in pain. From what I could see, the tree trunks below were stout and kinked cruelly, whipsawing in a struggle for space.

For a second, the entire forest seemed to be moving, tumbling down on me, and I felt myself losing balance.

After I restored equilibrium, a tight spot remained at the base of my throat.

I looked up at the trees again.

Robin had mentioned a subtle coolness drifting over the walls, but all I felt was an internal chill.

I hiked along the border, listening for sounds from the other side but hearing nothing. When I stopped, the same illusion of movement recurred and I placed both hands on the stone and breathed in deeply.

Probably low blood sugar. I hadn't eaten since breakfast.

I headed back. When I got to the grove, I picked up an orange, peeled it, and finished it in three bites, letting the juice run down my chin the way I'd done as a child.

Back in my office, I tackled another carton of medical files. More routine; the only psychological diagnoses Moreland had noted were stress reactions to physical illnesses.

I pulled down another box and found myself growing bored till a folder at the bottom made me take notice.

On the front cover Moreland had drawn a large, red question mark.

The patient was a fifty-one-year-old laborer named Joseph

Cristobal, with no history of mental disorder, who began to experience visual hallucinations – 'white worms' and 'white worm people' – and symptoms of agitation and paranoia.

Moreland treated him with tranquilizers and noted that Cristobal did have 'a fondness for drink but is not an alcoholic.' The symptoms didn't abate.

Two weeks later Cristobal died suddenly in his sleep, the apparent victim of a heart attack. Moreland's autopsy revealed no brain pathology but did discover an occluded coronary artery.

Then the doctor's final remark in large, bold print, the same red color as the question mark: '*A. Tutalo?*'

I figured that for a bacterium or virus but the medical dictionary he'd provided me didn't list it.

A drug? No citation in the *Physicians' Desk Reference*.

I returned to the storage room, squeezed my way past the columns of boxes, and searched the bookshelves.

Natural history, archaeology, mathematics, mythology, history, chemistry, physics, even a collection of antique travelogues.

One complete case devoted to insects.

Another to plant pathology and toxicology, which I went through carefully.

No mention of *A. Tutalo*.

Finally, in a dark, musty corner, the medical books.

Nothing.

I thought of the catwoman. Moreland's telling me about the case moments after we'd met.

Now another case of spontaneous death.

I'd reviewed perhaps sixty files. Two out of sixty was three percent.

An emerging pattern?

Time for another collegial chat.

When I reached the house, I saw Jo Picker near the fountain, watching Dennis Laurent's police car drive away. Water dotted her hair and face. As I came up to her she wiped her cheek and looked at the moisture on her hand. The spray continued to hit her. Slowly she moved out of its arc.

'That policeman came over to tell me what's going on.'

She rubbed her eyes. Her new tan had been replaced by mourner's pallor. 'They say Ly landed on the base and they're shipping him back today . . . I should've expected it, working in Washington. But when it happens to you . . . I've been calling his family.'

One of her hands rolled tight.

'I didn't really chicken out,' she said. 'Though that would have been rational.'

She looked at me. I nodded.

'I probably *would've* been stupid enough to go up even though I had bad feelings about it. But this time . . . he got mad at me, called me a . . . I just said to heck with it and walked away.'

She moved her face nearer to mine. Close enough to kiss but there was nothing seductive about it.

'Even so, I still probably would've relented. But he wouldn't let up . . . as I was walking through that bamboo I heard the plane engine start up and almost ran back. But instead I kept going. To the beach. Found a nice spot on the rocks and sat down and stared at the ocean. I was feeling pretty relaxed when I heard it.'

Our noses were nearly touching. Her breath was stale.

'I miss him,' she said, as if finding it hard to believe. 'You're with someone for a long time . . . I told his mother she could bury him in New Jersey near his father. We never made any plans for that kind of thing – he was forty-eight. When I get back we'll have some kind of service.'

I nodded again.

She noticed a stain on her shirt and frowned. 'My ticket out of Guam isn't for another two weeks. I guess I should say that I can't wait to get back, but the truth is, what's waiting for me? I might as well stay and finish up my work.'

Wetting her finger with her tongue, she rubbed the stain. 'That sounds cold to you, doesn't it?'

'Whatever helps you through it.'

'My *work* helps me. Coming here's the final leg of a three-year study – why throw it away?'

She backed away and drew herself up. 'Enough blubbering. Back to the old laptop.'

It was just before five. I strolled to the rose garden and watched through the boughs of a pine tree as the men in the mowers painted broad stripes in the lawn. I thought about sudden death.

The catwoman. White worms.

AnneMarie Valdos killed to be eaten.

Routine medical cases collected during a thirty-year practice.

Some routine.

I was probably making too much of it. After all, *I'd* initiated the conversation about the Valdos murder.

Though it had been Moreland who'd brought over the autopsy photos, sparing no detail.

Maybe the old man had a strong stomach and assumed I did too.

He'd implied as much during the tour of the bug zoo.

Research on predators.

I recalled the animation with which he'd discussed the history of cannibalism.

Not exactly your simple country doctor.

Milo had thought him spacey. Joked about Frankenstein monsters.

Milo was a self-admitted sultan of cynicism, but he was also a trained detective, his hunches more often right than wrong . . .

Neurotic, Delaware. Bunked down in Eden, getting paid handsomely to do a dream job and you just can't cope.

I returned to the house but couldn't get the catwoman out of my mind.

Her ordeal. Bound to a chair while her husband made love to another woman. The final scream . . .

Such cruelty.

Maybe *that* was it.

Over the years, Moreland had seen too much cruelty.

Radiation poisoning, the hopeless deterioration of the Bikini islanders.

The catwoman. Joseph Cristobal. The cargo cult leader.

Absorbing the pain the way sensitive people often do.

Confronting his helplessness but able to forget about it during dark hours in the bug zoo. His lab. His own private paradise.

Now, watching Aruk deteriorate – nearing the end of his own life – his defenses had been shaken.

He needed to make sense of the cruelty.

Needed someone to share it with.

15

That night at dinner, there were five places set.

Jo was last to come down. She wore a white blouse and a dark skirt; her face looked fresh and her hair was shiny and combed out.

'Go on with the small talk.' She sat and unfolded her napkin. 'Grapefruit, one of my favorites.'

The talk hadn't been small: Moreland giving a detailed lecture on the history of colonization. He'd seemed to lose his train of thought a couple of times.

Now there was silence, as Jo peered at the serrated edge of her grapefruit spoon. She cut a section from the fruit, and the rest of us picked up our utensils.

Moreland reached for a roll and spread it with apple butter. He closed his eyes and chewed.

'Dad?' said Pam.

His eyes opened and he looked around the table, as if trying to locate the sound.

'Yes, dear?'

'You were talking about the Spanish.'

'Ah, yes, machismo's finest hour. What gave the *conquistadores* a unique approach was the combination of risk taking and a strong religious commitment. When you believe you have God on your side, anything's possible. Hormones *and* God are unbeatable.'

He nibbled on the roll. 'Then, of course, there was the easy funding: outright theft, in the name of heaven. Señor Columbus's journeys were funded with the plunder of the Inquisition.'

'Hormones, religion, and money,' said Pam very softly. 'That just about sums up the world, doesn't it.'

Moreland stared at her for a second. A worried parental stare that he ended abruptly by shifting his attention to his bread. 'In toto, a force to be reckoned with, the Spanish. They came to the Pacific in the sixteenth century, set about trying to do precisely what they'd done in—'

He stopped and looked across the terrace. Gladys had come out of the house.

'I'm not sure we're ready for the next course, dear.'

'There's a phone call, Dr Moreland.'

'A medical call?'

'No, sir.'

'Well, then, please take a message.'

'It's Captain Ewing, sir.'

Moreland's stooped frame jerked forward, then he straightened. 'How curious. Please excuse me.'

After he was gone, Pam said, 'This is the first we've heard from Ewing in months. I spoke to him once over the phone. What a sour man.'

I repeated what Dennis had told me about Ewing's being exiled for the sex scandal.

'Yes, I heard that, too.'

Jo said, 'He's crating and shipping Lyman like luggage.'

Pam paled. 'I'm sorry, Jo.'

124

Jo dabbed at her lips. 'Government is like junior high. Your status depends upon whom you're able to persecute.'

'Maybe Dad can work something out with them.'

'I doubt it,' said Jo. 'I think they shipped him already.'

'Your connections don't help?' said Robin.

'What connections?'

'Working at the Defense Department.'

Jo's bosom heaved and she let out a barklike laugh. '*Thousands* of people work at the Defense Department. It's not exactly as if I'm the Secretary of Defense.'

'I just thought—'

'I'm *nothing*,' said Jo. 'Lowly G-12 nerds don't count.'

She stabbed the grapefruit, turned the spoon, freeing the last bits of pulp.

More silence, heavier, oppressive. Geckos racing along the rail would have been welcome, but they were keeping a low profile tonight.

Pam said, 'Gladys made lamb. It looks great.'

Moreland came back out, a loping skeleton.

'An invitation. To all of us. Dinner at the base, tomorrow night. Casual formal. I shall wear a tie.'

That night, I awoke at two in the morning and was unable to fall back asleep. As I got out of bed Robin turned away from me. I slipped into some shorts and a shirt and she rolled back.

'Y'okay, honey?'

'Think I'll just get up for a while,' I whispered.

She managed to mumble, 'Restless?'

'A little.'

If her head was clear enough, she was thinking: *Some things never change.*

I bent and kissed her ear softly. 'Maybe I'll take a little walk.'

'. . . not too late.'

I covered her shoulders, pocketed the room key, and slipped out of the bedroom. As I passed Spike's crate, he snored a greeting.

'Nighty-night, handsome.'

My bare feet were silent on the landing carpet. The stairs were sturdy, not a creak.

Down in the entry, the stone floor was cool and welcome as summer lemonade. All the lights were off and the island silence saturated the house. I opened the front door and stepped outside.

The moon was ice-white and the sky pulsed with stars. Starlight frosted the trees and the fountain, turning the spatter to glycerine, giving life to the gargoyle roof tiles.

I walked to the gates. They were open and I looked down the long, sloping road, matte-black till it hit the onyx of the ocean.

Something moved along the grass at the road's edge.

Something else skittered in response.

I turned back, fully awake now. Maybe I'd look over a few more charts. I headed for my bungalow, then stopped when I heard a door shut.

Footsteps from the rear of the house. The back door, leading from the kitchen to the gravel paths.

Slow, deliberate footseps. They ceased. Continued.

Someone came out into the open and stood looking up at the sky.

Moreland's unmistakable silhouette.

Not wanting to talk to him or anyone else – I retreated into the shadows and watched as he descended the path, landing thirty feet in front of me.

Something clunked in his hand. A doctor's bag.

Same clothes he'd worn at dinner plus a shapeless cardigan sweater. He headed for the outbuildings, passed my bungalow, and continued past Robin's.

Stopping at his office.

At the door, he put the bag down, fumbled in his pocket, finally found the key but had some trouble inserting it in the lock. Starlight filtered through trees slashed his face diagonally, highlighting a cucumber of nose, the deep pouches columning his downturned mouth.

The door swung open. He picked up his bag and entered.

The door closed silently.

The lights went on, then off. The room stayed dark.

16

The following morning brought cooler air and cotton-swab clouds drifting from the east.

'Rain,' said Gladys, as she poured our coffee. 'Five or six days.'

The clouds were translucent and filmy, not a hint of moisture.

'They pick up the water as they go,' she said, offering the bread basket. 'Sucking it up from the ocean. Do you like whole wheat?'

'Sure.'

'Dr Bill does too, but a lotta people don't. One time he had me bake rolls for the kids at school. They didn't eat too many.'

She tugged the corner of the yellow tablecloth. We were the only ones at breakfast.

'Kids like the soft stuff. We used to get lots of white bread on the supply boats. Now, when we get anything, it's stale. Were you planning on swimming again?'

'Yes.'

'Well, don't be fooled by those clouds: be sure to put on sunscreen. You got the nice olive skin, ma'am, but the doctor here, with those pretty blue eyes, he could burn.'

Robin smiled. 'I'll take good care of him.'

'Men think they're tough, but they need to be taken care of. How about some nice fresh-squeezed juice?'

At the lagoon, the fish were quick learners, approaching for a handout but swimming away quickly when we had nothing to give them. Robin managed to get one large, latecoming, pink-and-yellow wrasse to nibble at her fingers. Then it too realized she was all show, and it shot away to a high mound of coral, where it snaked through a hole and disappeared.

She followed, head turning constantly, her eye for detail in full play. When she stopped, paddled in place, and waved me over, I joined her.

A tiny bald head floated in the crack. Chinless. Gray-brown skull. Oversized eyes bright with intelligence.

A baby octopus, legs as thin and flaccid as boiled spaghetti. It kept staring, finally retreated, slithering into a crevice, turning impossibly small.

We pressed closer.

It squirted ink in our faces.

I laughed, got water in my tube, and had to tread water to clear it. The surface of the water was a clean metal plate. The beach was empty.

I went under again, tagging along with a school of yellow surgeonfish, watching the bony, sharp protrusions under their pectoral fins pivot at the sense of threat, feeling the calmness of their blank, black stares.

Paradise.

We were back at the house by two. Jo's door was closed and an untouched lunch tray sat on the floor nearby. I imagined her tapping her keyboard in hopes of blunting her grief.

Studying the wind. Something too vast to control.

Moreland, on the other hand, delighted in manipulating nature's small variables. Had he once harbored grand plans for the island? Was his own grief what had kept him up last night, sitting in the dark?

I worked. No medical oddities, no gore, and the only untimely death I found was a young woman with ovarian cancer.

Another two cartons, more routine. Then the name of a drowning victim caught my eye.

Pierre Laurent, a twenty-four-year-old sailor lost in a squall near the Mariana Trench. The body had been returned to Aruk, and Moreland had certified the death, making note of the eighteen-year-old widow, four months pregnant with Aruk's future police chief.

Right below, Dennis's birth chart. A ten-pound baby, healthy.

Two more hours of tedium.

I liked that.

Just as I was heading for the back room to fetch yet another box, Ben knocked and came in. 'Base just called. Navy copter's picking you up in an hour on South Beach.'

'VIP treatment?'

'It's either that or they send down a big ship or rowboats.' He took in the clutter of my desk and I thought I saw disapproval. 'Need anything by way of supplies?'

'No thanks. Are you coming tonight?'

'Nope. One hour, you'll all be leaving from here together.'

He started to leave and I said, 'Hold on, I'll walk back with you.'

He shrugged and we left together.

'How're the vaccinations coming along?' I said.

'All finished till next year.'

'Tough job?'

'Not really. It's for their own good.'

'You had a real rhythm going, yesterday.'

'That's me,' he said. 'Natural rhythm.'

The taste in my mouth matched his expression. We walked in silence toward the big house.

As we neared the fountain, he said, 'Sorry, that was out of line. I'm not like that . . . What I mean is, race isn't a big thing to me.'

'Me neither; forget it.'

'Guess I'm bushed. The baby was up all night.'

'How old?'

'Six months.'

'Boy or girl?'

'Girl. All of them slept great except her. Sorry. I mean it.'

'No problem. Dr Bill said the dinner was formal casual. What does that mean, tux jacket and jeans?'

His smile was grateful. 'Who knows? Typical military, give out rules without explaining them. You serve any time?'

'No,' I said.

'After a month in the Guard I knew it wasn't for me, but no choice by then. I told them I was interested in medicine, so they put me in a hospital on Maui, pulling sea urchin spines out of toes. Never even hit the water. I love the ocean.'

'Do you dive?'

'Used to. Used to sail, too. Had an old catamaran that Dennis and I took out the few days a year we had enough wind. What with the kids, though, no time. And Dr Bill keeps me busy. No complaints – it's what I like.'

He gave another smile – full and warm. An old, dented gray Datsun station wagon was parked near the front steps of the house. A Chinese woman got out of it.

Tiny, with a bone-porcelain face under very short hair, she wore a red blouse tucked into blue jeans. Her eyes were huge. She smiled at me and gave Ben a sandwich wrapped in wax paper.

'Tuna,' he said, kissing her cheek. 'Excellent. Dr Delaware, this is my wife, Claire. Claire Chang Romero, Dr Alex Delaware.'

We exchanged greetings.

'Everything okay?' said Ben. 'We still on for hibachi dinner?'

'After homework – addition practice for Cindy and composition for Ben Junior.'

He put his arm around her. He was a small man, but she made him look big. Walking her to the car, he held her door open. He looked happy. I left.

Casual formal for Robin was a long, sleeveless black dress with a mandarin collar and high slits on the side. Her hair was piled and mabe-pearl earrings glistened like small moons.

I put on the linen sportcoat she'd bought me for the trip, tropical wool slacks, blue shirt, maroon tie.

'Spiffy,' she said, patting my hair down.

Spike looked up at us with big eyes.

'What?' I said.

He began baying like a hound.

The give-me-attention-I'm-so-needy bit. Our dressing up was always a cue.

'And the Oscar goes to,' I said.

Robin said, 'Poor *baby*!' and bent down and mothered him for a while, then coaxed him into his crate with an extra-large biscuit and a kiss through the grill. He gave out a bass snort, then a whine.

'What is it, Spikey?

'Probably "I want my MTV,"' I said. 'His internal clock's telling him *The Grind*'s on in L.A.'

'Aw,' she said, still looking into the crate. 'Sorry, baby. No TV, here. We're roughing it.'

She took my arm.

No TV, no daily newspaper. The mail irregular, packed on the biweekly supply boats.

Cut off from the world. So far, I was surprisingly content.

How would it suit me, long term?

How did it suit the people of Aruk? Moreland's letters had emphasized the isolation and insulation. Preparing us, but there'd been a bit of boast to it.

A man who hadn't switched from rotary phones.

Doing it his way, in the little world he'd built for himself. Breeding and feeding his bugs and his plants, dispensing altruism on his own schedule.

But what of everyone else on the island? They had to know other Pacific islanders lived differently: during our stopover on Guam, we'd had access to newsstands, twenty-four-hour cable, radio bands of music and talk. The travel brochures I'd picked up there showed similar access on Saipan and Rota and the larger Marianas.

The global village, and Aruk was on the outside looking in.

Maybe Spike wasn't the only one who missed his MTV.

Creedman had said Moreland was extremely wealthy, and Moreland had confirmed growing up on ranchland in California wine country.

Why didn't he use his money to improve communication? There was no computer in his office. Journals arrived in the unpredictable mail. How did he keep up with medical progress?

Did Dennis Laurent have a computer? Without one, how could he do his police tracking?

Was the failure to find a repeat of the beach murder the result of inadequate equipment, and was *that* why Moreland was still worried?

'Alex?' I felt a tug at my sleeve.

'What, hon?'

'You all right?'

'Sure.'

'I was talking to you and you spaced out.'

'Oh. Sorry. Maybe it's contagious.'

'What do you mean?'

'Moreland spaces out all the time. Maybe it's island fever or something. Too much mellow.'

'Or maybe you're both working too hard.'

'Snorkel all morning and read charts for a couple of hours? I can stand the pain.'

'It's all expenditure of energy, darling. And the air. It does sap you. I find myself wanting to vegetate.'

133

'My little brussel sprout,' I said, taking her hand. 'So it'll be a real vacation.'

'For you too, doc.'

'Absolutely.'

She laughed. 'Meaning what? The body rests but the mind races?'

I tapped my forehead. 'The mind makes a pit stop.'

'Somehow I don't think so.'

'No? Watch me tonight. Pinkies out, hmph hmph, how about them Dodgers?' I went limp and rolled my eyes.

'Maybe I should bring a snorkel, then. In case you nod off in the soup.'

17

Moreland was sitting in the Jeep when we got there. Wearing an ancient brown blazer and a tie the color of gutter water.

'We're waiting on Pam,' he said, looking preoccupied. He started the car and gave it gas, and a moment later the little red MG sped up and screeched to a halt. Pam jumped out, flushed and breathless.

'Sorry.' She ran into the house.

Moreland frowned and looked at his watch. The first hint of paternal disapproval I'd seen. I hadn't noticed any closeness, either.

He checked the watch again. An old Timex. Milo would have approved. 'You look lovely, dear,' he said to Robin. 'As soon as she's ready, we'll get going. Mrs Picker's not coming, understandably.'

A few minutes later, Pam sprinted out, perfectly composed in a blazing white trouser suit, her hair loose and shining, her cheeks flushed.

'Onward,' said Moreland. When she kissed his cheek he didn't acknowledge it.

He drove the way he walked, maneuvering the Jeep slowly and awkwardly down toward the harbor, veering close to the edge of the road as he pointed out plants and trees.

At the bottom of the road, he turned south. The sun had been subdued all day, and now it was retiring; the beach was oyster-gray, the water old nickel.

So quiet. I thought of AnneMarie Valdos sectioned like a side of meat on the flat rocks.

We got out and waited silently near the edge of the road.

'How long of a copter ride is it?' I said.

'Short,' said Moreland.

A scuffing sound came from the top of the coastal road.

A man emerged from the shadow of the barrier and came toward us.

Tom Creedman, waving. He wore a blue pinstripe suit, white button-down shirt, yellow paisley tie, tasseled loafers. His black hair was slicked down and his mustache smiled in harmony with his mouth.

Moreland's eyes were furious. 'Tom.'

'Bill. Hi, Moreland *fille*. Doctor-and-Robin.'

Insinuating himself into the middle of our group, he tightened the knot of his tie. 'Pretty nifty, personal aerial escort and all that.'

'Not much choice if they want us there,' said Moreland.

'Well,' said Creedman, 'we could swim. You're a strong swimmer, Pam. I saw you today, taking those waves on the North End with Chief Laurent.'

Moreland blinked hard and snapped his head toward the water.

'Maybe I should try it one day,' said Pam. 'What is it, a few knots? Do you swim, Tom?'

'Not if I can avoid it.' Creedman chuckled, fished a wood-tipped cigarillo out of his jacket, and lit it with a chrome lighter.

Sucking in deeply, he examined the lagoon with a flinty stare and blew smoke through his nose. Foreign correspondent on assignment. I waited for theme music.

'Funny, isn't it?' he said. 'After all the enforced segregation, they decide it's party time – at least for the white folk. I see Ben and Dennis weren't included. What do you think, Bill? Is brown skin a disqualifying factor?'

Moreland didn't answer.

Creedman turned to Robin and me. 'Maybe it's in *your* honor. Any Navy connections, Alex?'

'I played with a toy boat in the bathtub when I was five.'

'Ha,' said Creedman. 'Good line.'

Pam said, 'You don't swim, you don't sun. What do you do all day, Mr Creedman?'

'Live the good life, work on my book.'

'What exactly is it about?'

Creedman tapped his cigarillo and gave a Groucho leer. 'If I told you, it would kill the suspense.'

'Do you have a publisher?'

His smile flickered. 'The best.'

'When's it coming out?'

He drew a finger across his lips.

Pam smiled. 'That's top secret, too?'

'Has to be,' said Creedman, too quickly. The cigarillo tilted and he pulled it out. 'The publishing business is vulnerable to leaks. Information superhighway; the commodity is . . . ephemeral.'

'Meaning everyone's out to steal ideas?'

'Meaning billions are invested in the buying and selling of concepts and everyone's looking for the *golden* idea.'

'And you've found it on Aruk?'

Creedman smiled and smoked.

'It's not like that in medicine,' she said. 'Discover something important, you've got a moral obligation to publicize it.'

'How noble,' said Creedman. 'Then again, you doctors chose your field *because* you're noble.'

Moreland said, 'I think it's coming.' His finger was up but he was still facing the ocean.

I heard nothing but the waves and bird chirps. Moreland nodded. 'Yes, definitely.'

Seconds later, a deep tom-tom rumble sounded from the east, growing steadily louder.

A big, dark helicopter appeared over the bluffs, sighted directly over us, hovered, then lowered itself on the road like a giant locust.

Double rotors, bloated body. Sand sprayed and we dropped our heads and cupped our hands over our mouths.

The rotors slowed but didn't stop. A door opened and a drop-ladder snapped down.

Hands beckoned.

We trotted to the craft, eating sand, ears bursting, and climbed into a cabin walled with canvas and plastic and reeking of fuel. Moreland, Pam, and Creedman took the first passenger row and Robin and I settled behind them. Piles of gear and packed parachutes filled the rear storage area. A pair of Navy men sat up front. Half-drawn pleated curtains allowed us a partial view of the backs of their heads and a strip of green-lit panel.

The second officer looked back at us for a moment, then straight ahead. He pointed. The pilot did something and the copter shuddered and rose.

We headed out to sea, hooking southeast and following the coastline. High enough for me to make out the bladelike shape of the island. South Beach was the point of the dagger, our destination the hilt.

The blockade was no more than a paper cut from this height. The mountaintops were a black leather belt, the banyans obscured by burgeoning darkness and the ring of mountains. The copter veered sharply and the east end of the island slid into view.

Concrete shore and choppy water, no trees or sand or reefs. The windward harbor was a generous soupspoon indentation.

Natural port. Ships large enough to look significant from these heights were moored there. Some of them moved. Strong waves – I could see the froth, piling up against a massive seawall.

We turned north toward the base: empty stretches of black veined with gray, toy-block assemblages that had to be barracks, some larger buildings.

The copter descended and we touched down perfectly, the trip as brief as an amusement park ride, the blockade's cruel efficiency clearer than ever. The pilot cut the engine and exited without a word. The second officer waited till the rotors had quieted before releasing our door.

We got out and were hit by a blast of humid air, stale and chemically tainted.

'The windward side,' said Moreland. 'Nothing grows here.'

A sailor in a contraption that resembled an oversize golf cart drove us through a sentry post and past the barracks, storehouses, hangars, empty airstrips. Concrete fields crowded with planes and copters and disassembled craft made me think of Harry Amalfi's aerial junkyard. Some of the planes were antiques, others looked new. One sleek passenger jet, in particular, would have done a CEO proud.

The harbor was blocked from view by the seawall, a monstrous thing of the same raw construction as the blockade. Above it, an American flag whipped and snapped like a locker-room towel. I could hear the ocean charging angrily, hitting the concrete with the roar of a gladiator audience.

Looking toward the base's western border, I saw the area where Picker must have gone down. At least half a mile away. Twenty-foot chain-link fencing completed the banyan's prison. Creedman had said the base was run by a skeleton crew, and there were very few sailors on the ground – maybe two dozen, walking, watching.

The golf cart veered across a nearly empty parking lot, through a small drab garden, up to a colonial building, three stories high, white board and brick, green shutters.

Next door was a one-story building of the same design. The officer's club.

Inside the club was a long walnut hallway – deep red wool carpeting patterned with crossed sabers, brass fixtures. The paneling was lined with roiling seascapes and model ships in glass cases.

Another sailor took us to a waiting room decorated with photo blowups of fighter jets and club chairs. A sailor in dress uniform stood behind a host's lectern. Glass doors opened to a dining room: soft lighting, empty tables, the smell of canned vegetable soup and melted cheese.

The sailors saluted one another, and the first one left without breaking step.

'This way,' said the one behind the lectern. Young, with clipped hair and a soft face full of pimples. He took us to an unmarked door. A sign hanging from the knob said Captain Ewing had reserved the room.

Inside were one long table under a hammered-copper chandelier and twenty bright blue chairs. A portrait of the President wearing an uneasy smile greeted us from behind the head chair. Three walls of wood, one blocked by blue drapes.

A new sailor came and took our cocktail order. Two different men brought the drinks.

Creedman sipped his martini and licked his lips. 'Nice and dry. Why can't we get vermouth like this in the village, Bill?'

Moreland stared at his tomato juice and shrugged.

'I asked the Trading Post to get me something dry and Italian,' said Creedman. 'Took a month and what I ended up with was some swill from Malaysia.'

'Pity.'

'Go to any duty-free in the booniest outpost and they've got everything from Chivas to Stoli, so what's the big deal about filling an order here? It's almost as if they want to do it wrong.'

'Is that the theme of your book?' said Pam. 'Incompetent islanders?'

Creedman smiled at her over his drink. 'If you're that curious about my book, maybe you and I should get together and discuss it. That is, if you've got any energy after your swims.'

Moreland walked to the blue drapes and parted them.

'Same view,' he said. 'The airfield. Why they put a window here, I'll never know.'

'Maybe they like to see the planes take off, Dad,' said Pam.

Moreland shrugged again.

'How long did you and Mom live here?'

'Two years.'

Three men came in. Two wore officer's garb – the first fiftyish, tall and thickset, with rough red skin and steel glasses; the other even taller, ten years younger, with a long, swarthy, rubbery face and restless hands.

The man between them had on a beautiful featherweight gray serge suit that trimmed ten pounds from his two hundred. Six feet tall, heavy shouldered and narrow hipped, with a square face, bullish features, slit mouth, rancher's tan. His shirt was soft blue broadcloth with a pin collar, his foulard a silver and wine silk weave. His hair was bushy and black on top, the temples snow-white. The contrast was almost artificial, as dramatic in real life as on TV.

He looked like Hollywood's idea of a senator, but Hollywood had nothing to do with his becoming one, if newspapers and magazines could be believed.

The story was a good one: born to a young widow in a struggling Oregon logging camp, Nicholas Hoffman had been tutored at home till the age of fifteen, when he'd lied about his age and enlisted in the Navy. By the end of the Korean War, he was a decorated hero who gave the military another 15 years of distinguished service before entering the real estate business, making his first million by 40 and running successfully for the Senate at forty-three. His doctrine was the avoidance of extremes; someone dubbed him Mr Middle-of-the-Road and it stuck. True believers on both ends tried to use it against him. The voters ignored them, and Hoffman was well into his third term after a no-contest race.

'Bill!' he said, barging ahead of the officers and stretching out a meaty hand.

'Senator,' said Moreland, softly.

'Oh, Jesus!' roared Hoffman. 'Cut the crap! How *are* you, man?'

He grabbed Moreland's hand and pumped. Moreland remained expressionless. Hoffman turned to Pam. 'You must be Dr Moreland, Junior. Christ, last time I saw you, you were in diapers.' He let go of her father and touched her fingers briefly. 'You *are* a doctor?'

She nodded.

'Splendid.'

Creedman stuck out his hand and announced himself.

'Ah, the press,' said Hoffman. 'Captain Ewing told me you were here, so I said invite him, show him open government in action or he'll make something up. On assignment?'

'Writing a book.'

'On what?'

'Nonfiction novel.'

'Ah. Great.'

'What brings *you* here, Senator?'

'Fact-finding trip. Not one of those sun-and-fun junkets. Real work. Downsizing. Appraising military installations.'

Unbuttoning his jacket, he patted his middle. He had a small, hard paunch that tailoring had done a good job of camouflaging.

'And you must be the doctors from California.' He stuck out his hand. 'Nick Hoffman.'

'Dr Delaware's a psychologist,' said Robin. 'I build musical instruments.

'How nice . . .' He glanced at the table. 'Shall we, Captain?'

'Certainly, Senator,' said the red-faced officer. His voice was

142

raspy. Neither he nor the swarthy man had budged during the introductions. 'You're at the head, sir.'

Hoffman strode quickly to his place and removed his jacket. The taller officer rushed to take it from him, but he'd already hung it on the back of the chair and sat down, removing his collar pin and loosening his tie.

'Drink, Senator?' the officer said.

'Iced tea, Walt. Thanks.'

The tall man left. The red-faced man remained in place near the door.

'Join us, Captain Ewing,' said Hoffman, motioning to one of the two empty chairs.

Ewing removed his hat and complied, leaving lots of space between his back and the chair.

'Can I assume everyone knows everyone, Elvin?' said Hoffman.

'I know everyone by name,' said Ewing. 'But we've never met.'

'Mr Creedman, Dr Pam Moreland, Dr and Mrs Delaware,' said Hoffman, 'Captain Elvin Ewing, base commander.'

Ewing put a finger to his eyeglasses. He looked as comfortable as a eunuch in a locker room.

The officer returned with Hoffman's tea. The glass was oversized and a mint sprig floated on top.

'Anything else, Senator?'

'No. Sit down, Walt.'

As he started to obey, Ewing said, 'Introduce yourself, lieutenant.'

'Lieutenant Zondervein,' said the tall man looking straight ahead.

'There,' said Hoffman. 'Now we're all friends.' Emptying most of the glass with one gulp, he picked out the mint sprig and chewed on a leaf.

'Are you traveling alone, Senator?' said Creedman.

Hoffman grinned at him. 'Just can't turn it off, can you? If you mean do I have an entourage no, just me. And yes, it's a leased government jet, but I rode along with the base supplies.'

The sleek craft I'd noticed.

'Actually,' continued Hoffman, 'there are three other leglislative luminaries assigned to this particular trip. Senators Bering, Petrucci, and Hammersmith. They're in Hawaii right now, arriving in Guam tomorrow, and I can't promise you they haven't been sunbathing.' Grinning. 'I decided to come early so I could revisit my old stomping grounds, see old friends. No, Mr Creedman, it didn't cost the taxpayers an extra penny, because my assignment is to assess facilities on several of the smaller Micronesian islands, including Aruk, and by coming alone I turned it into a cheap date.'

He finished the tea, crushed an ice cube, swallowed, and laughed. 'I got to sit up with the pilot. God, the instrumentation on these things. Might as well have been trying to play one of those damn computer games my grandkids are addicted to – did you know the average seven-year-old has more computer proficiency than his parents will ever achieve? Great eye-hand skills, too. Maybe we should train seven-year-olds to fly combat, Elvin.'

Ewing's smile was anemic.

'Let me get you a refill, Senator,' said Zondervein, starting to get up.

Hoffman said, 'No, thanks – anyone else?'

Creedman lifted his martini glass.

Lieutenant Zondervein took it and went to the door. 'I'll check on the first course.'

Hoffman unfolded his napkin and tucked it into his collar. 'Mafia style,' he said. 'But one wirephoto with grease spots on the tie and you learn. So what's on the menu, Elvin?'

'Chicken,' said Ewing.

'Does it bounce?'

'I hope not, sir.'

'Roast or fried?'

'Roast.'

'See that, Mr Creedman? Simple fare.'

He turned to Ewing. 'And for Dr Moreland?'

'Sir?'

Hoffman's lips maintained a smile but his eyes narrowed until they disappeared. 'Dr Moreland's a vegetarian, Captain. I believe I radioed you that from the plane.'

'Yes, sir. There are vegetables.'

'There are *vegetables*. Fresh ones?'

'I believe so, sir.'

'I hope so,' said Hoffman, too gently. 'Dr Moreland maintains a very healthy diet – or at least he used to. I assume that hasn't changed, Bill?'

'Anything's fine,' said Moreland.

'You were way ahead of your time, Bill. Eating right while the rest of us went merrily about, clogging our arteries. You look *great*. Been keeping up with the bridge?'

'No.'

'No? You had how many masters points – ten, fifteen?'

'Haven't played at all since you left, Nicholas.'

'Really.' Hoffman looked around. 'Bill was a great bridge player – photographic memory and you couldn't read his face. The rest of us were amateurs, but we did manage to put together some spirited matches, didn't we, Bill? You really quit? No more duplicate tournaments like the ones you used to play at the Saipan club?'

Another shake of Moreland's head.

'Anyone here play?' said Hoffman. 'Maybe we can get a game going after dinner.'

Silence.

'Oh, well . . . great game. Skill plus the luck of the draw. A lot more realistic than something like chess.'

Zondervein returned with Creedman's martini. Two sailors followed with a rolling cart of appetizers.

Honeydew melon wrapped in ham.

Hoffman said, 'Take the meat off Dr Moreland's.'

Zondervein rushed to obey.

The ham tasted like canned sausage. The melon was more starch than sugar.

145

Gladys had said Hoffman was a gourmet, but gourmand was more like it: he dug in enthusiastically, scraping honey-dew flesh down to bare rind and emptying his water glass three times.

'Dad's been writing to you,' said Pam. 'Did you receive his letters?'

'I did indeed,' said Hoffman. 'Two letters, right, Bill? Or did you send some I didn't get?'

'Just two.'

'Would you believe they just made their way to my desk? The filtering process. Actually only the second one got to me directly. Maybe the three times you wrote "personal" on the envelope did the trick. Anyway, I was tickled to receive it. Then I read the reference to your first letter and put out a search for it. Finally found it in some aide's office filed under "Ecology." You probably would have received a form letter in two or three months – where do you get the ham, Elvin? Not Smithwood or Parma, that's for sure.'

'It's through the general mess, sir,' said Ewing. 'As you instructed.'

Hoffman stared at him.

Ewing turned to Zondervein. 'Where's the ham from, Lieutenant?'

'I'm not sure, sir.'

'Find out ASAP. Before the senator leaves.'

'Yes, sir. I'll go to the kitchen right now—'

'No,' said Hoffman. 'Not important – see, Tom, we eat frugally when the public picks up the tab.'

'If you want great grub, Senator, come over to my house.'

'You cook, do you?'

'Love to cook. Got a great beef tournedos recipe.' Creedman smiled at Moreland. 'I'm into meat.'

'Get much meat on the island?' said Hoffman.

'I make do. It takes some creativity.'

'How about you, Pam? Do you like to cook?'

'Not particularly.'

146

'Only thing I can do is biscuits. Campside biscuits, recipe handed down from my great-grandmother – flour, baking soda, salt, sugar, bacon drippings.'

'How long will you be staying?' said Moreland.

'Just till tomorrow.'

'You've finished assessing Stanton?'

'The process began stateside.'

'Are you planning to close it down?'

Hoffman put down his fork and rubbed the rim of his plate. 'We're not at the decision stage, yet.'

'Meaning closure is likely.'

'I can't eliminate any possibilities, Bill.'

'If the base closes, what will happen to Aruk?'

'You're probably in a better position to say, Bill.'

'I probably am,' said Moreland. 'Do you remember what I wrote about the blockade of South Beach road?'

'Yes, I mentioned that to Captain Ewing.'

'Did Captain Ewing give you his reason?'

Hoffman looked at Ewing. 'Elvin?'

Ewing's red face was aflame. 'Security,' he rasped.

'Meaning?' said Moreland.

Ewing directed his answer at Hoffman. 'I'm not free to discuss it openly, sir.'

'The blockade was economic oppression, Nick,' said Moreland.

Hoffman cut free a white outer scrap of melon, stared at it, chewed, and swallowed.

'Sometimes things change, Bill,' he said softly.

'Sometimes they shouldn't, Nick. Sometimes under the guise of helping people we do terrible things.'

Hoffman squinted at Ewing again. 'Could you be a little more forthcoming for Dr Moreland, Elvin?'

Ewing swallowed. There'd been no food in his mouth. 'There was some local unrest. We appraised it given the data at hand, and the judgment was that it had the potential to escalate and pose a hazard to Navy security. Restricting contact between the men and the locals was deemed advisable in terms or risk management. The proper forms were sent to Pacific Command and approval was granted by Admiral Felton.'

'Gobbledygook,' said Moreland. 'A few kids got out of hand. I think the Navy can handle that without choking off the island's economy. We've exploited them all these years, it's immoral to simply yank out the rug.'

Ewing bit back comment and stared straight ahead.

'Bill,' said Hoffman, 'my memory is that *we* saved *them* from the Japanese. That doesn't make us exploiters.'

'Defeating the Japanese was in our national interest. Then we took over and imposed our laws. That makes the people our responsibility.'

Hoffman tapped his fork on his plate.

'With all due respect,' he said very softly, 'that sounds a little paternalistic.'

'It's *realistic*.'

Pam touched the top of his hand. He freed it and said: 'Local unrest makes it sound like some kind of uprising. It was nothing, Nick. Trivial.'

Ewing's lips were so tight they looked sutured.

'Shall I check on the second course, sir?' said Zondervein.

Ewing gave him a guillotine-blade nod.

'Actually, it's not quite that simple,' said Creedman. 'There was a murder. A girl raped and left cut up on the beach. The locals were sure a sailor had done it and were coming up here to protest.'

'Oh?' said Hoffman. 'Is there evidence a sailor was responsible?'

'None whatsoever, sir,' said Ewing, too loudly. 'They love rumors here. The locals got liquored up and tried to storm—'

'Don't make it sound like an insurgence,' said Moreland. 'The people had justification for their suspicions.'

'Oh?' said Hoffman.

'Surely you remember the people, Nick. How nonviolent they are. And the victim consorted with sailors.'

'Consorted.' Hoffman smiled, put his fingers together, and

148

looked over them. 'I knew the people thirty years ago, Bill. I don't believe Navy men tend to be murderers.'

Moreland stared at him.

Ewing was nearly scarlet. 'We were concerned about things getting out of hand. We still believe that concern was justified, given the facts and the hypotheticals. The order came from Pacific Command.'

'Nonsense,' said Moreland. 'The facts are that we're a colonial power and it's the same old pattern: islanders living at the pleasure of westerners only to be abandoned. It's a betrayal. Yet *another* example of abusing trust.'

Hoffman didn't move. Then he picked something out of his teeth and ate another ice cube.

'A betrayal,' repeated Moreland.

Hoffman seemed to be thinking about that. Finally, he said, 'You know that Aruk has a special place in my heart, Bill. After the war, I needed peace and beauty and something unspoiled.' To us: 'Anyone tells you there's anything glorious about war has his head jammed up his rectum so high he's been blinded. Right, Elvin?'

Ewing managed a nod.

'After the war I spent some of the best years of my life here. Remember how you and Barb and Dotty and I used to hike and swim, Bill? How we used to say that some places were better left untouched? Perhaps we were more prescient that we knew. Maybe sometimes nature has to run her course.'

'That's the point, Nicholas. Aruk *has* been touched. People's lives are at—'

'I know, I know. But the problem is one of population distribution. Allocation of increasingly sparse resources. I've seen too many ill-conceived projects that look good on paper but don't wash. Too many assumptions about the inevitable benefits of prosperity and autonomy. Look what happened to Nauru.'

'Nauru is hardly typical,' said Moreland.

'But it's instructive.' Hoffman turned to us. 'Any of you heard

149

of Nauru? Tiny island, southeast of here, smack in the center of Micronesia. Ten square miles of guano – bird dirt. Two hundred years of hands-off colonization by the Brits and the Germans, then someone realizes the place is pure phosphate. The Brits and the Germans collaborate on mining, give the Nauruans nothing but flu and polio. World War Two comes along, the Japanese invade and send most of the Nauruans to Chuuk as forced laborers. After the war, *Australia* takes over and the native chiefs negotiate a sweet deal: big share of the fertilizer profits *plus* Australian welfare. In sixty-eight Australia grants full independence and the chiefs take over the Nauru Phosphate Corporation, which is exporting two million tons of gull poop a year. A *hundred* million dollars in income; per-capita income rises to twenty-thousand-plus. Comparable to an oil sheikdom. Cars, stereos, and junk food for the islanders. Along with a thirty-percent national rate of diabetes. Think of that – one in three. Highest in the world. No special hereditary factors, either. It's clearly all the junk food. Same for high blood pressure, coronary disease, gross obesity – I met an Australian senator who called it "land o' lard." Throw in serious alcoholism and car crashes, and you've got a life expectancy in the fifties. And to top it off, ninety percent of the phosphate is gone. A few more years and nothing'll be left but insulin bottles and beer cans. So much for unbridled prosperity.'

'Are you advocating the virtues of poverty, Nick?'

'No, Bill, but the world's changed, some people think we need to stop looking at ourselves as the universal nursemaid.'

'We're talking about *people*. A way of life—'

Creedman said, 'Whoa. You make it sound as though everything was hunky-dory before the Europeans came over and colonization spoiled everything, but my research tells me there were plenty of diseases in the primitive world and that the people who didn't die of them would probably have died of famine.'

I expected Moreland to turn on him, but he continued to stare at Hoffman.

150

Hoffman said, 'There is some truth to that, Bill. As a doctor you know that.'

'Diseases,' said Moreland, as if the word amused him. 'Yes, there were parasitic conditions, but nothing on the scale of the misery that was brought over.'

'Come on,' said Creedman. 'Let's get real. We're talking primitive tribes. Pagan rituals, no indoor plumbing—'

Moreland faced him slowly. 'Are you a waste-disposal expert in addition to all your other talents?'

Creedman said, 'My resear—'

'Did your *research* tell you that some of those primitive rituals *ensured* impeccable cleanliness? Practices such as reserving mornings for defecation and wading out to the ocean to relieve oneself?'

'That doesn't sound very hygien—'

Moreland's hands rose and his fingers sculpted air. 'It was fine! Until the civilized *conquerors* came along and told them they needed to dig holes in the ground. Do you know what that ushered in, Tom? An era of *filth*. Cholera, typhoid, salmonellosis, lungworm fever. Have you ever *seen* someone with cholera, Creedman?'

'I've—'

'Have you ever held a dehydrated child in your arms as she convulses in the throes of explosive *diarrhea*?'

The gnarled hands dropped and slapped down on the table.

'Research,' he muttered.

Creedman sucked his teeth. He'd gone white.

'I bow, doctor,' he said softly, 'to your superior knowledge of diarrhea.'

The door opened. Zondervein and three sailors, kitchen smells, more food.

'Well,' said Hoffman, exhaling. *'Bon appétit.'*

18

O ther than Hoffman, no one ate much.
After his second dessert, he stood and ripped his napkin free. 'Come on, Bill, let's you and me catch up on old times. Nice to meet you all.'

A glance at Lieutenant Zondervein, who said, 'How about the rest of us head over to the rec room? There's a pool table and a big-screen TV.'

Outside in the hall, Ewing gave him a disgusted look. 'If you'll all excuse me.' He left swiftly.

'This way,' said Zondervein.

'Do you get cable?' Creedman asked.

'Sure,' said Zondervein. 'We get everything, have a satellite dish.'

'Excellent.'

'Isn't there a dish at the Trading Post?' I said.

Creedman laughed. 'Broke a year ago and no one's bothered to fix it. Does that tell you something about local initiative?'

* * *

Creedman and I played a couple of games of pool. He was good, but cheated anyway, moving the cue ball when he thought I wasn't looking.

The big-screen was tuned to CNN.

'News lite,' he said.

'Only thing I get from the news is depressed,' said Pam. She and Robin were sitting in chairs too big for them, looking bored. I caught Robin's eye. She waved and sipped her Coke.

A few minutes later, Zondervein brought Moreland back. He sagged with exhaustion.

Pam said, 'Dad?'

'Time to go.'

After we landed, Creedman walked away from us without a word. No one spoke during the ride back to the estate. When Moreland pulled up in front of the house it was nine-forty. 'I think I'll catch up on work. You all relax.' He patted Pam's arm. 'Have a good night, dear.'

'Maybe I'll go into town.'

'Oh?'

'I thought I might go for a night swim.'

He touched her arm again. Held on to it. 'That could be tricky, Pamela. Urchins, morays, you could run into trouble.'

'I'm sure Dennis can keep me out of trouble.'

He must have squeezed her arm because she winced.

'Dennis,' he said, just above a whisper, 'is engaged to a girl studying at the nursing school in Saipan.'

'Not anymore,' said Pam.

'Oh?'

'They broke up a few weeks ago.'

She touched his arm and he dropped it.

'A pity,' said Moreland. 'Nice girl. She would have been valuable to the island.' Fixing his eyes on his daughter: 'Dennis still is, dear. It would be best for all concerned if you didn't *distract* him.'

Turning on his heel, he walked down toward the bungalows.

Pam's mouth was wide open. She ran up to the house.

'Fun evening,' I said. We were up in our suite, sitting on the bed.

'The way he just acted,' said Robin. 'I know he's under stress, but . . .'

'Loves the natives but doesn't want them dating his daughter?'

'It sounded more like he was shielding Dennis from *her*.'

'It did. Maybe she's got an unfortunate history with men. The first time I saw her I noticed the sadness in her eyes.'

She smiled. 'Is that all you noticed?'

'Yes, she's good-looking but I don't find her sexy. There's something about her that sets up a clear boundary. I've seen it in patients: "I've been wounded. Stay away."'

'That obviously doesn't apply to Dennis.'

'The old man really lost it,' I said. 'Perfect capper to a charming dinner.'

She laughed. 'That base. Night of the uniformed dead. And Hoffman. Joe Slick.'

'Why do I get the feeling Hoffman's sole purpose for the dinner was the half hour he and Moreland spent alone?'

'Then why not just drop over here?'

'Maybe he wanted to be on his home turf, not Moreland's.'

'You make it sound like some sort of battle.'

'I can't help but think it was. The tension between them . . . as if the two of them have some issue that goes way back. At any rate, Moreland didn't get what he wanted for Aruk. Whatever that is.'

'What do you mean?'

'He puzzles me, Rob. Talks about helping the island, rejuvenating it. But if he's as rich as Creedman says, it seems to me there are things he could have already done. Like improve communication. Put some of his fortune into schooling, training. At the very least, more frequent shipping schedules. Instead, he pumps a fortune into his projects. Walled in here like some lord while the rest of the island molders. Maybe the islanders know that and that's why they're leaving. We certainly haven't seen any big show of civic pride. Not even a grass-roots movement to protest the barricade.'

She thought about that. 'Yes, he is very much the lord of the manor, isn't he? And maybe the islanders know something else: Hoffman's right about some places not being set up for development. Look at Aruk's geography. The leeward side has great weather but no harbor, the windward side has a natural harbor but rocks instead of soil. In between, you've got mountains and a banyan forest full of land mines. Nothing fits right. It's like a geographic joke. Maybe everyone gets it but Moreland.'

'And Skip and Haygood with their resort scheme. Which proves your point. Oh, well, looks like I signed on with Dr Quixote.'

She got up and rolled off her panty hose, frowning. 'It was so out of character, the way he just treated Pam. There doesn't seem to be much intimacy between them – which makes sense, with his being an absent father – but till tonight he's never been harsh.'

'He's the one who sent her to boarding school,' I said. 'And even with her M.D. he doesn't consider her a colleague. All in all, no candidate for father of the year.'

'Poor Pam. First time I saw her I thought, "homecoming queen." But you never know, do you?'

She unbuttoned her dress and stepped out of it. Folded it over a chair and touched her wrist.

'How does it feel?' I said.

'Excellent, actually. Are you working tomorrow?'

'Guess so.'

'Maybe I'll try to do something with those pieces of shell.'

She went into the bathroom. And screamed.

19

Three of them.

No, *four!*

Racing back and forth, light-panicked, on the white tile floor.

One scurried up the shower wall, pointed its antennae at us. Waved.

Robin was pressed into a corner, fighting another scream.

One crawled up the side of the tub, paused on the rim.

Lozenge shaped. Red-brown armored shell as long as my hand.

Six black legs.

The eyes, too damn smart.

It hissed.

They all began hissing.

Speeding toward us.

I pulled Robin out of the room and slammed the door behind us. Checked the space beneath the door. Tight fit, thank God.

My heart was hurtling. Sweat burst out of me and it leaked down in cold, itchy trails.

Robin's fingers bit into my back.

'Oh God, Alex! Oh God!'

I managed to say, 'It's okay, they can't get out.'

'Oh, God . . .' She gasped for breath. 'I walked in and something touched – my foot.'

She looked down at her toes and trembled.

I sat her down. She held onto my fingers, shaking.

'Easy,' I said, remembering the insect's face – stoic, intense.

'Get rid of them, honey. Please!'

'I will.'

'The light was off. I felt it before I saw it – how many were there?'

'I counted four.'

'It seemed like more.'

'I think four is all.'

'Oh, *God*.'

I held her tight. 'It's all right, they're confined.'

'Yucch,' she said. '*Yucch!*'

Spike was barking. When had he started?

'Maybe I should sic *him* on them.'

'No, no, I don't want him near them – they're disgusting. Just get them out of here, Alex! Call Moreland. I can take them in their cages, but please get them *out!*'

Gladys arrived first.

'Bugs?' she said.

'*Huge* ones,' said Robin. 'Where's Dr Bill?'

'Must be from the bug zoo. It never happened before.'

'Where *is* he, Gladys?'

'On his way. You poor thing. Where are they?'

I pointed to the bathroom.

She grimaced. 'Personally, I hate bugs. Nasty little things.'

'Little wouldn't be bad,' said Robin.

'Working here doesn't bother you?' I said.

157

'What, the zoo? I never go in there. No one goes in there but Dr Bill and Ben.'

'Well, something obviously comes out.'

'It never happened before,' she repeated.

Hissing from behind the door. I pictured the damn things chewing through the wood. Or escaping down the toilet and hiding in the pipes. Where the hell was Moreland?

'Did you see what they were?' said Gladys.

'They looked like giant cockroaches,' said Robin.

'Madagascar hissing cockroaches,' I said, suddenly remembering.

'Them I really hate,' said Gladys. 'Cockroaches in general. One of the things I like about Aruk is the dryness, we don't get roaches. Lots of bugs, period.'

'So we import them,' I mumbled.

'I keep my kitchen clean. Some of the other islands you've got bugs all over the place, got to spray all the time. Bugs bring disease – not Dr Bill's bugs, he keeps them real clean.'

'That's a comfort,' I said.

A knock sounded on the suite door and Moreland loped in carrying a large mahogany box with a brass handle and looking around.

'I don't see how . . . did you happen to notice what kind—'

'Madagascar hissing roaches,' I said.

'Oh . . . good. They can't seriously harm you.'

'They're in there.'

He advanced to the bathroom door.

'Careful,' said Robin. 'Don't let them out.'

'No problem, dear.' He turned the knob slowly and took something out of his pocket – a piece of chocolate cake that he compressed into a gummy ball. Spreading the door a crack, he tossed the bait, closed, waited.

A few seconds later, he opened the door again, peered through. Nodded, opened wider, slipped in.

'My new fudge loaf,' said Gladys.

Sounds came from inside the bathroom.

Moreland talking.

Soothingly.

He emerged moments later holding the mahogany box and giving the OK sign. Chocolate smears on his fingers. Crumbs on the floor.

Thumps from within the box.

Hiss.

'You're sure you got all of them?' said Robin.

'Yes, dear.'

'They didn't lay eggs or anything?'

He smiled at her. 'No, dear, everything's fine.'

It sounded patronizing and it got to me.

'Not really, Bill,' I said. 'How the hell did they get here in the first place?'

'I – don't know – I'm sorry. *Dreadfully* sorry. My apologies to both of you.'

'They're definitely from the insectarium?'

'Certainly, Aruk has no indig—'

'So how'd they get out?'

'I – suppose someone must have left the lid loose.'

'It's never happened before,' said Gladys.

'That's us,' I said. 'Trailblazers.'

Moreland tugged at his lower lip, rubbed his fleshy nose. Blinked. 'I suppose *I* must have left the lid off—'

'It's okay,' Robin said, squeezing my hand. 'It's over.'

'I'm *so* sorry, dear. Perhaps the scent of your dog food—'

'If it was food they were after,' I said, 'why didn't they head for the kitchen?'

'I keep my kitchen clean and shut up tight,' said Gladys. 'No flies, not even grain weevils.'

'Our door was locked,' I said, 'and the dog food's sealed in plastic bags. How did they get in, Bill?'

He went over to the door, opened and closed it a couple of times, kneeled and ran his hand over the threshold.

'There's some give to the carpet,' he said. 'They're very good at compressing themselves. I've seen them manage—'

'Spare the details,' I said. 'You probably knocked a year off our lives.'

'I'm terribly, terribly sorry.' He hung his head. The cockroaches bumped inside the box. Then the hissing began again. Louder . . .

'You did handle it perfectly,' he said. 'Locking them in. Thank you for not damaging them.'

'You're welcome,' I said. I'd turned phone solicitors down with a kinder tone.

Robin squeezed my hand again.

'It's okay, Bill,' she said. 'We're fine.'

Moreland said, 'An unforgivable laspse. I'm always so careful – I'll put double locks on the insectarium immediately. And door seals. We'll get working on it right now – Gladys, call Kamon and Carl Sleet, apologize for waking them up, and tell them I've got a job for them. Triple overtime pay. Tell Carl to bring the Swiss drill I gave him for Christmas.'

Gladys rushed out.

Moreland looked at the box and rubbed the oiled wood. 'Better be getting these fellows back.' He hurried to the door and nearly collided with Jo Picker as she padded in, wearing robe and slippers, rubbing her eyes.

'Is everything . . . okay?' Her voice was thick. She coughed to clear it.

'Just a little mishap,' said Moreland.

She frowned. Her eyes were unfocused.

'Took something . . . to sleep . . . did I hear someone scream?'

'I did,' said Robin. 'There were some bugs in the bathroom.'

'Bugs?'

The roaches hissed and her eyes widened.

'Go back to sleep, dear,' said Moreland, guiding her out. 'Everything's been taken care of. Everything's fine.'

When we were alone, we let Spike out and he raced around the room, circling. Sniffing near the bathroom before charging in head down.

'The dog food goes downstairs tomorrow,' said Robin.

Then she got up suddenly, pulled back the bedcovers, looked underndeath the box spring, and then stood. Smiling sheepishly.

'Just being careful,' she said.

'Are you going to be able to sleep?' I said.

'Hope so. How about you?'

'My heart's down to two hundred beats a minute.'

She sighed. Started laughing and couldn't stop.

I wanted to join in but couldn't manage more than a taut smile.

'Our little bit of New York,' she finally said. 'Manhattan tenement in our island hideaway.'

'Those things could *mug* New York roaches.'

'I know.' She put my hand on her breast. 'How many beats?'

'Hmm,' I said. 'Hard to tell. I need to count for a *long* time.'

More laughter. 'God, the way I shrieked. Like one of those horror movies.'

Her forehead was moist, curls sticking to it. I brushed them away, kissed her brow, the tip of her nose.

'So how long do we stay in bug-land?' I said.

'You want to leave?'

'Plane crash, unsolved murder, the zombie base, some fairly uncongenial people. Now this.'

'Don't leave on my account. I can't tell you I won't freak out if the same thing happens again, but I'm okay, now. Ms Adaptable. I pride myself on it.'

'Sure,' I said, 'but sometimes it's nice not having to adapt.'

'True . . . Maybe I'm nuts but I still like it here. Maybe it's my hand feeling better – a lot better, actually. Or even the fact that this may be our last chance to experience Aruk before the Navy turns it into a bomb yard or something. Even Bill – he's unique, Aruk is unique.'

She held my face and looked into my eyes. 'I guess what I'm saying, Alex, is I don't want to be back in L.A. next week, dealing with the house or some business hassle, and start thinking back with regrets.'

I didn't answer.

'Am I making sense, doctor?'

I touched my nose to hers. Curled my lip. Bared my teeth. Hissed.

She jumped up. Pounded my shoulder. '*Oh!* Maybe I should have Spike sleep in the bed and put *you* in the crate.'

Lights out.

A few self-conscious jokes about creepy-crawlies and she was sleeping.

I lay awake.

Trying to picture the roaches trekking all the way from the insectarium to our suite . . . marching in unison? The idea was cartoonish.

And even if the dog food *had* attracted them, why hadn't they stayed in the sitting room, near the bag?

Roaches were supposed to be smart, as bugs went. Why not head for an easier meal – the fruit from the orchard?

Instead, they'd taken a circuitous journey, scampering up the gravel paths, across the lawn, into the house somehow. Bypassing Gladys's kitchen. Up the stairs. Under our door.

All because of a sealed sack of kibble?

Despite Moreland's claim, the bathroom door seemed too snug to let them in or out. Had we left it open before leaving for dinner at the base?

Robin always left the bathroom door closed. Sometimes I didn't . . . Which of us had last used the lav?

Why hadn't they come running out when we arrived home? Or at least hissed in alarm?

An alternative scenario: they'd been placed in the bathroom and shut in.

Someone up to mischief during the dinner at Stanton. The house empty. Someone seizing the opportunity to send us a message: *Go away.*

But who and why?

Who had the opportunity?

Ben was the obvious choice, because he had access to the insectarium.

He'd said his evening was full, between fatherhood and a hibachi dinner with Claire.

Had he come back?

But why? Apart from the remark about natural rhythm, he'd shown no sign of hostility toward us. On the contrary. He'd gone out of his way to make us feel welcome.

Out of obligation to Moreland?

Were his own feelings something else?

I thought about it for a while, but it just didn't make sense.

Someone else on the staff?

Cheryl?

Too dull to be that calculating, and once again, what was her motive? Plus, she usually left after dinner, and no meal had been served tonight.

Gladys? Same lack of motive, and the idea of her purloining roaches seemed equally ludicrous.

There had to be at least a dozen groundskeepers and gardeners who came and went, but why would *they* resent us?

Unless the message had been meant for *Moreland.*

My surmise about his attitude of noblesse oblige and the resentment it might have generated in the villagers could be right on target.

The good doctor less than universally loved? His guests seen as colonial interlopers?

If so, it could be anyone.

Paranoia, Delaware. The guy had kept thousands of bugs for years, four had gotten out because he was old and absentminded and had forgotten to put a lid on tight.

Spacey, just as Milo had said.

Not a comforting thought, *considering* the thousands of bugs, but I supposed he'd be especially careful now.

I tried to empty my head and sleep. Thought of the way Jo Picker had come in: drowsy, asking if someone had screamed.

Robin's scream had sounded a full ten minutes before.

Why the delay?

The sleeping pill slowing her responses?

Or no need to hurry because she *knew*?

And *she'd* been alone upstairs all evening.

Paranoia run amok. What reason would a grieving widow have for malicious mischief?

She'd said she was squeamish about insects, had refused even to enter the bug zoo.

And there was no animosity between us. Robin had been especially kind to her . . . Even if she was a fiend, how could she have gained access to our room?

Her own room key – the lock similar to ours?

Or a simple pick. Most bedroom locks weren't designed for security. Ours back home could be popped with a screwdriver.

I lay there and listened for sounds through the wall.

Nothing.

What did I expect to hear, the click of her keyboard? Widow's wails?

I shifted position and the mattress rocked, but Robin didn't budge.

Teachers' voices from many years ago filtered through my brain.

Alexander is a very bright little boy, but he does tend to day-dream.

Is something wrong at home, Mrs Delaware? Alexander has seemed rather distracted lately.

A soft, liquid line of light oozed through a part in the curtains like golden paint freshly squeezed.

Playing on Robin's face.

She smiled in her sleep, curls dangling over one eye.

Take her example and *adapt*.

I relaxed my muscles consciously and deepened my breathing. Soon my chest loosened and I felt better.

164

Able to smile at the image of Moreland with his chocolate cake and schoolboy guilt.

My body felt heavy. Ready to sleep.

But it took a long time to fall under.

20

The next morning, the clouds were darker and moving closer, but still, remote.

We were ready to dive at ten. Spike was acting restless, so we decided to take him along. Needing something to shade him, we went to the kitchen and asked Gladys. She called Carl Sleet in from the rose garden, where he was pruning, and he trotted over carrying his shears. His gray work clothes, hair, and beard were specked with grass clippings, and his nails were filthy. He went to the outbuildings and came back with an old umbrella with a spiked post and a blue-and-white canvas shade that was slightly soiled.

'Want me to load it for you?'

'No, thanks. I can do it.'

'Put new locks on the bug house last night. Strong ones. Shouldn't be having any more problems.'

'Thanks.'

'Welcome. Got any fudge left, Gladys?'

'Here you go.' She gave him some and he returned to his work, eating.

Gladys walked us through the kitchen. 'Dr Bill feels awful about last night.'

'I'll let him know there are no hard feelings.'

'That would be . . . charitable – now you two have a good time.'

I pitched the umbrella on South Beach and realized we'd forgotten to bring drinks. Leaving Robin and Spike on the sand, I drove over to Auntie Mae's Trading Post. The same faded clothes were in the windows, which were fly-specked and cloudy. Inside, the place was barnlike, with wooden stalls lining a sawdust aisle and walls of raw board.

Most of the booths were empty and even those that were stocked weren't staffed. More clothing, cheap, out of date. Beach sandals, suntan lotion, and tourist kitsch – miniature thatched huts of bamboo and astroturf, plastic dancing girls, pouting tiki gods, coconuts carved into blowfish. The building smelled of cornmeal and seawater and a bit of backed-up bilge.

The only other human being was a young, plainfaced woman in a red tank top watching TV behind the counter of the third booth to the right. Her cash register was a scarred, black antique. Next to it were canisters of beef jerky and pickled eggs and a half-full bottle of Windex and a rag. The front case was filled with candy bars and chips – potato, corn, taro. On the rear wall were a swinging door and shelves holding sealed boxes of sweets. The television was mounted to the side wall that separated the stall from its neighbor, sharing space with a pay phone.

She noticed me but kept watching the screen. The image was fuzzy, streaked intermittently with bladelike flashes of white. A station from Guam. Long shot of a big room with polished wood walls, corporate logo of a hotel chain over a long banquet table.

Senator Nicholas Hoffman sat in the center behind a glass of water and a microphone. He wore a white-and-brown batik shirt and several brilliantly colored flower necklaces. The two white

167

men flanking him were dressed the same way. One I recognized as a legislator from the Midwest; the other was cut from the same hair-tonicked, hungry-smile mold. Four other men, Asians, sat at the ends of the table.

Hoffman glanced at his notes, then looked up smiling. 'And so let me conclude by celebrating the fact that we all share a vision of a more viable and prosperous Micronesia, a multicultural Micronesia that moves swiftly and confidently into the next century.'

He smiled again and gave a small bow. Applause. The screen flickered, went gray, shut off. The young woman turned it back on. Commercial for Island Fever Restaurant #6: slack-key guitar theme song, pupu platters and flaming desserts, 'native beauties skilled in ancient dances for your entertainment pleasure.' A caricature of a chubby little man in a grass skirt rolling his hips and winking.

'C'mon, brudda!'

The woman flicked the remote control. More black screen, then a ten-year-old sitcom. She watched as the credits rolled, then said, 'Can I help you?' Pleasant, almost childish voice. Twenty or so, with acne and short, wavy hair. No bra under the tank top. Not even close to pretty, but her smile was open and lovely.

'Something to drink, if you've got it.'

'I've got Coke and Sprite and beer in the back.'

'Two Cokes, two Sprites.' I noticed a couple of paperback books on the rear counter. 'Maybe something to read, too.'

She handed me the books. A Stephen King I'd read and a compact world atlas, both with curled covers.

'Any magazines?'

'Um, maybe under here.' She bent and stood. 'Nope. I'll check in back. You're the doctor staying with Dr Bill, right?'

'Alex Delaware.' I held out my hand and we shook. I noticed a diamond chip ring on the third finger.

'Bettina – Betty Aguilar.' She smiled shyly. 'Just got married.'

'Congratulations.'

'Thanks . . . he's a great man – Dr Bill. When I was a kid I

168

had a bad whooping cough and he cured me. Hold on, lemme get you your drinks and see about magazines.'

She went through the swinging door.

So much for rampant island hostility to Moreland.

She came back with four cans and a stack of periodicals. 'This is all we've got. Pretty old. Sorry.'

'Is it hard to get current stuff?'

She shrugged. 'We get whatever comes over on the supply boats, usually it's a couple of issues late. *People* and *Playboy* and stuff like that goes fast – any of this interest you?'

Half-year-old issues of *Ladies Home Journal, Reader's Digest, Time, Newsweek, Fortune*, and at the bottom, several copies of a large glossy quarterly entitled *Island World*. Gorgeous smiling black-haired girls and sun-blushed tropical vistas.

The publications dates, three to five years old.

'Boy, those really *are* old,' said Betty. 'Found 'em under a box. They used to publish it out of Guam but I don't think they do anymore.'

I flipped through tables of contents. Mostly boosterism. Then a title caught my eye.

'I'll take them,' I said.

'Really? Gee, they're so old I wouldn't know what to charge you. Here, take 'em for free.'

'I'll be happy to pay.'

'It's okay,' she insisted. 'You're my best customer today and they're just taking up space. Want some munchies to go with your drinks?'

I bought two bags of kettle-boiled Maui potato chips and some jerky. As she took my money, her eyes drifted back to the TV. Another blackout. She switched the set on automatically, as if used to it.

'Bad reception?'

'The satellite keeps going in and out, depending on the weather and stuff.' She counted out change. 'I'm having a baby. Dr Bill's gonna deliver it. In six months.'

'Congratulations.'

169

'Yeah . . . we're excited. My husband and me. Here you go . . . After the baby's born we'll probably be moving away. My husband works construction and there's no work.'

'Nothing at all?'

'Not really. This here is the biggest building in town. A few years back Dr Bill was thinking of redoing it, but no one else really cared.'

'Dr Bill owns the Trading Post?'

She seemed surprised that I didn't know. 'Sure. He's real good about it, doesn't charge rent, just lets people order their own stuff and sell it outta the booths. There used to be more business here, when the Navy guys still came in. Now most of the stallkeepers don't come in unless someone calls to order. It's actually my mom's stall, but she's sick – bad heart. I've got time, waiting for my baby, so I take over for her and my husband delivers – most of our stuff's delivery.'

She touched her still-flat belly.

'My husband would like a boy, but I don't care as long as it's healthy.'

Laugh-track noise from the TV. She turned her head and smiled along with the electronic joy.

'Bye,' I said.

She waved absently.

When I got back to the beach, Robin's snorkel was a tiny white duck bobbing near the outer edge of the reef. Our blankets were spread, and Spike was leashed to the umbrella post, barking furiously.

The object of his wrath was Skip Amalfi, stark naked, peeing a high, arcing stream into the sand, several yards away. Anders Haygood stood next to him, in knee-length baggies, watching. Skip's bleached-bone buttocks said skinnydipping wasn't a habit. His green trunks lay next to him like a heap of wilted salad.

Spike barked louder. Skip laughed and aimed the stream closer to the dog, shaking with glee as Spike growled and spat drool.

Then the arc dribbled and died. Spike shook himself off theatrically, and moved closer to them.

I ran. Haygood saw me and said something to Skip, who stopped and turned, offering a full frontal view. I kept coming.

Grinning, Skip looked over his shoulder at Robin's snorkel. His urine trail was drying quickly, a brown snake sinking into the sand. Spike was pawing the blanket, finally moving enough of it to reach sand and scatter it.

Skip stretched and yawned and massaged his gut.

'Is that going to be the official welcome at your resort?' I said, smiling.

His face darkened, but he forced himself to smile back. 'Yeah, living naturally.'

'Better watch the ultraviolet radiation. It can lead to impotence.'

'Whu?'

'The sun.'

'Your hard-on,' said Haygood, amused. 'What the man's trying to tell you is bruise it and lose it. Watch the UV on your tool or you'll be hauling limp wiener.'

'Fuck you,' Skip told him, but he looked at me edgily.

'It's true,' I said. 'Too much UV to the genitals heats up the scrotal plexus and weakens the neurotestostinal reflex.'

'Boil it and spoil it,' said Haygood.

'Fuck you in the *ass*,' said Skip. Looking for his trunks.

Haygood lunged, grabbed them up, and began running down the beach. Stocky but fast.

Skip went after him, potbelly quivering, holding his crotch.

Spike was still drooling and breathing hard. I sat down and tried to calm him. Robin had moved into shallower waters. She stood, lifted her face mask, and waved. Then she saw the two men running and came out of the water.

'What was that all about?'

I told her.

'How rude.'

'He was probably hoping you'd come out and see him playing fireman.'

'Shucks, I missed it.' She squatted and petted Spike. 'Mama's all right, sweetie. Don't worry about those turkeys. It's gorgeous down there, Alex. Come on in.'

'Maybe later.'

'Is something wrong?'

'Let me just stick around for a while in case they return. Though I may have traumatized old Skip.'

I recounted my UV warning and she cracked up.

'You probably ruined what little sex life he's got.'

'Reverse therapy. My education is now fully validated.'

'Don't worry about them, Alex – dive with me. If they come back, we'll give Spike a run at them.'

'Spike can be drop-kicked by a twelve-year-old.'

'They don't know that. Tell them he's a neurotestostinal pit bull.'

We visited every crag in the reef side by side and emerged an hour later to an undisturbed beach. Spike slept noisily, under a cloud of sand flies. The drinks had warmed, but we poured them down our throats. Then Robin stretched out on a blanket and closed her eyes, and I picked up the spring 1988 issue of *Island World*.

The article that had caught my eye was on page 113, after come-hither tourist pieces on Pacific Rim archaeological sites, choice dive spots, restaurants and nightclubs.

'Bikini: A History of Shame.'

The author was a man named Micah Sanjay, formerly a civilian official of the Marshall Islands' U.S. military government, now a retired high school principal living in Chalan Kanoa, Saipan.

His story was identical to the one Moreland had told me: failure to evacuate the residents of Bikini and Majuro and the neighboring Marshall atolls. Clandestine nighttime boat rides doling out compensation.

The *exact* same story, down to the amount of money paid.

Sanjay wrote matter-of-factly but his anger came through. A Majuro native, he'd lost relatives to leukemia and lymphoma.

No greater anger than when recounting the payoff.

Sanjay and six other civil servants assigned the job.

Six names, none of them Moreland.

I reread the article, searching for any mention of the doctor. Nothing.

If the old man had never been part of the payoff, why had he lied about it?

Something else he said the first night resonated:

Guilt is a great motivator, Alex.

Feeling himself culpable for the blast? He'd been a Navy officer. Had he known about the winds?

Was it *guilt* that had transformed him from a trust-fund kid in dress whites to a would-be Schweitzer?

Coming to Aruk to *atone*?

Not that his lifestyle had suffered – living in a grand estate, indulging his passions.

Aruk, his fiefdom . . . but his daughter couldn't be permitted to fraternize with the locals.

Did he *want* the villagers isolated? So he could enjoy Aruk on his own terms – an idealized refuge for noble savages with good hygiene and clean water?

Maybe I was judging him unfairly – residual anger about the cockroaches.

But it did appear that he'd lied to me about the Marshalls' compensation program, and that bothered me.

I looked over at Robin's beautiful, prone body, gleaming in the sun. Spike slept too.

I was hunched, fingers tight on the magazine.

Maybe Moreland had indeed been in those boats. Another payoff team, not Sanjay's.

One way to find out: talk to the author.

Sanjay had worked for the government forty years ago, then as a school principal, meaning he was Moreland's age or close to it.

Still alive? Still on Saipan?

Robin rolled over. 'Umm, this sun is great.'

'Sure is,' I said. 'Hot, too, and the drinks are all gone. I'll bop over to the Trading Post and get us some more.'

21

I jogged this time, veering from the beach to the docks where Skip and Haygood sat dangling fishing poles. Haygood watched me. Skip kept his eyes on the water. He had his trunks on and a T-shirt, the most clothes I'd seen him in.

Inside the Trading Post, Betty Aguilar was watching a game show and munching a Mars bar.

'Hi. Back so soon?'

'Couple of beers, two more Cokes.'

'You're *definitely* my best customer – hold on, I'll get them for you.'

'Does the pay phone work?'

'Usually, but if you want to call Dr Bill's place, I can let you use the one in back for free.'

'No, this is long distance.'

'Oh – do you need change?'

'I thought I'd use my calling card.'

'I think that'll work.' She went in back and I lifted the receiver.

Another rotary. It took a while to get a dial tone, a lot longer to work my way through several operators and finally obtain permission to use the card. Each successive connection was worse than the previous one, and by the time I reached Saipan Information, I was speaking through a hail of static and the echo of my own voice on one-second delay.

But Micah Sanjay was listed, and when I called his number an older-sounding man with a mild voice said, 'Yes?'

'Sorry to bother you, Mr Sanjay, but I'm a free-lance writer named Thomas Creedman, on temporary stopover in Aruk.'

'Uh-huh.'

'I just happened to come across your article in *Island World* on the nuclear testing in the Marshalls.'

'That was a long time ago.'

Unsure if he meant the disaster or the magazine piece, I pressed on. 'I thought it was very interesting and extremely well done.'

'Are you writing about Bikini, too?'

'I'm thinking about it, if I can get a fresh slant.'

'I tried to sell that article to some mainland magazines, but no one was interested.'

'Really?'

'People don't want to know, and those that do know want to forget.'

'Easier on the conscience.'

'You bet.' His voice had hardened.

'I think some of the most powerful scenes were your descriptions of the compensation process. Those nighttime boat rides.'

'Yes, that was tough. Sneaking around.'

'Were you and the six other men the entire compensation staff?'

'There were bosses who ordered it from behind a desk, but we did all the actual paying.'

'Do you remember the boss's names?'

'Admiral Haupt, Captain Ravenswood. Above them were people from Washington, I guess.'

176

'Are you still in touch with the other men on the team? If it would be possible for me to talk to them . . .'

'I'm not in touch but I know where they are. George Avuelas died a few years ago. Cancer, but I can't say for sure if it was related. The others are gone, too, except Bob Taratoa, and he lives in Seattle, has a boy there. But he had a stroke last year, so I'm not sure how much he could tell you.'

'So there's no one else still in the Marianas?'

'Nope, just me. Where'd you say you were from?'

'Aruk.'

'What is that, one of those small islands up north a bit from here?'

'That's it.'

'Anything to do there?'

'Sun and write.'

'Well, good luck.'

'There's a doctor who lives here named Moreland, says he was in the Navy when the tests went off. Says he treated some of the people who'd been exposed.'

'Moreland?'

'Woodrow Wilson Moreland.'

'Don't know him, but there were lots of doctors, some of them pretty good. But they couldn't do anything for the people even if they wanted to. Those bombs poisoned the air and the water, radioactivity got into the soil. No matter what they say, I'm convinced they'll never get the stuff out.'

As I left the post, I saw Jacqui Laurent and Dennis standing in front of the Chop Suey Palace. The mother was talking and the son was listening.

Scolding him. Being subtle about it – no hand gestures or raised voice – but her eyes flashed and the displeasure on her face was evident.

Dennis stood there and took it, his giant frame slightly bowed. She looked so young a casual observer might have thought it a lovers' spat.

She folded her hands over her chest and waited.

Dennis scuffed the ground. Nodded.

Similar look to the one Pam had worn after Moreland had reprimanded her.

Same issue?

Lord of the manor dropping in on one of his tenants this morning? Letting her know his displeasure about Dennis and Pam?

Dennis looked from side to side, saw me, and said something. Jacqui put a hand around his thick forearm and propelled him quickly inside.

Back at the estate, I sat through a lunch of broiled halibut and fresh vegetables, walked Robin and Spike down to the orchard, and headed for my office.

Moreland had left another folded card on my desk.

Alex:
> *Cannot locate catwoman file.*

> *Spirits overwrought*
> *Were making night do penance for a day*
> *Spent in a round of strenuous idleness.*
> *Wordsworth*

> *A fitting quote for that case, don't you think?*
> *Bill*

I sat at my desk. *Night do penance . . . strenuous idleness.*

The philandering husband?

Always riddles.

As if he were playing with me.

Why had he lied to me about the payoff?

Time to talk.

178

*   *   *

The door to his office was unlocked, but he wasn't in there, and the lab door was closed. I went over to knock and, passing his desk, noticed the reprints of my journal articles fanned like playing cards. Next to some newspaper clippings.

Clippings about me.

My involvement in a mass child-abuse case years ago.

My consultation to a grade school terrorized by a sniper.

Accounts of court testimony in several murder cases.

My name highlighted in yellow.

Milo's, too.

I remembered the message he'd written about Milo's call: *Detective Sturgis*. Off the job Milo generally didn't identify himself by title.

Researching him, too?

Thick pile of clippings. On the bottom, a homicide trial. My testimony for the prosecution, debunking the phony insanity plea of a man who'd savaged a dozen women.

Moreland's notation in the margin: *Perfect!*

So I'd been selected for something other than 'a fine combination of scholarliness and common-sense thinking.'

Moreland, definitely worried about the cannibal killer.

Had he lured me here under false premises in order to pick my brain?

Dr Detective. What the hell did I have to offer?

Did he have reason to believe the murderer was still on Aruk?

A crash from inside the lab made me jump, and my hand brushed the clippings to the floor. I picked them up quickly and ran to the inner door.

Locked.

I knocked hard.

A groan from inside.

'Bill?'

Another groan.

'It's Alex. Are you all right?'

179

A few seconds later, the knob turned and Moreland stood there rubbing his forehead with one hand. The other was palm down, dripping blood. He looked stunned.

'Fell asleep,' he said. Behind him, on the lab table, were brightly colored boxes, plastic cartons. Test tubes on the floor, reduced to jagged glass.

'Your hand, Bill.'

He turned his hand palm up. Blood had pooled and was trickling down his wrist and narrowing to a single red line that wiggled the length of his scrawny forearm.

I led him to the sink and washed the wound. Clean gash, not deep enough to require stitching but still oozing steadily.

'Where's your first-aid kit?'

'Underneath.' Pointing drowsily to a lower cabinet.

I applied antibiotic ointment and a bandage.

'Fell asleep,' he repeated, shaking his head. The colored boxes contained dehydrated potatoes and wheat pilaf, precooked peas, lentils, rice mix.

'Nutritional research,' said Moreland, as if he owed me an explanation.

His attention shifted to the broken glass and he bent.

I reached out to restrain him. 'I'll take care of it.'

'Working late,' he said, weakly. He glanced at the bandaged hand, rubbed his mouth, licked his lips. 'Usually I do some of my best work after dark. Got a late start, making sure those locks got installed correctly. I'm still mortified about what happened.'

'Forget it.'

He stretched out a hand. We shook and I felt his tremor.

'I must have left the lid off and the door unlocked. Inexcusable. Must remember to check every detail.'

He began massaging his temples very rapidly.

'Headache?'

'Sleep deprivation,' he said. 'I should know better, at my age . . . Are you aware that most so-called civilizations are *chronically* sleep deprived?'

'Because of electricity?'

180

He nodded emphatically. 'Before electricity, people lit a candle or two, then went to bed. The sun was their alarm clock; they were tuned to a natural cadence. Nine, ten hours of sleep a day. It's a rare civilized man who gets eight.'

'Do the villagers sleep well?'

'What do you mean?'

'There's not much technology on the island. Lousy TV reception, less to keep them up.'

'TV', he said, 'is multiple-choice rubbish. However, if you miss it, I can arrange something.'

'No, thanks, but I wouldn't mind a newspaper now and then. Just to stay in touch with the world.'

'I'm sorry, son, can't help you there. We used to get papers more often when the Navy let us ship things on their supply planes, but now we depend upon the boats. Don't you find the radio news sufficient?'

'I noticed some American papers on your desk.'

He blinked. 'Those are old.'

'Research?'

Our eyes locked. His were clear and alert now.

'Yes, I use a clipping service in Guam. If you'd like I can have them bulk-order some periodicals for you. And if you'd like to watch TV, I can get you a portable set.'

'No, it's not necessary.'

'You're sure?'

'Hundred percent.'

'Please tell me if there's anything more you need by way of creature comforts. I want your stay to be enjoyable.'

He ran his tongue under his right cheek and frowned. 'Has it been – enjoyable? Excepting last night, of course.'

'We're having a fine time.'

'I hope so. One tries . . . to be a good host.' He smiled and shrugged. 'My apologies again about the hissers—'

'Let's really forget it, Bill.'

'You're very gracious . . . I suppose I've been living here by myself so long that the niceties of social discourse elude me.'

181

Staring at the floor again. Holding his bandaged hand with the other and getting that absent look in his eyes.

Then he snapped out of it, stood suddenly, and surveyed the lab. 'Back to work.'

'Don't you think you should rest?'

'No, no, I'm tiptop. By the way, what was it you came here for?'

What I'd *come* for were piercing questions about Samuel H. and radiation poisoning. Payoffs, half-truths, and subterfuge. What, if anything, his role had been forty years ago.

Now something else: why was my involvement in crime cases 'perfect'?

I said, 'Just wanted to know if there were any specific cases you wanted me to look over.'

'Oh, no, I wouldn't presume. As I told you at the outset, you have total freedom.'

'I wouldn't mind reviewing any other nuclear fallout cases you might have. Neuropsychological sequellae of radiation poisoning. I don't think anyone's studied it. It could be a great opportunity for us to produce a unique theoretical base.'

His head retracted an inch and he put a hand on the counter. 'Yes, it could.'

He began arranging boxes of dried food, peering at ingredients, straightening a test-tube rack. 'Unfortunately, Samuel's is the only radiation chart I took with me. Till I came across it, I didn't know it was there. Or perhaps I left it there unconsciously. Wanting a reminder.'

'Of what?'

'The terrible, terrible things people do under the guise of authority.'

'Yes,' I said, 'authority can be horribly corrupting.'

Short, hard nod. Another burdened look.

He stared at me, then turned away and held a testtube of brown liquid up to the light. His arm tremored.

'It would have been an interesting paper, Alex. Sorry I haven't any more data.'

'Speaking of authority,' I said, 'I was at the Trading Post this morning and happened to catch the tail end of Hoffman's press conference in Guam.'

'Really?' He inspected another tube.

'He was talking about his plan to develop Micronesia.'

'He made his fortune building shopping centers, so I'm not surprised. That and so-called managed forestry. His father was a lumberjack, but he's responsible for more timber clearing than his father could have ever imagined.'

'He has a reputation for being ecologically minded.'

'There are ways.'

'Of what?'

'Of getting one's way without fouling one's own nest. He chopped down rain forest in South America but supported national parks in Oregon and Idaho. So the ecology groups gave him an excellent rating. A fact he reminded me of last night. As if that excused it.'

'Excused what?'

'What he's doing here.'

'Letting Aruk die?'

He put down the test tube and glared at me. 'A loss of vigor doesn't imply the terminal state.'

'So you have hope for the island?'

His hands dropped to his sides again, skinny and rigid as ski poles. Blood had seeped under the bandage and crusted.

'I always have hope,' he said, barely moving his lips. 'Without hope, there's nothing.'

He lit a Bunsen burner and I returned to my office. Why hadn't I been more forthright?

The fall? His seeming fragility?

Falling. Forgetfulness. Tremors.

Sleep deprivation as he claimed, or was he just an old man in decline?

Declining along with his island.

His reaction to my suggestion that Aruk was dying had been

sharp. The same type of frosty anger he'd shown Pam last night. I wondered if he'd once been a harder, colder man.

Without hope, there's nothing.

Hope was fine, but what was he *doing* about it? The same question: why not take heroic measures to revive things, rather than put his energy into the nutritional needs of bugs?

Because he was running *out* of energy?

Needed a universe he could *control?*

Lord of the Roaches . . .

Where did I fit in?

22

I left to find Robin but she found me first, coming up the path with Spike, looking troubled.

'What's wrong?'

'Let's go inside.'

We returned to the office and sat on the couch.

'Oh, boy,' she said.

'What is it?'

'I took another walk. To the northeast corner of the estate where it curves away from the banyan forest. Actually, I followed Spike. He kept pulling me there.'

She pushed curls away from her eyes and rested her head on the back of the sofa.

'The stone walls continue all around, but as the road curves there's a very thick planting of avocado and mango that blocks the border. Hundreds of mature trees, you have to really squeeze to get through. Spike kept huffing, really yanking me. After a hundred feet or so I figured out why: someone was crying. I ran to see.'

She took my hand and squeezed it.

'It was Pam, Alex. Lying on a blanket between the trees. Picnic stuff with her, a thermos, sandwiches. Lying on her back, wearing a sundress . . . oh, boy.'

'What?'

'The straps were down and one hand was here.' She cupped her own left breast. 'Her eyes were closed; the other hand was up her dress. We just burst in on her—'

'Crying from pleasure?'

'No, no, I don't think so. More like emotional pain. She'd been . . . touching herself, and for some reason it had made her *miserable*. Tears were running down her cheeks. I tried to leave before she saw us, but Spike started barking and she opened her eyes. I was *mortified*. She sat up and adjusted her clothes, and meanwhile Spike's running straight to her, licking her face.'

'Our little protector.'

'Lord, lord.'

'Poor you.'

'Can you imagine, Alex? The size of this place, you'd figure you could find a private spot without Sherlock Bones sniffing you out.'

'Rotten luck,' I agreed. 'Though I guess a really private spot would have been in her room with the door closed. How'd she react?'

'A split second of shock, then calm, ladylike, as if I was a neighbor dropping by to borrow sugar. She invited me to sit down. I wanted to be anywhere *but* there, but what could I say? No, thanks, I'll just leave you to whatever dark and depressing sexual fantasies you were having, ta ta? Meanwhile, Spike's sniffing the sandwiches and drooling.'

'The boy knows his priorities.'

'Oh, yeah, the world stops for ham and cheese. Actually, having him there was a good distraction. She played with him for a while, fed him, and we were doing a pretty good job of pretending it never happened. Then all of a sudden she burst into tears and stuff just started *pouring* out – how rotten her marriage had been, what an ugly divorce . . . I felt like a sponge, soaking up her pain – I don't know how you've done it all these years. I didn't say a thing, but she just kept going. It was almost as if she was glad I'd found her.'

'Maybe she was.'

'Or being discovered lowered her defenses.'

'What was so rotten about her marriage?'

'Her husband was also a doctor, a vascular surgeon, couple of years younger. Very brilliant, very good-looking, the med center's most eligible bachelor. Love at first sight, whirlwind courtship, but sex with him was – she couldn't respond, so she faked it. It had never been a problem for her before; she figured it would work itself out. But it didn't and eventually he realized it. At first he didn't care, as long as he got his. Soon, though, it began to bother him. Affront to his manhood, he started pressuring her. Interrogating her. Then it became an obsession: if she didn't come, it wasn't real lovemaking. Eventually, they started avoiding each other and he started having affairs. Lots of affairs, not even trying to hide it. With both of them working in the same place, she felt she was a laughingstock.'

'She just sat there and told you all this?'

'It was more as if she was talking to herself, Alex. She asked him to go into counseling. He refused, saying it was her problem. So she went into therapy by herself, and eventually things just broke down between them completely and she filed for divorce. At first he was really rotten – humiliating her with cracks about her being frigid, telling her about all the girls he was going out with. But then he had a change of heart and wanted to reconcile. She turned him down; he kept calling her, begging for another chance. She said no and pressed on with the divorce. A month later he died in a freak accident. Working out in his home gym, bench-pressing. The barbell fell on his chest and crushed him to death.'

'And she feels guilty.'

'Extremely guilty. Even though she knows it's not rational.

Because she feels he really did still love her. She can't get rid of the idea that he was overdoing the weightlifting because he was stressed out over her. And to think the first time I saw her I thought she was the girl with everything.'

'The girl with nothing left,' I said. 'So she packs up and returns here. And finds another man. Did the flap over Dennis come up?'

'No. But it sure looks like you were right about her having man problems, so maybe that's what Bill *was* reacting to. He doesn't want her hurt again so soon.'

'Maybe. C'mere.' She climbed onto my lap and I held her close. 'Looks like you missed your true calling.'

'That's what I'm concerned about. It's *not* my calling. You always talk about patients saying too much, too quickly, then growing hostile.'

'Honey,' I said, 'you weren't probing, you just listened. And you have no professional responsibility—'

'I know, Alex, but I like her – basically she seems to be a sweet woman who's experienced some horrible things. She was only three when her mother died and Bill sent her away – farming her out to relatives and then boarding schools. She says she doesn't blame Bill, he was doing his best. But it's got to hurt. Is there anything more I should be doing for her?'

'If she seeks you out, listen, as long as it doesn't make you feel uncomfortable.'

'I don't want *her* to feel uncomfortable. We're all living together in close quarters.'

'This place,' I said, 'is starting to feel like Eden *after* the fall from grace.'

'No,' she said, smiling. 'No serpents, just bugs.'

'Maybe we *should* think about cutting our stay short, Rob—no, wait, hear me out. There are things bothering me that I haven't told you.'

She shifted position and stared up at me. 'Like what?'

'Maybe I'm being paranoid, but I can't get rid of the idea

188

that someone planted those roaches.' I told her my suspicions.

'But what would be the motive, Alex?'

'The only thing I can think of is that someone wants us out of here.'

'Who and why?'

'I don't know, but I'm pretty sure Bill hasn't been totally straight about his reasons for bringing me over, so there may be something going on that we're totally unaware of.'

I told her about Moreland's fall in the lab, my seeing the crime clippings on his desk, his knowledge of my friendship with Milo.

'You think he wants help with a crime?' she said. 'The murder on South Beach?'

'He says it's the only major crime they've had in a long time.'

'What could he want from you?'

'I don't know, but he did show me the record of the autopsy, and he claims no one else has seen it other than Dennis. Each time I talk to him I get the feeling he's holding back. Either he's building up his courage or making sure he can trust me. The question is, will I ever be able to trust him? Because he lied to me about something else.'

I recounted the case of Samuel H.'s radiation poisoning and my conversation with Micah Sanjay.

'That is odd,' she said. 'But maybe there's an explanation. Why don't you just come out and ask him?'

'I was on my way to do just that. But after he fell and started bleeding, I guess I felt sorry for him. I'll deal with it.'

'And then we leave?' She looked sad.

I said, 'There are also things about the murder I haven't told you. It was more than just a gory killing. There was organ theft. Evidence of cannibalism.'

She lost color. Got off my lap, walked to a teak wall, and traced the wood's grain with her finger. 'You thought I couldn't handle it?'

'I didn't think it was necessary to expose you to every disgusting detail.'

She didn't answer.

'I wasn't patronizing you, Rob. But this was supposed to be a vacation. Would hearing about marrow being sucked out of leg bones have done you any good?'

'You know,' she said, facing me, 'when Pam started unloading, it was tough at first, but then it felt good. The fact that she trusted me. Breaking my routine and finding out my *sympathies* have been awakened isn't a bad thing. I've started to realize how much I use work to escape people.'

'I've always considered you great with peop—'

'I'm talking about relating in depth, Alex. Especially to other women. You know, I've never done much of that, growing up so close to my dad, always trying to please him by doing boy stuff. You always say we're an odd couple – the guy dealing with feelings, the girl wielding power tools.'

I got up and stood next to her.

'Being here,' she said, 'away from the grind, even for these few days, has been a . . . learning experience. Don't worry, I'm not going to give it all up to be a therapist. Two shrinks in one house would be too much to bear. But helping people gratifies me.'

She threw her arms around me and pressed her face against my chest. 'Welcome to Robin's epiphany – all that said, we can leave early if you're uncomfortable here.'

'No, there's no emergency – I'm probably letting my imagination get out of control, as usual.'

She kissed my chin. 'I like your imagination.'

'So you're okay with cannibals on the beach?'

'Hardly. But it happened half a year ago, and as you said, sex killers don't just stop. So I figure he is gone.'

'You're a tough kid, Castagna.'

She laughed. 'Not really. First thing I did this afternoon was check my shoes for creepy-crawlies. And if something else happens, you may just see me swimming for Guam.'

'I'll be right behind you. Okay, if you're fine, I am – hey, you calmed me down. You can be *my* therapist.'

'Nope.'

'Why not?'

'Ethical considerations. I want to keep sleeping with you.'

23

I went back to Moreland's bungalow, locked now, and no one answered.

The next time I saw him was at the dinner table that evening. The bandage on his hand was fresh, and he acknowledged me with a smile. Pam stood in a corner of the terrace, hands at her sides. She wore a blood-red Chinese silk dress and red sandals. Her hair was pinned and a yellow orchid rested above her left ear. Forced festivity?

She turned and gave us a wave. Robin looked at me and when I nodded went over to her

I sat down next to Moreland.

'How's the hand?'

'Fine, thank you. Some juice? Mixed citrus, quite delicious.'

I took some. 'There's a case I'd like to discuss with you.'

'Oh?'

'A man named Joseph Cristobal, thirty-year-old file. He complained of visual hallucinations – white worms, white worm people

– and then he died in his sleep. You found a blocked coronary artery and gave the cause of death as heart failure. But you also noted an organism called *A. Tutalo*. I looked it up but couldn't find any mention of it.'

He rubbed his crinkled chin. 'Ah, yes, Joseph. He worked here, gardening. Looked healthy enough, but his arteries *were* a mess. Loved coconut, maybe that contributed. He never complained of any cardiac symptoms, but even if he had there wouldn't have been much I could have done. Today, of course, I'd refer him for an angiogram, possible bypass surgery. It's the humbling thing about medicine. Acceptable practice inevitably resembles medieval barbering.'

'What about *A. Tutalo*?'

He smiled. 'No, it's not an organism. It's . . . a bit more complicated than that, son – ah, one second.'

Jo had come out, Ben and Claire Romero right behind her. Moreland sprang up, touched Jo's hand briefly, then continued on and gave Claire a hug. Looking over his shoulder, he said, 'Shall we continue our discussion after dinner, Alex?'

Jo seemed different – eyes less burdened, voice lighter, almost giddy, praising the food every third bite, informing the table that Lyman's body had reached the States and been picked up by his family. Then, waving off condolences, she changed the subject to her research, pronouncing that everything was 'proceeding grandly.'

The sky turned deep blue, then black. The rainclouds were gray smudges. They hadn't moved much since morning.

When Jo stopped talking, Moreland strode to the railing where some geckos were racing. When he waved a piece of fruit, they stopped and stared at him; dinnertime was probably a cue. He hand-fed them, then returned to the table and delivered a discourse on interspecies bonding. Avoiding my eyes, I thought.

A bit of small talk followed before the conversation settled upon Claire Romero, the way it often does with a newcomer.

She was well-spoken, but very quiet. The Honolulu-born

daughter of two high school teachers, she'd played violin in college and in several chamber groups and had considered a professional career in music.

'Why didn't you?' said Jo, nibbling a croissant.

Claire smiled. 'Not enough talent.'

'Sometimes we're not our own best judges.'

'I am, Dr Picker.'

'She's the only one who feels that way,' said Ben. 'She was a child prodigy. I married her and took her away from it.'

Claire looked at her plate. 'Please, Ben—'

'You *are* immensely talented, dear,' said Moreland. 'And it's been so long since you played for us – last year, wasn't it? On my birthday, in fact. What a lovely night that was.'

'I've barely played since, Dr Bill.' She turned to Robin. 'Have you ever built a violin?'

'No, but I've thought of it. I have some old Alpine spruce and Tyrolean maple that would be perfect, but it's a little intimidating.'

'Why's that?' said Jo.

'Small scale, subtle gradations. I wouldn't want to ruin old wood.'

'Claire's got a terrific old fiddle,' said Ben. 'French – a Guersan. Over a hundred years old.' He winked. 'In *fact*, it just happens to be down in the car.'

Claire glared at him.

He smiled back with mock innocence.

She shook her head.

'Well, then,' said Moreland, clapping his hands. 'You must play for us.'

'I'm really rusty, Dr Bi—'

'I'm willing to assume the risk, dear.'

Claire stared at Ben.

'Please, dear. Just a piece or two.'

'I'm warning you, get out the earplugs.'

'Warning duly noted. Would it be possible to play the piece you did for us last year? The Vivaldi?'

Claire hesitated, glanced at Ben.

'I saw the case,' he said. 'Just lying there in the closet. It said, "Take me along."'

'If you're hearing voices, perhaps you should have a long talk with Dr Delaware.'

'Dear?' said Moreland, softly.

Claire shook her head. 'Sure, Dr Bill.'

She played wonderfully, but she looked tense. Mouth set, shoulders hunched, swaying in time with the music as she filled the terrace with a rich, brocade of melody. When she was through, we applauded and she said, 'Thanks for your tolerance. Now, I've really got to get going. Science projects due tomorrow.'

Moreland walked her and Ben out. Pam nibbled a slice of mango, distracted. Robin took my hand.

'She *is* good, Alex.'

'Fantastic,' I said. But I was thinking about *A. Tutalo*. The other things I'd ask Moreland when he returned.

He didn't.

When Robin said, 'Let's go upstairs,' I didn't argue.

The moment we closed our suite door we were embracing, and soon we were in bed, kissing deeply, merging hungrily.

Afterward, I sank into a molasses vat of dreamless sleep, a welcome brain-death.

That made waking up in the middle of the night so much more unsettling.

Sitting up, sweating.

Noises . . . my head was fogged and I struggled to make sense of what I was hearing:

Rapid pounding – footsteps out in the hall . . .

Someone running?

A tattoo of footsteps; more than one person.

Fast.

Panic . . .

Then shouts – angry, hurried – someone insisting, '*No!*'

Spike barked.

Robin sat up, hair in her face. She grabbed my arm.

A door slammed.

'Alex—'

More shouts.

Too far away to make out words.

'*No!*' Again.

A man's voice.

Moreland.

We got up, threw on robes, opened our door carefully.

The chandelier over the entry was on, whitening the landing. My eyes ached, struggling to stay open.

Moreland wasn't there, but Jo was, her broad back to us, hands atop the banister. A door down the hall opened and Pam came running out, wrapped in a silver kimono, her face paper-white. The door stayed open and I had my first look at her room: white satin bedding, peach-colored walls, cut flowers. At the end of the landing, her father's door remained closed.

But I heard him again. Down in the entry.

We hurried next to Jo. She didn't turn, kept looking.

At Moreland and Dennis Laurent. The police chief stood just inside the front door, in full uniform, hands on his hips. A holstered pistol on his belt.

Moreland faced him, hands clenched. He had on a long white nightshirt, soft slippers. His legs were varicosed stilts, his hands inches from the police chief's impassive face.

'*Impossible, Dennis! Insane!*'

Dennis held out a palm. Moreland came closer anyway.

'Listen to me, Dennis—'

'I'm just telling you what we—'

'I don't care *what* you found, it's impossible! How could *you* of all—'

'Take it easy. Let's just go one step at a time and I'll do what I—'

'What you can do is *end* it! Right *now*! Don't even entertain

196

the possibility, and don't allow anyone *else* to. There's simply no *choice*, son.'

The policeman's eyes became black cuts. 'So you want me to—'

'You're the law, son. It's up to you to—'

'It's up to me to enforce the law—'

'Enforce it, but—'

'But not fully?'

'You know what I'm saying, Dennis. This must be—'

'Stop.' Dennis's bass voice hit a note at the bottom of his register. He stood even taller, bearing down on Moreland. Forced to look up, Moreland said, 'This is *psychotic*. After all you and—'

'I go with what I have,' said Dennis, 'and what I have looks bad. And it could get lots worse. I called the base and asked Ewing to keep his men under watch—'

'He took your call?'

'As a matter of fact, he did.'

'Congratulations,' said Moreland bitterly. 'You've finally arrived.'

'Doc, there's no reas—'

'There's no reason to continue this *insanity*!'

The police chief started to open the door. Moreland took hold of his arm. Dennis stared at Moreland's bony fingers until the old man let go.

'I've got things to do, doc. Stay here. Don't leave the estate.'

'How can you—'

'Like I said, I go with what I have.'

'And *I* said—'

'Stop wasting your breath.' Dennis made another attempt to leave, and once again Moreland reached for his arm. This time the big man shook him off and Moreland fell back.

Dennis caught him as Pam called out.

Dennis looked up at us.

'*Think*, son!' said Moreland. 'Does it make—'

'I'm not your damn *son*. And I don't need you to tell me what to think or how to do my job. Just stay up here till I tell you different.'

'That's house impris—'

'It's good *sense*. You're obviously not going to be of much help, so I'm calling over to Saipan and have them send me someone.'

'No,' said Moreland. 'I'll cooperate. I'm perfectly—'

'Forget it.'

'I'm the—'

'Not anymore,' said Dennis. 'Just stay here and don't cause problems.' Growling now. His enormous shoulders bunched.

He looked up at us again. Focused on Pam, then scanned the bannister from end to end, eyes darting like the geckos.

'What's going on?' I said.

He chewed his lip.

Moreland's head was down and he was holding it as if to keep it from falling off his neck.

Pam said, 'What's happened? What's happened, Dennis?'

Dennis seemed to consider an answer, then he looked back at Moreland, now leaning, face to the wall.

'A bad thing,' he said, putting one foot out the door. 'Daddy can tell you all about it.'

The door slammed and he was gone. Moreland remained in the entry, not moving. The chandelier turned his bald head metallic.

Pam rushed down to him and we followed.

'Dad?'

She put her arm around him. His color was bad. 'What is it, Dad?'

He mumbled something.

'What?'

Silence.

'Please, Daddy, tell me.'

He shook his head and muttered, 'As Dennis said. A bad thing.'

'What bad thing?'

More headshaking.

She guided him to an armchair in the front room. He sat reluctantly, remaining on the edge, one hand scratching a knobby knee, the other shielding most of his face. The visible part

198

was the color of spoiled milk and his lips looked like slices of putty.

'What's going on, Daddy? Why was Dennis so rude to you?'

Moreland coughed. 'Doing his job . . .'

'A crime? There was a *crime*, Dad?'

Moreland dropped both hands in his lap. Defeat had stripped his face of structure; each wrinkle was as black and deep as freshly gouged sculptor's clay.

'Yes, a crime . . . murder.'

'Who was murdered, Dad?'

No answer.

'*When?*'

'Tonight.'

I said, 'Another—'

He cut me off with a hand-slash. 'A terrible murder.'

'Who?' said Jo.

'A young woman.'

'Where, Dad?'

'Victory Park.'

'Who was the victim?' pressed Jo.

Long pause. 'A girl named Betty Aguilar.'

Pam frowned. 'Do we know her?'

'Ida Aguilar's daughter. She works Ida's stall at the Trading Post. She came in for a checkup last week, I introduced you to her when—'

'My God,' I said. 'I just spoke to her today. She was three months pregnant.'

Robin said, 'Oh, no.' She was holding onto the sash of my robe, eyes belladonna-bright.

'Well, *that's* certainly dreadful,' said Jo. Not a trace of slur. Off the sleeping pills?

'Yes, yes,' said Moreland. 'Very dreadful, yes, yes, yes . . .' He grabbed for the chair's arm. Pam braced him.

'I'm so sorry, Daddy. Were you close to her?'

'I—' He began to cry and Pam tried to hold him, but he freed

199

himself and looked over at the big dark windows. The sky was still deep blue, the clouds larger, lower.

'I *delivered* her,' he said. 'I was going to deliver her baby. She was doing so well with prenatal care – she used to smoke and . . .' He touched his mouth. 'She resolved to take good care of herself and stuck to it.'

'Any idea why she was killed?' said Jo.

Moreland stared at her. 'Why would I know that?'

'You knew her.'

Moreland turned away from her.

'Why does Dennis want you to stay up here?' I said.

'Not just me, all of us. We're all under house arrest.'

'Why, Daddy?' said Pam.

'Because . . . they – it's . . .' He listed forward then sat back heavily, both hands glued to the chair's arms. The fabric was a rose damask, silk, once expensive. Now I noticed the worn spots and the snags, a stitched-up tear, stains that could never be cleaned.

Moreland rubbed his temples the way he had after his fall in the lab. Then his neck. He winced and Pam put a finger under his chin and propped it. 'Why are we under house arrest, Daddy?'

He shuddered.

'Da—'

He reached up, removed her finger, held onto it. Shaking.

'*Ben,*' he said. 'They think *Ben* did it.'

24

He hid his face again.

Looking helpless, Pam left and returned with Gladys, who carried a bottle of brandy and glasses.

Seeing Moreland in that state frightened the housekeeper.

'Doctor Bill—'

'Please go back to bed,' said Pam. 'We'll need you in the morning.'

Gladys wrung her hands.

'Please, Gladys.'

Moreland said, 'I'm fine, Gladys,' in a voice that proved otherwise.

The old woman chewed her cheek and finally left.

'Brandy, Dad?'

He shook his head.

She filled a glass anyway and held it out to him.

He waved off the liquor but accepted some water. Pam took his pulse and felt his forehead.

'Warm,' she said. 'And you're sweating.'

'The room's hot,' he said. 'All the glass.'

The windows were open and scented air flowed through the screens. Chilly air. My hands were icy.

Pam wiped Moreland's brow. 'Let's get some fresh air, Dad.'

We moved to the terrace, Moreland offering no resistance as Pam put him at the head of the empty dining table.

'Here, have some more water.'

He sipped as the rest of us stood around. The sky was blue suede, the moon a slice of lemon rind. Droplets of light hit the ocean. I looked out over the railing, watching as lights switched on rapidly in the village.

I poured brandy all around.

Moreland's eyes were fixed and wide.

'Insane,' he said. 'How could they *think* it!'

'Do they have evidence?' said Jo.

'No!' said Moreland. 'They claim he – someone found him.'

'At the scene?' I said.

'Sleeping at the scene. Convenient, isn't it?'

'Who found him?' said Jo.

'A man from the village.'

'A credible man?' Something new in her voice – scientist's skepticism, an almost hostile curiosity.

'A man named Bernardo Rijks,' said Moreland. 'Chronic insomniac. Takes too many daytime naps.' He looked at the brandy. 'More water please, kitten.'

Pam filled a glass and he gulped it empty.

'Bernardo takes a walk late at night, has for years. Down from his home on Campion Way to the docks, along the waterfront, then back up. Sometimes he makes two or three circuits. Says the routine helps make him drowsy.'

'Where's Campion Way?' I said.

'The street where the church is,' said Pam. 'It's unmarked.'

'The street were Victory Park is.'

Moreland gave a start. 'Tonight when he passed the park he heard groans and thought there might be a problem. So he went to see.'

'What kind of problem?' I said.

'Drug overdose.'

'The park's a drug hangout?'

'Used to be,' he said angrily. 'When the sailors came into town. They'd drink themselves silly at Slim's or smoke marijuana on the beach, try to pick up local girls, then head for the park. Bernardo lives at the top of Campion. He used to call me to treat the stuporous boys.'

'Is he credible?' said Jo.

'He's a *fine* gentleman. The problem's not with him, it's—' Moreland ran his fingers through the white puffs at his temples. 'This is insane, just insane! Poor Ben.'

I felt Robin tense.

'What happened then?' said Jo. 'After this Bernardo went over to check the moaning?'

'He found . . .' Long pause. Moreland began breathing rapidly.

'Dad?' said Pam.

Inhaling and letting the air out, he said, 'The moaning was Ben. Lying there, next to . . . the foul scene. Bernardo ran to the nearest home, woke the people up – soon a crowd gathered. Among them Skip Amalfi, who pinned Ben down until Dennis got there.'

'Skip doesn't live nearby,' I said.

'He was down on the docks fishing and heard the commotion. Apparently he now fancies himself the great white leader, taking charge. He twisted Ben's arm and sat on top of him. Ben was no danger to anyone. He hadn't even regained consciousness.'

'Why was he unconscious?' I pressed.

Moreland studied his knees.

'Was *he* on drugs?' said Jo.

Moreland's head snapped up. 'They claim he was drunk.'

'Ben?' said Pam. 'He's as much a teetotaler as you, Dad.'

'Yes, he is . . .'

'Has he always been?' I said.

Moreland covered his eyes with a trembling hand. Touching his hair again, he twisted white strands. 'He's been completely sober for years.'

'How long ago did he have an alcohol problem?' I said.

'Very long ago.'

'In Hawaii?'

'No, no, before that.'

'He went to college in Hawaii. He had problems as a kid?'

'His problem emerged when he was in high school.'

'Teenage alcoholic?' said Pam, incredulous.

'Yes, dear,' said her father, with forced patience. 'It happens. He was vulnerable because of a difficult family situation. Both his parents were drinkers. His father was an *ugly* drunk. Died of cirrhosis at fifty-five. Lung cancer got his mother, though her liver was highly necrotic, as well. Stubborn woman. I set her up with oxygen tanks in her home to ease the final months. Ben was sixteen, but he became her full-time nurse. She used to yank off the mask, scream at him to get her cigarettes.'

'Poor genetics and environment,' pronounced Jo.

Moreland shot to his feet and staggered, shaking off help from Pam. 'Both of which he *overcame*, Dr Picker. After he was orphaned, I put him up here, exchanging work for room and board. He started as a caretaker, then I saw how bright he was and gave him more responsibility. He read through my entire medical library, brought his grades up, stopped drinking completely.'

Sadness had replaced Pam's surprise. Jealousy of his devotion to Ben or feeling left out because it was the first time she'd heard the story?

'Completely sober,' repeated Moreland. 'Incredible strength of character. That's why I financed the rest of his education. He's built a life for himself and Claire and the children . . . you saw him tonight. Was that the face of a psychopathic killer?'

No one answered.

'I tell you,' he said, slapping the tabletop, 'what they're claiming is *impossible*! The fact that it was a bottle of vodka near his hand proves it. He drank only beer. And I treated him with Antabuse,

204

years ago. The taste of alcohol's made him ill ever since – he despises it.'

'What are you saying?' said Jo. 'Someone poured it down his throat?'

The coolness in her voice seemed to throw him off balance. 'I – I'm *saying* he has no tolerance – or desire for alcohol.'

'Then that's the only alternative I can see,' she said. 'Someone forced him to drink. But who would do that? And why?'

Moreland gritted his teeth. 'I don't *know*, Dr Picker. What I do know is Ben's nature.'

'How was Betty killed?' I said.

'She . . . it was . . . a stabbing.'

'Was Ben found with the weapon?'

'He wasn't holding it.'

'Was it found at the scene?'

'It was . . . embedded.'

'Embedded,' echoed Jo. 'Where?'

'In the poor girl's throat! Is it necessary to *know* these things?'

Robin was squeezing my hand convulsively.

'The whole thing is absurd!' said Moreland. 'They claim Ben was right next to her – *sleeping* with her, his arms around her, his head on her . . . what was left of her abdomen. That he'd be able to sleep with her after something like that is – *absurd!*'

Robin broke away and ran to the railing. I followed her and covered her shoulders with my arms, feeling her shivers as she stared up at the bright yellow moon.

Back at the table, Jo was saying, 'He *mutilated* her?'

'I don't want to continue this discussion, Dr Picker. The key is to help Ben.'

Robin wheeled around. 'What about Betty? What about helping her family?'

'Yes, yes, of course that's . . .'

'She was *pregnant*! What about her unborn child? Her husband, her parents?'

Moreland looked away.

'What *about* them, Bill?'

Moreland's lips trembled. 'Of course they deserve sympathy, dear. I *ache* for them. Betty was my patient – I *delivered* her, for God's sake!'

'Whooping cough,' I said.

'What's that?'

'I spoke with her yesterday. She told me you treated her for whooping cough when she was a kid. She considered you a hero.'

He slumped and sat back down. 'Dear God . . .'

No one talked. Brandy got poured. It burned a slow, cleansing trail down my gullet, the only sensation in an otherwise numb body. Everyone looked numb.

'Anyone know the time?' I said.

Pam shot the sleeve of her kimono. 'Just after four.'

'Rise and shine,' said Jo, softly. 'I still don't see why we're all locked up here.'

'For our own safety,' said Moreland. 'At least that's the theory.'

'Who's out to get us?'

'No one.'

'But Ben is closely identified with this place,' I said, 'so people may start talking.'

Moreland didn't answer.

Jo frowned. 'Staying cooped up just makes us sitting targets. You've got no security here – anyone can walk right in.'

'I've never *needed* security, Dr Picker.'

'Do you keep any weapons around?' she said.

'No! If you're concerned with your safety, I suggest you—'

'No problem,' said Jo. 'Personally, I'm fine. It's the only good thing that came out of losing Ly. When your worst fantasy comes true, you find out you can handle things.'

She got up and shuffled toward the living room, tightening the robe of her belt, big hips shifting like the pans of a balance scale.

When she was gone, Robin said, 'She's got a gun. A little pistol. I saw it in an open drawer of her nightstand.'

Moreland's mouth worked. 'I despise firearms.'

Pam said, 'Hopefully she won't shoot someone by accident. Is there any way you can get some rest now, Dad? You're going to be needing your strength.'

'I'll be fine, dear. Thank you for your . . . ministrations, but I believe I'll stay up for a while.' He leaned over as if to kiss her, but patted her shoulder instead. 'Hopefully when the sun comes up, cooler heads will prevail.'

'There are some things I'd like to discuss with you,' I said.

He stared at me.

'Things we never got to last night.'

'Yes, certainly. In the morning, right after I call Dennis—'

'I'm staying up, too. We can talk now.'

He fidgeted with the neckband of his nightshirt. 'Of course. What say we leave the terrace to the ladies and move to my office?'

I squeezed Robin's hand and she squeezed back and sat next to Pam, who looked baffled. But the two of them were already talking as Moreland and I left.

'What's so urgent?' he said, flicking the lights on in the bungalow. The newspaper clippings were gone from his desk. So were all his other papers; the wood surface gleamed.

'We never talked about A. Tutalo—'

'Surely you can see why that wouldn't be a priority at this time—'

'There are other things.'

'Such as?'

'Murder. Ben. What's really going on with Aruk.'

He said nothing for a while, then, 'That's quite an agenda.'

'We've got nowhere to go.'

'Very well.' He pointed crossly to the sofa and I sat, expecting him to settle in a facing chair. Instead, he went behind the desk, lowered himself with a grimace, opened a drawer, and began searching.

'You don't believe Ben could have done this,' he said. 'Do you?'

'I don't know Ben very well.'

He gave a small, tired smile. 'Psychologist's answer . . . Very well, I can't expect you to follow me blindly; you'll see, he'll be vindicated. The notion of his butchering Betty is beyond ridiculous – all right, trivial things first. 'A. Tutalo.' You couldn't find an organism by that name because it's not a germ, it's a fantasy. A local myth. The '*A*' stands for 'Aruk.' 'Aruk Tutalo.' An imaginary tribe of creatures who live in the forest. Goes back years. A myth. No one's believed it for a long time.'

'Except Cristobal.'

'Joseph hallucinated. That's not belief.'

'You convinced him he hadn't seen anything?'

Pause. 'He was a stubborn man.'

'Have there been other sightings?'

'None since I've lived here. As I said, it's a primitive idea.'

'Creatures from the forest,' I said. 'What do they look like?'

'Pale, soft, hideous. A shadow society, living under the forest. Nothing unique to Aruk; all cultures develop fantasies of fanciful, lustful creatures in order to project forbidden desires – animal *instincts*. The minotaurs, centaurs, and satyrs of ancient Greece. The Japanese have a saucer-headed anthro-creature called the *kappa* who lurks by forest streams, abducting children and pulling their intestines through their anuses. Witch's rituals use animal masks to hide the faces of participants, the Devil himself is often thought of as the Great Beast with goat feet and a serpentine tail. Wood-demons, anthro-bat vampiric creatures, werewolves, the yeti, Bigfoot, it's all the same. Psychological defense.'

'What about the catwoman—'

'No, no, that was something totally different.'

'A response to trauma.'

'A response to *cruelty*.'

'Worm people,' I said.

'There are no mammals native to Aruk – one uses what's at hand. 'Tutalo' is derived from an ancient island word of uncertain

208

etymology: *tootali*, or wood-grub. From what I've gathered they're large, humanoid, with tentaclelike limbs, slack bodied but strong. And chalky *white*. I find that particularly interesting. Perhaps a covert indictment of colonizers: white creatures 'appearing' on the island and establishing brutal control.'

'Demonizing the oppressor?'

'Precisely.'

'Was Joseph Cristobal politically active?'

'On the contrary. A simple man. Illiterate. But fond of drink. I'm sure that had something to do with it. Today, your average villager would laugh at the notion of a Tutalo.'

'He was your gardener. Did he sight the Tutalo here?'

He licked his lips and nodded. 'He was working on the eastern walls, tying vines. Working overtime, everyone else had gone home. It was well after dark. Fatigue was probably a factor as well.'

'Where did he see the creature?'

'Making its way through the banyans. Waving its arms, then retreating. He didn't tell anyone right away. Too scared, he claimed, but I suspect he'd been drinking and didn't want to be thought of as a drunkard or old-fashioned.'

'So he suppressed the vision and began hallucinating at night?'

'It began as nightmares. He'd wake up screaming, see the Tutalo in his room.'

'Could the original sighting have taken place as he slept?' I said. 'Could he have dozed off on the job and made up the vision to cover up?'

'I wondered about that, but of course he denied it. I also wondered if he'd fallen off his ladder and hurt his head, but there were no bruises or swellings anywhere on his body.'

'Was he an alcoholic?'

'He wasn't a raving drunk but he did like his spirits.'

'Could the visions have been alcohol poisoning?'

'It's a possibility.'

'Bill, exactly how endemic is alcoholism on Aruk?'

He blinked and removed his glasses. 'In the past it was a serious problem. We've worked hard at education.'

'Who's we?'

'Ben and myself, which is why what's happened tonight is *madness*, Alex! You *must* help him!'

'What would you like me to do?'

'Speak to Dennis. Let him know Ben couldn't have done it, that he simply doesn't fit the profile of a psychopathic killer.'

'Why would Dennis listen to me?'

'I don't know that he would, but we must try everthing. Your training and experience will give you credibility. Dennis respects psychology, majored in it in junior college.'

'What profile don't you think Ben fits?'

'The FBI's two forms of lust-killer: he's neither the disorganized, low-intellect spree-murderer nor the calculating, sadistic psychopath.'

The FBI had earned a lot of TV time with patterns of serial killers obtained from interviews with psychopaths careless enough to get caught. But psychopaths lied for the fun of it, and profiles rarely if ever led to the discovery of a killer, occasionally confirming what police scutwork and luck had already accomplished. Profiles had been responsible for some serious fallacies: Serial killers never murdered across races. Till they did. Women couldn't be serial killers. Till they were.

People weren't computer chips. People had the uncanny ability to surprise.

But even if I'd had more faith in the orderly nature of evil, Ben wouldn't have been easily acquitted.

Right after Lyman Picker's death, Robin and I had discussed the hardness of his personality, and I recalled the cold, impersonal way he'd jabbed needles into the arms of the schoolchildren.

Family history of alcoholism.

Rough childhood, probably abuse from the 'ugly drunk' father.

A certain rigidity. Tight control.

Outwardly controlled men sometimes lost it when under the

influence of booze or drugs. A high percentage of serial killers committed their crimes buoyed by intoxication.

'I'll talk to him,' I said. 'But I doubt it'll do any good.'

'Talk to Ben, too. Try to make some sense of this. I'm shackled, son.'

'If I'm to succeed with Dennis, I need to be impartial, not Ben's advocate.'

He blinked some more. 'Yes, that makes sense. Dennis is rational and honest. If he responds to anything it'll be the rational approach.'

'Rational and honest,' I said, 'but you don't want him dating your daughter.'

It had slipped out like loose change.

He recoiled. Sank heavily into the desk chair. When he finally spoke, it was in a low, resigned voice:

'So you despise me.'

'No, Bill, but I can't say I understand you. The longer I stay here, the more inconsistent things seem.'

He smiled feebly. 'Do they?'

'Your love for the island and its people seems so strong. Yet you tongue-lash Pam for hanging around Dennis. Not that it's my business – you've devoted your life to Aruk and I'm just a visitor.'

He folded his arms across his chest and rubbed the sweat from his forehead.

'I know that this situation with Ben is terrible for you,' I said, 'but if I'm to stay here I need to know a few things.'

Looking away, he said, 'What else troubles you, son?'

'The fact that Aruk's so cut off from the outside world. That more of your energies haven't been spent opening it up. You say there's hope, but you don't *act* hopeful. I agree with you that TV's mostly garbage, but how can the people ever develop when their access to information is so limited? They can't even get mail on a regular basis. It's solitary confinement on a cultural level.'

His hands started to shake again and spots of color made his cheeks shine.

'Forget it,' I said.

211

'No, no, go on.'

'Do you want to respond to what I just said?'

'The people have books. There's a small library in the church.'

'When's the last time new books came in?'

He used a fingernail to scrape something off the desk top. 'What do you suggest?'

'More frequent shipping schedules. The leeward harbor's too narrow for big craft but couldn't the supply boats sail more often? And if the Navy won't allow planes to land on Stanton, why not build an airfield on the west side? If Amalfi won't cooperate, use some of your land.'

'And how is all this to be financed?'

'Your personal finances are none of my business, either, but I've heard you're very wealthy.'

'Who told you that?'

'Creedman.'

His laugh was shrill. 'Do you know what Creedman really does for a living?'

'He's not a journalist?'

'He's worked for a few minor papers, done some cable television work. But for the last several years he's written quarterly reports for corporations. His last client was Stasher-Layman. Have you heard of them?'

'No.'

'Big construction outfit, based in Texas. Builders of government housing and other tax-financed projects. They put up ticky-tack boxes, sell the management contract for high profits, and walk away. Instant slum. Creedman's scribblings for them made them sound like saints. If I hadn't thrown the reports out, I'd show them to you.'

'You researched him?'

'After we caught him snooping I thought it prudent.'

'Okay,' I said. 'So he's a corporate hack. Is he wrong about your wealth?'

He pulled on a long, pale finger till it cracked. Righted his glasses. Brushed nonexistent dust from the desk.

212

'I won't tell you I'm poor, but family fortunes recede unless the heirs are talented in business. I'm not. Which means I'm in no position to build airports or lease entire fleets of boats. I'm doing all I can.'

'Okay,' I said. 'Sorry for bringing it up, then.'

'No apology necessary. You're a passionate young man. Passionate but focused. It's rare when the two go hand in hand: "I may not hope from outward forms to win the passion and the life, whose fountains are within" – Coleridge said that. Another great thinker; even narcotics didn't still *his* genius . . . Your passion even comes through your scientific writing, son. *That's* why I asked you to join me.'

'And here I thought it was my experience with police cases.'

He sat back and let out another shrill laugh. 'Passionate *and* observant. Yes, your experience with criminal behavior was a bonus because to me it means you have a strict sense of right and wrong. I admire your sense of justice.'

'What does justice have to do with analyzing medical charts?'

'I was speaking in an abstract sense – doing things ethically.'

'Are you sure that's it?'

'What do you mean?'

'Has the cannibal murder remained on your mind, Bill? Have you been more worried about recurrence than you let on? Because if that's it, you're going to be disappointed. I've gotten involved in a few bloody things, mostly because of my friendship with Milo Sturgis. But he's the detective, not me.'

He took time to answer. Staring at his wife's watercolors. Twisting his fingers as if they were knitting needles.

'Worry's too strong a word, son. Let's just say the *possibility* of recurrence has remained in the back of my mind. AnneMarie's murder was my first real brush with this kind of thing, so I read up on it and learned that recurrence is the norm, not the exception. When I learned you had some experience with murder in addition to your scholarly achievements, I felt a great sense of . . . appropriateness.'

'How similar is Betty's murder to AnneMarie Valdos's?'

213

'Dennis claims there are . . . similarities.'

'Was Betty cannibalized?'

'Not . . .' He tapped the desk. The flutter of wings outside a window made us both start. Nightbirds or bats.

'Not yet,' he said. 'Nothing was missing. She was . . .' He shook his head. 'Decapitated and eviscerated, but nothing had been taken.'

'What about the long bones?'

'One leg was broken – hacked but not severed.'

'What kind of knife was used?'

He didn't reply.

'Bill?'

'Knives,' he said miserably. 'A set of surgical tools were found there.'

'Ben's?'

Headshake.

'Yours?'

'An old set I'd once owned.'

'Did you give it to Ben?'

'No. It was kept here – in the lab. In a drawer of this desk.'

'Where Ben had easy access.'

He nodded, almost crying. 'But you must believe me, Ben would never take anything without permission. Never! I know it sounds bad for him, but *please* believe me.'

'AnneMarie had a drinking problem,' I said. 'You implied Betty did too.'

'Did I?'

'Back in the house you said she used to smoke and . . . Then you trailed off and said she'd been taking excellent care of herself during her pregnancy.'

'The poor thing's dead. Why besmirch her memory?'

'Because it may be relevant. She's beyond hurt, Bill. Was she an alcoholic?'

'No, not an alcoholic. She was a . . . friendly girl. She smoked and drank a bit.'

'What does friendly have to do with it?'

214

'Friendly,' he said. 'To the sailors.'

'Like AnneMarie. One of those girls who went up to Victory Park. Was it common knowledge in the village?'

'I don't know *what's* common knowledge. I heard it from her mother.'

'Her mother complained about Betty's promiscuity?'

'Ida brought Betty in to be treated for a veneral infection.'

'Gonorrhea?'

He nodded.

'When?'

'A year ago. Before she became engaged. We kept it confidential from Mauricio – her boyfriend. Tested him, too, under a false pretense. Negative. Eventually they married.

'Maybe he found out anyway and reacted.'

'This? No, not Mauricio. What was done to her was beyond . . . no, no, impossible. Mauricio's not a . . . calculating sort. He'd never have thought to incriminate Ben.'

'Not smart enough?'

'He's simple. As was Betty.'

I remembered Betty's open manner and easy smile. Trusting me enough after meeting me to talk about herself. No bra under the tank top . . .

'Simple and trusting,' I said. 'A drinker, overly friendly with the boys. Sounds like a perfect victim. What was Ben's relationship with her?'

'They knew each other the way everyone on the island knows each other.'

'Did Ben know about her gonorrhea?'

He thought. 'I didn't discuss it with him.'

'But he could have found out – read it in the chart.'

'Ben was busy enough without sticking his nose where it didn't belong.'

'Maybe he came across it by accident. We both know you're not a compulsive filer.'

No answer. He got up and paced, twisting his fingers again, bobbing his neck.

I said, 'Learning that, he could have assumed she was easy.'

'I didn't record the diagnosis in my notes. I made sure to protect her.'

'What did you write?'

'Just that she had an infection that required penicillin.'

'Someone with Ben's medical sophistication could have figured it out, Bill. And what about the lab tests? Did you destroy the results?'

'I – don't believe so . . . but still it's not possible. Not Ben. Why are you *thinking* in these terms?'

'Because I have an open mind. If that upsets you, we can end the discussion.'

He gritted his teeth. 'This isn't the last time I'll be hearing these kinds of speculations. I might as well get used to it. Let's assume – for the sake of argument – that Ben did know she'd been infected. Why in the world would he murder her?'

'As I said, it could have led him to believe she was easy. One scenario is that they'd had a relationship for a while, or even that last night was a one-night stand. In either case, they went up to the park, got drunk, and things got out of hand.'

'That's ridiculous! You saw him with Claire tonight. He loves her, they've got so much going – the children.'

'Lots of psychopaths lead double lives.'

'No! Not Ben! And he's not a *psychopath*. He didn't kill AnneMarie and he didn't kill Betty!'

'Does he have an alibi for AnneMarie's murder?'

'He was never asked to present one. But I remember the way he reacted to the murder. Utterly *revolted*!'

'Did you tell him AnneMarie had been cannibalized?'

'No! Only Dennis and I knew. And now you.'

'But once again, Ben had access to the information. And Dennis knows AnneMarie's murder file is here. So even if Ben does develop an alibi for the first murder, Dennis may suspect he read up on the case and pulled a copycat. To disguise murdering Betty.'

216

'He's not a premeditated killer! This whole line of reasoning is spurious!'

'No one else knew about AnneMarie's wounds.'

'The killer knew – a killer who isn't Ben.'

'What about the fishermen who found AnneMarie's body?'

'Alonzo Rubino and Saul Saentz,' he said. 'They're even older than I. Saul's downright frail. And they didn't know the details.'

'Leaving only Ben, who might have.'

'You were at dinner tonight, son. Was that the demeanor of a cannibal butcher? Do you mean to tell me he drove Claire home, tucked her in bed, and left to commit murder?'

'He was in the park. What's his explanation for that?'

'Dennis hasn't interrogated him. Refuses to until there's an attorney present.'

'Ben's still free to offer an explanation. Has he?'

He paused. 'After Dennis and I had words, he was less than forthcoming.'

'When will Ben have an attorney?'

'Dennis has wired to Saipan for a court-appointed lawyer.'

'There are no lawyers on the island?'

'No. Until now that's been a plus.'

'How long will it take for the appointee to get over?'

'The next boat's due in five days. If the base allows a plane to land, it could be sooner.'

'Why would the base cooperate all of a sudden?'

'Because this is just what they want. Another nail in Aruk's coffin.' He made a fist and regarded it as if it belonged on someone else's arm. The fingers opened slowly. The bandage on his hand was soiled.

'Why is the Navy waging war on the island, Bill?'

'The Navy's a branch of the government, and the government wants to rid itself of responsibility. Ben's arrest is yet another reason to abandon ship: murderous savages. *Cannibals,* no less. And if the fiend who murdered AnneMarie was a Navy man, he's now off the hook, so Ewing's got a vested interest in having Ben prosecuted.'

217

'I thought you believed the killer had moved on.'

'Perhaps he left and returned. Corpsmen fly in and out all the time. A look at Navy flight records would be instructive, but try obtaining them. There's more than one kind of barricade, Alex.'

'You said Dennis never discovered any similar murders during the interim.'

'That's true. As far as it goes. But some of the places in the region – I've heard there's a restaurant in Bangkok that serves human flesh. Perhaps apocryphal, perhaps not. But there's no doubt things go on that we never hear about.'

He rubbed his head. 'Aruk has been abandoned, but I won't abandon Ben.'

'Does Senator Hoffman also have a vested interest in Aruk's decline?' I said.

'Most probably, strip away the veneer of political correctness and you've got a strip-mall builder.'

'In cahoots with someone like Creedman's employer – Stasher-Layman?'

'The thought has occurred to me.'

'Creedman's an advance man?'

'I've thought about that, too.'

'At dinner, Creedman and Hoffman acted as if they didn't know each other. But during the discussion of colonialism, Creedman rushed to defend Hoffman's point of view.'

'The *fool.*' He looked ready to spit. 'That *book* of his. No one's ever seen it and he won't be pinned down on details. Why else would Hoffman invite him to that abysmal dinner? Nicholas does nothing without a reason.'

'Have you found any connection between Hoffman and Stasher-Layman?'

'Not yet, but we mustn't get distracted. We must focus on Ben.'

'When Ben caught Creedman snooping, what was Creedman after?'

'I have no idea. There's nothing to hide.'

'What about the AnneMarie Valdos file? And not necessarily for nefarious reasons. Creedman's the one who told me about the murder. Said you did the autopsy, had the details. He sounded regretful. Maybe he smelled a good story.'

'No. As much as I'd like to attribute something malicious to him, he was snooping before AnneMarie's murder. Now let's—'

'One more thing: after you came back from speaking to Hoffman alone, you looked dejected. Why?'

'He refused to help Aruk.'

'Is that the only reason?'

'That's not enough?'

'I just wondered if there was some personal issue between the two of you.'

He sat straighter. Stood and smiled. 'Oh, there is. We dislike each other immensely. But that's ancient history, and I simply can't allow myself to be drawn into nostalgia. I acted stupidly with Dennis and now I'm persona non grata. But he may allow you to speak to Ben. Please call the police station tomorrow and ask his permission. If he grants it, use your professional skills to offer Ben psychological support. He's living a nightmare.'

He came around and rested a hand on my shoulder.

'Please, Alex.'

We hadn't gotten into his lie about being part of the Marshall Islands compensation, the nighttime boat rides. And he'd avoided explaining his reaction to Pam and Dennis's friendship. But the look in his eyes told me I'd taken things as far as I could tonight. Maybe there'd be another opportunity. Or maybe I'd be off Aruk before it mattered.

'All right,' I said. 'But let's get something straight: I'll give Ben the benefit of the doubt till the forensics come in. Unless I get into that cell and he tells me he murdered Betty – or AnneMarie. That happens, I'll march straight into Dennis's office and swear out a statement.'

He walked away from me and faced the wall. One of the watercolors was at eye level. Palms over the beach. Not unlike the one where Barbara Moreland had drowned.

Delicate strokes, washed-out hues. No people. A loneliness so intense . . .

'I accept your conditions,' he said. 'I'm glad to have you on my side.'

25

As we left for the house, he noticed a fat-petaled white flower and started to describe its pollination. 'Oh, shut up,' he told himself abruptly, and we continued in silence.

Inside, he gripped my hand. 'Thank you for your help.'

I watched him walk away quickly. Energized?

A man who studied *predation*.

Where had he come from the night I'd seen him with his doctor's bag? What had he been doing in the dark lab?

I'd phone the police station in the morning, but my first two calls would be to the airport at Saipan and the company that chartered the supply boats.

Upstairs, Spike's bark greeted me as I entered our suite. Robin wasn't back yet from talking with Pam. Four-fifty A.M. Someone else I might be able to reach.

The connection broke a few times before I finally got an international line. Wondering if anyone could listen in and deciding I didn't care, I told the desk officer at the West

L.A. station that I had urgent business with Detective Sturgis. He said, 'Yeah, I think he's here.'

A minute or so later, Milo barked his own name.

'Stanley? It's Livingstone.'

'Hey,' he said, 'buena afternuna – it's got to be what, five in the morning over there?'

'Just about.'

'What's up?'

'A bit of trouble.'

'Another cannibal?'

'As a matter of fact . . .'

'Shit, I was *kidding*. What the hell's going on?'

I told him about Betty's murder and everything else that had been on my mind.

'Jesus,' he said. 'After you told me about the first one, I got curious, so I played with the computers. Thankfully, cannibalism hasn't caught on big-time. Other than that Milwaukee moron only thing I came up with was a ten-year-old case, place called Wiggsburg, Maryland. Didn't sound that different from yours – neck slash, organ theft, legs cracked for the marrow – but they caught the bad guys, pair of eighteen-year-olds who decided Lucifer was their main man, he ordered them to carve up and dine on a local topless dancer.'

'Where are they now?'

'Jail, I assume. They were sentenced to life. Why?'

'There are two guys here who would have been around eighteen back then. They like to cut things up and they've been eyeing Robin.'

'But they're not suspects in the killing.'

'No, Ben does look good for it. But do you have the Maryland killers' names and descriptions, just to be thorough?'

'Got the fax right here . . . Wayne Lee Burke, Keith William Bonham, both caucs, brown and brown. Burke was six three, one seventy, Bonham five five, one fifty-two. Appendectomy—'

'I don't need any more, it doesn't match.'

'No big surprise. Things have gotten nuts but I don't see lads who suck out a young lady's bone marrow qualifying for early parole.'

'How far is Wiggsburg from Washington, D.C.?'

'About an hour's drive. Why?'

'There's another guy, here, D.C. background, also creepy.' I filled him in on Creedman.

'Sounds like a prince,' he said. 'Yeah, I've heard of Stasher-Layman 'cause they built public housing projects years ago in South Central, while I was riding a car at seventy-seventh Division. Bad plumbing, gang members hired to handle security. Immediate problems. They sold the management contract, then bailed. Had a deal to build a new jail, too, out in Antelope Valley, till the locals found out about their record, protested, and got it kaboshed. So what are they planning to build over there?'

'I don't know.'

'Not that it has anything to do with cannibals . . . so what's Dr Frankenstein's reaction to his protégé's predilection for intraspecies feasting?'

'Total denial. Ben was his project – rehabilitating a kid with a rotten background. Be interesting to know if that background includes any serious criminal activity Moreland didn't mention. If you've a mind to go back to the computer.'

'Sure, give me the particulars.'

'Benjamin Romero, I don't know if there's a middle name. He's thirty or so, born here, went to school in Hawaii and did Coast Guard duty there. Trained as a registered nurse.'

'I'll have a go at it. How's Robin handling all this?'

'She's a trooper but I want out. The next boats are due in around five days. If Chief Laurent allows us off the island, we'll be on one of them.'

'Why shouldn't he let you off?'

'Public opinion of Moreland and everything associated with

him isn't too high right now. We're all under informal house arrest.'

'Damned inconsiderate, not to say illegal. Want me to have a little cop-to-cop chat with him?'

'From what I saw tonight, that might make things worse. Moreland tried to influence him and he hardened his stance.'

'Maybe that's cause he's pissed at Moreland – "Not with my daughter, you don't."'

'Maybe, but I'll try to handle it myself first. If I have problems, believe me, you'll hear about it.'

'Okay . . . bugs and cannibals. Sounds almost as bad as Hollywood Boulevard.'

Feeling rancid, I showered. Robin returned as I was toweling off, and I summarized my talks with Moreland and Milo and told her I wanted to book us on the next boat out.

She said, 'It's too bad it had to end this way, but absolutely.' She sat down on the bed. 'What was that construction company?'

'Stasher-Layman.'

'I think Jo had something with their name on it in her room. Stack of computer printout – I assumed it was something to do with her research. The only reason it sticks in my mind is that when she saw me looking at it, she slid a book over it.'

'How sure are you it was Stasher Layman?'

'Very big Gothic initials – 'S-L,' then the name. I read it just before she covered it.'

An artist's eye.

'Jo and Creedman,' I said. 'Two people with D.C. connections. Two advance agents. I've had a weird feeling about her since the roaches. I didn't tell you because I thought I was just being paranoid, but I couldn't stop thinking that she was alone in the house that night. And the time lag between hearing your scream and coming in seemed odd. She excused it as drowsiness due to sleeping pills, but tonight she was out there before us, lucid as hell. Motive stumped me, but if she's doing dirty work for

224

Stasher-Layman and wants to get rid of distractions, that would serve nicely.'

'But then why not hide her gun, Alex? She kept it right out there on top of her suitcase, almost as if she wanted me to know she had it.'

'Maybe she did. Trying to intimidate you.'

'It didn't seem that way. There was absolutely no hostility between us. In fact, the more time I spent with her, the friendlier she got. As if I was helping her cope.'

And cope she had. Tranquilized widow to sharp-eyed interrogator in two days.

I said, 'She sure had an interest in the murder. Did you notice the way she was quizzing Moreland? That would also make sense if she's got an interest in Aruk's decline.'

'But if this company builds things, why would they want Aruk to decline?'

'Moreland said they build government projects. Milo's memory backs that up: low-income housing, prisons. Maybe they want the land cheap.'

'Low-income housing doesn't make sense,' she said, 'if the people are all leaving. But a prison might.'

'Yes, it might,' I said. 'No locals to protest. And what better place to dump felons than a remote island with no natural resources. It would be politically *beautiful*. Which is where Hoffman may fit in. What if Stasher-Layman paid him under the table to find a site and he chose Aruk because he remembered it from his days as base commander, knew there wasn't much of a constituency? If he embedded the prison, or whatever it is, in an extensive Pacific Rim revitalization – cash infusion for the bigger islands – who'd notice or mind? Other than Bill. But right now Bill's in a position to cause troubles for the deal because he owns so much of the island. Which could be the real reason Hoffman stopped over: making a final offer that Bill refused. So Hoffman pressured him, maybe threatened him with something.'

'Threatened him with what?'

'I don't know, but remember my feeling they had some issue between them that went way back? The first night I met Bill he said something about guilt being a great motivator. He could have done something years ago that he wants to forget. Something he's been trying to atone for all these years by being "the good doctor."'

She touched my arm. 'Alex, if he is holding up a giant deal he could be in serious danger. Do you think he's aware of what he's up against?'

'I don't know what he's aware of and what he chooses to deny. The man's a cipher and he's stubborn.'

'What about Pam? As his heir, she could also be in a treacherous position.'

'If she's his heir.'

'Why wouldn't she be?'

'Because she has no roots in Aruk, and Bill seems to view the *island* as his real child. He's excluded Pam from scientific discussion and just about everything else. You saw her surprise when he discussed Ben's family history. She's an outsider. So it wouldn't surprise me if he bequeathed his holdings to someone else. Someone with a strong commitment to Aruk.'

She stared at me. 'Ben?'

'In some ways he's Bill's *functional* son.'

'And being accused of murder gets *him* out of the way.'

'Sure, but nothing I've heard indicates he's not a murderer. In fact everything Bill told me just added to the picture of guilt: access to the weapon, Betty's medical records, and AnneMarie's autopsy file. And remember our discussion about his being a hard guy? No sympathy for Picker's crash. The way he vaccinated those children, mechanically. Add alcoholism and a rotten childhood and you've got a pretty good textbook history of a psychopath. Maybe even his outward devotion to Bill and the island is calculated. Maybe he's just after Bill's money.'

'Maybe . . . Yes, he is dispassionate. But he sat there

tonight at dinner with us, Alex, and I thought I saw a warmer side of him. As if Claire'd brought out something in him.'

'Could be acting. Psychopaths can turn it on at will.'

'You really think he could have been so lighthearted while planning to murder someone in a few hours? Planning to *mutilate* someone?'

'If he's a severe psychopath, he's got an extremely low level of anxiety. For all we know, sitting here listening to Claire play was part of the thrill.'

'Are you saying he killed both girls or just Betty?'

'It could go either way. AnneMarie could have been murdered by a sailor and Ben decided to do a copycat as a cover.'

'But why?'

'He and Betty could have been having an affair. Maybe the baby was his, he wanted out, permanently. When I talked to her, she seemed thrilled about the pregnancy; but who knows?'

'If he was so calculating, Alex, how'd he get caught so stupidly?'

'Screwing up's another psychopathic trait. Look at Bundy, escaping from Washington, where there's no death penalty, and murdering in Florida, where there is. Psychopaths walk a narrow line, all screwed up inside, constantly putting on a show. A psychiatrist named Cleckley labeled it perfectly: the mask of sanity. Eventually the mask falls off and shatters. Ben used booze to get rid of his.'

She shuddered. 'It's still hard to make sense of. I can see using alcohol to lower his inhibitions. But why stick around and get drunk *after* killing Betty?'

'It's possible he drank a little before meeting Betty, to take the edge off, had some more with Betty, killed her before the total effect set in, then boom. Bill said he'd always drunk beer. Vodka could have been too much to handle.'

'I guess so,' she said, rubbing her eyes. 'But he always seemed *decent*. I suppose I sound like one of those people who get interviewed on the news: he was such a quiet guy . . . well, at least the part about whose baby Betty was carrying can be tested. Who's doing the medical investigation?'

'Dennis is bringing a lawyer over from Saipan. I assume he'll call for a pathologist, too.'

She leaned against me heavily. 'What a horror.'

'How's Pam taking it?'

'At first she talked mostly about Bill – worried about him. Wanting to help, but feeling he pushes her away.'

'He does.'

'She's not ready to give up. She thinks she owes him.'

'For what?'

'Coming through for her during the divorce. She also talked more about herself. Said she'd had problems with men before her marriage – attracted to losers, guys who got rough with her, psychologically and physically. After the divorce she was so low she was having suicidal thoughts. Her therapist wanted to establish a support system, found out Bill was her only relative, and called him. To Pam's surprise, he flew out to Philadelphia, stayed with her, took care of her. Even apologized for sending her away. Said losing her mother had been too much to handle, he'd been overwhelmed, it had been a big mistake that he knew he could never make up for, but would she like to come back and give him another chance? But now that she's here . . .'

She looked at the clock. 'It's almost daybreak. Tell you one thing I've learned from all this. I could never be a therapist.'

'Most therapy cases aren't like this.'

'I know, but it's still not for me. I admire you.'

'It's a nasty job, but someone's got to do it.'

'I'm serious, honey.'

'Thank you. I admire you, too. And despite all that's happened, I have no regrets.'

'Me, neither.' She ran her fingers through my hair. 'In a few days when we're back in L.A., I'm going to remember being with you. Everything else good about this place. Frame it in my mind, like a picture.'

Psychic sculpting. I doubted I had the talent.

26

By ten A.M. the reservations were booked: back to Saipan in five days, LAX in a week. I'd try to find a good time to tell Moreland. If I didn't find one, I'd tell him anyway.

I phoned the Aruk police station. A man with a sibilant voice told me the chief was busy.

'When will he be free?'

'Who's this?'

'Dr Delaware. I'm staying at—'

'Knife Castle, yeah, I know. I'll give him your message.'

Robin was still sleeping and I went down to breakfast. Jo was there by herself, eating heartily.

'Morning,' she said. 'Get any sleep?'

'Not much.'

'It's something, isn't it? You come to an out-of-the-way place, think you're escaping big-city crime, and it runs after you like a mad dog.'

I buttered a piece of toast. 'True. Life can be a prison.

Sometimes, out-of-the-way places make the best prisons.'

She wiped her lips. 'I suppose that's one way of looking at it.'

'Sure,' I said. 'The isolation and poverty. For all we know there are all kinds of behavioral aberrations rampant.'

'Is that what you're looking for in your research?'

'I haven't gotten far enough to develop hypotheses. Looks like I won't; we're booked on the next boat out.'

'That so?' She placed a dollop of marmalade on a scone. The sun was behind her, crowning her with a rainbow aura.

'How long are you planning to stay?'

'Till I finish.'

'Wind research,' I said. 'What exactly are you looking at?'

'Currents. Patterns.'

'Ever hear of the Bikini atoll disaster? Atomic blast over in the Marshall Islands. Shifting winds showered the region with radioactive dust.'

'I've heard of it, but I study weather from a theoretical standpoint.' She nibbled the scone and gazed at the sky. 'There are wet winds coming, as a matter of fact. Lots of rain. Look.'

I followed her finger. The clouds had moved inland and I could see black patches behind the white fluff.

'When will the rain get here?'

'Next few days. It could delay your getting out. The boats won't sail if the winds are strong.'

'Are we talking winds or a storm?'

'Hard to say. The house probably won't fly away.'

'That's comforting.'

'It could be just rain, very little air movement. If the winds kick up, stay inside. You'll be fine.'

'The charter company didn't mention anything about delays.'

'They never do. They just cancel without warning.'

'Great.'

'It's a different way of life,' she said. 'People don't feel bound by the rules.'

'Sounds like Washington.'

231

She put the scone down and smiled, but held onto her butter knife. 'Washington has its own set of rules.'

'I'll bet. How long have you been working for the government?'

'Since I got out of grad school.' Her eyes returned to the clouds. 'As they get lower, they pick up moisture, then they turn jet-black and burst all at once. It's something to see.'

'You've been to the region before?'

She examined the cutting edge of the knife. 'No, but I've been other places with comparable patterns.' Another glance upward. 'It could come down in sheets. Only problem'll be if the cisterns fill too high for the filters to handle and the germ count rises.'

'I thought Bill had the water situation under control.'

'Not without access to the town he doesn't. But you heard Laurent. He's stuck here. All of us are. Guilt by association.'

'At least you've got your gun.'

She raised her eyebrows. Put the knife down and laughed. Pointing her finger at the coffeepot, she pulled an imaginary trigger.

'Crack shot?' I said.

'It was Ly's.'

'How'd he get it through baggage control?'

'He didn't. Bought it in Guam. He always traveled armed.'

'Exploring dangerous places?'

Filling her juice glass, she drank and looked at me over the rim. 'As you said, it's impossible to escape crime.'

'Actually, you said that. I said life could be a prison.'

'Ah. I stand corrected.' She put the glass down, snatched up the scone, bit off half, and chewed vigorously. 'It's incredible, being that close to a psychopathic killer. Ben seemed okay, maybe a little too *pukka sahib* with Bill, but nothing scary.' She shook her head. 'You never know what's inside someone's head. Or maybe *you* do.'

'Wish I did,' I said.

Dipping her hand into the pastry basket, she scooped up croissants, muffins, and rolls, and then broke off a cluster of grapes.

'Working lunch,' she said, standing. 'Good talking to you. Sorry you didn't have time to solve the mysteries of the island psyche.'

She headed for the doors to the house. When she got there, I said, 'Speaking of prisons, this place would make an especially good one, don't you think? U.S. territory, so there'd be no diplomatic problems. Remote, with no significant population to displace, and the ocean's a perfect security barrier.'

Her mouth got small. 'Like Devil's Island? Interesting idea.'

'And politically expedient. Ship the bad guys halfway around the world and forget about them. With the crime situation back home, I bet it would play great in Peoria.'

Crumbs trickled from her hand, dusting the stone floor. Squeezing the pastries. 'Are you thinking of going into the prison business?'

'No, just thinking out loud.'

'Oh,' she said. 'Well, you could take it one step further. When you get back home, write your congressman.'

Yet another folded card on my desk:

> *O let not Time deceive you,*
> *You cannot conquer Time.*
>
> *In the burrows of the Nightmare*
> *Where Justice naked is,*
> *Time watches from the shadow . . .*
>
> WH Auden

Below that: *A: Don't you think Einstein would agree? B.'*

What was he getting at now? The ultimate power of time . . . deceitful time . . . Einstein – time's relativity? The nightmare – death? Impending mortality?

An old man losing hope?

Making a typically oblique cry for help?

233

If so, I was in no mood to oblige.

I read a few more charts but couldn't concentrate. Returning to the house, I encountered Gladys coming out the front door.

'I'm glad I caught you, doctor. Dennis – Chief Laurent's on the phone.'

I picked it up in the front room. 'Dr Delaware.'

Dead air, then a click and background voices. The loudest was Dennis, giving orders.

I said, 'I'm here, Chief.'

'Oh – yeah. My man said you had something to tell me.'

'I was wondering if I could come into town to talk to Ben.'

Pause. 'Why?'

'Moral support. Dr Moreland asked me. I know it's a tall order—'

'No kidding.'

'Okay, I asked.'

'You don't want to do it?'

'I don't particularly want to mix in,' I said. 'Any idea when the rest of us will be allowed off the estate?'

'Soon as things quiet down.'

'Robin and I have reservations out in five days. Any problems with that?'

'No promises. No one's allowed off the island till we settle this.'

'Does that include the sailors on the base?'

He was silent. The noise in the background hadn't subsided.

'Actually,' he said, 'maybe you *should* come down to talk to him. He's acting nuts, and I don't want to be accused of not providing proper care, create any technicalities.'

'I'm not an M.D.'

'What are you?'

'Ph.D. psychologist.'

'Close enough. Check him over.'

'Pam's an M.D.'

'She's no head doctor. What, now that I want you, you're not interested?'

234

'Are you concerned about a suicide attempt?'

Another pause. 'Let's just say I don't like to see prisoners behave like this.'

'What's he doing?'

'Nothing. That's the point. Not moving or talking or eating. Even with his wife there. He wouldn't acknowledge her. I guess you'd call it catatonic.'

'Are his limbs waxy?'

'You mean soft?'

'If you position him, does he stay that way?'

'Haven't tried to move him – we don't want anyone claiming brutality. We just slide his food tray in and make sure he's got enough toilet paper. I'm bending over to protect his rights until his lawyer shows up.'

'When's that?'

'If Guam can free up a public defender and Stanton lets him fly in, hopefully in a couple of days – hold on.'

He barked more orders and returned to the line. 'Listen, you coming or not? If so, I'll send someone to pick you up and drive you back. If not, that's fine too.'

'Pick me up,' I said. 'When?'

'Soon as I can get someone over.'

'Thanks. See you then.'

'Don't thank me,' he said. 'I'm not doing it for your sake. Or his.'

He came himself, an hour later, emotions hidden behind mirrored shades, a shotgun clamped to the dash of the little police car.

As I walked out, he looked up at the gargoyle roof tiles and frowned, as if in imitation. I got in the car and he took off, speeding around the fountain and through the open gate, downshifting angrily and taking bumps hard. His head nearly touched the roof and he looked uncomfortable.

When we were out of sight of the estate, he said, 'I'll give you an hour, which is probably more than you need 'cause he's still playing statue.'

235

'Think he's faking?'

'You're the expert.' He grabbed the gearshift as we went around a sharp curve. His forearms were thick and brown, corded and veined and hairless. White crust flecked the corner of his mouth.

'He told me you two grew up together.'

Bitter smile. 'He was a couple of years older but we hung out. He was always small, I used to protect him.'

'Against who?'

'Kids making fun – his family was trash. He was too, didn't comb his hair, didn't like to bathe. Later, he changed so much you couldn't believe it.' He whipped his head toward the window, spat, returned his eyes to the road.

'After he moved in with Moreland?'

'Yeah. All of a sudden he got super-straight, studied all the time, preppy mail-order clothes, and Dr Bill bought him a catamaran. We used to go out sailing. I'd have a beer; he never touched it.'

'All that due to Moreland's influence?'

'Probably the military, too. We did that at the same time also. I was an MP in the Marines, he was Coast Guard. Then he got married, kids, all that good stuff. Probably decided it was a good idea to keep the straight life going.'

The next sentence came out a snarl: 'I *liked* the bastard.'

'Hard to reconcile that with what he did.'

He glanced at me and picked up speed. 'What're you trying to do? Put me on the couch? Dr Bill *tell* you to do that?'

'No. Sometimes I lapse into shoptalk.'

He shook his head and and put on more speed, turning the final dip to the harbor into a roller-coaster swoop.

The water enlarged as if at the hands of some celestial projectionist, blue, mottled platinum where the clouds hovered.

Laurent shoved the shift lever hard, yanked it back into neutral, gunned the engine, stopped so short I had to brace myself against the dash. My fingers landed inches from the shotgun and I saw his head swivel sharply. I put my hands in my lap and he chewed his cheek and stared out the windshield.

236

More people than usual on the waterfront, mostly men, milling around the docks and congregating in front of the Trading Post, which was closed. The only open establishment, in fact, was Slim's Bar, where a few more drinkers than usual loitered, smoked, and swigged from long-necks. I picked out Skip Amalfi's fair hair among the sea of black, then his father, hovering nervously at the back of the crowd.

Skip was animated, talking and gesturing and brushing hair out of his face. Some of the villagers nodded and gesticulated with their arms, slicing the air choppily, pointing up Front Street toward the road that led up to Victory Park.

Laurent put the car into gear and rolled down so fast I couldn't focus on anyone's face. Ignoring the stop sign on Front Street, he made a sharp right and raced toward the municipal center. The parking spaces facing the whitewashed building were all taken. Nosing behind a crumbling Toyota, he jerked the key out of the ignition, freed the shotgun, and got out carrying the weapon against his thigh. His size made it look like a toy.

Slamming the car door, he marched toward the center. Onlookers moved aside and I rode his wake, managing to get inside before the remarks to my back took form.

The front room was tiny, dingy, and hot, filled with the salty-fatty smell of canned soup. Nicked walls were covered with wanted posters, Interpol communiqués, lists of the latest federal regulations. Two desks, messy, with phones tilting on mounds of yet more paper. One held a hotplate.

The only spot of color was a tool company calendar over one of the workstations, starring a long-torsoed, pneumatic brunette in a red spandex bikini that could have been used for a handkerchief. A middle-aged deputy sat under sleek, tan thighs, writing and moving a toothpick around in his mouth. Skinny, he had a jutting stubbled chin and a sunken, lipless mouth. Lots of missing teeth. His hair was limp and graying, fringing unevenly over his collar. His uniform needed pressing but his engraved metal nameplate was shiny. *Ruiz*.

'Ed,' said Dennis. 'This is Dr Delaware, the psychologist from the castle.'

Ed pushed away from his desk and the legs of the folding chair groaned against the linoleum floor. The skin under his eyes was smudged. A pile of plastic-wrapped toothpicks was at his left hand. He lowered his head to the wastebasket and blew out the pick in his mouth, selected a new one, tore the plastic, rested the splinter on a ridge of bare gum, and laced his hands behind his head.

'Anything?' said Dennis.

'Uh-uh.' Ed manipulated the pick with his tongue and watched me.

'No action from the jokers at Slim's?'

'Nah, just big talk.' The sibilant voice. He touched the revolver in his belt with his left hand. I thought of something and filed it away.

'Why don't you take a walk up and down Front. Check things out.'

Ed shrugged and rose to a slumping five four. Pocketing more toothpicks, he ambled out the door.

Dennis said, 'You can sit in his chair.'

I took my place under Miss Redi-Lathe, and he settled half a buttock atop the other desk and folded his arms across his chest.

'Ed may not look like much to you, but he's reliable. Ex-Marine. In Vietnam he won enough medals to start a jewelry store.'

'Southpaw, too.'

He took off the mirrored glasses. His light eyes were clear and hard as bottle glass. 'So?'

'It reminded me that Ben's left-handed. I know because I saw him vaccinating the kids at the school. I read AnneMarie Valdos's file. Moreland said the killer was probably right-handed.'

'To me, "probably" means not for sure.'

I didn't answer.

Laurent's arms tightened and his biceps jumped. 'Moreland's no forensic pathologist.'

'He was good enough for the Valdos case.'

He chewed his cheek again and shot me a close-mouthed smile. 'Are you his rent-a-sherlock, supposed to raise doubts about my investigation?'

'The only thing he asked me to do was give Ben moral support. If my being here's a problem, take me back and I'll catch up on my sunbathing.'

Another bicep flex. Then the smile widened, flashing white. 'Look at that, I pissed you off. Thought shrinks didn't lose their tempers.'

'I came to Aruk to do some interesting work and get away from city life. Since I got here it's been nothing but weirdness, and now you're treating me like some kind of sleazeball. I'm not Moreland's surrogate and I don't enjoy being placed under house arrest. When those boats pull up, I plan to be on one.'

I stood.

He said, 'Take it easy, sit down. I'll make coffee.' Switching on the hotplate, he pulled packets of instant and creamer and styrofoam cups out of his desk.

'It ain't Beverly Hills café au lait. That okay?'

'Depends on what kind of conversation goes with it.'

Grinning, he went through a battered rear door. I heard water run and he returned with a metal coffeepot that he placed on the hotplate.

'You want to stand, suit yourself.'

I waited until the pot bubbled before sitting.

'Black or cream?'

'Black.'

'Tough guy.' Deep chuckle. 'No offense, just trying to take the tension off. Sorry if I rubbed you wrong before.'

'Let's just get through this.'

He fixed two cups, handed me one. Terrible, but the bitterness was what I needed.

'I know damn well Ben's a lefty,' he said. 'But all Moreland said in AnneMarie's case was that the killer was righthanded *if* she was grabbed from behind and done like this.' Tilting his head back, he exposed his Adam's apple and ran a hand

239

along his throat. 'If she was cut from the front, it could have been a lefty.'

He shifted his weight.

'Yeah, I know what you're thinking. We dropped it before it was finished. But it's not like some big city, tons of money to follow every lead.'

'Hey,' I said, 'big-city cops don't always follow through. I watched thugs burn L.A. down while the police sat around waiting for instructions from brain-dead superiors.'

'You don't like cops?'

'My best friend is one – seriously.'

He stirred creamer into his cup and sipped with surprising delicacy. 'I've got a pathologist flying in. Looking at AnneMarie's file as well as Betty's. I don't know if she'll be able to make any determination about how Betty got cut, because her head was taken clean off. Maybe, though. I'm no expert.'

Shifting again, he got up and sat behind the other desk, propping his feet up.

'Does your gut tell you Ben's guilty?' I said.

'My gut? What the hell's that worth?'

'My friend's a homicide detective. His hunches have led him to some good places.'

'Well,' he said, 'good for him. I'm just one third of a dinky-shit three-man police force on a dinky-shit island. Ed's my main backup and my other deputy's older than him.'

'You probably never needed more.'

'Till now I didn't . . . Do I think Ben's guilty? It sure as hell looks like it, and he's not bothering to deny it. Only one who thinks otherwise is Dr Bill, with his usual . . .'

He shook his head.

'His usual singlemindedness?' I said.

He forced a smile. 'My word was "fanaticism." Don't get me wrong, I think he probably could have won a Nobel Prize for something if he'd put his mind to it. He's helped my mother and me plenty, giving her a free lease on the restaurant till things get better, paying for my schooling. I felt like a *shithead*, mouthing off

240

to him last night. But you've got to understand, he's like a moray eel – gets hold of something and won't let go. What the hell does he want me to do? Let Ben walk on his say-so and watch the whole damn island explode?'

'Is the island near exploding?'

'Hotter than I've ever seen it – a lot worse than when AnneMarie got killed, and we had grumblings then.'

'The march up South Road?'

'No march, just a few kids shouting and waving sticks but look where it led. Now some people think they were fooled into believing a sailor did AnneMarie, and they're doubly pissed.'

'Fooled by Ben?'

'And Dr Bill. 'Cause Ben's seen as Dr Bill's boy. And even though people admire Dr Bill, they're also . . . nervous about him. You hear stories.'

'About what?'

'Mad scientist shit. Growing all this fruit and vegetables, bringing some into town, but rumor is he hoards it.'

'Is that true?'

'Who the hell knows? Guys who work the estate say he fools around with dehydration, nutritional research. But who cares? What's to stop anyone from growing their own stuff? My mother does. Dr Bill set her up years ago with soil and seeds, and she grows her own Chinese vegetables for the restaurant. But people get dependent, they like to piss and moan. Doesn't take much to get their tongues flapping. AnneMarie was a newcomer, no roots here, but everyone liked Betty.'

'Including the sailors.'

He turned toward me very slowly. 'Meaning?'

'Moreland said she'd socialized with them. As had AnneMarie.'

'Socialized . . . yeah, Betty liked to party before she got engaged, but for your own safety I wouldn't repeat that.'

'Any chance Betty and Ben had an affair?'

'Not that I heard, but who knows? But whatever Betty did, she was a nice kid. Didn't deserve to be ripped up like that.'

'I know. I spoke to her the morning before she died.'

He put his cup down. 'Where?'

'At the Trading Post. I bought drinks and magazines. She told me about her baby.'

He arced his feet off the desk and they hit the floor hard.

'Yeah, her mom said she loved the idea of having a baby.' Real pain clouded his eyes. 'Anyone who'd do that should have his nuts cut off and stuffed down his throat.'

The phone rang. He grabbed it. 'Yeah? No, not yet. No, not before his lawyer – I don't know.'

He slammed the phone down. 'That was Mr Creedman. Wants to do a story for the wire services.'

'Opportunity knocks,' I said.

'Meaning?'

'He's a writer. Now he's got a story.'

'What do you think of him?'

'Not much.'

'Me, neither. First day he got here, he hit on my mother. She straightened him out soon enough.'

He trained his eyes on me. He was a handsome man but I thought of a rhino, ready to charge.

'So tell me, doc, is Ben one of those guys, when you hear about his killing someone you say, "No way, couldn't be"?'

'I don't know him well enough to answer that.'

He laughed. 'Got my answer. Not that I've got any grudge against him. I've always admired him for the way he pulled himself up. I grew up without a father, but my mother's good enough for ten parents. Ben's mom was a dirty drunk and his dad was a real asshole, beat the hell out of him just for laughs. According to you guys, isn't that exactly the kind of thing that grows killers?'

'It helps,' I said. 'But there are plenty of abused kids who don't end up violent, and people from good homes who turn bad.'

'Sure,' he said, 'anything's possible. But we're talking odds. I took psychology, learned about early influences. Someone like Ben, I guess it's no surprise he cracked. I guess the big surprise is the time he had in between, acting normal.'

'In between what?'

242

Instead of answering, he finished his coffee. I'd barely touched mine and he noticed.

'Yeah, it's lousy – want some tea instead?'

'No, thanks.'

'The situation's really bad,' he said into his empty cup. 'Betty's family, Mauricio. Claire, her kids. Everyone thrown together, people can't escape each other.'

The phone rang again. He got rid of the caller with a couple of barks.

'Everyone wants to know everything.' He looked above me, at the bikini girl. 'I should take that down. Ed and Elijah like it, but it's disrespectful.'

He got up and came toward me. 'I've seen plenty, doctor, but never anything like what happened to those two women.'

'One thing you might want to know,' I said. 'After I read the Valdos file I called my detective friend. He ran a search for similar murders and came up with one, ten years old, in Maryland.'

'Why'd you ask him to look?'

'I didn't. He did it on his own.'

'Why?'

'He's a curious guy.'

'Checking out the island savages, huh? Yeah, I know about that one. Two satanists ate a working girl.' He shot out some details. 'My computer rarely works right, but I phone stuff in to the MPs on Guam and they hook into NCIC.'

'What do you think of the similarities?'

'I think satanic psychos have some sort of script.'

'Any evidence Ben was into satanism?'

'Nope.'

'Have you ever seen evidence of satanism on Aruk?'

'Not a trace, everyone's Catholic. But Ben was in Hawaii ten years ago – who knows what kind of shit he picked up?'

'Did he take any side trips to the mainland?'

'Like to Maryland? Good question. I'll look into it. For all I know, he killed girls in *Hawaii* and never got caught. For all I know, he was lucky the only thing they got him for was indecent exposure.'

The look on my face made him smile.

'That's what I meant by acting normal in between.'

'When?' I said.

'Ten years ago. He peeped in some lady's window with his pants down and his dick out. He was in the Guard and they handled it. Ninety days in the brig. That's how a lot of sex killers get started, isn't it? Watching and beating off, then moving on to the heavy stuff?'

'Sometimes.'

'*This* time.' He looked disgusted. 'Okay, have your hour with him. Give him his moral support.'

27

Behind the battered door was a warren of small, dim rooms and narrow corridors. At the back was a dented sheet-metal door bolted by a stout iron bar.

Laurent removed my watch and emptied my pockets, placed my belongings on a table along with his gun, then unlocked the bar, raised it, and pocketed the key. Pushing the door open, he let me pass, and I came up against grimy gray bars and the sulfur-stink of excreta.

A two-cell jail, a pair of three-pace cages, each with a cement floor, a grated, translucent window, a double bunk chained to the wall, a crusted hole with heel-rests for a toilet.

The ceilings were six and half feet high. Black mold grew in cracks and corners. The plaster had been scored by decades of fingernail calligraphy.

Laurent saw the revulsion on my face.

'Welcome to Istanbul West,' he said, with no satisfaction.

'Usually guys don't stay here for more than a few hours, sleeping off a drunk.'

The nearer cell was empty. Ben sat on the lower bunk of the other, chin in hand.

'Well, well, looks like we've had some movement,' said Laurent, loudly.

Ben didn't budge.

The keys jangled again and soon I was in the cell, locked in, and Laurent was outside saying, 'Trust me with your wallet and your watch, doc?'

I smiled. 'Do I have a choice?'

'Thanks for the vote of confidence. One hour.' Tapping his own watch. 'I'll leave the door open so you can shout.'

He left. Inside the cell, the stink was stronger, the heat almost unbearable.

I tried to find a place to stand that allowed me some distance from Ben, but the cramped space prevented it – so I contented myself with keeping maximum distance from the floor latrine as I scanned the graffiti. Names, dates, none of them recent. A large depiction of exaggerated female genitalia above the bunk. Sgraffito message: *Get me out of this hole!*

Ben didn't move. His eyes were unfocused.

'Hello,' I said softly. Though my five-ten height missed the ceiling by a few inches, I found myself hunching.

Silence. As complete as at the estate but not at all peaceful. After only seconds in here, my nerves screamed for some noise.

'Dr Bill sent me to see if there's anything I can do for you, Ben.'

He kept perfectly still, not even a blink, hair greasy, face streaked with sweat tracks. My armpits were already sodden.

'Ben?'

I took hold of his right arm and moved it from under his chin. Stiff and unyielding, as he resisted me.

No catatonia.

I let go. Repeated my greeting.

He continued to tune me out.

Three more attempts.

Five minutes passed.

'Okay,' I said. 'You're a political prisoner, giving the world the silent treatment as a protest against injustice.'

Still no response.

I waited some more. His cheeks were sunken – almost as hollow as Moreland's – and his eyes looked remote.

No eyeglasses. They'd been taken from him. Along with his shoelaces and belt and watch and anything else hard-edged. An angry boil had broken out on the back of his neck.

I kept staring at him, hoping my scrutiny would cause him to react. His nails were gnawed almost to the quick, one thumb bloody. Had he always been a biter? I'd never noticed. Or had Betty Aguilar resisted and snapped off some keratin? A clue he'd tried to conceal by chewing his other fingers?

I looked for nail bits on the floor. Nothing but inlaid dirt and scuffmarks, but they could have been tossed down the toilet hole. Big black ants single-filed under the bunk. After Moreland's zoo, they were laughable.

No scratches on his face and hands.

His color was bad, but he was unmarked.

'How well do you see without your glasses?'

Silence.

Slow count to one thousand.

'This isn't exactly the behaviour of an innocent man, Ben.'

Nothing.

'What about your family?' I said. 'Claire and the kids.'

No response.

'I know this has been a nightmare for you, but you're not helping yourself.'

Nothing.

'You're being a fool,' I said, loud as I could without attracting Dennis's attention. 'Pigheaded like Moreland, but sometimes it pays to think independently.'

Involuntary flinch.

Then back to stone-face.

'Sins of the father,' I went on. 'People are already making that connection.'

His lower lip twitched.

'Guilt by association,' I went on. 'That's why I had to come down here. Moreland's confined to the estate because Dennis is afraid of what people might do to him. We're all confined. It's gotten ugly.'

Silence.

'People are angry, Ben. It's only a matter of time before they start wondering about his being Dr Frankenstein, what he does in that lab. If maybe AnneMarie and Betty were *his* idea as well as yours.'

The lip dropped, then snapped shut.

I gave him a few more minutes, then came closer and spoke to his left ear.

'If you're really as loyal as you make out, tell me what happened. If you butchered Betty on your own, just admit it and let them know Moreland had nothing to do with it. If you have another story, tell it, too. You're not helping yourself or anyone else this way.'

Nothing.

'Unless Moreland *did* have something to do with it,' I said.

No movement.

'Maybe he did. All those late-night walks. God knows what he was up to. I saw him one night, two A.M., carrying his doctor's bag. Treating who? And those surgical tools were his.'

Another flinch. Stronger.

Flick of his head.

'What?' I said.

He clamped his mouth shut.

'He studies predators. Maybe his interest isn't limited to bugs.'

He blinked hard and fast. *Exactly* the way Moreland did when he was nervous.

'Is he in on it with you, Ben? Did he teach you – Aruk's own Dr Mengele?'

Half a headshake turned into a full one.

'Okay,' I said. 'So why clam up like this?'

Back to immobility.

'You want me to believe you did do it, alone. Okay, I'll buy it, for the moment. No surprise, I guess, given your family history.'

Silence.

'Your criminal history, too,' I added. 'Some sex killers start off as peepers. Some of them search for new ways to deal with their impotence. AnneMarie wasn't penetrated sexually, and I bet Betty wasn't, either.'

More blinking, as if to make up for lost time.

'Dennis told me about the Hawaii arrest. Soon everyone will know about it, including Claire and the kids. And Dr Bill. If he doesn't already.'

He let out hot, sour breath.

I forced myself to remain close.

'What else were you up to, back then? Ever travel to the mainland when you were in the Guard? See the sights – maybe Washington, D.C.?'

Blank look.

'Peeping Tom,' I said. 'Vivaldi on the terrace doesn't cancel it out. Whatever else you did over there will come out too, once they really start checking.'

No reaction.

'The reason I mentioned D.C. is it's not far from a place called Wiggsburg, Maryland.'

His eyes angled downward. Puzzled? Distressed? Then they were staring straight ahead, again, as unmoving as when I'd entered.

I was coated with sweat. Had become accustomed to the sulfur stench.

'The funny thing is, Ben, it's still hard for me to think of you that way. Despite the evidence. Do you actually like to *eat* people? Odd for someone raised by a vegetarian. Unless that's the *point*.'

249

He began breathing hard and fast.

'Is it your way of slapping Moreland in the face?'

He inhaled deeply, held his breath. His hands began curling and tightening, the knuckles almost glassy. I stepped back but kept talking:

'The brain, the liver. The bone marrow? How does something like that start? When did it start?'

He struggled to stay calm.

'Moreland taught you a lot about medicine. Did it include dissection?'

His chest swelled and his skin turned as gray as the cell floor.

Then he stopped.

Stilling his eyes.

Composing himself.

Another slow count. To two thousand.

I stood there watching him.

He pressed one hand against his breastbone.

His eyes, suddenly clear.

Not with insight.

Washed by tears.

He began shaking, flung his arms wide, as if welcoming crucifixion.

Staring at me.

I moved back further, my spine at the wall. Had I pushed it too far?

His arms fell.

Turning away, he whispered: 'Sorry.'

'For what, Ben?'

Long silence. 'Getting into this.'

'Getting into this?'

Slo-mo nod.

'Stupid,' he said, barely audible.

'What was?'

'Getting into this.'

'Killing Betty?'

250

'No,' he said, with sudden strength. He bent so low his brow touched his knees. The back of his neck was exposed, as if for the executioner's ax. The boil seemed to stare at me, a fiery cyclops eye.

'You didn't kill her?'

He shook his head and mumbled.

'What's that, Ben?'

'But . . .'

'But what?'

Silence.

'But what?'

Silence.

'But what, Ben?'

'No one will believe me.'

'Why?'

'You don't.'

'All I know are the facts that Dennis gave me. Unless you tell me different, why should I believe otherwise?'

'Dennis doesn't.'

'Why *should* he?'

He looked up, still bowed, face angled awkwardly. 'He knows me.'

'Then if you've got an alibi, give it to him.'

He straightened and returned his eyes to the wall.

Shaking his head.

'What is it?' I said.

'No alibi.'

'Then what's your story?'

More headshaking, then silence.

'What's your last memory before they found you with Betty?'

No answer.

'When did you start drinking last night?'

'I didn't.'

'But you were drunk when they found you.'

'They say.'

'You didn't drink but you were drunk?'

251

'I don't drink.'

'Since when?'

'A long time.'

'Since you cleaned up in high school?'

Hesitation. Nod.

'Were you drunk in Hawaii? The Peeping Tom bust?'

He started to cry again. Growled and stiffened and managed to hold it in check.

'What happened in Hawaii, Ben?'

'Nothing – it was a big . . . mistake.'

'You weren't peeping?'

Suddenly he laughed so heartily, it caused him to rock, rattling the bunk.

Taking hold of his cheeks, he tugged down and created a sad-clown face, horribly at odds with the laughter.

'Big mistake. Big, big, *big* mistake.'

After that, he stopped talking, fluctuating between long bouts of silence and incongruous laughter.

Some kind of breakdown?

Or faking it?

'I just don't understand it, Ben. You claim you didn't kill Betty, but you seem awfully comfortable being a suspect. Maybe it is something to do with Moreland. I'm going back to the estate to talk to *him*.'

I moved toward the cell door.

'You wouldn't understand,' he said.

'Try me.'

He shook his head.

'What's so damned profound that you can't part with it?' I said. 'The fact that you grew up low status and now you're being thought of as the scum of the earth again? Sure, it's a cruel irony, but what happened to those girls was a hell of a lot crueler, so forgive me if I don't shed tears.'

'I—' Shaking his head again.

'Everything comes round, Ben. Big insight. I'm a psychologist, I've heard it before.

'You – you're wasting your time. Dr Bill is. Best to cut me loose.'

'Why?'

'I – don't stand a chance. Because of who I am – what you just said. Scum family, scum child. Before Dr Bill took me in, they wanted to send me to reform school. I . . . used to do bad things.'

'Bad things?'

'That's why this makes sense to everyone. Dennis knows me, and *he* thinks I did it. When they brought me in, their faces – everyone's.'

He looked back at the wall. Put a finger to his mouth and tried to get a purchase on what remained of the cuticle.

'What about their faces?' I said.

The finger flew out. 'No! You're wasting your time! They *found* me there. *With* her. I know I wouldn't – couldn't have done it, but they *found* me. What can I say? I'm starting to think I . . .'

This time he let the tears come.

When his sobs subsided, I said, 'Have you ever done anything like this before?'

'No!'

'Did you kill AnneMarie Valdos?'

'*No!*'

'What about the Peeping Tom thing?'

'That was *stupid*! A bunch of us from the Guard were on weekend leave; we went to a club in Waikiki. Everyone was drinking and partying. Usually I had ginger ale, this time I thought I could . . . handle it. Had a beer. Stupid. *Stupid*. Then another . . . I'm a stupid asshole, okay? We tried to pick up some girls, couldn't, went to walk it off in some residential neighborhood. I had to take a . . . needed to urinate. Found a garage wall, behind some house. The window to the house was open. She heard. We got caught – I did. The others ran.'

He looked at me.

'That doesn't sound terrible,' I said. 'If that's really the way it happened.'

253

'It is. That's the only filthy thing I've ever done since . . . I reformed.'

'What was your relationship with Betty?'

'I knew her. Knew her family.'

'Did she have a reputation for fooling around?'

'I guess.'

'Did you fool around with her?'

'No!'

'No affair?'

'*No*! I *love* my wife – my life is *clean*!'

'Her baby wasn't yours?'

'*I love my wife! My life is clean!*'

'Repeating it won't make it so.'

He started to come toward me, stopped himself. 'It's true.'

'Did you know she had the clap?'

Surprise on his face. Genuine?

'I don't know about that. My life is clean.'

'So how'd you end up in the park with your head on Betty's entrails?'

'I – it's a . . . it's a crazy story, you'll never believe it.' Closing his eyes. 'Just go. Tell Dr Bill to forget about me. He's got important things to do.'

'You're pretty important to him.'

He shook his head violently.

'Tell me the story, Ben.'

The head kept shaking.

'Why not?'

He stopped. Another smile. Enigmatic. 'Too stupid. I couldn't even tell Claire – wouldn't believe it myself.'

'Try me. I'm used to strange stories.'

Silence.

'Keeping quiet just makes you look guilty, Ben.'

'Everything makes me look guilty,' he said. 'If you keep your mouth shut, you can't swallow flies.'

'Did Moreland tell you that? His quotations are usually a little more elegant.'

'No,' he said sharply. 'My . . . father.'

'What other words of wisdom did your father give you?'

Keeping his eyes closed, he tightened the lids.

Lying down on the bunk, face to the skimpy straw mattress.

'Okay,' I said. 'Maybe you should save it for your lawyer, anyway. Dennis has called for a public defender from Saipan. It'll take at least two days, maybe longer. Anything you want me to tell Moreland other than to abandon you?'

No movement.

I called out Dennis's name.

Deputy Ed Ruiz shuffled in and produced a key. 'Say anything?'

I didn't answer.

The toothless mouth creased in contempt. 'Figures. His old man never said anything either when we used to throw his ass in here. Just lie there, like he's doing. Like some damn piece of wood. Then, soon as the lights went out, he'd start having those drunk-dreams, screaming about things eating him alive.'

He put the key in the lock. 'When it got so loud we couldn't stand it, we'd hose him off and that would work for a while. Then he'd sleep again and go right back into those DTs. All night like that. Next morning, he'd be denying he did anything. Few days later, he'd be sauced up again, insult some woman or grab her, take a poke at some guy, and be back in here, the same damn thing all over.'

He came forward, pointing at Ben. 'Only difference is, Daddy used to sleep on the top bunk. We'd put him on the bottom, but he'd always find a way to get up there, no matter how drunk. Then, of course, he'd roll off in the middle of the night, fall on his ass, crack his head. But climb right back on top, the stupid shithead. *Stubborn*-stupid. Some people don't learn.'

He snickered and turned the key.

Behind me, Ben said, 'Hold on.'

28

Ruiz looked at him with disgust.

'Hey, killer.' Bracing one bony hand against the edge of the cell door. USMC tattoo across the top.

'How much time do I have left?' said Ben.

'The doctor here is ready to go.'

'I can wait,' I said. 'If he's got something to tell me.'

Ruiz mashed his lips and peered at his watch. 'Suit yourself. Eighteen minutes.'

He lingered near the door.

'We'll take all eighteen,' I said. He walked away, very slowly.

When I turned back to Ben, he was on his feet, next to the toilet hole, squeezing himself into a corner.

'This is the story,' he said in a dead voice. 'I don't care what you think of it, the only reason I'm telling you is so you'll pass it along to Dr Bill.'

'Okay.'

'Though you probably won't.'

'Why not?'

'You can't be trusted.'

'Why's that?'

'The way you talked about him before. He's a great man – you have no idea.'

'Hey,' I said. 'If you don't trust me to deliver the message, save it for your lawyer.'

'Lawyers can't be trusted, either.'

'The one in Hawaii didn't do well by you?'

'There was no trial in Hawaii,' he said. 'I pled guilty and the Guard gave me some brig time. They said it wouldn't go on my record. Obviously, they can't be trusted either.'

'Life's rough,' I said. 'I'm sure Betty's family thinks so too.'

He stared into the filthy pit.

I said, 'Sixteen minutes left.'

Without shifting position, he said, 'When we got home from dinner, Claire was upset with me. For pressuring her to play. She didn't show it, but that's the way she is. I shouldn't have done it.'

Wringing his hands.

'We had . . . a tiff. Mostly, she talked and I listened, then she went to bed and I stayed up, trying to read. To get rid of my anger. Sometimes that works for me . . . not that I'm angry a lot. And we don't have many tiffs. We get along great. I love her.'

Tears.

'What did you read?'

'Medical journals. Dr Bill gives me his when he's through. I like to educate myself.'

'Which journals?'

'*New England Journal, Archives of Internal Medicine, Tropical Medicine Quarterly.*'

'Do you remember any specific articles?'

'One on pyloric stenosis. Another on gallbladder disease.'

He rattled off more medical terminology, suddenly looking at ease.

'How long did you read?'

'Maybe an hour or two.'

'One hour or two? There's a big difference.'

'I – we got home around nine forty. The . . . tiff took maybe another ten minutes – mostly, it was cold silence. Then Claire was in bed by ten – so I guess a little over an hour. Maybe an hour and a half. Then the phone rang, some guy saying there was a medical emergency.'

'What time was this?'

'I don't know – when I'm not working I don't watch the clock. Bill taught me time was valuable, but when I'm home, not paying attention to time is my freedom.'

He looked at me in a new way. Childlike. Craving approval.

'I understand,' I said, thinking of the Auden poem Moreland had just left me.

O let not Time deceive you . . . burrows of the Nightmare . . . naked justice.

He scratched his cheek, then his chest. Gazed into the latrine as if he wanted to crawl in.

'It was probably eleven-thirty,' he said. 'Or around then.'

'Who called?'

'Some guy.'

'You don't know who?'

He shook his head.

'Small island like this,' I said, 'I'd think you'd know everyone.'

'At first I thought it was one of the gardeners at the estate, but it wasn't.'

'Which gardener?'

'Carl Sleet. But it wasn't. When I said "Carl" he didn't acknowledge, and this guy's voice was lower.'

'When you said "Carl" he didn't identify himself?'

'He was talking fast – very upset. And the connection was bad.'

'Like a long distance call?'

That surprised him. 'Why would anyone call me long distance? No, the worst calls are the local ones. The long distance ones if you get a satellite linkup, you're fine. But most of the island lines are old and corroded.'

'All right,' I said. 'Some guy you didn't recognize calls you sounding upset—'

'I've been wracking my brain to see if I could figure out who it was, but I can't.'

'Why was he upset?'

'He said there was an emergency, a heart attack on Campion Way, near the park, and they needed help.'

'He didn't say who had the heart attack?'

'No. It all happened very fast – as if he was panicked.'

'Why'd he call you instead of Moreland?'

'He said he had called Dr Bill and Dr Bill was on his way and told him to get me because I was closer to Campion. So I grabbed my stuff and went.'

'What stuff?'

'Crisis kit – paddles, epinephrine, other heart stimulants. I figured I'd start CPR till Dr Bill got there, then the two of us . . .'

'Then what happened?'

'I left the house—'

'Did Claire see you go?'

'No. I snu – left as quietly as possible. I didn't want to wake her or the kids.'

'Did she hear the phone ring?'

'I don't know . . . usually she doesn't. The phone's in the kitchen and there's no extension in the bedroom. We keep the ringer on low at night.'

'With no bedroom extension, how do you hear emergency calls?'

'I'm a light sleeper and we usually leave the bedroom door open. Tonight it was shut – Claire shut it 'cause she was mad. When it rang, I ran over and picked up on the first ring.'

Meaning no one could verify the call or the time frame.

'So you left with your medical kit,' I said.

'Yes.'

'Did you walk or drive?'

'Drove. I got to the park maybe five minutes after the call.'

259

'Close to midnight.'

'Must have been. It was really dark, there are no streetlights on the island except for Front Street. At first I couldn't see anything, was worried I'd run over the patient, so I parked and walked. As I got closer I saw someone lying by the side of the road.'

'Just one person? What about the caller?'

'No one else. I assumed whoever had called it in had chickened out. And I figured it would take another few minutes for Dr Bill to get there, so I went over, opening my kit, ready to start, and someone grabbed me.'

'Grabbed you how?'

'Like this.' Hooking his left arm around his neck, he did a rough imitation of a police chokehold.

'A left arm?'

'Uh – no, it came from this side.' Reversing the hold. 'I guess it was the right – I can't be sure. It was so sudden and I blacked out. Next thing I remember is Dennis's face staring down at me, looking really weird. *Angry.* Other people, all of them staring down at me, my head feels as if it's about to explode and my neck's stiff and I think something happened to me and they're there to rescue *me.* But their faces – their eyes are hard. Then someone I can't see calls me "killer." And they're all looking at me the way they used to look at me when I was – the way they did – before I *changed.*'

I waited a while before saying, 'Anything else?'

'That's it . . . great story, huh?'

'The one thing you can say for it is, if you killed her, it sure wasn't premeditated. If it had been, you'd have prepared something useful.'

His smile was rueful. 'Yeah, great planner. So what do I do?'

'Tell your lawyer the story and see what he says.'

'You'll tell Dr Bill? It's important to me – his knowing I'm innocent.'

'I'll tell him.'

'Thank you.'

I heard footsteps.

260

'Anything else I can do for you, Ben?'

He bit his lip. 'Have Dr Bill tell Claire I'm sorry. For pressuring her to play . . . for everything.'

'Do you want to see her?'

'No. Not like this – ask her to tell the kids something. That I'm away on a trip.' Once more, tears welled.

Ed Ruiz opened the metal door. 'Time's up.'

On the way back to the office he said, 'Have fun?'

'A real blast,' I said. 'Next time, I bring streamers and funny hats.'

He let me in. Dennis was at his desk. He put the phone down, looking annoyed.

'Time well spent?' he asked me.

I shrugged.

'Well, the screws are already turning. Dr Bill doing his thing.'

'What thing is that?'

'I just got a call from Oahu. Landau, Kawasaki and Bolt. High-powered law firm, senior partner's some motormouth named Alfred Landau. Flying over in a couple of days – scratch the public defender.'

'Flying into Stanton?'

'Nope, into Saipan by chartered jet, then a private yacht's taking him the rest of the way. If it can't fit into the keyhole harbor, I'm sure they'll find a way of getting him to shore.' He drummed the phone receiver. 'Must be nice to be rich. Let me take you back.'

As we stepped outside, Tom Creedman intercepted us. He was wearing a white polo shirt, white shorts, and tennis shoes. All that was missing was a racquet. Instead, he carried a thin black attaché case in one hand, a pocket tape recorder in the other. The crowd on the waterfront had dispersed somewhat. A few stragglers remained on the south end. Among them were Skip Amalfi and Anders Haygood. Skip pointing to the spot where AnneMarie Valdos had been found.

'Going to Wimbledon, Tom?' said Laurent.

'Yeah, me and the queen – got a minute, Dennis?'

'Not even half of one – come on, doctor.'

Creedman blocked me. 'See the suspect, Dr Delaware?'

'Let's go,' said Dennis, moving to his car.

Creedman didn't budge. 'Care for some coffee, Dr Delaware?'

'Sure,' I said.

Surprising both of them.

'Great,' said Creedman. 'Let's boogie.'

'I'm taking him back,' said Dennis. 'For his safety.'

'I'll take him back, Dennis.'

'No way—'

'I'll take the risk,' I said.

'It's not your risk to assume,' said Dennis.

'No?' I said. 'What law are you invoking to restrict my movement?'

He hesitated for a beat. 'Material witness.'

'To what?'

'You spoke to him.'

'With your permission. Let's call Mr Landau and see what he has to say about it.'

Dennis's huge shoulders spread even wider. He touched his belt, looked up and down Front Street.

'Fine,' he said savagely. 'You're on your own.'

Creedman and I walked past Campion Way to the next unmarked load. Past angry stares and mutters.

'Ooh,' he said. 'The natives are restless.'

'You're pretty relaxed about it.'

'Why not? I have nothing to do with good ol' Dr Bill. On the contrary, the fact that he evicted me works in my favor.'

He grinned, then continued, 'You, on the other hand, need to watch your back. But I'm here to stand up for you, buddy.' Unzipping the attaché, he peeled back a flap and revealed a chunky chrome automatic.

'Sixteen shots,' he said gaily. 'I'm sure that'll do the trick in the event of civil unrest. Very few of the natives own arms. Safe place and all that.'

'Do you usually carry?'

'Only during periods of stress.'

'Bring it over with you?'

'Bought it in Guam, bargain price. Owned by an Army lieutenant who ran up some debts. Took beautiful care of it.'

He zipped the case. 'I'm just up the hill.'

'Pretty close to the murder scene.'

'Not close enough.'

'What do you mean?'

'By the time I got there the crowd was thick – no chance to get close. I would have liked a close look at Mr Romero's face right after they caught him. Editors like that kind of immediacy. The emptiness in a psychopath's eyes.'

'I'm sure you can make something up.'

His smile died. 'That's not very kind, Alex.'

I winked.

His round face stayed angry, even after he restored the smile. 'But I understand. The cognitive dissonance must be painful for you. Coming here expecting Pleasure Island and getting Auschwitz. Did Ben have anything exculpatory to say?'

'Nothing an editor would be interested in.'

'What a sicko,' he continued. 'Cutting them up, then *eating* them.'

'Ever see that kind of thing before?'

The road had taken on a steeper slant, and though he kept up an athletic pace his breathing got louder. 'See what?'

'Cannibalism.'

'On other islands? No.'

'I meant back in the States, when you were on the crime beat.'

'Did I say I was ever on the crime beat?'

'I think you did. The first time we met.'

'I think I didn't. Not my meat – pardon the joke. No, Alex, I did politics. Dog eat *dog*.' He laughed. 'Have *you* seen it before?'

263

I shook my head.

'First time for everything,' he said.

We progressed up the hill, passing small houses, children, dogs, cats. Women with frightened eyes drew the children closer as we neared. Window shades lowered suddenly.

'Tsk, tsk,' he said. 'Paradise lost.'

29

His house was at the top, where the street dead-ended, a pale blue cottage with a full ocean view, hugged by pink oleander and yellow hibiscus. A Volkswagen bug sat at the end of a shattered-stone driveway. Much of the surrounding property was overrun by ivy and flowering vines. The nearest house was a hundred feet away, separated by a splintering wooden fence.

Inside was a different story: freshly painted white walls, black leather couches, oriental rugs that made the vinyl floor look better than it was, limited-edition posters, teak and lacquer furniture. In the closet-kitchen next to the dining area, a cast-iron ceiling rack bore expensive copper pots. German cutlery in a wooden case adorned a counter. All the appliances were European and they looked brand-new.

'Let me fix you a drink,' said Creedman, heading for a portable brass-and-glass bar.

'Just a Coke.'

He poured the soda and fixed a double scotch for himself. Johnny Black. Ice from a small, chrome-faced Swedish freezer.

I looked around. The main space was an office – living room. Computer and printer, thousand-watt battery pack, brass reflector telescope, stereo set, CD rack, German twenty-inch TV hooked up to a beefy cable that ran up through the ceiling.

'Had a dish,' he said, 'but a wind blew it down.'

'Looks like you've settled in for the long run.'

'I like to live well. Lime with that?'

'Sure.'

He brought the drinks and we sat down. The ocean was framed beautifully through a wide window.

'Best revenge,' he said, sipping. 'Living well.'

'Revenge against who?'

'Whoever deserves it.' He took a long, slow swallow and emptied his glass. Sucking in an ice cube, he moved it around his mouth.

'So what can I do for you?' I said.

'Nothing, Alex. Just trying to be friendly. Fellow ugly Americans, and all that. Too bad we didn't get much time together before you left.'

'Who said I'm leaving?'

He smiled. 'Aren't you?'

'Eventually. How about you?'

'I've got no schedule – one advantage of freelancing.'

'Sounds nice.'

'It is.'

We drank and he emptied his glass. 'Can I get you another one?'

'No, thanks.'

'Don't mind if I do.'

He poured himself a taller scotch and returned.

'It's really something, isn't it, this bloodfest. Guess I am on the crime beat now. Back in D.C. it never appealed to me because the vast majority of criminals were total shit-for-brains. The police and the prosecutors were no rocket scientists, either.'

'Are politicians smart?'

'Some of them.' He laughed. 'A few.'

'Nicholas Hoffman?'

He took a long, slow sip. 'Smart enough, from what I hear. So when are you packing out?'

'I'm not sure yet, Tom.'

'So what happens to your project with Moreland?'

'There isn't much of a project.'

'What was it all about, anyway?'

'Reviewing his files to see if we could find themes.'

'Themes?'

'Patterns of disease.'

'Mental disease?'

'All kinds.'

'That's it?'

'That's as far as it got.'

'And if you found patterns, then what?'

'We'd write it up for a medical journal. Maybe a book of our own. How's your own book going?'

'Great.'

'Going to add a chapter on the murders?'

'You better believe it . . . So how's Robin?'

'Fine.'

'Doggy okay, too?'

'Great.'

'Any chance Moreland put Ben up to killing those girls?'

I exaggerated my surprise. 'Why would he?'

He put the drink down, uncrossed his legs, scooted forward. 'Let's face it, Alex, the guy's strange.'

'He's a little different.'

'Like Norman Bates was different. That place – those bugs. And what the hell does he do all day in that lab? It sure ain't medicine, 'cause Ben handles most of the medical situations – or at least he used to. Till Pam came over. So what's the old guy up to all day?'

'I don't know.'

'Come on, you've been working with him.'

'In separate buildings.'

'What's he hiding?'

'I don't know that he's hiding anything.'

His mustache turned down. The black line was as flat as a grease-pencil scrawl, but he smoothed it anyway.

'He probably told you about the hassle Ben gave me. Probably made me out to be a thief.'

'He said you were looking for something. Were you?'

'Sure. Reporter's instincts. Because the minute I got to that place I started having a strange feeling.'

'About what?'

'Just general weirdness. And obviously I was right. All that do-gooding and his best boy's a serial killer. People are pissed, Alex. If you care about that pretty lady and that cute little pooch, you'll head back to lala land pronto.'

His voice had stayed low and even, but his eyes were holes burnt in linen.

'That sounds almost like a warning, Tom.'

'Word to the wise, Alex. Strategic assessment based upon the data at hand.'

I smiled. 'And *that* sounds kind of corporate. Almost like a quarterly report.'

He reached for the scotch. Missed, groped, got hold of it, drank. When he lowered the glass, his lower lip was wet and shiny. 'Guess I'd better be taking you back to Weird Castle.'

'Guess so.'

We left the house and he walked ahead of me and got into the VW. The engine squealed but it wouldn't turn over.

'Damn,' he said, without a trace of regret. 'Battery must have gone dead. I'd call Harry or Skip for a jump, but they're back in town with everyone else.'

'I'll walk.' I started down the road.

'I feel terrible,' he called after me. When I looked over my shoulder he was smiling.

*　　*　　*

The clouds had moved directly over the shoreline, and the air was warm and sticky.

I encountered no one on my way to the harbor, but a stray yellow mutt with a gray muzzle heeled for a while, then ran off as I reached Front Street. A group of young men standing near the intersection watched me over their cigarettes, grumbling as I passed and ignoring my 'good morning.'

Dennis's police car was still parked in front of the municipal center. He wouldn't want to play taxi.

I'd accepted Creedman's invitation in order to check him out. He'd wanted me there for the same reason.

Pumping me and warning me off.

Then stranding me.

His decor said someone was paying him well. His reaction to my crack about quarterly reports said it was probably Stasher-Layman.

Had it been a mistake to let him know I was onto that? No matter, I'd be gone soon.

I walked along the docks, ignoring stares. The municipal center's door opened and Dennis came out, followed by three small men, one middle-aged, the others in their twenties. They all wore thin shirts and jeans and talked wildly as Dennis tried to appease them.

The middle-aged man stamped a foot, waved a fist, and shouted. Dennis said something and the fist waved again. The man pointed and touched his heart. Dennis put a hand on his shoulder. The man shook it off angrily.

People started to move in from the street.

Dennis glared and they dispersed, very slowly.

The older man stamped and touched his heart again. One of the younger men turned and I got a look at his face: plain, round, acned.

Unmistakable resemblance to Betty Aguilar.

Dennis ushered them back inside and I continued south. I hadn't gone far before I heard footsteps behind me. A quick look back: some of the youths I'd passed at the intersection. Four of them, hands in pockets, advancing quickly.

I stopped, looked at them blankly and when that didn't stop them, tried to stare them down.

They kept coming.

I crossed the street, ending up in front of the Trading Post. The structure was sealed with yellow crime-scene tape. Some things were the same everywhere.

Slim's Bar was closed now too, but several beer swillers loitered in the gravel bed that served as the tavern's parking lot.

The four men behind me hesitated, then jogged across.

I reversed direction and headed back toward the center.

The youths picked up speed. One of them had something in his hand. A short wooden club – like a cop's billy, but sawn-off.

I ran.

They did too. Their mouths were open and their eyes were fixed.

The police station wasn't far, but the hangers-on at Slim's could be a problem.

As I got closer, they closed rank, forming a human wall.

Skip Amalfi among them, flushed, his lips pursed in an attempted belch. Anders Haygood, next to him, stolid and sober, the gray eyes amused.

The boys to my back shouted something.

The Slim's crowd moved forward.

Caught in the middle.

More shouts, loud murmuring, then someone's voice above it all: *'Idiots!'*

Jacqui Laurent had burst through the Slim's crowd. Taller than most of the men, she wore a grease-specked apron over her flowered dress and was waving something.

Big cast-iron frypan.

One of the Slim's crowd said something.

She cut him off: 'Shut up, you *moron*! What do you think you're *doing*?'

The four young men were close enough for me to hear their panting.

270

I whipped around.

The one with the club came forward, making small circles with the weapon. He had a feather beard and long hair. Some of his shirt buttons were missing, exposing a hairless chest.

Jacqui was at my side. *'Ignacio!'*

She grabbed for the club. Ignacio held on. She tugged.

Someone laughed.

She curled her lip. '*Big* shots. Big *heroes*. Ganging up on an innocent guy.'

'Who says he's innocent?' said one of the Slim's crowd. 'He lives up *there*.'

'*Yeah.*'

'*Yeah motherfu*—'

'So?' said Jacqui. 'So *what*?'

'So he's . . .'

'What?'

'A—'

'*What, Henry?* So he's a guest up at the castle? So what does that mean? That we act like animals?'

'*Someone's* been acting like an animal,' said Skip, 'and it ain't—'

'You *shut up* – look who's *talking*.'

Skip's nostrils opened. 'Hey—'

'Hey, *yourself*. Shut up and *listen*. *You're* an animal – and that animal's a *pig*.'

Skip moved forward. Haygood held him back, thick arms taut.

'Come on, big man,' said Jacqui, jerking the club. 'You going to *attack* me? A woman with a *frypan*? *That* how you get your jollies? Or is *peeing* at women your only thing?'

Skip's chinless face paled and he struggled in Haygood's grip.

Haygood said something and Skip made the sound of a hungry kid refused supper.

'*Big* shot,' said Jacqui. 'Big shot with your *bladder*. Every time a woman goes on the beach you follow her and pee near her blanket. Like a dog marking. Very brave.'

271

Skip lunged. Haygood restrained him, and some of the other men joined in holding him back.

'Easy, man,' said one of them.

'Come on,' said Jacqui, suddenly wresting the billy from Ignacio's grip and waving it along with the skillet. '*Go* at me, Skip. You like to get tough with women, right? Maybe *you* had something to do with Betty, tough guy.'

Skip snarled and Haygood did something to his shoulder that made his face go limp.

'Like a dog,' said Jacqui. 'Following every new woman around, peeing – you think that's funny?'

She ran her eyes over the other men: 'Any of *you* think that's funny? Peeing on the beach near a woman's blanket? Did it happen to any of your sisters? Or your mamas? 'Cause he did it to me when he first came over – remember that, Skip?'

Back to the others: '*That* your idea of brave, boys? Peeing on women and beating up on innocent men?'

Silence.

'*Big tough macho-men.* Gang up on a guest – what's his crime? Visiting? How do you think this island will ever get anywhere, you treat people like this?'

The men avoided her eyes.

Skip was rubbing his shoulder. Haygood turned him around and tried to move him away. Skip shoved Haygood's arm away but walked.

Jacqui stared at the Slim's crowd until it began to fall apart. Soon no one was left but the four youths who'd stalked me. The one named Ignacio stared at the billy in Jacqui's hand. She pointed the frypan at them.

'You should be ashamed of yourselves. I have a good mind to tell your mothers.'

One of the youths started to smirk.

'Think that's *funny*, Duane? I'll tell *your* mama *first*.'

'Go ahea—'

'Want me to? Really, Duane? First I'll tell her about what I saw on North Beach.'

Duane's mouth slammed shut. The other boys stared at him. 'Yeah, so?' he said.

'Yeah, so.' Jacqui tapped a firm thigh with the skillet. 'You really want me to do that, Duane?'

'Whu—?' said one of the other boys, giggling. 'Whud you do, Duane?'

'Nuthin'.'

'Sure *was* nothing,' said Jacqui, and Duane's nose twitched.

'Ah, fuck,' he said. 'Let's get the fuck out of here.'

'Good idea,' said Jacqui. 'All of you – scoot.'

They slunk away, the other boys surrounding Duane as he cursed them. When they were well past the center, Jacqui faced me.

'What did you think you were doing?'

'Walking home.'

'It's not a good time to play tourist.'

'I see that.'

She inspected the billy. Frowned and replaced it in her pocket. 'Walking all the way back to the castle?'

'My ride didn't come through.'

She gave me a puzzled look.

I told her about Creedman.

'What'd you want with *him*?'

'He invited me.'

Her expression said I was a cretin.

'Come on, I'll get Dennis or a deputy to drive you.'

'Dennis already offered,' I said. 'I turned him down, so I doubt he'll want to.'

She scraped something off the bottom of the frypan. Hefted the utensil as if considering braining me.

'Men,' she said. 'Why does everything have to be a contest? Come on, we'll go ask him again. He'll do it. He's been raised on the Fifth Commandment.'

Her fingers prodded the small of my back. Strong. Her skin was creamy and unlined, her body big and strong. She'd been eighteen when she'd given birth to Dennis, but even up close she could pass for his sister.

273

'Come on,' she said, 'I can't be here forever.'

She walked very fast, swinging the pan in a semicircle, big breasts heaving, mouth slightly parted.

I said, 'What did you see that boy Duane do on North Beach?'

She grinned.

'Never really saw him. *Heard* him.' Chuckle. 'Fooling around with his girlfriend.'

'Is that unusual?'

'Not for North Beach. Kids go there all the time.'

Avoiding South Beach because of the murder?

'So what was the big threat?' I pressed.

She laughed, high and girlish. It relaxed her face and made her seem even younger. Shifting closer to me, she said, 'The big *threat*, Dr Delaware, was that the boy was no *good* at it. His girlfriend was not very happy with him.'

More laughter as her hip nudged mine. 'You know, wham bam, thank you ma'am?'

'Ah,' I said.

'Ah.' She smiled, tightening the arc of the pan and scraping her flank. Her apron ruggled and her dress blew up, revealing brown leg. 'Ah.'

30

She went into the center first. I stuck my head in, saw Dennis huddled with Betty's family, and backed out quickly.

I waited next to the police car, keeping my eyes on the street. Quiet had settled over the waterfront. The rain clouds seemed to sag.

Deputy Ed Ruiz came out a few moments later and said, 'Let's go.'

The ride to the estate was silent. He stopped in front of the big gates. 'This far enough?'

'Thanks.' I got out.

'When you leaving Aruk?'

'Soon as the boats come in.'

He stuck his head out of the car. 'Listen, I've got nothing against Dr Bill. He helped my daughter out of a real bad situation a few years ago. Scraped herself on some coral, got this infection, we thought she'd lose the leg till he saved it.'

His toothless mouth folded inward.

'I'll forward your regards,' I said.

'But things change, you know? Not everyone's down on him. Some people know him better than others.'

'The ones he's helped directly?'

'Yeah. But others, they *don't* know.' He let the wheel spin back. 'Ben did those girls and you know it.'

'Let's say he did. What does Dr Bill have to do with it?'

Silence.

'You think he's somehow involved?'

He didn't answer.

'But people are saying he is?'

'People talk.'

'Maybe,' I said, 'someone wants Dr Bill to leave, and this is a golden chance to get rid of him.'

'Why?'

'Because he owns too much of the island.'

'That's the *point*,' he said angrily. 'He owns *too* damn much. Nothing much to go around and each year it's less. People get tired of wanting. Those that want, start thinking about those that got.'

Gladys was running a manual carpet sweeper over the second-floor landing, looking tired but moving quickly. As I approached the door to my suite, she put a finger to her lips.

'Robin's napping,' she whispered. 'That's why I'm using this instead of the Hoover.'

'Thanks for telling me,' I whispered back.

'Can I fix you some lunch?'

'No, thanks. Is Dr Bill around?'

'Somewhere. Claire came by to see him, brought KiKo for us to take care of. I've got him in a cage in the laundry room. Claire had the children with her – poor little things, so scared. Robin let them play with Spike.'

She looked ready to cry. 'Dennis promised to have someone watch them. So who does he send? Elijah Moon, everyone calls him Moojah. He's supposed to be a police deputy, but

276

he's my age, got a belly out to here. What good can a fat old man do?'

I started down the stairs, then stopped.

'Gladys?'

'Yes, doctor?'

'You cooked for Senator Hoffman when he was the base commander?'

'I was head cook, sailors working under me.' She frowned.

'Tough job?'

'He liked his food fancy. All sauced up, always had to be something new. We used to send over for that really expensive beef from Japan – cows that do nothing all day but sit around and eat rice.'

'Kobe beef.'

'Right. And vegetables you never heard of and oysters and all kinds of expensive seafood. Nothing local, mind you. Had his crabs shipped from Oregon – Dungeness crabs. New England lobster. Philippine scallops. He was always clipping recipes out of magazines and sending them over to me. "Try this, Gladys." Why do you ask?'

'I was just curious what kind of relationship he and Dr Bill had. The night we had dinner at the base, they talked privately and Dr Bill was really upset afterwards.'

'I know,' she said. 'The next day he didn't eat a thing for breakfast or lunch. And him so thin in the first place.'

'Any idea why?'

'No. But he never liked Hoffman.' Her eyes misted. 'I don't believe Ben did anything, sir.'

'The people down in the village do.'

'Then they're stupid.'

'For all Dr Bill's accomplished, there's a lot of resentment toward him.'

She gripped the sweeper and the soft flesh of her arms quivered. 'Ungrateful *welfare* bums! Dr Bill tried to get them to work, but they don't want to know about that, do they? Did you know he offered free leases on the Trading Post and hardly anyone was interested?

Even those that rented stalls hardly showed up except to cash those *welfare* checks. Government keeps sending those checks, why should anyone bother? The nerve, to resent him!'

Anger had pulled her voice out of a whisper. She slapped her hand over her mouth.

'What with Ben's troubles, it's too bad about Dr Bill and Hoffman,' I said. 'It would be good to have friends in high positions.'

'Lot of good he'd do,' she said. 'That one was always for himself. Used to come up here and eat Dr Bill's food and cheat at cards. Illegal bridge signals, can you believe that? He was no gentleman, doctor.'

'Did Dr Bill know he cheated?'

'Of course, that's how I know! He used to joke about it with me, saying, "Nicholas thinks he's fooling me, Gladys." I told him it was terrible, he should put an end to it. He laughed, said it wasn't important.'

'Cheating at bridge,' I said. 'So Hoffman's wife went along with it.'

'No, she – it was—' She colored. 'What a thing! Shameful! Half the time Hoffman invited himself. Played tennis and sunned, ordered food from the kitchen, like I was still working for him. Like *everything* here was his.' The hand clamped over her lips again. This time, she blushed behind it.

'Everything?' I said.

'You know, a big shot – used to having things his way. I'll tell you something else, Dr Delaware: the man was heartless. Back when I was still his cook, a plane full of sailors went down – men and their wives and children, returning to the States.' She dipped a hand.

The crash Moreland had mentioned after Picker's accident. Nineteen sixty-three.

'All those people,' she said. 'A tragedy. So what did Hoffman do? That evening, he sends over a crate of scallops on ice and orders me to fix him coquille St Jacques.'

She resumed sweeping. 'Miss Castagna said you'll be leaving

278

soon. I'm sorry. From the way you treat Miss Castagna I can tell you're a gentleman. And we need more kindness.'

'On Aruk?'

'In the whole world, doctor. But Aruk would be a good place to start.'

I was surprised to find Moreland in my office, slumped in an armchair, reading a pathology journal. He looked like a skeleton coated with wax.

Putting down the magazine, he sat up sharply. 'How's Ben?'

I summarized my time in the cell.

He said nothing. The journal's table of contents was on the front cover and he'd circled an article. 'Bloodstain evidence.'

'Defense research?' I said.

'Someone called him on an emergency? Someone who sounded like Carl?'

'That's what he said.'

His fingers looked frail as sparrow's feet. They cracked as he flexed them. 'Meaning you don't believe him?'

'Meaning it's not much of a story, Bill.'

A long time passed.

'Doesn't that indicate to you,' he said, 'that he's innocent? Surely someone as intelligent as Ben could concoct a *first*-rate story if his object was to get away with something.'

'He's intelligent but he's also highly troubled,' I said. 'Drink was once a problem for him, and he obviously reacts strongly to it now. And he's got at least one prior sexual offense. Indecent exposure in Haw—'

'I know about that,' he said. 'That was nonsense. I took care of that for him.'

I let the non sequitur stand.

He said, 'So even after speaking with him you judge him guilty.'

'Things look bad for him, but I try not to judge.'

'Yes, yes, of course. You're a *psychologist*.'

'Last time we spoke, that was why you wanted me to see him, Bill.'

279

He picked up the journal, rolled it, hefted it. Blinking.

'Forgive me, son. I'm on edge – you're certainly entitled to your opinion, though I wish you felt differently.'

'I'd love to change my opinion, Bill. If you've got information, I'm listening. More important, communicate it to the lawyer you hired.'

He bent low in the chair.

'Maybe you've done all you can do for the time being,' I said. 'Maybe you should start looking after your own interests. Down in the village there's a lot of hostility toward you.'

'Alfred Landau is the best,' he said, softly. His firm handled Barbara's will, after she died . . . She was a wealthy woman. What she left me enabled me to buy up more parcels of land. Alfred was . . . most helpful.'

'Did he handle Ben's arrest in Hawaii, too?'

'Minimally. That was a military affair. I made a few calls, used my former rank.'

He stood. 'You're absolutely right. I'd better call Alfred now.'

'You're not concerned about what I just told you? The anger down in the village?'

'It will pass.'

I told him about the near confrontation with the four boys and how Jacqui had stepped in.

'I'm sorry it came to that. Thank God you weren't harmed.'

'But *you're* not out of harm's way, Bill. Betty's family is enraged. Lots of idle talk's circulating about you.'

That seemed to genuinely perplex him.

'You're a have among have-nots, Bill.'

'I've always shared.'

'Despite that, you're still lord of the manor. And the serfs aren't doing well.'

'I – it's hardly the feudal system—'

'Isn't it?' I said. 'Betty's murder is the spark that lit tinders, but it's obvious to me after just a few days here that things were heating up well before.'

He shook his head. 'The people are good.'

'But their lives are falling apart, Bill. Their entire society is shutting down – when's the last time the gas station pumps worked?'

'I've put in for a shipment.'

'You own that, too?'

'And I ration my personal vehicles the same way I do theirs. They know that—'

They also know how you live, and measure it against their own existence. More people leave than stay. Betty and her *husband* were planning to leave. Perfect climate for provocateurs, and you've got some: Skip Amalfi's been having fun whipping up the crowd. And I wouldn't be surprised if Tom Creedman starts to take a more active role. I was up at his place after visiting Ben, and he—'

'You didn't tell him anything, I hope.' His eyes were bright with alarm.

'No,' I said, trying to hold onto my patience. 'He asked, but I played dumb.'

'Asked about what?'

'If Ben had told me anything significant; what you and I were working on. He also clearly wanted to convince me to leave, which makes sense if he's working for Stasher-Layman and they want to control Aruk. Have you seen the interior of his house?'

He shook his head.

'Rooms full of brand-new furniture, computer equipment, expensive appliances.'

'Yes, I remember he received a large shipment shortly after he arrived. Right after I asked him to leave here.'

'Meaning he'd planned all along to settle down in his own place, came up here to snoop. What was he looking for, Bill?'

'I told you I don't know.'

'Not a clue?'

'None.' Taking hold of the journal, he rolled it again and let it unfurl.

'Jo Picker has something to do with Stasher-Layman, too.'

That nearly lifted him off the sofa. 'What – how do you know?'

'Robin saw their literature in her room. She's another one from Washington and she was here alone the night the roaches ended up in our room.'

'I – we've already established that was my fault. Leaving the cage open.'

'Do you actually remember leaving it open?'

That absent look came into his eyes. 'No, but . . . I . . . you really believe she could be working for them, too?'

'I think it's likely, and I'm bringing it up to warn you. Because you'll be dealing with her after I'm gone. Which is what I came to tell you: Robin and I are leaving on the next boat.'

He took hold of the chair. It slid forward and he lost his footing. I shot up and got hold of him just before he tumbled.

'Clumsy oaf,' he said, jerking away and pulling at his shirt as if trying to rip it off. 'Clumsy goddamned old *fool*.'

It was the first time I'd heard him swear. I managed to sit him back down.

'Pardon my language – the next boat is when, a week?'

'Five days.'

'Ah . . . well,' he said in a clogged voice, 'you must do what you feel is best. There's a time for everything.'

'Time is important to you,' I said.

He stared at me.

'Ben told me that. It made me think of your last note. The Auden poem – time's deceit. Your question about Einstein. What exactly were you getting at?'

He looked up at the ceiling. 'What do you think it meant?'

'To take time seriously but to understand that it's relative? What kind of deceit were you referring to?'

More of the absent look. Then: 'Einstein . . . in his own way, he was a magician, wouldn't you say? Turning the universe on its end, as if reality was one big illusion. Forcing us all to look at reality in a new way.'

'Unencumbered by time.'

'Unencumbered by prior *assumptions*.'

He lowered his gaze and met mine.

'And you want me to do that, Bill?'

'What I want really doesn't matter, does it, son?'

'A new way,' I said. 'Being skeptical about reality?'

'Reality is . . . to a good extent what we *want* it to be.'

He got up, inhaled, stretched and cracked more joints.

'The great thinkers,' I said.

'Always something to learn from them,' he answered, as if we were reciting responsively.

'I still don't understand the note, Bill.'

He came up to me, moving into my personal space the way he had with Dennis. A big, clumsy, intrusive bird. I felt as if I was about to be pecked and had to control myself from retreating.

'The note,' he said. 'Actually, you did very well with the note, son. *Bon voyage.*'

31

The rain came just before Milo called.

Robin and I were reading in bed when I felt the air turn suddenly heavy and saw the sky crack.

The windows were open and a burnt smell drifted through the screen. For one knife-stab moment, I thought of fire, but as I looked out, the water began dropping.

Panes of plate glass, filming the view. The burnt smell turned sweet – gardenias and old roses and cloves. Spike began barking and circling and the room got dimmer and warmer. I shut the windows, blocking out some but not all of the sound.

Robin got up and stared through a now filmy pane.

The phone rang.

'How's everything?' said Milo.

'Bad and getting worse.' I told him about my experiences in the village. 'But we're booked for home.'

'Smart move. You can always stop over in Hawaii for a real vacation.'

'Maybe,' I said, but I knew we'd be jetting back to L.A. as quickly as possible.

'Robin there? Got some house stuff to tell her.'

I handed over the phone and Robin listened. Her smile told me things were going well.

When I got back on, he said, 'Now *your* stuff, though now that you're leaving, who cares?'

'Tell me anyway.'

'First of all, both Maryland cannibals are still locked up. The asshole who only cut the victim is eligible for parole but has been refused. The asshole who cut *and* dined isn't going anywhere. Thank God it wasn't an L.A. jury, right? L.A. jury couldn't convict Adolf Hitler. What's that sound? Static on your end?'

'Rain,' I said. 'Think of a shower on high and triple it.'

'Typhoon?'

'No, just rain. Supposedly they don't get typhoons here.'

'Supposedly they didn't get crime, either.'

I moved closer to the window. Only the tops of the trees were visible through the downpour. Above the rain clouds, the sky was milk-white and peaceful.

'Nope, no wind. Just lots of water. I hope it lets up in time for the boats to come get us.'

'Daylight come and you wanna go home, huh? Well, when you hear the rest, you'll wish it were sooner. Guess who covered the cannibal case for a local rag?'

'Creedman.'

'Didn't even have to look for him, his name was right there on the articles. Then someone else took over mid-case and that made me a little curious, so I dug deeper. No one at the paper remembers Creedman specifically, but I found out there'd been some hassle with the local police around the same time he got pulled off the story: officers leaking information to his paper and others for money. A bunch of cops got fired.'

'Did reporters get fired, too?'

'Couldn't find that out, but it's a good bet. Anyway, Creedman's next gig of record was at a D.C. cable station, some kind of business show, but he only lasted three months before getting hired by Stasher-Layman Construction's D.C. office. Communications officer. The company issued a press release describing major balance-sheet problems. Their stock went way down and the owners bought it all up and went private. Next year profits went way, way higher.'

'Manipulation?'

'Maybe the owners are just a couple of lucky guys. And maybe lawyers go to heaven.'

'Who are the owners?'

'Two brothers from Oregon, inherited it from their daddy, moved to Texas. Big liberals on paper – funding ecology research, humane solutions to crime.'

'Oregon,' I said. 'Hoffman's constituents. Was he part of the buyout?'

'If he was, it didn't hit the news, but they did contribute big to his last reelection.'

'How big?'

'Three hundred thou – what they call soft money, gets around the spending limits. Seeing as Hoffman didn't have to put out much – he was a shoo-in – that's very sweet. So it wouldn't surprise me if he's backing them on some island project. He chairs a committee that considers big federal development grants, has the power to let things through or hold them up. But I can't find anything smelly.'

'The cops who got fired,' I said. 'Were the leaks directly related to the cannibal murder?'

'I had trouble getting details. The press doesn't believe in full disclosure when it comes to the press. But the firings took place right after the arrest.'

'Did you get any names of fired cops?'

I heard paper rustling. 'White, Tagg, Johnson, Haygood, Ceru—'

'Anders Haygood?'

'That's what it says.'

'He lives here. One of the guys who likes to cut things up. His

286

buddy's been whipping the crowd up against Ben. Likes to pee when women are watching.'

'Wonderful.'

'So he and Creedman got booted at the same time – they know each other. Ten to one they're both on Stasher-Layman's payroll. Same for my next-door neighbor. She claims to be a botanist, but both she and Creedman are carrying guns that they picked up in Guam.'

'Jesus, Alex. Just sit tight till the boat comes in. Don't try to find out any more.'

'All right,' I said. 'But now I'm starting to think Moreland *could* be right about Ben being innocent. Not that he's got much of a story.'

'"I wuz framed"?'

'Ten points for the detective.'

'It's always "I wuz framed" unless it's "I blacked out" or "He started it."'

'Ben's two for three, claims he was choked out, the rest is blank.'

'Brilliant.'

I told him the rest of Ben's account.

'Beyond lame,' he said. 'Needs a four-prong walker. You know, Alex, a *real* bad smell's coming though the line. Even with Creedman and Haygood in cahoots over some development deal, that doesn't get Benjy off the hook – hell, for all you know *he's* on Stasher's payroll, too. You watch your back.'

'What should I do about the info on Creedman and Haygood?'

'Nothing. If the lawyer Moreland hired is really so sharp, let *him* do something with it. I'll tell him, not you. Name?'

'Alfred Landau. Honolulu.'

'When's he getting over there?'

'Two or three days.'

'Perfect timing. I'll wait till you've left.'

'Meanwhile Ben sits there rotting?'

'Ben ain't going anywhere no matter what anyone says or does. They found him *lying* on the goddamn body.'

287

'Convenient, isn't it?'

'Or stupid,' he said. 'But that just makes it typical. I had an idiot last month carjacked and killed some citizen, then drove the car for a couple of days before taking it to the dealer to complain about the fucking brakes. Funny, except the citizen's just as dead. Don't deal with it, Alex. I'll call Landau as soon as you're off the island. And don't feel bad about Ben. From what you're telling me, that jail cell may well be the safest place for him right now.'

'I'm not sure of that. We're not talking maximum security, just a hole at the back of the building. The victim's family visited the police station today. I saw the look in their eyes. It wouldn't take much of a mob to pull him out.'

'Sorry about that, but where else can he go? How's security at the estate?'

'Nonexistent.'

'Just stay *put*, Alex. Stay in your goddamn room – pretend it's a second honeymoon and you don't even *want* to come out.'

'Okay.'

'You definitely have your passage booked?'

'Definitely.' If the storm didn't stall things.

'See you soon. Enough of this paradise shit.'

Cheryl brought dinner up to our room and we picked at it. Darkness made its entrance virtually unnoticed. The rain got stronger, relentless, slapping the sides of the house.

But still warm. No lightning. The air was flat, deenergized.

As I sat there and did nothing, time's edges melted.

Time . . . *Einstein a magician . . . bending reality*.

Relativity – Moreland, a *moral* relativist?

Trying to *excuse* himself for something?

'Guilt's a great motivator.'

All these years – all his accomplishments – propelled by a troubled conscience?

Milo was right. It wasn't my battle.

Robin smiled from across the room. I'd told her what Milo had learned and she'd said, 'So it's good we're leaving.'

She was curled up now with some old magazines that had come with the suite. Spike snored at her feet. Peaceful scene, damned domestic. Pretending was fun.

I pointed to a wet window. 'Listen to it.'

She let her hand drop to Spike's head. 'It was a dark and stormy night.'

I laughed, went over, and kissed her hair.

She put the *Vogue* on her lap and reached up to stroke my face. 'This isn't so bad, huh? When you get down to it, making the best of a bad situation is the heart of creativity.'

She teased my tongue with hers. Our mouths collided. All the electricity, here.

We were slow-dancing toward the bed, fumbling with buttons, when the knocks on the door added thunder.

32

Pam's voice on the other side: 'Is anyone in there?'
We opened the door.

'Is Dad with you?' She stood, dripping, in a khaki raincoat drenched black, face shiny-wet under a snarl of run makeup.

'No,' said Robin.

'I can't find him anywhere! All the cars are here, but he isn't. We were supposed to get together an hour ago.'

'Maybe Dennis or one of the deputies picked him up,' I said.

'No, I called Dennis. Dad's not in town. I've searched all the outbuildings and every square inch of the house except your room and Jo's.'

She hurried next-door. Jo answered her knock quickly. She had on a bathrobe but looked wide awake.

'Is Dad with you?'

'No.'

'Have you seen him at all this evening?'

'Sorry. Been in all day – touch of the stomach bug.' She placed a hand on her abdomen. Her hair was combed out and her color was still good. When she noticed me studying her, she stared back hard.

'Oh God,' said Pam. 'This weather. What if he's outside and fell?'

'Older people do tend to spill,' said Jo. 'I'll help you look.' She went inside and returned wearing a tentlike transparent slicker over a black shirt and black jeans, matching hat, rubber boots.

'When's the last time you saw him?' she said. I followed her eyes down to the entry. Water had pooled there. Gladys and Cheryl were standing next to it, looking helpless.

'Around five,' said Pam. 'He was in his office, said he just had a little work, would be in soon. We were supposed to have dinner together at seven and it's already eight-thirty.'

'I spoke to him just before that,' I said, thinking of Moreland's tumble in the lab.

'Hmm,' said Jo. 'Well, I'm sorry, haven't noticed a thing. Been out of commission since noon.'

'Bad stomach,' I said.

She gave me another challenging look. 'Could he have gone off the grounds?'

'No,' said Pam, wringing her hands. 'He must be out there – Gladys, get me a flashlight. A big powerful one.'

She started for the stairs.

'Let's look for him in a group,' I said. 'Is anyone else here?'

'No, Dad sent the staff home early so they wouldn't get caught in the rain.' To the maids: 'Did anyone stay behind?'

Gladys shook her head. Cheryl watched her mother, then imitated the gesture. Her usual stoicism was replaced by a rabbity restlessness: sniffing, rubbing her fingers together, tapping a foot.

A sharp glance from Gladys stilled her.

'Okay,' said Jo, 'let's do it logically—'

'Did you check the insectarium?' I said.

'I tried to get in,' said Pam, 'but couldn't. The new locks – do *you* have the keys, Alex?'

'No.'

'The lights were out and I pounded hard on the door, no answer.'

'Doesn't he work in the dark sometimes?' said Jo. 'Doesn't he keep things dark for the bugs?'

'I guess so,' said Pam. Panic stretched her sad eyes. 'You're right, he could *be* in there, couldn't he? What if he's lying there hurt? Gladys, any idea where we can find a duplicate key?'

'I checked all the ones on the rack, ma'am, and it's not there.'

Cheryl grunted, then lowered her head.

Gladys turned to her. 'What?'

'Nothing, momma.'

'Do *you* know where Dr Bill is, Cheryl?'

'Uh-uh.'

'Have you seen him?'

'Just in the morning.'

'When?'

'Before lunchtime.'

'Did he say anything to you about going somewhere tonight?'

'No, momma.'

Gladys lifted her daughter's chin. 'Cheryl?'

'Nothin,' momma. I was in the kitchen. Cleaning the oven. Then I made lemonade. You said it had too much sugar, remember?'

Gladys's face tightened with irritation, then resignation set in. 'Yes, I remember, Cher.'

'Damn, damn,' said Pam. 'You're sure about the keys on the rack.'

'Yes, ma'am.'

'He probably forgot. As usual.'

'He gave it to Ben,' said Cheryl. 'I saw it. Shiny.'

'Lot of good that does,' said Pam. 'All right, I'm going back over to the insectarium and try to get in through one of those windows.'

'The windows are high,' said Jo. 'You'll need a ladder.'

'Gladys?' said Pam. Her voice was so tight the word was a squeak.

'In the garage, ma'am. I'll go get it.'

'I'll come with you,' said Jo. 'I can hold the ladder or climb it myself.'

'You're sick,' I said. 'Let me.'

She closed her door and positioned herself between Pam and me. 'I'm fine. It was just a twenty-four-hour thing.'

'Still—'

'No problem,' she said firmly. 'You probably don't have rainclothes, right? I do. Come on, let's not waste any more time.'

She and Pam hurried down, picked up Gladys, and headed toward the kitchen.

Cheryl remained alone in the entry. Fidgeting again. Looking everywhere but up at us.

Then right up at us.

At me.

'What is it, Cheryl?' I said.

'Um . . . can I get you something? Lemonade – no, too sweet . . . coffee?'

'No, thanks.'

She nodded as if expecting the answer. Kept bobbing her head.

'Is everything okay, Cheryl?' said Robin.

The young woman jumped. Forced herself to stand still.

Robin went down to her. 'What's the matter, hon?'

Cheryl kept looking up at me.

'It's pretty scary,' I said. 'Dr Bill disappearing like this.'

She began rubbing her thighs, over and over. I followed Robin down.

'What is it, Cheryl?' said Robin.

Cheryl looked at her guiltily. Turned to me. One hand kept rubbing her leg. The other patted a pocket.

293

'I need *you*,' she said, on the verge of tears.

I looked at Robin and she went to the far end of the front room. The rain was beating out a two-two rhythm, smearing the picture windows.

Cheryl's rubbing had intensified and her face was compressed with anxiety.

Sweating.

Conflict.

Then I remembered that Moreland had used her to deliver Milo's phone message.

'Did Dr Bill give you something for me, Cheryl?'

Running her eyes in all directions, she took a folded white card out of her pants pocket and thrust it at me. Stapled shut on all four corners.

I started to pull it open.

'*No!* He said it's for *secret*!'

'Okay, I'll look at it in secret.' I palmed the card. She started to leave, but I held her back.

'When did Dr Bill give it to you?'

'This morning.'

'To deliver tonight?'

'If he didn't come to the kitchen.'

'If he didn't come to the kitchen by a certain time?'

She looked confused.

'Why would he come to the kitchen, Cheryl?'

'Tea. I fix the tea.'

'You fix tea for him every night at a special time?'

'*No!*' Distraught, she tried to pull loose again. Staring at my pocket, as if expecting the paper to burst through.

'Gotta go!

'One second. Tell me what he told you.'

'*Give* it to you.'

'If he didn't want tea.'

Nod.

'When do you usually make him tea?'

'When he *tells* me.'

294

She started to whimper. Looked down at my hand on her arm.

I let go. 'Okay, thanks, Cheryl.'

Instead of running off, she held back. 'Don't tell momma?'

Moreland's trusty courier. He'd figured her limited intelligence would keep her on track, eliminate moral dilemmas.

Wrong.

'All right,' I said.

'Momma will be *mad.*'

'I won't tell her, Cheryl. I promise. Go on now, you did the right thing.'

She hurried away and I took the card to Robin. It was too dark to read and I didn't want to put on the lights. Hurrying back up to our suite, I popped the staples.

Moreland's familiar handwriting:

DISR. 184: 18

'What?' said Robin. 'A library catalogue number?'

'Some kind of reference – probably a volume or page number. He's been leaving cards since we got here. Quotes from great writers and thinkers: Stevenson, Auden, Einstein – the last one was something about time and justice. The only great thinker I can come up with who matches "DISR" is Disraeli. Did you notice a book by him up here?'

'No, only magazines. Maybe there's an article on Disraeli.'

'Architectural Digest?,' I said. 'House and Garden?'

'Sometimes they run features on ancestral homes of famous people.'

She divided the magazines and we started scanning tables of contents.

'French *Vogue*,' I muttered. 'Yeah, that'll be it. What Disraeli wore when addressing parliament: Now available at Armani Boutique. What the hell's he getting at? Even at his darkest hour the old coot's playing games.'

She discarded an *Elle*, started scrutinizing a *Town and Country*.

'Using poor Cheryl as a messenger,' I said. 'If he had something to tell me, why couldn't he just come out and say it?'

'Maybe he feels it's too dangerous.'

'Or maybe he's just going off the deep end.' I picked up a six-year-old *Esquire*. 'Everything he does is calculated. I feel like a character in a play. *His* script. Even this disappearance. Middle of the night, so damned *theatrical*.'

'You think he faked it?'

'Who knows what goes on in that big, bald head? I sympathize with the fact that his life's falling apart, but the logical thing would have been to beef up security and wait until Ben's lawyer arrives. Instead, he lets the staff go home early and puts his daughter through this.'

Rain hit the window so hard it shook the casement.

I ran my finger down another contents page, tossed it. 'Why choose *me* to play Clue with?'

'He obviously trusts you.'

'Lucky me. It makes no sense, Rob. He knows we're leaving. I told him this afternoon. Unless in his own nutty way he thinks this'll keep us here.'

'Maybe that or something else spurred him to action. But he could also be in real trouble. Knew he was in danger and left a message for you because you're the only one he's got left.'

'What kind of trouble?'

'Someone could have gotten in here and abducted him.'

'Or he fell, like he did in the lab.'

'Yes,' she said. 'I've noticed he loses his balance a lot. And the absentmindedness. Maybe he's sick, Alex.'

'Or just an old man pushing himself too hard.'

'Either way, his being out there on a night like this isn't a pleasant thought.'

The rain kept sloshing. Spike listened, tense and fascinated.

We finished the magazines. Nothing on Disraeli.

'There are books in your office,' she said. 'In back, where the files are.'

'But they're not categorized,' I said. 'Thousands of volumes, no system. Not too efficient if he's really trying to tell me something.'

'Then what about that library off the dining room?' she said. 'The one he told us wouldn't interest us. Maybe he said that because he was hiding something.'

'A book on or by Disraeli? What is this, Nancy Drew and Joe Hardy's blind date?'

'Let's at least check. What could it hurt, Alex? All we've got is time.'

We went downstairs again. The house was a scramble of streaks and shadows, hidden angles and blind corners, ripe with charged air.

We passed through the front room and the dining room. The library door was closed but unlocked.

Once inside, I turned on a crystal lamp. Dim light; the salmon moiré walls looked brown and the dark furniture muddy.

Very few books. Maybe a hundred volumes housed in the pair of cases.

Unlike the big library, this one *was* alphabetized: fiction to the left, nonfiction to the right, the former mostly *Reader's Digest* condensed editions of best-sellers, the latter art books and biographies.

I found the Disraeli quickly: an old British edition of a novel called *Tancred*. Inside was a rose-pink, lace-edged bookplate that said EX LIBRIS: *Barbara Steehoven Moreland*. The name inscribed in a calligraphic hand, much more elegant than Moreland's.

I turned hurriedly to page 184.

No distinguishing marks or messages.

Nothing noteworthy about line eighteen or word eighteen or letter eighteen.

Nothing noteworthy about anything in the book.

I read the page again, then a third time, handed it to Robin.

She scanned it and gave it back. 'So maybe "DISR" stands for something else. Could it be something medical?'

Shrugging, I flipped through the book again. No inscriptions anywhere. The pages were yellowed but crisp at the edges, as if never handled.

I put it back, pulled out another volume at random. *Gone With the Wind*. Then *Forever Amber*. A couple of Irving Wallaces. All with Barbara Moreland's bookplate.

'Her room,' said Robin. 'So he probably thinks of the big one as his. Leaving something there makes more sense – it's right behind your office. Maybe he pulled something out and left it for you.'

'This isn't exactly strolling weather.'

She wagged a finger at me. 'And someone forgot to bring his *rain* slicker!'

'Unlike the always-prepared Dr *Picker*. Wonder if she packed her little gun under that giant condom. I should have insisted on going with her and Pam. Maybe I should go over to the bug zoo and see what the two of them are up to.'

'No,' she said. 'If Jo *is* armed, I don't want you out there in the dark. What if she mistakes you for an intruder?'

'Or pretends to.'

'You really suspect her?'

'At the very least she's working for Stasher-Layman.'

She frowned. 'And Pam's out there with her – let's go see if Bill left anything for you.'

'Two targets in the dark? Forget it.' I buttoned my shirt at the neck and raised the collar. 'You go back and lock yourself in the room, and I'll dash over. I'll circle around from the back and avoid the bug house.'

She grabbed my arm. 'No way are you leaving me alone. Waiting for you to return will drive me batty.'

'I'll be quick. If I don't find anything in ten minutes, I'll forget about it.'

'No.'

'You'll get drenched.'

'We'll get drenched together.'

'Let's just forget the whole thing, Rob. If Moreland wanted to send a message, he should have used Western Union.'

'Alex, please. You know if I wasn't here, you'd be running to that bungalow.'

'I don't know that at all.'

'Come on.'

'The point is you *are* here. Let me go in and out or forget about it, Nancy.'

'Please, Alex. What if he's in danger and our not helping leads to tragedy?'

'There's already been plenty of tragedy, and what can Disraeli have to do with helping him?'

'I don't know. But like you said, he's got reasons for everything. He may play games, but they're serious ones. Come on, let's make a quick run for it.'

'You'll catch a cold, young lady.'

'On the contrary. It's a warm rain – think of it as showering together. You always like that.'

We were soaked immediately. I held her arm, and rain-blinded and slick-footed, concentrated on staying on the paths.

No worries about the gravel-crunch; the downpour blocked it out.

Vertical swimming; new Olympic event.

The downpour felt oily as it rolled off our skin.

Slow going till I spotted the yellow light over my office door. I stopped, looked around. No one in sight, but an army could have been hiding, and I knew if Moreland was out there it would be nearly impossible to find him before morning.

I glanced toward the insectarium. Lights still off. Pam and Jo hadn't gotten in.

The rain chopped our necks and our backs. Deep-tissue

massage. I tapped Robin's shoulder and the two of us made a dash for the bungalow. The door was unlocked, as I'd left it. I got Robin inside, then myself, and flipped on the weakest light in the room — a glass-shaded desk lamp.

Water flooded the hardwood floor. Our clothes clung like leotards and we sounded like squeegees when we moved.

Books and journals on my desk.

Piles of them that hadn't been there this afternoon.

Medical texts. But nothing by or about Disraeli.

No references beginning 'DISR.'

Then I found it, hefty and blue, on the bottom of the stack.

The Oxford Dictionary of Quotations.

I flipped to page 184. Samples of the wisdom of Benjamin Disraeli.

Line 18:

'Justice is truth in action.'

All that for this? The crazy old bastard.

Robin read the quote out loud.

I tried to recall the Auden quote . . . *naked justice, justice is truth.*

Wanting me do something to ensure justice?

But what?

Suddenly I felt tired and useless. Dropping a sodden sleeve onto the desk, I started to close the book, then noticed a tiny handwritten arrow on the bottom of page 185.

Pointing to the right.

Instruction to turn the page?

I did.

A notation in Moreland's handwriting parallel to the spine. I rotated the book:

214: 2

That turned out to be the wisdom of Gustave Flaubert.

Two quotations.

One about growing beards, the other demeaning the value of books.

More games . . . Moreland had been reading Flaubert the day he'd shown me the office. *L'Éducation sentimentale*. In the original French. Sorry, Dr Bill, I took Latin in high school . . . tapping the book, I felt something hard under the righthand leaf.

Ten pages down. Wedged into the spine and taped to the paper.

A key. Brass, shiny new.

I removed it. Underneath was another handwritten inscription, the letters so tiny I could barely make them out:

> *Thank you for persisting.*
> *Gustave's girl will be assisting.*

'Gustave's girl?' said Robin.

'Gustave Flaubert,' I said. 'The girl who comes to my mind is Madame Bovary. I told Bill I'd read the book years ago.'

'Meaning what?'

'I thought Madame Bovary was married to a doctor, got bored, had affairs, ruined her life, ate poison, and died.'

'A doctor's wife? Barbara? Is he trying to tell us she committed suicide?'

'He told me she drowned, but maybe. But why bring that up, now?'

'Could that be what he feels guilty about?'

'Sure, but it still doesn't make sense, making such a big deal about that now.'

I tried to reel the book's plot through my mind.

Then the truth came at me nastily and unexpectedly, like a drunk driver.

'No, not his wife,' I said. I shut the book.

Stomach turning.

'What is it, Alex?'

'Another Emma,' I said, 'is going to help us. A girl with eight legs.'

33

'Something hidden near her cage?' said Robin. 'Or in it?'

'He may have hidden it in the bug zoo to keep it from Jo. She claimed to be queasy about bugs, and this afternoon I told him my suspicions of her.'

'She's there right now.'

'Holding the ladder for Pam. Be interesting to see if she actually goes in.'

'What could he be hiding?'

'Something to do with either the murders or Stasher-Layman's plan. Ben's arrest made him realize things are bad and he has to play whatever cards he's got.'

The door opened suddenly and Jo and Pam sloshed in. I closed the book of quotations and tried to look casual. Dropped the shiny key into my pocket as the two women wiped the water from their eyes.

Pam shook her head despondently.

Jo fixed her gaze on me and shut the door. 'What are you folks doing out?'

'We wanted to help,' said Robin. 'Started looking around the grounds, but it got to be too much so we ducked in. Any luck at the insectarium?'

Pam shook her head miserably.

Jo scanned the room. 'The windows are bolted shut and layered with wire mesh. I managed to break the glass with the flashlight, but the wire wouldn't bend, so all I could do was shine it around and look in as best I could. Far as I could see, he's not there.'

'He didn't answer my shouts,' said Pam. 'We got a pretty good look.'

'Can't break the door, either,' said Jo. 'Three locks, plate steel and the hinges are inside.'

She removed her hat. Rain had gotten underneath and her hair was limp.

'I'm going back out,' said Pam.

'Reconsider,' Jo told her. 'Even if he is out there, with this kind of limited visibility, I don't see how you'd spot him.'

'I don't care.'

As she rushed for the door, Jo stared at me. 'What about you?'

'We'll stay here for a while, then return to the house. Let us know if you find him.'

Pam left. Jo put her hat back on.

'Are you armed?' I said.

'Excuse me?'

'Are you carrying your gun?'

She smiled. 'No. Weather like this, it could flood. Why? Think I need protection?'

'Anyone could be out there. The hostility down in the village . . . the rain'll probably keep people away, but who knows? We're all pretty vulnerable traipsing around.'

'So?' said Jo.

'So we need to be careful.'

'Fine, I'll be careful.' She threw the door open and was gone.

*   *   *

304

I opened the door a crack and watched as she melted into the downpour.

'Why'd you do that?' said Robin when I closed it.

'To let her know I was on to her. Maybe it'll prevent her from trying something, maybe not.'

We stood there, then I cracked the door again and looked outside. Nothing, no one. For what that was worth.

'Now what?' said Robin.

'Now we either go back to our room and wait till daylight or you go back and wait and I use the key and see what Gustave's girl can do for us.'

She shook her head. 'Third option: we both go visit Emma.'

'Not again.'

'I'm the one who had the pet tarantula.'

'That's some qualification.'

'What's yours?'

'I'm nuts.'

She touched my arm. 'Think about it, Alex: where would you rather I be? With you, or alone with Jo next door? There's no reason for her to think we have any way of getting in there. It's the last place she'll look for us, especially if she really is bug-phobic.'

'Nancy,' I said. 'Nancy, Nancy, Nancy.'

'Am I wrong? He's a strange old man, Alex, but in a crazy way he's left a logical trail. Maybe we should see the rest of it, Mr *Hardy*.'

I checked again twice. Waited. Checked again. Finally we snuck out.

Staying out of the path-lights as much as we could, we took a tortuously slow, route to the big building. Stopping several times to make sure we weren't being followed.

The rain kept battering us. I was so wet I forgot about it.

There, finally.

The three new locks were dead bolts.

The key fit all of them.

One final look around.

I pushed the steel door and we slipped in.

It closed on total darkness – the windowless anteroom.

Safe to turn on the light.

The space was exactly as I recalled: empty, the white tiles spotless.

And dry.

No one had entered recently.

We squeezed out our clothes. I shut off the lights and pushed open the door to the main room.

Cold metal handrails.

Robin's hand even colder.

A softer darkness in the zoo, speckled by pale-blue dots in some of the aquariums.

Muted moonlight struggled through the two windows Jo and Pam had broken. Each was dead center of the long walls, the glass punched out but the wire mesh remaining. Water shot through on both sides, making a whooshing noise, hitting the sill, and running down to the concrete floor, collecting in shiny blots.

Something else shiny – window shards, sharp and ragged as ice chips.

We waited, giving our eyes time to adjust.

The same rotten produce odor. Peat moss, overrripe fruit.

Steps down. Thirteen, Moreland had said.

I took in the central aisle, rows of tables on each side, the work space at the far end where he concocted insect delicacies.

Movement from some of the tanks, but again, the rain overpowered the sounds.

Thirteen steps. He'd said it twice, then counted each one out loud.

Making a point? Knowing this night would eventually come and preparing us for a descent in the dark?

I took Robin's hand. What I could see of her expression was resolute. Step number one.

Now I could hear it. Scurrying and slithering as we got closer to the tanks.

Even as we searched for Moreland, I knew we wouldn't find him. He had something else in mind.

Welcome to my little zoo.

Gustave's girl will be assisting . . .

The little glass houses were dark, and identical. Where was the tarantula . . . On the left side, toward the back.

As I tried to pinpoint the spot, Robin guided me to it.

The cage was dark, the mulch floor still.

Nothing on the table nearby.

Maybe Moreland had removed the creature and left something in its place.

I stooped and looked through the glass.

Nothing for a moment. Maybe I'd misunderstood. I started to hope – Emma shot up out of the moss and leaves, and I fell back.

Eight bristly legs drummed the glass frantically.

The spider's body segments pulsed.

Half a foot of body.

Slow, confident movements.

She's spoiled . . . eats small birds, lizards . . . immobilizes . . . crushes.

'Good evening, Emma,' I said.

She kept stroking, then scooted back down and sat in the mulch. Light from a neighboring tank hit her eyes and turned them to black currants.

Focused black currants.

Looking at Robin.

Robin put her face up against the glass. The spider's lipless mouth compressed, then formed an oval, as if pushing out a sound.

Robin tickled the glass with one fingertip.

The spider watched.

Robin made a move for the top lid and I held her wrist.

The spider shot up again.

'It's okay, Alex.'

307

'No way.'

'Don't worry. He said she wasn't venomous.'

'He *said* she wasn't venomous enough to kill *prey*, so she *crushes*.'

'I'm not worried – I have a good feeling about her.'

'Women's intuition?'

'What's wrong with that?'

'I just don't think this is the time to test theory.'

'Why you and not me?'

'Who says it has to be anyone?'

'Why would Bill put us in danger?'

'His being reasonable isn't something I'd take to the bank.'

'Don't worry.'

'But your hand—'

'My hand's fine. Though you're starting to hurt my wrist.'

I let go and before I could stop her, she nudged the lid back half an inch and was dangling her fingers in the tank – that damned dexterity.

The spider watched but didn't move.

I cursed to myself and kept still. Sweat mixed with the rain on my skin. I itched.

The spider pulsed faster.

Robin's entire hand was in the tank now, hanging limply. The spider caressed its own mouth again.

'Enough. Pull it out.'

Her face expressionless, Robin let her fingers come to rest near the spider's abdomen.

Touching tentatively, then with greater confidence.

Stroking.

The tarantula turned languidly, spreading to accept the caresses.

Nudging up against Robin's undulating fingers.

Covering them.

Encompassing Robin's hand.

Robin let the animal rest there for several moments, then slowly lifted her hand out of the aquarium.

Wearing the spider like a grotesque hairy glove.

Bending her knees, she placed her palm flat on the table. The spider extended one leg, then another. Stretching again . . . testing the surface. Peering back toward its home, it walked off the hand. Then back on.

Nosing Robin's fingertips.

Robin smiled. 'Hey, fuzzy one. You feel a little like Spike.'

As if encouraged, the spider continued up Robin's forearm and came to rest on her upper sleeve, its weight pulling down at the fabric.

'My, Emma, you've been eating well.'

The spider curled around Robin's bicep, hugging the arm, then inched forward, like a steeplejack scaling a pole.

Coming to a stop on Robin's shoulder.

Nuzzling the side of Robin's neck.

Stopping right near the jugular. All the while, Robin talked and stroked.

'See, Alex, we're buddies. Why don't you see if there's anything in the tank?'

I started to put my hand in, then stopped – was there another one in there? *Mr* Emma?

Oh hell, hadn't I read somewhere that the females were the tough ones? Removing the glass lid completely, I peered down, saw nothing, and plunged in. My hand groped leaves and soil and branches. Then something hard and grainy – lava rock.

Something underneath. Paper.

I pulled it out. Another folded card.

Too dark to read. I found a tank whose blue light was strong enough.

> *Impressive though Emma may be at first sight,*
> *Everything's relative – size as well as time.*

Relative.

Something bigger than the tarantula?

My eyes drifted to the last row of tanks.

One aquarium, larger than the others.

Twice as large.

A big piece of slate resting atop the lid.

What lived there was *twice* Emma's length.

My brontosaurus . . . significantly more venomous.

Over a foot of flat-bodied leather whip. Spiked-tail, antennae as thick as linguini.

Scores of legs . . . I remembered how the front ones had pawed the air furiously as we approached.

The flat, cold hostility.

I haven't quite trained it to love me.

Sadistic old bastard.

Robin was reading over my shoulder, Emma still resting on hers.

'Oh,' she said.

Before she could get brave again, I ran to the back of the zoo.

The centipede was just where it had been the first time, half out of its cave, the rear quarters concealed.

It saw me before I got there, antennae twitching like electrified cables.

All the front legs pawing this time.

Battling the air.

Everything's relative.

Including my willingness to go along with his little game.

I was about to leave when I noticed another difference about the large aquarium.

The entire tank was raised off the table.

Resting on something. More pieces of slate.

When I'd seen it a few nights ago, it had sat flush.

I ran my hand along the surface of the table. Dust and chips.

Moreland remodeling.

Creating a miniature crawlspace – it looked just wide enough to accommodate my hand.

As I extended my arm, the centipede coiled. As my fingers touched the edge of the slate platform, the creature attacked the glass. A cracking sound made me jump back.

The pane was intact, but I could swear I heard the glass hum.

Robin behind me now.

I tried again, and once more the monster lunged.

Kept lunging.

Using its knobby head to butt the glass while snapping its body into foot-long curlicues.

Something oily oozed down the glass.

Like that rattler-in-a-jar game in old Westerns; I knew I was safe, but each blow sent a jolt to my heart.

Robin made a small, high, wordless sound. I turned to see the spider doing pushups on her shoulder.

Jammed my hand under the slate and kept it there.

The centipede kept hurling itself. More cracking sounds. More venomous exudate.

Then something coarse and throaty I could have sworn was a growl came from inside the aquarium, rising above the rain.

I groped hyperactively. Touched something waxy and yanked back.

The centipede stopped attacking.

Tired, finally?

It glared and started again.

Crack, crack, crack . . . I was back in. The waxy thing felt inert, but God knew . . . *predators* . . . pull it out. Stuck.

Crack.

Right angles . . . more paper? Thicker than the card.

The centipede continued to tantrum and secrete.

I clawed the wax thing, got a purchase with my nails and pulled hard enough to feel it in my shoulder.

The wax thing slipped out of reach and I fell back, kept my balance, and crouched, eye to eye with the centipede.

Separated from its maniacal thrusts by a quarter inch of glass that trembled with each impact.

Its primitive face dead as rock. Then an infusion of rage turned it nearly human.

Human like a death-row resident.

The tank rocked.

I found the corner of the wax thing again, pinched, clawed, scraped . . . *crack* . . . missed, tried again – it moved, then resisted.

Stuck to the tabletop? Taped. The *bastard*.

Hooking a nail under the tape, I tugged upward, felt it give.

One more yank and the damned thing came out.

Thick wad of waxy paper, the edges crumbling between my fingers as I stepped away as fast as I could.

Robin followed me. So did Emma's black eyes.

Crack, crack . . . the beast reared up against the lid, trying to force it off. Noble in its own way, I supposed. A hundred-legged Atlas, fighting for liberation. I could *smell* its fury, bitter, steaming, hormonally charged.

Another push. The slate atop the lid bounced and I worried it would break the glass.

Spotting a flowerpot at the end of the aisle, filled with dirt, I used it for ballast.

The centipede continued lunging. The entire front of the aquarium was filmy with slime.

Crack.

'Nighty-night, you prick.'

Taking Robin by the hand, I hurried back to the front of the insectarium, stopping at a spot where the light through one of the broken windows was strongest. Then I realized Emma was still with us – why had I ever worried about *her*?

Everything's relative . . . time, too.

Moreland's point: nothing was what it seemed . . . I unfolded the wax paper. More pieces flaked off.

Dry. Old. Dark paper – black or deep blue, oversized, scored with light lines.

Blueprints.

Squares and circles, semicircles and rectangles. Symbols I couldn't understand.

Lines tipped with arrow points. Directional angles?

An aerial layout. The rectangles and squares were probably buildings.

The largest structure on the south side. Nearby a round thing
– water waves within.

The front fountain.

The main house.

Oriented, I located the insectarium with its thirteen steps and
central spine, lots of small rectangles angling off like verterbrae.

The baths . . .

I found my office, Moreland's, the other outbuildings.

To the east, a mass of overlapping amorphous shapes that had
to be treetops. The edges of the banyan forest.

A map of the estate's center.

But what did he want me to *see*?

The longer I studied the sheet, the more confusing it got.
Networks of lines, as dense as the streets on an urban map.
Shapes that had no meaning.

Words.

In Japanese.

34

'The original construction plans,' said Robin. 'Can you make any sense of it?'

She took the blueprints and studied them. All those months at the jobsite in L.A. reading plans . . .

She traced lines, came to a stop.

'Maybe this?'

Guiding my hand to a rough spot – a pimpling of the paper, like Braille.

'Pinhole,' I said.

'Right in the center of this building here – his office. And look at this leading out of the office.' She ran her finger along a solid line that continued off the paper.

Due east. Out of his bungalow, through the neighboring buildings, past the border of the property, straight into the banyans.

'A tunnel?' I said.

'Or some kind of underground power cable,' she said,

flipping the sheet and examining the back. 'This *has* to be it.'

A circle had been drawn around the pinhole.

'A tunnel under his office,' I said. 'That explains the night I saw him go in there and turn the lights off. He went underground.'

She nodded. 'He's got a secret hiding place, and he's inviting us to see it.'

She lifted Emma from her shoulder, talked soothingly to the spider, and stroked its belly. Eight limbs relaxed and stayed that way as the animal was returned to its home. Pausing a moment, Robin smiled.

'Nothing like new friends,' I said.

'Careful or I'll take her home with us.'

I folded the blueprints, tucked them in my waistband under my jacket, and we edged out of the insectarium.

The rain had lightened a bit and I could make out the shapes of shrubs and trees.

Nothing two-legged . . . then I heard something from behind and froze. Scraping – a tree branch rubbing against something.

We pressed ourselves against the wall and waited.

No human movement.

Moreland's bungalow was just a short walk under swaying trees. Off in the distance the main house was visible – lights on. Pam and Jo back?

We made a run for it.

The door was unlocked, probably from Pam's initial search. Or had Moreland left it that way for us?

Double-sided key lock. Once inside, I tried to bolt it with the key to my office and when that didn't fit, the new one. No go. We'd have to leave it open, too.

And the lights off.

The door to the lab was closed. Moreland's desk was

315

clear as it had been this afternoon, except for a single shiny object.

His penlight.

Robin took it and we crouched behind the desk and, shielded by wood, spread the blueprints on the floor. She shined the light on the plans. The ink had run. Our hands were indigo.

'Yes,' she said, 'definitely from behind there.' Pointing to the lab door.

She gave an uneasy smile.

'What is it?'

'All of a sudden I have visions of something disgusting on the other side.'

'I was just there, and there was nothing but test tubes and food samples. Nutritional research.'

'Or,' she said, 'he's feeding something.'

The lab looked untouched. Keeping the penlight low, Robin walked around, pausing to consult the blueprints, then resuming.

Finally, she stopped in the center of the room and stared, puzzled, at a black-topped lab table with a cabinet below.

'Whatever's down there would have to start here.'

A rack full of empty test tubes and an empty beaker sat on the counter. I placed the glassware on a nearby bench, then pushed the table. It didn't budge.

Wheels at each corner, but they weren't functional.

No sink, so no plumbing.

But attached, somehow, to the floor.

I opened the cabinet below as Robin aimed the penlight. Nothing but boxes of paper towels. Removing them revealed a metal rod running the height of the rear wall.

Springs, a handle.

I pulled down, encountered some resistance, then the rod lowered into place with a click.

The table shifted, rolled, and Robin was able to push it away easily.

Underneath was more concrete floor. A five by two rectangle. Etched. Deep seams.

A concrete trapdoor?

But no handle.

I stepped down on a corner of the rectangle, pressed and removed my foot, testing it. The slab rocked a fraction of an inch, then popped back into place, giving off a deep resonant sound, like a huge spinning top.

'Maybe it needs more weight,' said Robin. 'Let's do it together.'

'No. If Moreland can move it by himself, I can too. I don't want to trigger it too hard and have it slam up in our faces.'

I toed another corner. A bit more give, the slab bounced back again.

Pressure on the third corner caused it to yield further and I caught a view of the slab's side, at least half a foot thick. More metal underneath – some kind of pulley system.

Moving to the fourth corner, I felt myself being lifted and jumped off.

The slab rocked hard, stopped, then began rotating, very slowly. Barely making a full arc before continuing until it was perpendicular with the floor.

It came to a halt, shaking the floor. I tried to move it; locked into place.

Rectangular opening, four feet by two.

Dark, but not black – distant illumination from below.

I got down on my belly and peered down. Concrete steps, similar to those in the insectarium. Thirteen again, but these were striped with green.

Astroturf.

Leading to grayness.

'Guess this is why they call spies "moles",' I said.

Robin's smile was a faint courtesy. She brushed wet curls away from her face and took a deep breath.

Stepped toward the opening.

I blocked her and went in first.

The tunnel was seven feet high and not much wider, tubular walls of reinforced concrete, trowel seams marked by steel studs. The light I'd seen from above came from a caged mining fixture wired to the ceiling forty paces in the distance.

The astroturf lay over dirt, ending at the beginning of a single railroad track that bisected the tube.

Narrow track with polished pine ties. Too small for a train. Probably designed for a handcar, but none was in sight.

No rain sounds. I touched the ground. The soil was hardpacked and dry. Perfect seal.

Rapping the walls produced no tone either. The concrete had to be yards thick.

I told Robin to wait and returned to the tunnel's mouth. The slab loomed like a gigantic stiff lip. From down here the lab was a black hole.

I climbed the stairs, tested the slab a second time. Just as immobile – set into place by a mass of gears and counterweights, responsive to a special series of pressures.

Probably a safety feature installed by the Japanese army to prevent crushed fingers or accidental imprisonment. Probably some way to close it safely from below, but I didn't know it and we had no choice but to leave the entry exposed.

Maybe the best thing was to get out of here and wait till morning.

I climbed back down to Robin and offered her the choice.

'We've come this far, Alex. Let's at least follow it for a while and see where it leads.'

'If it extends past the property line, we'll be under the banyans. Land mines.'

'If there are mines.'

'You have doubts?' I said.

'If you wanted to hide something, what better way to discourage intruders than a rumor like that?'

318

'You want to test that hypothesis.'

'He's down here.' She gazed into the tunnel. 'He clearly wants us there too. Why would he want to hurt us?'

'He wants *me*,' I said. 'He brought me *over* for this.'

'Whatever, it's important to him. Look at all the precautions he took.'

'Cryptic messages. Voices of wise ones . . . bugs – he's like a big kid playing games.'

'Hide and seek,' she said. 'Maybe I'm way off but I don't think he's a bad man, Alex. Just a secretive one.'

I thought of Moreland and Hoffman and their wives playing bridge on the terrace. Hoffman cheating. Moreland never letting on.

'All right,' I said. 'Let's play.'

We walked along the tracks, passing under the glow of the caged light and slipping into darkness. A hundred paces later, the glint of an identical fixture came into view. Then another.

The monotony became pleasant – the *tunnel* was more pleasant than I'd imagined: warm, dry, silent. No bugs.

'What do you think it was, originally?' said Robin. 'An escape route for the Japanese?'

'Or some kind of supply channel.'

We reached the second light and were nearly out of its glow when we saw something against the wall.

Cardboard boxes. Scores of them, piled neatly in columns. Just like the case files in the storeroom.

Confidential files? Was this what Moreland wanted me to see?

I pulled down a box. The flaps were folded closed but unsealed.

Inside, zip-locked plastic bags.

Dried fruit and vegetables.

I tried another carton. More food.

A third contained pharmaceutical samples and bottles of pills – antibiotics, antifungals, vitamins, minerals, dietary supplements.

Then bottles of something clear – tonic water. The antimalarial properties of quinine.

Another carton. More dried fruit. Gatorade.

'Dr Bill's secret stash,' I said. 'He grows stuff in his garden, preserves it, and brings it down here. Maybe we're dealing with a survivalist. The question is, what's his Armageddon?'

Robin shook her head and fished out canned goods from another box. Beef stew, chicken and rice.

'So much for vegetarianism,' I said.

She looked sad. 'Maybe Armageddon's the destruction of the island. Could be he's planning to stay underground.'

'Under the forest,' I said. 'Protected by those mines, real or phony. It's pretty nuts, but there are bunkers full of folks just like that all over the States. The problem is, they also tend toward hair-trigger paranoia. A lust for the big battle.'

'That doesn't seem like Bill.'

'Why? Because he says he despises weapons? Everything the man's said or done is suspect – including his altruism. Aruk imports food at two, three times the usual cost. Bill helps out with occasional handouts but stockpiles all this stuff for himself. If he's been planning to go under for a while, that would explain why he hasn't been more aggressive promoting business for the island. Maybe he's given up on Aruk – on reality. Maybe he's concentrating on creating his own little subterranean world. Came up with the idea after finding the blueprints somewhere in the house. Eventually, he discovered the tunnel: instant caveman.'

She took something else out of the box. A foil packet with a white label.

'"Freeze-Dried Combat Meal,"' she read aloud. '"Segment B: reconstituted carrots, beets, peas, lima and string beans, soya protein' . . . then a whole bunch of vitamins . . . United States Navy issue . . . oh, boy.'

'What?'

'The date.'

Tiny numbers at the bottom of the label. February 1963.

'Sixty-three was his last year in the Navy,' I said. 'He bought the estate that year – he's been doing this for thirty years.'

'Poor man,' she said.

'He's obviously quite content. Damned proud of what he's accomplished.'

'Why do you say that?'

'Because now he wants to show it off.'

Six more ceiling lights, two more large caches of food and medicine.

We kept walking, automatically, like soldiers, drained of further conjecture, tracks and ties slipping past hypnotically.

My watch said we'd been underground nearly half an hour, but it felt both longer and briefer.

Time's deceit.

Another caged bulb.

Then a patch of green just beyond.

Another astroturf strip.

Another flight of stairs, fifty yards ahead.

Thirteen steps up to a metal door.

No handles or locks. I pushed, expecting ponderous weight, another tricky leverage system. It opened so easily I had to stop myself from falling forward.

On the other side was an upsloping concrete ramp lit by a weak bulb.

We climbed till we came to yet another door.

Metal grillwork – radiating circles of iron crisscrossed by spokes. Beyond it total darkness.

I knocked and pushed but this one didn't give. Then my brain put the grill design in context.

A web. What had Moreland called webs – *a beautiful deceit.*

Enough.

I turned to head back down the ramp.

Saw the first door closing behind us, rushed to catch it and failed.

It slammed shut, refused to yield.

321

Trapped in the ramp.

Ensnared.

Moreland's thin face appeared in my head. Long, loose limbs, fleshy snout, pouchy eyes, loping walk – arachnid walk.

Not a camel or a flamingo.

Predators . . .

Robin put her hand to her mouth. I stopped breathing; panic became a tight necktie.

Then light appeared behind the web, letting in a draft of very cool air.

The same chill I'd felt coming over the walls from the banyan forest.

The webbed door swung open. I saw walls of hewn stone, then blackness.

A cave.

The choice was to stay there and risk another entrapment or step through and take our chances with whatever was on the other end.

I stepped through.

A hand settled lightly on my shoulder.

I spun around. 'Damn you, Bill!'

But the eyes that stared back weren't Moreland's.

Dark slits – at least, the left one was. Its mate was a wide-open, milky-white crescent, drooping heavily, tugging at a ragged lid.

No iris. The white was shot through with capillaries.

The face around the orb was white, too.

The eyes lower than mine, set into an elliptical, neckless head that rested on meager, sloping shoulders.

Misshapen and hairless except for three patches of color-less down.

Ridges of skin in place of ears.

A mouth opened. Less than a dozen teeth, some of them no more than yellow buds. Framing them was a pouchlike, puckered aperture: no lower lip, the upper one thick, cracked, liverish – a smile? Why wasn't I screaming?

I smiled back. The hand so light on my shoulder . . . an inch of downy skin separated the mouth from a nose that was two black holes under a nub of pink-white flesh, twisted like a pig's tail.

Wens and scabs, keloid tracks, and crater scars danced across the face, a moonscape in closeup. A sharp smell fumed from the skin. Familiar smell . . . hospital corridors – antibiotic ointment.

The hand on my shoulder sat so delicately, I barely felt it.

I looked at it.

Four stumpy, broad-tipped fingers, the thumb clubbish and spatulate, no nail on the index finger. More of that soft, downy hair. Dimpled knuckles.

The wrist thin and frail, laced with baby-blue veins and scabbed heavily, disappearing into the cuff of a white shirt.

Clean, white oxford button-down.

Khaki trousers cinched tight around a thin waist, the cuffs rolled thick.

A man, I supposed . . . protruding from under the cuffs, brown loafers that looked new.

A boy-sized man – five feet tall if that, maybe eighty pounds.

'Hhh,' he said. *'Hhhii.'*

Whispery rasp. I'd heard voices like that before: burn victims, the larynx and vocal cords seared, learning to talk from the gut.

The pouch-mouth stayed open, as if struggling for speech. More medicinal smell – mouthwash. The single eye watched my face. The pouch twisted upward in what might have been a smile.

'Hi,' I said.

The eye studied me some more. Blinked – winked? No eyebrows, but the skin above the sockets creased into deep dual crescents that simulated brows.

Neckless, chinless, that congealed-fat complexion. But soft . . . I thought of the baby octopus in the lagoon.

The hand slid off my shoulder, slowly, gracefully.

The mouth closed and pouted – sad?

Had I done something wrong?
I tried smiling again.
The arm hung loosely.
Very loose. An invertebrate grace.
Fingers curling in ways that normal fingers couldn't.
Serpentine – no, even a snake had more firmness.
White and flaccid –
Wormlike.

35

He scratched a thigh, a cuff rode up, and I saw something shiny atop a loafer. Brand-new penny.

He saw something behind me and his head lowered shyly.

'Hi,' I heard Robin say.

Then I saw something behind *him*.

Another man emerging from the shadows, even smaller, so severely hunchbacked his head seemed to protrude from his chest.

Red-and-black plaid button-down, blue jeans, high-top sneakers.

Two good eyes. One ear. The eyes soft.

Innocent.

Curling a finger, he turned his back on us and stepped further into the cave.

The first man's forehead creased again and he followed.

We tagged along, tripping and stumbling as our feet snagged on bits of rock.

The little soft men had no trouble at all.

Gradually, the cave turned from black to charcoal to dove-gray to gold as we stepped out into a huge, domed cavern lit by several more of the caged fixtures.

Rock formations too blunt to be stalagmites rose from the floor. A bank of refrigerators filled one wall. Ten of them, smallish, a random assortment of colors and brands. Avocado. Gold. Hues fashionable thirty years ago. The wires met at a junction box attached to a thick black cable that ran behind a crag and out of the room.

In the center of the cavern were two wooden picnic tables and a dozen chairs. Shag area rugs were scattered over a spotless stone floor. A whirring, humming noise came from behind the junction box – a generator.

The rain slightly audible, now. A tinkle. But everything was dry.

Moreland came in and sat at the head of the table, behind a large bowl of fresh fruit. He wore his usual white shirt and his bald head looked oiled. His hands took hold of a grapefruit.

Four more small, soft people filed in and sat around him. Two wore cotton dresses and had finer features. Women. The others were dressed in plaid shirts and jeans or khakis.

One of the men had no eyes at all, just tight drums of shiny skin stretched across the sockets. One of the women was especially tiny, no larger than a seven-year-old.

They looked at us, then back at Moreland, their ruined faces even whiter in the full light.

Place settings before each of them. Fruit and biscuits and vitamin pills. Glasses of bright orange and green and red liquid. Gatorade. Empty bottles were grouped in the center of the table, along with plates full of rinds and pits and cores.

The two men who'd brought us stood with their hands folded.

Moreland said, 'Thank you, Jimmy. Thank you, Eddie.'

Rolling the grapefruit away, he motioned. The men took their places at the table.

Some of the others began to murmur. Deformed hands trembled.

Moreland said, 'It's all right. They're good.'

Runny eyes settled upon us, once again. The blind man waved his hands and clapped.

'Alex,' said Moreland. 'Robin.'

'Bill,' I answered, numbly.

'I'm sorry to put you through such a rigamarole, son – and I didn't know *you'd* be coming, dear. Are you all right?'

Robin nodded absently, but her eyes were elsewhere.

The tiny woman had engaged her visually. She had on a child's pink party dress with white lace trim. A white metal bracelet circled a withered forearm. A child's curious eyes.

Robin smiled at her and hugged herself.

The woman licked the place where her lips should have been and kept staring.

The others noticed her concentration and trembled some more. The generator kept up its song. I took in details: framed travel posters on the walls – Antigua, Rome, London, Madrid, the Vatican. The temples at Angkor Wat. Jerusalem, Cairo.

More cartons of food lined up neatly across from the refrigerators. Portable cabinets and closets, a couple of dollies.

So many refrigerators because they had to be small enough to fit down the hatch. I pictured Moreland wheeling them through the tunnel. Now I knew where he'd gone that night with his black bag. Where he'd gone so many nights, all these years, barely sleeping, working to the point of exhaustion. The fall in the lab . . .

A sink in the corner was hooked up to a tank of purified water. Gallon bottles stood nearby.

No stove or oven – because of poor ventilation?

No, the air was cool and fresh, and the rain sound was faint but clear, so there had to be some kind of shaft leading up to the forest.

No fire because the smoke would be a giveaway.

No microwave, either – probably because Moreland had doubts about the safety. Worries about people who'd already been damaged.

327

His lie about being part of the nuclear coverup a partial truth?

Lots of partial truths; right from the beginning he'd swaddled the truth in falsehood.

Events that had happened but in other places, other times.

Einstein would approve . . . it's all relative . . . time's deceit.

Everything a symbol or metaphor.

The other quotes . . . all for the sake of justice?

Testing me.

I looked at the scarred faces huddled around him.

White, wormlike.

Joseph Cristobal, tying vines to the eastern walls, hadn't hallucinated thirty years ago.

Three decades of hiding puncuated by only one mishap?

One of them going stir-crazy, emerging aboveground and heading toward the stone walls?

Cristobal sees, is gripped by fright.

Moreland diagnoses hallucinations.

Lying to Cristobal . . . for justice's sake.

Soon after, Cristobal gives one last scream and dies.

Just like the catwoman . . . what had *she* seen?

'Please,' said Moreland. 'Sit down. They're gentle. They're the gentlest people I know.'

We squeezed out our soaked clothes and took our places around the table as Moreland announced our names. Some of them seemed to be paying attention. Others remained impassive.

He cut fruit for them and reminded them to drink.

They obeyed.

No one spoke.

After a while, he said, 'Finished? Good. Now please wipe your faces – very good. Now please clear your plates and go into the game room to have some fun.'

One by one they stood and filed out, slipping behind the refrigerators and disappearing around a rock wall.

Moreland rubbed his eyes. 'I knew you'd manage to find me.'

'With Emma's help,' I said.

'Yes, she's a dear . . .'

'Time's deceit. Including the deceit you used to bring me over. You've been leading up to this since the first day I got here, haven't you?'

He blinked repeatedly.

'Why now?' I said.

'Because things have come to a head.'

'Pam's up there looking for you, scared to death.'

'I know – I'll tell her . . . soon. I'm sick, probably dying. Nervous system deterioration. Neck and head pain, things go blank . . . out of focus. I forget more and more, lose equilibrium . . . remember my tumble in the lab?'

'Maybe that was just lack of sleep.'

He shook his head. 'No, no, even when I *want* to sleep it rarely comes. My concentration . . . wanders. It may be Alzheimer's or something very similar. I refuse to put myself through the indignities of diagnosis. Will you help me before there's nothing left of me?'

'Help you how?'

'Documentation – this must be recorded for perpetuity. And taking care of them – we must figure out something so they'll be cared for after I'm gone.'

He stretched his arms out. 'You've got the training, son. And the character – commitment to justice.'

'Mr Disraeli's justice? Truth in action?'

'Exactly . . . there is *no* truth without action.'

'The great thinkers,' I said.

His eyes dulled and he threw back his head and stared at the cavern's ceiling. 'Once upon a time I thought *I* might develop into a significant thinker – shameless youthful arrogance. I loved music, science, literature, yearned to be a Renaissance man.' He laughed. '*Medieval* man would be more like it. Always mediocre, occasionally evil.'

329

He ruminated some more, snapped back to the present, licking his lips and staring at us.

Robin hadn't stopped glancing around the room. Her eyes were huge.

'Truth *is* relative, Alex. A truth that hurts innocents and causes injustice is no truth at all, and an evasive action that's rooted in compassion and leads to mercy can be justified – can you see that?'

'Did the second nuclear tests take place near Aruk? Because I know you lied about Bikini. If so, how was the government able to conceal them?'

'No,' he said. 'That's not it at all.'

Standing, he walked around the table. Stared at the boxes against the wall.

'Nothing you do is accidental,' I said. 'You told me about the nuclear blast and Samuel H. for a reason. You held on to Samuel's file for a reason. "Guilt's a great motivator." What are you atoning for, Bill?'

Putting his hands behind his back, he laced his fingers.

Long arms. Spidery arms.

'I *was* in the Marshalls during the blast,' he said. 'Perhaps that's why I'm dying.' Looking down. 'Now have I lied?'

'You didn't participate in the payoffs. I know. I spoke to a man who did.'

'True,' he said.

'So what's the point? What were the blasts a metaphor for—'

'Yes,' he said. 'Exactly. A metaphor.'

He sat back down. Retrieved the grapefruit. Rolled it.

'Injections, son.'

'Medical injections?'

Long slow nod. 'We'll never know exactly what they used, but my guess is some combination of toxic mutagens, radioactive isotopes, perhaps cytotoxic viruses. Things the military was experimenting with for decades.'

'Who's *they*?'

330

He jerked forward, bony chest pressing against the table edge.

'*Me. I* put the needle in their arms. When I was chief medical officer at Stanton. I was told it was a vaccination research program – confidential, voluntary – and that as chief medical officer, I was responsible for carrying it out. Trial doses of live and killed viruses and bacteria and spirochetes developed in Washington for civil defense in the event of nuclear war. The ostensible goal was to develop a single supervaccine against virtually every infectious disease. The "paradise needle" they called it. They claimed to have gotten it down to a series of four shots. Provided me experimental data. Pilot studies done at other bases. All false.'

He took hold of the white puffs over his ears. Compared to the soft people, his hair was luxuriant.

'Hoffman,' he said. 'He gave me the data. Brought the vials and the hypodermics to my office, personally. The patient list. Seventy-eight people – twenty families from the base. Sailors, their wives and children. He told me they'd agreed to participate secretly in return for special pay and privileges. Safe study, but classified because of the strategic value of such a powerful medical tool. It was imperative the Russians never get hold of it. Military people could be trusted to be obedient. And they were. Showing up for their injections right on time, rolling up their sleeves without complaint. The children were afraid, of course, but their parents held them still and told them it was for their own good.'

He pulled at his hair again and strands came loose.

'When exactly did this happen?' I said.

'The winter of sixty-three. I was six months from discharge, had fallen in love with Aruk. Barbara and I decided to buy some property and build a house on the water. She wanted to paint the sea. She told Hoffman, and he informed us the Navy was planning to sell the estate. It wasn't waterfront, but it was magnificent. He'd make sure we got priority, a bargain price.'

'In return for conducting the vaccination program secretly.'

'He never stated it as a quid pro quo, but he got the message

331

across and I was eager to receive it. Blissful, stupid ignorance until a month after the injections, when one of the women who'd been pregnant gave birth prematurely to a limbless, anencephalic stillborn baby? At that point, I really didn't suspect anything. Those things happen. But I felt we should be doing some monitoring.'

'Pregnant women were included in the experiment?'

He looked down at the table. 'I had doubts about that from the beginning, was reassured by Hoffman. When I reported the stillbirth, he insisted the paradise needle was safe – the data proved it was.'

He bent low, talking to the table: 'That baby . . . no brain, limp as a jellyfish. It reminded me of things I'd seen on the Marshalls. Then one of the children got sick. A four-year-old. Lymphoma. From perfect health to terminally ill nearly overnight.'

He raised his head. His eyes had filled with tears.

'Next came a sailor. Grossly enlarged thyroid and neurofibromas, then rapid conversion to anaplastic carcinoma – it's a rare tumor, you generally only see it in old people. A week later he had myelogenous leukemia as well. The rapidity was astonishing. I started to think more about the nuclear tests in the Marshalls. I knew the symptoms of poisoning.'

'Why'd you tell me you were part of the payoff?'

'Couching my own guilt . . . actually, I was *asked* by my superior to participate, but managed to get out of it. The idea of placing a monetary value on human life was repulsive. In the end, the people who did participate were clerks and such. I'm not sure they had a clear notion of the damage.'

Craving confession for years, wanting some sort of absolution from me.

But not trusting me enough to go all the way. Instead, he'd used me the way a defensive patient uses a brand-new therapist: dropping hints, exploiting nuance and symbol, embedding facts in layers of deceit.

'I suppose,' he said, sounding puzzled, 'I was hoping this

332

moment would arrive eventually. That you'd be someone I could
. . . communicate with.'

His eyes begged for acceptance.

My tongue felt frozen.

'I'm sorry for lying to you, son, but I'd do it all over again if it
meant getting to this point. Everything in its time – everything has
a time and place. Life may seem random, but patterns emanate.
Like a child tossing stones in a pond. The waves form predictably.
Something sets off events, they acquire a rhythm of their own . . .
Time is a like a dog chasing its tail – more finite than we can
imagine, yet infinite.'

He wiped his eyes and bit back more tears.

I took Robin's hand. 'After the other illnesses did you go back
to Hoffman?'

'Of course. And I expected him to become alarmed, take some
action. Instead, he *smiled*. Thirty years old but he had an evil old
man's smile. A *filthy* little smile. Sipping a martini. I said, "Perhaps
you don't understand, Nick: something we did to these people
is making them deathly ill – *killing* them." He patted me on the
back, told me not to worry, people got sick all the time.'

He gave a sudden, hateful look.

'A baby without a brain,' he said. 'A toddler with end-stage
cancer, that poor sailor with an old person's disease, but he
could have been dismissing a case of the sniffles. He said he was
sure it had nothing to do with the vaccines, they'd been tested
comprehensively. Then he smiled again. The same smile he gave
when he cheated at cards and thought he was getting away with
it. Wanting me to understand that he'd *known* all along.

'I'd planned to conduct an autopsy on the baby the next day,
decided to do it right then. But when I got to the base mortuary,
the body was gone. All the records were gone, too, and the sailor
who'd been my assistant had been replaced by a new man – from
Hoffman's staff. I stormed back to Hoffman and demanded
to know what was going on. He said the baby's parents had
requested a quick burial, so he'd granted compassionate leave
and flown them to Guam the previous night. I went over to

333

the flight tower to see if any planes had left. None had for seventy-two hours. When I got back to my office, Hoffman was there. He took me for a walk around the base and began talking about the estate. It seemed all of a sudden some other buyers had surfaced, but he'd managed to keep my name at the top of the list *and* to lower the price. It was all I could do not to rip out his throat.'

He put on his glasses.

'Instead,' he said. The word tapered off. He put a hand on his chest and inhaled several times. '*Instead*, I thanked him and smiled back. Invited the bastard and his wife to my quarters the next night for bridge. Now that I knew what he was capable of, I felt I needed to protect Barbara. And Pam – she was only a baby herself. But on the sly, I began checking the others who'd been injected. Most looked fine, but a few of the adults weren't feeling well – vague malaise, low-grade fevers. Then some of the children began spiking *high* fevers.'

He dug a nail into his temple. 'There I was, the kindly doctor, reassuring them. Dispensing analgesics and ordering them to drink as much as they could in the hope some of the toxins would be flushed out. But unable to tell them the *truth* – what good would it have done? What curse is worse than knowing your own death is near? Then *another* child died suddenly of a brain seizure. Another family supposedly flown out overnight, and this time Hoffman informed me my involvement with the paradise needle was terminated, I was to attend to all base personnel *except* the vaccinated families. *New* doctors had arrived for them, three whitecoats from Washington. When I protested, Hoffman ordered me to begin a new project: reviewing twenty years of medical files and writing a detailed report. Busy-work.'

'Sounds familiar.'

He smiled weakly. 'Yes, I'm a horrid sneak; being direct has always been difficult for me. I used to rationalize it as the result of growing up an only child in a very big house. One wanders about alone, acquires a taste for games and intrigue. But perhaps it's just a character flaw.'

334

'What happened to the rest of the vaccinated patients?' said Robin.

'More were growing ill, and rumors had finally gotten out on the base about some kind of mysterious epidemic. Too much to keep secret, so the doctors from Washington issued an official memo: an unknown island organism had infiltrated Stanton, and strict quarantine was imposed. The sick people were all isolated in the infirmary, and quarantine signs were nailed to the doors. Understandably, everyone gave the place a wide berth. Then I heard a rumor that all the vaccinated families would be shipped back to the Walter Reed Hospital in Washington for evaluation and treatment. I had a pretty good idea what that meant.'

He pulled down on his cheeks.

'I sneaked over to the infirmary one night after midnight. One attendant was on guard at the front door, smoking, not taking the job seriously. Which was typical of the base. Nothing ever happened here. Everyone had a slipshod attitude. I managed to sneak in through a rear door, using a skeleton key I'd lifted from Hoffman's office. The smug bastard hadn't even bothered to put on a new lock.'

Reaching out, he grabbed the grapefruit, clawing so hard juice flowed through his fingers.

'Some of them,' he said, softly, 'were already dead. Lying in cots . . . unconscious, rotting. Others were on the verge of losing consciousness. Sloughed skin was everywhere . . . limbs . . . the room stank of gangrene.'

He began crying, tried to stop, then to hide it. It took a while before he resumed, and then, in a whisper.

'Bed after bed, crammed together like open coffins . . . I could still recognize a few of their faces. No attempt was being made to treat them – no food or medication or I.V. lines. They were being *stored*.'

The grapefruit, a mess of pulp and rind.

'The last ward was the worst: dozens of dead children. Then, a miracle: some of the babies were still alive and looking relatively healthy. Dermal lesions, malnutrition, but conscious

335

and breathing well – their little eyes *followed* me as I stood over their layettes . . . I counted. Nine.'

He stood again and circled the room unsteadily.

'I still don't understand it. Perhaps the relatively low dosage had protected them, or something in their newborn immune systems. Or maybe there is a God.'

Wringing his hands, he walked to the refrigerators and faced a copper-colored Kenmore.

'Sometimes it's good to be a sneak. I got them out. Four the first time, five the second. Swaddled in blankets so their cries would be muffled, but it wasn't necessary. They *couldn't* cry. All that came out was *croaking.*'

Facing us.

'The vaccine, you see, had burned their vocal cords.'

He picked up his pace, stalking an invisible victim.

'I had no place to take them but the forest. Thank God it was winter. Winter here is kind, warm temperatures, dry. I'd discovered the caves hiking. Had always liked caves.' Smile. 'Secretive places. Used to spelunk when I was at Stanford, did a senior thesis on bats . . . I didn't think anyone else knew of them, and there was nowhere else to go.'

'What about the land mines?' I said.

He smiled. 'The Japanese had plans to lay mines, but they never quite got around to it.'

'The night of the knives?'

He nodded.

'You spread the rumor?' I said.

'I planted the seed. When it comes to rumors, there's never a shortage of gardeners . . . where was I? . . . I placed them in a cave. Not this one, I didn't know about this one. Or the tunnel. Once they were secreted, I checked them over, cleared them up, gave them water and electrolytes, returned to the infirmary, disassembled their layettes, scattering the parts in the hope they wouldn't be missed. And they weren't. The entire place was a charnel house, corpses and dying people had slid onto the floor, lying on top of one another, body fluids dripping. I'll never forget the sound. Even now, when it drizzles . . .'

His face took on that absent look and for a moment I thought he'd slip somewhere else. But he started talking again, louder:

'Then, a complication: one of the adults had survived, too. A man. As I was finishing with the layettes he came in, reaching for me, *falling* on me. I nearly died of fright – he was . . . putrid. I knew who he was. Aircraft mechanic, huge fellow, enormously strong. Perhaps that's why the symptoms hadn't take him over as rapidly. Which isn't to say he wasn't gravely ill. His skin was pure white – as if bleached, one arm gone, no teeth, no hair. But able to stagger. He hadn't been a good man. A bully, really, with a vicious temper. I'd patched up men he'd beaten. I was worried he'd have enough strength to somehow set off an alarm, so I dragged him out too. It nearly killed me. Even starved, he must have weighed a hundred and eighty pounds. It took so long to get him across the base, I was sure some sentry would see me. But I finally made it.

'I put him in another cave, away from the babies, and tended to him as best I could. He was shaking with chills, skin starting to slough. Trying to talk and growing enraged at his inability . . . He kept looking at the stump where his arm had been and screaming – a silent scream. *Rabid* anger. His eyes were wild. Even in that condition, he frightened me. But I calculated it would only be hours.'

Lurching toward a chair, he sat.

'I was wrong. He lasted five days, fluctuating between stupor and agitation. He'd actually get up and lurch around the cave, injuring himself horribly but remaining on his feet. His premorbid strength must have been superhuman. It was on the fifth day that he managed to escape. I'd been at the base, got back that night and he wasn't there. At first I panicked, thinking someone had discovered everything, but the babies were still in their cave. I finally found him lying under one of the banyans, semiconscious. I dragged him back. He died two hours later.'

'But not before Joseph Cristobal saw him,' I said.

He nodded. 'The next day, Gladys came to my office and told me about Joe. One of the other workers at the estate had told her Joe had a fit, claimed to have seen some kind of forest devil.'

'A Tutalo.'

'No,' he smiled. 'I made that up, too. *Tootali* is the old word for "grub," but there's no myth.'

'Planting the seed,' I said. 'So Joe's story wasn't taken seriously?'

'Joe had always been odd. Withdrawn, talked to himself, especially when he drank. What concerned me were his chest pains. They sounded suspiciously like angina, but with anxiety, it was hard to know. As it turned out, his arteries *were* in terrible shape. There was nothing I could have done.'

'You're saying the sighting had nothing to do with his death?'

'Perhaps,' he said, 'his condition was complicated by fright.'

'Did you let him go on believing there *were* monsters?'

He blinked. 'When I tried to discuss it with him, he covered his ears. Very stubborn man. Very rigid ideation – not schizophrenic, but perhaps schizoid?'

I didn't answer.

'What should I have done, son? Told him he'd really seen something and endanger the babies? *They* were my priority. Every spare moment was spent with them. Checking on them, bringing blankets, food, medicine. Holding them in my arms . . . Despite everything I did, two of them got progressively worse. But every night that passed without one of them dying was a victory. Barbara kept asking me what was wrong. Each night I left her . . . a light dose of sleeping medicine in her bedside water helped . . . shuttling back and forth, never knowing what I'd find when I got there. Do you understand?'

'Yes,' I said, 'but all these years, they haven't come above-ground?'

'Not unsupervised they haven't. They need to stay out of the sunlight – extreme photosensitivity. Similar to what you see in some porphyric patients, but they have no porphyria and I've

338

never been able to diagnose, never been able to find out what they were gi – where was I?'

Looking baffled.

'Shuttling back and forth,' said Robin.

'Ah, yes – after a week or so it finally got to me. I fell asleep at my desk, only to be shaken awake by a loud roar. I knew the sound well: a large plane taking off. Seconds later, there was a tremendous explosion. A Navy transport had gone down over the ocean. Something about the fuel tanks.'

The 1963 crash. Hoffman ordering Gladys to prepare coquille St Jacques that night. Celebrating . . .

'With the quarantined patients on board,' I said. 'Eliminating any witnesses.'

'The doctors from Washington, as well,' said Moreland. 'Plus three sailors who'd guarded the infirmary assigned as flight attendants, and two medics.'

'My God,' said Robin.

'The patients would have died anyway,' said Moreland. 'Most probably *were* dead when they loaded them on – an airborne hearse. But the doctors and the medics and the flight crew were sacrifices – all in the name of God and country, eh?'

'Why weren't you eliminated?' said Robin.

He put his hands together and studied the table.

'I've thought about that many times. I suppose it was because I bought myself some insurance. The day of the crash, I invited Hoffman over for drinks in my quarters. No wives, just us fellas in our snappy dress whites, veddy dry martinis – back then I was still indulging. As he picked pimiento out of his olive, I told him I knew exactly what he'd done and had made a detailed written record that I'd filed somewhere very safe with instructions to make it public if anything happened to me or any member of my family. That I was willing to forget the whole thing and move on if he was.'

'He bought that?'

'It was a theatrical little stunt, I got the idea from one of those stupid detective shows Barbara used to watch. But apparently, it did the trick. He smiled and said, "Bill, your imagination's been working overtime. Pour me another one." Then he drank up and left. For months I slept with a gun under my pillow – dreadful thing, I still hate them. But he never moved against me. The way I see it, he decided to deal because he believed me and felt it was the easy way out. Evil people have little trouble believing everyone else lacks integrity. The next day, a sailor delivered a sealed envelope to my quarters: discharge papers, three months early, and the deed to the estate. *Excellent* price, including all the furniture. The Navy moved us in, and we were provided with a year of free electricity and water. The pretense continued. Even our *bridge* games continued.'

'Along with his cheating,' I said.

'His cheating *and* my pretending not to know. That's as apt a metaphor for civilization as any, isn't it?'

He gave an unsettling laugh.

'Meanwhile, my real life continued at night, and any other time I could get away without attracting too much notice. I hadn't discovered the tunnel yet, and I hid a ladder so I could climb the wall. The two babies who'd deteriorated passed away, as did another. The first was a little girl named Emma – hers was the only name I actually knew, because I'd treated her as a newborn for herniated umbilicus. Her father had made jokes about how she'd look in a bikini and I told him that should be his biggest problem . . .'

He looked ready to cry again, managed to blink it away.

'She died of malnutrition. I buried her and conducted a funeral service as best I could. A month later, a second little girl left me. Bone marrow disease. Then a little boy, from pneumonia that wouldn't respond to antibiotics. The other six survived. You've just met them.'

'What's their health status?' I said. 'Physically and mentally?'

'None of them have normal intelligence, and they have no speech. I taught myself the rudiments of IQ testing, administered the nonverbal components of the Wechsler tests and the Leiter. They seem to fall in the fifty-to-sixty range, though Jimmy and

Eddy are a bit brighter. Their nervous systems are grossly abnormal: seizures, motor imbalance, sensory deficits, altered reflexes. Poor muscle tone, even when I can get them to exercise. Then there's the photosensitivity – the slightest bit of UV exposure eats up their skin. Even living down here hasn't managed to protect them completely. You saw their eyes, ears, fingers. Extensive fibrosing, probably something autoimmune – the actual process isn't unlike leprosy. They're not in danger of imminent wasting, but the erosion continues steadily. They're sterile – a blessing, I suppose. Not much libido, either. *That's* made my life easier.'

'I still don't see how you've managed to keep them down here all these years.'

'At first it was difficult, son. I had to . . . confine them. Now it's not a serious problem. They may not be normal, but they've learned what the sun does to them. Half an hour outside and they're in pain for days. I've made every effort to provide them with as rich a life as possible. Here, let me show you.'

He took us to an adjoining room, slightly smaller than the dining area. Beanbag chairs and homemade cases full of toys and picture books. A phonograph connected to a battery pack. Next to it, a stack of old 45s. The top one: Burl Ives singing children's songs. 'Jimmy Crack Corn' . . . A model train set in disarray on the shag carpet. Some of the soft people sat on the floor fooling with the tracks. Others reclined on the chairs, fingering dolls.

They greeted him with smiles and raspy cries. He went to each of them, whispered in their ears, hugged and patted and tickled.

When he turned to leave, one of them – the larger woman – took hold of his hand and tugged.

He pulled back. She resisted.

Giggles all around. A familiar game.

Finally, Moreland tickled her under the arm and she gave a silent, wide-mouthed laugh and let go, tumbling backward. Moreland caught her, kissed the top of her head, pulled a Barbie doll out of the case and gave it to her.

'Look, Suzy: *Movie* Star Barbie. Look at this beautiful, fancy *dress.*'

The woman turned the figurine, suddenly engrossed. Her features were saurine but her eyes were warm.

'Be right back, kids,' said Moreland.

We left the room and walked down a narrow stone passage.

'How often do you come down here?' I asked.

'Optimally, two to five times a day. Less frequent than that and things get out of hand.' His thin shoulders sagged.

'It sounds impossible,' said Robin.

'It's . . . a challenge. But I keep my other obligations to a minimum.'

Virtually no sleep.

No wife.

Sending his own daughter away as a toddler.

Allowing the island to decay . . . his one recreation the insects. A small world he could control.

Studying predators in order to forget about victims.

We came to a third room: six portable chemical toilets and two sinks attached to large water tanks outfitted with sterilization kits. A cloth partition halved the space. Three latrines and one basin on each side. Cutouts of men pasted on the stalls to the left, women to the right.

A strong wave of disinfectant.

Moreland said, 'I've toilet trained each of them. It took some time, but they're quite dependable now.'

Next were the sleeping quarters – three smaller caves, each with two beds. More books and toys. Piles of dirty clothes on the floor.

'We still have a ways to go on neatness.'

'Who does their laundry?' said Robin.

'We handwash, everything's cotton. They enjoy laundry time, I've turned it into a game. The clothes are old but good. Brooks Brothers and similar quality, brought in years ago on several boatloads. I couldn't order too much at a time, didn't want to attract attention . . . Come, come, there's more.'

342

He led us back into the passageway. It narrowed and we had to turn sideways. At the end was another webbed door. He saw me looking at it.

'Japanese ironwork. Beautiful, isn't it?'

On the other side was an exit ramp, descending steeply, its terminus out of view. The door was fastened with an enormous lock.

The soft people confined forever.

Moreland produced a key, rammed it into the lock, pushed the door open, and the three of us walked to the bottom of the ramp.

'Sometimes, when it's very dark and I can be sure they'll behave themselves, I take them up to the forest for nighttime picnics. Moonlight is kind to them. They love their picnic time. Mentally they're children, but their bodies are aging prematurely. Arthritis, bursitis, scoliosis, osteoporosis, cataracts. One of the boys has developed significant atherosclerosis. I treat him with anticoagulants, but it's a bit tricky because he bruises so easily.'

He stopped. Stared at us.

'I've learned more about medicine than I ever believed possible.'

'Do you have any idea of their life expectancy?' said Robin.

Moreland shrugged. 'It's difficult to say. They're deteriorating, but they've survived so many crises, who knows? With good care, all or most of them will probably outlive me.'

He leaned against the wall. 'And that is the issue. That's why I must arrange something for them.'

'Why haven't you gone public and gotten them care?' she said.

'What would that accomplish, dear? Subjecting them to the scrutiny of scientists and *doctors*? Scientists condemned them to this life. How long would they last out in the monstrosity we call the real world? No, I couldn't allow that to happen.'

'But surely they—'

'They'd wither and die, dear,' said Moreland, straining for patience.

343

He reached for the open door and took hold of one of the bars. 'What they need is *continuity*. A transfer of care.'

His eyes moved from Robin to me. Studying. Waiting.

I could hear music from the game room. A scratchy record. *Lou, Lou, Skip to My Lou.*

He said, 'I want you to be their guardians once I'm gone.'

'I'm not a physician,' I said. As if that was the only reason.

'I can teach you what you need to know. It's not that difficult, believe me. I've been composing a manual . . .'

'You just pointed out how tricky it—'

'You can *learn,* son. You're a smart man.'

Raising his voice. When I didn't answer, he turned to Robin.

'Bill,' she said.

'Hear me out,' he said. 'Don't close your minds. Please.'

'But why me?' I said. 'Give me the real answer, this time.'

'I already have – your dedication to—'

'You don't even *know* me.'

'I know enough. I've *studied* you! And now that I've met Robin, I'm even more convinced. With two people, sharing the challenge, it would be—'

'How did you really find me, Bill?'

'Coincidence. Or fate. Choose your nomenclature. I was in Hawaii taking care of some legal matters with Al Landau. My hotel delivered the daily paper. Despite my aversion to what passes for news, I skimmed it. The usual corruption and distortions, then I came across an article about a case in California. A little girl in a hospital, poisoned to simulate illness. You helped bring the matter to resolution. References were made to other cases you'd been involved in – abused children, murders, various outrages. You sounded like an interesting fellow. I researched you and learned you were a serious scholar.'

'Bill—'

'Please, son, listen: intellectual vigor and humanity don't always go together. One can be an A student but a D person. And you have *drive*. I need someone with *drive*. And *you*, dear. You're his soulmate in every way.'

I tried to find words. The look on his face said no language existed that would work.

'Mind you, I'm not proposing a one-way deal. Care for my kids properly, and the entire estate and all my other property holdings on Aruk will be yours, in addition to excellent real estate in Hawaii and California, securities, a bit of cash. What I told you about my family fortune dwindling was true, but it's still substantial. Of course, I'll have to give a generous inheritance to Pam as well as some stipends to trusted individuals, but the rest would be yours. Once the kids are all gone. You can see why I need someone with integrity. Someone who wouldn't kill them to get to the money. I now trust you – both of you. When your duties are through, you'll be wealthy and free to enjoy your wealth in any way that pleases you.'

Robin said, 'Pam's a doctor. Why don't you want her to take over?'

He shook his head so vigorously his glasses fell off his nose.

Retrieving them, he said, 'Pam's a wonderful girl, but not equipped. She has . . . vulnerabilities. My fault. I don't deserve the title "father." She needs to get out in the world. To find someone who values her – the kind of relationship you two have. But you *will* have assistance. From Ben.'

'Ben knows?'

'I let him into my confidence five years ago. The kids have come to adore him. He's been a tremendous help, taking shifts as my strength ebbs.'

'You don't want him to take over?' said Robin.

'I considered it, but he has his own family. My kids need full-time parents.'

Single-minded, isolated parents. As he'd been after Barbara died and Pam was sent away.

What he wanted was *philosophical cloning*. I felt stunned and sick.

'Ben will continue to pitch in,' he said. 'Between the three of you the task is do-able.'

'Ben's in no position to help anyone,' I said.

345

'He will be once we get past this nonsense. Al Landau's brilliant, especially when defending an innocent man. *Please*. Accept my offer. I've taken you into my confidence. I'm at the mercy of your good graces.'

He picked up Robin's hand and held it in both of his.

'A woman's touch,' he said. 'It would be so good for them.'

Smiling. 'Now you know everything.'

'Do we?' I said.

He let go of her hand. 'What's the problem, son?'

'The written report you threatened Hoffman with. Does it exist?'

'Of course.'

'Where is it?'

He blinked hard. 'In a safe place. If we progress, you'll know the precise location.'

'And you want us to believe it's the only reason he let you live all these years.'

He thumbed his chest and smiled. 'I'm here, am I not?'

'I think there's more, Bill. I think Hoffman's always known you wouldn't expose him because he's got something on *you*.'

The smile evaporated. He took a step up the ramp and ran his hand over the rough stone wall.

'My guess is the two of you are locked together,' I went on. 'Like rams, with tangled horns. Hoffman can't move in and destroy Aruk overnight because you might expose him. But he's still able to grind the island down gradually because he's younger than you, confident he'll survive you and eventually have his way. And I'll bet controlling Aruk's important to him on two levels: the money from the development project, *and* he wants to erase what he did thirty years ago from his mind.'

'No, no, you're giving him way too much credit. He's got no conscience. He simply wants to exploit for profit.' He turned around suddenly. 'You have no idea what he has in mind for Aruk.'

'A penal colony like Devil's Island?'

346

His mouth stayed open and he managed to work it into another smile. 'Very good. How did you figure it out?'

'He's in with Stasher-Layman, and in addition to instant slums they build prisons. Aruk's location is perfect. The dregs of society shipped and warehoused far, far away, with nowhere to escape.'

'Very good,' he repeated. 'Very, very good. The bastard told me the details that night at dinner. He wants to call it "Paradise Island." Clever, eh? But there's more: the waters surrounding Aruk will be used to sink other dregs: barrels of radioactive waste. He's confident of receiving environmental clearance because of Aruk's obscurity and because once the economy shuts down completely and the island's depopulated, there'll be no one to protest.'

'Nuclear dumpsite,' I said. 'Perfect complement to the prison: toxic water's another escape deterrent. If Hoffman pulls it off, he manages to fight crime and pollution on the mainland and pocket big cash payoffs from Stasher-Layman. Cute.'

'"Cute" is not an adjective I'd apply to him.'

Different music drifted from the game room. A woman singing, *This old man, he plays two* . . .

'When did you first suspect he was involved?'

'When the Navy started treating us differently. Ewing's predecessor was no saint but he was civil. Ewing has the demeanor of an assassin – did you know he was sent here as punishment for lewd behavior? Tied a woman down and took photographs . . . From the moment I met him, I knew he'd been sent to punish *Aruk*. And that Hoffman had to be behind it. Who else even knew about the place? I wrote to him, he never answered. Then Ben caught Creedman snooping in my files and I asked Al Landau to do some research. He learned the skunk had worked for Stasher-Layman and what they were all about. But I had no idea it was a dumpsite till Hoffman bragged about it after dinner. Apologizing for not answering, he'd been *so* busy. Then that same *smile*.'

'Were your letters threatening?' I said.

'Poo! Give me credit, son. I was discreet. Nuances, not threats.'

'Nuances that he ignored.'

'He said he hadn't wanted to put anything in writing. That's why he'd come personally.'

'Why'd he invite all of us to dinner?'

'For cover. But you notice that he got me alone. That's when he boasted and made his offer.'

'To buy you out?'

'At a laughable price. I refused and reminded him of my little diary.'

'What did he say?'

'He simply smiled.'

'If he's worried about the diary, why can't you get him to stop the project?'

'I – we negotiated. He pointed out that stopping completely would be impractical. Things have gone too far. To reverse what's already been done would call attention to Aruk.'

'And you agreed to consider it because of the kids.'

'Exactly! Though the bastard thinks it's my own lifestyle I don't want jeopardized.' He grimaced. 'You're right, he and I are stalemated: he doesn't want publicity and neither do I. My only goal is to let my kids live out their lives in peace – how long do they *really* have? Five years, maybe six or seven. Hoffman's project will take years to complete even under the best of circumstances – you know the government. So hopefully, he and I can achieve some sort of compromise. I'll sell off token bits of land to the government, take my time, delay things without seeming unduly obdurate.'

'The Trading Post, and your other waterfront holdings.'

He nodded. 'And the money will be set aside for you two.'

'A compromise,' I said. 'As you both let Aruk die.'

He sighed. 'Aruk's been good to me, but I'm an old man and I know my limitations. Priorities must be set. What I've demanded from Hoffman was to slow things *down*.'

'Did he agree?'

'He didn't refuse.'

'The man coldbloodedly murdered six dozen people. Why would he give in to you?'

'Because of my insurance.'

'I still don't understand why, if you can ruin him, you don't have more power.'

He scratched the tip of his nose. 'I've told you everything, son.'

He reached out to pat my shoulder and I backed away.

'No, I don't think so,' I said. 'When you returned from talking to him you looked shellshocked. Not like someone who'd negotiated a compromise. Hoffman reminded *you* about something, didn't he?'

No answer.

'What's he holding over you, Bill?'

He stepped further into the ramp.

'First things first,' he said. 'My offer.'

'First answer my question?'

'These things are irrelevant!'

'Honesty's irrelevant? Oh, I forgot, the truth is relative.'

'Truth is *justice*! Getting into irrelevant areas that bring about injustice is *deceitful*!'

This old man, he plays ten . . .

'All right,' I said. 'You're entitled to your privacy.'

I looked at Robin. She cocked her head very slightly, toward the cavern.

'Goodbye, Bill.'

He held me back. 'Please! Everything in due time! Please be patient!'

His crinkled chin shook so hard his teeth knocked. 'I'll tell you everything when the time's right, but first I must have your commitment. I believe I've earned it! What I'm offering you would enrich your lives!'

'We can't give you an answer just like that.'

He climbed further up the ramp. 'Meaning you think I'm mad and your answer is no.'

'Let's get back and clear our heads. You, too. Pam needs to know you're safe.'

'No, no, this isn't right, son. Leaving an old man in the lurch after I've . . . flayed my soul open for you!'

'I'm sorry—'

He clutched my arm. '*Why not just agree?* You're young, robust, so many years ahead of you! Think of what you can do with all that wealth.' His eyes brightened. 'Perhaps *you* could figure out a way to save Aruk! Think of the meaning *that* would bring to your lives! What else *is* there to life but finding some kind of meaning?'

I removed his fingers from my arm. The record in the game room had caught. The old man playing ten, over and over . . .

'I was wrong,' he said, behind me. 'You're not the compassionate boy I thought you were.'

'I'm not a boy,' I said. 'And I'm not your son.'

The retort bursting out of me, the same way it had out of Dennis Laurent.

The look on his face . . . I *felt* like a bad son.

A maddening man.

Mad or on the brink of it.

'No, you're not,' he whispered. 'Indeed, you're not.'

Robin took my hand and we both left the ramp. Moreland watched us, not budging.

After we'd gone a few steps, he turned his back on us.

Robin stopped, tears in her eyes.

'Bill,' she said, just as sound came from the top of the ramp.

Moreland looked up and almost lost his balance.

Another noise – hollow, metallic – came from above, just as he straightened.

Then rapid, muffled footsteps.

Two figures in black rain slickers barreled down the ramp. One grabbed Moreland. The other stopped for a fraction of a second, then came toward us.

Glossy wet slickers, galoshes. All that rubber buffed brighter by moisture.

Like giant seals.

Anders Haygood splashed water on us as he waved the automatic.

36

His heavy face was calm, the lower half shadowed by stubble. Wide mouth set, gray eyes as dead as pebbles.

'Against the wall.' Practiced boredom. Ex-cop's familiarity with rousting suspects.

He frisked me, then Robin. She gave out a high-pitched sound of surprise. Not reacting was agonizing.

From where I was standing I could see Tom Creedman with his grip on Moreland. From the way his fingers hooked, it must have hurt, but Moreland wasn't showing it. Staring at Creedman, as if trying to snag his eyes. Creedman's face was rain specked and sweating, his gun jammed against Moreland's rib cage.

'The boys from Maryland,' I said. 'Off on a South Seas lark.'

Creedman's black mustache arced in surprise. Haygood flipped me around with a surprisingly light touch. His cleft chin looked rough enough to hone a blade.

I smiled. 'Why'd you pull me over, officer?'

A muscle in his cheek jumped.

He put his gun against my heart and chucked Robin's chin. His hand dropped lazily onto her chest. Brushing. Squeezing.

Robin's eyes closed. Haygood continued to touch her, studying me.

I looked at Creedman. The water rolling off the top of his hat and into his eyes. He flinched, and Haygood finally let go of Robin.

'Never met a cannibal before,' I said. 'Who did the surgery? Or was it both of you?'

'Fuck off,' said Creedman.

Haygood said, 'Chill,' but it was unclear who he was addressing. Creedman frowned but shut up.

The rain, louder; they'd opened some kind of hatch above-ground. Found the tunnel with the help of all the doors I'd had to leave open. The slab sticking out of the laboratory floor.

They'd probably climbed down and walked some distance before figuring out where it led. Unable to broach the webbed door, they'd retraced their steps, made it over the wall, and come in from the other end.

The rain blocked out the music from the game room. I could still hear the nagging drone of the generator.

'The boys from Maryland,' I repeated. 'Reporter buys information from cop on a murder case, gets them both fired. Reporter finds a job with Stasher-Layman and procures cop a position there, too. Must be a close friendship.'

Creedman wanted to say something, but a look from Haygood silenced him. Haygood the pro . . . he kept his gun steady while exmaining the cavern with all the passion of a camera.

'You've done lots of cute things for the company,' I said, 'so now you get a sun-and-fun assignment. But does the home office have any idea you handled it by replicating the murder that got you into trouble in the first place? Slicing up women and pretending to *eat* them? Or maybe you *didn't* pretend. You did say you were a gourment cook, Tom.'

'What is this?' said Haygood. 'A bomb shelter or something?'

'If I know about Maryland, don't you think others do?'

Creedman looked at Haygood.

Haygood continued to inspect the cavern.

'What they don't know,' I said, 'is the part of it that's wishful thinking, Tom. Telling me it was a rape-murder when it wasn't. A few problems in the *potency* area?'

Creedman turned red and tightened his grip on Moreland.

Haygood repeated, 'A bomb shelter?'

'Japanese supply tunnel,' said Moreland. 'My little sanctuary.'

Keeping his eyes away from the game room.

'What do you have down here?'

'Old furniture, clothes, a few books.'

'Let's take a look.'

'There's nothing interesting, Anders.'

'Let's take a look, anyway.' Haygood waved us forward with the gun and told Creedman: 'Bring him over.'

Creedman poked Moreland and the old man tripped forward.

'You two, out,' said Haygood, when they'd passed. He looked down the narrow opening and frowned. 'Don't surprise me, doctor. You go in front, Tom. Anything happens, kill the girl.'

Creedman didn't argue. I'd have pegged him as the one in charge. Class snobbery. Haygood's police experience gave him the edge.

I thought back to the day we'd arrived. Haygood on the dock, butchering the shark with quiet authority.

Haygood and Skip Amalfi.

Was Skip just a cover, allowing Haygood to come across as the aimless beachbum? All along, Haygood's attitude toward him had been a mixture of patience and contempt. Watching, amused, as Skip peed on the sand. Remaining in the background as Skip harangued the villagers.

Tolerating him the way you tolerate a dull sibling.

Skip, stupid enough to get sucked into a fantasy of running a resort. The dream probably planted by Haygood.

Skip peeing in front of women . . . Had he also been involved in the cannibal murders? Probably not; too unstable.

But he *had* served his purpose the night of Betty Aguilar's killing: fishing on the docks, as Haygood knew he did most every night. There to hear Bernardo Rijks's cries of alarm, rushing over to subdue Ben.

Haygood and Creedman had murdered both girls. First AnneMarie Valdos on the beach, a rehearsal for Betty and setting up Ben. And the stimulus to local unrest that had justified the blockade.

Then, Betty in Victory Park – what had they used to lure her? Dope? Money? One last fling before motherhood?

Cutting her throat and carrying out the mutilation. Drawing Ben out with a bogus emergency call, then choking him out, pouring vodka down his throat, and positioning him with the corpse.

An ex-cop would know how to pull off a perfect choke hold.

An ex-cop would know about positioning corpses.

The park because it was secluded and a common spot for partying. And because Rijks the insomniac walked by every night.

Even if Rijks hadn't heard the moans, he could have been led to it by a night-strolling Creedman. Not as neat, but no reason for anyone to catch on.

Because Ben came from trash and Betty had been promiscuous.

Ben lying asleep on the carnage. An absurd alibi.

Skip's outrage, genuine. Hostile to Moreland because his father resented the old man, he'd eagerly whipped up the villagers' anger.

Framing Ben had killed three birds with one stone: damaging Moreland irreparably, getting rid of his protégé, and causing another deep rip in Aruk's social fabric.

Hastening the exodus from the island.

Hoffman's and Stasher-Layman's war of attrition. Perhaps Hoffman had decided to speed things up after coming face to face with the old man, his stubbornness . . .

Believing Moreland cared about the island, when all he really wanted was a few years of peace for the *kids.*

Moreland willing to do anything to prevent Hoffman from finding out about the kids. Willing to let Aruk die, buying time.

The two of them circling like wrestlers, waiting for an opening.

Still, the same thing bothered me: if Moreland had that kind of power over Hoffman, why not bargain harder?

Creedman stepped in front of me. 'Stay back.' The thin mustache was beaded with perspiration.

'Sure, Tom. But when this is over, share some gourmet recipes with me. How about *girl* bourguignon?'

Creedman's nostrils opened. From behind, Haygood cleared his throat and Creedman grabbed Moreland and cuffed him through the passage. Then he turned sideways and squeezed in himself. When he was several paces ahead of us, Haygood cupped Robin's buttock, squeezed, and shoved.

'Go, babe.'

Then the heel of his hand hit me in the lower back.

We filed out. When the passage widened, Creedman stopped and Haygood herded us into the center. The dead eyes shifted as he heard something.

Music from the game room. The broken record removed. Something new asserting itself above the generator.

The wheels on the bus go round and round . . .

'What the . . . ?' said Creedman.

The game room was less than thirty feet away, the door partially open.

Haygood said, 'What's with the music?'

'I like music,' said Moreland. 'As I said, it's my refuge.'

'Kiddie music?' said Creedman. 'You *are* one buggy old fart.' His eyes brightened: 'Do you bring little girls down here to play?'

Moreland blinked. 'Hardly.'

'*Hardly*,' Creedman imitated. 'Maybe you bring kiddies down here to play *doctor*.'

The doors on the bus go open and shut . . .

'Projection,' said Moreland.

'What's that?'

'A Freudian term. Projecting one's own impulses onto someone else. That's what you just did, Tom.'

'Oh, fuck off, you self-righteous bag of shit.' To us: 'Bet you

356

didn't know Dr *Bill* here was once the ace pussy-hound of the U.S. Navy. Big-time stud, chased everything in a skirt, the younger the better. Remember those days, Dr *Bill*? Chasing and bagging, dark meat, light meat, *any* kind of meat? Just couldn't control your pecker, could you? Drove poor *Mrs* Bill to one-way surfing.'

Moreland said nothing, did nothing. That blank look . . .

'Turned herself to shark chum,' said Creedman, 'because Dr *Bill* here couldn't stop playing doctor with the local pussy. Nice advantage, that M.D. Knock some little thing up, do your own abortion—'

'Unlike you,' I said. 'Assault with a dead weapon.'

Creedman snarled. Haygood clicked his tongue and said, 'Check out all these doors.'

'Maybe *you* should,' said Creedman. 'You're the expert.'

Haygood shrugged and pushed Robin, Moreland, and me close together. Backing away, he said, 'Not the stomach, the head,' and Creedman raised his gun till it was half a foot from Robin's right eye.

'Any problems,' he said, 'I want to see her brains on the wall.'

He stepped back some more, pausing a few feet from the entrance to the latrine, then flattening himself against the wall the way cops do and inching toward the opening, gun first.

Waiting. Looking back at us. Waiting some more.

He peeked in. Took a long, slow look.

The broad face puzzled.

Moving to the next door, just as carefully.

'Wait,' I said. 'It's rigged – that door and the others. He's got it booby-trapped.'

Haygood turned.

'He *is* nuts,' I said. 'Stockpiling food and clothes and survival gear, preparing for the end of the world. I'd let you blow yourself up, but he's rigged enough explosives to turn us all into soup.'

'That so?' said Haygood.

'Tell him, Bill.'

'Nonsense,' said Moreland. 'Utter nonsense.'

Haygood thought a while. 'What doors are you saying are rigged?'

'That one for sure,' I said. 'The room where the music's coming from has a package of dynamite hooked up to the record player. The cable runs into another room. Connected to a generator – listen.'

The drone.

'He's got it set up so if the record arm's lifted, boom. There are probably other traps, too, but that's the one he showed us.'

'Ridiculous,' said Moreland. 'Go take a look, Anders.'

'How about *you* go in there,' Haygood told him. 'Turn off the music while I watch you.'

Moreland blinked. 'I'd rather not.'

'Why not?'

'Because it's silly,' said Moreland.

'Come over here,' said Haygood.

Moreland ignored him.

'Come over here, *piss*ant.'

Moreland closed his eyes and moved his lips silently.

Creedman took hold of his shirt and yanked him forward. 'Move, you crazy asshole!'

Moreland passed within Haygood's reach and Haygood got behind him.

'Go,' he said, shoving the old man.

Moreland stumbled and stopped. 'I'd rather not.'

'Go or I'll kill you, sir.'

'I'd rather—'

'Okay,' said Haygood, smiling at me. 'Thanks for the tip, doc. What else should we know about?'

'I wish I knew.'

The driver on the bus says, 'Move on back . . .'

'Fucking maniac,' said Creedman. 'Let's shoot all of them right now and get the hell out of here, Anders.'

'I don't think so,' said Haygood.

Ordered by his bosses to keep Moreland alive. Till the insurance policy was found . . . Hoffman going along with the stalemate for thirty years, willing to wait a while longer.

Thirty years of silence from Moreland had convinced him the paradise needle had been forgotten. So he'd felt safe in refocusing his energies on Aruk. Wanting to destroy the island, depopulate it, rebuild it in his own image.

Moreland claimed it was simply greed, but I doubted it.

I visualized Hoffman at a D.C. power lunch with the brothers from Stasher-Layman. 'Soft money' changing hands, a discussion of potential sites for a multibillion-dollar project, with Hoffman getting a chunk of the profits.

Storing human garbage along with plutonium and cobalt and strontium.

The need for an isolated spot. A remote place with no political constituency.

Hoffman smiling and coming up with one.

Finding out that Moreland still lived on Aruk, but that the doctor was unable or unwilling to reverse the island's economic problems. The population sliding, the welfare checks coming in regularly; what little commerce there was, dependent upon the Navy base.

Send in the advance team: Creedman, Haygood, the Pickers. Probably others. The goal: hasten the decline and isolate Moreland so that the old man would sell out cheap.

Then Moreland starts writing letters, and the team's told to speed things up.

Creedman and Haygood coming up with a grisly touch – perverse mastery over the case that had ruined their careers. A side benefit: slaking their own hatred for women.

The team . . . Lyman Picker's plane crash an accident or had his big mouth offended the higher-ups?

Haygood, living on Harry Amalfi's airfield, had been in a perfect position to mess with the plane.

Creedman . . . the crash had taken place just after Robin and I finished drinking with him outside the restaurant. Creedman and

Jacqui had both gone inside the restaurant, but after the explosion only Jacqui had come out.

Creedman not bothering because he'd *known*.

Someone else had known, too: Jo, opting out at the last minute. Opting out of the base dinner, too, to plant the roaches. And now she was up there with Pam . . .

'Okay, let's get out of here,' said Haygood, pointing back to the rear ramp.

'Those boxes in the tunnel,' said Creedman. 'There could be something important in them.'

'They could also be rigged. We'll check it out later.'

'I opened a few boxes,' I said. 'All I saw was food and drugs and bottled water. Like I said, he's planning for Armaggedon.'

'Stop being so helpful,' said Creedman. 'It won't do you any good.'

Haygood said, 'Come on, folks. Out.' He might have been guiding a tour.

He turned his back on the music room and began to herd us forward.

'Actually,' I said. 'He does have some kids down here.'

A strangled noise rose from Moreland's throat.

Haygood stopped. 'That so?'

'Right in there.' I pointed to one of the sleeping areas. Haygood's eyes followed. 'Want to see?'

Before he could answer, I shouted, *'Kids! Kids! Kids!'*

Creedman cursed and Haygood's hand tightened around his gun. But he stayed calm and kept his eyes on the sleeping-room entrance.

Nothing happened. Haygood smiled. 'Very funny, sir. Onward.'

Then a small white face appeared in the doorway to the music room. Two others.

Three, four, five, six. All of them, openmouthed and wide-eyed with wonder.

Except the blind one. He was making quick little circles with his hands.

Lesions and scars bright as strip-joint neon.

Haygood's calm finally shaken.

Creedman's face lost its color. 'Oh, shit,' he said, and took his eyes off me. I hit him hard under his nose, grabbed for his gun as he went down, but missed. Shoving Robin out of the way, I threw myself on top of him.

Haygood wheeled around. The soft people began croaking and rasping, looking at Moreland, moaning that burn-victim moan.

Moreland ran toward them. Haygood aimed his gun at the old man's back. The soft people kept coming and Haygood's bafflement gave way to revulsion and fear as he stepped back.

I had Creedman's gun now and was punching blindly at his face.

Haygood charged Moreland, shoved him to the floor, kicked at his head, aimed at me. The soft people were between us. I crouched low. They kept coming at Haygood and he struck out at them wildly as they cowered and moaned. Retreating closer to the door he believed was rigged to blow, he stopped. Trapped, confused.

Brassy hair visible above the throng. I pointed Creedman's gun at it.

But I was an easy target, too, and he raised his gun arm high while fending off the soft people with his free hand.

I shifted sharply to the right, trying to stay clear of the soft people so they wouldn't be caught in the middle.

Haygood lost sight of me, as he shoved and circled.

Moreland got to his feet, hurled himself at Haygood.

Haygood turned reflexively at the movement and fired. Moreland's left arm turned red and he fell.

The people converged upon his prone form. Haygood looked for me, but I was behind him.

I shot him five times.

His black slicker exploded. He stood there for a second. Collapsed.

The soft people were all over Moreland, croaking and moaning as he bled.

Robin was shouting my name and pointing.

361

Creedman trying to get up, holding his face. Blood gushed through his fingers. One eye was swollen shut and his nose was already blackening.

I put the gun to his forehead. He sank back down.

Robin pressed herself against the wall, staring at me. All the blood.

Moreland struggled to stand, the wounded arm dangling, dripping, the other arm trying to shield the soft people.

They were entranced by Haygood's corpse. Gray skin, eyes really dead now, dull and empty as the shark's. Gaping mouth leaking pink vomitus.

Blood spread from under him, settling in the crevices of the stone floor.

I'd turned him into a sieve.

I felt big as a building, sick to my stomach.

I'd never owned a firearm, never imagined killing anyone.

Robin, being there to see it.

37

Moreland's blood took me away from those thoughts. His sleeve was dyed crimson, and red drops hit the floor with a soft plunk.

He seemed unaware, kept trying to calm his kids.

As Robin ran to him, he said, 'It's all right, dear. Right through the muscle – the latissimus – and I'm leaking not spurting, so the brachial artery's been spared. Probably the basilic vein . . . I'll be fine. Get me a clean shirt from the basket in there and I'll staunch it.'

He smiled down at the smaller of the men who'd met us at the end of the tunnel. 'A little booboo, Eddie. Daddy's going to be just fine. Go help Gordon.' Pointing to the blind man who was up against a wall, grimacing and threshing the air.

'Go, Eddie. Tell him everything's okay.'

The little hunchback obeyed. Robin came back with a plaid shirt and Moreland pressed it against his arm. Smiling at me, he said, 'Wonderful bluff. We're a good team.'

One of the soft women looked at Haygood's body and started to whimper.

'Bad *man*,' said Moreland. 'Bad, bad *man*. All *gone*, Sally. He'll *never* come back.'

Creedman gasped. His face was ballooning. I yanked him to his feet.

'Let's get out of here,' said Robin.

'There's still Jo to consider,' I said. 'Where is she, Tom?'

Creedman stared at me. More shock than defiance, and his eyes were glassy. Had I hit him that hard?

I repeated the question. He cried out in pain, held his head, started to go loose. When I saw his eyes roll back, I propped him up.

Moreland had managed to quiet the soft people and was guiding them back into the game room. Despite the wound he looked revitalized.

'Play some more music, kids. How do the *daddies* on the bus go?'

Silence.

'Come on, now: "The daddies on the bus go . . ."'

'*Ee ee ee.*'

'Right! *Read read read* – you should read, too. It'll make you smart – go get some books down, Jimmy. Give everyone a book. I'll be right back.'

He smiled, closed the game room door, bolted it.

From inside, the music resumed.

'All right,' he said, eyes full of fear.

'Is there another way out besides the two ramps?' I said.

'I'm afraid not.'

'So either way, we could be walking into something.'

'But we're trapped down here, too,' said Robin. 'The longer we stay down, the more dangerous it gets, and you're still bleeding, Bill.'

'I'll be fine, dear.'

'Taking the rear ramp,' I said, 'will lead us into the forest and zero visibility, so I vote for the tunnel.'

Moreland didn't argue.

I shook Creedman back to consciousness. Holding him by the scruff, I pushed him past the smaller rooms and into the large entry cavern. His weight dragged. The hand I'd pummeled him with was beginning to throb.

'Stay behind me,' I told Robin and Moreland. 'If she's waiting for us at the hatch, Mr Gourmet here will be her first course.'

The return trip seemed a lot quicker, Moreland maintaining a good pace despite his age and his injury. Silent, no attempts to convince us of anything.

The one time our eyes met, his begged.

To let go? Forget about the things he hadn't revealed?

Creedman was limp with dejection, but conscious. He tried to get me to do all the work, and I had to shove him every other step. The silence of the tunnel emptied my head, until I thought of Haygood, perforated.

Remembering what he'd done to AnneMarie and Betty helped . . . the shark, the molding of bleached white jaws nailed over the door.

Trophies. I didn't want one.

Fifty feet from the hatch, I ordered Creedman to stay silent. His face was so bloated that his eyes could barely open, and his nose leaked filmy, blood-streaked mucus.

We reached the astroturfed steps and the open hatch. The lab above was a square yellow sun.

Someone had turned the lights on.

No choice but to go on. Motioning Moreland and Robin back, I propelled Creedman up, one step at a time. His rain boots squeaked but he kept quiet. Then, as we approached the top, he began to struggle.

A sharp jab of the gun in his back stopped him.

Three more steps. We waited.

Quiet from above.

Two more steps. One.

365

No sign of Jo.

We were in.

The room was just as we'd left it. Except for the doorway to the front office.

A man sat there, bound to a chair, gagged.

Thin, scraggly gray beard, spiked hair.

Carl Sleet. The gardener whose voice had drawn Ben to the park.

His eyes zoomed to Creedman, pupils constricted. His fingers flexed below wrists secured to the chair legs with plastic ties. The kind policemen used. Had Haygood taken care of him first?

But no: Creedman looked as confused as I was.

I stood there trying to figure out what to do next.

Jo's face appeared in the doorway, hands up. No weapon.

'Don't shoot,' she said cheerfully. 'Now, how about I move *my* scumbag out of the way so you can get *your* scumbag through.'

Her gun sat atop the books on Moreland's desk, well out of reach.

She produced something out of nowhere and held it up.

White card in a black leatherette holder, next to a silver badge. Some sort of government seal on the card, but I was too far away to read the small print.

'Where're Robin and Dr Moreland?' she said.

'Waiting for me to give them the okay.'

'I heard shots. Anyone actually hit?'

'Moreland was wounded.'

'I heard six shots. One, then five more.'

I said nothing. She laughed and waved the card. 'Don't worry, it's genuine. Except for the name.'

I stepped closer.

Department of Defense, a numbered division that meant nothing to me. JANE MARCIA BENDIG, SENIOR INVESTIGATOR.

I stood there, gripping Creedman. Wishing I had three more arms and a weapon for each.

'Look, I can understand your being wary,' she said. 'But if I wanted to shoot you, you'd be dead. I *am* a crack shot.'

I didn't respond.

'Okay,' she said. 'I can get in big trouble for this, but would giving you my gun make you feel better?'

'Maybe.'

'Suit yourself.' She stepped back and I managed to keep my gun on Creedman and pocket hers.

'Happy?' she said.

My laugh scared me. 'Ecstatic.'

'Okay, you're the guy in charge now. Why don't you give your friends the word.'

Moreland and Robin came up.

Jo said, 'Looks like that arm needs attention, doctor.'

'I'm fine.'

'Doesn't look fine to me.'

'You're not a physician.'

Carl Sleet made a noise.

'Put a lid on it,' she said, and Sleet obeyed.

Moreland said, *'Carl?'*

'Carl's been naughty,' said Jo. 'Pilfering petty cash, tools, your old surgical kit. Putting cockroaches in people's rooms. When he thinks no one's looking he tends to skulk around places he shouldn't be. I've had my eye on him for some time. Tonight, instead of leaving with the other members of the staff, he stayed in one of the storage sheds. Thought *he* was watching *me.*'

She smiled.

'After I dropped Pam off, I went back and watched him some more. Did you know that you hum when you're bored, Carl? Not advisable when skulking.'

Sleet writhed in the chair.

She turned to me. 'When you and Robin showed up at the bug zoo, he was off in the bushes, watching you. After you went in, he waited then made a call from the lab phone, right here. His pals got over in a jiff – probably waiting down the road, outside the gates. They left him here to stand watch, went into the lab, were gone for a long time, and came back. Then they headed for the walls, and that was the last I saw of them. I decided to take Carl's place. I'd like my gun now, please. I have others in my room, but like I said, I could get in real big trouble.'

I hesitated.

'Pretty please?' she said, in a harder voice.

I handed her the automatic.

'Thanks. I'll take custody of your scumbag now. Producing more plastic ties.

I gave her Creedman, and she bound his wrists behind him and moved him closer to Carl Sleet.

'Carl,' said Moreland, sadly.

Sleet refused to look at him.

'Okay,' said Jo, 'let's get these losers locked up and see to that arm.

'After all these years, Carl,' said Moreland.

'All these years, Carl's been bearing a grudge against you, doc. Or at least that's his excuse – I'm sure the money they paid him didn't hurt.'

'A grudge?' said Moreland.

Sleet still avoided looking at him.

Jo said, 'Something about a cousin who saw a monster and died of a heart attack. Carl says you told the guy he was crazy instead of giving him heart medication.'

'That's not true. His arteries were clogged. Highly advanced athero—'

'You don't have to convince me.' Freeing Sleet's limbs from the chair, she stood him up, placed him face to the wall, and flipped Creedman around in the same position.

'Did Sleet say anything about calling Ben to the park?' I said.

'No.'

I summarized Ben's alibi.

'Well,' she said, 'I'm sure old Carl will be forthcoming when he finds out what it's like to be charged with multiple murder.'

Creedman stiffened, and she said, 'Watch it. Can I assume some of the five shots went into Haygood?'

'All five,' I said.

'Dead? Or did you leave him to bleed down there?'

'Dead.'

'Nothing worse than a bad cop,' she said. 'Even before he got busted in Maryland he was a suspect in some burglaries. He and Mr Creedman have been doing bad things for a long time.'

'Who pays the bills?' I said. 'Stasher-Layman?'

'You won't find their name on any checks. All cash. Mr Creedman here is the bursar. Haygood's really dead, huh?'

Big smile for a split second, then it was gone. Slip of professionalism. Something personal.

Haygood monkeying with the plane.

'Your husband—'

'He wasn't my husband. Though we did have a . . . relationship.'

'Was he also—'

'He was a botanist, just like he said. Keeping me company.'

She frisked Creedman. 'I tried to talk him out of going up in that heap. Traveling with me was always tough for him – okay, let's put these morons somewhere safe and see to that arm. Does the tunnel lead all the way into the forest?'

'Yes,' said Moreland.

'What do you keep down there, Dr M.?'

Moreland didn't answer.

She frowned. 'C'mon, I'm one of the good guys.'

'It's a long story,' I said. 'It's a very long story.'

We moved Sleet and Creedman to the house, locking them in separate basement closets, and put Moreland on a sofa in the front room. Gladys ran in from the kitchen, stared at the bloody sleeve, and put her hand to her mouth.

'He's been shot but it's not serious,' said Jo. 'Tell Pam to bring her medical stuff.'

369

Gladys ran up the stairs, and Pam came rushing down seconds later, carrying a black bag.

Moreland waved at her from the couch. 'Hello, kitten.'

She supressed a cry, unsnapped the bag, and crouched next to him.

'Oh, Daddy.'

'I'm all right, kitten.'

Pulling scissors from the bag, she began cutting away at the sleeve.

'Clean through the lattisimus. No arterial . . .'

Jo hooked a finger at Robin and me.

As we left, Moreland called out my name.

I stopped.

'Thank you, Alex.' Another beseeching look.

Once in the living room, Jo took an armchair under Barbara Moreland's beautiful, sad face.

'Tell me what's down there,' said Jo.

We did.

She tried to maintain her composure, but each revelation knocked it looser. When we were through, she was pale. 'Unbelievable – six of them, down there all these years?'

'Locked up for their own good,' said Robin.

'Twilight Zone . . . unbelievable. Think he's crazy? I'm asking you professionally now.'

'Obsessive,' I said. 'And a hero of sorts. Everyone else went down on that plane.'

'That plane . . . they like plane crashes, don't they? . . . Must have somehow heard Defense was sending someone here and figured it was Ly. All he wanted to do was see the trees, bring some photos back for his pals. But they assumed *he* was the agent, me the tag-along – top of everything else, they're sexist pigs.'

Cold laugh.

'Six of them,' she said. 'Crazy . . . are they – is there any danger going down there?'

'They're harmless,' said Robin. 'But sick.'

She described some of their physical anomalies.

Jo said. 'And what did he call this toxic injection?'

'The "paradise needle."'

She repeated it. 'Talk about a Christmas gift. For years, we've been watching the financial angles, but this is *gorgeous* – Moreland actually kept records of the injections?'

'So he says.'

Her eyes sparkled. 'These . . . people. They're all retarded?'

'Yes,' I said.

'But not vegetables.'

'No. More like small children.'

'Any way they could testify in court?'

'I don't see how. Apart from mental incompetence, they can't speak. Damaged vocal chords.'

She winced. 'Still . . . just the visual impact – we can video them, get Moreland to list all their problems. A whole other line of evidence. Thank you, Dr M.'

'Are you after Hoffman?' I said. 'Or the entire Stasher-Layman organization?'

She smiled. 'Let's just say we've been working on this for a long time.'

'Major financial angle.'

'The kind of thing that raises everyone's taxes by a couple of bucks but the taxpayers never find out about . . . I've got to go down there and see them with my own eyes. Start documenting. I'm going upstairs to get my camera, then I'd appreciate it if one of you would take me back.'

'I wouldn't approach them without Moreland,' I said. 'Apart from what they just went through, they've got all sorts of physical problems – sensitivities.'

'Such as?'

'He mentioned sunlight, there may be others.'

'What does sunlight do to them?'

'Destroys their skin.'

'My flash isn't UV.'

'At the least, they'll panic when they see you. They've been

371

down there so long, let's hold off till we're sure we can't hurt them.'

She thought. 'All right . . . but I've got to see this. If he's right about the arm only being a flesh wound, he should be able to take me himself.'

She tapped her leg very fast, checked her watch, and stood. 'Let's go see how he's doing.'

'His whole purpose in life all these years has been sheltering them,' said Robin. 'He's not going to use them.'

'I understand the man's got principles. But things change, you have to adapt.'

A strand of hair looped over one eye and she shoved it away. The gun was in her waistband. She ran a finger over the butt. 'Things change quickly.'

38

Moreland's arm was bandaged and it rested on his chest. A thermometer protruded from his mouth.

Pam read it. 'A hundred. Are you comfortable there, Daddy, or should we try to get you up to your bed?'

'This is fine, kitten.' He saw us. 'I used to call her that when she was little.'

Pam's look said it was another lost memory. She snapped her doctor's bag shut.

'How're we doing?' said Jo. I thought of how she'd waited upstairs, knowing we were down there with Creedman and Haygood.

Using us. But I'd just shot a man in the back, and there was no anger left in me.

'I'll survive,' said Moreland. He stole a glance at me.

Jo said, 'I know about what you've got down there, Dr Moreland. Whenever you're ready to show it to me.'

'He's not going anywhere,' said Pam.

'It's something of an emergency. A lot's at stake. Right, doctor?'

Moreland didn't answer.

'What are you talking about?' said Pam.

'It's complicated,' said Jo. 'I think I can help your father in a big way if he can help me.'

'What's going on, Daddy?'

Moreland held out a hand to her and grasped her fingers. 'She's right, it is complicated, kitten. I should get down there—'

'Down *where*?'

Moreland blinked.

Pam said, 'Who's she to tell you what to do, Daddy?'

No answer.

'Who are you, Jo?'

Jo flashed her badge.

Pam stared at it.

'Long story,' said Jo. 'Come with me for a sec.'

She put her arm around Pam just as she'd done a few hours ago. Pam shook her off angrily.

'I'm not leaving him alone.'

'It's . . . fine,' said Moreland. 'Thank you for taking care of me. Go with her. Please. For my sake.'

'I don't *understand*, Daddy.'

'Robin,' said Moreland, 'could you go along and help explain things?'

Robin said, 'Sure.'

'Why can't *you* tell me, Daddy?'

'I will, kitten, all in due time. But right now I need some rest. Go with them. Please, darling.'

The three women left and Moreland beckoned me closer. The rain was hitting the picture windows sharply, like buckshot on metal.

He stared up at me. Chewed his lip. Blinked. 'Your questions down there, about what Hoffman had over me . . . the things Creedman said about me down there. There's some truth to them.'

374

Moving with difficulty, he faced the back of the sofa.

'I was a different man back then, Alex. Women – *having* them – meant so much to me.'

Forcing himself to face me, he said, 'I've made mistakes. Big ones.'

'I know. Dennis thinks the man who died at sea was his father, but he's wrong.'

He tried to speak, couldn't.

'I'm not judging you, Bill.'

Though the room was dim, I could see dark spots on the white couch. Spots of his blood. His eyes were sunken and dry.

'When did you figure it out?'

'You paid for Dennis's schooling – Ben's too, but Ben gave you something in return. And you got upset about Dennis and Pam getting close. So upset you spoke to Jacqui about it and she called Dennis off. I didn't think you were a racist. Then, after what Creedman said, it made sense. It must have been hard since Pam came back.'

'Oh,' he said, more exhalation than word. 'As a father, I'm a disgrace. They've both turned out better than I deserve. I sent Pamela away because I didn't – couldn't cope after Barbara died.'

Propping himself up.

'No, that's not all of it. I sent her away because of the guilt.'

'About Jacqui?'

'And the others. Many others. I *did* serve as my own abortionist. Barbara had never been a happy woman, I made her miserable.'

He sank back down again.

'The bastard was right, I *was* a repugnant lecher. Lecher with surgical training . . . but Jacqui refused to terminate . . . Barbara's death made me realize . . . how could I hope to raise a daughter?'

'And you already had kids.'

He closed his eyes. 'I put the needle in their arms . . . my life since then's been a quest for redemption, but I doubt I'm redeemable . . . Jacqui was such a *beautiful* thing. Barely eighteen, but mature. I was always . . . hungry – not that it's an excuse, but Barbara was . . . a *lady*. She had . . . different drives.'

A woman alone on the sand, the day before she died.

'It was the baby that drove her to it,' he said. 'The fact that I'd actually let it get that far.'

'How did she find out?'

'Someone told her.'

'Hoffman?'

'Had to be. He and Barbara were chums – bridge partners. A young man paying her attention.'

'So Barbara went along with his cheating.'

He smiled. 'I suppose she can be forgiven that tiny revenge.'

'Did their playing go beyond bridge?'

'I truly don't know – anything's possible. But as I said, Barbara wasn't inclined to the physical . . . toward the end, she hated me fiercely. And she always liked *him* – found his interest in cuisine and tailoring *charming*.'

'Then why did he tell her about Jacqui?'

'To wound me. After our dinner at the base, we spoke of several things. Including the fact that he'd seen Barbara in Honolulu the day before she died. *He* took the picture I showed you. I'd never known. It was mailed from her hotel, compliments of the manager, I'd always thought it a courtesy.'

'Did she go to Honolulu to be with him?'

'He claimed not, that their running into each other was a coincidence. At the hotel bar, he was there on Navy business. Maybe it's true, Barbara did like to drink . . . he told her about Jacqui and Dennis, she cried on his shoulder about my whore and my little bastard. *Shattered*, was his exact word. Then he smiled – *that* smile.'

'But how did *he* find out?'

'Back in those days, I was less than discreet – discretion wasn't part of being a first-rate cocksman. So Hoffman or a member of his staff could easily have heard something, or even seen something. There was an empty hangar on the north end of the base. Little unused offices we officers used, to be with girls from the village. "Play rooms" we called them. Mattresses and liquor and portable radios for mood music. We still thought of ourselves as war heroes – entitled.'

'Did Hoffman bring girls there?'

'Not that I saw. His only lust is for power.'

'And when Jacqui gave birth to a fair-haired baby he figured it out.'

'A beautiful baby – a beautiful woman.'

'Was it only Aruk you fell in love with, Bill?'

He smiled. 'Jacqui and I – she's a very strong woman. Independent. Over the years we've reached an understanding. A fine friendship. I believe it's been good for both of us.'

Thinking of the oil over the mantel, I said, 'Strong – unlike your wife. Did Barbara have a history of depression?'

He nodded. 'She'd been chronically depressed for years, taken shock treatment several times. In fact, the trip to Hawaii was for her to consult yet another psychiatrist. But she never showed up for her appointment. Probably spent her time drinking with Hoffman instead. He sensed her vulnerability, told her what I'd done, and the next morning she walked into the ocean.'

Some of his weight shifted onto the wounded arm and his breath caught. I helped him find a comfortable position.

'So you see, that's the hold he has over me: keeping it secret from Pam. I killed her mother and so did he. In that sense we *are* partners. Rams locking horns, just as you said. Beautiful analogy, my friend – are you offended by my thinking of you as a friend?'

'No, Bill.'

'All these years, I've yearned to expose him. Convinced myself the reason I haven't done it is the kids' safety. Then, tonight, you began asking questions and I was forced to confront reality. I acquiesced because I knew it would ruin Pam. I sent her away because I was overwhelmed and guilty, but also because I didn't want her here on the chance that she and Dennis . . . so what happens? She comes back. And it starts . . .' He grabbed my arm and held tight. 'What do I do? There's no escape.'

'Tell her.'

'How can I?'

'In due time you'll be able to.'

'Men have mistreated her because I abandoned her! She'll despise me!'

'Give her some credit, Bill. She loves you, wants to get closer to you. Being unable to is the biggest source of her pain.'

He covered his face. 'It never ends, docs it?'

'She loves you,' I repeated. 'Once she realizes the good things you've done, gets to really know you, she may be willing to pay the price.'

'The price,' he said weakly. 'Everything has its price . . . the microeconomics of existence.'

He looked up at me. 'Is there anything *else* you need to know?'

'Not unless there's something else you want to tell me.'

Long silence. The eyes closed. His lips moved.

Incoherent mumbles.

'What's that, Bill?'

'Terrible things,' he said, barely louder. 'Time deceives.'

'You've made mistakes,' I said, 'but you've also done good.' Ever the shrink.

His face contorted and I took his cold, limp hand.

'Bill?'

'Terrible things,' he repeated.

Then he did sleep.

39

It was a big beautiful room in a big beautiful hotel. One glass wall looked out to white beach and furious surf. Yesterday, I'd seen dolphins leaping.

The three walls were koa panels so densely figured they seemed to tell a story. Crystal chandeliers hung above black granite floors. Up in front was a banquet table laden with papayas and mangoes, bananas and grapes, and thick, wet wedges of the kind of orange-yellow, honey-sweet pineapple you get only when you harvest it ripe.

Sterling silver coffeepots were set every six feet, their shine blue-white.

Other tables, too, round, seating ten, interspersed around the hall. Hundreds of men and a few women, eating and drinking coffee, and listening.

Robin and I watched it on TV, from a suite upstairs. Room service and suntan lotion and every newspaper and magazine we could get our hands on.

'Here he goes,' she said.

Hoffman stood up at the center of the big table, dressed in a mocha suit, white shirt and yellow tie.

A banner at his back.

He talked, paused for applause, smiled.

The banner said: PACIFIC RIM PROGRESS: A NEW DAWN.

Another one-liner. Laughter.

He continued talking and smiling and pausing for applause.

Then he stopped and only smiled.

Something changed in his eyes. A shutter-snap flicker of confusion.

If I hadn't been looking for it, I probably wouldn't have noticed.

If I hadn't been looking for it, I wouldn't have been tuned to C-Span.

The camera left him and swung to the back of the room.

A tall, gaunt old man in a brand-new charcoal-gray suit walked toward the front.

Next to him walked a woman I'd known first as Jo Picker, then as Jane Bendig, official-looking in a navy-blue suit and high-necked white blouse. Fox the last three days she'd worked nearly twenty-four hours a day. The easy part: using Tom Creedman's computer to send bogus messages by e-mail. The hard part: convincing Moreland he could redeem himself.

The doctors and psychologists at the medical center had helped some. Examining the kids with care and compassion, assuring the old man they were clinicians, not technocrats.

Jane shared her grief with him, talked numbers, morality, absolution.

Eventually, she just wore him down.

Now he walked ahead of her.

Behind the two of them, six men in blue suits flanked a massive black thing, like pallbearers.

Black thing with legs, a shuffling variant of the circus horse.

Stirring and confusion at the other tables, too.

Moreland and Jo kept marching. The black cloth seemed to float in midair.

Some men next to Hoffman began to move, but other men stopped them.

Zoom on Hoffman's face, still smiling.

He mouthed something – an order – to a man standing behind him, but the man had been restrained.

Moreland reached Hoffman.

Hoffman started to speak, smiled instead.

Someone shouted, 'What's going on?' and that seemed to shake Hoffman out of it.

'I'm sorry, ladies and gentlemen, this man's quite disturbed and he's been harassing me for quite a—'

The men in blue suits flicked their wrists, and the black cloth seemed to fly away.

Six soft, misshapen people stood there, hands at their side, placid as milk-sated babies. Ruined skin highlighted mercilessly by the chandelier. The doctors at the medical center had established that only UV was a threat. The black sheet protecting them from the stares of gawkers.

Gasps from the room.

The blind one began bouncing and waving his hands, staring up at the light with empty sockets.

'My God!' said someone.

A glass dropped on the granite and shattered.

Two blue-suited men took hold of Hoffman's arms.

Moreland said, 'My name is Woodrow Wilson Moreland. I'm a doctor. I have a story to tell.'

Hoffman stopped smiling.

40

A few days later, on the plane back to L.A., it hit me. First-class flight, seats like club chairs, the Defense Department's generosity allowing Spike's crate a seat of its own.

Dinner had been salmon stuffed with sole mousse. I'd indulged in half a bottle of Chablis and fallen asleep. Robin had finished only a third of a glass, but she'd drifted off too. Now her head was heavy on my blanketed shoulder.

Sweet sleep, but I came out of it thinking about Haygood – who he'd been as a child. Was there a mother out there who'd mourn him?

Stupid thoughts, but inevitable. I tried to shake myself out of it, thinking of the good I'd been part of.

Ben freed. Some limited hope for Aruk.

The 'kids' liberated and well cared for.

Moreland hospitalized, too, and evaluated. No Alzheimer's, no obscure neurological disease, just an exhausted old man.

I'd visited him an hour before we left. He hadn't told Pam or Dennis yet.

Holding back. His entire life, after the paradise needle, a struggle against impulse.

Heroism thrust upon him, he'd reinvented himself.

A thirty-year transformation, from a cruel womanizer to the patron saint of Aruk.

But yet he felt guilty.

Other sins?

Things for which there was no atonement?

As I'd left his hospital room, he'd called out, 'Time deceives.'

The same thing he'd told me as he bled on the white couch.

Another confession?

Well, that's it. Is there anything else you need to know?

Cold hands . . . still afraid.

Not unless there's something else you want to tell me.

A long silence before he'd closed his eyes and mumbled.

Terrible things . . . Time deceives.

Offering himself to me – defenses down, his world unraveling.

The first time, I'd comforted him instead of pursuing it. The second time, I'd just kept walking.

Not wanting to know?

Terrible things.

Time's deceit.

His unique *brand* of deceit. Presenting a veiled truth while changing time and context.

Telling me about cannibal cargo cults because he suspected AnneMarie's death had been part of a money-driven conspiracy.

Recounting the nuclear blast because he'd been part of another technological horror.

Discussing Joseph Cristobal's vision and 'A. Tutalo' because he yearned to unload the secret of his kids.

And something else.

The first case he'd discussed with me, moments after we'd met.

Discussing in great detail, but unable to locate the file.

Because there'd never been a file?

The catwoman.

A 'lovely lady . . . sweet nature . . . clean habits.' Thirty years old, her mother was morose . . .

Abused and humiliated by a philandering husband – forced to watch him make love to another woman.

The husband dead, years later. Eaten away by lung cancer.

A ravaged chest . . .

I'm all right, kitten.

Kitten, kitten . . . I used to call her that when she was little.

Pam not remembering.

Sent away too young to remember anything.

But *Moreland* remembered everything.

He'd exiled her to the best schools, turned her into an orphan who'd become a woman demeaned by men.

Marrying a philandering abuser. Turning off sexually.

Humiliated . . . had she, too, watched her husband rut with a lover?

Those sad eyes. Driven to depression. To the brink of suicide, she'd admitted to Robin.

So fragile, her therapist searched for family support, located and phoned Moreland.

To Pam's surprise, he flew to Philadelphia. Offered a shoulder to cry on – and more?

Had she told him the details of the humiliation?

Or had he assigned one of his lawyers to find out the facts?

Little kitten . . . pouring her heart out to Daddy.

The truth torturing Daddy. Because of his guilt about sending her away.

Guilt about having once been exactly the kind of man who hurt her.

A few days later, the philandering husband dies in a freak accident.

Falling barbell. Ravaged chest.

And 'kitten' returns to her birthplace.

Is there anything else you need to know?

Not unless there's something else you want to tell me.

Had Moreland stalked the young surgeon? Or had he hired

someone to make things right? He was a wealthy man with the means to arrange things. The obsessive's talent for rationalizing extreme measures . . .

The barbell hovering over that arrogant chest . . .

The man who'd hurt his 'kitten' so deeply.

Or maybe it *had* been an accident and I was letting things get away from me.

Terrible things, he'd said.

Had to be . . .

I'd never know.

Did I care?

At that moment, I did. Maybe one day I wouldn't.

Robin's breath reached my nostrils, hot, tinged with coffee and wine.

A pretty, dark-haired flight attendant smiled as she walked down the aisle.

'Comfy, doctor?'

'Fine, thanks.'

'Going home?'

'Yup.'

'Well, that's nice – unless you'd rather still be on vacation.'

'No,' I said. 'I'm ready to get back to reality.'

Bad Love

1

It came in a plain brown wrapper.

Padded envelope, book-rate, book-sized. I assumed it was an academic text I'd forgotten ordering.

It went onto the mail table, along with Monday's bills and announcements of scholarly seminars in Hawaii and St. Croix. I returned to the library and tried to figure out what I was going to do in ten minutes when Tiffani and Chondra Wallace showed up for their second session.

A year ago their mother had been murdered by their father up on a ridge in the Angeles Crest Forest.

He told it as a crime of passion and maybe he was right, in the very worst sense. I'd learned from court documents that absence of passion had never been a problem for Ruthanne and Donald Dell Wallace. She had not been a strong-willed woman and, despite the ugliness of their divorce, she had held onto 'love feelings' for Donald Dell. So no one had been surprised when he cajoled her into taking a night ride with sweet words, the promise of a lobster dinner, and good marijuana.

Shortly after parking on a shaded crest overlooking the forest, the two of them got high, made love, talked, argued, fought, raged, and finally clawed at one another. Then Donald Dell took his buck-knife to the woman who still bore his name, slashed and stabbed her thirty-three times and kicked her corpse out of his pickup, leaving behind an Indian-silver clip stuffed with cash and his membership card in the Iron Priests motorcycle club.

A docket-clearing plea bargain landed him in Folsom Prison on a five to ten for second-degree murder. There he was free to hang out

1

in the yard with his meth-cooking Aryan Brotherhood bunkmates, take an auto mechanics course he could have taught, accrue good behavior brownie points in the chapel, and bench-press until his pectorals threatened to explode.

Four months into his sentence, he was ready to see his daughters.

The law said his paternal rights had to be considered.

An L.A. family court judge named Stephen Huff – one of the better ones – had asked me to evaluate. We met in his chambers on a September morning and he told me the details while drinking ginger ale and stroking his bald head. The room had beautiful old oak paneling and cheap county furniture. Pictures of his own children were all over the place.

'Just when does he plan on seeing them, Steve?'

'Up at the prison, twice a month.'

'That's a plane ride.'

'Friends will chip in for the fare.'

'What kind of friends?'

'Some idiocy called The Donald Dell Wallace Defense Fund.'

'Biker buddies?'

'Vroom vroom.'

'Meaning it's probably amphetamine money.'

His smile was weary and grudging. 'Not the issue before us, Alex.'

'What's next, Steve? Disability payments because he's stressed out being a single parent?'

'So it smells. So what else is new? Talk to the poor kids a few times, write up a report saying visitation's injurious to their psyches and we'll bury the issue.'

'For how long?'

He put down the ginger ale and watched the glass raise wet circles on his blotter. 'I can kabosh it for at least a year.'

'Then what?'

'If he puts in another claim, they can be re-evaluated and we'll kabosh it again. While time's on their side, right? They'll be getting older and hopefully tougher.'

'In a year they'll be ten and eleven, Steve.'

He picked at his tie. 'What can I tell you, Alex? I don't want to see these kids screwed up, either. I'm asking you to evaluate because you're tough-minded – for a shrink.'

'Meaning someone else might recommend visitation?'

'It's possible. You should see some of the opinions your colleagues render. I had one the other day, said the fact that a mother was severely depressed was good for the kid – teach her the value of true emotions.'

'Okay,' I said. 'But I want to do a real evaluation, not some rubber-stamp. Something that may have some use for them in the future.'

'Therapy? Why not? Sure, do whatever you want. You are now shrink of record. Send your bill straight to me and I'll see you get paid within fifteen working days.'

'Who's paying, our leather-clad friends?'

'Don't worry, I'll make sure they divvy up.'

'Just as long as they don't try to deliver the check in person.'

'I wouldn't worry about it, Alex. Those types shy away from insight.'

The girls arrived right on time, just as they had last week, linked, like suitcases, to the arms of their grandmother.

'Well, here they are,' Evelyn Rodriguez announced. She remained in the entry and pushed them forward.

'Morning,' I said. 'Hi, girls.'

Tiffani smiled uneasily. Her older sister looked away.

'Have an easy ride?'

Evelyn shrugged, twisted her lips and untwisted them. Maintaining her grip on the girls, she backed away. The girls allowed themselves to be tugged, but they put their weight into it, like nonviolent protesters. Feeling the burden, Evelyn let go. Crossing her arms over her chest, she coughed and looked away from me.

Rodriguez was her fourth husband. She was Anglo, stout, bottom-heavy, an old fifty-eight, with dimpled elbows and knuckles, nicotine skin, and lips as thin and straight as a surgical incision. Talk came hard for her and I was pretty sure it was a character trait that preceded her daughter's murder.

This morning she wore a sleeveless, formless blouse – a faded mauve and powder blue floral print that reminded me of a decorative tissue box. It billowed, untucked, over black stretch jeans piped with red. Her blue tennis shoes were speckled with bleach spots. Her hair was short and wavy, corn-colored above dark roots. Earring slits creased her lobes but she wore no jewelry. Behind bifocals, her eyes continued to reject mine.

She patted Chondra's head and the girl pressed her face against a thick, soft arm. Tiffani had walked into the living room and was staring at a picture on the wall, tapping one foot fast.

Mrs. Rodriguez said, 'Okay, then, I'll just wait down in the car.'

'If it gets too hot, feel free to come up.'

'The heat don't bother me.' She raised a forearm and glanced at a too-small wristwatch. 'How long we talking about this time?'

'Aim for an hour, give or take.'

'Last time was twenty minutes.'

'I'd like to try for a little longer today.'

She frowned. 'Okay . . . can I smoke down there?'

'Outside the house? Sure.'

She muttered something.

'Anything you'd like to tell me?' I said.

'Me?' She freed one finger, poked a breast and smiled. 'Nah. Be good, girlies.'

Stepping out on the terrace, she closed the door. Tiffani kept examining the picture. Chondra touched the doorknob and licked her lips. She had on a white Snoopy t-shirt, red shorts, and sandals with no socks. A paper-wrapped Fruit Roll-Up extended from one pocket of the shorts. Her arms and legs were pasty and chubby, her face broad and puggish, topped by white-blond hair drawn into very long, very tight pigtails. The hair gleamed, almost metallic, incongruous above the plain face. Puberty might turn her pretty. I wondered what else it might bring.

She nibbled her lower lip. My smile went unnoticed or unbelieved.

'How are you, Chondra?'

She shrugged again, kept her shoulders up, and looked at the floor. Ten months her sister's senior, she was an inch shorter and seemed less mature. During the first session, she hadn't said a word, content to sit with her hands in her lap as Tiffani talked on.

'Do anything fun this week?'

She shook her head. I placed a hand on her shoulder and she went rigid until I removed it. The reaction made me wonder about some kind of abuse. How many layers of this family would I be able to peel back?

4

The file on my nightstand was my preliminary research. Before-bed reading for the strong-stomached.

Legal jargon, police prose, unspeakable snapshots. Perfectly typed transcripts with impeccable margins.

Ruthanne Wallace reduced to a coroner's afternoon.

Wound depths. Bone rills . . .

Donald Dell's mug shot, wild-eyed, black-bearded, sweaty.

'And then she got mean on me — she knew I didn't handle *mean but that didn't stop her. No way. And then I just — you know — lost it. It shouldn'ta happened. What can I say.'*

I said, 'Do you like to draw, Chondra?'

'Sometimes.'

'Well, maybe we'll find something you like in the playroom.'

She shrugged and looked down at the carpet.

Tiffani was fingering the frame of the picture. A George Bellows boxing print. I'd bought it, impulsively, in the company of a woman I no longer saw.

'Like the drawing?' I said.

She turned around and nodded, all cheekbones and nose and chin. Her mouth was very narrow and crowded with big, misaligned teeth that forced it open and made her look perpetually confused. Her hair was dishwater, cut institutionally short, the bangs hacked crookedly. Some kind of food stain specked her upper lip. Her nails were dirty, her eyes an unremarkable brown. Then she smiled and the look of confusion vanished. At that moment she could have modeled, sold anything.

'Yeah, it's cool.'

'What do you especially like about it?'

'The fighting.'

'The fighting?'

'Yeah,' she said, punching air. 'Action. Like WWA.'

'WWA,' I said. 'World wrestling?'

She pantomimed an uppercut. 'Pow poom.' Then she looked expecting support.

Chondra didn't move.

'Pow poom,' said Tiffani, advancing toward her. 'Welcome to WWA fighting, I'm Crusher Creeper and this is The Red Viper in a grudge Match of the Century. *Ding!*' Bellpull pantomime.

She laughed, nervously. Chondra chewed her lip and tried to smile.

5

'Aar,' said Tiffani coming closer. She pulled the imaginary chord again. 'Ding. Pow poom.' Hooking her hands, she lurched forward with Frankenstein-monster unsteadiness. 'Die, Viper! *Aaar!*'

She grabbed Chondra and began tickling her arms. The older girl giggled and tickled back, clumsily. Tiffani broke free and began circling, punching air. Chondra started chewing her lip, again.

I said, 'C'mon, guys,' and took them to the library. Chondra sat immediately at the play table. Tiffani paced and shadow-boxed, hugging the periphery of the room like a toy on track, muttering and jabbing.

Chondra watched her, then she plucked a sheet of paper off the top of the stack and picked up a crayon. I waited for her to draw, but she put the crayon down and watched her sister.

'Do you guys watch wrestling at home?' I said.

'Roddy does,' said Tiffani, without breaking step.

'Roddy's your grandmother's husband?'

Nod. Jab. 'He's not our grampa. He's Mexican.'

'He likes wrestling?'

'Uh huh. Pow poom.'

I turned to Chondra. She hadn't moved. 'Do you watch wrestling on t.v., too?'

Shake of the head.

'She likes "Surfriders" ' said Tiffani. 'I do, too, sometimes. And "Millionaire's Row".'

Chondra bit her lip.

'"Millionaire's Row",' I said. 'Is that the one where rich people have all sorts of problems?'

'They *die*,' said Tiffani. 'Sometimes. It's really for real.' She put her arms down and stopped circling. Coming over to us, she said, 'They die because money and materials are the roots of sins and when you lay down with Satan, your rest is never peaceful.'

'Do the rich people on "Millionaire's Row" lay down with Satan?'

'Sometimes.' She resumed her circuit, striking out at unseen enemies.

'How's school?' I asked Chondra.

She shook her head and looked away.

'We didn't start, yet,' said Tiffani.

'How come?'

'Gramma said we didn't have to.'

6

'Do you miss seeing your friends?'

Hesitation. 'Maybe.'

'Can I talk to Gramma about that?'

She looked at Chondra. The older girl was peeling the paper wrapper off a crayon.

She nodded. Then: 'Don't do that, they're his.'

'It's okay,' I said.

'You shouldn't destroy other people's stuff.'

'True,' I said. 'But some things are meant to be used up. Like crayons. And these crayons are here for you.'

'Who bought them?' said Tiffani.

'I did.'

'Destroying's Satan's work,' said Tiffani, spreading her arms and rotating them in wide circles.

I said, 'Did you hear that in church?'

She didn't seem to hear. Punched the air. 'He laid down with Satan.'

'Who?'

'*Wallace*.'

Chondra's mouth dropped open. 'Stop,' she said, very softly.

Tiffani came over and dropped her arm over her sister's shoulder. 'It's okay, he's not our dad anymore, remember? Satan turned him into a bad spirit and he got all his sins wrapped up like one. Like a big burrito.'

Chondra turned away from her.

'Come on,' said Tiffani, rubbing her sister's back. 'Don't worry.'

'Wrapped up?' I said.

'Like one,' Tiffani explained to me. 'The Lord counts up all your good deeds and your sins and wraps them up. So when you die, He can look right away and know if you go up or down. *He's* going down. When he gets there, the angels'll look at the package and know all he done. And then he'll burn.'

She shrugged. 'That's the truth.'

Chondra's eyes pooled with tears. She tried to remove Tiffani's arm from her shoulder but the younger girl held fast.

'It's okay,' said Tiffani. 'You got to talk about the truth.'

'Stop,' said Chondra.

'It's okay,' Tiffani insisted. 'You got to talk to him.' She looked at me. 'So he'll write a good book for the judge and *he'll* never get out.'

Chondra looked at me.

I said, 'Actually, what I write won't change how much time he spends in jail.'

'Maybe,' insisted Tiffani. 'If your book tells the judge how evil he is, then *maybe* he could put him in longer.'

'Was he ever evil to you?'

No answer.

Chondra shook her head.

Tiffani said, 'He *hit* us.'

'A lot?'

'Sometimes.'

'With his hand or something else?'

'His hand.'

'Never a stick, or a belt or something else?'

Another headshake from Chondra. Tiffani's was slower, reluctant.

'Not a lot, but sometimes,' I said.

'When we were bad.'

'Bad?'

'Making a mess – going near his bike – he hit Mom more. Right?' Prodding Chondra. 'He *did*.'

Chondra gave a tiny nod, grabbed the crayon and started peeling again. Tiffani watched but didn't stop her.

'That's why we left him,' she said. 'He hit her all the time. And then he came after her, with lust and sin in his heart and killed her – tell the judge that, you're rich, he'll listen to you!'

Chondra began crying. Tiffani patted her and said, 'It's okay, we got to.'

I got a tissue box. Tiffani took it from me and wiped her sister's eyes. Chondra pressed the crayon to her lips.

'Don't eat it,' said Tiffani. 'It's poison.'

Chondra let go and the crayon flew out of her hand and landed on the floor. Tiffani retrieved it and placed it neatly alongside the box.

Chondra was licking her lips. Her eyes were closed and one soft hand was fisted.

'Actually,' I said, 'it's not poisonous, just wax with color in it. But it probably doesn't taste too good.'

Chondra opened her eyes. I smiled and she tried to smile, producing only a small mouth.

Tiffani said, 'Well, it's not food.'

'No, it isn't.'

She paced some more. Boxed and muttered.

I said, 'Let me go over what I told you last week. You're here because your father wants you to visit him in jail. My job is to find out how you feel about that, so I can tell the judge.'

'Why doesn't the judge ask us?'

'He will,' I said. 'He'll be talking to you, but first he wants me to –'

'Why?'

'Because that's my job – talking to kids about their feelings. Finding out how they really –'

'We don't *want* to see him,' said Tiffani. 'He's an insumet of Satan.'

'An –'

'An *insumet*! He laid all down with Satan and became a sinful spirit. When he dies, he's going to burn in Hell, that's for sure.'

Chondra's hands flew to her face.

'Stop!' said Tiffani. She rushed over to her sister, but before she got there, Chondra stood and let out a single, deep sob. Then she ran for the door, swinging it open so hard it almost threw her off balance.

She caught it, then she was out.

Tiffani watched her go, looking tiny and helpless.

'You got to tell the truth,' she said.

I said, 'Absolutely. But sometimes it's hard.'

She nodded. Now her eyes were wet.

She paced some more.

I said, 'Your sister's older but it looks like you take care of her.'

She stopped, faced me, gave a defiant stare, but seemed comforted.

'You take good care of her,' I said.

Shrug.

'That must get hard sometimes.'

Her eyes flickered. She put her hands on her hips and jutted her chin.

'It's okay,' she said.

I smiled.

'She's my sister,' she said, standing there, knocking her hands against her legs.

I patted her shoulder.

She sniffed, then walked away.

'You got to tell the truth,' she said.

'Yes, you do.'

Punch, jab. 'Pow poom . . . I wanna go home.'

Chondra was already with Evelyn, sharing the front seat of the thirty-year-old, plum-colored Chevy Caprice. The car had nearly bald blackwalls and a broken antenna. The paint job was homemade, the color nothing GM had ever conceived. One edge of the car's rear bumper had been broken off and it nearly scraped the ground.

I got to the driver's window as Tiffani made her way down the steps from the landing. Evelyn Rodriguez didn't look up. A cigarette drooped from her lips. A hardpack of Winstons sat on the dashboard. The driver's half of the windshield was coated with greasy fog. Her fingers were busy tying a lanyard keychain. The rest of her was inert.

Chondra was pressed up against the passenger door, legs curled beneath her, staring at her lap.

Tiffani arrived, making her way to the passenger side while keeping her eyes on me. Opening the rear door, she dove inside.

Evelyn finally took her eyes off her work, but her fingers kept moving. The lanyard was brown and white, a diamond stitch that reminded me of rattlesnake skin.

'Well, that was quick,' she said. 'Close that door now, don't kill the battery.'

Tiffani scooted over and slammed the door.

I said, 'The girls haven't started school yet.'

Mrs. Rodriguez looked at her for a second, then turned to me. 'That's right.'

'Do you need any help with that?'

'Help?'

'Getting them started. Is there some kind of problem?'

'Nah, we been busy – I make 'em read at home, they're okay.'

'Planning to send them soon?'

'Sure, when things calm down – so what's next? They have to come again?'

'Let's try again tomorrow. Same time okay?'

'Nope,' she said. 'Matter of fact, it isn't. Got things to do.'

'What's a good time for you, then?'

She sucked the cigarette, adjusted her glasses and placed the lanyard on the seat. Her slash lips twitched, searching for an expression.

'There are no good times. All the good times already been rolled.'

She started the car. Her lips were trembling and the cigarette bobbed. She removed it and turned the wheel sharply without shifting out of *Park*. The car was low on steering fluid and shrieked in protest. The front swung outward and scraped the asphalt.

'I'd like to see them again fairly soon,' I said.

'What for?'

Before I could answer, Tiffani stretched herself out along the back seat, belly down, and began kicking the door panel with both feet.

'Cut that *out*!' said Mrs. Rodriguez, without looking back. 'What for?' she repeated. 'So we can be told what to do and how to do it, as usual?'

'No, I –'

'The problem is, things are upside *down*. *Nonsensical*. Those that *should* be dead *aren't*, and those that *are*, shouldn't *be*. No amount of talking's gonna change that, so what's the difference? Upside down, completely, and now I got to be a mama all over again.'

'He can write a book,' said Tiffani. 'So that –'

Evelyn cut her off with a look. 'You don't worry yourself about things. We got to be heading back – if there's time, I'll get you an ice cream.'

She yanked the gear lever down. The Chevy grumbled and bucked, then drove off, rear bumper flirting with the road.

I stood there a while, sucking up exhaust fumes, then went back up to the house, returned to the library, and charted:

'Strong resistance to eval. on part of m.g.m. T overtly angry. Hostile to father. Talks in terms of sin, retribution. C still not communic. Will follow.'

Profound.

I went to the bedroom and retrieved Ruthanne Wallace's file.

Big as a phone book.

'Trial transcripts,' Milo had said, hefting it as he handed it over. 'Sure isn't because of any hotshot detection. Your basic moron murder.'

He'd pulled it from Foothill Division *Closed* files, filling my

11

request without question. Now, I flipped pages, not knowing why I'd asked for it. Closing the folder, I took it into the library and crammed it down into a desk drawer.

Ten in the morning and I was already tired.

I went to the kitchen, loaded some coffee into the machine and started going through the mail, discarding junk mail, signing checks, filing paper, then coming to the brown-wrapped package that I'd assumed was a book.

Slitting the padded envelope, I stuck my hand in, expecting the bulk of a hardcover. But my fingers touched nothing and I reached deeper, finally coming upon something hard and smooth. Plastic. Wedged tightly in a corner.

I shook the envelope. An audio cassette fell out and clattered onto the table.

Black, no label or markings on either side.

I examined the padded envelope. My name and address had been typed on a white sticker. No zip code. No return address either. The postmark was four days old, recorded at the Terminal Annex.

Curious, I took the tape into the living room, slipped it into the deck, and sank back into the old leather couch.

Click. A stretch of static-fuzzed nothing started me wondering if this was some sort of practical joke.

Then a shock of noise killed that theory and made my chest tighten.

A human voice. Screaming.

Howling.

Male. Hoarse. Loud. Wet – as if gargling in pain.

Unbearable pain. A terrible incoherence that went on and on as I sat there, too surprised to move.

A throat-ripping howling interspersed with trapped-animal panting.

Heavy breathing.

Then more screams – louder. Ear-clapping expulsions that had no shape or meaning . . . like the soundtrack from the rancid core of a nightmare.

I pictured a torture chamber, shrieking black mouths, convulsing bodies.

The howling bore through my head. I strained to make out words amid the torrent but heard only the pain.

Louder.

I leaped up to turn down the volume on the machine. Found it already set to *Low*.

I started to turn it off but before I did, the screaming died.

More static-quiet . . .

Then a new voice.

Soft. High-pitched. Nasal.

A child's voice:

> *'Bad love. Bad love.*
> *Don't give me the bad love.'*

Child's timbre – but with no childish lilt.

Unnaturally flat – *robot*like.

> *'Bad love. Bad love.*
> *Don't give me the bad love. . .'*

Repeating it. Three times. Four.

A chant, Druidish and mournful – so oddly metallic.

Almost like a prayer.

> *'Bad love. Bad love . . .*

No, too hollow for prayer – too faithless.

Idolatrous.

A prayer for the dead.

By the dead.

2

_____

I turned the recorder off. My fingers were stiff from clenching, my heart thumped and my mouth was dry.

Coffee smells drew me to the kitchen. I filled a cup, returned to the living room, and rewound the tape. When the spool filled, I turned the volume to near-inaudible and pressed PLAY. My gut knotted in anticipation. Then the screams came on.

Even that soft, it was hideous.

Someone being *hurt*.

Then the child's chant again, even worse in replay. The robotic drone conjured a gray face, sunken eyes, a small mouth barely moving.

'Bad love. Bad love . . .'

What had been done to strip the voice so completely of emotion?

I'd heard that kind of voice before – on the terminal wards, in holding cells and shelters.

Bad love . . .

The phrase was vaguely familiar, but why?

I sat there for a long time, trying to remember, letting my coffee go cold and untouched. Finally I got up, ejected the tape and took it into the library.

Down into the desk drawer, next to Ruthanne's file.

Dr. Delaware's Black Museum.

My heart was still chopping away. The screams and chants replayed themselves in my mind.

14

The house felt too empty. Robin was not due back from Oakland till Thursday.

At least she hadn't been home to hear it.

Old protective instincts.

During our years together I'd worked hard at shielding her from the uglier aspects of my work. Eventually, I realized I'd erected the barrier higher than it needed to be and had been trying to let her in more.

But not this. No need for her to hear this.

I sank lower into my desk chair, wondering what the damned thing meant.

Bad love . . . what should I do about it?

A sick joke?

The child's voice . . .

Bad love . . . I knew I'd heard the phrase before. I repeated it out loud, trying to trigger a memory. But the words just hovered, chattering like bats.

A psychological phrase? Something out of a textbook?

It did have a psychoanalytic ring.

Why had the tape been sent to me?

Stupid question. I'd never been able to answer it for anyone else.

Bad love . . . most likely something orthodox Freudian. Melanie Klein had theorized about good breasts and bad breasts – perhaps there was someone out there with a sick sense of humor and a side interest in neo-Freudian theory.

I went to my bookshelves, pulled out a dictionary of psychological terms. Nothing. Tried lots of other books, scanning indices.

Not a clue.

I returned to the desk.

A former patient taunting me for services poorly rendered?

Or something more recent – Donald Dell Wallace, festering up in Folsom, seeing me as his enemy and trying to play with my head?

His attorney, a dimwit named Sherman Bucklear, had called me several times before I'd seen the girls, trying to convince me his client was a devoted father.

'*It was Ruthanne neglected them, doctor. Whatever else Donald Dell did, he cared about them.*'

'*How was he on child support?*'

15

'Times are rough. He did the best he could – does that prejudice you, doctor?'

'I haven't formed an opinion yet, Mr. Bucklear.'

'No, of course not, no one's saying you should. The question is, are you willing to form one at all or do you have your mind made up just because of what Donald Dell did?'

'I'll spend time with the girls, then I'll form my opinion.'

''Cause there's a lot of potential for prejudice against my client.'

'Because he murdered his wife?'

'That's exactly what I mean, doctor – you know I can always bring in my own experts.'

'Feel free.'

'I feel very free, doctor. This is a free country. You'd do well to remember that.'

Other experts . . . was this bit of craziness an attempt to intimidate me so that I'd drop out of the case and clear the way for Bucklear's hired guns? Donald Dell's gang, the Iron Priests, had a history of bullying rivals in the meth trade, but I still didn't see it. How could anyone assume I'd make a connection between screams and chants and two little girls?

Unless this was only the first step in a campaign of intimidation . . . even so, it was almost clownishly heavyhanded.

Then again, Donald Dell's leaving his I.D. at the murder scene didn't indicate finesse.

I'd consult an expert of my own. Dialing the West L.A. police station, I was connected to Robbery Homicide where I asked for Detective Sturgis.

Milo was out of the office, no big surprise. He'd endured a demotion and six months' unpaid suspension for breaking the jaw of a homophobic lieutenant who'd put his life in danger, then a butt-numbing year as a computer clerk at Parker Center. The department hoped inertia would finally drive him into disability retirement; the LAPD still denied the existence of gay cops and Milo's very presence was an assault upon that ostrich logic. But he'd stuck it out and finally gotten back into active service as a Detective II. Back on the streets now, he was making the most of it.

'Any word when he'll be back?' I asked the detective who answered.

'Nope,' he said, sounding put-upon.

I left my name. He said, 'Uh huh,' and hung up.

I decided nothing further could be gained by worrying, changed into a t-shirt, shorts, and sneakers, and trotted out the front door, ready for a half-hour run, knees be damned.

Bounding down the steps, I jogged across the motor court, passing the spot where Evelyn Rodriguez' car had leaked oil. Just as I rounded the eugenia hedge that blocked my house from the old bridle path winding above the Glen, something stepped in front of me and stopped.

And stared.

A dog, but I'd never seen one like it.

Small dog – about a foot high, maybe twice that in length. Short, black coat brindled with yellow hairs. A lot of muscle crammed into the compact package; its body bulged and gleamed in the sunlight. It had thick legs, a bull neck, a barrel chest and a tight, tucked-in belly. Its head was disproportionately wide and square, its face flat, deeply wrinkled and pendulously jowled.

Somewhere between frog, monkey, and extra-terrestrial.

A strand of drool dangled from one flew.

It continued to look me straight in the eye, arching forward, as if ready to spring. Its tail was an inch of stub. Male. Neutered.

I stared back. He snorted and yawned showing big, sharp, white teeth. A banana-sized tongue curled upward and licked meaty lips.

A diamond of white hair in the center of it, his chest throbbed with cardiac excitement. Around his beefy neck was a nailhead-studded collar, but no tag.

'Hi, fella.'

His eyes were light brown and unmoving. I thought I detected a softness that contradicted the fighter's stance.

Another yawn. Purple maws. He panted faster and remained rooted in place.

Some kind of bulldog or mini-mastiff. From the crust around his eyes and the heaving of his chest, the early autumn heat wasn't doing him any good. Not a pug, considerably bigger than a pug, and the ears stood upright, like those of a Boston Terrier – in fact, he looked a bit like a Boston. But shorter and a lot heavier – a Boston on steroids.

An exotic dwarf fighter bred to go for the kneecaps, or a pup that would turn massive?

He yawned again, and snorted harshly.

We continued to face off.

A bird chirped.

The dog cocked his head toward the sound for half a second, then peered back at me. His eyes were preternaturally alert, almost human.

He licked his lips. The drool strand stretched, broke, and fell to the pavement.

Pant, pant, pant.

'Thirsty?'

No movement.

'Friend or foe?'

Another display of teeth that seemed more smile than snarl, but who knew?

Another moment of standoff, then I decided letting something this pint-sized obstruct me was ridiculous. Even with the bulk, he couldn't weigh more than twenty or twenty-five pounds. If he did attack, I could probably puntkick him onto the Glen.

I took a step forward, then another.

The dog came toward me deliberately, head lowered, muscles meshing, in a rolling, pantherish gait. Wheezing.

I stopped. He kept going.

I lifted my hands out of mouth-range, suddenly aware of my exposed legs.

He came up to me. Up to my legs. Rubbed his head against my shin.

His face felt like hot suede. Too hot and dry for canine health.

I reached down and touched his head. He snorted and panted faster, letting his tongue loll. I lowered my hand slowly and dangled it, receiving a long lick on the palm. But my skin remained bone-dry.

The pants had turned into unhealthy-sounding clicks.

He tremored for a second, then worked his tongue over his arid face.

I kneeled and patted his head again, feeling a flat plate of thick, ridged bone beneath the glossy coat. He looked up at me with a bulldog's sad-clown dignity. The crust around his eyes looked calcified. The folds of his face were encrusted, too.

The nearest water source was the garden-hose outlet near the pond. I stood and gestured toward it.

'Come on, buster, hydration.'

The dog strained but stayed in place, head cocked, letting out

18

raspy breaths that grew faster and faster and began to sound labored. I thought I saw his front legs quaver.

I began walking to the garden. Heard soft pad and looked behind me to see him following a few paces behind. Keeping to the left – a trained heeler?

But as I opened the gate to the pond, he hung back, remaining well outside the fence.

I went in. The pond water was greening due to the heat, but still clear. The koi were circling lazily. A couple of them saw me and approached the rim for feeding – babies who'd survived the surprise spawn of two summers ago. Most were over a foot long, now. A few were colored brilliantly.

The dog just stood there, nose pointed at the water, suffering.

'Come on, pal.' I picked up the hose.

Nothing.

Uncoiling a couple of feet, I opened the valve. The rubber hummed between my fingers.

'C'mere. H-2-O.'

The dog stared through the gateway, panting, gasping, legs bowed with fatigue. But he didn't budge.

'C'mon, what's the problem, sport? Some kind of phobia or don't you like seafood?'

Blink. He stayed in place. Swayed a bit.

The hose began to dribble. I dragged it out the gate, sprinkling plants as I walked.

The dog stood his ground until the water was an inch from his fleshy mouth. Then he craned his neck and began lapping. Then gulping. Then bathing in it, shaking his head and showering me before opening his maw and heading in for more.

Long time since the last tipple.

He shook and sprayed me again, turned his head away from the water and sat.

When I returned from replacing the hose, he was still there, settled on his ample haunches.

'What now?' I said.

He ambled up to me, jauntily, a bit of roll in his stride. Putting his head against my leg, he kept it there.

I rubbed him behind the ears and his body went loose. He stayed relaxed as I used my handkerchief to wipe the crust from his face. When I was through, he let out a grumble of contentment.

19

'You're welcome.'

He put his head against my leg once more, blowing out breath as I petted.

What a morning. I sighed.

He snorted. A reply?

I tried it again, sighing audibly. The dog produced an adenoidal grunt.

'A conversationalist,' I said. 'Someone talks to you, don't they? Someone cares about you?'

Grunt.

'How'd you get here?'

Grumble.

My voice was loud against the quiet of the Glen, harsh counterpoint to the flow of the waterfall.

Nut-mail and talking to a dog. This is what it's come to, Delaware.

The dog gazed up at me with a look I was willing to classify as friendship.

You take what you can get.

He watched as I pulled the Seville out of the carport and when I opened the passenger door, he jumped in as if he owned the vehicle. For the next hour and a half, he looked out the window as I drove around the canyon, watching for *Lost Dog* posters on trees and talking to neighbors I'd never met. No one belonged to him and no one recognized him, though the check-out girl at the Beverly Glen market opined that he was 'a little stud,' and several other shoppers concurred.

While I was there, I bought a few groceries and a small bag of kibble. When I got home, the dog bounced up the stairs after me and watched as I unloaded the staples. I poured the kibble into a bowl and set it on the kitchen floor, along with another bowl of water. The dog ignored it, choosing instead to station himself in front of the refrigerator door.

I moistened the kibble but that had no effect. This time the stubby tail was wagging.

I pointed to the bowl.

The dog began nudging the fridge door and looking up at me. I opened the door and he tried to stick his head in. Restraining him by the collar, I scrounged and found some left-over meatloaf.

The dog jumped away from my grasp, leaping nearly to my waist.

'A gourmet, huh?'

I crumbled some meatloaf into the kibble and mixed it with my fingers. The dog was snarfing before my hand was free, coating my fingers with a slick layer of drool.

I watched him feast. When he finished, he cocked his head, stared at me for a moment, then walked toward the back of the kitchen, circling and sniffing the floor.

'What now? Sorbet to clean your palate?'

He circled some more, walked to the service porch door and began butting and scratching at the lower panel.

'Ah,' I said, bounding up. I unlatched the door and he zipped out. I watched him race down the stairs and find a soft, shaded spot near a juniper bush before squatting.

He climbed back up, looking content and dignified.

'Thank you,' I said.

He stared at me until I petted him, then trailed me into the dining room, settling next to my leg, frog-face lifted expectantly. I scratched him under his chin and he promptly flipped onto his back, paws upright.

I scratched his belly and he let out a long, low, phlegmy moan. When I tried to stop, one paw pressed down on my hand and bade me continue.

Finally he turned back on his belly and fell asleep, snoring, jowls shaking like mudflaps.

'Someone's got to be looking for you.'

I slid the morning paper across the table. Plenty of *Lost Dog* ads in the classifieds, but none of the animals remotely matched the creature stretched out on the floor.

I got Animal Control's number from Information, and told the woman who answered it what I'd found.

'He sounds cute,' she said.

'Any idea what he is?'

'Not offhand – could be some kind of bulldog, I guess. Maybe a mix.'

'What should I do with him?'

'Well,' she said, 'the law says you have to try to return him. You could bring him in and leave him with us, but we're pretty crowded and I can't honestly tell you he'll get anything more than basic care.'

'What if you have him and no one claims him?'

'Well . . . you know.'

'What're my alternatives?'

'You could put an ad in the paper – 'Founds' are sometimes free. You might also want to take him to a vet – make sure he's not carrying anything that could cause you problems.'

I thanked her, called the newspaper and placed the ad. Then I pulled out the Yellow Pages and looked under Veterinarians. There was an animal hospital on Sepulveda near Olympic that advertised 'Walk-ins and Emergencies'.

I let the dog sleep for an hour, then took him for another ride.

The clinic was a milky blue, cement-block building set between a wrought iron foundry and a discount clothing barn. The traffic on Sepulveda looked angry so I carried my guest to the front door, upping the weight estimate to thirty pounds.

The waiting room was empty except for an old man wearing a golf-cap, comforting a giant white German Shepherd. The dog was prone on the black linoleum floor, weeping and trembling from fright. The man kept saying, 'It's okay, Rexie.'

I tapped on a frosted glass window and registered, using my name because I didn't know the dog's. Rex was summoned five minutes later, then a college-age girl opened the door and called out, 'Alex?'

The bulldog was stretched on the floor, sleeping and snoring. I picked him up and carried him in. He opened one eye but stayed limp.

'What's the matter with Alex, today?' said the girl.

'Long story,' I said and followed her to a small exam room outfitted with lots of surgical steel. The disinfectant smell reminded *me* of traumas gone by, but the dog stayed calm.

The vet arrived soon after – a young, crewcut, Asian man in a blue smock, smiling and drying his hands with a paper towel.

'Hi, I'm Dr. Uno – ah, a Frenchie, don't see too many of those.'

'A what?'

He one-handed the towel into a waste-bin. 'A French Bulldog.'

'Oh.'

He looked at me. 'You don't know what he is?'

'I found him.'

'Oh,' he said. 'Well, that's a pretty rare dog you've got there –

22

someone'll claim him.' He petted the dog. 'These little guys are pretty expensive and this one looks like a good specimen.' He lifted a flew. 'Well cared-for, too – these teeth have been scaled pretty recently and his ears are clean – these upright ears can be receptacles for all kinds of stuff . . . anyway, what seems to be your problem with him?'

'Apart from a fear of water, nothing,' I said. 'I just wanted him checked out.'

'Fear of water? How so?' I recounted the dog's avoidance of the pond.

'Interesting,' said the vet. 'Probably means he's been perimeter-trained for his own safety. Bulldog pups can drown pretty easily – real heavy-boned, so they sink like rocks. Top of that, they have no nose to speak of so they have trouble getting their head clear. Another patient of mine lost a couple of English bull babies that way. So this guy's actually being smart by shying away.'

'He's housebroken and he heels, too,' I said.

The vet smiled and I realized something very close to owner's pride had crept into my voice.

'Why don't you put him up here on the table and let's see what else he can do.'

The dog was probed, vaccinated and given a clean bill of health.

'Someone definitely took good care of him, ' said Uno. 'The basic thing to watch out for is heatstroke, especially now, when the temperature is rising. These brachycephalic dogs are really prone to it, so keep him out of the heat.'

He handed me some brochures on basic dog-care, reiterated the heat danger and said, 'That's about it. Good luck finding the owner.'

'Any suggestions along those lines?'

'Put an ad in the paper, or if there's a local Frenchie club, you could try getting in touch with them.'

'Do you have a list of club addresses?'

'Nope, sorry, we do mostly E.R. work – maybe the AKC, American Kennel Club, could help. They register most of the purebreds.'

'Where are they?'

'New York.'

He walked me to the door.

'These dogs generally have good temperament?' I said.

He looked down at the dog, who was staring up at us and wagging his stub.

'From the little I've heard and read, what you're seeing right now is pretty much it.'

'They ever attack?'

'Attack?' He laughed. 'I guess if he got attached to you he might try to protect you, but I wouldn't count on it. They're really not good for much but being a friend.'

'Well, that's something,' I said.

'Sure it is,' he said. 'That's where it's at, bottom line, right?'

3

I drove away from the clinic stroking the dog and thinking of the child's voice on the tape. I wasn't hungry but figured I'd need some lunch eventually. Spotting a hamburger stand further up on Sepulveda, I bought a take-out half-pounder. The aroma kept the dog awake and drooling all the way home, and a couple of times he tried to stick his nose in the bag. Back in the kitchen, he convinced me to part with a third of the patty. Then he carried his booty to a corner, sat, masticated noisily and promptly went to sleep, chin to the floor.

I phoned my service and found out Milo had called back. This time he answered at Robbery-Homicide. 'Sturgis.'

'How's it going, Joe Friday?'

'The usual buckets of blood. How's by you?'

I told him about receiving the tape. 'Probably just a prank, but imagine getting a kid to do that.'

I expected him to slough it off, but he said, '"Bad love"? That's weird.'

'What is?'

'Those exact same words popped up in a case a couple of months ago. Remember that social worker who got murdered at the mental health center? Rebecca Basille?'

'It was all over the news,' I said, remembering headlines and soundbites, the smiling picture of a pretty, dark-haired young woman butchered in a soundproof therapy room. 'You never said it was your case.'

'It wasn't really anyone's case because there was no investigation to speak of. The psycho who stabbed her died trying to take another caseworker hostage.'

'I remember.'

'I got stuck filling out the paperwork.'

'How did bad love pop up?'

'The psycho screamed it when he ran out after cutting Becky. Clinic director was standing in the hall, heard him before she ducked into her office and hid. I figured it was schizo-talk.'

'It may be something psychological – jargon that he picked up somewhere in the mental health system. Cause I think I've heard it, too, but I can't remember where.'

'That's probably it,' he said. 'A kid, huh?'

'A kid chanting in this strange, flat voice. It may be related to a case I'm working on, Milo. Remember that file you got me – the woman murdered by her husband?'

'The biker?'

'He's been locked up for six months. Two months ago he started asking for visitation with his daughters – around the same time as the Basille murder, come to think of it. If Becky's murderer screaming "bad love" *was* in the news, I guess he could have taken notice and filed it away for future use.'

'Intimidate the shrink – maybe remind you of what can happen to therapists who don't behave themselves?'

'Exactly. There'd be nothing criminal in that, would there? Just sending a tape.'

'Wouldn't even buy him snack bar demerits, but how could he figure you'd make the connection?'

'I don't know. Unless this is just an appetizer and there's more coming.'

'What's this fool's name, again?'

'Donald Dell Wallace.'

He repeated it and said, 'I never read the file. Refresh me on him.'

'He used to hang out with a biker gang called the Iron Priests – small-time Tujunga bunch. In between prison sentences, he worked as a motorcycle mechanic. Dealt speed on the side. I think he's a member of the Aryan Brotherhood.'

'Well, there's a character reference for you. Let me see what I find out.'

'You think this is something I should worry about?'

'Not really – you might think of locking your doors.'

'I already do.'

'Congratulations. You going to be home tonight.?'

'Yup.'

'How's Robin?'

'Fine. She's up in Oakland, giving a seminar – medieval lutes.'

'Smart kid, working with inanimate objects – all right, I'll come by, rescue you from your hermitude. If you want me to I can fingerprint the tape, check it against Wallace's. If it's him, we'll report him to his keepers, at least let him know you're not going to roll over.'

'Okay – thanks.'

'Yeah . . . don't handle it anymore, hard plastic's a real good surface for preservation. . . . *Bad love*. Sounds like something out of a movie. Sci-fi, splatter flick, whatever.'

'I couldn't find it in any of my psych books, so maybe that's it. Maybe that's where Becky's murderer got it, too – all of us are children of the silver screen. The tape was mailed from the Terminal Annex, not Folsom. Meaning if Wallace *is* behind it, someone's helping him.'

'I can check the rest of his gang, too. At least the ones with records. Don't lose any sleep over it, I'll try to get by around eight. Meanwhile, back to the slaughter.'

'Buckets of blood, huh?'

'Big *sloshing* buckets. Every morning I wake up, praise the Lord and thank Him for all the iniquity – how's that for perverse?'

'Hey,' I said, 'you love your work.'

'Yeah,' he said. 'Yeah, I do. Demotion never felt so goddamn glorious.'

'Department treating you well?'

'Let's not lapse into fantasy. The Department's *tolerating* me, because they think they've wounded me *deeply* with their pissanty pay cut and I'll eventually cave in and take disability like every other goldbricking pension-junkie. The fact that one night of moonlighting more than makes up for the difference in take-home has eluded the brass. As has the fact that I'm a contrary bastard.'

'They're not very observant, are they?'

'That's why they're administrators.'

After he hung up, I called Evelyn Rodriguez's house in Sunland. As the phone rang, I pictured the man who'd carved up her daughter playing with a tape recorder in his cell.

No one answered. I put the phone down.

27

I thought of Rebecca Basille, hacked to death in a soundproof room. Her murder had really gotten to me – gotten to lots of therapists. But I'd put it out of my head until Milo reminded me.

I drummed my fists on the counter. The dog looked up from his empty bowl and stared. I'd forgotten he was there.

What happens to therapists who don't behave themselves . . .

What if Wallace had nothing to do with the tape? Someone else, from my past.

I went into the library and the dog followed. The closet was stacked with boxes of inactive patient files, loosely alphabetized with no strict chronological order, because some patients had been treated at several different time periods.

I put the radio on for background and started with the A's, looking for children whom I'd tagged with psychopathic or antisocial tendencies and cases that hadn't turned out well. Even long-term deadbeats I'd sent to collections.

I made it halfway-through. A sour history lesson with no tangible results: nothing popped out at me. By the end of the afternoon, my eyes hurt and I was exhausted.

I stopped reading, realized grumbly snores had overpowered the music. Reaching down, I kneaded the bulldog's muscular neck. He shuddered but remained asleep. A few charts were fanned on the desk. Even if I came up with something suggestive, patient confidentiality meant I couldn't discuss it with Milo.

I returned to the kitchen, fixed kibble and meatloaf and fresh water, watched my companion sup, burp, then circle and sniff. I left the service door open and he bounced down the stairs.

While he was out, I called Robin's hotel in Oakland again, but she was still out.

The dog came back. He and I went into the living room and watched the evening news. Current events were none too cheerful, but he didn't seem to mind.

The doorbell rang at eight-fifteen. The dog didn't bark, but his ears stiffened and tilted forward and he trailed me to the door, remaining at my heels as I squinted through the peephole.

Milo's face was a wide-angle blur, big and pocked, its paleness turned sallow by the bug light over the doorway.

'Police. Open up or I'll shoot.'

He bared his teeth in a Halloween grimace. I unlocked the door and he came in, carrying a black briefcase. He was dressed for work: blue hopsack blazer, gray slacks, white shirt stretched tight over his belly, blue and gray plaid tie tugged loose, suede desert boots in need of new soles.

His haircut was recent, the usual: clipped short at side and backs, long and shaggy on top, sideburns down to the earlobes. Country yokels had looked that way back in the fifties. Melrose Avenue hipsters were doing it nowadays. I doubted Milo was aware of either fact. The black forelock that shadowed his forehead showed a few more gray streaks. His green eyes were clear. Some of the weight he'd lost had come back; he looked to be carrying at least 240 pounds on his seventy-five inches.

He stared at the dog and said, '*What?*'

'Gee, Dad, he followed me home. Can I keep him?'

The dog gazed up at him and yawned.

'Yeah, I'm bored, too,' Milo told him. 'What the hell *is* it, Alex?'

'French bulldog,' I said. 'Rare and pricey, according to a vet. And this one's a damned good specimen.'

'Specimen.' He shook his head. 'Is it civilized?'

'Compared to what you're used to, very.'

He frowned, patted the dog gingerly, and got slurped.

'Charming,' he said, wiping his hand on his slacks. Then he looked at me. 'Why, Marlin Perkins?'

'I'm serious, he just showed up this *morning*. I'm trying to locate the owner, have an ad running in the paper. The vet said he's been well cared for. It's just a matter of time before somebody claims him.'

'For a moment I thought this tape stuff had gotten to you and you'd gone out and bought yourself some protection.'

'This?' I laughed, remembering Dr. Uno's amusement. 'I don't think so.'

'Hey,' he said, 'sometimes bad things come in small packages – for all I know it's trained to go for the gonads.'

The dog stood on his hind legs and touched Milo's trousers with his forepaws.

'Down, Rover,' he said.

'What's the matter, you don't like animals?'

'Cooked, I do. Didja name it yet?'

I shook my head.

'Then Rover will have to do.' He took his jacket off and tossed it onto a chair. 'Here's what I've got so far on Wallace. He keeps a low profile in slam and has some associations with the Aryan Brotherhood, but he's not a full-member. In terms of what kind of hardware he's got in his cell, I don't know yet. Now where's the alleged tape?'

'In the alleged tapedeck.'

He went over and turned on the stereo. The dog stayed with me.

I said, 'You know where the meatloaf comes from, don't you?'

He cocked his head and licked my hand.

Then the screams came on and the hairs rose on the back of his neck.

Hearing it the third time was worse.

Milo's face registered revulsion but after the sound died, he said nothing. Taking his briefcase over to the deck, he switched it off, ejected the tape and removed it by inserting a pencil in one of the reel-holes.

'Black surface,' he muttered. 'Ye olde white powder.'

Placing the cassette atop the plastic cover of my turntable, he removed a small brush and a vial from the case. Dipping the brush into the vial, he dusted the cassette with a pale, ash-like powder, squinting as he worked.

'Well, looks like we've got some nice ridges and swirls,' he said. 'But they could all be yours. Your prints are on file with the medical board, right, so I can check?'

'They printed me when I got my license.'

'Meaning a week or two going through channels in order to pry it loose from Sacramento – non-criminal stuff's not on PRINTRAK yet. You haven't been arrested for anything recently, have you?'

'Nothing I can remember.'

'Too bad ... okay, let's get a quick fix on your digits right now.'

He took an inkpad and fingerprint form from the case. The dog watched as he inked my fingers and rolled them on the form. The audio-cassette was near my hand and I looked at the concentric white patches on its surface.

'Keep that pinkie loose,' said Milo. 'Feel like a scumbag felon yet?'

'I don't say squat without my lawyer, pig.'

He chuckled and handed me a cloth. As I wiped my fingers, he took a small camera out of the case and photographed the prints on the tape. Flipping the cartridge over with the pencil, he dusted, raised more prints on the other side and took pictures of them, muttering, 'Might as well do it right.' Then he lowered the cassette into a small box lined with cotton, sealed the container and put it into the case.

'What do you think?' I said.

He looked at my print form, then at the tape, and shook his head. "They always look the same to me. Let the lab deal with it.'

'I meant about the tape. Sound like any movie you know?'

He ran his hand over his face, as if washing without water. 'Not really.'

'Me neither. Didn't the kid's voice have a brainwashed quality to it?'

'More like brain*dead*,' he said. 'Yeah, it was ugly. But that doesn't make it real. Far as I'm concerned, it's still filed under B for Bad Joke.'

'Someone getting a child to chant as a joke?'

He nodded. 'We're living in weird times, Doc.'

'But what if it is real? What if we're dealing with a sadist who's abducted and tortured a child and is telling me about it in order to heighten the kick?'

'The *screamer* was the one who sounded tortured, Alex. And that was an adult. Someone's messing with your head.'

'If it's not Wallace,' I said, 'maybe it's some psychopath picking me as his audience because I treat kids and sometimes my names gets in the papers. Someone who read about Becky's murderer screaming "bad love" and got an idea. And for all I know, I'm not the only therapist he's contacted.'

'Could be. When was the last time you *were* in the papers?'

'This summer – when the Jones case went to trial.'

'Anything's possible,' he said.

'Or maybe it's more direct, Milo. A former patient, telling me I failed him. I started going through my files, got halfway and couldn't find anything. But who knows? My patients were all children. I have no idea what kind of adults they turned into.'

'If you found anything funny, would you give me the names?'

'Couldn't,' I said. 'Without some kind of clear danger, I couldn't justify breaking confidentiality.'

He scowled. The dog watched him unwaveringly.

31

'What're *you* staring at?' he demanded.

Wag, wag.

Milo began to smile, fought it, picked up his case, and put a heavy hand on my shoulder.

'Listen, Alex, I still wouldn't lose any sleep over it. Let me take these to the lab right now instead of tomorrow, see if I can get some night-shifter to put some speed on. I'll also make a copy and start a case file – private one, just for my eyes. When in doubt, be a goddamn clerk.'

After he left, I tried to read a psychology journal but couldn't concentrate. I watched the news, did fifty pushups and had another go at my charts. I made it through all of them. Kids' names, vaguely remembered pathologies. No allusions to bad love. No one I could see wanting to frighten me.

At ten, Robin called. 'Hi, honey.'

'Hi,' I said. 'You sound good.'

'I am good, but I miss you. Maybe I'll come home early.'

'That would be great. Just say when and I'll be at the airport.'

'Everything okay?'

'Peachy. We've got a visitor.'

I described the bulldog's arrival.

'Oh,' she said, 'he sounds adorable. Now I definitely want to come home early.'

'He snorts and drools.'

'How cute. You know, *we* should get a dog of our own. We're nurturant, right? And you had one when you were a kid. Don't you miss it?'

'My father had one,' I said. 'A hunting cur that didn't like children. It died when I was five and we never got another, but sure, I like dogs – how about something big and protective?'

'Long as it's also warm and furry.'

'What breeds do you like?'

'I don't know – something solid and dependable. Let me think about it and when I get back we can go shopping.'

'Sounds good, bowwow.'

'We can do other stuff, too,' she said.

'Sounds even better.'

*　　*　　*

32

Just before midnight, I fashioned a bed for the dog out of a couple of towels, placed it on the floor of the service porch and turned out the light. The dog stared at it, then trotted over to the fridge.

'No way,' I said. 'Time to sleep.'

He turned his back on me and sat. I left for the bedroom. He heeled along. Feeling like Simon Legree, I closed the door on his supplicating eyes.

As soon as I got under the covers I heard scratching, then heavy breathing. Then something that sounded like an old man choking.

I jumped out of bed and opened the door. The dog raced through my feet and hurled himself up on the bed.

'Forget it,' I said and put him on the carpet.

He made the choking sound again, stared, and tried to climb up.

I returned him to the floor.

A couple more tries and he gave up, turning his back on me and staying hunkered against the dust ruffle.

It seemed a reasonable compromise.

But when I awoke in the middle of the night, thinking about pain-screams and robot-chants, he was right next to me, soft eyes full of pity. I left him there. A moment later, he was snoring and it helped put me back to sleep.

4

The next morning I woke up tasting the metal and bite of bad dreams. I fed the dog and called the Rodriguez house again. Still no answer, but this time a machine fed me Evelyn's tired voice over a background of Conway Twitty singing 'Slow Hand'.

I asked her to call me. She hadn't by the time I finished showering and shaving. Neither had anyone else.

Determined to get outdoors, I left the dog with a big biscuit and walked the couple of miles to the university campus. The computers at the BioMed library yielded no references to 'bad love' in any psychological journals and I returned home at noon. The dog licked my hand and jumped up and down. I petted him, gave him some cheese and received a drool-covered hand by way of thanks.

After boxing my charts, I carried them back to the closet. A single carton had remained on the shelf. Wondering if it contained files I'd missed, I pulled it down.

No patient records; it was crammed with charts and reprints of technical articles I'd set aside as references. A thick roll of papers bound with a rubber band was wedged between the folders. The word 'PROFUNDITIES' was scrawled across it, in my handwriting. I remembered myself younger, angrier, sarcastic.

Removing the band from the roll, I flattened the sheaf and inhaled a snootful of dust.

More nostalgia: a collection of articles I'd authored, and programs from scientific meetings at which I'd presented papers.

I leafed through it absently until a brochure near the bottom caught my eye. Strong black letters on stiff blue paper, a coffee stain on one corner.

34

GOOD LOVE/BAD LOVE

Psychoanalytic Perspectives and
Strategies in A Changing World

November 28-29, 1979 – Western Pediatric Medical Center
Los Angeles, California

A Conference Examining the Relevance to and Application
of de Boschian theory to Social and Psychobiological Issues
and Commemorating Fifty Years of
Teaching, Research, and Clinical Work by

ANDRES B. DE BOSCH, Ph.D.

Co-sponsored by WPMC
and
The de Bosch Institute and Corrective School,
Santa Barbara, California

Conference Co-Chairs

Katarina V. de Bosch, Ph.D.   Practicing Psychoanalyst and Acting
Director, The de Bosch Institute and Corrective School
Alexander Delaware, Ph.D.   Assistant Professor of Pediatrics and
Psychology, WPMC
Harvey M. Rosenblatt, M.D.   Practicing Psychoanalyst and Clini-
cal Professor of Psychiatry, New York University School of
Medicine

Headshot photos of all three of us. Katarina de Bosch thin and
brooding, Rosenblatt and I, bearded and professorial.

The rest was a list of scheduled speakers – more photos – and
details of registration.

Good Love/Bad Love. I remembered it clearly now. Wondered
how I could have forgotten.

Nineteen seventy-nine had been my fourth year on staff at Western
Peds, a period marked by long days and longer nights on the cancer
ward and the genetic unit, holding the hands of dying children and
listening to families with unanswerable questions.

In March of that year, the head of psychiatry and the chief
psychologist both chose to go on sabbatical. Though they weren't

on speaking terms and the chief never returned, their last official cooperative venture was designating me interim chief.

Slapping my back and grinding their teeth around their pipe bits, they worked hard at making it sound like a stepping stone to something wonderful. What it had amounted to was more administrative chores and just enough of a temporary pay raise to kick me into the next tax bracket, but I'd been too young to know any better.

Back then, Western Peds had been a prestigious place, and I learned quickly that one aspect of my new job was fielding requests from other agencies and institutions wanting to associate with the hospital. Most common were proposals for jointly-sponsored conferences, to which the hospital would contribute its good name and its physical premises in return for continuing education credits for the medical staff and a percentage of the box office. Of the scores of requests received yearly, a good many were psychiatric or psychological in nature. Of those, only two or three were accepted.

Katarina de Bosch's letter had been one of several I received, just weeks after assuming my new post. I scanned it and rejected it.

Not a tough decision – the subject matter didn't interest me or my staff: the front-line battles we were waging on the wards placed the theorizations of classical psychoanalysis low on our want list. And, from my readings of his work, Andres de Bosch was a middleweight analyst – a prolific but superficial writer who'd produced little in the way of original thought and had parlayed a year in Vienna as one of Freud's students and membership in the French Resistance into an international reputation. I wasn't even sure he was still alive; the letter from his daughter didn't make it clear. And the conference she proposed had a memorial flavor to it.

I wrote her a polite letter.

Two weeks week later I was called in to see the medical director, a pediatric surgeon named Henry Bork who favored Hickey-Freeman suits, Jamaican cigars, and sawtooth abstract art, and who hadn't operated in years.

'Alex.' He smiled and motioned to a Breuer chair. A slender woman was sitting in a matching nest of leather and chrome, on the other side of the room.

She looked to be slightly older than me – early thirties – but her face was one of those long, sallow constructions that would always seem aged. The beginnings of worry lines suggested themselves at crucial junctures, like a portrait artist's initial tracings. Her lips were chapped – all of her looked dry – and her only makeup a couple of grudging lines of mascara.

Her eyes were large enough without the shadowing, dark, heavy-lidded, slightly bloodshot, close-set. Her nose was prominent, down-tilted, and sharp, with a small bulb at the tip. Full wide lips were set sternly. Her legs were pressed together at the knees, feet set squarely on the floor.

She wore a coarse, black, scallop-necked wool sweater over a pleated black skirt, stockings tinted to mimic a Caribbean tan, and black loafers. No jewelry. Her hair was straight, brown, and long, drawn back very tightly from a low, flat brow, and fastened above each ear with wide, black, wooden barettes. A houndstooth jacket was draped over her lap. Near one shoe was a black leatherette attaché case.

As I sat down, she watched me, hands resting upon one another, spindly and white. The top one was sprinkled with some sort of eczematous rash. Her nails were cut short. One cuticle looked raw.

Bork stepped between us and spread his arm preparing to conduct a symphony.

'Dr. Delaware. Dr. Katarina de Bosch. Dr. de Bosch, Alex Delaware, our acting chief psychologist.'

I turned to her and smiled. She gave a nod so tiny I might have imagined it.

Bork backed away, rested a buttock on his desk and cupped both his hands over one knee. The desk surface was twenty square feet of lacquered walnut shaped like a surfboard, topped with an antique padded leather blotter and a green marble inkwell. Centered on the blotter was a single rectangle of stiff blue paper. He picked it up and used it to rap his nuckles.

'Do you recall Dr. de Bosch writing to you suggesting a collaborative venture with your division, Alex?'

I nodded.

'And the disposition of that request?'

'I turned it down.'

'Might I ask why?'

'The staffs been asking for things directly related to inpatient management, Henry.'

Looking pained, Bork shook his head, then handed the blue paper to me.

A program for the conference, still smelling of printer's ink. Full schedule, speakers, and registration.

My name was listed below Katarina de Bosch's as co-chair. My picture below, lifted off the professional staff roster.

My face broiled. I took a deep breath. 'Looks like a fait accompli, Henry.' I tried to hand him the brochure but he put his hands back on his knees.

'Keep it for your records, Alex.' Standing, he sidled in front of the desk, taking tiny steps, like a man on a ledge. Finally, he managed to get behind the surfboard and sat down.

Katarina de Bosch was inspecting her knuckles.

I considered maintaining my dignity but decided against it. 'Nice to know what I'm doing in November, Henry. Care to give me my schedule for the rest of the decade?'

A small, sniffing sound came from Katarina's chair. Bork smiled at her, then turned to me, shifting his lips into neutral.

'An unfortunate misunderstanding, Alex – a snafu. Something Naturally Always Fouls Up, right?'

He looked at Katarina again, got nothing in return, and lowered his eyes to the blotter.

I fanned the blue brochure.

'Snafu,' Bork repeated. 'One of those interim decisions that had to be made during the transition between Dr. Greiloff's and Dr. Franks' sabbaticals and your stepping in. The Board offers its regrets.'

'Then why bother with a letter of application?'

Katarina said, 'Because I'm polite.'

'I didn't know the Board got involved in scheduling conferences, Henry.'

Bork smiled. 'Everything, Alex, is the province of the Board. But you're right. It's not typical for us to get directly involved in that type of thing. However . . .'

He paused, looked again at Katarina, who gave another tiny nod. Clearing his throat, he began fingering a cellophaned cigar – one of a trio of Davidoffs sharing pocket space with a white silk handkerchief.

'The fact that we *have* gotten involved should tell you something, Alex,' he said. His smile was gone.

'What's that, Henry?'

'Dr. de Bosch – *both* Dr. de Bosches are held in extremely high esteem by . . . Western's medical community.'

Are. So the old man was still alive.

'I see,' I said.

'Yes, indeed.' The color had risen in his cheeks and his usual glibness had given way to something tentative, shaky.

He removed the cigar from his pocket and held it between his index fingers.

From the corner of my eye I saw Katarina. Watching me.

Neither of them spoke; I felt as if the next line was mine and I'd flubbed it.

'High esteem,' said Bork, finally, sounding tense.

I wondered what was bugging him, then remembered a rumor of a few years ago. Doctors' dining room gossip, the kind I tried to avoid.

A Bork problem child, the youngest of four daughters. A chronic truant with learning disorders and a tendency toward sexual experimentation, sent away, two or three summers ago, hush-hush, for some kind of live-in remediation. The family tight-lipped with humiliation . . .

One of Bork's many detractors had told the story with relish.

The de Bosch Institute and Corrective School . . .

Bork was watching me. The look on his face told me I shouldn't push it any further.

'Of course,' I said.

It sounded hollow. Katarina de Bosch frowned.

But it made Bork smile again. 'Yes,' he said. 'So obviously, we're eager for this conference to take place. Expeditiously. I hope you and Dr. de Bosch will enjoy working together.'

'Will I be working with both Drs. de Bosch?'

'My father isn't well,' said Katarina, as if I should have known it. 'He had a stroke last winter.'

'Sorry to hear that.'

She stood, smoothed her skirt with brief, flogging movements, and picked up her attaché. In the chair she'd seemed tall – willowy – but upright she was only five two or three, maybe ninety-five bony pounds. Her legs were short and her feet pointed out. The skirt hung an inch below her knees.

'In fact, I need to get back to take care of him,' she said. 'Walk

39

me back to my car, Dr. Delaware, and I'll give you details on the conference.'

Bork winced at her imperiousness, then looked at me with some of that same desperation.

Thinking of what he was going through with his daughter, I stood and said, 'Sure.'

He put the cigar in his mouth. 'Splendid,' he said. 'Thank you, Alex.'

She said, 'Henry,' without looking at him and stomped toward the door.

He rushed from behind his desk and managed to get to it soon enough to hold it open for her.

He was a politician and a hack – a skilled physician who'd lost interest in healing and had lost sight of the human factor. In the coming years he never acknowledged my empathy of that afternoon, never displayed any gratitude or particular graciousness to me. If anything, he became increasingly hostile and obstructive and I came to dislike him intensely. But I never regretted what I'd done.

The moment we were out the door, she said, 'You're a behaviorist, aren't you?'

'Eclectic,' I said. 'Whatever works. Including behavior therapy.'

She smirked and began walking very fast, swinging the attaché in a wide, dangerous arc, through the crowded hospital corridor. Neither of us talked all the way to the glass doors that fronted the building. She moved her short legs furiously, intent upon maintaining a half-step advantage. When we reached the entrance, she stopped, gripped the attaché with both hands and waited until I held one of the doors open, just as she'd done with Bork. I pictured her growing up with servants.

Her car was parked right in front, in the *No Stopping* ambulance zone – a brand new Buick, big and heavy, black with a silver vinyl top, buffed shiny as a general's boot. A hospital security guard was standing watch over it. When he saw her approaching he touched his hat.

Another door held open. I half-expected to hear a bugle-burst as she slid into the driver's seat.

She started the car with a sharp twist, and I stood there, looking at her through a closed window.

She ignored me, gunned the engine, finally looked at me and raised an eyebrow, as if surprised I was still there.

The window lowered electrically. 'Yes?'

'We were supposed to discuss details,' I said.

'The *details*,' she said, 'are, I'll do everything. Don't worry about it, don't complicate things, and it will all fall into place. All right?'

My throat got very tight.

She put the car into Drive. 'Yes, *ma'am*,' I said, but before the second word was out she'd roared off.

I went back into the hospital, got coffee from a machine near the Admittance desk and took it up to my office, trying to forget about what had happened and determined to focus myself on the day's challenges. Later, seated at my desk, charting the morning's rounds, my hand slipped and some of the coffee spilled on the blue brochure.

I didn't hear from her again until a week before the conference, when she sent a starchily phrased letter inquiring if I cared to deliver a paper. I called and declined and she sounded relieved.

'But it would be nice if you at least welcomed the attendees,' she said.

'Would it?'

'Yes.' She hung up.

I did show up on the first day to offer brief words of welcome, and, unable to escape graciously, remained on stage for the entire morning, with the other co-chair – Harvey Rosenblatt, the psychiatrist from New York. Trying to feign interest as Katarina strode to the podium, wondering if I'd see another side of her, softened for public consumption.

Not that there was much of a public. Attendance was thin – maybe seventy or eighty therapists and graduate students in an auditorium that seated four hundred.

She introduced herself by name and title, then read a prepared speech in a strident monotone. She favored complex, meandering sentences that lost meaning by the second or third twist and soon the audience was looking glazed. But she didn't seem to care, didn't seem to be talking to anyone but herself.

Reminiscing about her father's glory days.

Such as they were.

Anticipating the symposium, I'd taken the time to review Andres de Bosch's collected writings and it hadn't raised my opinion of him.

His prose style was clear but his theories about childrearing – the good love/bad love spectrum of maternal involvement his daughter had used to title the conference seemed nothing more than extensions and recombinations of other people's work. A little Anna Freud here, a little Melanie Klein there, tossed with croutons of Winnicott, Jung, Harry Stack Sullivan, Bruno Bettelheim.

He leavened the obvious with clinical anecdotes about the children he'd treated at his school, managed to work both his Vienna pilgrimage and his war experiences into his summaries, name-dropping and adopting the overly casual manner of one truly self-impressed.

Emperor's new clothes; the audience wasn't showing any great excitement. But from the rapt look on Faithful Daughter's face, she thought it was cashmere.

By the second day of the conference, attendance was down by half and even the speakers on the dais – three L.A.-based analysts – looked unhappy to be there. I might have felt sorry for Katarina but she seemed unaware of it all, continuing to flash slides of her father, dark-haired and goateed in healthier days – working at a big, carved desk surrounded by talismans and books, drawing in crayon with a young patient, writing in the brandied light of a Tiffany lamp.

Then another batch: posing with his arm around *her* even as a teenager, she'd looked old, and they could have been lovers – followed by shots of a blanket-swaddled old man sunk low in an electric wheelchair, positioned atop a high, brown bluff. Behind him the ocean was beautiful and blue, mocking his senescence.

A sad variation upon the home-movie trap. The few remaining attendees looked away in embarrassment.

Dr. Rosenblatt seemed especially pained; I saw him shade his eyes and study some scribbled notes that he'd already read from.

A tall, shambling, gray-bearded fellow in his forties, he'd struck up a conversation with me as we waited for the afternoon session to begin. His warmth seemed more than just therapeutic veneer. Unusually forthcoming for an analyst, he talked easily about his practice in mid-Manhattan, his twenty-year marriage to a psychologist, and the joys and challenges of raising three children. The youngest was a fifteen-year-old boy whom he'd brought with him.

'He's back at the hotel,' he said, 'watching movies on pay t.v. – probably the dirty ones, right? I promised to get back in an hour and take him out to Disneyland – do you have any idea how late they're open?'

'During the winter, I think only till six or so.'

'Oh.' He frowned. 'Guess we'll have to do that tomorrow, hopefully Josh can deal with it.'

'Does he like arcade games?' I said.

'Does a duck quack?'

'Why don't you try the Santa Monica pier. It's open late.'

'Okay – that sounds good, thanks. Do they have good hot dogs by any chance?'

'I know they have hot dogs, but I can't vouch for them being gourmet.'

He smiled. 'Josh is a hot dog connoisseur, Alex. We go out to Nathan's all the time – that's Coney Island. They've got great dogs, there.'

He puffed his cheeks and smoothed his beard. 'Too bad about Disneyland. I hate to disappoint him.'

'Challenges of parenthood, huh?' I said.

He smiled. 'He's a sweet kid. I brought him with me hoping to turn it into a semi-vacation for both of us. I try to do that with each of them when they're old enough. It's hard to reconcile working with other people's kids when you can't find time for your own – you have any?'

I shook my head.

'It's an education, believe me. Worth more than ten years of school.'

'Do you treat only children?' I said.

'Half and half. Actually, I find myself doing less and less child work as time goes on.'

'Why's that?'

'To be honest, kid-work's just too non-verbal for me. Three hours in a row of play therapy makes my eyes narcissistic, I know, but I figure I'm not doing them much good if I'm fading away. My wife, on the other hand, doesn't mind. She's a real artist with it. Great mom, too.'

We walked to the cafeteria, had coffee and donuts and chatted for a while about other places he could take his son. As we headed back to the auditorium, I asked him about his connection to the de Bosches.

'Andres was my teacher,' he said, 'in England. I did a fellowship

43

eleven years ago at Southwick Hospital – near Manchester. Child psychiatry and pediatric neurology. I'd toyed with the idea of working for the government and I wanted to see how the Brits ran their system.'

'Neurology?' I said. 'Didn't know de Bosch was interested in the organic side of things.'

'He wasn't. Southwick was heavily biological – still is – but Andres was their token analyst. Kind of a . . .' He smiled. 'I was about to say throwback, but that wouldn't be kind. It's not as if he was some sort of relic. Quite vital, actually, gadfly to the hard-wire boys, and don't we all need gadflies.'

We entered the conference room. Ten minutes until the next speech and the place was nearly empty.

'Was it a good year?' I said after we were seated.

'The fellowship? Sure. I got to do lots of long-term depth work with kids from poor and working class families, and Andres was a wonderful teacher – great at communicating his knowledge.'

I thought: It's not genetic. I said, 'He is a clear writer.'

Rosenblatt nodded, crossed his legs and looked around the deserted auditorium.

'How's child analysis accepted here?' he said.

'It's not used much,' I said. 'We deal mostly with kids with serious physical illnesses so the emphasis is on short-term treatment. Pain control, family counseling, compliance with treatment.'

'Not much tolerance for delayed gratification?'

'Not much.'

'Do you find that satisfying – as an analyst?'

'I'm not an analyst.'

'Oh.' He blushed around his beard. 'I guess I assumed you were – then how'd you get involved in the conference?'

'Katarina de Bosch's powers of persuasion.'

He smiled. 'She can be a real ball-breaker, can't she. When I knew her back in England she was just a kid – fourteen or fifteen – but even then she had a forceful personality. She used to attend our graduate seminars. Spoke up as if she was a peer.'

'Daddy's girl.'

'Very much so.'

'Fourteen or fifteen,' I said. 'So she's only twenty-five or -six?'

He thought for a moment. 'That's about right.'

'She seems older.'

44

'Yes, she does,' he said, as if coming up with an insight. 'She has an old soul, as the Chinese say.'

'Is she married?'

He shook his head. 'There was a time I thought she might be gay, but I don't think so. More likely asexual.'

I said, 'The temptation to think Oedipally is darn near irresistible, Harvey.'

'For girls it's Elektra,' he said, wagging a finger with amusement. 'Get your complexes straight.'

'She drives one, too.'

'What?'

'Her car's an Electra – a big Buick.'

He laughed. 'There you go – now if that doesn't convert you to fervid belief in Freud I don't know what will.'

'Anna Freud never married, either, did she?' I said. 'Neither did Melanie Klein.'

'What, a neurotic pattern?' he said, still chuckling.

'Just presenting the data, Harvey. Draw your own conclusions.'

'Well, *my* daughter's damned *boy* crazy, so I wouldn't get ready to publish just yet.' He turned serious. 'Though I'm sure the impact of such a powerful paternal – '

He stopped talking. I followed his gaze and saw Katarina heading toward us from the left side of the auditorium. Carrying a clipboard and marching forward while looking at her watch.

When she reached us, Rosenblatt stood.

'Katarina. How's everything going?' There was guilt in his voice – he'd make a very bad liar.

'Fine, Harvey,' she said, looking down at her board. 'You're up in two minutes. Might as well take your place on stage.'

I never saw either of them again, and the events of that autumn soon faded from memory, sparked briefly, the following January, by a newspaper obituary of Andres de Bosch. Cause of death was suicide by overdose – prescription tranquilizers. The 80-year-old analyst was described as despondent due to ill health. His professional achievements were listed in loving, inflated detail and I knew who'd provided them.

Now, years later, another spark.

Good love/*Bad love*. De Bosch's term for mothering gone bad.

45

The psychic damage inflicted when a trusted figure betrays the innocent . . .

So Donald Dell Wallace probably wasn't behind it. Someone else had picked me – because of the *conference*?

Someone with a long, festering memory? Of what? Some transgression committed by de Bosch? In the name of de Boschian therapy?

My co-chairmanship made me seem like a disciple but that was my only link . . .

Some kind of grievance. Was it even real, or just a delusion?

A psychotic sitting at the conference, listening, boiling . . .

I thought back to the seventy strangers in the auditorium. A collective blur.

And why had Becky Basille's murderer howled bad love?

Another madman?

Katarina might have had the answer, but she hadn't had much use for me back in seventy-nine and there was no reason to believe she'd talk to me now.

Unless she'd gotten a tape, too, and was frightened.

I punched 805 Information. There was no Santa Barbara listing for either the de Bosch Institute or the Corrective School. Neither was there an office number for Katarina de Bosch, Ph.D. Before the operator could get away, I asked her to check for a home number. Zilch.

I hung up and pulled out the latest American Psychological Association directory. Nothing there, either. Retrieving some older volumes, I finally found Katarina's most recent entry. Five years ago. But the address and number were those of the Santa Barbara school. On the offchance the phone company had messed up, I called.

A woman answered, 'Taco Bonanza.' Metallic clatter and shouts nearly drowned her out.

I cut the connection and sat at my desk, stroking the top of the bulldog's head and gazing at the coffee stain on the brochure. Wondering how and when enlightenment had given way to enchiladas.

Harvey Rosenblatt.

Half past one made it four-thirty in New York. I got the number for NYU'S med school and asked for the department of psychiatry. After a couple of minutes on hold, I was informed that there was no Dr. Harvey Rosenblatt on either the permanent or the part-time clinical staff.

'We do have a *Leonard* Rosenblatt,' said the secretary. 'His office is out in New Rochelle – and a Shirley Rosenblatt in Manhattan, on East Sixty-Fifth Street.'

'Is Shirley an M.D. or a Ph.D.?'

'Um – one second – a Ph.D. She's a clinical psychologist.'

'But no Harvey?'

'No, sir.'

'Do you have any old rosters on hand? Lists of staff members who've retired?'

'There may be something like that somewhere, sir, but I really don't have the time to search. Now if you'll – '

'Could I have Dr. Shirley Rosenblatt's number please?'

'One moment.'

I copied it down, called *Manhattan* Information for a listing on Harvey Rosenblatt, M.D., learned there was none, and dialed Shirley, Ph.D'S exchange.

A soft, female voice with Brooklyn overtones said, 'This is Dr. Shirley Rosenblatt. I'm in session or out of the office, and can't come to the phone. If your call is a true emergency, please press One. If not, please press Two, wait for the beep and leave your message. Thank you and have a lovely day.'

Mozart in the background . . . *beep*.

'Dr. Rosenblatt, this is Dr. Alex Delaware, from Los Angeles. I'm not sure if you're married to Dr. Harvey Rosenblatt or even know him, but I met him several years ago at a conference out here and wanted to touch base with him on something – for research purposes. If you can help me reach him, I'd appreciate your passing along my number.'

I recited the ten digits and put the phone back in its cradle. The mail came a half hour later. Nothing out of the ordinary, but when I heard it drop into the bin, my hands clenched.

5

I went down to feed the fish and when I got back, the phone was ringing.

The operator at my service said, 'This is Joan, Dr. Delaware, are you free? There's someone on the line about a dog, sounds like a kid.'

'Sure.'

A second later a thin, young voice said, 'Hello?'

'Hi, this is Dr. Delaware.'

'Um . . . this is Karen Alnord. My dog got lost and you said in the paper that you found a bulldog?'

'Yes, I did. He's a little French Bulldog.'

'Oh . . . mine's a Boxer.' Dejected.

'Sorry, this one's not a Boxer, Karen.'

'Oh . . . I just thought – you know, sometimes people think they're bulldogs.'

'I can see the resemblance,' I said. 'The flat face – '

'Yeah.'

'But the one I've found's much smaller than a boxer.'

'Mine's a puppy,' she said. 'He's not too big yet.'

I put her age at between nine and eleven.

'This one's definitely full-grown, Karen. I know because I took him to the veterinarian.'

'Oh . . . um . . . okay, thank you, sir.'

'Where'd you lose your dog, Karen?'

'Near my house. We have a gate, but somebody left it open and he got out.'

'I'm really sorry. Hope you find him.'

'I will,' she said, in a breaking voice. 'I've got an ad, too, and I'm calling all the other ads, even though my mom says none of them are probably the right one. I'm paying a reward, too – twenty dollars, so if you do find him you can get it. His name's Bo and there's a bone-shaped tag on his collar that says Bo and my phone number.'

'I'll keep an eye out, Karen. Whereabouts do you live?'

'Reseda. On Cohasset between Sherman Way and Saticoy. His ears haven't been cropped. If you find him here's my phone number.'

I wrote it down, even though Reseda was over the hill to the north, fifteen or twenty miles away.

'Good luck, Karen.'

'Thank you, sir. I hope your bulldog finds his owner.'

That reminded me that I hadn't yet called the Kennel Club. Information gave me the number in New York and another one in North Carolina. Both answered with recorded messages and told me business hours were over.

'Tomorrow,' I told the bulldog.

He'd been observing me, maintaining that curious, cocked head stance. The fact that someone was probably grieving for him bothered me, but I didn't know what else to do other than take good care for him.

That meant food, water, shelter. A walk, when it got cool enough.

A walk meant a leash.

He and I took a drive to a pet store in south Westwood and I bought a lead, more dog food, biscuits in various flavors, and a couple of nylon bones the salesman assured me were excellent for chewing. When we returned, it seemed temperate enough for a stroll if we stayed in the shade. The dog stood still, tail wagging rapidly, while I put the leash on. The two of us explored the Glen for half an hour, hugging the brush, walking against traffic. Like regular guys.

When I got back, I called my service. Joan said, 'There's just one from a Mrs. Rodriguez – hold on, that's your board . . . there's someone ringing in right now.'

I waited a moment, and then she said, 'I've got a Mr. Silk on the line, says he wants to make an appointment.'

'Thanks, put him on.'

Click.

'Dr. Delaware.' Silence.

'Hello?'

Nothing.

'Mr. Silk?'

No answer. Just as I was about to hang up and redial the service, a low sound came through the receiver. Mumbles no. Laughter.

A deep, throaty giggle.

'Huh huh huh.'

'Who is this?' I said.

'Huh huh huh.' Gloating.

I said nothing.

'Huh huh huh.'

The line went dead. I got the operator back on the line.

'Joan, that guy who just called. Did he leave anything other than his name?'

'No, he just asked if you treated adults as well as children and I said he'd have to speak to you about that.'

'And his name was Silk? As in the fabric.'

'That's what I heard. Why, doctor, is something wrong?'

'He didn't say anything, just laughed.'

'Well that's kind of crazy . . . but that's your business, isn't it, doctor?'

Evelyn Rodriguez answered on the first ring. When she heard my voice, hers went dead.

'How's everything?' I said.

'Fine.'

'I know it's a hassle for you, but I would like to see the girls.'

'Yeah, it's a hassle,' she said. 'Driving all the way out there.'

'How about if I come out to you?'

No answer.

'Mrs. Rodriguez?'

'You'd do that?'

'I would.'

'What's the catch?'

'No catch, I'd just like to make this whole thing as easy as possible for you.'

'Why?'

To show Donald Dell Wallace I can't be intimidated. 'To help the girls.'

'Uh huh . . . *they're* paying for your time, right? His . . . bunch a heathens.'

'The judge made Donald Dell responsible for the costs of the evaluation, Mrs. Rodriguez, but as we talked about the first time, that doesn't obligate me to him in any way.'

'Uh huh.'

'Has that been a problem for you?' I said. 'The fact that he's paying?'

She said nothing for a moment, then: 'Bet you're charging plenty.'

'I'm charging my usual fee,' I said, realizing I sounded like a Watergate witness.

'Bet it includes your driving time and all. Door to door, just like the lawyers.'

'Yes, it does.'

'Good,' she said, stretching the word. 'Then *you* can drive instead of me – drive *slow*. Keep your meter running and make them devils *pay*.'

Angry laughter.

I said, 'When can I come out?'

'How 'bout right now? They're running around like wild Injuns, maybe you can settle 'em down. How about you drive out here right this *minute* and see 'em? You ready for that?'

'I can probably be there in forty-five minutes.'

'Whenever. We'll be right here. We're not taking any vacations to Honolulu.'

She hung up before I could ask for directions. I looked up her address in my case file – the ten thousand block of McVine Terrace in Sunland – and matched it to my Thomas map. Setting the dog up with water, food and a bone, I left, not at all unhappy about running up the Iron Priests' tab.

The 405 Freeway deposited me in a scramble of northbound traffic just beginning to clot, facing hills so smogged they were no more than shrouded, gray lumps on the horizon. I did the L.A. stop-and-go boogie for a while, listening to music and trying to be patient, finally made it to the 118 East, then the 210, and cruised into the high desert northeast of the city, picking up speed as both the road and the air got clearer.

Exiting at Sunland, I hooked north again and got onto a commercial stretch of Foothill Boulevard that ran parallel to the mountains:

auto parts barns, body shops, unfinished furniture outlets, and more roofers than area.

I spotted McVine a few minutes later and turned left. The street was narrow, with grass growing down to the curb instead of sidewalks, and planted haphazardly with eucalyptus and willow. The curb-grass was dry and yellow. The houses behind it were small and low, some of them no more than trailers on raised foundations.

The Rodriguez residence was on a northwest corner, a boxcar of mocha stucco with a gutterless, black composition roof and a flat, porchless face broken by windows. One of the windows was blocked by a tilting sheet of lattice. The squares were broken in spots, warped in others, and a few dead branches wormed around them. A high, pink block wall enveloped the rear of the property.

I got out and walked up a hardpack lawn stippled with blemish-like patches of some sort of low-growing succulent and split by a foot-worn rut. Evelyn's plum-colored Chevy was parked to the left of the pathway, next to a red half-ton pickup with two stickers on the bumper. One sang the praises of the Raiders, the other dared me to keep kids off drugs. A stick-on sign on the door said *R and R Masonry*.

I pressed the bell and a wasp-buzz sounded. A woman opened the door, and looked at me through the smoke vining upward from a freshly lit Virginia Slim.

In her late twenties, five seven and lanky, she had dirty blonde hair gathered in a high, streaked ponytail and pale skin. Slanted, dark eyes and broad cheekbones gave her a Slavic look. The rest of her beginning to pinch. Her shape was perfect for the hardbody era: sinewy arms, high breasts, straightedge tummy, long legs leading up to flaring hips just a little wider than a boy's. She wore skintight, low-riding jeans and a baby-blue, sleeveless midriff top that showcased an apostrophe of a navel some obstetrician should have been mighty proud of. Her feet were bare. One of them tapped arhythmically.

'You the doctor?' she said, in a husky voice, talking around the cigarette, just the way I'd seen Evelyn Rodriguez do.

'Dr. Delaware,' I said, and extended my hand.

She took it and smiled – amusement rather than friendliness – gave a hard squeeze, then dropped it.

'I'm Bonnie. They're waiting for you, c'mon in.'

The living room was half the width of the boxcar and smelled like a drowned cigar. Carpeted in olive shag and paneled with knotty pine it was darkened by drawn drapes. A long, brown corduroy sofa ran along the back wall. Above it hung a Born Again fish symbol. To the left was a console t.v. topped with some sort of cable decoder and a VCR and a beige velveteen recliner. On a hexagonal table, an ashtray brimmed over with butts.

The other half of the front-space was a kitchen-dining area combo. Between the two rooms was an ochre-colored door. Bonnie pushed it open, letting in a lot of bright, Western light and took me down a short, shagged hall. At the end was a den, walled in grayish, mock-birch and backed by sliding glass doors that looked out to the backyard. More recliners, another t.v., porcelain figurines on the mantle, below three mounted rifles.

Bonnie slid open a glass door. The yard was a small, flat square of scorched grass surrounded by the high pink walls. An avocado tree grew at the rear, huge and twisted.

Barely out of its shade was an inflatable swimming pool, oval and bluer than anyone's heaven. Chondra sat in it, splashing herself without enthusiasm. Tiffani was in a corner of the property, back to us, jumping rope.

Evelyn Rodriguez sat between them in a folding chair, working on her lanyard and smoking. She had on white shorts, a dark blue t-shirt and rubber beach sandals. On the grass next to her was her purse.

Bonnie said, 'Hey,' and all three of them looked up.

I waved. The girls stared.

Evelyn said, 'Go get him a chair.'

Bonnie raised her eyebrows and went back into the house, putting some wiggle in her walk.

Evelyn shaded her face, looked at her watch and smiled. 'Forty-two minutes. Couldn't ya have stopped for coffee or something?'

I forced a chuckle.

'Course,' she said, 'don't really matter what you actually do, you can always *say* you done it, right? Just like a lawyer. You can say anything you *please*.'

She stubbed her cigarette out on the grass.

I went over to the pool. Chondra returned my 'Hi,' with a small, silent smile. Some teeth this time: progress.

Tiffani said, 'You write your book yet?'

'Not yet. I need more information from you.'

She nodded gravely. 'I got lots of truth – we don't want to ever see him.'

She grabbed hold of a branch and started swinging. Humming something.

I said, 'Have fun,' but she didn't answer.

Bonnie came out with a folded chair. I went and took it from her. She winked and went back into the house, rear twitching violently. Evelyn wrinkled her nose and said, 'Well, does it?'

I unfolded the chair. 'Does it what?'

'Does it matter? What actually happens? You're just gonna do what you want to, write what you want to anyway, right?'

I sat down next to her, positioning myself so I could see the girls. Chondra was motionless in the pool, gazing at the trunk of the avocado.

Evelyn humphed. 'You ready to come out?'

Chondra shook her head and began splashing herself again, doing it slowly, as if it were a chore. Her white pigtails were soaked the color of old brass. Above the pink walls the sky was static and blue, bottomed by a soot-colored cloud bank that hid the horizon. Someone in the neighborhood was barbecuing and a mixture of scorching fat and lighter fluid spread its cheerful toxin through the autumn heat.

'You don't think I'll be honest, huh?' I said. 'Been burned by other doctors, or is it something about me?'

She turned toward me slowly and put her lanyard in her lap.

'I think you do your job and go home,' she said. 'Just like everyone else. I think you do what's best for *you*, just like everyone else.'

'Fair enough,' I said. 'I'm not going to sit here and tell you I'm some saint who'd work for free or that I really know what you've been going through, 'cause I don't, thank God. But I think I understand your rage. If someone had done it to my child, I'd be ready to kill him, no question about it.'

She took her Winstons out of her pocket and knocked a cigarette loose. Sliding it out and taking it between two fingers, she said, 'Oh you would, would you? Well that would be revenge and the Bible says revenge is a negational action.'

She lit up with a pink disposable lighter, inhaled very deeply and held it. When she let the smoke out, her nostrils twitched.

Tiffani began jumping very fast. I wondered if we were within her earshot.

Evelyn shook her head. 'Gonna break her head one of these days.'

'Lots of energy,' I said.

'Apple don't fall far.'

'Ruthanne was like that?'

She smoked, nodded, and started to cry, letting her tears drip down her face and wiping with short, furious movements. Her torso pushed forward and for a moment I thought she was going to leave.

'Ruthanne was *just* like that when she was little. Always moving. I never felt I could . . . she had spirit, she was – she had . . . wonderful spirit.'

She tugged her shorts down and sniffed.

'Want some coffee?'

'Sure.'

'Wait right here.' She went into the house.

'Hey, girls,' I called out.

Tiffani kept jumping. Chondra looked up. Her mouth hung slightly open and water droplets bubbled her forehead, like oversized sweat.

I went over to her. 'Swim a lot?'

She gave a very small nod and splashed one arm, turning away, and facing the avocado tree. Young fruit hung from the branches, veiled by a cloud of whiteflies. Some of it was blackened with disease.

Tiffani waved at me. Then she began to chant in a loud voice:

> 'I went to the Chinese Restaurant,
> to get a loaf of bread bread bread,
> a man was there with a big mustache,
> and this is what he said said said.
> El eye el eye chicholo beauty, pom-pom cutie . . .'

Evelyn came back holding a couple of mugs. Bonnie marched behind her carrying a small plate of sugar wafers. The look on her face said she'd been created for better things.

I walked back to the lawn chairs.

Bonnie said, 'Here you go,' handed me the plate and sashayed off.

Evelyn gave me a mug. 'Black or cream?'

'Black.'

We sat and sipped. I balanced the cookie plate on my lap.

'Have one,' she said, 'or are you one of those health-food types?'

I took a wafer and chewed on it. Lemon-flavored and slightly stale.

'I dunno,' she said, 'Maybe I shoulda been a health fooder. I always gave my kids sugar and stuff, whatever they wanted, maybe I shouldnta. Got a boy went AWOL over in Germany two years ago, don't even *know* where he is, the baby don't know *zero* about what she wants to do with her life, and Ruthie . . .'

She shook her head and looked over at Tiffani. 'Watch your head on that branch, you!'

'Bonnie's the baby?' I said.

Nod. 'She got all the brains and the looks. Just like her daddy – he coulda been a movie star. Only time I ever went gaga for the looks, and boy what a mistake *that* was.'

She gave a full smile. 'He cleaned me out thirteen months after we were married. Left me with the baby in diapers and went down to Louisiana to work the deep sea rigs. Got killed soon after in a fall that they *said* was an accident. Never took out the right insurance for himself so I got nothing.'

She smiled wider. 'He had a temper on him. All my men do. Roddy's got a fuse on him, though it takes a while to get it lit. He's a Mexican, but he's the best of the lot.'

She patted the t-shirt pocket that held the cigarette pack. 'Sugar and bad tempers and cancer sticks. I really go for all the good things in life, huh?'

Her eyes watered again. She lit up.

'All the good things,' she said. 'All the blessed good things.'

She kept the cigarette in her mouth, busied her hands by squeezing them together, letting go, repeating the motion. The lanyard lay on the grass, neglected.

'There's no room for your guilt,' I said.

She yanked the cigarette out of her mouth and stared at me. '*What'd* you say?'

'There's no room for your guilt. All the guilt belongs to Donald Dell. One hundred per cent of it.'

She started to say something, but I stopped her.

I said, 'No one else should carry that burden, Evelyn. Not Ruthanne for going with him that night, and certainly not you for the way you raised her. Junk food had nothing to do with what happened. Neither did anything but Donald Dell's impulses. It's *his* cross to bear now.'

Her eyes were on me, but wavering.

I said, 'He's a bad guy, he does bad things, no one knows why. And now you're having to be a mom, all over again, when you weren't planning on it. And you're going to do it without complaining too much and you're going to do your best. No one's going to pay you or give you any credit, so at least give *yourself* some.'

'You talk sweet,' she said. 'Telling me what I want to hear.' Wary, but not angry. 'Sounds like you got a temper on you, too.'

'I talk straight. For my own sake – you're right about that. All of us do what we think's best for us. And I do like to make money – I went to school a long time to learn what I do, I'm worth a high fee so I charge it. But I also like to sleep well at night.'

'Me, too. So what?' She smoked, coughed, ground out the cigarette with disgust. 'Been a long time since I slept peacefully.'

'Takes time.'

'Yeah . . . how long?'

'I don't know, Evelyn.'

'Least you're honest.' Smile. 'Maybe.'

'What about the girls?' I said. 'How do they sleep?'

'Not good,' she said. 'How could they? The little one wakes complaining she's hungry – which is a laugh, 'cause she eats all day, though you wouldn't know it to look at her, would you? I used to be like that, believe it or not.' Squeezing her thigh. 'She gets up two, three times a night, wanting Hersheys and licorice and ice cream.'

'Does she ever get those things??'

'Hel— heck no. There's a *limit*. I give her a piece of orange or something – maybe a half a cookie – and send her right back. Not that it stops her the next time.'

'What about Chondra?'

'*She* don't get up, but I hear her crying in her bed under the blanket.' She looked over at the older girl, who was sitting motionless in the center of the pool. 'She's the soft one. Soft as jelly.'

She sighed and and looked down at her coffee with disdain. 'Instant. Shoulda made real stuff.'

'It's fine,' I said, and drank to prove it.

'It's okay, but it's not great – don't see great around here too often.

My second husband – Brian's dad – owned a big place up near Fresno – table grapes and alfalfa, some quarter horses. We lived up there for a few years – that was *close* to great, all that space. Then he went back to his drinking – Brian Senior – and it all went to – straight down the tubes. Ruthie used to love that place – especially the horses. There's riding stables around here, out in Shadow Hills, but it's expensive. We always said we'd get over there but we never did.'

The sun dropped behind the cloud bank and the yard dimmed.

'What're you gonna do to us?' she said.

'To you?'

'What's your plan?'

'I'd like to help you.'

'If you wanna *help* them, keep them away from him, that's all. He's a devil.'

'Tiffani called him an instrument of Satan.'

'I told her that,' she said defiantly. 'You see something wrong with that?'

'Not at all.'

'It's my faith – it props me up. And he is one.'

'How'd Ruthanne meet him?'

Her shoulders dropped. 'She was waitressin' at a place out in Tujunga – okay, it was a bar. He and his *bunch* hung out there. She went out with him for months before tellin' me. Then she brought him home and the first look I got I said no, no no – my experiences, I can spot a bad apple like that.' Snap of fingers. 'I warned her, but that didn't do no good. Maybe I gave up too easy, I don't know. I was havin' problems of my own and Ruthie didn't think I had a single intelligent thing to say to her.'

She lit another cigarette and took several hard, fast drags. 'She was stubborn. That was her only real sin.'

I drank more coffee.

'Nothing to say anymore, doc? Or am I boring you?' She flicked ashes onto the dirt.

'I'd rather listen.'

'And they pay you all that money for that? Good racket you got there.'

'Beats honest labor,' I said.

She smiled. First friendly one I'd seen.

'Stubborn,' she said. She smoked and sighed and called out, 'Five more minutes, then into the house for homework, botha you!'

58

The girls ignored her. She kept looking at them. Drifted off, as if she'd forgotten I was there. But then she turned and looked at me.

'So, Mr. Easy Listener, what *do* you want from me and my little girls?'

Same question she'd asked me the first time she met me. I said, 'Enough time to find out exactly how they've been affected by their mom's death.'

'How do you *think* they've been affected? They loved their mama. They're crushed to dirt.'

'I need to get specific for the court.'

'What do you mean?'

'I need to list symptoms that prove they're suffering psychologically.'

'You gonna say they're crazy?'

'No, nothing like that. I'll talk about symptoms of anxiety – like the sleep problems, changes in appetite, things that make them vulnerable to seeing him. Otherwise they're going to get swept up in the system. Some of it you can tell me, but I'll also need to hear things directly from them.'

'Won't that mess them up more, talking about it?'

'No,' I said. 'Just the opposite – keeping things inside is more likely to create problems.'

She gave a skeptical look. 'I don't see them talkin' to you much, so far.'

'I need time with them – need to build up their trust.'

She thought about that. 'So what do we do, just sit here, jawing?'

'We could start with a history – you telling me as much as you remember about what they were like as babies. Anything else you think might be important.'

'A history, huh?' She took a deep drag, as if trying to suck maximum poison out of the cigarette. 'So now we've got a history . . . yeah, I've got *plenty* to tell you. Why don't you get out a pencil and start writing?'

6

She talked as the sky darkened further, letting the girls play on as she recounted nightmares and weeping spells, the terrors of orphanhood. At five-thirty Bonnie came out and switched on floodlights that turned the yard sallow. It stilled her mother's voice and Evelyn stood and told the girls, 'Go in the house, you.'

Right after they did, a man came out, rubbing his hands together and sniffing the air. Five three or so, in his late fifties or early sixties, low-waisted, dark-skinned and weak-chinned, with long, tattooed arms. Bowlegs gave him a tottering walk. His eyes were shadowed by thick, gray thatches and a drooping, iron-colored Zapata mustache obscured his mouth. His bushy gray hair was slicked straight back. He wore a khaki workshirt and blue jeans with hand-rolled cuffs. His hands were caked with plaster and he rubbed them more vigorously as he approached.

Evelyn saluted him.

He returned the gesture and looked at me, stretching to stand taller.

'This here's that doctor,' she said. 'We been having a nice talk.'

He nodded. The shirt was embroidered with a white oval tag that said 'Roddy' in red script. Up close I saw that his face was severely pockmarked. A couple of crescent-shaped scars ran down his chin.

I held out a hand.

He looked at his palm, gave an embarrassed smile and said, 'Dirty.' His voice was soft and hoarse. I put my hand down. He smiled again and saluted me.

'Dr. Delaware.'

'Roddy. Pleased to meetchu.' Boyle Heights accent. As he lowered his fingers, I noticed tattooed letters across the knuckles. L.O.V.E. Homemade job. On the other hand was the inevitable H.A.T.E. In the fold between his thumb and forefinger, was a crude blue crucifix. Next to that, a tiny red-eyed spider climbed a tiny web above the legend NR.

He put his hands in his pocket.

'How's your day?' Evelyn asked him. She looked as if she wanted to touch him.

'Okay.' He sniffed.

'Hungry?'

'Yeah, I could eat.' The tattooed hands emerged and rubbed together. 'Gotta wash up.'

'Sure, *patron*.'

He went into the house.

'Well,' she told me, 'I'd better get into the kitchen. Guess it's too late for you to talk to them, but you can come back tomorrow.'

'Great.'

We walked inside. Chondra and Tiffani were on the sofa in the rear den, watching cartoons on t.v. A cat was being cheerfully decapitated. Tiffani held the remote control.

'Bye, girls.'

Glazed eyes.

'Say bye to the doctor.'

The girls looked up. Small waves and smiles.

'I'm leaving now,' I said. 'I'll be coming out here tomorrow, maybe we can get a chance to talk.'

'See you,' said Tiffani. She nudged her sister. Chondra said, 'Bye.'

Evelyn was gone. I found her out in the kitchen, pulling something out of the freezer. Rodriguez was stretched back in the velveteen recliner, eyes closed, a beer in his hand.

'See you tomorrow.'

'One sec.' Evelyn came over. The package in her hand was a diet frozen entrée. Enchilada Fiesta. 'Better be the day after – I forgot there's some things I got to do.'

'Okay. Same time?'

'Sure.' She looked at the frozen package, and shook her head.

'How 'bout New York steak?' she called out to her husband.

'Yeah,' he said, without opening his eyes.

'He likes his steak,' she said quietly. 'For a fella his size, he's a real meat-eater.'

She followed me all the way out to the front lawn. Looked at the t.v. dinner in her hand. 'No one likes this one, maybe I'll have it.'

I hit bad traffic on the western end of the 210 and by the time I pulled into the carport, it was after seven. When I got in the house, the dog greeted me, but he had his head down and looked subdued. I smelled the reason first, then saw it, on the service porch floor near the door.

'Oh,' I said.

He drooped lower.

'My mistake for locking you in.' I rubbed his neck and he gave me a grateful lick, then trotted over to the fridge.

'Let's not push things, bucko.'

I cleaned up the mess, reflecting on the responsibilities of pet foster-parenthood, and phoned in for messages, wondering if anyone had responded to my ad. No one had. Nothing from Shirley Rosenblatt, Ph.D., either. Or Mr. Silk. The operator gave me a few business calls. I decided to put the tape out of my mind, but the child's chant stayed there and I couldn't sit still.

I fed the dog and was contemplating what to do about my own dinner when Milo called at eight-ten.

'No prints on the tape but yours. Any mail problems today?' He sounded tired.

'No, but I did get a call.' I told him about the giggling man.

'Silk, huh? Well, that's a pisser.'

'What is?'

'Sounds like you've got a nutcase on your hands.'

'You don't think it's serious?'

Pause. 'Most of these guys are cowards, like to stay in the background. But to be honest, Alex, who knows?'

I said, 'I think I may have found what bad love means,' and filled him in about the symposium.

'Seventy-nine,' he said. 'Nut with a real long memory.'

'Think that's a bad sign?'

'I – let's put our heads together and hash it out. You eat yet?'

'Nope.'

'I'm over in Palms, got to finish up a few things. I could meet you at that place on Ocean in about half an hour.'

'Don't think I'd better,' I said. 'Left my guest alone too long already.'

62

'What guest? Oh, him. Why can't you leave him? Is he lonely and depressed?'

'It's more of a gastrointestinal issue,' I said, rubbing the dog behind the ears. 'He just ate and will be needing easy ingress and egress.'

'Ingr— oh . . . *fun*. Well, get a dog door, Alex. Then, get a *life*.'

'A dog door means sawing a hole. He's only a short-term lodger.'

'Suit yourself.'

'Fine,' I said. 'I'll put a door in – Robin wants a dog anyway. How about you bring one over, I'll install it, and then we can go out.'

'Where the hell am I gonna find a dog door at this hour?'

'You're the detective.'

Slam.

He arrived at nine-fifteen, pulling an unmarked Ford into the carport. His tie was loose, he looked wilted, and he carried two bags – one from a pet store, the other from a Chinese restaurant.

The dog came up and nuzzled his cuffs and he gave the animal a grudging pat and said, 'Ingress the egress.'

Removing a metal and plastic contraption out of the pet store bag, he handed it to me. 'Seeing as I don't feel like manual labor before dinner and the *handy* resident of this household is out of town, I figured we'd better do takeout.'

He went over to the fridge, dog following.

Watching his slow trudge, I said, 'You look wiped. New blood buckets?'

He got a Grolsch, opened it, and nodded. 'Armed robbery, what I was working on in Palms. Little mom-and-pop grocery. Pop died a few months ago, mom's eighty, barely hanging on. Two little shits came in this afternoon, flashed knives, and threatened to rape her and cut off her breasts if she didn't hand over the cashbox. Old lady puts them at around thirteen or fourteen. She's too shook to say much else, chest pains, shortness of breath. They admitted her to St. John's for observation.'

'Poor thing. Thirteen or fourteen?'

'Yeah. The timing of the robbery might mean the little assholes waited till after school to do it – how's that for your extracurricular activities? Or maybe they're just your basic truant psychopaths out for a fun day.'

'Urban Huck and Tom,' I said.

'Sure. Smoke a corncob of crack, gangbang Becky Thatcher.'

He sat down at the table and sniffed the top of the beer bottle. The dog had remained at the refrigerator and was looking at him, as if contemplating approach, but Milo's tone and expression stilled him and he came over and settled at my feet.

I said, 'So no one else's prints were on the tape.'

'Not a one.'

'What does that mean? Someone took the trouble to wipe it clean?'

'Or handled it with gloves. Or there *were* prints and they got smeared when you touched the tape.' He stretched his legs. 'So show me this brochure you found.'

I went to the library, got the conference program, and gave it to him. He scanned it, 'No one named Silk here.'

'Maybe he was in the audience.'

'You look intense,' he said, pointing to my photo. 'That beard – kind of rabbinic.'

'Actually, I was bored.' I told him how I'd become a co-chair.

He put down his bottle. 'Nineteen seventy-nine. Someone carrying around a grudge all this time?'

'Or something happened recently that triggered a recollection from seventy-nine. I tried calling Katarina and Rosenblatt, to see if maybe they'd gotten anything in the mail, but she's closed up shop in Santa Barbara and he's no longer practicing in Manhattan. I found a psychologist in New York who may be his wife and left her a message.'

He examined the brochure again. 'So what could the grudge be about?'

'I have no idea, Milo. Maybe it's not even the conference, maybe it's someone who sees himself as victimized by the therapist – or the therapy. Maybe the grievance isn't even real – something paranoid – a delusion that would never occur to you or me.'

'Meaning we're normal?'

'Everything's relative.'

He smiled. 'So you can't remember anything weird happening at the conference.'

'Nothing at all.'

'This de Bosch – was he controversial in any way? The kind to make enemies?'

'Not that I know, but my only contact for him was through his writings. They're not controversial.'

'What about the daughter?'

I thought about that. 'Yeah, she could have made enemies – a real sourpuss. But if she's the target of someone's resentment, why would I be? My only link to her was the conference.'

He waved the brochure. 'Reading this, someone could believe you were esteemed colleagues. She hemmed you in, huh?'

'Expertly. She had clout with the medical director of the hospital. My guess was that it was because she'd treated one of his daughters – a kid with problems – and called in a marker. But it could have been something else completely.'

He put his beer bottle down on the coffee table. The dog looked up then lowered its chin to the floor.

'The kid's voice on the tape,' I said. 'How does that figure in? And the guy who killed Becky Basille – '

'Hewitt. Dorsey Hewitt. Yeah, I know, what does he have to do with it?'

'Maybe he was treated by the de Bosches, too. Maybe "bad love" was a phrase they used in therapy. But what does that mean? A whole slew of therapy graduates freaking out – getting back at their doctors?'

He handed the brochure back to me. 'Wonder if Donald Wallace was ever treated by the de Bosches – still waiting for more info from the prison. How're those girls doing?'

'The kinds of problems you'd expect, documenting a good case against visitation shouldn't be a problem. The grandmother's opening up a bit, too. I went out to the house this afternoon. Her latest husband looks like a retired cholo – lots of homemade tattoos.'

I described Rodriguez's skin art.

'Dealing with the elite,' he said. 'You and me both.' He crossed his legs and glanced down at the dog: 'C'mere, Rove.'

The dog ignored him.

'Good dog,' he said, and drank his beer.

He left at ten-thirty. I decided to put off installing the dog door till the next day. Robin called at ten-fifty and told me she'd decided, definitely, to come home early tomorrow evening at nine. I wrote down her flight number and said I'd be at LAX to pick her up, told her I loved her and went to sleep.

I was dreaming about something pleasantly sexual when the dog woke me just after three in the morning, growling and pawing the dust ruffle.

I groaned. My eyes felt glued shut.

He pawed some more.

'What?'

Silence.

Scratch scratch.

I sat up. 'What is it?'

He did the old-man-choking-bit.

Ingress and egress . . .

Cursing myself for not installing the door, I forced myself out of bed and made my way, blindly, through the dark house, to the kitchen. When I opened the porch door, the dog raced down the stairs. I waited, yawning and groggy, muttering, 'Make it fast.'

Instead of stopping to squat near the bushes, he kept going and was soon out of sight.

'Ah, exploring new ground.' I forced one eye to stay open. Cool air blew in through the door. I looked outside, couldn't see him in the darkness.

When he didn't return after a minute or so, I went down to get him. It took a while to find him, but I finally did – sitting near the carport, as if guarding the Seville. Huffing, and moving his head from side to side.

'What is it, guy?'

Pant, pant. He moved his head faster but didn't budge his body.

I looked around some more, still unable to see much. The mixed smells of night-blooming plants hit my nose and the first spray of dew moistened my skin. The night sky was hazy, just a hint of moonlight peeking through. Just enough to turn the dog's eyes yellow.

'Hound of the Basketballs,' I said, remembering an old *Mad* magazine sketch.

The dog scratched the ground and sniffed, started turning his head from side to side.

'*What?*'

He began walking toward the pond, stopping several feet from the fence, just as he had during our first encounter. Then he came to a dead halt.

The gate was closed. It had been hours since the timed lights had shut off. I could hear the waterfall. Peering over the fence,

I caught a glimpse of moonstreaked wetness as my eyes started to accommodate.

I looked back at the dog.

Still as a rock.

'Did you hear something?'

Head cock.

'Probably a cat or a possum, pal. Or maybe a coyote, which might be a little too much for you, no offense.'

Head cock. Pant. He pawed the ground.

'Listen, I appreciate your watchfulness, but can we go back up now?'

He stared at me. Yawned. Gave a low growl.

'I'm bushed, too,' I said, and headed for the stairs. He did nothing until I'd gotten all the way up, then raced up with a swiftness that belied his bulk.

'No more interruptions, okay?'

He wagged his stub, cheerfully, jumped on the bed and sprawled across Robin's side.

Too exhausted to argue, I left him there.

He was snoring long before I was.

Wednesday morning I assessed my life: crank letters and calls, but I could handle that if it didn't accelerate. And my true love returning from the wilds of Oakland. A balance I could live with. The dog licking my face belonged in the plus column, too, I supposed. When I let him out, he disappeared again and stayed out.

This time he'd gotten closer to the gate, stopping only a couple of feet from the latch. I pushed it open and he took another step.

Then he stopped, stout body angling forward.

His little frog face was tilted upward at me. Something had caused it to screw up, the eyes narrowing to slits.

I anthropomorphized it as conflict – struggling to get over his water phobia. Canine self-help hampered by the life-saving training some devoted owner had given him.

He growled and jutted his head toward the gate.

Looking *angry*.

Wrong guess? Something near the pond bothering him?

The growls grew louder. I looked over the fence and saw it.

One of my koi – a red and white *kohaku*, the largest and prettiest of the surviving babies – was lying on the moss near the water's edge.

A jumper. Damn.

Sometimes it happened. Or maybe a cat or coyote *had* gotten in. And that's what he'd heard . . .

But the body didn't look torn up.

I opened the gate and went in. The bulldog stepped up to the gatepost and waited as I kneeled to inspect the fish.

It *had* been torn. But no four-legged predator had done it.

Something was sticking out of its mouth – a twig, thin, stiff, a single shriveled red leaf still attached.

A branch from the dwarf maple I'd planted last winter.

I glanced over at the tree, saw where the bough had been cut off, the wound oxidized almost black.

Clean cut. Hours old. A knife.

I forced my eyes back to the carp.

The branch had been jammed down its gullet and forced down through its body, like a spit. It exited near the anus, through a ragged hole, ripping through beautiful skin and letting loose a rush of entrails and blood that stained the moss cream-gray and rusty brown.

I filled with anger and disgust. Other details began to leap out at me, painful as spattering grease.

A spray of scales littering the moss.

Indentations that might have been footprints.

I took a closer look at them. To my untrained eye, they remained characterless gouges.

Leaves beneath the maple, where the branch had been sheared.

The fish's dead eyes stared up at me.

The dog was growling.

I joined in and we did a duet.

7

I dug a grave for the fish. The sky was Alpine-clear and the beauty of the morning was a mockery of my task.

I thought of another beautiful sky – Katarina de Bosch's slide show. Azure heavens draping her father's wheelchaired form.

Good love/bad love.

Definitely more than just a sick joke now.

Flies were divebombing the koi's torn corpse. I nudged the body into the hole and shoveled dirt over it as the bulldog watched.

'Should have taken you more seriously last night.'

He cocked his head and blinked, brown eyes gentle.

The dirt over the grave was a small umber disc that I tamped with my foot. After taking one last look, I dragged myself up to the house. Feeling like a dependent child, I called Milo. He wasn't in and I sat at my desk, baffled and angry.

Someone had trespassed my property. Someone had watched me.

The blue brochure was on my desk, my name and photo the perfect logic of trumped-up evidence.

Reading this, someone could believe you were esteemed colleagues.

I phoned my service. Still no callback from Shirley Rosenblatt, Ph.D. Maybe she wasn't Harvey's wife . . . I tried her number again, got the same recorded message and slammed down the phone in disgust.

My hand started to close around the brochure, crumpling it, then my eyes dropped to the bottom of the page and I stopped and smoothed the stiff paper.

Other names.

The three other speakers.

WILBERT HARRISON, M.D., FACP,
Practicing Psychoanalyst
Beverly Hills, California

GRANT P. STOUMEN, M.D., FACP,
Practicing Psychoanalyst
Beverly Hills, California

MITCHELL A. LERNER, M.S.W., ACSW
Psychoanalytic Therapist
North Hollywood, California.

Harrison, chubby, around fifty, fair, and jolly-looking, with dark-rimmed glasses. Stoumen older, bald and prunefaced with a waxed, white mustache. Lerner, the youngest of the three, Afroed and turtlenecked, full-bearded, like Rosenblatt and myself.

I had no memory beyond that. The topics of their papers meant nothing to me. I'd sat up on the dais, mind wandering, angry about being there.

Three locals.

I opened the phone book. Neither Harrison nor Lerner were in there but Grant P. Stoumen, M.D. still had an office on North Bedford Drive – Beverly Hills couch row. A service operator answered, 'Beverly Hills Psychiatric, this is Joan.'

Same service I used. Same voice I'd just spoken to.

'It's Dr. Delaware, Joan.'

'Hi, Dr. Delaware! Fancy talking to you so soon.'

'Small world,' I said.

'Yeah – no, actually, it happens all the time, we handle lots of psych docs. Who in the group are you trying to reach?'

'Dr. Stoumen.'

'Dr. Stoumen?' Her voice lowered. 'But he's gone.'

'From the group?'

'From – uh . . . from life, Dr. Delaware. He died six months ago, didn't you hear?'

'No,' I said. 'I didn't know him.'

70

'Oh . . . well, it was really pretty sad. So unexpected, even though he was pretty old.'

'What did he die of?'

'A car accident. Last May, I think it was. Out of town, I forget exactly where. He was at some kind of convention and got run over by a car. Isn't that terrible?'

'A convention?'

You know, one of those medical meetings. He was a *nice* man, too – never lost patience the way some of the – ' Nervous laugh. 'Scratch *that* comment, Dr. D. Anyway, if you're calling about a patient, Dr. Stoumen's were divided up among the rest of the doctors in the group and I can't be sure which one took the one you're calling about.'

'How many doctors are in the group?'

'Carney, Langenbaum, and Wolf. Langenbaum's on vacation but the other two are in town, take your pick.'

'Any recommendations?'

'Well . . .' Another nervous laugh. 'They're both – all right. Wolf tends to be a little better about returning calls.'

'Wolf'll be fine. Is that a him or a her?'

'A him. Stanley Wolf, M.D. He's in session right now. I'll put a message.'

'Thanks a lot, Joan.'

'Sure bet, Dr. D. Have a nice day.'

I installed the dog door, making slow progress because I kept pausing between saw-swings and hammer blows, convinced I'd heard footsteps in the house or unwarranted noise out on the terrace.

A couple of times I actually went down to the garden and looked around, hands clenched.

The grave was a dark ellipse of dirt. Dried fishscales and a slick gray-brown stain marked the pond bank.

I went back up, did some touch-up painting around the door-frame, cleaned up and had a beer. The dog tried his new passageway, ingressing and egressing several times and enjoying himself.

Finally, tired and panting, he fell asleep at my feet. I thought about who'd want to scare me or hurt me. The dead fish stayed in my head, a cognitive stench, and I remained wide awake. At eleven, he awoke and raced for the front door. A moment later, the mailchute filled.

Standard-sized envelopes that I sorted through. One had a Folsom POB return address and an eleven digit serial number hand-printed above it in red ink. Inside was a single sheet of ruled notebook paper, printed in the same red.

Doctor A. Delaware, Ph.D.

Dear Dr. Delaware, Ph.D.:

I am writing to you to express my feelings about seeing my daughters, namely Chondra Wallace and Tiffani Wallace, as their natural father and legal guardian.

Whatever was done to our family including done by myself and no matter how bad is in my opinion, water under the bridge. And such as it is, I should not be denied permission and my paternity rights to see my lawful, legal daughters, Chondra Wallace and Tiffani Wallace.

I have never done anything to hurt them and have always worked hard to support them even when this was hard. I don't have any other children and need to see them for us to have a family.

Children need their fathers as I'm sure I don't have to tell a trained doctor like yourself. One day I will be out of incarceration. I am their father and will be taking care of them. Chondra Wallace and Tiffani Wallace need me. Please pay attention to these facts.

Yours sincerely,
Donald Dell Wallace

I filed the letter in the thick folder, next to the coroner's report on Ruthanne. Milo called at noon and I told him about the fish. 'Makes it more than a prank, doesn't it?'

Pause. 'More than I expected.'

'Donald Dell knows my address. I just got a letter from him.'

'Saying what?'

'One day he'll be out and wanting to be a full-time dad, so I shouldn't deny him his rights now.'

'Subtle threat?'

'Could you prove it?'

'No, he could have gotten your address through his lawyer – you're reviewing his claim, he'd be entitled to it legally. Incidentally, according to my sources he doesn't have an audio-recorder in his cell. T.V. and VCR, yes.'

'Cruel and unusual. So what do I do?'

'Let me come over and check out your pond. Notice any footprints or obvious evidence?'

'There were some prints,' I said, 'though they didn't look like much to my amateur eyes. Maybe there's some other evidence that I wasn't sophisticated enough to spot. I was careful not to disturb anything – oh, hell, I buried the fish. Was that a screw-up?'

'Don't worry about it, it's not like we're gonna do an autopsy.' He sounded uneasy.

'What's the matter?' I said.

'Nothing. I'll come by and have a look as soon as I can. Probably the afternoon.'

He spoke the last words tentatively, almost turning the statement into a question.

I said, 'What is it, Milo?'

'What it is, is that I can't do any full court press for you on this. Killing a fish just isn't a major felony – at the most we've got trespassing and malicious mischief.'

'I understand.'

'I can probably take some footprint-molds myself,' he said. 'For what it's worth . . .

'Look,' I said, 'I still don't consider it a federal case. This is cowardly bullshit. Whoever's behind it probably doesn't want a confrontation.'

'Probably not,' he said. But he still sounded troubled and that started to rattle me.

'Something else,' I said. 'Though it's also probably no big deal. I was looking at the conference brochure again and tried to contact the three local therapists who gave speeches. Two weren't listed, but the one who was had been killed this past summer. Car crash while attending a psychiatric symposium. I found out because his answering service just happens to be the same one I use and the operator told me.'

'Killed here in L.A.?'

'Out of town, she didn't remember where. I've got a call in to one of his associates.'

'Symposium,' he said. 'Curse of the conference?'

'Like I said, it's probably nothing – the only thing that is starting to bug me is I can't reach anyone associated with the de Bosch meeting. Then again, it's been a long time, people move.'

'Yeah.'

'Milo, *you're* bugged about something. What is it?'

Pause. 'I think given everything that's been happening, putting it all together and you'd be justified getting a little – watchful. No paranoia, just extra-careful.'

'Fine,' I said. 'Robin's coming home early – tonight. I'm picking her up at the airport. What do I tell her?'

'Tell her the truth, she's a tough kid.'

'Some welcome home.'

'What time are you picking her up?'

'Nine.'

'I'll get over well before then and we'll put our heads together. You want, I can stay at the house while you're gone. Just feed me and water me and tell Rover not to make demands.'

'Rover's who heard the intruder.'

'Yeah, but there was no *follow-through*, Alex. Instead of *eating* the sucker, he just stood around and watched. What you've *got* is a four-legged bureaucrat.'

'That's cold,' I said. 'Didn't you ever watch *Lassie*?'

'Screw that, my thing was *Godzilla*. There's a useful pet.'

By three, no one had returned my calls and I felt like a cartoon man on a desert island. I did paperwork and looked out the window a lot. At three thirty, the dog and I hazarded a walk around the Glen and when I arrived back home, there were no signs of intrusion.

Shortly after four, Milo arrived, looking hurried and bothered. When the dog came up to him, he paid no mind.

He held an audiocasette in one hand, his vinyl attaché case in the other. Instead of making his usual beeline to the kitchen, he went into the living room and loosened his tie. Putting the case on the coffee table, he handed me the tape.

'The original's in my file, this is your copy.'

Seeing it brought back the screams and the chants. That child . . . I put it in my desk and we went down to the pond, where I showed him the footprints.

He kneeled and inspected for a long time. Stood, frowning. 'You're right, these are useless. Looks to me like someone took the time to mess them up.'

He checked around the pond area some more, taking his time, getting his pants dirty. 'Nope, nothing here worth a damn. Sorry.'

That same troubled tone in his voice that I'd heard over the phone. He was holding back something, but I knew it was useless to probe.

Back in the living room, I said, 'Something to drink?'

'Later.' He opened the vinyl case and took out a brown, plastic box. Removing a videocasette from it, he bounced it against one thigh.

The tape was unmarked but the box was printed with the call letters of a local t.v. station. Rubber-stamped diagonally across the label was the legend PROPERTY LAPD: EVIDENCE RM. and a serial number.

'Dorsey Hewitt's last stand,' he said. 'Definitely not for prime time but there's something I want you to check out – if your stomach can take it.'

'I'll cope.'

We went into the library. Before inserting the cartridge into the VCR, he peered into the machine's load slot.

'When's the last time you lubricated this?'

'Never,' I said. 'I hardly use it except to record sessions when the court wants visuals.'

He sighed, slid the cartridge in, picked up the remote control, pressed PLAY and stood back, watching the monitor with his hands folded across his waist. The dog jumped up on a big leather chair, settled, and regarded him. The screen went from black to bright blue and a hiss filtered through the speakers.

A half minute more of blue, then the t.v. station logo flashed over a digital date, two months old.

Another few moments of video-stutter were followed by a long shot of an attractive, one-story brick building, with a central arch leading to a courtyard and wood-grilled windows. Tile roof, brown door to the right of the arch.

Close up on a sign: *Los Angeles County Mental Health Center. Westside.*

Swing-back to longshot: two small, dark-garbed figures crouched on opposite sides of the arch – toy-like. G.I. Joe figurines holding rifles.

A side shot revealed police barriers fencing the street.

No sound other than static but the dog's ears had perked and pitched forward.

Milo raised the volume and a soup of incomprehensible background speech could be heard above the white noise.

Nothing for a few seconds, then one of the dark figures moved, still squatting, and repositioned itself to the left of the door. Another figure came from around a corner and lowered itself to a deep crouch, both hands on its weapon.

A close-up inflated the new arrival, turning dark cloth into navy blue, revealing the bulk of protective vesting, white letters spelling out LAPD across a broad back. Combat boots. Blue ski mask revealing only eyes; I thought of Munich terrorists and knew something bad was going to happen.

But nothing did for the next few moments. The dog's ears were still stiff and his breathing had quickened.

Milo rubbed one shoe with another and ran his hand over his face. Then the brown door on the screen swung open on two people.

A man, bearded, long-haired, scrawny. The beard, a matted frenzy of blond and gray corskcrews. Above a blemished, knotted forehead, his hair haloed in spiky clumps, recalling a child's clumsily drawn sun.

The camera moved in on him, highlighting dirty flesh, sunken cheeks, bloodshot eyes so wide and bulging they threatened to shoot off the shaggy launchpad of his face.

He was naked from the waist up and sweating furiously. The wild eyes began rotating madly, never blinking, never settling. His mouth was agape, like a dental patient's, but no sound issued forth. He appeared to be toothless.

His left arm was clamped around a heavy black woman, imbedded so tightly in her soft, skirted waist that the fingers disappeared.

The skirt was green. Over it the woman wore a white blouse that had come partially untucked. She was around thirty-five and her face was wet, too – perspiration and tears. *Her* teeth were visible, lips stretched back in a rictus of horror.

The man's right arm was a bony yoke around her neck. Something silvery flashed in his hand as he pressed it up against her throat.

She closed her eyes and kept them clenched.

The man was leaning her back, pressing her to him, convexing her neck and revealing the full breadth of a big, shiny carving knife. Red-stained hands. Red-stained blade. Only her heels touched the pavement. She was off-balance, an unwilling dancer.

The man blinked, darted his eyes and looked at one of the SWAT cops. Several rifles were aimed at him. No one moved.

The woman trembled and the collaring hand moved involuntarily and brought forth a small red mark from her neck. The blotch stood out like a ruby.

She opened her eyes and stared straight ahead. The man screamed something to her, shook her, and they closed again.

The camera stayed on the two of them, then shifted smoothly to another of the SWAT men.

No one moved.

The dog was standing on the chair, breathing hard.

The bearded man's knife elbow quivered.

The man closed his mouth, opened it. Looked to be screaming at the top of his lungs, but the sound wasn't carrying.

The woman's mouth was still open. Her wound had already coagulated – just a nick.

The man propelled her onto the sidewalk, very slowly. One of her shoes came off. He didn't notice it, was looking from side to side, cop to cop, screaming nonstop.

All at once the sound came on. Very loud. New microphone.

The dog began barking.

The man with the knife screamed, a howling, hoarse and wet.

Panting. Wordless.

Pain-scream.

My hands dug into my thighs. Milo faced the screen, immobile.

The bearded man shifted his head from side to side some more, faster, harder, as if being slapped. Screaming louder. Pressing the knife up under the woman's chin.

Her eyes shot open.

The dog's barks turned to growls, guttural and bearish, loud enough to be scary and a lot more threatening than the warning sounds he'd uttered last night.

The man with the knife was directing his screams at a SWAT man to his left, haranguing wordlessly, as if the two of them were friends turned hateful.

The cop might have said something because the madman upped his volume.

Roaring. Shrieking.

The man backed away, hugging the woman more tightly, concealing his face behind hers as he dragged her into the doorway.

Then a smile and a short, sharp twist of his wrist.

Another spot of blood – larger than the first – formed on the woman's throat.

She raised her hands reflexively, trying to bend out from under the knife, losing her balance and stumbling.

Her weight and the movement surprised the man and for one brief moment, as he tried to keep her upright and haul her backward, he lowered his right arm.

A quick, sharp sound like a single handclap and a red dot appeared on the man's right cheek.

He spread his arms. Another dot materialized, just left of the first one.

The woman fell to the pavement as a rain of gunfire sounded – corn popping in an echo chamber. The man's hair blew back. His chest burst, and the front of his face turned into something amoebic and rosy – a pink and white kaleidoscope that seemed to unfold as it imploded.

The hostage was face down, fetal. Bloodspray showered down on her.

The man, now faceless, slumped and sagged, but he remained on his feet for one hellish second, a gore-topped scarecrow, still gripping the knife as red juice poured out of his head. He had to be dead but he continued to stand, bending at the knees, his ruined head shadowing the hostage's shoulder.

Then all at once he let go of the knife and collapsed, falling on the woman, limp as a blanket. She twisted and struck out at him, finally freed herself and managed to rise to her knees, sobbing and covering her head with her hands.

Policemen ran to her.

One of the dead man's bare feet was touching her leg. She didn't notice it but a cop did and he kicked it away. Another officer, still ski-masked, stood over the faceless corpse, legs spread, gun pointed.

The screen went black. Then bright blue.

The dog was barking again, loud and insistent.

I made a shushing sound. He looked at me, cocked his head. Stared at me, confused. I went over to him and patted his back. His back muscles were jumping and drool trickled from his flews.

'It's okay, fella.' My voice sounded false and my hands were cold. The dog licked one of them and looked up at me.

'It's okay,' I repeated.

Milo rewound the tape. His jaw was bunched.

How long had the scene lasted – a few minutes? I felt as if I'd aged watching it.

I stroked the dog some more. Milo stared at the numbers on the VCR's counter.

'It's him, isn't it?' I said. 'Hewitt. Screaming on my tape?'

'Him or a good imitation.'

'Who's the poor woman?'

'Another social worker at the center. Adeline Potthurst. She just happened to be sitting at the wrong desk when he ran out after killing Becky.'

'How is she?'

'Physically, she's okay – minor lacerations. Emotionally?' He shrugged. 'She took disability leave. Refused to talk to me or anyone else.'

He ran a hand along the edge of a bookshelf, grazing book-spines and toys.

'How'd you figure it out?' I said. 'Hewitt on the "bad love" tape?'

'I'm not sure what I figured, actually.'

He shrugged. His forelock cast a hat-brim shadow over his brow and in the weak light of the library, his green eyes were drab.

The tape ejected. Milo put it on an end table and sat down. The dog waddled over to him and this time Milo looked pleased to see him.

Rubbing the animal's thick neck, he said, 'When I first heard *your* tape, something about it bugged me, reminded me of something. But I didn't know what it was so I didn't say anything to you. I figured it was probably "bad love" – Hewitt's using the phrase, my reading about it in the clinic director's witness report.'

'Had you watched the video before?'

He nodded. 'But at the station with half an ear, a bunch of other detectives sitting around, cheering when Hewitt bit it. Splatter's never been my thing, I was filling out forms, doing paperwork . . . When you told me about the tape, it still didn't trigger, but I wasn't that bugged. I figured what you did – a bad joke.'

'The phone call and the fish make it more than a joke, don't they?'

'The phone call, by itself, is stupidity – like you said, cowardly shit. Someone coming on your property in the middle of the night and *killing* something *is* more. All of it put *together* is more. How *much* more I don't know, but I'd rather be a little paranoid than get taken by surprise. After we spoke on the phone this afternoon I really wracked my brains about what was bothering me. Went back into the Basille files, found the video and watched it. And I realized it wasn't the phrase that I remembered, it was the *screams*. Someone had stuck Hewitt's screams on your little gift.'

He pulled his wet hand away from the dog's maws, looked at it, wiped it on his jacket.

'Where'd the video come from?' I said. 'T.V. station's raw footage?'

He nodded.

'How much of it was actually broadcast?'

'Not much at all. This t.v. station has a twenty-four-hour crimewatch van with a scanner – anything for the ratings, right? They got to the scene first and were the only ones to actually record the whole thing. Their total footage is ten minutes or so, mostly no-action standoff before Hewitt comes out with Adeline. What you just saw is thirty-five seconds.'

'That's all? It seemed a lot longer.'

'Seemed like a goddamn eternity, but that's what it was. The part that actually made it to the six o'clock news was *nine* seconds. Five of Hewitt with Adeline, three of Rambo closeups on the SWAT guys, and one second of Hewitt down. No blood, no screaming, no standing dead man.'

'Wouldn't sell deodorant,' I said, pushing the image of the teetering corpse out of my head. 'Why was the sound off for most of it? Technical difficulties?'

'Yup. Loose cable on their parabolic mike. The sound man caught it midway through.'

'What did the other stations broadcast?'

'Postmortem analysis by the department mouthpiece.'

'So if the screams on my tape were lifted, the source had to be this particular piece of footage.'

'Looks that way.'

'Meaning what? Mr. Silk's an employee of the t.v. station?'

'Or a spouse, kid, lover, pal, significant other, whatever. If you give me your patient list, I can try to get hold of the station's personnel records and crosscheck.'

'Be better if you give me the personnel list,' I said. 'Let me check it against my patients so I can preserve confidentiality.'

'Fine. Another list you might try to get is the one for your Bad

Love conference. Anyone who attended. It was a long time ago, but maybe the hospital keeps records.'

'I'll call them tomorrow.'

He got up and touched his throat. '*Now*, I'm thirsty.'

We went into the kitchen, opened beers, and sat at the table, drinking and brooding.

The dog positioned himself between us, licking his lips.

Milo said, 'He doesn't get to go for the gusto?'

'Teetotaler.' I got up and slid the water bowl over. The dog ignored it.

'Bullshit, he wants hops and malt,' said Milo. 'Looks like he's closed a few taverns in his day.'

'*There's* a marketing opportunity for you,' I said. 'Brew a hearty lager for quadrupeds. Though I'm not sure you could set your criteria too high for a species that imbibes out of the toilet.'

He laughed. I managed a smile. Both of us trying to forget the videotape. And everything else.

'There's another possibility,' I said. 'Maybe Hewitt's voice wasn't lifted from the video footage. Maybe he was taped simultaneously by someone at the mental health center. Someone who happened to have a recorder handy the day of the murder and switched it on during the standoff. There'd probably be machines lying around the center, for therapy.'

'You're saying there's a therapist behind this?'

'I was thinking more of a patient. Some paranoids make a fetish of keeping records. I've seen some lug tape recorders around with them. Someone who'd been bearing a grudge since seventy-nine could very well be highly paranoid.'

He thought about that. 'Nutcase with a pocket Sony, huh? Someone you once treated who ended up at the mental health center?'

'Or just someone who remembered me from the conference and ended up at the center. Someone tying me in with bad love whatever it means to him. Probably anger at bad therapy. Or therapy he perceived as bad. De Bosch's theory has to do with bad mothers letting their kids down. Betrayal. If you think of therapists as surrogate parents, the stretch isn't hard to make.'

He put down his bottle and looked at the ceiling. 'So we've got a nut, one of your old patients, gone downhill, can't afford private treatment so he's getting county help. Happens to be at the center the day Hewitt freaks out and butchers Becky. Recorder in his pocket – keeping tabs on all the people talking behind his back. He hears the screams, presses *Record* . . . I guess it's possible – anything's *possible* in this city.'

'If we're dealing with someone who's been stewing for a long time, witnessing Becky Basille's murder and the SWAT scene could have set him off. Hearing Hewitt screaming about bad love could have done it, too, if he'd had experiences with de Bosch or a de Boschian therapist.'

He rolled the bottle between his palms. 'Maybe. But two nuts with a "bad love" fixation just *happening* to show up at the same place on the same day is too damned cute for my taste.'

'Mine, too,' I said.

He drank some more.

'What if it wasn't a coincidence at all, Milo? What if Hewitt and the taper *knew* each other – even shared a common rage about bad love, de Bosch, therapists in general? If the mental health center's typical, it's a crowded place, patients waiting for hours. It wouldn't be that strange for two disturbed people to get together and discover a mutual resentment, would it? If they were paranoid to begin with, they could have played upon each other's fears and delusions. *Confirming* for each other that the way they saw the world was valid. The taper might even be someone who wouldn't have been violent under different circumstances. But seeing Hewitt murder *his* therapist and then seeing Hewitt's face blown off could have pushed him over.'

'So now he's ready to do his own therapist? So what's the tape and the call and the fish?'

'Preparing the scene. Or maybe he won't go any further, I don't know. And something else: I might not even be his only target. He might have a current therapist who's in danger.'

'Any idea who it could be? From your patient list?'

'No, that's the thing. There's no one who fits. But my patients were all kids. Lots can happen over time.'

He sat back in his chair and looked up at the ceiling.

'Speaking of kids,' he said. 'Where does the kid's voice fit in with your two-nut scenario?'

'I don't know, dammit. Maybe the taper's got a kid. Or he's abducted one – God, I hope not, but that voice stank of coercion, didn't it? So flat – did *Hewitt* have any children?'

'Nope, the report has him as unmarried, unemployed, unevery-thing.'

'Be good to know who he hung out with at the center. We could also try to verify that my tape was taken from the video footage. Because if it wasn't, we wouldn't have to bother cross-referencing the station personnel list.'

He smiled. 'And you wouldn't have to expose your patient list, right?'

'Right. That would be a major betrayal. I still can't justify it.'

'You're sure it's not any of them?'

'No, I'm not sure, but what am I going to do? Call hundreds of people and ask them if they've grown up to be hate-crazed nuts?'

'No Mr. Silk in your past, huh?'

'Only silk I know is in my ties.'

'One thing I can tell you, your tape's not an *exact* lift off the video. The footage has Hewitt screaming for just over twenty-seven seconds out of the thirty-five, and your segment only lasts sixteen. I had a brief go at it before I came over here – tried running both tapes simultaneously on two machines to see if I could pick out any segments that coincided exactly. I couldn't – it was tricky, going from machine to machine, on-off, on-off, trying to synchronize. And it's not like we're dealing with words, here – doesn't take long before all the screaming starts to sound the same.'

'What about doing some kind of voiceprint analysis? Trying to get an electronic match.'

'From what I know, you need actual words for a match. And the Department doesn't do voiceprints anymore.'

'Why not?'

'Probably not enough call. What they're useful for, mostly, is kidnapping ransom calls, and that's usually the FBI's game. Also phone scams, bunco stuff, which is low-priority with all the buckets of blood. I think one guy at the Sheriff's is still doing them. I'll find out.'

The dog finally put its head in the bowl and began slurping water. Milo lifted his bottle, said 'Cheers' and emptied it.

'Why don't you and I try a little bit of low-tech teamwork right now,' I said. 'You take audio, I'll take video – '

'And I'll be in Screamland afore ye.'

*   *   *

He took the portable tapedeck into the library and loaded the video. We sat across from one another, listening to screams, trying to shut out the context. Even with two people it was difficult – hard to divide the howls into discreet segments.

We played and rewound, doing it over and over, trying to locate the sixteen seconds of the bad love tape amid the pain and noise of the longer video segment. The dog tolerated only a minute or so before scooting out of the room.

Milo and I stayed and sweated.

After half an hour, a triumph of sorts.

A discrepancy.

A second or two of sing-song, wordless jabber at the tail end of my tape that didn't materialize anywhere on the soundtrack of the video.

Ya ya ya . . . the screamer lowering his volume just a bit, a barely discernible shift not much longer than an eyeblink. But once I pointed it out, it mushroomed, as obvious as a billboard.

'Two separate taping sessions,' I said, as stunned as Milo looked. 'Has to be, otherwise why would the shorter tape have something on it that's missing from the longer segment?'

'Yeah,' he said quietly, and I knew he was angry at himself for not catching it first.

He sprang to his feet and paced. Looked at his Timex. 'When'd you say you were going to the airport?'

'Nine.'

'If you're comfortable leaving the place unguarded, I could go get something done.'

'Sure,' I said, rising, 'What?'

'Talk to the clinic director about Hewitt's social life.'

He collected his things and we walked to the door.

'Okay, I'm off,' he said. 'Got the Porsche and the cellular, so you can always reach me if you need to.'

'Thanks for everything, Milo.'

'What're friends for?'

Ugly answers flashed in my head, but I kept them to myself.

8

_____

Just as I was preparing to head out for LAX, Dr. Stanley Wolf returned my call. He sounded middle-aged and spoke softly and hesitantly, as if doubting his own credibility.

I thanked him and said I'd called about Dr. Grant Stoumen.

'Yes, I got the message.' He asked several torturous questions about my credentials. Then: 'Were you a student of Grant's?'

'No, we never met.'

'Oh . . . what do you need to know?'

'I'm being harassed by someone, Dr. Wolf, and I thought Dr. Stoumen might be able to shed some light on it.'

'Harassed?'

'Annoying mail. Phone calls. It may be linked to a conference I co-chaired several years ago. Dr. Stoumen delivered a paper there.'

'A conference? I don't understand.'

'A symposium on the work of Andres de Bosch entitled "Good Love/Bad Love." The term "bad love" was used in the harassment.'

'How long ago was this?'

'Seventy-nine.'

'De Bosch – the child analyst?'

'Did you know him?'

'No, child analysis is outside of my . . . purview.'

'Did Dr. Stoumen ever talk about de Bosch – or this particular conference?'

'Not to my recollection. Nor did he mention any . . . annoying mail?

'Maybe annoying's too mild,' I said. 'It's fairly nasty stuff.'

'Uh hm.' He didn't sound convinced.

I said, 'Last night it went a little further. Someone trespassed my property. I have a fish pond. They took a fish out, killed it and left it for me to see.'

'Hmm. How ... bizarre. And you think this symposium's the link?'

'I don't know, but it's all I've got so far. I'm trying to contact anyone who appeared on the dais, to see if they've been harassed. So far everyone I've tried to reach has moved out of town. Do you happen to know a psychiatrist named Wilbert Harrison or a social worker named Mitchell Lerner?'

'No.'

'They also delivered papers. The co-chairs were de Bosch's daughter, Katarina, and a New York analyst named Harvey Rosenblatt.'

'I see ... well, as I mentioned I'm not a child analyst. And unfortunately, Grant's no longer with us, so I'm afrai— '

'Where did his accident take place?'

'Seattle,' he said, with sudden strength in his voice. 'At a conference as a matter of fact. And it wasn't a simple accident. It was a hit-and-run. Grant was heading out for a late night walk, he stepped off the curb in front of his hotel, and was struck down.'

'I'm sorry.'

'Yes, it was terrible.'

'What was the topic of the conference?'

'Something to do with child-welfare – the Northwest Symposium on Child Welfare, I believe. Grant, always an advocate for children.'

'Terrible,' I said. 'And this was in May?'

'Early June. Grant was on in years, his eyesight and hearing weren't too good. We prefer to think he never saw it or heard it coming.'

'How old was he?'

'Eighty-nine.'

'Was he still in practice?'

'A few old patients stopped by from time to time and he kept an office in the suite and insisted on paying his share of the rent. But mostly he traveled. Art exhibitions, concerts. And conferences.'

'His age made him a contemporary of Andres de Bosch,' I said. 'Did he ever mention him?'

'If he did, I don't recall it. Grant knew lots of people. He was in practice for almost sixty years.'

'Did he treat especially disturbed or violent patients?'

'You know I can't discuss his cases, Dr. Delaware.'

'I'm not asking about specific cases, just the general tenor of his practice.'

'The little that I saw was pretty conventional – children with adjustment problems.'

'Okay, thanks. Is there anyone else who could talk to me about him?'

'Just Dr. Langenbaum and he knows about as much as I.'

'Did Dr. Stoumen leave a widow?'

'His wife died several years ago and they had no children. Now I really do have to get going.'

'Thanks for your time, Dr. Wolf.'

'Yes . . . hmm. Good luck on . . . working this through.'

I got my car keys, left a lot of lights on in the house, and turned on the stereo to loud jazz. The dog was sleeping noisily on his blanket bed but he roused himself and followed me to the door.

'Stay and guard the homefront,' I said and he harumphed, stared for a moment, finally sat down.

I walked out, closed the door, listened for a protest and when I didn't hear any, went down to the carport. The night had cooled, massaged by a sea current. The waterfall seemed deafening and I drove away listening to it diminish.

As I coasted down toward the Glen, a sense of dread dropped over me, dark and smothering, like a condemned man's hood.

I paused at the bottom of the road, looking at black treetops and slate-sky. A faint bit of light from a distant house blinked through the foliage like an earthbound star.

No way to gauge its distance. I had no real neighbors because an acre-wide strip of county land, unbuildable due to a quirky water table, cut through this section of the Glen. Mine was the only buildable site on the plot plan.

Years ago the isolation had been just what I wanted. Now a nosy streetmate didn't seem half-bad.

A car sped down the Glen from the north, appearing suddenly around a blind curve, going too fast, its engine flatulent with power.

I tensed as it passed, took another look backward, and hooked right, toward the Sunset on-ramp of the 405 South. By the time I got on the freeway, I was thinking of Robin's smile and pretending nothing else mattered.

Slow night at the airport. Cabbies circled the terminals and skycaps looked at their watches. I found a space in the passenger loading zone and managed to stay there until Robin came out, toting her carry-on.

I kissed her and hugged her, took the suitcase and put it in the trunk of the Seville. A man in a Hawaiian shirt was looking at her over cigarette smoke. So were a couple of kids with backpacks and surfer hair.

She had on a black silk t-shirt and black jeans, and over that a purple and red kimono-type shirt tied around her waist. The jeans were tucked into black boots with tooled silver toes. Her hair was loose and longer than ever – well past her shoulder blades, the auburn curls bronzed by the light from the baggage claim area. Her skin gleamed and her dark eyes were clear and peaceful. It had been five days since I'd seen her, but it seemed like a long separation.

She touched my cheek and smiled. I leaned in for a longer kiss.

'Whoa,' she said, when we stopped, 'I'll go away more often.'

'Not necessary,' I said. 'Sometimes there is gain without pain.'

She laughed and hugged me and put her arm around my waist. I held the door open as she got in the car. The man in the Hawaiian shirt had turned his back on us.

As I drove away she put her hand on my knee and looked over at the back seat. 'Where's the dog?'

'Guarding hearth and home. How was your talk?'

'Fine. Plus I may have sold that archtop guitar I did last summer – the one Joe Shah defaulted on. I met a jazz musician from Dublin who wants it.'

'Great,' I said. 'You put a lot of time into that one.'

'Five hundred hours, but who's counting?'

She stifled a yawn and put her head on my shoulder. I drove all the way to Sunset before she woke up, shaking her curls. 'Boy . . . must have hit me all of a sudden.' Sitting up, she blinked at the streets of Bel Air.

'Home sweet home,' she said.

I waited until she'd roused herself before telling her the bad news.

She took it well.

'Okay,' she said, 'I guess it goes with the territory. Maybe we should move out for a while and stay at the shop.'

'Move out?'

'At least till you know what's going on.'

I thought of her studio, separated from the mean streets of Venice by a thin veneer of white windows and locks. Saws and drills and wood shavings on the ground floor. The sleeping loft in which we'd made love so many times . . .

'Thanks,' I said, 'but I can't stay away indefinitely, the house needs maintenance. Not to mention the fish that're left.'

That sounded trivial, but she said, 'That poor fish. And you worked so hard to keep them alive.'

She touched my cheek.

'Welcome home,' I said glumly.

'Don't worry about *that*, Alex. Let's just figure out how to deal with this stupidity until it's resolved.'

'I don't want to put you in any danger. Maybe *you* should move to the shop – '

'And leave you alone in the middle of this?'

'I just want to make sure you're okay.'

'How okay do you think I'm going to be, worrying every minute about you? I mean, the fish are wonderful, Alex, but you can hire someone to feed them. Hire someone to look after the whole house, for that matter.'

'Pack up the wagons and head out?'

'What's wrong with being a little cautious, honey?'

'I don't know . . . it just seems awfully drastic – all that's really happened is malicious mischief.'

'So why were you so upset when you told me about it?'

'Sorry. I didn't want to upset you.'

'Of *course* it upsets me,' she said. 'Someone sending you weird tapes, sneaking in and . . . ' She put her arm around my shoulder. The light changed to green and I turned left.

'Goes with the territory,' she repeated. 'All those troubled people you've worked with over the years. All that misdirected passion. The surprising thing isn't that it happened. It's how long it took.'

'You never said it worried you.'

'It wasn't a matter of worry – I didn't obsess on it. Just thought about it from time to time.'

'You never said anything.'

'What would have been the point? I didn't want to upset you.'

I lifted her hand from my shoulder and kissed it. 'Okay,' she said, 'so we protect each other, Curly. Ain't that what true love's all about?'

I pulled up in front of the house. No obvious signs of intrusion.

I said, 'Just let me check around for a sec before you get out.'

'Oh, really,' she said. But she stayed in the car. gave the pond a quick inspection. The fish moved with nighttime languor, and none was missing.

I jogged up the stairs to the landing, checked the front door, peered in through the living room window. Something moved as the drapes parted. The dog's face pressed against the glass, wetting it. I raised my hand in greeting. He pawed the window. I could hear the jazz through the redwood walls.

By the time I got back down, Robin was lifting her valise from the trunk. When I tried to take it from her, she said, 'I've got it,' and headed for the steps.

As I unlocked the front door, she said, 'We could at least get an alarm. Everyone else has one.'

'Never been a slave to fashion,' I said, but when she didn't smile, I added, 'Okay. I'll call a company tomorrow.'

We walked in and almost tripped over the bulldog, who'd positioned himself on the welcome mat. He stared from Robin to me, then back to her where he lingered, with Churchillian dignity.

Robin said, 'My God.'

'What?' I said.

'He *invented* cute, Alex. Come here, sweetie.' She bent down to his level with one hand extended, palm down.

He trotted forward without hesitation, jumped up, put his paws on her shoulders and embarked on a lick-fest.

'Ooh!' She laughed. 'What a *handsome* boy you are, what a cutie – look at those *muscles*!'

She stood, wiping her face, still laughing. The dog continued to nuzzle and paw her legs. His tongue was out and he was panting.

She placed a hand on my shoulder and gave me a grave look. 'Sorry, Alex, there is now another man in my life.' Bending she rubbed him behind the ears.

'Crushed,' I said, placing a hand over my heart. 'And you might reconsider – he doesn't have gonads.'

'Them's the breaks,' she said, smiling. 'Look at that *face*!'

'Also, he snores.'

'So do you, once in a while.'

'You never told me.'

She shrugged. 'I kick you and usually you stop – well, just look at *you*, you little hunk. Apathy's not *your* problem, *is* it?'

She knelt back down and got her face re-bathed. 'What a doll!'

'Think of the ramifications on your social life,' I said. 'Meatloaf and kibble by candlelight.'

She laughed again and roughed the dog's fur.

As the two of them played, I picked up the suitcase and carried it into the bedroom, checking rooms as I passed, trying not to be obvious. Everything looked fine. I took Robin's clothes out and arranged them on the bed.

When I got back, she was on the leather couch, the dog's head in her lap. 'I know this is heartless, Alex, but I hope his owner never calls – how long, legally, do you have to run the ad?'

'I'm not sure.'

'There's got to be a limit, right? Some sort of statute of limitations?'

'Probably.'

Her smile disappeared. 'With my luck someone'll show up tomorrow and cart him off.'

She covered another yawn. The dog looked at her, fascinated.

'Tired?' I said.

'A little. Everything okay around here? I'm sure you looked.'

'Perfect.'

'I'll get unpacked.'

'Did it,' I said. 'Why don't you run a bath and I'll put your stuff away then join you.'

'That's sweet of you, thanks.' She looked at the dog. 'See, he really is a nice guy, our Dr. D. How 'bout you – you like baths, too?'

'As a matter of fact, he hates the water. Won't even get near it. So it's just you and me, kid.'

'How Machiavellian of you – where does he sleep?'

'Last night he slept in the bed. Tonight he moves back into the kitchen.'

She pouted.

I shook my head. 'Uh uh, no way.'

'Oh, c'mon, Alex. It's just temporary'

'Do you want those eyes watching us?'

'Watching us do what?'

'The crossword puzzle.'

'He'll be lonely out there, Alex.'

'All of a sudden we're into voyeurism?'

'I'm sure he's a gentleman. And as you so unkindly pointed out, he has no . . .'

'Balls or no balls, he's a *nudist*, Robin. And he's got the hots for you. The kitchen.'

She tried a bigger pout.

I said, 'Put it out of your mind.'

'Cruel,' she said. 'Heartless and cruel.'

'Sounds like a law firm. Heartless, Cruel and Horny – think I'll put 'em on retainer.'

The dog posted himself at the bathroom door as Robin stepped into the suds. She soaped up, I picked him up and carried him, grumbling, to his blanket-bed. The moment I put him down, he tried to escape. I closed the kitchen doors, gave him a milk-bone and as he began chewing, I snuck out.

He fussed for a while, attempting a sonorous rendition of the old-man-choking bit, but I applied sound behavior theory principles and ignored him, while trying to suppress my guilt. After a minute or so he calmed down and soon I heard him galumping in two-four time.

When I got back, Robin looked at me reproachfully. Her hair was up and the water's soapy surface reached just below her nipples.

'He's fine.' I got out of my clothes. 'Enjoying the slumber of the truly virtuous.'

'Well,' she said, putting her arms behind her head and watching, 'I suppose it's best.'

'Forgiven?' I said, sinking into the heat of the bath.

She contemplated. Breathed in. Smiled.

'I don't know . . .'

92

I kissed her. She kissed back. I touched one breast, kissed a soapy nipple.

'Umm,' she said, breaking away. 'Well . . .'

'Well, what?'

'You can forget Mr. Cruel and Mr. Heartless, but I think it's time to take a meeting with their partner – what's his name?'

9

Thursday morning she was up and out of the shower by six-fifteen. When I got to the kitchen I expected to see her dressed for work, that restless look in her eyes.

But she was still in her robe, drinking coffee and reading *ArtForum*. She'd set out food for the dog and only a few bits remained. He was at her feet and looked up at me only briefly before returning his head to the side of her leg.

She put the magazine down and smiled up at me.

I kissed her and said, 'You can get going, I'll be fine.'

'What if I just want to be with you?'

'That would be great.'

'Of course, if *you* have other plans . . .'

'Nothing till the afternoon.'

'What's then?'

'Patient appointment out in Sun Valley at three-thirty.'

'Making a house call?'

I nodded. 'Custody case, some resistance and I want to see the kids in their natural environment.'

'Three-thirty? That's good. We can hang out together till then.'

'Terrific.' I poured myself a cup, sat down and pointed to the magazine. 'What's new in the art world?'

'The usual foolishness.' She closed it and pushed it aside. 'Actually I have no idea what's going on in the art world or anywhere else. I can't concentrate, Alex. Woke up in the middle of the night, thinking about everything that's been happening to you and that poor psychiatrist up in Seattle. Do you really think there is a connection?'

'I don't know. It was a hit-and-run but he was eighty-nine and couldn't see or hear well. Like Freud said, sometimes a cigar is just a cigar – did you get any sleep?'

'A bit.'

'Was I snoring?'

'No.'

'Would you tell me if I was?'

'Yes!' She gave my hand a gentle cuff.

'Why didn't you wake me to talk?' I said.

'You were deep asleep. I didn't have the heart.'

'Next time wake me.'

'We can talk right now, if you want. This whole thing's giving me very definite creeps the more I think about it. I'm worried about you – what will the next call or mail delivery bring?'

'Milo's looking into it,' I said. 'We'll get to the bottom of it.'

I took her hand and squeezed it. She squeezed back hard. 'You can't think of anyone who'd want to get back at you? Out of all the patients you've known?'

'Not really. I worked at the hospital, I saw physically ill kids. In practice, it was basically normal children with adjustment problems.' The same kinds of patients Grant Stoumen had treated.

'What about your legal cases? All that custody garbage?'

'Anything's possible, theoretically,' I said. 'But I've gone through my files and found nothing. The conference has to be the link – bad love.'

'What about that madman – Hewitt. Why was he shouting it?'

'I don't know,' I said.

She let go of my hand. 'He killed his therapist, Alex.'

'Guess I could switch careers. But I'm really not good for anything else.'

'Be serious.'

'Okay – what happened to Becky Basille is the extreme. It's a long way from tapes and a crank call and a mangled carp to murder.'

The look on her face made me add: 'I'll be careful scout's honor. I'll call an alarm company – get a referral from Milo.'

'You won't consider moving out – just for a while?'

'Let's just see what happens over the next few days.'

'What are you waiting for, Alex? Things to get worse – oh, never mind, let's not bicker.'

She got up, shaking her head, and went to the coffee pot for a refill. Stayed there drinking and looking out the window.

'Honey, I'm not trying to tough it out,' I said. 'I just want to see what Milo comes up with before I shake up our lives completely. Let's at least give him a day or two to look into it, okay? If he doesn't we'll move to the studio temporarily.'

'A day or two? You've got a deal.' The dog padded over to her. She smiled at him, then at me. 'Maybe I'm overdoing it. Was the tape that bad?'

'Bizarre,' I said. 'Like some kind of sick gag.'

'It's the *sick* part that bothers me.'

The dog snorted and jangled his collar. She took some cheese out of the fridge, told him to sit and rewarded his obedience with small bites. He gobbled noisily and licked his flews.

'What do you call this?' she said. 'Operant conditioning?'

'A-plus,' I said. 'Next week's topic is stress management.'

She grinned. The last bit of cheese disappeared amid the soft folds of the dog's mouth. Robin washed her hands. The dog continued to sit and stare at her. 'Shouldn't we give him a name, Alex?'

'Milo calls him Rover.'

'Figures.'

'I've stuck with "hey you" because I keep expecting someone to call and claim him.'

'True . . . why get attached . . . are you hungry? I can dish something up.'

'Why don't we go out?'

'Go out?'

'Like normal people.'

'Sure, I'll go change.'

The sparkle in her eyes made me say, 'How about changing into something semi-fancy and we can hit the Bel Air?'

'The Bel Air? What are we celebrating?'

'The new world order.'

'If only there was one. What about him?'

'Milk bone *en le kitchen*,' I said. 'I don't have a suit that fits him.'

*   *   *

She put on a silver crêpe de Chine blouse and a black skirt and I found a lightweight sportcoat, brown turtleneck and khaki slacks that looked decent. I told my service where I'd be and we took Sunset to Stone Canyon Road and drove up the half mile to the Bel Air Hotel. Pink-shirted valets opened our doors and we walked across the covered bridge to the main entrance.

Swans glided below in the still, green pond, cutting through the water in blissful ignorance. A white lattice marriage canopy was being set up on the banks. Huge pine and eucalyptus umbrellaed the grounds, air-conditioning the morning.

We passed through the pink stucco arcade hung with black and white photos of monarchs gone by. The stone pathways had been freshly watered, the ferns dripped dew, and the azaleas were in bloom. Room Service waiters rolled carts to sequestered suites. An emaciated, androgynous, long-haired thing in brown velvet sweats walked past us unsteadily, carrying the *Wall Street Journal* under one atrophied arm. Death was in its eyes and Robin bit her lip.

I held her arm tighter and we entered the dining room, exchanged smiles with the hostess, and were seated near the French doors. Several years ago – soon after we'd met – we'd lingered right here over dinner and seen Bette Davis through those same doors, gliding across the patio in a long, black gown and coronation-quality diamonds, looking as serene as the swans.

This morning, the room was nearly empty and none of the faces had a measurable Q-rating, though all looked well-tended: an Arab in an ice cream suit drank tea, alone, at a corner table. An elderly, dewlapped couple who could have been pretenders to a minor throne whispered to each other and nibbled on toast. In a big booth, on the far end, half a dozen dark suits sat listening to a crewcut, white-haired man in a red t-shirt and khakis. He was telling a joke, gesturing expansively with an unlit cigar. The other men's body language was half humble servant, half Iago.

We had coffee and took a long time deciding what to eat. Neither of us felt like talking. After a few moments, the silence began to feel like a luxury and I relaxed.

We finished a couple of fresh grapefruit juices and put in our breakfast order, holding hands until the food came. I'd just taken the first bite of my omelet when I spotted the hostess approaching. Two steps ahead of someone else.

A tall, broad someone, easily visible over her coiffure. Milo's jacket was light blue – a tint that clashed with his aqua shirt. Pigeon-gray pants and brown and blue striped tie rounded off the ensemble. He had his hands in his pockets and looked dangerous.

The hostess kept her distance from him, clearly wanting to be somewhere else. Just before she reached our table, he stepped ahead of her. After kissing Robin, he took a chair from another table and pulled it up perpendicular to us.

'Will you be ordering, sir?' said the hostess.

'Coffee.'

'Yes, sir.' She walked away hastily.

Milo turned to Robin. 'Welcome home. You look gorgeous, as ever.'

'Thank you, Milo – '

'Flight okay?'

'Just fine.'

'Every time I'm up in one of those things I wonder what gives us the right to break the Law of Gravity.'

Robin smiled. 'To what do we owe the pleasure?'

He ran his hand over his face. 'Has he told you about what's going on?'

She nodded. 'We're thinking of moving into the shop until things clear up.'

Milo grunted and looked at the tablecloth.

The waiter brought the coffee and a place setting. Milo unfolded the napkin over his lap and drummed a spoon on the table. As the coffee was being poured, he glanced around the room, lingering on the suits in the far booth.

'Meals and deals,' he said, after the waiter left. 'Either showbiz or crime.'

'There's a difference?' I said.

His smile was immediate but very weak – it seemed to torment his face.

'There's a new complication,' he said. 'This morning I decided to have a go at the computer, tracking down any references to "bad love" in the case files. I really didn't expect to find anything, just trying to be thorough. But I did. Two unsolved homicides, one three years old, the other five. One beating, one stabbing.'

'Oh God,' said Robin.

He covered her hand with his. 'Hate to spoil your breakfast, kids, but I wasn't sure when I'd be able to catch both of you. Service said you were here.'

'No, no, I'm glad you came.' She pushed her plate away and gripped Milo's hand.

'Who got killed?' I said.

'Does the name Rodney Shipler mean anything to you?'

'No. Is he a victim or a suspect?'

'Victim. What about Myra Paprock?'

He spelled it. I shook my head.

'You're sure?' he said. 'Neither of them could have been old patients?'

I repeated both names to myself. 'No – never heard of them. How does "bad love" figure into their murders?'

'With Shipler – he was the beating – it was scrawled on a wall at the crime scene. With Paprock, I'm not sure what the connection is yet. The computer just threw out "bad love" under "miscellaneous factors" – no explanation.'

'Did the same detectives work both cases?'

He shook his head. 'Shipler was in Southwest Division, Paprock over in the Valley. Far as I can tell, the cases were never cross-referenced – two years apart, different parts of the city. I'm going to try to get the actual case-files this afternoon.'

'For what it's worth,' I said, 'I spoke to Dr. Stoumen's associate last night. The accident was hit and run. It happened in Seattle, in June of last year.'

Milo's eyebrows rose.

'It may have just been a hit and run,' I said. 'Stoumen was almost ninety, couldn't see or hear well. Someone ran into him as he stepped off a curb.'

'At a psych conference?'

'Yes, but unless Shipler or Paprock were therapists, what link could there be?'

'Don't know what they were yet. The computer doesn't give out that level of detail.'

Robin's head had dropped, curls spilling onto the table. She looked up, clear-eyed. 'So what do we do?'

'Well,' said Milo, 'you know I'm not Mr. Impulsive, but with everything we've got here – nut mail, nut call, dead fish, two cold-case homicides, hazardous conferences.' He looked at me. 'Moving's not a bad idea. At least till we find out what the hell's going on. But I wouldn't go to the shop. Just in case whoever's bothering Alex has done enough research on him to know the location.'

She looked out the window and shook her head. He patted her shoulder.

She said, 'I'm fine. Let's just figure out where we're going to live.' She looked around. 'This place ain't shabby, too bad we're not oil sheiks.'

'As a matter of fact,' said Milo, 'I think I've got an option for you. Private client of mine – investment banker I moonlighted for last year. He's in England for a year, put his house up for rent and hired me to keep an eye on the premises. It's a nice size place and not that far from you. Beverly Hills PO, off Benedict Canyon. It's still empty – you know the real estate market – and he's coming back in three months, so he unlisted it. I'm sure I can get his permission for you to use it.'

'Benedict Canyon.' Robin smiled. 'Close to the Sharon Tate house?'

'Not far, but the place is as safe as you're gonna get. The owner's security conscious – has a big art collection. Electric gates, closed circuit t.v., screaming siren alarm.'

It sounded like prison. I didn't say a thing.

'The alarm's hooked up to Beverly Hills PD,' he went on. 'And their response time's averaging two minutes – maybe a little longer up in the hills, but still damn good. I'm not going to tell you it's home, chillun, but for temporary lodgings you could do worse.'

'And this client of yours won't mind?'

'Nah, it's a piece of cake.'

'Thanks, Milo,' said Robin. 'You're a doll.'

'No big deal.'

'What do I do about my work? Can I go to the shop?'

'Wouldn't hurt to avoid it for a few days. At least until I found out more about these unsolveds.'

She said, 'I had orders piled up before I went to Oakland, Milo. The time I spent up there already set me back.' She grabbed her napkin and crushed it. 'I'm sorry, here you are getting threatened, baby, and I'm griping . . .'

I took her hand and kissed it.

Milo said, 'In terms of work, you could set up shop in the garage. It's a triple and there's only one car in it.'

'That's big enough,' said Robin. 'But I can't just pack up the table saw and the band saw and cart them over.'

'I may be able to help you with that, too,' said Milo.

'An alternative,' I said, 'would be moving to the studio and hiring a guard.'

'Why take a chance?' said Milo. 'My philosophy is when trouble calls, don't be there to answer the doorbell. You can even take Rover with. Owner keeps cats – a friend's taking care of them now, but we're not talking pristine environment.'

'Sounds good,' I said, but my throat had gone dry and a refugee numbness was rising up from my feet. 'As long as we're talking critters, there're the rest of the koi. The pond maintenance people can probably board them for a while – time to get organized.'

Robin began folding her napkin, over and over, ending up with a small, thick wad that she pressed between her hands. Her knuckles were ivory knobs and her lips were clamped together. She gazed over my shoulder, as if peering into an uncertain future.

The waiter came over with the coffee pot and Milo waved him away.

From the big booth came the sound of male laughter. The levity had probably been going on for a while but I heard it now because the three of us had stopped talking.

The Arab got up from his table, smoothed his suit, put cash on the table, and left the dining room.

Robin said, 'Guess it's time to hitch up the wagons,' but she didn't move.

'This whole thing seems so unreal,' I said.

'Maybe it'll turn out we've hassled for nothing,' Milo said, 'but you two are among the few humans I hold any positive regard for, so I do feel an obligation to protect and serve.'

He looked at our barely-touched food and frowned. 'This'll set you back some.'

'Have some.' I pushed my plate toward him.

He shook his head.

'The stress diet,' I said. 'Let's write a book and hit the talk-show circuit.'

*　　*　　*

101

He followed us home in an unmarked Ford. When the three of us stepped into the house, the dog thought it was a party and began jumping around.

'Take a Valium, Rover,' said Milo.

'Be nice to him,' said Robin, kneeling and holding her arms out. The dog charged her and she tussled with him for a second, then stood. 'I'd better figure out what I'm going to need to take.'

She left for the bedroom, dog at heel.

'True love,' said Milo.

I said, 'Is there anything more you want to tell me?'

'You mean, am I shielding her from gory details? No. Didn't figure I should.'

'No, of course not,' I said. 'I just – I guess I still want to protect her . . .'

'Then you're doing the right thing by moving.'

I didn't answer.

'Nothing to be ashamed of,' he said. 'The protective instinct. I keep my work out of Rick's face, he does the same for me.'

'If anything happened to her . . .' From the back of the house came Robin's footsteps, rapid and intermittent.

Pause and decision.

Dull sounds as clothing hit the bed. Soft, sweet words as she talked to the dog.

I paced some more, circling, trying to focus . . . what to take, what to leave . . . looking at things I wouldn't be seeing for a while.

'Ring around the rosy,' he said. 'Now you're looking like me when I'm uptight.'

I ran my hand over my face. He laughed, unbuttoned his jacket and pulled a notepad and pen out of an inner pocket. He was wearing his revolver in a brown cowhide hip holster.

'Do *you* have any more details for me?' he said. 'Like about the psychiatrist – Stoumen?'

'Just the approximate date – early June – and the fact that the conference was the Northwest Symposium on Child Welfare. I'm pretty sure it's sponsored by the Child Welfare League and they have an office here in town. Maybe you can pry an attendance roster out of them.'

'You have a go at the Western Pediatric roster yet?'

'No. I'll try right now.'

I called the hospital and asked for the Office of Continuing Education. The secretary told me records of past symposia were only kept for one year. I asked her to check anyway and she did.

'Nothing, doctor.'

'There're no archives or anything?'

'Archives? With our budget problems we're lucky to get bedpans, doctor.'

Milo was listening in. When I hung up, he said, 'Okay, scratch that. Onward. I'm going to hook up with the FBI's violent crime data bank and see if "bad love" shows up on any out-of-town homicides.'

'What about Dorsey Hewitt?' I said. 'Could he have killed Shipler and Paprock?'

'Let me try to find out if he was living in L.A. during their murders. I'm still trying to get hold of Jean Jeffers, the clinic director – see if Hewitt had clinic buddies.'

'The taper,' I said. 'You know, that second session could have taken place the day of the murder – someone taping Hewitt right after he killed Becky. Before he ran out and the t.v. mikes picked him up. That's pretty damn cold – almost premeditated. Same kind of mind who could turn a child's voice robotic. What if the taper knew exactly what Hewitt was going to do and was ready to tape him.'

'An accomplice?'

'Or at least a knowing confederate. Someone who knew Becky was going to die but didn't stop it.'

He stared at me. Grimaced. Wrote something down. Said, 'Ready to start packing, now?'

It took an hour or so for Robin and me to throw together suitcases, plastic shopping bags, and cardboard cartons. A smaller collection than I would have expected.

Milo and I carried all of it into the living room then I called my pond maintenance people and arranged for them to collect the fish.

When I returned to the pile, Milo and Robin were staring at it. She said, 'I'm going to go over to the shop and get the small tools and the breakable things together – if that's okay.'

'Sure, just be careful,' said Milo. 'Anyone weird hanging around, just turn around and come back.'

'Weird? This is Venice we're talking about.'

'Relatively speaking.'

'Gotcha.' She took the dog with her. I walked her down to her truck and watched as they drove away. Milo and I had a couple of Cokes, then the doorbell rang and he went to get it. After looking through the peephole, he opened the door and let in three men – boys, really, around nineteen or twenty.

They were thick-faced and had power lifter's rhino physiques. Two white, one black. One of the white ones was tall. They wore perforated tank tops, knee-length baggies in nauseating color combinations and black, lace-up boots that barely closed around their tree-stump calves. The white boys had their hair cut very short, except at the back, where it fringed around their excessive shoulders. The black's head was shaved clean. Despite their bulk, all three seemed awkward – intimidated.

Milo said, 'Morning, campers, this is Dr. Delaware. He's a psychologist so he knows how to read your minds. Doctor, this is Keenan, Chuck and DeLongpre. They haven't figured out what to do with their lives yet, so they abuse themselves over at Silver's Gym and spend Keenan's money. Right, boys?'

The three of them smiled and cuffed one another. Through the open door I saw a black van parked near the carport. Jacked-up suspension, black-matte reversed hubcaps, darkened windows, diamond-shaped bulb of black plastic set into the side panel, a skull and bones decal just below that.

'Tasteful, huh?' said Milo. 'Tell Dr. Delaware who recovered your wheels for you, after a miscreant scumbag junkie made off with it because you left it on Santa Monica Boulevard with the key in the ignition?'

'You did, Mr. Sturgis,' said the shorter white boy. He had a crushed nose, puffy lips, a very deep voice and a slight lisp. The confession seemed to relieve him and he gave a big grin. One of his canines was missing.

'And who didn't charge you his usual private fee because you'd run out of trust-fund that month, Keenan?'

'*You* didn't, sir.'

'Was that a gift?'

'No, sir.'

'Am I a chump?'

Shake of the thick head.

'What did I demand in return, boys?'

'Slave labor!' they shouted in unison.

He nodded and rapped the back of one hand against the palm of the other. 'Payoff time. All this stuff goes into the Deathmobile. The really heavy gear's over in Venice – Pacific Avenue. Know where that is?'

'Sure,' said Keenan. 'Near Muscle Beach, right?'

'Very good. Follow me there and we'll see what you're made of. Once you're finished, you'll keep your mouths shut about it. Period. Understood?'

'Yes, sir.'

'And be careful with it – pretend it's bottles of liver shake or something.'

10

We met up with Robin and loaded her pickup. Watching her shop empty made her blink but she wiped her eyes quickly and said, 'Let's go.'

We set up a caravan – Milo in the lead, Robin and the dog in the truck, me in the Seville, the van trailing – and headed back to Sunset, passing Beverly Glen as if it was someone else's neighborhood, entering Beverly Hills and driving north onto Benedict Canyon.

Milo turned off on a narrow road, poorly paved and sided with eucalyptus. A cheerless, white iron gate appeared fifty feet up. He slipped a card-key into a slot and it opened. The caravan continued up a steep pebbled drive hedged with very high columns of Italian cypress that looked slightly moth-eaten. Then the road kinked and we descended another two or three hundred feet, toward a shallow bowl of an unshaded lot maybe half an acre wide.

A low, off-white, one-story house sat in the bowl. A long, straight, concrete drive led to the front door. As I got closer I saw that the entire property was hilltop, the depression an artificial crater, scalped from the tip.

Canyon and mountain-views surrounded the property. Lots of brown slopes and a few green spots, flecked with the lint of occasional houses. I wondered if mine could be seen from up here, looked around but couldn't get my bearings.

The house was wide and free of detail, roofed too heavily with deep brown aluminum tile supposed to simulate shake, and windowed with aluminum-cased rectangles.

A flat-topped, detached garage was separated from the main

building by an unfenced paddle tennis court. A ten-foot satellite dish perched atop it, aimed at the cosmos.

A few cacti and yuccas grew near the house but that was it in terms of landscaping. What could have been front lawn had been converted to concrete pad. An empty terracotta planter sat next to the coffee-colored double doors. As I got out of the car, I noticed the t.v. camera above the lintel. The air was hot and smelled sterile.

I got out and went over to Robin's truck.

She smiled. 'Looks like a motel.'

'Long as the owner's not named Norman.'

The black van dieseled as its ignition shut down. The three beef-boys exited and threw open the rear doors. Tarped machines filled the cabin. The boys did some squats and grunts and began unloading.

Milo said something to them, then waved to us. His jacket was off and but he still wore his gun. The heat had returned.

'Crazy weather,' I said.

Robin got out and lifted the dog out of the pickup. We walked to the front door and Milo let us into the house.

The floor was white marble streaked with pink, the furniture teakwood and ebony and bright-blue velour. The far wall was taken up by single light French doors. All the others were covered with paintings – hung frame-to-frame, so that only scraps of white plaster were visible.

The doors looked out onto a yard encircled by invisible fence – glass panes in thin iron frames. A strip of sod-grass separated a cement patio from a long, narrow lap pool. The pool had been dug at the edge of the lot – someone aiming for a merge-with-the-sky effect. But the water was blue and the sky was gray and the whole thing ended up looking like an off-balance cubist sculpture.

The dog ran to the French doors and tapped the glass with his paws. Milo let him out and he squatted in the grass before returning.

'Make yourself right at home, why don't you.' To us: 'Called London, everything's set up, there'll be a token rent, but you don't have to worry about it until he gets back.'

We thanked him. He dusted off one of the couches and I studied the art. Impressionist pictures that looked French and important nudged up against pre-Raphaelite mythology. Syrupy, Orientalist harem scenes neighbored with English hunt paintings. Modern pieces too: a Mondrian, a Frank Stella chevron, a Red Grooms subway cartoon, something amorphous fashioned out of neon.

The dining area was all Maxfield Parish: cobalt skies, heavenly forests and beautiful blond boys.

Lots of nude male statuary, too. A lamp whose black granite base was a limbless, muscular torso – Venus de Milo in drag. A framed cover from *The Advocate* commemorating the Christopher Street riot side by side with a Paul Cadmus drawing of a reclining Adonis. A framed Arrow Man shirt ad from an old issue of Colliers kept company with a black and white gelatin print of a Paul Newman lookalike in nothing but a g-string. I felt less comfortable than I would have expected. Or maybe it was just the suddenness of the move.

Milo brought us back to the door and demonstrated the closed circuit surveillance system. Two cameras – one in front, the other panning the rear of the house, two black and white monitors mounted over the door. One of them captured the three behemoths, shlepping and swearing.

Milo opened the door and shouted, 'Careful!' Closing it, he said, 'What do you think?'

'Great,' I said. 'Plenty of space – thanks a lot.'

'Beautiful view,' said Robin. 'Really gorgeous.'

We followed him into the kitchen and he opened the door of a Sub-Zero cooler. Empty except for a bottle of cooking sherry. 'I'll get you some provisions.'

Robin said, 'Don't worry, I can take care of that.'

'Whatever . . . let's get you a bedroom – you've got your choice of three.'

He took us down a wide, windowless hallway lined with prints. A wall clock in a mother of pearl case read two thirty-five. In less than an hour, I was expected in Sunland.

Robin read my mind: 'Your afternoon appointment?'

'What time?' said Milo.

'Three thirty,' I said.

'Where?'

'Wallace's mother-in-law. I'm supposed to see the girls out there. No reason not to go, is there?'

He thought for a moment. 'None that I can see.'

Robin caught the hesitation. 'Why should there be a reason?'

'This particular case,' I said, 'is potentially ugly. Two little girls, their father killed their mother and now wants visitation rights.'

'That's absurd.'

'Among other things. The court asked me to evaluate and make a recommendation. In the very beginning Milo and I talked about the father possibly being behind the tape. Trying to intimidate me. He's got a criminal record and hangs with an outlaw motorcycle gang that's been known to use strongarm tactics.'

'This creep's walking free?'

'No, he's locked up in prison. Maximum security at Folsom. I just got a letter from him telling me he was a good father.'

'Wonderful,' she said.

'He's not behind this. It was just a working guess, until I learned about the Bad Love symposium. My problems have something to do with de Bosch.'

She looked at Milo. He nodded.

'All right,' she said, taking hold of my jacket lapel and kissing my chin. 'I'm going to stop being Mama Bear and go about my business.'

I held her around the waist. Milo looked away.

'I'll be careful,' I said.

She put her head on my chest.

The dog began pawing the floor.

'Oedipus Rover,' said Milo.

Robin pushed me away gently. 'Go help those poor little girls.'

I took Benedict into the Valley and picked up the Ventura Freeway at Van Nuys Boulevard. Traffic was hideous all the way to the 210 and beyond, and I didn't make it to McVine until three-forty. When I got to the Rodriguez house, no cars were parked in front and no one answered my ring.

Evelyn showing her displeasure at my tardiness?

I tried again, knocked, then harder, and when that brought no response, went around to the back. Managing to hoist myself up high enough to peer over the pink block wall, I scanned the yard.

Empty. Not a toy or a piece of furniture in sight. The inflatable pool had been put away, the garage was shut and drawn drapes blocked the rear windows.

Returning to the front, I checked the mailbox and found

yesterday's and today's deliveries. Bulk stuff, coupon giveaways, and something from the gas company.

I put it back and looked up and down the street. A boy of around ten zoomed by on rollerblade skates. A few seconds later, a red truck came speeding down from Foothill and for an instant I thought it was Roddy Rodriguez's. But as it passed, I saw that it was lighter in shade than his, and a decade newer. A blond woman sat in the driver's seat. A big yellow dog rode in the bed, tongue out, watchful.

I returned to the Seville and waited for another twenty-five minutes but no one showed up. I tried to recall the name of Rodriguez's masonry company and finally did – R and R.

Driving back to Foothill Boulevard, I headed east until I spotted a phone booth at an Arco station. The directory had been yanked off the chain so I called Information and asked for R and R's address and phone number. The operator ignored me and switched over to the automated message, leaving only the number. I called it. No one answered. I tried Information a second time and got a street address – right on Foothill, about ten blocks east.

The place was a gray-topped lot, forty or fifty feet behind a shabby, brown building. Surrounded by barbed link, a green clapboard beer bar on one side, a pawn shop on the other.

The property was empty except for a few brick fragments and some paper litter. The brown building looked to have once been a double garage. Two sets of old-fashioned hinge doors took up most of the front. Above them, ornate yellow letters shouted *R and R Masonry*: *Cement*. *Cinder and Custom Brick*. Below that: *Retaining Walls Our Specialty* followed by an overlapping R's logo meant to evoke Rolls Royce fantasies.

I parked and got out. No signs of life. The padlock on the gate was the size of a baseball.

I went over to the pawnshop. The door was locked and a sign above a red button said, 'Press and Wait.' I obeyed and the door buzzed but didn't open. I leaned in close to the window. A man stood behind a nipple-high counter, shielded by a Plexi Glas window.

He ignored me.

I buzzed again.

He made a stabbing motion and the door gave.

110

I walked past cases filled with cameras, cheap guitars, cassette decks and boomboxes, pocket knives and fishing rods.

The man was managing to examine a watch and check me over at the same time.

He was sixty or so, with slicked, dyed-black hair and a pumpkin-colored bottle tan. His face was long and baggy.

I cleared my throat.

He said, 'Yeah?' through the plastic and kept looking at the watch, turning it over with nicotined fingers and working his lips as if preparing to spit. The window was scratched and cloudy and outfitted with a ticket-taker remote speaker that he hadn't switched on. The store had soft, wooden floors and stank of WD-40, sulfur matches, and body odor. A sign over the gun display said *No Loonies*.

'I'm looking for Roddy Rodriguez next door,' I said. 'Have some work for him to do on a retaining wall.'

He put the watch down and picked up another.

'Excuse me,' I said.

'Got something to buy or sell?'

'No, I was just wondering if you knew when Rodriguez was – '

He turned his back on me and walked away. Through the Plexi Glas I saw an old desk full of papers and other timepieces. A semi-automatic pistol served as a paperweight. He scratched his butt and held the watch up to a fluorescent bulb.

I left and walked over to the bar two doors down. The greenboard was rubbed to raw timber in spots and the front door was unmarked. A sun-shaped neon sign said 'Sunny's Sun Valley.' A single window below it was filled with a Budweiser sign.

I walked in, expecting darkness, billiard-clicks, and a cowboy juke box. Instead, I got bright lights, ZZ Top going on about a Mexican whore, and a nearly empty room not much larger than my kitchen.

No pool table – no tables of any kind. Just a long, pressed-wood bar with a black vinyl bumper and matching stools, some of them patched with duct tape. Up against the facing wall were a cigarette machine and a pocket comb dispenser. The floor was grubby concrete.

The man working the bar was thirtyish, fair, balding, stubbled. He wore tinted eyeglasses and one of his ears was double-pierced, hosting a tiny gold stud and a white-metal hoop. He had on a soiled white apron over a black t-shirt and his chest was flabby. His arms were soft-looking, too, white and tattooed. He wasn't doing much when I came in and continued along those lines. Two men sat at the bar, far from each other. More tattooes. They didn't move either. It looked like a poster for National Brain Death Week.

I took a stool between the men and ordered a beer.

'Draft or bottle?'

'Draft.'

The bartender took a long time to fill a mug and as I waited I snuck glances at my companions. Both wore billed caps, t-shirts, jeans and work shoes. One was skinny, the other muscular. Their hands were dirty. They smoked and drank and had tired faces.

My beer came and I took a swallow. Not much head and not great, but not as bad as I'd expected.

'Any idea when Roddy'll be back?' I said.

'Who?' said the bartender.

'Rodriguez – the masonry guy next door. He's supposed to be doing a retaining wall for me and he didn't show up.'

He shrugged.

'Place is closed,' I said.

No answer. I said, 'Guy's got my goddamned deposit.'

The bartender began soaking glasses in a gray plastic tub.

I drank some more.

ZZ gave way to a disc jockey's voice, hawking car insurance for people with bad driving records. Then a series of commercials for ambulance-chasing lawyers polluted the air some more.

'When's the last time you've seen him around?' I said.

The bartender turned around. 'Who?'

'Rodriguez.'

Shrug.

'Has his place been closed for a while?'

Another shrug. He returned to soaking.

'Great,' I said.

He looked over his shoulder. 'He never comes in here, I got nothing to do with him, okay?'

'Not much of a drinker?'

Shrug.

'Fucking asshole,' said the man on my right.

The skinny one. Sallow and pimpled, barely above drinking age.

His cigarette was dead in the ashtray. One of his index fingers played with the ashes.

I said, 'Who? Rodriguez?'

He gave a depressed nod. 'Fucking greaser don't pay.'

'You worked for him?'

'Fucking A, digging his fucking ditches. Then the roach coach comes by for lunch and I wanna advance so's to get a burrito, he says sorry, amigo, not till payday. So I'm *adios, amigo*, man.'

He shook his head, still pained by the rejection.

'Asshole,' he said, and returned to his beer.

'So he shafted you, too,' I said.

'Fucking A, man.'

'Any idea where I can find him?'

'Maybe Mexico, man.'

'Mexico?'

'Yeah, all a them beaners got second homes there, got they extra wives and they little taco-tico kids, send all they money there.'

I heard a metallic click to the left, looked over and saw the muscular man light up a cigarette. Late twenties or early thirties, two-day growth of heavy beard, thick, black fu-manchu mustache. His cap was black and said CAT. He blew smoke toward the bar.

I said, 'You know Rodriguez, too?'

He gave a long, slow headshake and held out his mug. The bartender filled it then extended his own hand. The mustachioed man jostled the pack until a cigarette slid forward. The bartender took it, nodded and lit up.

Guns 'n' Roses came on the radio. The bartender looked at my half-empty mug. 'Anything else?'

I shook my head, put money down on the bar and left.

'Asshole,' said the skinny man, raising his voice to be heard over the music.

I drove back to the Rodriguez house. Still dark and empty. A woman across the street was holding a broom and she began looking at me suspiciously.

I called over: 'Any idea when they'll be back?'

She went inside her house. I drove away and got back on the freeway, exiting on Sunset and heading north on Beverly Glen. I realized my error just as I completed the turn, but continued on to my house, anyway, pulling up in front of the carport. Looking over my shoulder with paranoid fervor, I decided it was safe to get out of the car.

I walked around my property, remembering. Though it made no sense, the house already looked sad.

You know how places get when they're empty . . .

I took a quick look at the pond. The fish were still there. They swam up to greet me and I obliged with food.

'See you guys,' I said and left, wondering how many would survive.

11

I made it to Benedict a few minutes later.

The black van and the unmarked were gone. Two of the three garage doors were open and I saw Robin inside, wearing work-clothes and goggles, standing behind her lathe.

She saw me coming and turned off the machine. A gold BMW coupe was parked in the third garage. The rest of the space was a near duplicate of the Venice shop.

'Looks like you're all set up,' I said.

She pushed her goggles up on her forehead. 'This isn't too bad, actually, as long as I leave the door open for ventilation. How come you're back so soon?'

'No one home.'

'Flake out on you?'

'It looks like they're gone for a while.'

'Moved out?'

'Must be the week for it.'

'How could you tell?'

'Two days' mail in the box and her husband's business was padlocked.'

'Considerate of her to let you know.'

'Etiquette isn't her strong suit. She wasn't thrilled about my evaluation in the first place, though I thought we were making progress. She probably took the girls out of state – maybe Hawaii. When I spoke to her yesterday she made a crack about a Honolulu vacation. Or Mexico. Her husband may have family there . . . I'd better call the judge.'

'We set up an office for you in the one of the bedrooms,' she said, leaning over and pecking my cheek. 'Gave you the one with the best view plus there's a Hockney on the wall – two guys showering.' She smiled. 'Poor Milo, he was a little embarrassed about it – started muttering about the "atmosphere". Almost apologizing. After all he did to help us. I sat him down and we had a good talk.'

'About what?'

'Stuff – the meaning of life. I told him you could handle the *atmosphere*.'

'What'd he say to that?'

'Just grunted and rubbed his face the way he does. Then I made coffee and told him if he ever learned to play an instrument I'd build one for him.'

'Safe offer,' I said.

'Maybe not. When we were talking it came up that he used to play the accordion when he was a kid. And he sings – have you ever heard him?'

'No.'

'Well, he sang for me this afternoon. After some prodding. Did an old Irish folk song and guess what? He's got a really nice voice.'

'Basso profundo?'

'*Tenor*, of all things. He used to be in the church choir when he was a little boy.'

I smiled. 'That's a little hard to picture.'

'There's probably a lot about him you don't know.'

'Probably,' I said. 'Each year I get in touch with more of my ignorance . . . speaking of grunts, where's our guest?'

'Sleeping in the service porch. I tried keeping him here while I worked but he kept charging the machines – he was ready to take on the bandsaw when I got him out of here and locked him in.'

'Tough love, huh? Did he do his little strangulation routine?'

'Oh, sure,' she said. She put her hand around her throat and made a gagging sound. 'I yelled at him to be quiet and he stopped.'

'Poor guy. He probably thought you were going to be his salvation.'

She grinned. 'I may be sultry and sensual, but I ain't easy.'

*   *   *

I let the dog loose, gave him time to pee outside and took him into my new office. A chrome glass-topped desk was pushed up against one wall. My papers and books were piled neatly on a black velour couch. The view was fantastic, but after a few minutes, I stopped noticing it.

I phoned Superior Court, got Steve Huff in his chambers and told him about Evelyn Rodriguez's no-show.

'Maybe she just forgot,' he said. 'Denial, avoidance, whatever.'

'I think there's a good chance she's gone, Steve.' I described Roddy Rodriguez's locked yard.

'Sounds like it,' he said. 'There goes another one.'

'Can't say that I blame her. When I saw her two days ago, she really opened up about the girls' problems. They're having plenty of them. And Donald wrote me a letter – no remorse, just tooting his own horn as a good dad.'

'Wrote you a *letter*?'

'His lawyer's been calling me, too.'

'Any intimidation?'

I hesitated. 'No, just nagging.'

'Too bad. No law against that . . . no, can't say that I blame her either, Alex – off the record. Do you want to wait and try again, or just write up your report now – document all the crap she told you?'

'What's the difference?'

'The difference is how quickly you want to get paid versus how much lead time you want to give her, if she *has* hightailed it. Once you put it in writing and I receive it, I'm obligated to send it over to Bucklear. Even with reasonable delays he gets it in a couple of weeks or so, then *he* files paper and gets warrants out on her.'

'A murderer gets warrants on a grandmother taking her grandkids out of town? Do we file that under I for Irony or N for Nuts?'

'Do I take that to mean you'll wait?'

'How much lead time can I give her?'

'A reasonable period. Consistent with typical medical psychological practice.'

'Meaning?'

'Meaning what shrinks normally do. Three, four, even five weeks wouldn't chafe any hides, you guys are notorious for being sloppy about your paperwork. You might even stretch it to six or seven –

but you never heard that from me. In fact, we never had this talk, did we?'

'Judge who?' I said.

'Attaboy – oops, bailiff's buzzing me to be Solomonic again, bye-bye.'

I put the phone down. The bulldog placed his paws on my knees and tried to get up on my lap. I lifted him and he settled on me like a warm lunk of clay. At *least* thirty pounds.

The Hockney was right in front of me. Great painting. As was the Benton drawing on the opposite wall – a mural study depicting hyper-muscular workmen cheerfully constructing a WPA dam.

I looked at both of them for a while and wondered what Robin and Milo had talked about. The dog stayed motionless as a little furry Buddha. I rubbed his head and his jowls and he licked my hand. A boy and his dog . . . I realized I hadn't gotten the number for the bulldog club, yet. Almost five p.m. Too late to call AKC.

I'd do it tomorrow morning.

Denial, avoidance, whatever.

That night I slept fitfully. Friday morning at eight, I phoned North Carolina and got an address for the French Bulldog Club of America in Rahway, New Jersey. A post office box. No phone number was available.

At eight-ten, I called the Rodriguez house. A phone company recording said that line had been disconnected. I pictured Evelyn and the girls barreling over a dirt road in Bahia, Rodriguez following in his truck. Or maybe the four of them, wandering through Waikiki with glazed tourists eyes. If only they knew how much we had in common now . . .

I began unpacking books. At eight thirty-five, the doorbell rang and Milo appeared on one of the t.v. monitors, tapping a foot and carrying a white bag.

'Breakfast,' he said, as I let him in. 'I already gave Ms. Castagna hers, God, that woman works – what've you been doing?'

'Getting organized.'

'Sleep okay?'

'Great,' I lied. 'Thanks a lot for setting us up.'

He looked around. 'How's the office?'

'Perfect.'

'Great view, huh?'

'To die for.'

We went into the kitchen and he took some onion rolls and two Styrofoam cups of coffee out of the bag.

We sat at a blue granite table. He said, 'What's your schedule like today?'

'It's pretty open now that the Wallace thing's on hold. Looks like Grandma decided to take matters into her own hands.'

I recounted what I'd found in Sunland.

He said, 'They're probably better off. If you feel like taking on a little assignment, I've got one for you.'

'What?'

'Go over to the Mental Health Center and talk to Ms. Jean Jeffers. I finally got through to her – she actually called me back last night, which I thought was pretty cool for a bureaucrat. Better attitude than I expected, too. Down to earth. Not that she shouldn't cooperate, after what happened to Becky. I told her we'd come across some harassment crimes – didn't go into specifics – that we had reason to believe might be coming from one of her patients. Someone we also had reason to believe was a buddy of Hewitt's. Mentioning *his* name got her going – she went on about how Becky's murder had traumatized all of them. Still sounds pretty shook up.'

He tore an onion roll into three pieces, placed the segments on the table like monte cards, picked one up and ate it.

'Anyway, I asked her if she knew who Hewitt hung out with and she said no. Then I asked her if I could look at her patient roster and she said she wanted to help but no the confidentiality thing. So I threw Tarasoff at her, hoping she didn't know the law that well. But she did: no specific threat against a specific victim, no Tarasoff obligation. At *that* point, I played my trump card: told her the department had a consultant doing some profiling work for us on psycho crimes – a genuine *Pee Aitch Dee* who respected confidentiality and would be discreet and I gave her your name, in case maybe she heard of you. And guess what, she thought she had. Especially after I told her you were semi-famous.'

'Hoo hah.'

'Hoo hah to the max. She said she couldn't promise anything but she'd be willing to at least talk to you, maybe there'd be some way to work something out. The more we talked, the friendlier she got. My feeling is she wants to help but is afraid of being burned by more publicity. So be gentle with her.'

'No brass knucks,' I said. 'How much do I tell her?'

He ate another piece of roll. 'As little as possible.'

'When can she see me?'

'This afternoon, here's the number.' He took a scrap of paper out of his pocket, gave it to me, and stood.

'Where you going?' I said.

'Over the hill. Van Nuys. Try to find out what I can about who cut up Myra Paprock five years ago.'

After he was gone, I called in for messages – still nothing from Shirley Rosenblatt in New York – then wrote a letter to the bulldog club informing them I'd found what might possibly be a member's pet. At nine-thirty, I phoned Jean Jeffers and was put through to her secretary, who sounded as if she'd been expecting me. An appointment with Ms. Jeffers was available in an hour if I was free.

I grabbed a roll, put on a tie, and left.

The center was in a block of cheerless, pastel-colored apartments, in a quiet part of West L.A. not far from Santa Monica. An old, working-class district, near an industrial park whose galloping expansion had been choked off by hard times. Constructus interruptus had left its mark all over the neighborhood – half-framed buildings, empty lots dug out for foundations and left as dry sumps, pigeon-specked *For Sale* signs, boarded-up windows on condemned pre-war bungalows.

The clinic was the only charming bit of architecture in sight. Its front windows were barred but boxes filled with begonias hung from the iron. The spot on the sidewalk where Dorsey Hewitt had fallen dead was clean. But for a couple of trash-chocked shopping carts in front, it could have been a private sanitarium.

A generous lot next door was two-thirds empty and marked *Employees Only. No Patient Parking*. I decided a consultant qualified as someone's employee, and parked there.

I made my way back to the front of the building, passing the section of wall that had been obsessed upon by the t.v. camera. A cement corner-stone etched with names of forgotten politicos stated that the building had been dedicated as a Veterans Clinic in 1919. The door Hewitt had come out of was just to the right, unmarked and locked – two locks, each almost as large as the one sealing Roddy Rodriguez' brickyard.

The main entrance was dead center, through a squat arch that led to a courtyard with an empty fountain. A loggia to the right of the fountain – the path Hewitt would have taken to get to the unmarked door – was sectioned off by a thick steel mesh that looked brand-new. An open hallway on the opposite side led me around the fountain to glass-paned doors.

A blue-uniformed guard stood behind the doors, tall, old, black, chewing gum. He looked me over and unlatched one of the doors, then pointed to a metal detector to his left – one of those walk-through airport things. I set it off and had to give the guard my keys before passing silently.

'Go 'head,' he said, handing them back.

I walked up to a reception desk. A young black woman sat behind more mesh. 'Can I help you?'

'Dr. Delaware for Ms. Jeffers.'

'One minute.' She got on the phone. Behind her were three other women at desks, typing and talking into receivers. The windows behind them were barred. Through the bars, I saw trucks, cars, and shadows – the gray, graffitied walls of an alley.

I was standing in a small, unfurnished area painted light green and broken only by a single door to the right. Claustrophobic. It reminded me of the sally port at the County Jail and I wondered how a paranoid schizophrenic or someone would handle it. How easy it would be for someone with a muddled psyche to make it from the No Parking Lot, through the metal detector, to this holding cell.

The receptionist said, 'Okay, she's all the way down at the end,' and pressed a button. The door buzzed – not quite as loudly as the one at the pawn shop, but just as obnoxious – and I opened it and stepped into a very long, cream-colored hall marked by lots of doors. Thick, gray carpeting covered the floor. The light was very bright.

Most of the doors were blank, a few were labeled THERAPY, even fewer bore slide-in signs with people's names on them. The cream paint smelled fresh; how many coats had it taken to cover up the blood?

The corridor was silent except for my footsteps – the kind of womb-like damping that only comes from real soundproofing. As I made my way to the end, a door on the left opened, spilling out people but no noise.

Three people, two women and a man, poorly dressed and

shuffling. Not a group; each walked alone. The man was lantern-jawed and stooped, the women heavy and red-faced, with cracked swollen legs and stringy hair. All of them looked down at the carpet as they passed me. They grasped small white pieces of paper, Rx stamped at the top.

The room they'd exited was classroom-sized and crowded with another thirty or so people queued up before a metal desk. A young man sat at the desk, talking briefly to the person before him, then filling out a prescription blank and handing it over with a smile. The people in line scuffed forward as automatically as cans on a conveyor belt. Some of them held out their hands in anticipation before they got to the doctor. None of them left without paper, none seemed cheered.

I resumed walking. The door at the end had a slide-in that said *Jean Jeffers, MSW, LCSW. Director.*

Inside was a five-by-five secretarial area occupied by a young, full-faced, Asian woman. Her desk was barely big enough to hold a PC and a blotter. The wall behind her was so narrow, a dark, mock-wood door almost filled it. A radio on an end table played soft-rock almost inaudibly. A nameplate in front of the computer said *Mary Chin.*

She said, 'Dr. Delaware? Go right in, Jean will see you.'

'Thank you.'

She began to open the door. A woman caught it from the other side and pulled it all the way back. Forty-five or so, tall and blond. She wore a crimson shirtdress gathered at the waist by a wide, white belt.

'Doctor? I'm Jean.' She held out her hand. Almost as big as mine, lanolin soft. The left one bore a ruby solitaire ring on the index finger over a broad, gold wedding band.

More white in her teardrop earrings and a mock ivory bracelet around one wrist. A sensible-looking watch encircled the other.

She had a strong frame and carried no extra fat. The belt showed off a firm waist. Her face was long, lightly tanned, with soft, generous features. Only her upper lip had been skimped upon by Nature – not much more than a pencil-line. Its mate was full and glossed. Dark blue eyes studied me from under black lashes. Gold-framed half-glasses hung from a white cord around her neck. Her hair was frosted almost white at the tips, clipped short in back and layered back at the sides. Pure utility except for a thick, Veronica

Lake flap in front. It swooped to the right, almost hiding her right eye. A handsome woman.

She flipped her hair and smiled.

'Thanks for seeing me,' I said.

'Of course, doctor. Please have a seat.'

Her office was the standard twelve-by-twelve setup, with a real wood desk, two upholstered armchairs, a three-drawer double file, a nearly empty bookcase and some paintings of seagulls. On the desk were a pen, a memo pad, and a short stack of file-folders.

A photo in a standup frame was centered on one of the shelves – she and a nice-looking, heavyset man about her age, the two of them in Hawaiian shirts and bedecked with leis. Social work diplomas made out to Jean Marie LaPorte were propped on another shelf, all from California colleges. I scanned the dates. If she'd graduated college at twenty-two, she was exactly forty-five.

'You're a clinical psychologist, right?' she said, sitting behind the desk.

I took one of the chairs. 'Yes.'

'You know, when Detective Sturgis mentioned your name I thought I recognized it, though I still can't figure out from where.'

She smiled again. I returned it.

She said, 'How does a psychologist come to be a police consultant?'

'By accident, really. Several years ago I was treating some children who'd been abused at a day care center. I ended up testifying in court and getting involved in the legal system. One thing led to another.'

'Day care center – the man who took pictures? The one involved with that horrible molesters' club?'

I nodded.

'Well, that must be where I remember your name from. You were quite a hero, weren't you?'

'Not really. I did my job.'

'Well,' she said, sitting forward and pushing hair out of her eyes, 'I'm sure you're being modest. Child abuse is so – to tell you the truth, I couldn't work with it myself. Which may sound funny considering what we deal with here. But children – ' She shook her head. 'It would be too hard for me to find any sympathy for the abusers even if they were once victims themselves.'

123

'I know what you mean.'

'To me that's the lowest – violating a child's trust. How do you manage it?'

'It wasn't easy,' I said. 'I saw myself as the child's ally and tried to do whatever helped.'

'Tried? You don't do abuse work anymore?'

'Occasionally, when it comes up as part of a custody case. Mostly I consult to the court on trauma and divorce issues.'

'Do you do any therapy at all?'

'Not much.'

'Me, neither.' She sat back. 'My main goal in school was to become a therapist but I can't remember the last time I actually did any real therapy.'

She smiled again and shook her head. The wave of hair covered her eyes and she flipped it back – a curiously adolescent mannerism.

'Anyway,' she said, 'about what Detective Sturgis wants, I just don't know how I can really help. I really need to safeguard our people's confidentiality – despite what happened to Becky.' She folded her lips inward, lowered her eyes and shook her head.

I said, 'It must have been terrifying.'

'It happened too *quickly* to be terrifying – the *terrifying* part didn't hit me until after it was over – seeing her . . . what he . . . now I really know what they mean by post-traumatic stress. No substitute for direct experience, huh?'

She pressed the skinny upper lip with one finger, as if keeping it still.

'No one knew what he was doing to her. I was right here, going about my business the whole time he was – the treatment rooms are totally soundproofed. He – ' She removed her finger. A white pressure circle dotted her lip, then slowly faded.

'Then I heard noise from the hall,' she said. 'That horrible screaming – he just kept *screaming*.'

'"Bad love,"' I said.

Her mouth remained open. The blue eyes dulled for a second. 'Yes. . . he . . . I went out to Mary's office and she wasn't there, so I opened the door to the hall and saw him. Screaming, waving it – the knife – *splashing* blood, the wall – he saw me – I saw his eyes settle on me – focusing – and he kept screaming. I slammed the door, shoved Mary's desk up against it and ran back into my office. Slammed *that* door and blocked it. I hid behind my chair

124

the whole time it was . . . it wasn't till later that I found out he'd grabbed Adeline.' She wiped her eyes. 'I'm sorry, you don't need to hear this.'

'No, no, please.'

She glanced at her message pad. Blank. Picking up the pen, she wrote something on it.

'No, that's it – I've told it so many times . . . no one knows how long he – if she suffered for a long time. That's the one thing I *can* hope. That she didn't. The thought of her trapped in there with him . . .' She shook her head and touched her temples. 'They soundproofed the rooms back in the sixties, when this place was a Viet Nam veteran's counseling center. We sure don't need it.'

'Why's that?'

'Because *no* one does much therapy around here.'

She took a deep breath and slapped her hands lightly on the desk. 'Life goes on, right? Would you like something to drink? We've got a coffee machine in the other wing, I can have Mary go get some.'

'No thanks.'

'Lucky choice.' Smile. 'It's actually pretty vile.'

'How come no one does much therapy?' I said. 'Too disturbed a population?'

'Too disturbed, too poor, too many of them. They need food and shelter and to stop hearing voices. The treatment is Thorazine. And Haldol and Lithium and Tegretol and whatever else chases the demons away. Counseling would be a nice luxury, but with our caseload it ends up being a very low priority. Not to mention funding. That's why we don't have any psychologists on our staff, just caseworkers, and most of them are SWA's – assistants. Like Becky.'

'On the way in I saw a doctor giving out prescriptions.'

'That's right,' she said. 'It's Friday, isn't it? That's Dr. Wintell, our once-a-week psychiatrist. He's just out of his residency, a real nice kid. But when his practice builds up, he'll be out of here like all the others.'

'If no one does therapy, what was Becky doing with Hewitt in the therapy room?'

'I didn't say we never *talk* to our people, just that we don't do much *insight* work. Sometimes we get cramped for space and the workers use the treatment rooms to do their paperwork. Basically, all of us use what's on hand. As to what Becky was doing with *him*, it could have been anything. Giving him a voucher for an SRO hotel, telling him where to get deloused. Then again, maybe she *was* trying to get into his head – she was that kind of person.'

'What kind is that?'

'An optimist. Idealistic. Most of us start out that way, don't we?'

I nodded. 'Did Hewitt have a history of violence?'

'None that was listed in our files. He'd been arrested just a few weeks before for theft and was due to stand trial – maybe she was counseling him about that. There was *nothing* on paper that would have warned us. And even if he was violent, there's a good chance the information would have never gotten to us, with all the red tape.'

She put down her pen and looked at me. Flipped her hair. 'The truth is, he was exactly like so many others who come in and out of here – there's still no way to know.'

She picked up one of the folders.

'This is his file. The police confiscated it and returned it, so I guess it's not confidential, anymore.'

Inside were only two sheets, clipped to each other. The first was an intake form listing Dorsey Hewitt's age as thirty-one and his address as NONE. Under *Reason For Referral* someone had written MULTIPLE SOCIAL PROBLEMS. Under *Diagnosis*: PROB. CHRON. SCHIZ. The rest of the categories *Prognosis. Family Support. Medical History. Other Psych. Treatment* – had been left blank. Nothing about 'bad love'.

At the bottom of the form were notations of referral for food stamps. The signature read: R. Basille, SWA.

The facing page was white and smooth, marked only with the notation 'Will follow as needed, R.B., SWA.' The date was eight weeks prior to the murder. I handed the folder back.

'Not much,' I said.

She gave a sad smile. 'Paperwork wasn't Becky's forte.'

'So you have no idea how many times she actually saw him?'

'Guess that doesn't say much for my administrative skills, does it? But I'm not one of those people who believes in riding the staff, checking out every little picayune detail. I try to find the best people I can, motivate them and give them room to move. Generally it works out. With Becky. . .'

She threw up her hands. 'She was a doll, a really sweet person. Not much for rules and regulations, but so what?'

She shook her head. 'We'd talked about it – helping her get her paperwork in on time. She promised to try, but to tell the truth, I didn't harbor much hope. And I didn't care. Because she was *productive* where it counted – getting on the phone all day with agencies and arguing for every last penny for her cases. She stayed late, did whatever it took to help them. Who knows, maybe she was going that extra mile for Hewitt.'

She picked up the phone. 'Mary? Coffee please . . . no, just one.'

Putting it down, she said, 'The *real* horror is that it could happen again. We have a steel corral, now, to direct them out onto the street after they get their meds. The County finally sent us a guard and the detector, but you tell me how to predict which of them is going to blow.'

'We're not very good prophets under the best of circumstances.'

'No, we're not. Hundreds of people file in here each week, for meds and vouchers. We've *got* to let them in. We're the court of last resort. Any of them could be another Hewitt. Even if we wanted to lock them up, we couldn't. The state hospitals that haven't been shut down are filled to capacity – I don't know what your theory is about psychosis, but mine is that most psychotics are born with it – it's biological, like any other illness. But instead of treating them, we demonize them or idealize them and they get caught in the squeeze between the do-gooders who think they should be allowed to run free, and the skinflints who think all they need is to pull themselves up by the bootstraps.'

'I know,' I said. 'When I was in grad school the whole community psych thing was in full bloom – schizophrenia as an alternative lifestyle, liberating patients from the back wards and empowering them to take over their own treatment.'

'Empowering.' She laughed without opening her mouth.

'I had a professor who was a fanatic on the subject,' I said. 'Studied the mental health system in Belgium or somewhere and wrote a book on it. He had us do a paper on de-institutionalization. The more I researched it, the less feasible it seemed. I started to wonder what would happen to psychotics who needed medication and couldn't be counted upon to take it. He handed the paper back with one comment: "Medication is mind control" and gave me a C minus.'

'Well, *I* give you an A. Some of *our* patients can't be counted upon to feed themselves, let alone calibrate dosage. In my opinion, de-institutionalization's the major culprit in the homeless problem.

Sure some street people are working folks who hit the skids, but at least thirty or forty percent are severely mentally debilitated. They belong in hospitals, not under some freeway. And now with all the weird street drugs out there, the old cliché that the mentally ill aren't violent just isn't true anymore. Each year it gets uglier and uglier, Dr. Delaware. I pray there won't be another Hewitt, but I don't count on it.'

'Do you try at all to identify which patients are violent?'

'If we have police records, we take them seriously, but like I said, that's rare. We've got to be our own police here. If someone goes around making threats, we call Security. But most of them are quiet. Hewitt was. Didn't really relate to anyone else that I'm aware of – that's why we're probably not going to be much help to Detective Sturgis. What exactly is he after, anyway?'

'Apparently he suspects Hewitt had a friend who may be harassing some people, and he's trying to find out if the friend was a patient here.'

'Well, after Sturgis called me I asked some of the other workers if they'd seen Hewitt with anyone and none of them had. The only one who might have known was Becky.'

'Is she the only one who worked with him?'

She nodded.

'How long had she been working here?'

'A little over a year. She got her assistantship from junior college last summer and applied right afterward. One of those second careers – she'd worked as a secretary for a while, decided to go back to school in order to do something socially important – her words.'

Her eyes flickered and her mouth set – the lower lip compressing and making her look older.

'Such a sweet girl,' she said. She shook her head, then looked at me. 'You know – I just thought of something. Hewitt's attorney – the one defending him on that theft thing? *He* might know if Hewitt had any friends – I think I've got his name tucked away somewhere – hold on.'

She went to the file, opened the middle drawer and began flipping. 'Just one second, so much junk in here. . . he called me – the attorney – after Becky's murder. Wanting to know if there was anything he could do. I think he wanted to talk – to get his own guilt off his chest . . . I didn't have time for . . . ah, here we go.'

She pulled out a piece of cardboard stapled with business cards. Working a staple, free with her fingernails, she removed a card and gave it to me.

Cheap, white paper, green letters.

Andrew Coburg
Attorney at Law
The Human Interest Law Center
1912 Lincoln Avenue
Venice, California

'Human interest law,' I said.

'I think it's one of those storefront things.'

'Thanks,' I said pocketing the card. 'I'll pass it along to Detective Sturgis.'

The door opened and Mary came in with the coffee.

Jean Jeffers thanked her and told her to tell someone named Amy that she'd be ready to see her in a minute.

When the door closed, she began stirring her coffee.

'Well,' she said, 'it was nice talking to you, sorry I couldn't do more.'

'Thanks for your time,' I said. 'Is there anyone else I could talk to who might be able to help?'

'No one I can think of.'

'What about the woman he took hostage?'

'Adeline? Now there's a *really* sad story. She'd transferred over here a month before from a center in South Central because she had high blood pressure and wanted a safer environment.'

She threw up her hands again and gave a sour laugh.

'Any particular reason Hewitt grabbed her?' I said.

'You mean did she know him?'

'Yes.'

She shook her head. The hair flap obscured her eye and she left it there. 'Just pure bad luck. She happened to be sitting at a desk in the hall working just as he was running out and he grabbed her.'

She walked me to the door. People kept coming out of the psychiatrist's office. She looked at them.

'How can you ever know someone like that, anyway?' she said. 'When you get down to it, how can you ever really know anyone?'

12

I decided to drive to Andrew Coburg's office and tender an appeal to his human interest. Getting onto Pico, I drove to Lincoln and headed south into Venice.

The Human Interest Law Center turned out, indeed, to be a storefront – one of three set into an old mustard-colored, one-story building. The brick façade was chipped. Next door was a liquor store advertising screwtop wine on special. The other side was vacant. On the window was painted DELI *** LUNCH & DINNER.

The law office window was papered with wrinkled silverfoil. An American flag hung over the doorway. Printed on one of the white stripes was 'Know Your Rights.'

The door was closed but unlocked. As I pushed it open, a bell tinkled but no one came out to greet me. In front of me was a particle-board partition. A black arrow pointed left and handpainted signs said 'Welcome!' and 'Bienvenidos!' A mass of noise – voices, phone rings, clicking typewriter keys – came from the other side.

I followed the arrow around the partition to a single large room, long and narrow. The walls were gray-white and crowded with bulletin boards and posters, the ceiling a high, dark nest of ductwork, electrical wiring and stammering fluorescent tubes.

No secretary or receptionist. Eight or nine mismatched desks were spread around the room, each equipped with a black dial phone, a typewriter and a facing chair. Behind each chair was a U-shaped construction of PVC tubing. White muslin curtains hung from the frame – the kind used for mock privacy in hospitals. Some of the curtains were drawn, others accordioned open. Shoes and cuffs were visible beneath the hem of the drawn drapes.

Young people sat behind the desks, talking into phones or to people in the chairs. The clients were mostly black or Hispanic. Some looked asleep. One of them – an old man of indeterminate race – held a terrier mutt on his lap. A few small children wandered around looking lost.

The desk nearest to me was occupied by a dark-haired man wearing a green plaid suit jacket, white shirt and bolo tie. He needed a shave, his hair was greased, and his face was sharp as an icepick. Though the phone receiver was cradled under his chin, he didn't appear to be talking or listening and his eyes drifted over to me.

'What can I do for you?'

'I'm looking for Andrew Coburg.'

'Back there.' Making a small, meaningless movement with his head. 'But I think he's with someone.'

'Which desk?' I said.

He put the phone down, swiveled and pointed to a station in the center of the room. Drapes drawn. Dirty sneakers and an inch of hairy shin below the hem of the muslin.

'Okay if I wait?'

'Sure. You an attorney?'

'No.'

'Sure, wait.' He picked up the phone and began dialing laboriously. Someone must have answered because he said, 'Yeah, hi, it's Hank, over at H.I. Yeah, me too – yeah.' Laughter. 'Listen, what about that *nolo* we talked about? Go and check – yeah, I think so. Yeah.'

I stood against the partition and read the posters. One featured a bald eagle on crutches and said HEAL OUR SYSTEM. Another was printed in Spanish – something to do with *immigracion* and *liberacion*.

The sharp-faced man started talking in lawyer's jargon, jabbing the air with a pen and laughing intermittently. He was still on the phone when the curtains at Andrew Coburg's station parted. An emaciated man wearing a filthy cableknit sweater and cutoff shorts got up. He was bearded and had matted hair and my chest tightened when I saw him because he could have been Dorsey Hewitt's brother. Then I realized I was seeing the brotherhood of poverty and madness.

He and Coburg shook hands and he left, eyes half-closed. As he passed me I backed away from the stench. He passed close to the man named Hank, too, but the lawyer didn't notice, kept talking and laughing.

Coburg was still standing. He wiped his hands on his pants, yawned and stretched. Early thirties, six one, two hundred. Pear-shaped, fair-haired, arms slightly too short for his long-waisted body. His hair was brass-colored, thinning, worn full at the sides with no sideburns. He had a soft face, fine features and rosy cheeks, had probably been a beautiful baby.

He wore a chambray work shirt with the sleeves rolled to the elbows, loosened paisley tie five years too narrow, rumpled khakis, saddle shoes. The laces on one shoe were untied.

Stretching again, he sat, picked up his phone and began dialing. Most of the other lawyers were on the phone now. The room sounded like a giant switchboard.

I walked over to him. His eyebrows rose as I sat down but he didn't show any signs of annoyance. Probably used to walk-ins.

He said, 'Listen, gotta go,' into the phone. ' – what's that? Fine – I accept that, just as long as we have a clear understanding, okay? What . . . no, I've got someone here. Okay. Bye. Cheers.'

He hung up and said, 'Hi, how can I help you?' in a pleasant voice. His tie was clipped with an unusual bit of jewelry: red guitar pick glued to a silver bar.

I told him who I was and that I was trying to locate any friends of Dorsey Hewitt.

'Dorsey. One of my triumphs,' he said, all the pleasantness gone. He sat back, crossed his legs. 'So what paper do you work for?'

'I'm a psychologist. Just like I said.'

He smiled. 'Really?'

I smiled back. 'Scout's honor.'

'And a police consultant, too.'

'That's right.'

'You don't mind if I see some I.D., do you?'

I showed him my psych license, my med school faculty card and my old LAPD consultant's tag.

'The police,' he said, as if he still couldn't believe it. 'Is that a problem for you?'

'In what way?'

'Working with the police mentality? All that intolerance – the authoritarianism.'

'Not really,' I said. 'Police officers vary, like anyone else.'

'That hasn't been my experience,' he said. There was a jar of licorice sticks near his typewriter. He took one and held out the container.

'No thanks.'

'High blood pressure?'

'No.'

'Licorice raises it,' he said, chewing. 'Mine tends to be low – I'm not saying they're intrinsically bad – the police. I'm sure most of them start out as okay human beings. But the job corrupts – too much power, too little accountability.'

'I guess the same could be said for doctors and lawyers.'

He smiled again. 'That's no comfort.' The smile stayed on his face but it began to look out of place. 'So. Why does a police consultant need to know anything about Dorsey's *friends*?'

I gave him the same explanation I'd offered Jean Jeffers.

Midway through, his phone rang. He picked it up, said, 'What? Okay, sure . . . hi, Bill, what is it? What? *What*? You've got to be kidding! No walkie, no talkie – I *mean* it. This is a bullsquat misdemeanor we're talking about – I don't care what else he's – okay, you do that. Good idea. Go ahead. *Talk* to him and get back to me, bye.'

He put the phone down. 'Where were we – oh yeah, harassment. What kind?'

'I don't know all the details.'

He pulled his head back and squinted. His neck was thick, but soft. His short arms folded over his abdomen and didn't move. 'Cops ask you to consult but don't let you in on the details? Typical. I wouldn't take the gig.'

Not seeing any way out of it, I said, 'Someone's been sending people harassing tapes with what may be Hewitt's voice on them – screaming "bad love" – the same thing he screamed after he murdered Becky Basille.'

Coburg thought for a minute. 'So? Someone taped him off the t.v. No shortage of strange souls out there. Keeps both of us busy.'

'Maybe,' I said. 'But the police think it's worth looking into.'

'Who's getting these tapes?'

'That I don't know.'

'Must be someone important for the cops to go to all this trouble.'

I shrugged. 'You could ask them.' I recited Milo's name and number. He didn't bother to write it down.

Taking another licorice stick from the jar, he said, 'Tapes. So what's the big deal?'

'The police are wondering if Hewitt might have had a close friend – someone influenced by what he did. Someone with the same dangerous tendencies.'

'Influenced?' He looked puzzled. 'What, some kind of harassment club? Street people going after good citizenry?'

'Hewitt wasn't exactly harmless.'

He began twisting the licorice stick. 'Actually, he was. He was *surprisingly* harmless when he took his medicine. On one of his good days, you might have met him and found him a nice guy.'

'Was he off his medicine when he committed the murder?'

'That's what the coroner says. Too much alcohol, not enough thorazine. Given the biochemistry, he must have stopped eating pills a week or so before.'

'Why?'

'Who knows? I doubt it was a conscious decision – h'mm, guess I won't take my meds this *morning* and let's see how the day goes. More likely he ran out, tried to get a refill and ran into such a hassle he gave up. Then, as he got crazier and crazier, he probably forgot all about the pills and why he was taking them in the first place. Happens all the time to people at the bottom. Every detail of daily living's a struggle for them, but they're expected to remember appointments, fill out forms, wait in line, follow a schedule.'

'I know,' I said. 'I've been to the center. Wondered how the patients coped.'

'Not well is how they cope. Even when they play by the rules they get turned away – Mean old Mr. Recession. Do you have any idea how hard it is for a sick person without money to get help in this city?'

'Sure do,' I said. 'I spent ten years at Western Pediatric hospital.'

'Over in Hollywood?'

I nodded.

'Okay,' he said, 'so you *do* know. Not that I'm glossing over what Dorsey did – that poor girl, every attorney's nightmare, I still lose sleep thinking about it. But he was a victim, too – as sappy and knee-jerk as that sounds. He should have been taken care of, not forced to fend for himself.'

'Institutionalized?'

His eyes turned angry. I noticed their color for the first time: very pale brown, almost tan.

'Taken *care* of. Not *jailed* – oh, hell, even jail wouldn't have been bad if that would have meant treatment. But it never does.'

'Had he been psychotic for a long time?'

'I don't know. He wasn't someone you just sat down and had a chat with – so tell me your life history, pal. Most of the time he was somewhere else.'

'Where was he from, originally?'

'Oklahoma, I think. But he'd been in L.A. for years.'

'Living on the street?'

'Since he was a kid.'

'Any family?'

'None that I know of.'

He took hold of the licorice, touched it to his lip, and used his other hand to caress his tie. Somewhere else, himself.

When he touched his phone I knew he was ready to break off the conversation.

'What kind of music do you play?' I glanced at the guitar-pick clasp.

'What? Oh, this? I just noodle around on weekends.'

'Me, too. I worked my way through college playing guitar.'

'Yeah? Guess lots of guys did.' He pulled the front end of the tie down and looked at the ceiling. I felt his interest continue to slip.

'What do you do mostly, electric or acoustic?'

'Lately I've been getting into electric.' Smile. 'So what's this? Gaining rapport with the subject? Got to hand it to you. At least you didn't get into the usual police/prosecutor rap – guilt-tripping me for what Dorsey did, asking me how can I live with myself defending scum.'

'That's because I don't have a problem with that,' I said. 'It's a good system and you're an important part of it – and no, I'm not patronizing you.'

He held out his hands. 'Whoa.'

I smiled.

'Actually, it's an *okay* system,' he said. 'I'll bet if you met the Founding Fathers, you wouldn't think they were such great guys. Slaveowners, fat cats, and they sure didn't think much of women and kids.'

The phone rang again. He took the call while gnawing on the remains of the licorice, talking lawyerese, bartering some defendant's future, never raising his voice.

When he hung up, he said, 'We try to make the system work for the people the Founding Fathers didn't care about.'

135

'Who funds you?'

'Grants, donations – interested in contributing?'

'I'll think about it.'

He grinned. 'Sure you will. Either way, we'll get by – bad salaries, no expense accounts. That's why most of these people'll be gone by next year – soon as they start thinking home equity and German cars.'

'What about you?'

He laughed. 'Me? I'm a veteran. Five years and thriving. Because it's a heck of a lot more satisfying than drawing up wills or defending polluters.'

He turned serious, looked away from me.

'Sure it gets ugly,' he said, as if responding to a question. 'What Dorsey did was as ugly as it gets.' Eye flicker. 'Jesus, what a . . . it was a tragedy, how else can you put it? A goddamn stupid tragedy. I know I couldn't have done anything differently, but it shouldn't have happened – it just stinks, but what can you do when society keeps lowering itself to the brutal denominator? Dorsey'd never shown me any signs of violence. *Nothing*. I was serious when I said you would have liked him. Most of the time he was pleasant – soft-spoken, passive. One of my easier clients, actually. A little paranoid, but it was always low-key, he never got aggressive with it.'

'What kind of delusions did he have?'

'The usual. Voices in his head telling him to do stuff – cross the street six times one day, drink tomato juice the next, I don't remember exactly.'

'Did the voices make him angry?'

'They annoyed him, but no, I wouldn't call it anger. It was as if he accepted the voices as being a part of him. I see that a lot in the long-timers. They're used to it, deal with it. Nothing aggressive or hostile, that's for sure.'

'As long as he took his medication.'

'I assumed he was taking it because he was always okay with me.'

'How well did you know him?'

'I wouldn't call it knowing. I did some basic legal stuff for him.'

'When did you meet him?'

He looked up at the ductwork, again. 'Let's see . . . it would have to be around a year ago.'

'Walk-in?'

'No, he was referred by the court.'

'What kind of theft were you defending him on?'

136

Smile. 'Cops didn't tell you?'

'I don't get involved in more than I need to.'

'Smart. *Theft* is an overstatement. He lifted a bottle of gin from a liquor store, and a couple of sticks of beef jerky. Did it in plain sight of the clerk and got busted. I'm sure he didn't even mean it. Clerk nearly broke his arm restraining him.'

'What defense were you planning?'

'What do you think?'

'Plea bargain.'

'What else? He had no prior record other than petty stuff. The way the jails are crowded it would have been a slam-dunk.'

He sat up and inserted five fingers into his thick hair. Massaging his scalp, he said, 'Gritz.'

'Pardon me?'

'It's a name. Gritz.'

'As in hominy?'

'With a z. The closest I can come to someone who might be called Dorsey's friend.'

'First name or last?'

'Don't know. He came by here a couple of times with Dorsey. Another homeless guy. The only reason I know his name is because I noticed him hanging around over there – ' pointing to the partition – 'asked Dorsey who he was and Dorsey said "Gritz". First thing I said was what you just did: as in hominy? That went right over Dorsey's head, and I tried to explain it. Spelled "grits", told him what they were, asked him if it was a last name or a first name. He said no, it was a *name* and it was spelled with a z. He spelled it for me. Really slowly – he always talked slow. G-R-I-T-Z. Like it was profound. For all I know he was making it up.'

'Did he tend to do that?'

'He was schizophrenic, what do you think?'

'Did he ever mention the term "bad love" to you?'

He shook his head. 'First time I heard about that was from the police. Asking me why Dorsey had screamed it, as if I'd know.'

Pushing himself away from the desk, he wheeled back in his chair, then sat up. 'And that's about all she wrote.'

'Can you describe this Gritz fellow?'

He thought. 'It was a while ago . . . about the same age as Dorsey – though with street people you can't really tell. Shorter than Dorsey, I think.' He looked at his watch. 'There's a call I've got to make.'

137

I got up and thanked him for his time.

He waved it off and picked up the phone.

'Any idea where this Gritz might be located?' I said, as he dialed.

'Nope.'

'Where did Dorsey hang out?'

'Wherever he could – and I'm not being flip. When it was warm, he liked to go down by the beach – Pacific Palisades Park, all up and down the beaches on PCH. When it cooled down, I was able to get him into a shelter or an SRO a couple of times, but he actually preferred sleeping outdoors – lots of times he bunked down in Little Calcutta.'

'Where's that?'

'Freeway overpass, West L.A.'

'Which freeway?'

'San Diego, just past Sepulveda. Never saw it?'

I shook my head.

He shook his, too, smiled, and put down the phone. 'The invisible city . . . there used to be these little hovels there called Komfy Kort – built God knows when, for Mexican workers doing the day-labor pickup thing on Sawtelle.'

'Those I remember,' I said.

'Did you happen to notice they're not there anymore? City tore them down a few years ago and the street people moved onto the property. Nothing to tear down with *them*, so what could the city do but keep chasing them out? And what with voodoo economics taking hold, *that* became too expensive. So the city let them stay.'

'Little Calcutta.'

'Yeah, it's a great little suburb – you look like a West Side kind of guy – live anywhere near there?'

'Not that far.'

'Go by and take a look, if you can spare the time. See who your neighbors are.'

13

I drove east to the overpass Coburg had described. The freeway formed a concrete ceiling over a fenced dirt lot, an arcing canopy of surprising grace supported by columns that would have challenged Samson. The shade it cast was cool and gray. Even with my windows closed I could hear the roar of unseen cars.

The lot was empty and the dirt looked fresh. No tents or bedrolls, no signs of habitation.

I pulled over across the street, in front of a storage facility the size of an army base, and idled the Seville.

Little Calcutta. The fresh dirt suggested a bulldozer party. Maybe the city had finally cleared it.

I drove further, slowly, past Exposition Boulevard. The west side of the street was lined with apartment buildings, the freeway concealed by ivied slopes. A few more empty spots peeked behind the usual chain link, then a couple of overturned shopping carts that made me stop and peer into the shadows.

Nothing.

I cruised several more blocks, until the freeway twisted out of sight, then turned around.

As I neared Exposition, again, I spied something shiny and huge – a white-metal mountain, some sort of factory or plant. Giant canisters, duodenal twists of pipe, five-story ladders, valves that hinted at monstrous pressure.

Running parallel to the machineworks was a blackened length of railroad track. Bordering the rails was a desert-pale table of sand.

Twenty years in L.A., and I'd never noticed it before.

Invisible city.

I headed toward the tracks, getting close enough to read a small red and blue sign on one of the giant towers. *Avalon Gravel and Asphalt.*

As I prepared to reverse direction again, I noticed another fenced lot catercornered to the plant – darker, almost blackened by the freeway, blocked from street-view by green-gray shrubs. The chain-link fence was obscured by sections of bowed, graffitied plywood, the wood nearly blotted out by the hieroglyphics of rage.

Pulling to the curb, I turned off the engine and got out. The air smelled of dust and spoiled milk. The plant was as still as a mural.

The only other vehicle in sight was the burnt-out chassis of something two-doored, with a crushed roof. My Seville was old and in need of a paint job but here it looked like a royal coach.

I crossed the empty street over to the plywooded fence and looked through an unblocked section of link. Shapes began forming in the darkness, materializing through the metal diamonds like holograms.

An overturned chair bleeding stuffing and springs.

An empty lineman's spool stripped of wire and cracked down the middle.

Food wrappers. Something green and shredded that might once have been a sleeping bag, And always the overhead roar, constant as breath.

Then movement – something on the ground, shifting, rolling. But it was submerged deeply in the shadows and I couldn't tell if it was human, or even real.

I looked up and down the fence, searching for an entrance to the lot, had to walk a ways until I found it: a square hatch cut into the link, held in place with rusty bailing wire.

Prying the wires loose took a while and hurt my fingers. Finally, I bent the flap back, squatted and passed through, re-tying one wire from the other side. Making my way across the soft dirt, my nostrils full of shit-smell, I dodged chunks of concrete, Styrofoam food containers, lumps of things that didn't bear further inspection. No bottles or cans – probably because they were recyclable and redeemable. Let's hear it for Green Power.

But nothing green here. Just blacks, grays, browns. Perfect camouflage for a covert world.

A vile smell overcame even the excremental stench. Hearing the buzz of flies, I looked down at a cat's carcass that was so fresh the maggots hadn't yet homesteaded, and gave it a wide berth. Onward, past an old blanket, clumps of newspaper so sodden they looked like printed bread dough . . . no people that I could see, no movement. Where had it come from?

I arrived back at the spot where I thought the thing had rolled, toward the back of the covered lot, just a few feet from the inner angle of a canted concrete wall.

Standing again, I focused. Waited. Felt my back itch.

Saw it again.

Movement. Hair. Hands. Someone lying rolled up in a sheet – several sheets, a mummy-wrap of frayed bedlinens. Twitchy movements below.

Lovemaking – no. No room for two people in the swaddle.

I walked toward it slowly, making sure I approached head-on, not wanting to startle.

My shoes kicked something hard. The impact was inaudible over the roar, but the figure in the sheeting sat up.

A young dark Latina, bare-shouldered. Soft shoulders, a large vaccine crater on one arm.

She stared at me, pressing the sheets up to her chest, long hair wild and sticky-looking.

Her mouth was open, her face round and plain, scared and baffled.

And humiliated.

The sheet dropped a bit and I saw that she was naked. Something dark and urgent scuffed at her breast – a small head.

A baby. The rest of it concealed by the filthy cotton.

I backed away, smiled, held up my hand in greeting.

The young mother's face was electric with fear.

The baby kept suckling and she placed one hand over its tiny skull.

Near her feet was a small, cardboard box. I got down and looked inside. Disposable diapers, new and used. More flies. A can of condensed milk and a rusty opener. A nearly empty bag of potato chips, a pair of rubber sandals and a pacifier.

The woman tried to nourish her baby while rolling away from me, unraveling more of the sheets and exposing a mottled thigh.

As I started to turn away, the look in her eyes changed from fear to recognition and then to another type of fear.

I whipped around and found myself face to face with a man.

A boy, actually, seventeen or eighteen. Also Latin, small and flimsily built, with a fuzz mustache and a sloping chin so weak it seemed part of his skinny neck. His eyes were downslanted and frantic. His mouth hung open; a lot of his teeth were gone. He had on a torn, checked, flannel shirt, stretched-out doubleknit pants and unlaced sneakers. His ankles were black with dirt.

His hands trembled around an iron bar.

I stepped away. He hesitated then came toward me.

A high sound pierced the freeway din.

The woman screaming.

Startled, the boy looked at her and I moved in, grabbed the bar and twisted it out of his grip. The inertia threw him backwards onto the ground so easily that I felt like a bully.

He stayed there, looking up at me, shielding his face with one hand, ready to be beaten.

The woman was up, tripping out of the sheets, naked, the baby left squalling on the dirt. Her belly was pendulous and stretchmarked, her breasts limp as a crone's, though she couldn't have been much older than twenty.

I threw the bar as far as I could and held out both hands in what I hoped was a gesture of peace.

The two of them looked at me. Now I felt like a bad parent.

The baby was open-mouthed with rage, clawing the air and kicking. I pointed to it.

The woman rushed over and picked it up. Realizing she was naked, she crouched and hung her head.

The chinless boy's hands were still shaking. I tried another smile and his eyes drooped, tugged down by despair.

I took out my wallet, removed a ten, walked over to the woman and held it out to her.

She didn't move.

I put the bill in the cardboard box. Went back to the boy, took out another ten and showed it to him.

More of that same hesitation he'd shown before coming at me with the bar. Then he took a step, biting his lip and teetering like a high-wire artist, and snatched the money.

Holding out yet another bill, I headed for the place where I'd broken through the fence. Checking my back as I trotted through the muck.

142

After a few steps the boy started following me. I picked up the pace and he tried to catch up, but couldn't. Walking was an effort for him. His mouth was open and his limbs looked rubbery. I wondered when he'd last eaten.

I made it to the flap, untied the wire and walked out to the sidewalk. He came through several moments later, rubbing his eyes.

The light hurt my pupils. He appeared to be in agony.

He finally stopped rubbing. I said, '*Habla Ingles?*'

'I'm from Tucson, man,' he said, in unaccented English.

His hands were fisted but the tremor and his small bones mocked his fighter's stance. He started to cough, dry and wheezing. Tried to bring up phlegm and couldn't.

'Didn't mean to scare you,' I said.

He was looking at the money. I extended my arm and he snatched the bill and crammed it under his waistband. The pants were much too big for him and held together with a plastic belt. One of his sneakers was patched with cellophane tape. As his hand balled up around the bill, I saw that the pinky of his left hand was missing.

'Gimme more,' he said. I didn't say anything.

'Gimme more. But she won' fuck you, anyway.'

'I don't want her to.'

He flinched. Thought a moment. 'I won', neither.'

'I'm not interested in that, either.'

He frowned, put a finger inside his mouth and rubbed his gums.

I gave a quick look around, saw no one and took out a fourth ten.

'Whu'?' he said, yanking his hand free and making a grab for it.

Holding it out of reach, I said, 'Is that Little Calcutta?'

'Huh?'

'The place we just were. Is that Little Calcutta?'

'Maybe.'

'Maybe?'

'Yeah.' He coughed some more, hit his chest with the four-fingered hand.

'How many people live there?'

'I dunno.'

'Are there others in there right now? People I didn't see?'

He considered his answer. Shook his head.

'Are there ever others?'

143

'Sometimes.'

'Where are they now?'

'Around.' He looked at the money, worked his tongue against his cheek and came closer.

'She fucks you, it's twenty bucks.'

I put the bill in my pocket.

'Hey!' he said, as if I'd cheated at a game.

'I don't want to fuck anyone,' I said. 'I just want some information. Answer my questions and you'll get paid, okay?'

'Why, man?'

'Because I'm a curious guy.'

'Cop?'

'No.'

He flexed his shoulders and rubbed his gums some more. When he removed his hand, the fingers were bloody.

'Is the baby yours?' I said.

'Tha's what you wanna know?'

'Is it?'

'I dunno.'

'It needs to be looked at by a doctor.'

'I dunno.'

'Is she your woman?'

He smiled. 'Sometimes.'

'What's your name?'

'Terminator Three.' Glaring. Challenging me to mock him.

'Okay,' I said. 'Are there more people in there?'

'I told you, man. Not now, just at night.'

'They come back at night?'

'Yuh.'

'Every night?'

He looked at me as if I were stupid. Shook his head slowly. 'Some nights – it changes places, I dunno.'

'It moves from place to place?'

'Yeah.'

Tent City as a concept. Some New Wave journalist would have a ball with it.

'What about a guy named Gritz?'

'Huh?'

'Gritz.' I began the description Coburg had given me and to my surprise, he broke in: 'Yeah.'

144

'You know him?'

'I seen him.'

'Does he live there?'

The hand went back into his mouth. He fiddled, twisted, pulled out a tooth and grinned. The root was inky with decay. He spit blood onto the pavement and wiped his mouth

'Does Gritz hang out here?'

He didn't hear me, was looking at the tooth, fascinated. I repeated the question. He kept staring, finally dropped the tooth into his pocket.

'Not no more,' he said.

'When's the last time you saw him?'

'Dunno.'

'Days? Weeks?'

'Dunno.'

He reached out to touch the sleeve of my jacket. Fifteen-year-old Harris tweed. The cuffs were starting to fuzz.

I stepped back.

'Wool?' he said.

'Yeah.'

He licked his lips.

'What do you know about Gritz?'

'Nuthin'.'

'But you definitely know him?'

'I seen him around.'

'When's the last time you saw him around?'

He closed his eyes. Opened them. 'A week.'

'A week definitely, or a week, maybe?'

'I think – I dunno, man.'

'Any idea where he is now?'

'To get rich.'

'To get rich?'

'Yeah, what's what he said – he was drinking and partying, you know. And singing – sometimes he liked to sing – and he was singing about hey, man I'm gonna get rich soon. Gonna get me a car and a boat – that kind of shit.'

'Did he say how he was going to get rich?'

'Nah.' A hint of threat sharpened his eyes. Fatigue wiped it out. He slumped.

'He didn't say how?' I repeated.

'No, man, he wuz partying and singing – he was nuts, that's *it*, man.'

'Is Gritz a first name or a last name?'

'*Dunno*, man.' He coughed, hit his chest, wheezed, 'Fuck.'

'If I told you to see a doctor, you'd shine me on, wouldn't you?'

Gap-toothed grin. 'You gonna pay me to go?'

'What if you had a disease you could give her – or the baby?'

'Gimme more money.' Holding out a hand again.

'The baby needs to see a doctor.'

'Gimme more money.'

'Who'd Gritz hang out with?'

'No one.'

'No one at all?'

'I dunno, man, gimme more money.'

'What about a guy named Hewitt?'

'Huh?'

'A guy named Dorsey Hewitt? Ever see Gritz with him?'

I described Hewitt. The boy stared – not that much blanker than his general demeanor, but enough to tell me his ignorance was real.

'Hewitt,' I repeated.

'Don' know the dude.'

'How long have you been hanging out here?'

'Hunerd years.' Phlegmy laugh.

'Hewitt killed a woman. It was on the news.'

'Don't got cable.'

'A social worker named Rebecca Basille – at the Westside Mental Health Center?'

'Yeah, I heard something.'

'What?'

Grin. 'Music. In my head.' He tapped one ear and smiled. 'It's like rock and soul, man. The def cool no-fool.'

I sighed involuntarily.

He brightened, latching onto my frustration like a buzzard on carrion. 'Gimme *money*, man.' Cough. '*Gimme*.'

'Anything else you want to tell me?'

'Yeah.'

Tapping one foot. Waiting for the straight man.

'What?' I said.

146

'The baby's mine.' Smile. His remaining teeth were pink with fresh blood.

'Congratulations.'

'Got a cigarette?'

'I don't smoke.'

'Then gimme *money*. I aks around for you, man. You come back and I tell you everything I aksed.'

I counted what I had in my wallet.

Two twenties and three singles. Gave him all of it. The jacket, too.

14

———

He scrambled back through the fence, and disappeared. I hung around until his footsteps died, then walked back to the car. The air had cooled – sudden shifts were becoming the rule this autumn – a soft wind from the east was nudging scraps of garbage off the sidewalk.

I gassed up the Seville at a station on Olympic and used the pay phone to get the number of the nearest Social Services office. After being put on hold several times and transferred from bureaucrat to bureaucrat, I managed to reach a supervisor and tell her about the infant living under the freeway.

'Was the baby being mistreated, sir?'

'No.'

'Did the baby look malnourished?'

'Actually, no, but – '

'Were there bruises or scars anywhere visible on the baby's body or other signs of abuse?'

'Nothing,' I said. 'The mother was caring for the baby, but they're living in filthy conditions out there. And the boy who might be the baby's father has a cough that sounds tubercular.'

'Was the *baby* coughing?'

'Not yet.'

'For a tuberculosis investigation, you'd have to call Public Health. Ask for a Communicable Disease Officer.'

'There's nothing you can do?'

'Doesn't sound like there's anything we should be doing, sir.'

'How 'bout getting the baby some shelter?'

'They'd have to ask, sir.'

'The baby would?'

'The legal guardians. We don't just go out looking for people.'

Click.

The dial tone was as loud as the freeway. I felt nuts. How did the certifiable psychotics handle it?

I wanted to call Robin. Then I realized I hadn't memorized my new phone number, didn't even know the name of the house's owner. I called Milo. He was at his desk and gave me the seven digits, then said, 'Before you hang up, I just got through with Myra Paprock's file. She wasn't a therapist. Real estate agent, killed on the job. Showing a house and somebody cut her, robbed her, raped her, and wrote "bad love" on the wall with her lipstick.'

'Oh, Jesus.'

'Yeah. In the photos, the lipstick looks like blood.'

'Real estate agent,' I said. 'That's sometimes a second career. Maybe she worked as some kind of therapist first.'

'If she did it's not down here in the file, and the Van Nuys guys seem to have done a pretty thorough job. Plus Shipler – the beating victim – wasn't a shrink, either, so I don't see any obvious mental health connection, here.'

'What did he do?'

'Janitor. Night custodian at Jefferson High. I haven't gotten his file yet but I had a records clerk over at Central give me the basics.'

'Was he killed on the job, too?'

'Nope, in the comfort of his own home.'

'Where'd he live?'

'Budlong Avenue – South L.A.'

'Black?'

'Yeah.'

'What happened to him?'

'Pounded to mush and the house was trashed.'

'Robbery?'

'Doubtful. His stereo, t.v. and some jewelry were left behind.'

'What, then? Someone looking for something?'

'Or someone got really angry. I want to read the whole file, got a call in for it.'

'Real estate agent and janitor,' I said. 'Doesn't make any sense. Any connection between them?'

'Other than "bad love" on the wall, there doesn't seem to be any.

Nothing matches. She was thirty-five, he was sixty-one. He was killed early morning – right after he finished work on the nightshift – and she got it in the middle of the day. She was stabbed, he was clubbed. There were even differences in what the killer used to write "bad love". Shipler's was done in molasses from his fridge.'

'In both cases the killer was opportunistic – used something of the victim's.'

'Weapons, too,' he said. 'She was killed with a kitchen knife from the house she was showing, Shipler with a fireplace poker that was identified as his. So?'

'I don't know, maybe it indicates some kind of power thing – dominance over the victims – turning the victims against themselves. Like using my tree branch on the koi. Were there any bondage or S & M overtones to either murder?'

'Paprock's bra was wrapped around her neck, but the coroner said it was done when she was already dead. Far as I can tell there were no sexual overtones at all to Shipler.'

'Still,' I said, 'the message was important. It must mean something to the killer.'

'It sure does,' he said, without enthusiasm.

'Did Shipler live alone?'

'Yeah, divorced.'

'What about Paprock?'

'No match there, either. Married, two kids.'

'If nothing was taken from Shipler's house,' I said, 'what was the assumed motive?'

'A gang thing – there was lots of activity in Shipler's neighbor-hood, even back then. Lots more, now. Like you said before, a trashed house could mean someone looking for something. Central figured dope. Figured Shipler was involved on some level and "bad love" was some sort of gangbanger slogan they hadn't heard of yet. They checked it out with the CRASH detail and *they* hadn't heard of it, but new stuff comes up all the time.'

'Did Shipler turn out to be involved in gangs or dope?'

'Far as I can tell he had no record, but plenty of scrotes slip through the cracks. In terms of there being no burglary, Southwest figured it was punks panicking and leaving before they could take anything. Which is consistent with gang-wannabees – new recruits out on a virgin adventure.'

'An initiation thing?'

'Yeah, they start 'em young. Automatics in the diapers. Speaking of which, I caught my little truant bastards on the Palms robbery – thirteen and fifteen. No doubt they'll get referred for some kind of therapy. Want a referral?'

'No thanks.'

'Cynic.'

'Was there gang activity where Paprock was killed?'

'A little, on the fringes. It's mostly working-class tough – north end of Van Nuys. No one made the gang assumption in that one, but maybe if Van Nuys had . . . Southwest, they would have. Neither of them knew about the other case – still don't.'

'Going to tell them?' I said.

'First I'm gonna read Shipler's file thoroughly, see what I can pull out of it. Then, yeah, I'll have to tell them, do the old network blah blah. Both cases are real cold, be interesting to see what kind of a response I get. Hopefully the whole thing won't deteriorate into endless memories. Though if "bad love" shows up anywhere in *Stoumen*'s file, we've got interstate blah blah.'

'Hear from Seattle, yet?'

'Very briefly. They're sending down records, it'll probably take a week or so. Both detectives on that one are retired and unavailable. Probable translation: burnouts gone fishing. If anything provocative comes up in the file, I'll bug 'em anyway.'

'What about the FBI records on other "bad love" murders?'

'Not yet, *them* gears grind slowly.'

'A real estate agent, a janitor, and "bad love," ' I said. 'I still think it has something to do with that conference. Or de Bosch, himself – Paprock and Shipler could have been his patients.'

'So why would someone kill them?'

'Maybe it's another patient, mad about something.'

'Then what's *your* connection?'

'I don't know . . . nothing makes sense, dammit.'

'You learn anything from Jeffers?'

'No one at the Center remembers Hewitt having any friends. But she referred me to Hewitt's lawyer and he gave me a name and possible address.' I described my encounter with the people under the freeway.

'Grits,' he said. 'As in hominy.'

'With a z. Could be first name or last, or just a nickname.'

'I'll run it through.'

151

'The kid I spoke to said he's been gone about a week. He also said Gritz was talking and singing about getting rich.'

'Singing?'

'That's what he said.'

'Oh those romantic hoboes, strumming around the campfire.'

'Maybe Gritz had some kind of job lined up, or maybe it's baloney. The kid could very well have been putting me on. For what it's worth, he said he'd ask around, I should come back later.'

'Getting rich,' he said. '*Everyone* talks and sings about it. That Calcutta place might be the dregs, but it's still L.A.'

'True,' I said. 'But wouldn't it be interesting if Gritz really did expect to get paid for something – like killing my koi, and other nasties?'

'Hitman on a fish? So who's doing the hiring?'

'The anonymous bad guy – I know, it's a ridiculous idea?'

'At this point, nothing's ridiculous, Alex, but if someone was looking to hire a nighttime skulker would they choose a homeless nutcase?'

'True . . . maybe what Gritz was hired for was to scream on tape – to imitate Hewitt because he knew what Hewitt sounded like.'

'Imitate?' he said. 'Those voice tracks sounded identical to me, Alex. Though we may never be able to verify it. I talked to the voiceprint guy over at the Sheriff's and screams *are* useless, legally. In order to make a match that can be used in court, you need two samples, minimum of twenty words on each and the exact same phrases. Even then, it gets challenged a lot and thrown out.'

'What about for non-admissible comparison?'

'Matching screams is still an iffy-business. It's words that have unique characteristics. I asked the Sheriff to give a listen, anyway, he said he's backlogged but would try to get to it eventually . . . why would someone want to imitate Hewitt?'

'I don't know – I can't help but think the tape's part of a ritual. Something ceremonial that only means something to the killer.'

'What about the kid on the tape?'

'Could be a homeless kid – someone from Little Calcutta or some place like it. Living down there could explain the robot quality of the voice despair. You should have seen it, Milo. The boy's gums were bleeding, he had a tubercular cough. The girl was naked, wrapped up in a sheet, trying to feed the baby. If I'd offered enough money, I probably could have *bought* the baby.'

'I've seen it,' he said softly.

'I know you have. I have, too. It's all around. But I haven't really let it register for a while.'

'What're you gonna do, solve everyone's problems? Plenty of your own to deal with, for the time being. You get names on the freeway people?'

'Not the girl. *He* calls himself Terminator Three.'

He laughed. 'No one else down there besides them and the baby?'

'No one I could see and I was flashing ten-dollar bills.'

'Real smart, Alex.'

'I watched my back.'

'Yeah.'

'The kid said the place fills up at night. I could go back after dark and see if anyone else knows Gritz.'

'You're really in the mood to get your throat cut, aren't you?'

'If I had a macho cop with me I'd be safe, right?'

'Don't count on it . . . yeah, okay, it's probably a waste of time, but that makes me feel *right* at home.'

Robin was still working in the garage, hunched over her bench, wielding shiny sharp things that resembled dental picks. Her hair was tied up and her goggles were lodged in her curls. Under her overalls, her t-shirt was tightened by perspiration. She said, 'Hi, doll,' as her hands continued to move. The dog was at her feet and he stood and licked my hand as I looked over Robin's shoulder.

A tiny rectangle of abalone was clamped to a padded section of the bench. The edges were beveled and the corners were inlaid with bits of ivory and gold wire. She'd traced the shell with minuscule curlicue-shapes, cut out some of them, and was in the process of excising another.

'Beautiful,' I said. 'Fretboard inlay?'

'Uh-huh. Thanks.' She blew away dust and cleaned the edge of a pick with a fingernail.

'You do root canal, too?'

She laughed and hunched lower. The tools clicked as she carved out a speck of shell. 'Headstock inlay – kind of baroque for my taste, but it's for a stockbroker who can't play very well and wants a showpiece for his wall.'

She worked some more, finally put the tools down and wiped her forehead. 'Enough for one day, I'm cramping up.'

'Everything okay?' I rubbed her neck.

'Nice and quiet. How about you?'

'Not bad.'

I kissed her. The wind got stronger and drier, ruffling the cypress trees and shooting a cold stream through the open garage. Robin unclamped the abalone, and put it in her pocket. Her arms were goosebumped. I put mine around them and the two of us headed for the house. By the time we got to the door, the wind was whipping the trees and stirring the dust, causing the bulldog to blink and sniff.

'Santa Ana?' she said.

'Too cold. Probably something Arctic that barely made it down here.'

'Brr,' she said, unlocking the door. 'Leave your jacket in the car?'

I shook my head. We went inside.

'You were wearing one, weren't you?' she said, rubbing her hands together. 'That baggy brown tweed.'

Artist's eye.

I said, 'Uh huh.'

'Did you lose it?'

'Not exactly.'

'Not exactly?'

'I gave it away.'

She laughed. 'You what?'

'No big deal. It was fraying.'

'Who'd you give it to?'

I told her about Little Calcutta. She listened with her hands on her hips, shaking her head, and went into the kitchen to wash her hands. When she came back, her head was still moving from side to side.

'I know, I know,' I said. 'It was a bleeding heart reflex, but they really were pitiful – it was a cheap old thing, anyway.'

'You wore it the first time we went out. I never liked it.'

'You didn't?'

'Nope. Too philosophy prof.'

'Why didn't you tell me?'

She shrugged. 'It wasn't that important.'

'Snoring, poor taste in haberdashery. What else don't you like that you haven't informed me about?'

'Nothing. Now that you've ditched the coat, you're perfect.'

She ruffled my hair, walked to the French doors, and looked out at the mountains. They were shimmering, denuded in patches, where the foliage was brushed back like blowdried hair. The pool water was choppy, the surface gritty with leaves and dirt.

Robin loosened her hair. I hung back and kept looking at her.

Perfect female statuary, rock-still against the turbulence.

She unsnapped one overall strap, then the other, letting the baggy denim collapse around her feet, and stood there in t-shirt and panties.

Half-turning, hands on hips, she looked back at me. 'How 'bout giving *me* something, big boy?' she said, in a Mae West voice.

The dog grumbled. Robin cracked up. 'Quiet, you! You're wrecking my timing.'

'*Now*, it feels like a home,' she said, snuggling under the covers. 'Though I do prefer our little love nest, be it ever so humble. So what'd you find out today?'

My second summation of the day. I did it quickly, adding what Milo'd told me about the murders and leaving out the gross pathology. Even sanitized, it was bad, and she turned quiet.

I rubbed her lower back, allowing my hand to linger on swells and dimples. Her body loosened, but only for a moment.

'You're sure you've never heard of those other two people?' she said, stilling my hand.

'I'm sure. And there doesn't even seem to be any connection between the two of *them*. The woman was a white real estate agent, the man a black janitor. He was twenty years older, they lived on opposite ends of the city, were killed in different ways. Nothing in common but "bad love". Maybe they were patients of de Bosch.'

'They couldn't be old patients of *yours*?'

'No way,' I said. 'I've been through every one of my case files. To be honest, I don't see the patient angle as too likely, period. If someone has a hangup with de Bosch, why go after the people he treated?'

'What about group therapy, Alex? Things can get rough in groups, can't they? People lashing out at one another? Maybe someone got dumped badly and never forgot it.'

'I guess it's possible,' I said, sitting up. 'A good therapist always tries to keep a handle on the group's emotional climate, but things can get out of control. And sometimes there's no way to know someone's feeling victimized. Once, at the hospital, I had to calm down the father of a kid with a bone tumor who brought a loaded pistol onto the ward. When I finally got him to open up, it came out that he'd been boiling for weeks. But there was no warning at all – till then he'd been a really easy-going guy.'

'There you go,' she said. 'So maybe some patient of de Bosch sat there and took it and never told anyone. Finally, years later, he decided to get even.'

'But what kind of therapy group would bring together a real estate agent from the Valley and a black janitor?'

'I don't know – maybe *they* weren't the patients, maybe their kids were. A parents group for problem kids – de Bosch was basically a *child* therapist, wasn't he?'

I nodded, trying to imagine it. 'Shipler was a lot older than Paprock – I suppose she could have been a young mother and he an old father.'

We heard scratching and thumping at the door. I got up and opened it and the dog bounded in. He headed straight for Robin's side of the bed, stood on his hind legs, put his paws on the mattress and began snorting. She lifted him up and he rewarded her with lusty licks.

'Settle down,' she said. 'Uh oh – look, he's getting excited.'

'Without testicles, yet. See the effect you have on men?'

'But of *course*.' She batted her lashes at me, turned back to the dog and finally got him to lie still by kneading the folds of flesh around his jowls. He lapsed into sleep with an ease that I envied. But when I leaned over to kiss her, he opened his eyes, snuffled and insinuated himself between us, curling atop the covers and licking his paws.

I said, 'Maybe Milo can get hold of Paprock's and Shipler's medical histories, see if De Bosch's name or the Corrective School appears on them. Sometimes people conceal psych treatment, but with the cost, it's more likely there's some kind of insurance record. I'll ask him when I see him tonight.'

'What's tonight?'

'We were planning on going back to the freeway, try to talk to more of the homeless people in order to get a handle on this Gritz character.'

'Is it safe going back there?'

'I'll have Milo with me. Whether or not it's productive remains to be seen.'

'All right,' she said uneasily. 'If you want it to be productive, why don't you stop at a market and get those people some food?'

'Good idea. You're full of them today, aren't you?'

'Motivation,' she said. She turned serious, reached up and held my face in both of her hands. 'I want this to be over. Please take care of yourself.'

'Promise.' We managed to maintain a convoluted embrace despite the dog.

I fell asleep, smelling perfume and kibble. When I woke up my stomach was sour and my feet were sore. Inhaling and letting out the air, I sat up and cleared my eyes.

'What is it?' Robin mumbled, her back to me.

'Just thinking.'

'About what?' She rolled over and faced me.

'Someone in a therapy group, getting wounded and keeping it inside all these years.'

She touched my face.

'What the hell do *I* have to do with it?' I said. 'Am I just a name on a damned brochure, or did I hurt someone without ever knowing it?'

15

I heard the unhealthy-sounding engine from inside the house. Milo's Fiat, reduced to a squat, little toy on the monitor.

I went outside. The wind had stopped. The car expelled a plume of smoke, then convulsed. It didn't look as if it would survive the evening.

'Figured it would blend in where we're going,' he said, getting out. He carried a large, white plastic bag and was wearing work clothes. The bag smelled of garlic and meat.

'More food?' I said.

'Sandwiches – Italian. Just consider me your official LAPD delivery boy.'

Robin was back in the garage, working under a funnel of fluorescence. The dog was there, too, and he charged us, heading straight for the bag.

Milo lifted it out of reach. 'Sit. Stay – better yet, go away.'

The dog snorted once, turned his back on us, and sank to his haunches.

Milo said, 'Well, one out of three ain't bad.' He waved at Robin. She raised a hand and put down her tools.

'She looks right at home,' he said. 'How 'bout you, Nick Danger?'

'I'm fine. Anything on Gritz in the records?'

Before he could answer, Robin came over.

'He's brought us dinner,' I said.

'What a prince.' She kissed his cheek. 'Are you hungry right now?'

'Not really,' he said, touching his gut and looking down at the ground. 'Had a little appetizer while I waited.'

'Good for you,' she said. 'Growing boy.'

'Growing the wrong way.'

'You're fine, Milo. You've got *presence*.' She patted his shoulder. From the way her fingers were flexing I knew she was eager to get back to her bench. I was itchy, too, thinking of the freeway people. The dog continued to sulk.

'How 'bout you, hon?' she said to me, and thinking – or pretending – it was meant for him, the dog came over.

'I can wait.'

'Me, too. So let me stick this in the fridge and when you guys get back, we'll chow down.'

'Sounds good.' Milo gave her the bag. The dog tried to lick it and she said, 'Relax, I've got a milk bone for you.'

Above the roofline, the sky was black and empty. Lights from the houses across the canyon seemed a continent away.

'You'll be okay?' I said.

'I'll be fine. Go.' She gave me a quick kiss and a small shove.

Milo and I headed for the Fiat. The dog watched us drive away.

The sound of the gate clanking shut made me feel better about leaving her up there. Milo coasted to Benedict, shifted to first, then upward, squeezing as much speed as possible out of the little car. Shifting roughly, big hands nearly covering the top of the steering wheel. As we headed south, I said, 'Anything on Gritz?'

'One possible citation – thank God it's an unusual name. Lyle Edward, male white, thirty-four years old, five six, one-thirty, I forget the color of his eyes.'

'Coburg said he was shorter than Hewitt.'

He nodded. 'Bunch of drunk and disorderlies from back when we still bothered with those, possession of narcotics, couple of shoplifting busts, nothing heavy.'

'When did he come to L.A.?'

'First arrest was fourteen years ago. The computer gives him no known address, no parole officer, either. He got probation for some of his naughties, lived at County Jail for the others and paid his debt in full.'

'Any mention of mental illness?'

'There wouldn't be unless he was a mentally disordered sex offender or committed some other kind of violent psycho crime.'

159

'I'll call Jean Jeffers Monday, see if I can find out if he ever got treated at the center.'

'Meanwhile, we can talk to the Off-rampers, for what it's worth. All he is, is a name, so far.'

'Robin suggested we should bring them food. Increase the rapport.'

He shrugged. 'Why not. There's a mini-market over on Olympic.'

We drove a bit more. He frowned and rubbed his face with one hand.

'Something the matter?' I said.

'Nah . . . just the usual. Justice got raped again – my truant scumbags. The old lady died this afternoon.'

'I'm sorry. Does that make it murder?'

He pumped his gas pedal leg. 'It makes it *shit*. She had badly clogged arteries and a big tumor growing in her colon. Autopsy said it was just a matter of time. That, her age, and the fact that the kids never actually touched her means the D.A.'s office doesn't want to bother to prove it was an unnatural death. Once they hospitalized her, she was never well enough to get even a deathbed declaration and without her testimony, there's not much of a case against the little bastards even for robbery. So they probably get a stern lecture and walk. Wanna make a bet by the time they start shaving, someone else'll be dead?'

He got to Sunset and joined the smooth, fast traffic flowing west from Beverly Hills. Amid the Teutonic tanks and cigarillo sports jobs, the Fiat looked like a mistake. A Mercedes cut in front of us and Milo swore viciously.

I said, 'You could give him a ticket.'

'Don't tempt me.'

A mile later, I said, 'Robin came up with a possible link between Paprock and Shipler. Both could have been in group therapy with de Bosch. Treatment for themselves, or some kind of parents group to talk about problem kids. The killer could also have been in the group, gotten treated roughly – or thought he had – and developed a grudge.'

'Group therapy . . .'

'Some kind of common problem – what else would draw two people from such different backgrounds to de Bosch?'

'Interesting . . . but if it was a parents group, de Bosch didn't run it. He died in eighty and Paprock's kids are six and seven years old,

160

now. So they weren't alive when he was. In fact, at the time Myra died, they were only babies. So what kind of problems could they have had?'

'Maybe it was a child-rearing program. Or some kind of chronic illness support group. And are you sure Paprock was only married once?'

'According to her file she was.'

'Okay,' I said. 'So maybe *Katarina* was the therapist. Or someone else at the school – maybe the killer believes in collective guilt. Or it could have been an *adult* treatment group. Child therapists don't always limit themselves to kids.'

'Fine. But now we're back to the same old question: What's *your* link?'

'Has to be the conference. The killer's gotten severely paranoid – let his rage get out of control. To him, anyone associated with de Bosch is guilty and where better to start than a bunch of therapists paying public homage to the old man? Maybe Stoumen's hit-and-run was no accident.'

'What? Major-league mass murder? The killer's going after patients *and* therapists?'

'I don't know – I'm just grasping.'

He heard the frustration in my voice. 'It's okay, keep grasping, doesn't cost the taxpayers a dime. For all I know, we're dealing with something so crazy, it'll never make sense.'

We rode in silence for a while. Then he said, 'De Bosch's clinic was private, expensive. How could a janitor like Shipler afford getting treatment there?'

'Sometimes private clinics treat a few hardship cases. Or maybe Shipler had good health insurance through the school system. What about Paprock? Did she have money?'

'Nothing huge, as far as I can tell. Husband worked as a car salesman.'

'Can you get hold of their insurance records?'

'If they had any, and haven't been destroyed.'

I thought of two motherless grade-school children and said, 'How old, exactly, were Paprock's children at the time of her murder?'

'Don't remember exactly – little.'

'Who raised them?'

'I assume the husband.'

'Is he still in town?'

'Don't know that either, yet.'

'If he is, maybe he'll be willing to talk about her, tell us if she was ever a therapy patient at de Bosch's clinic.'

He hooked a finger toward the rear seat. 'Got the file right there, check out the address.'

I swung around toward the darkened seat and saw a file box.

'Right on top,' he said. 'The brown one.'

Colors were indistinguishable in the darkness, but I reached over, groped around and came up with a folder. Opening it, I squinted.

'There's a penlight in the glove compartment.'

I tried to open the compartment but it was stuck. Milo leaned across and slammed it with his fist. The door dropped open and papers slid to the floor. I stuffed them back in and finally found the light. Its skinny beam fell on a page of crime-scene photos stapled to the right-hand page. Lots of pink and red. Writing on a wall: A closeup of BAD LOVE in big, red, block letters that matched the blood on the floor. . . neat lettering . . . a bloody thing below.

I turned to the facing page. The name of Myra Paprock's widower was midway through the intake data.

'Ralph Martin Paprock,' I said. 'Valley Vista Cadillac. The home address is in North Hollywood.'

'I'll run it through DMV, see if he's still around.'

I said, 'I need to keep looking for the other conference people to warn them.'

'Sure, but if you can't tell them who and why, what does that leave? "Dear Sir or Madam, this is to inform you might be bludgeoned, stabbed, or run over, by unidentified revenge-crazed psycho"?'

'Maybe one of them can tell me the who and why. And I know I'd have liked to have been warned. The problem is finding them. None of them are working or living where they were at the time of the conference. And the woman I thought might be Rosenblatt's wife hasn't returned any of my calls.'

Another stretch of silence.

'You're wondering,' he said, 'if they've been visited, too.'

'It did cross the mind. Katarina's not listed in the APA directory since five years ago. She could have just stopped paying dues, but it doesn't seem like her to just drop out of psychology and close up the school. She was ambitious, very much taken with carrying on her father's work.'

'Well,' he said, 'it should be easy enough to check tax rolls and

Social Security records on all of them, find out who's breathing and who ain't.'

He reached Hilgard and turned left, passing the campus of the university where I'd jumped through academic hoops for so many years.

'So many people gone,' I said. 'Now the Wallace girls. It's as if everyone's folding up their tents and escaping.'

'Hey,' he said, 'maybe they know something we don't.'

The strip-mall at Olympic and Westwood was dark except for the flagrant white glare from the mini-mart. The store was quiet and a turbaned Pakistani was drinking Gatorade behind the counter.

We stocked up on overpriced bread, canned soup, lunch and milk. The Pakistani eyed us unpleasantly as he tallied up the total. He wore a company shirt printed repetitively with the mart's parent company in lawn-green. The nametag pinned to his breast pocket was blank.

Milo reached for his wallet. I got mine out first and handed the clerk cash. He continued to look unhappy.

'Whatsamatter?' said Milo. 'Too much cholesterol in our diet?'

The clerk pursed his lips and glanced up at the video camera above the door. The machine's cyclops eye was sweeping the store slowly. The screen below filled with milky gray images.

We followed his gaze to the dairy case. An unkempt man stood in front of it, not moving, staring at cartons of half-and-half. I hadn't noticed him while shopping and wondered where he'd come from.

Milo eyed him for a long moment, then turned back to the clerk.

'Yeah, police work's strenuous,' he said in a loud voice. 'Got to shovel in those calories in order to catch the bad guys.'

He laughed even louder. It sounded almost mad.

The man at the dairy case twitched and half-turned. He glared at us for a second, then returned to studying the cream.

He was gaunt and hairy, wearing a dirt-blackened army jacket, jeans and beach sandals. His hands shook and one clouded eye had to be blind.

Another member of Dorsey Hewitt's extended family.

He slapped the back of his neck with one hand, turned again, tried to match Milo's stare.

Milo gave a salute. 'Evening, pal.'

The man didn't move for a second. Then he shoved his hands into his pockets and left the store, sandals slapping the vinyl floor.

The clerk watched him go. The cash register gave a computer burp and expelled a receipt. The Pakistani tore off the tape and dropped it into one of the half-dozen bags we'd filled.

'Got a box for all this?' said Milo.

'No, sir,' said the clerk.

'What about in back?'

Shrug.

We carried the food out. The gaunt man was at the far end of the lot, kicking asphalt and walking from store to store staring at black glass.

'Hey,' Milo called out. No response. He repeated it, pulled a cereal variety pack out of one of the bags and waved it over his head.

The man straightened, looked toward us, but didn't approach. Milo walked ten feet from him and underhanded the cereal.

The man shot his arms out, missed the catch, sank to his knees, and retrieved it. Milo was heading back to the car and didn't see the look on the man's face. Confusion, distrust, then a spark of gratitude that fizzled just short of ignition.

The gaunt man hobbled off into the darkness, fingers ripping at the plastic wrapping, sprinkling cereal onto the pavement.

Milo said, 'Let's get the hell out of here.' We got into the Fiat and he drove around toward the back of the mall where three dumpsters sat. Several empty cartons were piled up loosely against the bins, most of them torn beyond utility. We finally found a couple that looked and smelled relatively clean, put the bags in them and stashed the food in back of the car, next to Myra Paprock's homicide file.

A sliver of moon was barely visible behind a cloud-veil, and the sky looked dirty. The freeway was a stain topped with light and noise. After we rounded Exposition, Little Calcutta continued to elude us – the darkness and the plywood barrier concealed the lot totally. But the place on the sidewalk where I'd talked to Terminator Three was just within the light of an ailing streetlamp and I was able to point it out to Milo.

We got out and found gaps in the plywood. Through them, blue tongues quivered – thin gaseous alcohol flames.

'Sterno,' I said.

Milo said, 'Frugal gourmets.'

164

I took him to the spot along the fence where I'd unhinged the makeshift hatch a few hours before. Extra wires had been added since then, rusty and rough, wound too tightly to unravel by hand.

Milo took a Swiss army knife out of his trouser pocket and flipped out a tiny plier-like tool. Twisting and snipping, he managed to free the hatch.

We went back to the car, took out the boxes of groceries and stepped through. Blue lights began extinguishing, as if we'd brought a hard wind.

Milo reached into his trousers again and pulled out the penlight I'd used in the car. I'd replaced it in the glove compartment and hadn't seen him pocket it.

He removed something from one of the grocery bags and shined the light on it. Plastic-wrapped bologna slices.

He held it up and shouted, 'Food!'

Barely audible over the freeway. Fires continued to go out.

Training his beam more directly on the bologna he waved the meat back and forth. The package and the hand that held it seemed suspended in mid-air, a special effect.

When nothing happened for several more seconds, he placed the meat on the ground, making sure to keep the penlight trained on it, then removed more groceries from his bag and spread them out on the dirt. Walking backwards, toward the hatch, he created a snaky trail of food that led out to the sidewalk.

'Goddamn Hansel and Gretel,' he muttered, then he slipped back out.

I followed him. He was standing against the Fiat, had emptied one bag and crumpled it and was tossing it from hand to hand.

As we stood there and waited, cars rocketed overhead and the concrete hummed. Milo lit up a bad panatella and blew short-lived smoke rings.

A few minutes later, he stubbed out his cigar and jammed it between his fingers. Walking back to the hatch, he stuck his head through, didn't move for a second, then beckoned me to follow him through.

We stopped just a few feet from the hatch and he aimed the penlight upward, highlighting movement about fifteen feet up.

Frantic, choppy, a scramble of arms.

Squinting, I managed to make out human forms. Down on their

knees, scooping and snatching, just as the man at the mini-mart had done.

Within seconds they were gone and the food had vanished. Milo cupped his hands around his mouth and shouted over the freeway: 'Lots more, folks.'

Nothing.

He clicked his light off and we retreated to the other side of the fence again.

It seemed like a game – a futile one. But he looked at ease.

He began emptying another bag, placing food on the streetlit patch of sidewalk, just out of reach of the hatch. Then he returned to the car, sat on the rear-deck causing the springs to groan, and relit his cigar.

Luring and trapping – *enjoying* the hunt.

More time passed. Milo's eyes kept shifting to the fence, then leaving it. His expression didn't change, the cigar tilted as he bit down on it.

Then he stayed on the fence.

A large, dark hand was reaching out, straining to grab a loaf of white bread.

Milo went over and kicked the package away and the hand drew back.

'Sorry,' said Milo. 'No grain without pain.'

He took his badge out and shoved it at the hatch.

'Just talk, that's it,' he said.

Nothing.

Sighing, he picked up the bread, tossed it through the hatch. Picking up a can of soup he wiggled it.

'Make it a balanced meal, pal.'

A moment later, a pair of unlaced sneakers appeared in the opening. Above them, the frayed cuffs of greasy-looking plaid pants and the bottom seam of an army blanket.

The head above the cloth remained unseen, shielded by darkness.

Milo held the soup can between thumb and forefinger. New Orleans Gourmet Gumbo.

'Lots more where this came from,' he said. 'Just for answering a few questions, no hassles.'

One plaid leg angled forward through the opening. A sneaker hit the pavement, then the other.

A man emerged into the streetlight, wincing.

He had the blanket wrapped around him to the knees, covering his head like a monk's cowl and shrouding most of his face.

What showed of the skin was black and grainy. The man took an awkward step, as if testing the integrity of the sidewalk, and the blanket dropped a bit. His skull was big and half-bald, above a long, bony face that looked caved-in. His beard was a kinky gray rash, his skin cracked and caked. Fifty or sixty or seventy. A battered nose so flat it almost merged with his crushed cheeks, spreading like melted tar. His eyes squinted and watered and didn't stop moving.

He had the white bread in his hand and was looking at the soup.

Milo tried to give it to him.

The man hesitated, working his jaws. His eyes were quieter, now.

'Know what a gift horse is?' said Milo.

The man swallowed. Drawing his blanket around himself, he squeezed the bread so hard the loaf turned into a figure eight.

I went over to him and said, 'We just want to talk, that's it.'

He looked into my eyes. His were jaundiced and clogged with blood vessels, but something shone through – maybe intelligence, maybe just suspicion. He smelled of vomit and alcohol-belch and breath-mints and his lips were as loose as a mastiff's. I worked hard at standing my ground.

Milo came up behind me and covered some of the stench with cigar smoke. He put the soup up against the man's chest. The man looked at it, finally took it but continued to stare at me.

'You are not police.' His voice was surprisingly clear. 'You are definitely not police.'

'True,' I said. 'But he is.'

The man glanced at Milo and smiled. Rubbing the part of the blanket that covered his abdomen, he shoved both hands under it, secreting the bread and the soup.

'A few questions, friend,' said Milo. 'Simple stuff.'

'Nothing in life is simple,' said the man.

Milo hooked a thumb at the bags on the sidewalk. 'A philosopher. There's enough there to feed you and your friends – have a nice little party.'

The man shook his head. 'It could be poison.'

'Why the hell would it be poison?'

Smile. 'Why not? The world's poison. A while back someone

gave someone a present and it was full of poison and some-one died.'

'Where'd this happen?'

'Mars.'

'Seriously.'

'Venus.'

'Okay,' said Milo, blowing smoke. 'Suit yourself, we'll ask our questions elsewhere.'

The man licked his lips. 'Go ahead. I've got the virus, makes no difference to me.'

'The virus, huh?' said Milo.

'Don't believe me, you can kiss me.'

The man flicked his tongue. The blanket fell to his shoulders. Underneath, he wore a greasy Bush-Quayle T-shirt. His neck and shoulders were emaciated.

'I'll pass,' said Milo.

The man laughed. 'Bet you will – now what? Gonna beat it *out* of me?'

'Beat what out of you?'

'Whatever you want. You've got the power.'

'Nah,' said Milo. 'This is the new LAPD. We're New Age Sensitive Guys.'

The man laughed. His breath was hot and emetic. 'Bearshit. You'll always be savages – got to be to keep order.'

Milo said, 'Have a nice day,' and began to turn.

'What do you want to know, anyway?'

'Anything about a citizen named Lyle Edward Gritz, ' said Milo. 'You know him?'

'Like a brother.'

'That so?'

'Yup,' said the man. 'Unfortunately, this day and age, families deteriorating and all, that means not well at all.'

Milo looked over at the hatch. 'He in there, now?'

'Nope.'

'See him recently?'

'Nope.'

'But he did hang out here.'

'From time to time.'

'When was the last time?'

The man ignored the question and began staring at me again.

168

'What *are* you?' he said. 'Some kind of journalist riding along?'

'He's a doctor,' said Milo.

'Oh yeah?' Smile. 'Got any penicillin? Things get pretty infectious down here. Amoxycillin, erythromycin, tetracycline – anything to zap those little cocci boogers.'

'I'm a psychologist.'

'Ooh,' said the man, as if wounded. He closed his eyes and shook his head. When he opened them they were dry and focused. 'Then you're not worth a damn to me – pardon my linguistics.'

'Gritz,' said Milo. 'Can you tell me anything about him?'

The man appeared to be contemplating. 'White trash, juicehead, low IQ. But able-bodied. He had no excuse ending up down here. Not that I do – you probably think I was some kind of white collar over-achiever don't you? 'Cause I'm black and I know grammar.'

Smiling.

I smiled back.

'Wrong,' he said. 'I collected *garbage*. Professionally. City of Compton. Good pay, you wear your gloves, it's fine, terrific benefits. My mistake was leaving and starting my own business. Vinyl flooring. I did good work, had six people working for me. Did fine until business slumped and I let the dope comfort me.'

He produced one arm from under the blanket. Raised it and let the plaid sleeve fall back from a bony forearm. The underside of the limb was knotted with scars and abscesses, keloided and bunched, raw in spots.

'This is a fresh one,' he said, eyeing a scab near his wrist. 'Got off just before sundown. I waive my rights, why don't you take me in, give me a bunk for the night?'

'Not my thing,' said Milo.

'Not your thing?' The man laughed. 'What are you, some kind of liberal?'

Milo looked at him and smoked.

The man put his arm back. 'Well, at least get me a *real* doctor, so I can get hold of some methadone.'

'What about the county?'

'County ran out. Can't even get antibiotics from the county.'

169

'Well,' said Milo. 'I can give you a lift to an emergency room if you want.'

The man laughed again, scornfully. 'For what? Wait around all night with gunshots and heart attacks? I've got no active diagnosis – just the virus, no symptoms yet. So all they'll do is keep me waiting. Jail's better – they process you faster.'

'Here,' said Milo, dipping into his pocket for his wallet. He took out some bills and handed them to the man. 'Find a room, keep the change.'

The man gave a warm, broad smile and tucked the money under his blanket. 'That's real nice, Mr. Policeman. You made this po', unfortunate, homeless individual's evening.'

Milo said, 'Was Gritz into dope, too?'

'Just juice. Like I said, white trash. Him and his hillbilly singing.'

'He liked to sing?'

'All the time, this yodely white-trash voice. Wanted to be Elvis.'

'Any talent?'

The man shrugged. 'Who am I to judge?'

'Did he ever get violent with anyone?'

'Not that I saw.'

'What else can you tell me about him?'

'Not much. Stuck to himself – we all do. This is Little Calcutta, not some hippie commune.'

'He ever hang out with anyone?'

'Not that I saw.'

'How about Dorsey Hewitt?'

The man's lips pursed. 'Hewitt, Hewitt . . . The one that did that caseworker?'

'You knew him?'

'No, I read the paper – when that fool did that, I was worried. Backlash. Citizens coming down here and taking it out on all us po' unfortunates.'

'You never met Hewitt?'

'Nope.'

'Don't know if he and Gritz were buddies?'

'How would I know that if I never met him?'

'Someone told us Gritz talked about getting rich.'

'Sure, he always did, the fool. Gonna cut a record. Gonna be the next Elvis. Pour a bottle down his gullet and he was Number One on the charts.'

The man turned to me. 'What do you think my diagnosis is?'

'Don't know you well enough,' I said.

'They – the interns over at County – said I had an affective disease – severe mood swings. Then they cut off my metha-done.'

He clicked his teeth together and waited for me to comment. When I didn't, he said, 'Supposedly I was using stuff self-medicate – being my own psychiatrist.' He laughed. 'Bearshit. I used it to be *happy*.'

Milo said, 'Back on track: what else do you know about Gritz?'

'That's it.' Smile. 'Do I still get to keep the money?'

'Is Terminator Three still here?' I said.

'Who?'

'A kid from Arizona. Missing pinky, bad cough. He has a girlfriend and a baby.'

'Oh yeah, Wayne. He's calling himself *that*, now?' Laughter. 'Nah, they all packed up this afternoon. Like I said, people come and go – speaking of which . . .'

He hooded himself with the blanket and, keeping his eyes on us, began edging toward the fence.

'What about your room for the night?' said Milo.

The man stopped and looked back. 'Nah, I'll camp out tonight. Fresh air.' Grin.

Milo laughed a little bit with him, then eyed the food. 'What about all this?'

The man scrutinized the groceries. 'Yeah, I'll take some of that Gatorade. The Pepsi, too.'

He picked up the beverages and stashed them under the blan-ket.

'That's it?' said Milo.

'On a diet,' said the man. 'You want you can bring the rest of it inside, I'm sure someone'll take it off your hands.'

The hooded man led us through the darkness, walking unsteadily but without hesitation, like a well-practiced blind man.

Milo and I stumbled and fought to keep our balance, hauling boxes with only the skimpy guidance of the penlight beam.

As we progressed, I sensed human presence, the heat of fear. Then the petrol-sweetness of Sterno.

Urine. Shit. Tobacco. Mildew.

The ammonia of fresh semen.

The hooded man stopped and pointed to the ground.

We put the boxes down and a blue flame ignited. Then another.

The concrete wall came into focus, in front of it bedrolls, piles of newspaper. Bodies and faces blue-lit by the flames.

'Supper-time, chillun',' shouted the man over the freeway. Then he was gone.

More lights.

Ten or so people appeared, faceless, sexless, huddled like storm victims.

Milo took something out of the box and held it out. A hand reached out and snatched it. More people collected around us, blue-tinted, rabbity, open-mouthed with expectation.

Milo leaned forward, moving his mouth around his cigar. What he said made some of the people bolt. Other stayed to listen, a few talked back.

He fed them some more.

I joined in, feeling hands brush against mine. Finally our boxes were empty and we stood, alone.

Milo swung the penlight around the lot, exposing cloth heaps, lean-tos, people eating.

The hooded man, sitting with his back up against the freeway wall, plaid legs splayed. One naked arm stretched out over one of them, bound at the bicep by a coil of something elastic.

A beautiful smile on his face, a needle buried deep in his flesh.

Milo snapped his head away and lowered the beam.

'C'mon,' he said, loud enough for me to hear.

He headed west rather than back toward Beverly Hills, saying, 'Well, that was a big goddamn zero.'

'None of them had anything to say?'

'The consensus, for what it's worth, is that Lyle Gritz hasn't been seen for a week or two, and that it's no big deal, he drifts in and out. He did, indeed, mouth off a bit about getting rich before he split, but they've all heard that before.'

'The next Elvis.'

He nodded. 'Music fantasies, not fish-murder. I pressed for details and one of them claimed to have seen him get into someone's car

172

a week or so ago – across the street, over at the cement yard. But that same person seemed rather addled and had absolutely no clue as to make, model, color, or any other distinguishing details. And I'm not sure he didn't just say it because I was pushing. I'll see if Gritz's name shows up on any recent arrest files, you can ask Jeffers if he was ever a patient at the center. If he was, maybe you can get her to point you in any direction he may have gone. But even if we do find him, I'm not convinced it means a damn thing. Now you up for a little rest-stop? I'm still smelling that hell-hole.'

He drove to a cocktail lounge on Wilshire, in the drab part of Santa Monica. Neon highball glass above a quilted door. I'd never been there but the way he pulled into the parking lot told me he knew it well.

Inside, the place wasn't much brighter than the overpass. We washed our hands in the men's room and took stools at the bar. The decor was red vinyl and nicotine. The resident rummies seemed to be elderly and listless. A few looked dead asleep. The jukebox helped things along with low-volume Vic Damone.

Milo scooped up a handful of bar-nuts and fed his face. Ordered a double Chivas and didn't comment when I asked for a Coke.

'Where's the phone?' I said.

He pointed to a corner.

I called Robin. 'How's it going?'

'Not bad,' she said. 'The other man in my life and I are cuddled up watching a sit-com.'

'Funny?'

'I don't think so, and he's not laughing – just drooling. Any progress?'

'Not really, but we did give away lots of food.'

'Well,' she said, 'good deeds don't hurt. Coming home?'

'Milo wanted to stop for a drink. Depending on his mood, I may need to drive him home. Go ahead and eat without us.'

'Okay ... I'll leave a light in the window and a bone in your dish.'

16

Though Milo seemed coherent by the time we reached Benedict Canyon, I suggested he sack out in one of the bedrooms and he agreed without protest. When I awoke Saturday morning at seven, he was gone and the bed he'd slept in was in perfect order.

At nine, my pond maintenance people called to confirm they'd be moving the fish at two p.m.

Robin and I had breakfast then I drove to the BioMed Library.

I looked up Wilbert Harrison in the psychiatric section of the *Directory of Medical Specialists*. His most recent listing was ten years old – an address on Signal Street in Ojai, no phone number. I copied it down and read his bio.

Medical education at Columbia University and the Menninger Clinic, a fellowship in Social Anthropology at UC Santa Barbara and a clinical appointment at the De Bosch Institute and Corrective School.

The anthro training was interesting, suggesting interests that stretched beyond private practice. But he'd had no academic appointments and his fields of specialty were *psychoanalysis* and *the treatment of impaired physicians and health professionals*. His birthdate made him sixty-five. Old enough to have retired – the move to Ojai from Beverly Hills and the lack of a phone listing implied a yearning for the quiet life.

I flipped forward to the R's and found Harvey Rosenblatt's citation, complete with the NYU affiliation and an office on East Sixty-Fifth Street in Manhattan. Same address as the Shirley I'd been trying to reach. Had she ignored my call because they were no longer together – divorced? Or something worse?

I read on. Rosenblatt had graduated from NYU, done his clinical training at Bellevue, the Robert Evanston Hale Psychoanalytic Institute in Manhattan, and Southwick Hospital in England. *Psychoanalysis and psychoanalytic psychotherapy.* Fifty-eight years old.

He was listed in the next volume of the directory, too. I worked my way forward in time, until his name no longer appeared.

Four years ago.

Right between the Paprock and Shipler murders.

You're wondering if they've been visited, too.

One way to check: Like most house organs, the Journal of the American Medical Association ran obituaries each month. I went up to the stacks and retrieved bound copies, four and five years old for Rosenblatt, ten and eleven for Harrison.

There were no notices on either psychiatrist. But maybe they hadn't bothered to join the AMA.

I consulted the American Journal of Psychiatry. Nothing there either. Perhaps neither man had been a member of the specialty guild.

Bound copies of the *American Psychological Association Directory* were just a few aisles over. The five-year-old listing on Katarina de Bosch that I'd found in my volume at home was indeed her last.

No death notice on her, either.

So maybe I was working myself up for nothing.

I thought of another possible way to locate addresses – by-lines on scientific publications. The *Index Medicus* and *Psychological Abstracts* revealed that Katarina had co-authored a couple of articles with her father, but nothing since his death. One of them had to do with child-rearing and contained a reference to *bad love*:

The process of mother-child bonding forms the foundation for all intimate relationships, and disruptions in this process plant the seed of psychopathology in later life. Good love – the nurturant, altruistic, psychosocial 'suckling' by the mother/parenting figure, contributes to the child's sense of security and, hence, molds his ability to form stable attachments. Bad love – the abuse of parental authority – creates cynicism, retribution from the breast that has failed him.

Retribution. The abuse of parental authority. Someone had been failed. Someone was seeking revenge.

I checked for articles by Harrison and Rosenblatt. Neither had published a word.

No great surprise, most practitioners never get into print. But it still seemed odd that I couldn't locate any of them.

One therapist to go: the social worker, Mitchell Lerner.

He'd been last counted a member in good standing of the national social work organization six years ago. I made a note of his office address on Laurel Canyon, and the accompanying phone number. B.A. from Cal State Northridge, MSW from Berkeley, clinical training at San Francisco General Hospital, followed by two years as a staff social worker at the Corrective School.

Another disciple. Under specialties he'd listed *family therapy and substance abuse.*

Not hoping for much, I took the stairs back up to the stacks and pulled out six- and seven-year-old bound volumes of the social work journal.

No obits on him either, but a paragraph just below the death notices in a December issue caught my eye.

SUSPENSIONS

A list followed. Thirteen clinical social workers dropped by the organization because of ethics violations. Dead center among the names:

Lerner, Mitchell A.

No details were given about his or any of the others' sins. The state board of Behavioral Science Examiners was closed for the weekend so I jotted down the date he'd been expelled, and made a note to call first thing Monday morning.

Figuring I'd learned as much as I could from books, I left the library. Back at the house on Benedict, Robin was working and the dog looked bored. He followed me into the house and slavered as I fixed myself a sandwich. I did some paperwork and shared my lunch with him, and he tagged along as I walked outside to the Seville.

'Where to?' said Robin.

'The house. I want to make sure the fish get transfered okay.'

She gave a doubtful look but said nothing.

176

'There'll be plenty of people around,' I said.

She nodded and looked over at the car. The dog was pawing the front bumper. It made her smile.

'Someone's in a traveling mood. Why don't you take him along?'

'Sure, but pond drainage isn't his thing – the water phobia.'

'Why don't you try some therapy with him?'

'Why not,' I said. 'This could be the start of a whole new career.'

The four-man crew had arrived early and when I got there, the pond was half-empty, the waterfall switched off, and the fish transfered to aerated, blue vats that sat in the bed of a pickup truck. Workers uprooted plants and bagged them, shoveled gravel and checked the air-lines to the vats.

I checked in with the crew boss, a skinny brown kid with blond rasta locks and a dyed white chin beard. The dog kept his distance, but followed me as I went up to the terrace to pick up two days' worth of mail.

Lots of stuff, most of it routine. The exception was a long white envelope.

Cheap paper that I'd seen before.

Sherman Bucklear, Attorney at Law above a return address in Simi Valley.

Inside was a letter informing me that Petitioner Donald Dell Wallace had good reason to believe that I had knowledge of the whereabouts of said petitioner's legal offpsring, Chondra Starr Wallace and Tiffani Nicolette Wallace and was demanding that I pass along said information to said petitioner's attorney, without delay, so that said petitioner's legal rights would not be abridged.

The rest consisted of threats in legalese. I put the letter back in the envelope and pocketed it. The dog was scratching at the front door.

'Nostalgic already?' I unlocked the door and he ran ahead of me, straight into the kitchen. Straight to the refrigerator.

Milo's spiritual son.

Scratch, scratch, pant, pant.

I realized that, in all the haste of moving, I'd forgotten to remove the perishables from the fridge.

I did a quick visual survey of the shelves, spilled out milk and dumped cheese that had turned and fruit that was beginning to brown. Putting the unspoiled food in a bag, I thought of the people under the freeway.

Some meatloaf remained in a plastic container. It smelled okay and the dog looked as if he'd seen the Messiah.

'Okay, okay.' I put it in a bowl and set it down before him, bagged the good fruits and vegetables and brought them down to the car.

The pond crew was finishing up. The koi in the truck all seemed to be swimming fine.

The crew boss said, 'Okay, we've got the sump running, it'll take another hour or so to drain off. You want us to wait, we can, but you're paying us by the hour, so you can stick around and turn it off yourself.'

'No problem,' I said, glancing at the truck. 'Take care of them.'

'Sure. When do you think you'll be wanting 'em back?'

'Don't know, yet.'

'Some kind of long vacation?'

'Something like that.'

'Cool.' He handed me a bill ahd got behind the wheel of the truck. A moment later, they were gone and all I heard was the slow gurgle of draining water.

I said down on the banks of what was now a muddy hole, waiting and watching the level drop. The heat and the quiet combined to lull me, and I wasn't sure how long I'd been there when someone said, 'Hey.'

I jerked up, groggily.

A man stood in the gateway, holding a tire iron.

Late twenties or early thirties, heavy growth of dark stubble, thick black fu manchu that drooped to his chin.

He had on greasy jeans and Wellington boots with chains, a black t-shirt under a heavy black leather vest. Black, thinning hair, gold hoop earring, steel chains around his neck. Big tattooed arms. Big, hard belly, bowlegs. Maybe six-one, two hundred.

Red-rimmed eyes.

At Sunny's Sun Valley, next door to Rodriguez's masonry yard, he'd been wearing a black cap that said CAT.

The muscular guy at the bar who hadn't said much.

He whistled once and came closer. Let one hand drop from the iron. Lowered the metal, swung it parallel to his leg in a slow, small arc and came a few steps closer. Looked at my face. He wore a slow, lazy smile of recognition.

'Retaining wall, huh?'

'What do you want?'

'Donald's kids, man.' Deep slurry voice. He sounded as if he'd come straight from the bar.

'They're not here.'

'Where, man?'

'I don't know.'

The iron arc widened. I said, 'Why would I know?'

'You were lookin' for the little brown brother, man. Maybe you found him.'

'Maybe you *did*, man.' Stepping forward. Just a few feet away, now. Lots of missing teeth. Mustache clogged with dandruff. An angry pus pimple had erupted under his left eye. The tattoos were badly done, a green-blue riot of bloody blades and gothic lettering.

I said, 'I already got a letter from Wallace's lawyer – '

'Fuck *that*.' He came within swinging range, smelling like the bottom of a clothes hamper that needed emptying.

I backed up. Not much room to maneuver. Behind me was shrubbery – hedges and the maple tree whose branch had been used to skewer the koi.

'You're not helping Donald Dell,' I said. 'This won't look good for him.'

'Who gives a fuck, man? You're off the case.'

He swung the iron listlessly, pointing downward and hitting the dirt. Looking at the pond just for a second, then back at me. I searched the area for possible weapons.

Slim pickings: oversized polyethylene bags left behind by the pond crew. Lengths of rubber hosing. A couple of sheets of scummy filter screen. Maybe the koi net. Six feet of stout oak handle below a steel-mesh cup – but it was out of reach. 'Since when?' I said.

'*What*?'

'Since when am I off the case?'

'Since we said so, man.'

'The Iron Priests?'

'Where're the kids, man?'

'I told you. I don't know.'

He shook his head and advanced. 'Don't get hurt over it, man. It's just a job, what the fuck.'

'You like fish?'

'Huh?'

'Fish. Finny creatures. Seafood. Piscinoids.'

'Hey, ma— '

'You like to sneak around, spearing 'em? Breaking branches off trees and doing the old rotisserie bit?'

'*What?*'

'You've been here before, haven't you? Sportfishing carp, you sick fuck.'

Confusion tugged at his face, zipping it up into something peevish and tight and offering a hint of what he'd look like on the off-chance he made it to old age. Then anger took its place – a brattish resentment – and he lifted the iron and took a poke at my middle.

I danced away.

'Hey,' he said, annoyed. He jabbed again, missed. Sloshed, but not enough to stagger, and there was force in his movements. 'Here, chickie chick.' He laughed.

I kept moving away from his blows, managed the rock rim of the pond. The stones were slick with algae and I used my arms for balance. That made him laugh some more. He shouted, came after me, clumsy and slow. Caught up in the game as if it were what he'd come for.

He began making barnyard clucks.

I split my focus between the iron and his eyes. Readying myself for the chance to use surprise and his own weight against him. If I missed, my hand would get shattered.

'Boom, boom, boom,' he said. 'Chickie-chick.'

'C'mon, stupid,' I said.

His face puffed up and reddened. Two-handing the iron, he made a sudden swing for my knees.

I jumped back, stumbled, pitched forward onto the pond rim, breaking my fall with my palms.

The iron landed on rock and clanged. He raised it high over his head.

The next sounds came from behind him.

Deep bark.

Angry snorts.

Padded gallop.

He wheeled toward it, holding the iron in front of his own chest in instinctive defense. Just in time to see the bulldog racing toward him, a little black bullet, its teeth bared in a pearly grimace.

Just in time for me to spring to my feet and throw my arms around.

Not enough force to knock him over, but I got my hands on the ends of the iron and slammed it hard into his ribcage. Something cracked.

He said, 'Ohh,' sounding curiously girlish. Buckled. Bent.

The dog was on him, now, fixing his teeth on denim leg, shaking his head from side to side, growling and spraying spit.

The man's back was pushing against me. I pressed up on the iron, sharply, forcing it under his chin. Got it against his adam's apple and pulled in steadily until he made gagging noises and started to loosen his grip.

I held on. Finally, he stopped moving and let his full weight fall against me. Struggling to remain on my feet, I let him sink to the ground, hoping I hadn't destroyed his larynx but not torturing myself over it.

The dog stayed on him, grunting and eating denim.

The man sank to the dirt. I felt for a pulse. Nice and steady and he was already starting to move and groan.

I looked for something to bind him with. The polyethylene bags. Telling the dog, 'Stay,' I ran to get them. I tied them together, managed to fashion two thick, plastic ropes, and used one to secure his hands behind his back, the other his legs.

The dog had stepped back to watch me, head cocked. I said, 'You did great, Spike, but you don't get to eat this one. How about a sirloin instead – it's higher grade.'

The man opened his eyes. Tried to speak but produced only a retching cough. The front of his neck was swollen and a deep blue bruise that matched his tattoos was starting to blossom.

The dog padded over to him.

The man's eyes electrified. He turned his head away and grimaced in pain.

I said, 'Stay, Spike. No blood.'

The dog looked up at me with soft eyes that I hoped wouldn't betray him.

The man coughed and choked.

The dog's nostrils opened and shut. Saliva dripped from his maws and he growled.

'Good boy, Spike,' I said. 'Watch him for a sec and if he gives you any problem, you're allowed to rip out his throat for an appetizer.'

17

'What an idiot,' said Milo, putting his notepad away. 'His name's Hurley Keffler and he's got a sheet, but not much of one. More of a bad guy wannabee. We found his bike parked down the road. He wasn't stalking you, got here just as the pond people drove away and decided to have a talk.'

'Just one of those impulsive weekend jaunts, huh?'

'Yeah.'

We were up on the landing, watching the police cars drive away. The dog watched, too, sticking his flat face through the slats of the railing, ears pricked.

'I found a letter from the Wallaces' lawyer in my mailbox,' I said. 'He wanted to know where the girls were and threatened me with legal action if I didn't tell him. Looks like the Priests decided not to wait.'

'It might not be an official Priest mission,' he said. 'Just Keffler having a few too many and deciding to improvise. His dinky record, he's probably low-man in the gang, trying to impress the hairy brothers.'

'What are you booking him on?'

'ADW, trespassing, if his blood alcohol's high enough to prove he drove over here soused. If the Priests go his bail, he'll probably be out within a few days. I'll have a talk with them, tell them to lock him in the house. What a clown.'

He chuckled. 'Bet your little chokehold didn't do much for his powers of comprehension, either. What'd you use, one of those karate things I'm always ribbing you about?'

'Actually,' I said, bending and patting the dog's muscular neck, 'he gets the credit. Pulled a sneak attack from the back that allowed me to jump Keffler. Plus he overcame his water phobia – ran right up to the pond.'

'No kidding?' Smile. 'Okay, I'll put him up for sainthood.' He bent, too, and rubbed the dog behind the ears. 'Congrats, St. Doggus, you're a K-9 hero.'

The driver of one of the black-and-whites looked up at us and Milo waved him on.

'Good boy,' I said to the dog.

'Seeing as he's saved your kneecaps, Alex, don't you think he deserves a real name? My vote's still for Rover.'

'When I was trying to intimidate Keffler, I called him Spike.'

'Very manly.'

'Only problem is,' I said, 'he's already got a name – someone's bound to come get him. What a drag. I'm getting kind of attached to him.'

'What?' He elbowed my ribs, gently. 'We're afraid of getting hurt, so we don't reach out for intimacy? Give him a goddamn name, Alex. *Empower* him so he can fulfill his doggy potential.'

I laughed and rubbed the dog some more. He panted and put his head against my leg.

'Keffler's not the one who killed the koi,' I said. 'When I mentioned it, he fuzzed over completely.'

'Probably,' he said. 'That tree branch was too subtle for the Priests. They would have taken out all the fish and mashed 'em up, maybe eaten them and left the bones.'

'Back to our bad love fiend,' I said. 'Anything new on Lyle Gritz?'

'Not yet.'

'I was over at the library this morning, checking out the professional directories. No current listings on Rosenblatt or Katarina de Bosch. Harrison moved to Ojai and has no phone number, which sounds like retirement – and the social worker, Lerner, was suspended from the social work organization for an ethics violation.'

'What kind of violation?'

'The directory didn't say.'

'What's it usually mean? Sleeping with a patient?'

'That's the most common, but it could also be financial shenanigans, betrayal of confidentiality, or a personal problem, like drug or alcohol addiction.'

He rested his arms on the top of the railing. The squad cars were gone now. My pond was a dry hole and the sump pump was sucking air. I went down to the garden, dog at my heels, and turned it off.

When I got back, Milo said, 'If Lerner was a bad boy, he could have done something that pissed off a patient.'

'Sure,' I said. 'I looked up de Bosch's writings on "bad love". Specifically, it refers to abuse of parental authority leading to alienation, cynicism and in extreme cases, violence. De Bosch actually used the term "retribution". But, pardon the whining, I still don't know what the hell I could have done.'

'Why don't you try to get in touch with Harrison in Ojai, see if he has any idea what's going on. If his number's unlisted, I can get it for you.'

'Okay,' I said. 'And Harrison may be a good source for another reason. When therapists are suspended, they're usually required to get therapy. One of Harrison's specialties was treating impaired therapists. Wouldn't it be interesting if he treated Lerner? It's not that farfetched. Lerner turning to someone he knew. Get me that number right now, and I'll call.'

He went to his car and got on the radio. Returned ten minutes later and said, 'No listing at all, even though the address is still on the tax roles. Can you spare the time for a little drive? Ojai's nice this time of year. Cute little shops, antiques, whatever. Take the lovely Miss C for a cruise up the coast, combine business with pleasure.'

'Get out of town for a while?'

He shrugged.

'Okay,' I said. 'And Ojai's close to Santa Barbara, I can extend my trip. De Bosch's school is defunct, but it might be interesting to see if any of the neighbors remember it. Maybe there was some kind of scandal. Something that closed it down and left someone with a long-term grudge.'

'Sure, snoop around. If Robin can stand it, who am I to try and stop you.'

He slapped my back. 'I'm off.'

'Where to?'

'A little more research on Paprock and Shipler.'

'Anything new?'

'Nope. I'm planning to drop in on Paprock's husband tomorrow. He's still a car salesman at the Cadillac place, and Sunday's a good day for those guys.'

'I'll go with you.'

'Thought you were cruising to Ojai.'

'Monday,' I said. 'Monday's a good day for psychologists.'

'Oh, yeah? Why's that?'

'Blue day for everyone else. We get to concentrate on other people's problems and forget our own.'

I went back into the house and looked through the freezer. In our haste to move, we hadn't emptied it and there were several steaks in the top compartment. I took out a choice-cut rib-eye and put it in the oven to broil. The dog's eyes were glued to my every move. As the aroma of broiling meat filled the kitchen, his nose started to go crazy and he got down on the floor in a supplicative posture.

'Restrain the caballos,' I said. 'All good things come to those who salivate.'

I petted him and called my service for messages. Only one, from Jean Jeffers. The clinic director had called at eleven a.m. leaving an 818 return number.

'Did she say what it was about?' I asked the operator.

'No, just to call her, doctor.'

I did and got an answering tape with a friendly-sounding male voice backgrounded by Neil Diamond. I was starting to leave a message when Jean's voice broke in.

'Hi, thanks for calling back.'

'Hi, what's up?'

I thought I heard her sigh. 'I've got some . . . I think it would be best if we met personally.'

'Something about Hewitt?'

'Somethi— I'm sorry, I'd rather just talk about it in person, if you don't mind.'

'Sure. Where and when would you like to meet?'

'Tomorrow would be okay for me.'

'Tomorrow's fine.'

'Great,' she said. 'Where do you live?'

'West L.A.'

'I'm in Studio City, but I don't mind coming over the hill on the weekend.'

'I can come out to the Valley.'

'No, actually, I like to come out when it's not for work. Never get a chance to enjoy the city. Whereabouts in west L.A.?'

'Near Beverly Hills.'

'Okay . . . how about Amanda's, it's a little place on Beverly Drive.'

'What time?'

'Say one p.m.?'

'One it is.'

Nervous laughter. 'I know this must seem strange coming out of the blue, but maybe . . . oh, let's just talk about it tomorrow.'

I gave the dog a few bits of steak, wrapped the rest in plastic and pocketed it. Then we drove to the pet store where I let him sniff around the food bags. He lingered at some stuff that claimed to be scientifically formulated. Organic ingredients. Twice the cost of any of the others.

'You earned it,' I said, and I purchased ten pounds along with several packets of assorted canine snacks.

Going home, he munched happily on a bacon-flavored pretzel.

'Bon appetit, Spike,' I said. 'Your real name's probably something like Pierre de Cordon Bleu.'

Back at the house on Benedict Canyon, I found Robin reading in the living room. I told her what had happened with Harley Keffler and she listened, quiet and resigned, as if I were a delinquent child with no hope of rehabilitation.

'What a good friend you turned out to be,' she said to the dog. He jumped up on the couch and put his head in her lap.

'So what are they going to do with him – this Keffler?'

'He'll be in jail for a while.'

'How long's a while?'

'Probably not long. His gang's likely to make his bail.'

'And then?'

'And then he'll be out, but he won't know this address.'

'Okay.'

'Want to take a drive up to Ojai and Santa Barbara, next couple of days?'

'Business or pleasure?'

'Both.' I told her about Lerner and Harrison, my wanting to speak to the Corrective School's neighbors.

'Love to, but I really shouldn't, Alex. Too much work down here.'

'Sure?'

'I am, hon. Sorry.' She touched my face. 'There's so much piled up and even though I've got all my gear set up, it feels different here – I'm working slower, need to get back on the track.'

'I'm really putting you through it, aren't I?'

'No,' she said, smiling and mussing my hair. 'You're the one being put through.'

The smile lingered and grew into a soft laugh.

'What's funny?' I said.

'The way men think. As if our going through some stress together would be putting me *through* it. I'm worried about you, but I'm glad to be here with you – to be part of it. Putting me *through* it means something totally different.'

'Such as?'

'Constantly diminishing me – condescending to me, dismissing my opinions. Anything that would make me question my worth. Do those kinds of things to a woman and she may stay with you, but she'll never think the same of you.'

'Oh.'

'Oh,' she said, laughing and hugging me. 'Pretty profound, huh? Are you mad at me for not wanting to go to Ojai?'

' No, just disappointed.'

'You go anyway. Promise to be careful?'

'I promise.'

'Good,' she said. 'That's important.'

18

We had dinner at an Indian place near Beverly Hills' eastern border with L.A., washing the meal down with clove tea and driving home feeling good. Robin went to run her bath and I phoned Milo at home and told him about Jean's call.

'She has something to tell me but wouldn't elaborate over the phone – sounded nervous. My guess is she found something about Hewitt that scares her. I'm meeting her at one, I'll ask her about Gritz. When were you planning to see Ralph Paprock?'

'Right around then.'

'Care to make it earlier?'

'The dealership opens at ten, I suppose we could catch him just as he comes in.'

'I'll pick you up.'

Sunday morning I drove to West Hollywood. Milo's and Rick's place was a small, perfectly kept Spanish house at the end of one of those short, obscure streets that hide in the grotesque shadow of the Design Center's blue-green mass. Cedars-Sinai was within walking distance. Sometimes Rick jogged to work. Today, he hadn't; the white Porsche was gone.

Milo was waiting outside. The small front lawn had been replaced by ground cover and the flowers were blooming bright orange.

He saw me looking at it and said, 'Drought resistant,' as he got into the car. 'That "environmental designer" I told you about. Guy would upholster the world in cactus, if he could.'

I took Laurel Canyon up into the Valley, passing stiltbox houses and post-modern cabins, the decaying Palladian estate where

Houdini had done tricks for Jean Harlow. A governor had once lived right around there. None of the magic had rubbed off.

At Ventura, I turned left and traveled two miles to Valley Vista Cadillac. The showroom was fronted by twenty-foot slabs of plate glass and bordered by a huge outdoor lot. Banners were strung on high-tension wire. The lights were off but morning sun managed to get in and bounce off the sparkling bodies of brand-new coupes and sedans. The cars out on the lot were blinding.

A trim black man in a well-cut navy suit stood next to a smoke-gray Seville. When he saw us get out of my seventy-nine, he went over to the front door and unlocked it, even though business hours hadn't begun. When Milo and I stepped in, his hand was out and his smile was blooming brighter than Milo's lawn.

He had a perfectly trimmed pencil mustache and a pincollar shirt as white as an avalanche. Off to the side of the showroom, beyond the cars, was a warren of cubicles, and I could hear someone talking on the phone. The cars were spotless and perfectly detailed. The whole place smelled of leather and rubber and conspicuous consumption. My car had smelled that way once, even though I'd bought it used. Someone had told me the fragrance came in aerosol cans.

'That's a classic you've got,' said the man, looking through the window.

'Been good to me,' I said.

'Keep it and garage it, that's what I'd do. One of these days you'll see it appreciate, like money in the bank. Meanwhile, you can be driving something new for everyday. Good lines this year, don't you think?'

'Very nice.'

'Got those foreign deals beat hands down. Get folks in to actually test drive, they see that. You a lawyer?'

'Psychologist.'

He gave an uncertain smile and I found a business card in my hand.

John Allbright
Sales Executive

'Got a real good suspension this year, too,' he said. 'With all due respect to your classic, I think you'll find it a whole other

190

world, drive-wise. Great sound system, too, if you go for the Bose option and – '

'We're looking for Ralph Paprock,' said Milo.

Allbright looked at him. Squinted. Put his hand to his mouth and compressed his smile manually.

'Ralph,' he said. 'Sure. Ralph's over there.'

Pointing to the cubicles, he walked away, fast, ending up in a glass corner, where he lit up a cigarette and stared out at the lot.

The first two compartments were empty. Ralph Paprock sat behind a desk in the third. He was in his late forties, narrow and tan, with sparse gray-blond hair on top and a bit more of it on the sides, combed over his ears. His double-breasted suit was the same cut as Allbright's, olive green, just a bit too bright. His shirt was cream with long-point collar, his tie crowded with parrots and palm trees.

He was hunched over some papers. The tip of his tongue protruded from the corner of his narrow mouth. The pen in his right hand tapped his blotter very fast. His nails were shiny.

When Milo cleared his throat, the tongue zipped in and an eager grin took hold of Paprock's face. Despite the smile, his face was tired, the muscles loose and droopy. His eyes were small and amber. The suit gave them a khaki tint.

'Gentlemen. How can I help you?'

Milo said, 'Mr. Paprock, I'm Detective Sturgis, Los Angeles police,' and handed him a card.

The look that took hold of the salesman next – *what are you hitting me with this time?* – made me feel lousy. We had nothing to offer him and plenty to take.

He put his pen down.

I caught a side view of a photo on his desk, propped up next to a mug printed with the Cadillac crest. Two round-faced, fair-haired children. The younger one, a girl, was smiling, but the boy seemed on the verge of tears. Behind them hovered a woman of around seventy with butterfly glasses and cold-waved white hair. She resembled Paprock, but she had a stronger jaw.

Milo said, 'Sorry to bother you, Mr. Paprock, but we've come across another homicide that might be related to your wife's and wondered if we could ask you a few questions.'

'Another – a *new* one?' said Paprock. 'I didn't see anything on the news.'

'Not exactly, sir. This crime occurred three years ago –'

'Three years ago? Three *years* and you've just come *across* it? Did you finally get him?'

'No, sir.'

'Jesus.' Paprock's hands were flat on the desk and his forehead had erupted in sweat. He wiped it with the back of one hand. 'Just what I need to start off the week.'

There were two chairs facing his desk. He stared at them but didn't say anything else.

Milo motioned me into the office and closed the door behind us. There was very little standing room. Paprock held a hand out to the chairs and we sat. A certificate behind the desk said he'd been a prize-winning salesman. The date was three summers ago.

'Who's the other victim?' he said.

'A man named Rodney Shipler.'

'A man?'

'Yes, sir.'

'A man – I don't understand.'

'You don't recognize the name?'

'No. And if it was a man what makes you think it has anything to do with my Myra?'

'The words "bad love" were written at the crime scene.'

'Bad love,' said Paprock. 'I used to dream about that. Make up different meanings for it. But still . . .'

He closed his eyes, opened them, took a bottle out of his desk drawer. Enteric aspirin. Popping a couple of tablets, he dropped the bottle into his breast pocket, behind the colored handkerchief.

'What kind of meanings?' said Milo.

Paprock looked at him. 'Crazy stuff – trying to figure out what the hell it meant. I don't remember, what's the difference?'

He began moving his hands around, stirring the air very quickly, as if searching for something to grab. 'Was there any – some sign of – was this Shipler . . . what I'm getting at is, was there something sexual?'

'No, sir.'

Paprock said, ' 'Cause that's what *they* told me they thought it might mean. The first cops. Some psychotic thing – using sex in a bad way, some sort of sex nut. A pervert *bragging* about what he did – bad love.'

Nothing like that had been in Myra Paprock's file.

Milo nodded. 'A man,' said Paprock. 'So what are you telling me? The first cops had it all *wrong*? They went and looked for the *wrong* thing?'

'We don't really know much at all at this point, sir. Just that someone wrote "bad love" at the scene of Mr. Shipler's homicide.'

'Shipler.' Paprock squinted. 'You're opening the whole thing up again, 'cause of him?'

'We're taking a look at the facts, Mr. Paprock.'

Paprock closed his eyes, opened them, and took a deep breath. 'My Myra was taken *apart*. I had to identify her. To you that kind of thing's probably old hat, but . . .' Shake of the head.

'It's never old hat, sir.'

Paprock gave him a doubtful look. 'After I did it – identified her – it took me a long time to be able to remember her the way she used to be . . . even now . . . the first cops said whoever . . . did those things to her, did them after she was dead.' Alarm brightened his eyes. 'They were right about *that*, weren't they?'

'Yes, sir.'

Paprock's hands gripped the edge of his desk and he wheeled forward. 'Tell me the truth, detective, I *mean* it. I don't want to think of her suffering, but if – no forget it, don't tell me a damn thing, I don't *want* to know.'

'She didn't suffer, sir. The only thing new is Mr. Shipler's murder.'

More sweat. Another wipe.

'Afterwards,' said Paprock. 'After I identified her – I had to go tell my kids. The older one, anyway, the little one was just a baby. Actually, the older one wasn't much more than a baby, either, but he was asking for her, I had to tell him something.'

He knocked the knuckles of both hands together. Shook his head, tapped the desk.

'It took a helluva long time to get it set in my mind what had happened. When I went to tell my boy, all I could think of was what I'd seen in the morgue – imagining her . . . and here he is asking for Mommy. "Mommy, Mommy" – he was two and a half. I told him Mommy got sick and went to sleep forever. When his sister got old enough, I gave *him* the job of telling *her*. They're great kids, my mother's been helping me take care of them, she's close to eighty and they don't give her any problems. So who needs to change that? Who needs Myra's name in the papers and digging it all up? There was a time, finding out who did it was *all* that mattered to me, but I got over that. What's the difference, anyway? She's not coming back, right?'

I nodded. Milo didn't move.

Paprock touched his brow and opened his eyes wide, as if exercising the lids.

'That it?' he said.

'Just a few questions about your wife's background,' said Milo.

'Her *background*?'

'Her work background, Mr. Paprock. Before she became a real estate agent, did she do anything else?'

'Why?'

'Just collecting facts, sir.'

'She worked for a bank, okay? What kind of work did this Shipler do?'

'He was a janitor. What bank did she work for?'

'Trust Federal, over in Encino. She was a loan officer, that's how I met her. We used to channel our car loans through there and one day I went down there on a big fleet sale and she was at the loan desk.'

Milo took out his notepad and wrote.

'She would have probably made Vice President,' said Paprock. 'She was smart. But she wanted to work for herself, had enough of bureaucracies. So she studied for her broker's license at night, then quit. Was doing real well, lots of sales . . .'

He looked off to one side, fixing his gaze on a poster. Two perfect-looking, tennis-clad people getting into a turquoise Coupe De Ville with diamond-bright wire wheels. Behind the car, the marble and glass façade of a resort hotel. Crystal chandelier. Perfect-looking doorman smiling at them.

'Bureaucracies,' said Milo. 'Did she deal with any others before the bank?'

'Yeah,' said Paprock, still turned away. 'She taught school – but that was before I met her.'

'Here in L.A.?'

'No, up near Santa Barbara – Goleta.'

'Goleta,' said Milo. 'Do you remember the name of the school?'

Paprock faced us again. 'Some public school – why? What does her work have to do with anything?'

'Maybe nothing, sir, but please bear with me. Did she ever teach in L.A.?'

'Not to my knowledge. By the time she moved down here, she was fed up with teaching.'

'Why's that?'

'The whole situation – kids not interested in learning, lousy pay – what's to like about it?'

'A public school,' I said.

'Yeah.'

Milo said, 'What subjects did she teach?'

'All of them, I guess. She taught fifth grade, or maybe it was fourth, I dunno. In elementary school, you teach all the subjects, right? We never really had any detailed discussions about it.'

'Did she teach anywhere before Goleta?' said Milo.

'Not as far as I know. I think that was her first job out of school.'

'When would that be?'

'Let's see, she graduated at twenty-two, she'd be forty this May.' He winced. 'So that would have been what, eighteen years ago. I think she taught maybe four or five years, then she switched to banking.'

He looked at the poster again and wiped his forehead.

Milo closed his pad. The sound made Paprock jump. His eyes met Milo's. Milo gave as gentle a smile as I'd seen him muster. 'Thanks for your time, Mr. Paprock. Is there anything else you want to tell us?'

'Sure,' said Paprock. 'I want to tell you to find the filthy fuck who killed my wife and put me in a room with him.' He rubbed his eyes. Made two fists and opened them and gave a sick smile. 'Fat chance.'

Milo and I stood. A second later, Paprock rose, too. He was medium-sized, slightly round-backed, almost dainty.

He patted his chest, removed the aspirin bottle from his breast pocket and passed it from hand to hand. Walking around the desk, he pushed the door open and held it for us. No sign of John Allbright or anyone else. Paprock walked us through the showroom, touching the flanks of a gold Eldorado in passing.

'Whyncha buy a car, as long as you're here,' he said. Then he colored through his tan, and stopped.

Milo held out his hand.

Paprock shook it, then mine.

We thanked him again for his time.

'Look,' he said, 'what I said before – about not wanting to know? That's bullshit. I still think about her. I got married again, it lasted three months, my kids hated the bitch. Myra was . . . special. The kids, some day they're gonna have to know. I'll handle it. I can handle it. You find something, you tell me, okay? You find *anything*, you tell me.'

I headed for Coldwater Canyon and the drive back to the city.

'Public school near Santa Barbara,' I said. 'Lousy pay, so maybe she moonlighted at a local private place.'

'A reasonable assumption,' said Milo. He lowered the Seville's passenger window, lit up a bad cigar and blew smoke out at the hot Valley air. The city was digging up Ventura Boulevard and sawhorses blocked one lane. Bad traffic usually made Milo curse. This time he kept quiet, puffing and thinking.

I said, 'Shipler was a school janitor. Maybe he worked at de Bosch's school, too. That could be our connection: they were both staffers, not patients.'

'Twenty years ago . . . wonder how long the school district keeps records. I'll check, see if Shipler transfered down from Santa Barbara.'

'More reasons for me to drive up there,' I said.

'When are you doing it?'

'Tomorrow. Robin can't make it – all for the best. Between trying to find remnants of the school and looking for Wilbert Harrison in Ojai, it won't be a pleasure trip.'

'Those other guys – the therapists at the symposium – they worked at the school, too, right?'

'Harrison and Lerner did. But Rosenblatt didn't – he trained with de Bosch in England. I'm not sure about Stoumen, but he was a contemporary of de Bosch, and Katarina asked him to speak, so there was probably some kind of relationship.'

'So, one way or the other, it all boils down to Bosch . . . anyone seen as being close to him is fair game for this nut . . . bad love – destroying a kid's sense of trust, huh?'

'That's the concept.'

I reached Coldwater and started the climb. He drew on his cigar and said, 'Paprock was right about his wife. You saw the pictures – she *was* taken apart.'

'Poor guy,' I said. 'Walking wounded.'

'What I told him, about her being dead when she was raped? True. But she suffered, Alex. Sixty-four stab wounds and plenty of them landed before she died. That kind of revenge rage? Someone must have gotten fucked up bigtime.'

19

I made it to Beverly Hills with five minutes to spare for my one o'clock with Jean Jeffers. Parking was a problem and I had to use a city lot two blocks down from Amanda's, waiting at the curb as a contemplative valet decided whether or not to put up the *Full* sign.

He finally let me in and I arrived at the restaurant five minutes late. The place was jammed and it reeked of Parmesan cheese. A hostess was calling out names from a clipboarded list and walking the chosen across a deliberately cracked white marble floor. The tables were marble, too, and a gray faux-marble treatment had been give to the walls. The crypt look, nice and cold, but the room was hot with impatience and I had to elbow my way through a cranky crowd.

I looked around and saw Jean already seated at a table near the back, next to the south wall of the restaurant. She waved. The man next to her looked at me but didn't move.

I recalled him as the heavyset fellow from the photo in her office, a little heavier, a little grayer. In the picture, he and Jean had been wearing leis and matching Hawaiian shirts. Today, they'd kept the Bobbsy twin thing going with a white linen dress for her, white linen shirt for him, and matching yellow golf sweaters.

I waved back and went over. They had half-empty coffee cups in front of them and pieces of buttered olive bread on their bread plates. The man had an executive haircut and an executive face. Great shave, sunburnt neck, blue eyes, the skin around them slightly bagged.

Jean rose a little as I sat down. He didn't, though his expression was friendly enough.

'This is my husband, Dick Jeffers. Dick, Dr. Alex Delaware.'

'Doctor.'

'Mr. Jeffers.'

He smiled as he shot out his arm. 'Dick.'

'Alex.'

'Fair enough.'

I sat down across from them. Both their yellow sweaters had crossed tennis-racquet logos. His bore a small, gold masonic pin.

'Well,' said Jean. 'Some crowd, hope the food's good.'

'Beverly Hills,' said her husband. 'The good life.'

She smiled at him, looked down at her lap. A large, white purse sat there and one of her arms was around it.

Dick Jeffers said, 'Guess I'll be going, Jeanie. Nice to meet you, doctor.'

'Okay, honey,' said Jean.

Cheek pecks, then Jeffers stood. He seemed to lose balance for a second, caught himself by resting one palm on the table. Jean looked away from him as he straightened. He shoved the chair back with the rear of his thighs and gave me a wink. Then he walked off, limping noticeably.

Jean said, 'He has one leg, just got a brand new prosthesis and it's taking a while getting used to.' It sounded like something she'd said many times before.

I said, 'That can be tough. Years ago, I worked with children with missing limbs.'

'Did you?' she said. 'Well, Dick lost his in an auto accident.'

Pain in her eyes. I said, 'Recently?'

'Oh, no, several years ago. Before anyone really appreciated the value of seat belts. He was driving a convertible, was unbelted, got hit from behind and thrown out. Another car ran over his leg.'

'Terrible.'

'Thank God he wasn't killed. I met him when he was in rehab. I was doing a rotation at Rancho Los Amigos and he was there for a couple of months. He made a great adjustment to his appliance – always has until it started bothering him a few months ago. He'll get used to the new one. He's a good guy, very determined.'

I smiled.

'So,' she said, 'how are you?'

'Fine. And intrigued.'

'By?'

'Your call.'

'Oh.' The sheet of hair fell over her eye. She let it stay there. 'Well, I didn't mean to be overly dramatic, it's just – ' She looked around. 'Why don't we order first, and then we can talk about it.'

We read the menu. Someone in the kitchen had a thing for balsamic vinegar.

When she said, 'Well, I know what I want,' I waved over a waiter. Asian kid, around nineteen, with a waist-length pony tail and ten stud earrings rimming the outer cartilage of his left ear. It hurt to look at him and I stared at the table as Jean ordered an *insalata* something or other. I asked for linguini marinara and an iced tea. Ruined Ear came back quickly with the drink and a refill of her coffee.

When he left, she said, 'So you live pretty close to here?'

'Not far.'

'For a while Dick and I thought about moving over the hill, but then prices started to go crazy.'

'They've slid quite a bit recently.'

'Not enough.' She smiled. 'Not that I'm complaining. Dick's an aerospace engineer and he does well, but you never know when the government's going to cancel a project. The place we've got in Studio City is really pretty nice.' She looked at her watch. 'He's probably over at Rudnicks now. He likes to shop there for sweaters.

'He's not having lunch?'

'What I need to talk about is confidential. Dick understands that. So why did I bring him with me, right? To be honest it's because I'm still shaky. Still haven't gotten used to being alone.'

'I don't blame you.'

'Don't you think I should be past it by now?'

'I probably wouldn't be.'

'That's a very nice thing to say.'

'It's the truth.'

Another smile. She reached over and touched my hand, just for a second. Then back to her coffee cup.

'I'm *sleeping* a little better,' she said, 'but still far from per-fect. In the beginning I'd be up all night, heart pounding away, nauseated. Now I can *get* to sleep, but sometimes I still wake up all in a knot. Sometimes the thought of going to work makes me just want to crawl back in bed. Dick works in Westchester near the airport, so sometimes we take one car and he drops me off and picks me up. I guess I've become pretty dependent on him.'

She gave a small smile. The unspoken message: *for a change*.

'Meanwhile, I'm telling the staff and the patients there's nothing to worry about. Nothing like consistency.'

Ear brought the food.

'This looks yum,' she said, pushing her fork around in her salad bowl. But she didn't eat, and one arm stayed around her purse.

I tried a little linguini. Memories of school lunch. She nibbled on a piece of lettuce. Dabbed at her mouth. Looked around. Unsnapped the purse.

'You have to promise me to keep this absolutely confidential,' she said. 'At least where you got it from, okay?'

'Does it relate to Hewitt?'

'In a way. Mostly – it's nothing that can help Detective Sturgis – not that I can see, anyway. I shouldn't even be showing it to you. But people are being harassed and I know what it's like to feel besieged. So if this does lead anywhere, please keep me out of it – please?'

'All right,' I said.

'Thank you.' She inhaled, shoved her hand into the purse, and drew out a legal-size envelope. White, clean, unmarked. She held onto it. The paper made her nails look especially red.

'Remember how sketchy Becky's notes on Hewitt were?' she said. 'How I made excuses for her, saying she'd been a good therapist but not big on paperwork? Well, it bothered me more than I let on. Even for Becky that was cursory – I guess I just didn't want to deal with anything related to her murder. But after you left, I kept thinking about it and went looking to see if she'd taken any other notes that had somehow been misfiled. With all the upheaval right after, housekeeping wasn't exactly a high priority. I didn't find anything, so I asked Mary – my secretary. She said all Becky's active charts had been distributed to other caseworkers, but it was possible some of her inactive files might have ended up in our storage room. So she and I took some time on Friday and looked around for a few hours, and sure enough, stuck in a corner was a box with Becky's initials on it – RB. Who knows how it got there. Inside was junk that had been removed from her desk – pens, paper clips, whatever. Underneath all that, was this.'

Her hand shook slightly as she handed me the envelope.

I removed the contents. Three sheets of horizontal-ruled chart-paper, slightly grimy and bearing deep foldmarks, each partially filled with typed notations.

The first was dated six months ago:

Saw DH today. Still hearing vcs, but meds seem to hlp. Still dealing w strss of strt-life. Cam in with G, both strssed.
BB, SWA

Three weeks later:

D lots better. Snstv, too. Just meds, or me? Ha ha. Maybe some hope?
BB, SWA

Then:

D showing feelngs, more and more. Tlking lots, too. Very good! Yeah, thrpy! Success. But keep limits.
BB, BWA

D cohrnt – hr brshed, totally clean! But still late. Talk re childhd, etc. Some p-c, but approp. G there, waiting. A bit hostl? Jealous? Follow
BB

D a diff prsn. Open, vrbal, affectnt. Still late. A bit more p-c. Approp? Set lmts? Talk to JJ? Wrth the progrss? Yes!
BB

D late, but less – 15 min. Some anx. Hrng vcs? Denies, says strss, achl – drinking with G. Talked re G, re rel bet D and G. Some anx, defens, but also open-mind. More p-c but ok, relieves anx. O.K.
BB

D looking happy. Vry vrbl, no angr, no hrng vcs. G not there. Conflct bet G and D? P-c, tried to kiss, no hostil when I say no. Good! Approp soc skll! Rah rah!
BB

The final note was dated three weeks before Becky's murder:

D early – positv change! Yeah! G waits in hall. Definit hostil. Rel bet D and G straind? Re me? D's growth a stress on G? More p-c. Kss, but quick. Much affectn. Talk re this. Boundaries, lmits, etc. D a little down, but dealt w it, approp.
BB

'P-c,' I said, putting the papers down.

'Physical contact,' she said, miserably. 'I went over and over it and it's the only thing that makes sense.'

I reread the notes. 'I think you're right.'

'Hewitt was getting attached to her. Progressively more physical.' She shuddered. 'Look at the last one. She let him *kiss* her. She must have totally lost control of the situation. I had no idea, she never told me.'

'She obviously thought of telling you – "talk to JJ".'

'But she didn't follow through. Look what she wrote right after that.'

I read out loud: '"Worth the progress? Yes!" Sounds like she convinced herself she was helping him.'

'She convinced herself she knew what she was *doing*.' She shook her head and looked down at the table. 'My God.'

'Beginner's euphoria.'

'She was such a sweet thing – so naive. I should have kept a closer eye on her. Maybe if I had, it could've been prevented.' She pushed her salad away. Her hair hung in a sheet. Her head rested in her hands and I heard her sigh.

I said, 'Hewitt was psychotic, Jean. Who knows what set him off.'

She looked up. 'Letting him *kiss* her sure didn't help! She talks about setting limits but he probably saw it as rejection, what with his paranoia!'

She'd allowed her voice to climb. The man at the next table looked up from his cappuccino. Jean smiled at him, picked up her napkin and wiped her face.

I scanned the notes again. *Yeah, therapy! Rah rah!*

She held out her hand. 'I need them back.'

I gave her the papers and she slipped them back in the envelope.

I said, 'What are you going to do with them?'

'Destroy them. Can you just imagine what the media would do with it? Blaming Becky, turning the whole thing into something sleazy? Please, Alex, keep it to yourself. I don't want to see Becky victimized a second time.' She flipped her hair again. 'Also, to be perfectly honest, I don't want to be blamed for not supervising her.'

'It took guts for you to show it to me,' I said.

'Guts?' She laughed softly. 'Stupidity, maybe, but for some reason

I trust you – I don't even know why I did show it to you – getting it off my chest, maybe.'

She shook her head again.

'How could she have let it *happen*? She talks about *him* trying to touch her and kiss her, but what I got between the lines was her developing some sort of feelings for *him*. All that p-cing, as if it was a cute little game. Don't you agree?'

'Fondness for him definitely comes across,' I said. 'Whether or not it was sexual, I don't know.'

'Even if it was plain *affection*, it was irrational. The man was psychotic, couldn't even keep himself *clean*. And this G person she keeps mentioning, I still have no idea who *that* is. Probably Hewitt's girlfriend – some other psychotic he met on the street and dragged in with him. Becky was getting herself involved with a love triangle with *psychotics*, for God's sake. How could she? She was naive, but she was bright – how could she have shown such poor judgment?'

'She probably didn't think she was doing anything wrong, Jean. Otherwise why would she have kept notes?'

'But if she thought what she was doing was okay, why not keep those notes right in Hewitt's chart?'

'Good point,' I said.

'It's a mess. I should have supervised her more closely. I should have been more in touch . . . I just can't understand how she could have let him get that close to her.'

'Countertransference,' I said. 'Happens all the time.'

'With someone like that?'

'Prison therapists get attached to convicts. Who knows what causes attraction?'

'I should have known.'

'No sense blaming yourself. No matter how closely you supervise some, you can't be with them twenty-four hours a day. She was trained, Jean. It was up to her to tell you.'

'I *tried* to supervise her. I made appointments, but she broke more than she kept. Still, I could have clamped down further – I should've. If I'd had any *idea* . . . she never gave a *hint*. Always had a smile on her face, like one of those kids who works at Disneyland.'

'She was happy,' I said. 'She thought she was curing him.'

'Yup.' Lifting the bowl, she removed the envelope and dropped it back in her purse. 'What a mess . . . I probably showed it to you because you were sympathetic and I'm still so uptight over what happened, I thought I could talk to you.'

'You can.'

'I appreciate that,' she said wearily, 'but let's be honest. What good will more talking do? Becky's dead and I'm going to have to live with the fact that I might have been able to prevent it.'

'I don't see it that way. You did all you could.'

'You're sweet.' She looked at my hand, as if ready to touch it again. But she didn't move and her eyes shifted to her salad.

'Happy lunch,' she said glumly.

'Jean, it's possible the notes might be relevant to Detective Sturgis.'

'How?'

'"G" may not be a woman.'

'You *know* who it is?' This time her hand did move. Covering mine, taking hold of my fingers. Ice-cold.

'That lawyer whose card you gave me – Andrew Coburg? I went over to see him and he told me Hewitt had a friend named Gritz. Lyle Edward Gritz.'

No reaction.

I said, 'Gritz is a heavy drinker, and he has a criminal record. He and Hewitt hung out together and now no one can find him. A week or two ago, Gritz told some street people he expected to get rich, then he disappeared.'

'Get rich? How?'

'He didn't say, though in the past he'd talked about becoming a recording star. For all I know, it was drunk talk and has nothing to do with Becky. But if "G" does refer to him, it indicates tension between him and Becky.'

'Gritz,' she said. 'I assumed G was a woman. Are you saying Hewitt and this Gritz had something homosexual going on and Becky stepped in the middle of it – oh, God, it just keeps getting worse, doesn't it?'

'Maybe there was nothing sexual between Gritz and Hewitt. Just a close friendship that Becky intruded upon.'

'Maybe . . .' She pulled out the envelope, removed the notes, ran her finger down the page and read. 'Yes, I see what you mean. Once you think of 'G' as a man you don't have to see it that way, at all

. . . just friendship . . . but whatever the reason, Becky felt G was hostile to her.'

'She was getting between them,' I said. 'The whole therapy process was challenging whatever Hewitt had with Gritz. How did Becky phrase it in that last note?'

'Let me see – here it is: "Relationship between D and G strained. Me? D's growth?" Yes, I see what you mean. Then right after that, she mentions about p-c – the session where he actually kissed her . . . you know, you could read this and feel almost as if she was seducing him.' She crumpled the notes. 'God, what a travesty – why you interested in this Gritz? You think he could be the one harassing people?'

'It's possible.'

'Why? What else has he done, criminally?'

'I'm not sure of the details, but the harassment involved the words "bad love" – '

'What Hewitt screamed . . . does that actually mean something? What's going on?'

Her fingers had become laced with mine. I looked at them and she pulled away and fooled with her hair. The flap covered one eye. The exposed one was alive with fear.

I said, 'I don't know, Jean. But given the notes, I have to wonder if Gritz played a role in getting Hewitt to murder Becky.'

'Played a *role*? How?'

'By working on Hewitt's paranoia – telling Hewitt things about Becky. If he was a close friend, he'd know which buttons to push.'

'Oh, God,' she said. 'And now he's missing . . . it's not over, is it?'

'Maybe it is, this is all conjecture, Jean. But finding Gritz would help clear it up – any chance he was a patient at the center?'

'The name doesn't ring a bell . . . bad love . . . I thought Hewitt was just raving, now you're saying maybe he was reacting to something that had gone on between him and Becky? That he killed her because she rejected him.'

'Could be,' I said. 'I found a reference to "bad love" in the psych literature. It's a term coined by a psychoanalyst named Andres de Bosch.'

She stared at me. Nodded slowly. 'I think I've heard of him. What did he say about it?'

'He used it to describe poor child-rearing – a parent betraying a child's trust. Building up faith and then destroying it. In extreme cases, he theorized, it could lead to violence. If you consider the therapist–patient relationship similar to child-rearing, the same theory could be applied to cases of transference gone really bad. Hewitt may have heard about "bad love" somewhere – probably from another therapist, or even from Gritz. When he felt Becky had rejected him, he fell apart, became a betrayed child – and lashed out violently.'

'Betrayed child?' she said. 'You're saying his killing her was a *tantrum*?'

'A tantrum heated to the boiling point by Hewitt's delusions. And by his failure to take his medication. Who knows, Gritz may have convinced him not to take it.'

'Gritz,' she said. 'How do you spell it?'

I told her. 'Be good to know if he was one of your patients.'

'I'll comb the files first thing tomorrow, take that damned storage room *apart* if I have to. If he's anywhere in there, I'll call you right away. We need to know for our own safety.'

'I'll be out of town tomorrow. You can leave a message with my service.'

'All day tomorrow?' A touch of panic in her voice.

I nodded. 'Santa Barbara and back.'

'I love Santa Barbara. It's gorgeous. Taking some vacation time?'

'De Bosch used to have a clinic and a school up there. I'm going to try and find out if Hewitt or Gritz were ever patients.'

'I'll let you know if he was ours. Call me back, okay? Let me know what you find.'

'Sure.'

She looked at her salad again. 'I can't eat.'

I waved Ear over and got the bill.

She said, 'No, I invited *you*,' and tried to take it, but she didn't put up much of a fight and I ended up paying.

She stashed the notes in her purse and glanced at her watch. 'Dick's not coming back for another half an hour.'

'I can wait.'

'No, I won't keep you. But I wouldn't mind some fresh air.'

Just outside the restaurant she paused to button her sweater and smooth her hair. The first time, the buttons were out of line and she had to redo them.

We walked to the city lot without speaking. She looked in shop windows but seemed uninterested in the wares they displayed. Waiting until I'd redeemed the keys from the attendant, she accompanied me to the Seville.

'Thanks,' I said, shaking her hand. I opened the driver's door.

She said, 'What I said before still stands, right? About keeping all this quiet?'

'Of course.'

'It's nothing Detective Sturgis could ever use, anyway,' she said. 'Legally speaking – what does it really prove?'

'Just that people are fallible.'

'Oh, boy, are they.'

I got into the car. She leaned in through the window. 'You're more than just a consultant on this, aren't you?'

'What makes you say that?'

'Your passion. Consultants don't go this far.'

I smiled. 'I take my work seriously.'

She moved her head back, as if I'd blown garlic in her face. 'So do I,' she said. 'Sometimes I wish I didn't.'

20

Monday morning at nine, I set out for Ojai, taking the 405 to the 101 and making it to the strawberry fields of Camarillo in less than an hour. Migrant workers stooped in the stubby, green rows. The crop became blue cabbage and the air turned bitter. Kissy-face billboards boosted housing developments and home equity loans.

Just past the Ventura County Fairgrounds, I turned onto the 33 North, speeding by an oil refinery that resembled a giant junkyard. Another few miles of trailer parks and mower rental sheds and things got pretty: two lanes draped by eucalyptus, black mountains off to the northwest, the peaks flesh-colored where the sun hit.

The town of Ojai was a quarter of an hour further, announced by a bike/equestrian trail, orange groves, and signs directing the motorist to the Ojai Palm Spa, the Humanos Theosophic Institute, Marmalade Hot Springs. To the south were the clean, green slopes of a country club. The cars were good-looking and so were the people.

Ojai, proper, was quiet and slow-moving, with one traffic light. The main drag was Ojai Avenue, lined with the kind of low-rise, neo-Spanish architecture that usually means tight zoning laws. Unrestricted parking, plenty of spaces. Tans and smiles, organic fibers and good posture.

On the left side of the avenue, a colonnaded, tile-roofed building was filled with storefronts. Native American art and antiques, body wraps and herbal facials, a Little Olde Tea Shoppe. Across the street was an old theater, freshly adobed. Playing tonight: The Leningrad Cowboys.

I had my Ventura County Thomas Guide on the passenger seat, but I didn't need it. Signal was a couple of intersections up, and 800 North meant a left turn.

Big trees and small houses, residential lots alternating with olive groves. A drainage ditch paved with fieldstones ran alongside the left side of the street, spanned every few yards by one-stride foot bridges. Wilbert Harrison's address was near the top, one of the last houses before open fields took over.

It was a shingle-roofed wooden cottage painted an odd purplish-red and nearly hidden behind unruly snarls of agave cactus. The purple was vivid and it shone through the agave's sawtooth leaves like a wound. Atop a steep, dirt driveway, a Chevy station wagon was parked up against a single garage. Four stone steps led up to the front porch. The screen door was shut, but the wooden one behind it was wide open.

I knocked on the frame while looking into a small, dark living room, plank-floored and crowded with old furniture, shawls, throw pillows, an upright piano. A bay window was lined with dusty bottles.

Chamber music came from another room.

I knocked louder.

'One minute.' The music turned off and a man appeared from a doorway to the right.

Short. Chubby as in his old picture and white-haired. He had on a polyester jumpsuit the same purplish red as the house. Some of the furniture was upholstered that color, too.

He opened the screen door and gave me a curious but friendly look. His eyes were gray, but they picked up magenta accents from his surroundings. There was a softness to his face, but no weakness.

'Dr. Harrison?'

'Yes, I'm Bert Harrison.' His voice was a clear baritone. The jumpsuit was zipped in the front and had large, floppy lapels. Short-sleeved, it exposed white, freckled arms. His face was freckled, too, and I noticed reddish-blond tints in his white hair. He wore a pinky ring set with a violet cabochon, and a bolo tie with leather thongs held together by a big, shapeless purple rock. Sandals on his feet, no socks.

'My name is Alex Delaware. I'm a clinical psychologist from Los Angeles and I wondered if I could talk to you about Andres de Bosch and "bad love".'

The eyes didn't change shape or hue, but they became more focused.

He said, 'I know you. We've met somewhere.'

'Nineteen seventy-nine,' I said. 'There was a conference at Western Pediatric Hospital on de Bosch's work. You presented a paper and I was a co-chair, but we never actually met.'

'Yes,' he said, smiling. 'You were there as the hospital's representative, but your heart wasn't in it.'

'You *remember* that?'

'Distinctly. The entire conference had that flavor – ambivalence, all around. You were very young – you wore a beard then, didn't you?'

'Yes,' I said, amazed.

'The beginnings of old age,' he said, still smiling. 'Distant memories become clearer but I can't remember where I put my keys.'

'I'm still impressed, doctor.'

'I remember the beard vividly, perhaps because I have trouble growing one. And your voice. Full of stress. Just as it is right now. Well, come in, let's take care of it. Coffee or tea?'

There was a small kitchen beyond the living room and a door that led to a single bedroom. The little I could see of the sleeping chamber was purple and book-lined.

The kitchen table was birch, not more than four feet long. The counters were old white tile trimmed with purple-red bullnoses.

He fixed instant coffee for both of us and we sat. The scale of the table put us close together, elbows nearly touching.

'In answer to your unasked question,' he said, whitening his with lots of cream then adding three spoonfuls of sugar, 'it's the only color I can see. A rare genetic condition. Everything else in my world is gray, so I do what I can to brighten it.'

'Makes sense,' I said.

'Now that that's out of the way, tell me what's on your mind concerning Andres and bad love – that was the title of the conference, wasn't it.'

'Yes. You don't seem surprised that I just popped in.'

'Oh, I am. But I like surprises – anything that breaks up routine has the ability to freshen our lives.'

'This may not be a pleasant surprise, Dr. Harrison. You may be in danger.'

His expression didn't change. 'How so?'

I told him about the 'bad love' tape, my revenge theory, the possible links to Dorsey Hewitt and Lyle Gritz.

'And you think one of these men may have been a former patient of Andres'?'

'It's possible. Hewitt was thirty-three when he died and Gritz is a year older, so either of them could have been his patients as children. Hewitt killed one psychotherapist, perhaps under influence by Gritz, and Gritz is still out there, possibly still trying to get even.'

'What would he be trying to avenge?'

'Some kind of mistreatment – by de Bosch, himself, or a disciple. Something had happened at the school.'

No response.

I said, 'Real or imagined. Hewitt was a paranoid schizophrenic. I don't know Gritz's diagnosis, but he may be delusional, as well. The two of them might have influenced each other's pathology.'

'Symbiotic psychosis?'

'Or at least shared delusions – playing on each other's paranoia.'

He blinked hard. 'Tapes, calls . . . no I haven't experienced anything like that. And the name of this person who giggled over the phone was Silk?'

I nodded.

'Hmm. And what role do you think the conference played?'

'It may have triggered something – I really don't know, but it's my only link to de Bosch. I felt an obligation to tell you because one of other speakers – Dr. Stoumen – was killed last year – and I haven't been able to loca— '

'Grant?' he said, leaning forward close enough for me to smell the mint on his breath. 'I heard he died in an auto accident.'

'A hit and run accident. While attending a conference. He stepped off the curb and was knocked down by a car. It was never solved, Dr. Harrison. The police put it down to Dr. Stoumen's old age – poor vision, faulty hearing.'

'A conference,' he said. 'Poor Grant – he was a nice man. Formal, but nice.'

'Did he ever work at the school?'

'He did occasional consultations. Coming up summers for a week or two – combining vacation with business. Hit and run . . .' He shook his head.

'And as I was saying, I can't locate any of the other speakers or co-chairs.'

'You've located me.'

'You're the only one, Dr. Harrison.'

'Bert, please. Just out of curiosity, how did you find me?'

'From the Directory of Medical Specialists.'

'Oh. I suppose I forgot to cancel it.' He looked troubled.

'I didn't want to impose on your privacy, but – '

'No, no, that's fine, you're here for my own good . . . and, to tell the truth, I welcome visitors. After thirty years in practice, it's nice to talk to people rather than just listen.'

'Do you know where any of the others are? Katarina de Bosch, Mitchell Lerner, Harvey Rosenblatt.'

'Katarina is just up the coast, in Santa Barbara.'

'She's still there?'

'I haven't heard that she's moved.'

'Do you have her address?'

'And her phone number. Here, let me call it for you.'

He reached over, pulled a crimson rotary phone from the counter and put it on the table. As he dialed I wrote down the number on the phone. He held the receiver to his ear for a while, before putting it down.

'No answer,' he said.

'When's the last time you saw her?'

He thought. 'I suppose about a year or so. By coincidence. I was in a bookstore in Santa Barbara and ran into her, browsing.'

'Psychology?'

He smiled. 'No, fiction, actually. She was in the science-fiction section. Would you like her address?'

'Please.'

He wrote it down and gave it to me. Shoreline Drive.

'The ocean side,' he said. 'Just up from the marina.'

I remembered the slide Katarina had shown. Blue skies behind a wheelchair. The ocean.

'Did she live there with her father?' I said.

'Since the two of them came to California.'

'She was very attached to him, wasn't she?'

'She worshipped him.' He continued to look preoccupied.

'Did she ever marry?' He shook his head.

'When did the school close?' I said.

'Not long after Andres died – eighty-one, I believe.'

'Katarina didn't want to keep it going?'

He put his hands around his coffee cup. He had hammer thumbs and his other digits were short. 'You'd have to ask her about that.'

'Does she do any kind of psychological work, now?'

'Not to my knowledge.'

'Early retirement?'

He shrugged and drank. Put his cup down and touched the stone on his bolo tie. Something bothering him.

I said, 'I only met her twice, but I don't see her as someone with hobbies, Bert.'

He smiled. 'You encountered the force of her personality.'

'She was the reason I was at the conference against my will. She pulled strings with the Chief of Staff.'

'That was Katarina,' he said. 'Life as target practice: set your sights, aim, and shoot. She pressured me to speak, too.'

'You were reluctant?'

'Yes, but let's get back to Grant, for a moment. Hit-and-run isn't really the same as premeditated murder.'

'Maybe I'm wrong, but I still can't find anyone who was up on that dais.'

He grabbed the cup with both hands. 'I can tell you about Mitch – Mitchell Lerner. He's dead. Also the result of an accident. Hiking. Down in Mexico – Acapulco. He fell from a high cliff.'

'When?'

One year before Stoumen, one year after Rodney Shipler. Fill in the gaps . . .

' . . . the time,' he was saying, 'I had no reason to assume it was anything *but* an accident. Especially in view of it being a fall.'

'Why's that?'

He worked his jaws and his hands went flat on the table. His mouth twisted a couple of times. Anxiety and something else – dentures.

'Mitchell had occasional balance problems,' he said.

'Alcohol?'

He stared at me.

'I know about his suspension,' I said.

'I'm sorry, I can't talk any more about him.'

'Meaning he was your patient – your bio mentioned your specialties. Impaired therapists.'

Silence that served as affirmation. Then he said, 'He was trying to ease his way back into work. The trip to Mexico was part of that. He was attending a *conference* there.'

He put his finger in his mouth and fooled with his bridgework. 'Well,' he said, smiling, 'I don't go to conferences anymore, so maybe I'm safe.'

'Does the name Myra Paprock mean anything to you?'

He shook his head. 'Who is she?'

'A woman who was murdered five years ago. The words "bad love" were scrawled at the murder scene in her lipstick. And the police have found one other killing where the phrase was written. A man named Rodney Shipler, beaten to death *three* years ago.'

'No,' he said, 'I don't know him either. Are they therapists?'

'No.'

'Then what would they have to do with the conference?'

'Nothing that I know of, but maybe they had something to do with de Bosch. Myra Paprock was working as a real estate agent at the time but before that she was a teacher in Goleta. Maybe she moonlighted at the Corrective School. This was before she married, so her surname would have been something other than Paprock.'

'Myra,' he said, rubbing his lip. 'There *was* a Myra who taught there when I was consulting. A young woman, just out of college . . . blonde, pretty . . . a little . . .' He closed his eyes. 'Myra . . . Myra . . . what was her name – Myra *Evans*, I think. Yes, I'm pretty sure that's what it was. Myra Evans. And now you're saying she was murdered . . .'

'What else were you going to say about her, Bert?'

'Excuse me?'

'You just said she was blond, pretty, and something else . . .'

'Nothing really,' he said. 'I just remembered her as being a little hard. Nothing pathologic – the dogmatism of youth.'

'Was she rough on the kids?'

'Abusive? I never saw it. It wasn't that kind of place – Andres' force of personality was enough to maintain a certain level of . . . order.'

'What was Myra's method for maintaining order?'

'Lots of rules. One of those everything-by-the-rules types. No shades of gray.'

'Was Dr. Stoumen like that? Is that what you meant when you said he was formal?'

'Grant was . . . orthodox. He liked his rules. But he was an extremely gentle person – somewhat shy.'

'And Lerner?'

'Anything but rigid. *Lack* of discipline was his problem.'

'Harvey Rosenblatt?'

'Don't know him at all. Never met him before the conference.'

'So you never saw Myra Evans come down too hard on a child?'

'No . . . I barely remember her – these are just impressions, they may be faulty.'

'I doubt it.'

He moved his jaws from side to side. 'All these murders. You actually think . . .' Shaking his head.

I said, 'How important was the concept of "bad love" to de Bosch's philosophy?'

'I'd say it was fairly central,' he said. 'Andres was very concerned with justice – he saw achieving consistency in our world as a motive. Saw many symptoms as attempts to accomplish that.'

'The search for order.'

Nod. 'And good love.'

'When did you become disillusioned about him?'

He looked pained.

I held my gaze and said, 'You said Katarina pressured you to speak at the symposium. Why would a faithful student have to be pressured?'

He got up, turned his back on me and rested his palms on the counter. A little man in ridiculous clothing, trying to bring color to his world.

'I really wasn't that close to him,' he said. 'After I began my anthropology studies, I wasn't around much.' Taking a couple of steps, he wiped the counter with one stubby hand.

'Your own search for consistency?'

He stiffened but didn't turn.

'Racism,' he said. 'I heard Andres making remarks.'

'About who?'

'Blacks, Mexicans.'

'Were there black and Mexican children at the school?'

'Yes, but he didn't malign them. It was the workers – hired laborers. There was acreage behind the school. Andres hired people down on lower State Street to come clear the weeds every month or so.'

216

'What did you hear him say about them?'

'The usual garbage – that they were lazy, stupid. Genetically inferior. He called the blacks one half-step up from apes, said the Mexicans weren't much better.'

'He said this to your face?'

Hesitation. 'No. To Katarina. I overheard it.'

I said, 'She didn't disagree with him, did she?'

He turned around. 'She *never* disagreed with him.'

'How did you happen to overhear their conversation?'

'I wasn't eavesdropping,' he said. 'That would almost have been better. I walked in on the middle of the conversation and Andres didn't bother to interrupt himself. That really troubled me – the fact that he thought I would laugh along with it. And it wasn't just once – I heard him say those things several times. Almost taunting me. I didn't respond. He was my teacher and I became a worm.'

He returned to his chair, slumping a bit.

I said, 'Did Katarina respond at all to his remarks?'

'She laughed . . . I was disgusted. Lord knows I'm no paragon of virtue, I've done my share of pretending to listen to patients when my mind was elsewhere. Pretending to care. Been married five times, never longer than twenty-six months. When I finally achieved enough insight to realize I should stop making women's lives miserable, I opted for the solitary life. I drew plenty of blood along the way, so I don't put myself up on any moral pedestal. But I *have* always prided myself on racial tolerance – part of it is personal. I was born with multiple anomalies. Other things besides the lack of color vision.'

He looked away, as if considering his choices. Held out his short fingers and waved them. Pointing at his mouth, he said, 'I'm completely edentulous. Born without adult teeth. My right foot has three toes, the left one is clubbed. I'm unable to sire children and one of my kidneys atrophied when I was three. Most of my childhood was spent in bed due to severe skin rashes and a hole in the ventricular septum of my heart. So I guess I'm a little sensitive to discrimination. But I didn't speak up, just left the school.'

I nodded. 'Did de Bosch's intolerance come out in other ways?'

'No, that's the thing. On a day-to-day basis, he was extremely liberal. *Publicly*, he was liberal – took in minority patients, most of them charity cases, and seemed to treat them as well as the others.

And in his writings, he was *brilliantly* tolerant. Have you ever read his essay on the Nazis?'

'No.'

'Brilliant,' he repeated. 'He composed it while fighting in the French Resistance. Taking the bastards' own pseudotheories of racial superiority and throwing it all back in their faces with good, sound science. That was one of the things that attracted me to him when I was a resident. The *combination* of social conscience and pyschoanalysis. Too many analysts live in a twelve-foot-square world – the office as universe, rich people on the couch, summers in Vienna. I wanted more.'

'Is that why you studied anthropology?'

'I wanted to learn about other cultures. And Andres supported me in that. Told me it would make me a better therapist. He *was* a great mentor, Alex. That's why it was so crushing to hear him sneer at those field-hands – like seeing one's father in a disgusting light. I swallowed it in silence several times. Finally, I resigned and left town.'

'For Beverly Hills?'

'I did a year of research in Chile, then caved in and returned to my own twelve-foot-square world.'

'Did you tell him why you were leaving?'

'No, just that I was unhappy, but he understood.' He shook his head. 'He was an intimidating man. I was a coward.'

'It had to take force of personality to dominate Katarina.'

'Oh yes, and he did dominate her. . . . After I returned from Chile, he called me just once. We had a frosty conversation, and that was that.'

'But Katarina wanted you at the conference, anyway.'

'She wanted me because I was part of his past – the glory years. By then he was a vegetable and she was *resurrecting* him. She brought me pictures of him in his wheelchair. "You abandoned him once, Bert. Don't do it again." Guilt's a great motivator.'

He looked away. Worked his jaws.

'I don't see any obvious tie-ins,' I said, 'but Rodney Shipler, the man who was beaten to death, was black. At the time of the murder, he was a school janitor in L.A. Do you have any memory of him at all?'

'No, that name isn't familiar.' He looked back at me. Edgy – guilty?

'What is it, Bert?'

'What's what?'

'Something's on your mind.' I smiled. 'Your face is full of stress.'

He smiled back and sighed. 'Something came into my mind. Your Mr. Silk. Probably irrelevant.'

'Something about Lerner?'

'No, no, this is something that happened after the Bad Love conference – soon after, a couple of days, I believe.' He closed his eyes and rubbed his forehead, as if coaxing forth memories.

'Yes – it was two or three days,' he said, working his jaws again. 'I received a call in my office. After hours. I was on my way out and I picked up the phone before the answering service could get to it. A man was on the other end, very agitated, very angry. A young man – or at least he sounded young. He said he'd sat through my speech at the conference and wanted to make an appointment. Wanted to go into long-term psychoanalysis with me. But the way he said it – hostile, almost sarcastic – brought my guard up and I asked him what kinds of problems he was experiencing. He said there were many – too many to go into over the phone and that my speech had reminded him of them. I asked him how, but he wouldn't say. His voice was *saturated* with stress – real suffering. He demanded to know if I was going to help him. I said, of course, I'd stay late and see him right away.'

'You considered it a crisis?'

'At the least, a borderline crisis – there was real pain in his voice. An ego highly at risk. And,' he smiled, 'I had no pressing engagements other than dinner with one of my wives – the third one, I think. You can see why I was such a poor matrimonial prospect . . . anyway, to my surprise, he said no, right now wasn't a good time for him, but he could come in the evening. Stand-offish, all of a sudden. As if *I'd* come on too strong for *him*. I was a bit taken aback, but you know patients – the resistance, the ambivalence.'

I nodded.

He said, 'So we made an appointment for the following afternoon. But he never showed up. The phone number he'd given me was out of order and he wasn't listed in any local phone books. I thought it odd, but, after all, odd is our business, isn't it? I thought about it for a while, then I forgot about it. Until today. His being at the conference . . . all that anger.' Shrug. 'I don't know.'

'Was his name Silk?'

'This is the part I hesitate about, Alex. He never became my patient, formally, but in a sense, he was. Because he asked for help and I counseled him over the phone – least I attempted to.'

'There was no formal treatment, Bert. I don't see any problem, legally.'

'That's not the point. Morally, it's an issue – moral issues transcend the law.' He slapped his own wrist and smiled. 'Gawd, doesn't that sound self-righteous.'

'There *is* a moral issue,' I said. 'But weigh it against the alternatives. Two definite murders. Three if you include Grant Stoumen. Maybe four, if someone pushed Mitchell Lerner off that cliff. Myra Paprock was raped, as well. Taken apart physically. She left two small children. I just met her husband. He still hasn't healed.'

'You're quite good at guilt yourself, young man.'

'Whatever works, Bert. How's that for a moral stance?'

He smiled. 'No doubt you're a practical therapist . . . no, his name wasn't Silk. Another type of fabric. Merino.'

'First name?'

'He didn't give one. Called himself "mister." Mr. Merino. It sounded pretentious in someone so young. Awful insecurity.'

'Can you pinpoint his age?'

'Twenties – early twenties would be my guess. He had a young man's impetuousness. Poor impulse control to call like that and make demands. But he was stressed and stress causes regression, so maybe he was older.'

'When was the Corrective School established?'

'Nineteen sixty-two.'

'So if he was in his twenties in seventy-nine, he could easily have been a patient. Or one of the field hands – Merino's an Hispanic name.'

'Or someone with no connection to the school at all,' he said. 'What if he was just someone with deep-seated problems who sat in on the conference and reacted to it for one reason or the other?'

'Could be,' I said, calculating silently: Dorsey Hewitt would have been around eighteen in nineteen seventy-nine. Lyle Gritz, a year older.

'All right,' I said, 'thanks for telling me and I won't give out the information unless it's essential. Is there anything else you remember that might help?'

'No, I don't think so. Thank you. For warning me.'

He looked around his small house with longing. I knew the feeling.

'Do you have a place to go?' I said.

Nod. 'There are always places. New adventures.'

He walked me to my car. The heat had turned up a bit and the air was thick with honeybees.

'Off to Santa Barbara now?' he said.

'Yes.'

'Give Katarina my best when you see her. The easiest way is Highway 150. Pick it up just out of town and take it all the way, it's no more than a half-hour drive.'

'Thanks.'

We shook hands.

'One more thing, Bert?'

'Yes?'

'Mitchell Lerner's problems. Could they have resulted in any way from his work at the school – or did they *cause* problems, there?'

'I don't know,' he said. 'He never spoke about the school. He was a *very* closed person – highly defensive.'

'So you did ask him about it?'

'I asked him about every element of his past. He refused to talk about anything but his drinking. And even then, just in terms of getting rid of a bad habit. In his own work, he despised behaviorism, but when it came to his therapy, he wanted to be reconditioned. Overnight. Something short-term and discreet – hypnosis, whatever.'

'You're an analyst. Why did he come to you?'

'Safety of the familiar.' He smiled. 'And I've been known to be pragmatic from time to time.'

'If he was so resistant, why'd he bother to go into therapy in the first place?'

'As a condition of his probation. The Social Work ethics committee demanded it, because it had affected his work – missed appointments, failure to submit insurance forms so his patients could recover. I'm afraid he acted the same way as a patient. Not showing up, very unreliable.'

'How long did you see him?'

'Obviously, not long enough.'

21

There seemed little doubt that Myra Evans and Myra Paprock were the same person. And that her murder and the deaths of others were related to de Bosch and his school.

Silk. Merino.

The conference putting someone in touch with his problems . . . some sort of trauma.

Bad love.

Taken apart.

A child's voice chanting.

I felt a sudden stab of panic about leaving Robin alone, stopped in the center of Ojai and called her from a pay phone. No one home. The Benedict number had been channeled through my answering service and on the fifth ring an operator picked up.

I asked her if Robin had left word where she was going.

'No, she didn't, doctor. Would you like your messages?'

'Please.'

'Just one, actually, from a Mr. Sturgis. He called to say Van Nuys will be getting to your tape soon – got a broken stereo, Dr. Delaware?'

'Nothing that simple,' I said.

'Well, you know how it is, doctor. They keep making things more complicated so people have to feel stupid.'

I picked up the 150 a few miles out of town and headed northwest on two curving lanes. Lake Casitas meandered parallel to the highway, massive and gray under a listless sun. The land side was mostly avocado groves, gold-tipped with new growth. Halfway to Santa

Barbara, the road reconnected with the 101 and I traveled the last twelve miles at freeway speed.

I kept thinking about what Harrison had told me about de Bosch's racism and wondered what I'd tell Katarina when I found her, how I'd approach her.

I got off the highway without an answer, bought gas and called the number Harrison had given me. No answer. Deciding to delay confrontation for a while I looked through my Thomas Guide for the site where the Corrective School had once been. Near the border with Montecito, several miles closer than Shoreline Drive – an omen.

It turned out to be a straight, shady street lined with gated properties. The eucalyptus there grew huge, but the trees looked dried out, almost dessicated. Despite the fire risk, shake roofs were in abundance. So were Mercedes.

The exact address corresponded to a new-looking tract behind high, stone walls. A sign advertised six custom homes. What I could see of them was massive and cream-colored.

Across the way was a pink and brown tudor mansion with a sign out in front that said *The Bancroft School*. A semi-circular, gravel drive girdled the building. A black Lincoln was parked under a spreading live oak.

A man got out of the car. Mid-sixties – old enough to remember. I drove across the road, pulled up next to his driver's side and lowered my window.

His expression wasn't friendly. He was big and powerful looking, dressed in tweeds and a light blue sweater vest despite the heat, and he had very white, very straight hair and knocked-about features. A leather briefcase – an old one with a brass clasp – dangled from one hand. The leather had been freshly oiled – I could smell it. Several pens were clasped to his breast pocket. He looked the Seville over with narrow, dark eyes, then had a go at my face.

'Excuse me,' I said, 'was the Corrective School once across the street?'

Scowl. 'That's right.' He turned to leave.

'How long has it been gone?'

'Quite a while. Why?'

'I just had a few questions about it.'

He put his briefcase down and peered into the car. 'Are you an . . . alumnus?'

'No.'

He looked relieved.

'Do alumni come back frequently?' I said.

'No, not frequently, but . . . you do know what kind of school it was.'

'Troubled children.'

'A bad lot. We were never happy with it – we were here first, you know. My father broke ground thirty years before *they* came.'

'Really.'

'We were here before most of the houses. This was all agricultural back then.'

'Did the students from the Corrective School cause problems?'

'And what's your interest in that?'

'I'm a psychologist,' I said, and gave him a card. 'I'm doing some consulting to the Los Angeles police department and there's some evidence one of the alumni is involved in something unpleasant.'

'Something unpleasant. Well, that's not much of a surprise, is it?' He scowled again. His eyebrows were bushy, low-set, and still dark, giving him a look of perpetual annoyance. 'What kind of unpleasantness?'

'I'm sorry but I can't go into detail – is it Mr. Bancroft?'

'It certainly is.' He produced a card of his own, white, heavy stock, a heraldic shield in one corner.

The Bancroft School
Est. 1933 by Col. C.H. Bancroft (Ret.)
'Building Scholarship and Character'
Condon H. Bancroft, Jr., B.A., M.A., Headmaster

'By unpleasant do you mean criminal?' he said.

'It's possible.'

He gave a knowing nod

I said, 'Why did the place close down?'

'He died – the Frenchman – and no one was left to run it. It's an art, education.'

'Didn't he have a daughter?'

His eyebrows arched. 'She offered me the place, but I turned her down. Error on my part – I should have done it for the land alone. Now they've come and built *those*.' He cast a glare at the stone wall.

'They?'

'Some sort of foreign group. Asians, of course. She offered me all of it, lock, stock. But she wanted an outlandish amount of money and refused to negotiate. For *them*, money's no object.'

'She's still here in town, isn't she?'

'She's in Santa *Barbara*,' he said.

I wondered where he thought he was, then I answered my own question: Montecito Wannabee.

'This unpleasantness,' he said. 'It isn't anything that would . . . *impinge* upon my school, is it? I don't want publicity, the police traipsing around.'

'Did de Bosch's students ever impinge?'

'No, because I made sure they didn't. For all practical purposes, this property line was as impermeable as the Berlin Wall.' He drew a line in the gravel with the toe of one wingtip. 'Some of them had been to reform school. Fire-setters, bullies, truants – all sorts of miscreants.'

'Must have been difficult being this close.'

'No, it wasn't *difficult*,' he reprimanded. 'If they chanced to wander, I sent them hopping right back.'

'So you *never* had any problems?'

'Noise was a problem. There was always too much noise. The only *untoward* thing occurred after they were gone. One of them showed up and made quite a nuisance of himself.' Smile. 'His condition didn't speak well of the Frenchman's methods.'

'What condition was that?'

'A *tramp*,' he said. 'Unwashed, uncombed, high on drugs – his eyes had that look.'

'How do you know he was an alumnus?'

'Because he told me he was. Said it in those words: "I'm an alumnus." As if that should have impressed me.'

'How long ago was this?'

'Quite a while – let's see, I was interviewing the Crummer boy. The youngest one, and he applied around ten years ago.'

'And how old was this tramp?'

'Twenties. A real churl. He barged right into my office, past my secretary. I was interviewing young Crummer and his parents – a fine family, the elder boys had attended Bancroft quite successfully. The scene *he* created dissuaded them from sending the youngest lad here.'

'What did he want?'

'*Where* was the school? *What* had happened to it? Raising his voice and creating a scene – poor Mrs. Crummer. I thought I'd have to call the police, but I was finally able to convince him to leave by telling him the Frenchman was long dead.'

'That satisfied him?'

The eyebrows dipped. 'I don't know *what* it did to him but he left. Lucky for him, I'd had my fill.' A big fist shook. 'He was insane – *must* have been on drugs.'

'Can you describe him?'

'Dirty, uncombed – what's the difference? And he didn't have a car, walked away on foot – I watched him. Probably on his way to the highway. God help anyone who picked him up.'

He watched me leave, too, standing with his arms folded across his chest as I drove away. I realized I hadn't heard or seen any children at his school.

Bullies and firesetters. A tramp in his twenties.

Trying to dig up the past.

The same man who'd called Harrison?

Merino.

Silk. A thing for fabrics.

Hewitt and Gritz, two tramps who would have been in their twenties back then.

Myra Paprock was killed five years ago. Two years after that, Shipler. Then Lerner. Then Stoumen. Was Rosenblatt still alive?

Katarina was, just a few miles up this beautiful road. That gave us something in common.

I was ready to talk to her.

Cabrillo Boulevard swept up past the ocean, cleansed of the weekend tourist swarm and the bad sidewalk art. The wharf looked depopulated and its far end disappeared in a bank of fog. A few cyclists pumped in the bike lane and joggers and speed-walkers chased immortality. I passed the big new hotels that commandeered the prime ocean views and the motels that followed them like afterthoughts. Passed a small seafood place where Robin and I had eaten shrimp and drunk beer. People were eating there now, laughing, tan.

Santa Barbara was a beautiful place, but sometimes it spooked me.

226

Too much psychic space between the haves and the have-nots and not enough geography. A walk up State Street took you from welfare hotels and mean bars to custom tailors, and two-buck-a-scoop ice cream. The fringes of Isla Vista and Goleta were as hard as any inner city but Montecito was still a place where people ate cake. Sometimes the tension seemed murderous.

I pictured Andre de Bosch trolling lower State for day laborers. His daughter listening and laughing as he dehumanized those he'd found . . .

Cabrillo climbed higher and emptied of pedestrians and I caught an eyeful of endless Pacific. Sailboats were out in force at the marina, most of them floundering as they searched for a tailwind. Nearer to the horizon, fishing scows sat, still as artists' models. The boulevard flattened once again, turned into Shoreline and got residential. I began checking the numbers on the curb.

Most of the houses were fifties rancheros, several of them in renovation. I remembered the neighborhood as well-planted. Today, lots of the plants were gone and the ones that remained looked discouraged. The drought had come hard to this town kissed by salt water.

The lawns were suffering the most, most of them dead or dying. A few were vivid-green – too green.

Spray paint.

Santa Barbara, trying to free itself from dependence on Sierra snowpack, had declared mandatory rationing long before L.A. Now the town was returning to desert but the addiction to emerald was hard to shake.

I reached Katarina's house. Older than its neighbors and considerably smaller, a pale blue, country English cottage with two turrets, a slate roof that needed mending and a big dirt expanse in front. A privet hedge rimmed the plot, uneven, and picked-apart in spots. What had once been a rose garden was now a collection of trellised sticks.

An old-fashioned wire-link gate was fastened across an asphalt driveway, but as I pulled up I could see it was unlocked. I got out and pushed it open and walked up the drive. The asphalt was old and cracked, stretching a hundred feet to the tail end of a small, pale Japanese car.

Drapes whited all the windows of the house. The front door was paneled oak, its varnish bubbling, a Neighborhood Watch sticker affixed just below the lion's head knocker. Below that was another one, bearing the name of an alarm company.

I rang the bell. Waited. Did it again. Waited some more. Used the lion. Nothing.

No one was around. I could hear the ocean.

I went around the side, past the little white car and a high-peaked garage with sagging swivel doors left half-open. The backyard was twice the size of the front plot and denuded. The borders with its neighbors were obscured by thick plantings of dead citrus and dead avocado. On the ground were shapeless patches of lifeless shrubbery. Even the weeds were struggling.

But a couple of giant pines toward the back had survived nicely, their roots deep enough to tap into ground water. Their trunks yearned for the ragged cliff that overlooked the ocean beach. Through their boughs, the ocean was gray lacquer. The property was at least a hundred feet up but the tide was a drum roll, loud enough to block out every other sound.

I looked at the rear of the house. Buttoned up and curtained. Near the cliff was an old redwood table and two chairs, guano-specked and faded to ash. But half of the table was covered with a white tablecloth and on the cloth were a cup and saucer, and a plate.

I walked over. Coffee dregs in the cup, crumbs on the plate and an orange smear that looked like ossified marmalade.

The ocean grumbled and seabirds shrieked in response. I walked to the edge of the cliff. To the spot where Katarina had photographed her father, slumped in his wheelchair.

Dry dirt. No fence, easy fall. I peered over and a splinter of vertigo pierced my chest. When it subsided, I looked over again. The hillside was gouged with erosion – giant fingermarks that traced a dead drop down to the rocky beach.

The gulls screamed again – a reprimand that reminded me I was trespassing.

The coffee and crumbs said Katarina was in town. Probably gone out for an errand.

I could wait here, but the more efficient thing would be to call Milo and catch him up on Becky Basille's notes, Harrison, and Bancroft.

As I started to leave, I passed the garage once again and saw the rear end of another car, parked in front of the little white sedan. Bigger and darker – black. The distinctive vertical slash taillights of a Buick Elektra. Same car I'd seen at the front of the hospital, in seventy-nine.

Something near the rear tire.

Fingers. White and thin. A hand, the top speckled by an eczematous rash.

No, another kind of speckling.

Darker than eczema.

She was lying on the cement floor, face-up, parallel to the Buick, nearly concealed under the chassis. The other hand was over her head, palm exposed, gouged with deep cuts. Tendons looped from some of the wounds, curling like tired elastic bands.

Defense cuts.

She had on a pink housedress under a white terrycloth robe. The robe was splayed open and the dress was pushed up past her waist, nearly reaching her chin. Her feet were bare, the soles grimed by garage dirt. Her eyeglasses were a few feet away, one of the sidepieces twisted nearly off, one of the lenses cracked.

Her neck was cut, too, but most of the damage had been done to her abdomen. It was black and red – ripped apart, a jumble of viscera – but oddly bloated.

The vertigo returned. I wheeled around then, checked my back. Then I faced the body again and felt myself grow weirdly calm. Time slowed and an internal rush-and-roar filled my head, as if the ocean had been transplanted there.

Something missing. Where was the inevitable message?

I forced myself to look for red letters.

Searching for two words . . . nothing. Nothing in the garage but the car and Katarina and a small, metal workbench off to one side, backed by a pegboard panel.

A workbench liked Robin's, but cluttered with paint cans, tools, gluepots, jars of shellac. Hanging from the pegboard, hooks bearing hammers, gouges, chisels – one of the chisel hooks empty.

A knife on the table, its blade glazed red.

Birchwood handle. Wide tapered blade. Everything glazed . . . the bench stained, but no words, just a spatter of stains.

Old paint blotches. New ones. All mixed in with the telltale red/brown.

Dribs and droplets but no proclamation.

Something white underneath the handle of the killing tool.

A scrap of paper. Not white – almost white, beige. A nice, classy shade of ecru.

Business card.

Confident-looking brown letters said:

S.D.I. Inc.
9817 Wilshire Boulevard
Suite 1233
Beverly Hills, Ca. 90212

Something else.

In the upper right.

Tiny.

Hand-printed by ballpoint.

Printed neatly, the characters identical to the lettering on my tape-package.

So much pressure on the pen that the stiff paper had been torn through in spots.

BL!

22

I ran down the driveway, threw myself into the car and sped down to the marina. There was a pay phone on the boat moorings, near some trash cans. The stench was welcome.

I tried Robin again. Still no answer.

A detective at West L.A. Robbery Homicide said, 'He's not in.'

'It's an emergency.'

'Sorry, don't know where he is.'

'Maybe he's out in his car,' I said. 'Could you try radioing him?'

His voice hardened: 'Who is this?'

'Assistant Chief Murchison,' I said without thinking, marveling at the ease of the lie.

Second of silence. Something that might have been a gulp. 'One moment, sir.'

Thirty seconds later: 'Sturgis.'

'It's me, Milo —'

Pause.

'Alex,' I said.

'You palmed yourself off as *Murchison?*'

'Katarina's dead. I just found her body.' I gave him the details, describing the crime scene in a rapid word-storm. The card with the bad love message.

'Same printing as the package the tape came in.'

'SDI,' he said.

'It's right there in Beverly Hills. Maybe he chose to use it for the message for a reason.'

'SDI . . . sure as hell not the strategic defense initiative.'

'Could you check on Robin? I know the place is secure, but the

231

killer's picking up speed and the idea of her being alone up there . . . I tried calling her twice but she's not in.'

'Probably went out to do some shopping, but I'll stop by.'

'Thanks. What do I do now? I haven't even called the local police yet.'

'Where are you?'

'Pay phone, a few minutes from the house.'

'Okay, go back there. Stay away from the actual crime scene and just wait. I'll call Santa Barbara PD, tell 'em you're kosher, then I'll head up there myself – what time is it – three-thirty . . . I should be there by six, the latest.'

I waited near the cliff, far from the garage as I could be. Staring at the ocean, inhaling brine, and trying to make sense of things.

Two young uniforms showed up first. One stayed with the body and the other took a superficial report from me – name, rank, serial number, time and place – listening courteously and just a bit suspiciously.

Twenty minutes later, a pair of detectives arrived. One was a woman named Sarah Grayson, tall, slim, attractive, in her forties. Her eyes were slightly slanted, colored an even brown. They moved slowly but frequently. Taking things in. Reserving judgment.

Her partner was a big, heavy man named Steen, with a bushy dark mustache and not much hair. He went straight into the garage and left me with Grayson.

Somehow we'd ended back near the cliff-edge. I told her tape recorder everything I knew and she listened without interruption. Then she pointed at the water and said, 'There's a seal flipping around out there.'

I followed her arm and made out a small black dot, ten breast-strokes from the tideline, cutting a perpendicular line through the breakwaters.

'Or a sea lion,' she said. 'Those are the ones with the ears, right?'

I shrugged.

'Let's go over it again, doctor.'

When I finished, she said, 'So you were looking for Dr. de Bosch to warn her about this revenge-nut?'

'That, and I wanted to find out if she could tell me anything about why he's out for revenge.'

'And you think it has something to do with this school?'

'She and her father ran it. It's the only thing I can come up with.'

'What was the exact name of the school?' she said.

'The de Bosch Institute and Corrective School. It closed in eighty-one.'

'And you thought she'd know what happened because she was the owner's daughter.'

I nodded and looked at the rear of the house. 'There could be records in there. Therapy notes, something about an incident that traumatized one of the students enough to set him off years later.'

'What kind of students went to this school?'

'Emotionally disturbed. Mr. Bancroft, the owner of the school across the street, described them as antisocial fire-setters, truants and miscreants.'

She smiled. 'I know Mr. Bancroft. So when do you think this traumatic episode might have occurred?'

'Some time before nineteen seventy-nine.'

'Because of that conference?'

'That's right.'

She thought for a while. 'And how long was the school around?'

'From nineteen sixty-two to eighty-one.'

'Well, that's verifiable,' she said, more to herself than me. 'Maybe if there was a trauma we'll have a record of it. Assuming something happened.'

'What do you mean?'

'You just told me you think this guy's crazy, doctor – this supposed avenger.' She kept her eyes on me and turned one of her earrings. 'So maybe he cooked it all up in his head.'

'Maybe, but being psychotic doesn't mean being totally delusional – most psychotics have periods of lucidity. And psychotics can be traumatized, too. Plus, he might not even be psychotic. Just extremely disturbed.'

She smiled again. 'You sound like an expert witness.'

'I've been to court.'

'I know – Detective Sturgis told me. And I discussed you with Judge Stephen Huff, too, just to play it safe.'

'You know Steve?'

'Know him well. I used to work Juvenile down in L.A. Steve was handling that kind of thing, back then. I know Milo, too. You keep good company, doctor.'

She looked at the house. 'This victim down in L.A. – Ms. Paprock. You think she taught at the school?'

'Yes, under the name of Evans. Myra Evans. Her day job was with the public school system in Goleta. There might still be records of that. And the male victim, Rodney Shipler, worked as a school janitor in L.A., so he may have had a similar job up here.'

'Shipler,' she said, still looking at the house. 'Whereabouts in L.A. do you practice?'

'Westside.'

'Child counseling?'

'I do mostly forensic work now. Custody evaluations, injury cases.'

'Custody – *that* can get mean.' She turned her earring again. 'Well, we'll go and look around in the house soon as the tech team and the coroner come and okay it.'

She gazed at the ocean some more, brought her eyes back to the redwood table and lingered on the coffee cup.

'Having her breakfast,' she said. 'The dregs still haven't solidified, so my guess is this is from this morning.'

I nodded. 'That's why I thought she was home. But if she was eating out here and he surprised her, wouldn't the house be open? Look how sealed-up it looks. And why didn't anyone hear her scream?'

Holding up a finger, she slung her purse over her shoulder and went to the garage. She and Steen came out a few minutes later. He was holding a metal tape measure and camera, listening to her and nodding.

She took something out of her purse. Surgical gloves. After shaking them out, she donned them and tried a rear door. It opened. She stuck her head inside for a moment then drew it back.

Another conference with Steen.

Back to me.

'Total mess,' she said, wrinkling her nose.

'Another body?'

'Not that I can see so far . . . look, doctor, it's going to take a long time to get things sorted out here. Why don't you just try to relax until Detective Sturgis gets here. Sorry you can't sit on these chairs, but if you don't mind the grass, get yourself a place over on that side.' Indicating the south end of the yard. 'I already checked it for footprints and it's okay – ah, look, there's another sea lion. It's real pretty up here, isn't it?'

*   *   *

Milo made it by five forty-eight. I'd staked out a position in a corner of the yard and he walked straight to it, after talking to Grayson.

'Robin was still out when I checked,' he said. 'Her truck and her purse were gone and so was the dog and she'd written down something on the fridge pad about salad, so she probably went shopping. I saw absolutely nothing wrong. Don't worry.'

'Maybe she should stay with you.'

'Why?'

'I'm not safe to be around.'

He looked at me. 'Okay, sure, if it helps your peace of mind. But we'll *keep* you safe.'

He put a hand on my shoulder for a moment, then entered the garage and stayed there for twenty minutes or so. The coroner had come and gone and so had the body, and the technicians were still working, dusting and peeking and making casts. I watched them until Milo came out.

'Let's go,' he said.

'Where?'

'Out of here.'

'They don't need me anymore?'

'Did you tell Sally everything you know?'

'Yup.'

'Then let's go.'

We left, passing the garage. Steen was on his knees by a chalk body outline, talking into a tape recorder. Sarah Grayson was standing near him, writing in a notepad. She saw me and waved, then returned to her work.

'Nice lady,' I said, as we walked away.

'She was one of Central Juvey's best investigators, used to be married to one of the watch commanders – real asshole, mean drunk. Rumor had it he was rough on her and the kids.'

'Physically rough?'

He shrugged. 'I never saw bruises, but he had a vicious temper. Finally, they got divorced, and a couple of months later he came over to her place, raising a ruckus, and ended up shooting himself in the foot and losing a toe.' Smile. 'Whole big investigation. Afterward, Sally moved up here and the asshole retired on disability and packed out to Idaho.'

'In the foot,' I said. 'Not exactly a marksman.'

He smiled again. 'Actually, he was a crack shot, had once been a range instructor. A lot of people found it hard to believe he'd done it to himself, but you know how it is with chronic alcohol abuse. All that loss of *muscle* control. No telling.'

We reached the street. Santa Barbara police cars were parked at the curb, sandwiching the Seville. Neighbors were pressing up against the crime scene tape and a t.v. van was driving up. I looked in vain for Milo's Fiat or an unmarked.

'Where's your car?'

'Back in L.A. I took a chopper.'

'To where?'

'The airport.'

'How'd you get here from there?'

'Santa Barb uniform picked me up.'

'Status,' I said. 'Hoo-hah.'

'Yeah,' he said. 'Sally used to live in Mar Vista. I was the detective on her ex's toe job.'

'Oh.'

'Yeah. Oh. Now *you* drive me, let's split before the press-leeches start sucking.'

I headed down Cabrillo. He said, 'Are you too wiped out or grossed out to eat?'

'I haven't eaten since breakfast. I can probably hold something down, or at least watch you.'

'Voyeur – this looks okay, pull in.' He pointed to a small seafood place tucked next to one of the beach motels. Inside was a scattering of oilcloth-draped tables with abalone-shell ashtrays, sawdust floors, netted walls, a live bar and a self-order counter. The special of the day was salmon and chips. Both Milo and I ordered it, took a number, and sat down at a window table. We tried to look through the traffic at the water. A young waitress inquired if we wanted anything to drink, brought us two beers and left us alone.

I called Robin again, using a phone at the back, next to a cigarette machine. Still out. When I got back to the table, Milo was wiping foam from his upper lip.

'Katarina was pregnant,' he said. 'Coroner actually saw the fetus *hanging* out of her.'

'God,' I said, remembering the mess and the bloated abdomen. 'How far along was she?'

'Five to six months. Coroner could tell it was a boy.'

236

I tried to push aside my revulsion. 'Harrison said she never married and she lived alone. Who could the father have been?'

'Probably some med student with a Mensa membership. SDI stands for Seminal Depository and Inventory.'

'A sperm bank?'

'This particular one claims to screen its donors for both brains and brawn.'

'Designer babies,' I said. 'Yeah, I can see Katarina going for something like that. Artificial insemination would give her total control over the childrearing, no emotional entanglements . . . at five months she'd probably be showing. That's why the killer concentrated on her belly – focused his anger there. Wiping out de Bosch's line.'

He frowned.

I said, 'Maybe the sperm bank's card was chosen for the message for that same reason. The way it was pinned under the murder weapon was deliberate – setting the scene. It's all a big ritual for him.'

The waitress brought the food. A look at our faces erased the smile on hers.

I said, 'He's trying to obliterate everything associated with de Bosch. And once again, he used a weapon he found on hand. Turning the victim against himself – insult *and* injury. Trying to reverse what he thinks was done to him. But he must have brought another weapon with him, to intimidate her.'

'His fists could have been all he needed for that. Lots of bruises around her eyes.'

'Did he hit her hard enough to knock her out?'

'Hard to tell without an autopsy, but Sally said the coroner didn't think so.'

'If she was conscious, why didn't anyone hear her scream?'

'Sometimes people don't scream,' he said. 'Lots of times they freeze and can't get a sound out. Or the head blows could have stunned her. Even if she did scream, it might not have helped. Neighbors on both sides are away and the ocean blocks out lots of sound to begin with.'

'What about other neighbours? Didn't anyone see someone enter the property?'

'No one's come forward, yet. Sally and Steen are gonna do a door-to-door canvass.'

'Sally said the house was a mess. Did he mean poor housekeeping or a toss?'

'A toss. There was overturned furniture, ripped upholstery.'

'Rage,' I said. 'Or he could have been looking for old school records. Something that might incriminate him.'

'Getting rid of the evidence? He's been bumping off people for years, why start covering now?'

'Maybe he's getting more nervous.'

'My experience is just the opposite,' he said. 'Killers acquire a taste for it, enjoy it more and more and get careless.'

'Hope he did get careless and you find something in there.'

'It'll take a couple of days to do a thorough forensic work-over.'

'From the outside, the place looked sealed up. If I hadn't seen the breakfast dishes, I would have assumed Katarina was out of town. The killer must have closed the drapes after he killed her, then tossed in peace.'

'Like you said, it's a ritual, something he sets up carefully.'

'So we're not dealing with a raving psychotic. Everything that's happened is too calculated for a schizophrenic: traveling around to conventions, simulating accidents. Skewering my fish. Taping Hewitt screaming. Stalking, delaying gratification for years. This is calculated cruelty, Milo. Some kind of psychopath. Becky's notes mean we have to look at Gritz carefully. If he's Silk/Merino, his street-bum-alkie thing may be a disguise. The perfect disguise, when you think about it, Milo. The homeless are everywhere, part of the scenery. To most of us they all look alike. I remember seeing a guy at Coburg's office. He looked so similar to Hewitt, it startled me. All Bancroft really remembered about his intruder, besides age, was dirt and hair.'

He thought. 'How many years ago did Bancroft say this guy barged in?'

'Around ten. The guy was in his twenties, so he'd be in his thirties now, which would fit Gritz. Bert Harrison's Mr. Merino fits that time-frame, too. Both Merino and Bancroft's tramp were agitated. Merino talked about the conference putting him in touch with his problems. A few years later, the tramp returned to his old school, trying to dig up his past. So it could be the same guy, or maybe there are lots of Corrective School alumni wandering around, causing a scene trying to put their lives together. Whatever the case, something *happened* there, Milo. Bancroft called the

Corrective students miscreants and fire-setters. He denied there'd been any major problems that he couldn't handle, but he could have been lying.'

'Well,' he said, 'local records can be checked and Sally'll be talking to Bancroft again, see if she can get more details.'

'Good luck to her. He doesn't suffer the middle class lightly.'

He smiled and lifted his glass. 'That's okay. Sally doesn't suffer assholes lightly.'

He drank some beer but didn't touch his food. I looked at mine. It appeared well-prepared but had all the appeal of fried lint.

I said, 'Myra Paprock taught school here during the late sixties to the mid seventies, so that's probably the time-frame we're looking at. Lyle Gritz would have been around ten or eleven. Harrison remembers Myra as being young and very dogmatic. So maybe she got heavy-handed with discipline. Something a child could perceive as bad love. Shipler could have worked there, too, as a janitor. Got involved, somehow, in whatever happened. And most of the conference speakers were on the staff then, too. I've got the exact dates in my notes back home – let's finish up here, get back to L.A. and check.'

'You check, ' he said. 'I'll be staying up here for a day or two, working with Sally and Bill Steen. Leave messages at her desk.' He gave me a business card.

I said, 'The killer's been accelerating his pace. One year between victims, now only a few months between Stoumen and Katarina.'

'Unless there are other victims we don't know about.'

'True. I still can't find Harvey Rosenblatt and his wife hasn't returned my call. Maybe she's a widow who just doesn't want to deal with it. But I've got to keep trying. If Rosenblatt's alive, I need to warn him – need to warn Harrison, too. Let me call him right now and tell him about Katarina.'

I returned to the pay phone, and dialed Ojai while reading the warning label on the cigarette machine. No tape. I hoped it was because Harrison's self-preservation instincts were sharp. The little man would make an easy, crimson target.

When I returned to the table, Milo still hadn't eaten.

'Gone,' I said. 'Maybe he's hiding already. He said he had somewhere to go.'

'I'll ask an Ojai cop to stop by. What about Becky Basille? How do you fit her into this? Hewitt screaming "bad love", the killer taping Hewitt?'

'Maybe Hewitt was a Corrective alumnus, too. Or maybe the killer indoctrinated Hewitt about "bad love". If "G" is our guy, Becky's notes imply a close relationship of some kind between him and Hewitt. If I'm right about the killer not being psychotic, he'd have been the more put-together partner – the dominant one. Able to push Hewitt's buttons. Feed Hewitt's paranoia, get him off his medication, and turn him against his therapist. Because of *his* hatred of therapists. Plus, he had another reason to hate Becky: Hewitt was getting attached to her.'

He began cutting salmon with his fork. Stopped and ran his hand over his face.

'I'm still looking for Mr. Gritz. Pulled his complete sheet and it's all minor league.'

'He told the Calcutta folks he was going to get rich. Could there be some kind of profit motive to these murders?'

'Maybe he was just bragging. Psychopaths do that.'

'He looked at his food and shoved his plate away. 'Who'm I kidding.'

'The kid on the tape,' I said. 'Any record of Gritz having children?'

He shook his head.

'The chant,' I said, '"bad love, bad love, don't give me the bad love." *Sounds* like something an abused kid might say. Having a child recite it could be part of the ritual. Reliving the past, using de Bosch's own terminology. God only knows what else he's done, trying to work through his pain.'

He took out his wallet, pulled out cash and put it on the table. Tried to catch the waitress's attention, but her back was to us.

'Milo,' I said, 'Becky might still be a link. She could have talked to someone about Hewitt and "G".'

'Like who?'

'A relative, a friend. Did she have a boyfriend?'

'You're saying she broke confidentiality?'

'She was a beginner and we already know she wasn't that careful.'

'Don't know about any boyfriend,' he said. 'But why would she not tell Jeffers then go and gab to a lay-person?'

'Because telling Jeffers would have meant getting pulled off

Hewitt's case. And she could have talked without feeling she was breaching confidentiality. Leaving out names. But she might have said something to someone that can give us a lead.'

'The only member of her family I ever met was her mother, and that was just once, to listen to her cry.'

'A mother can be a confidante.'

He looked at me. 'After that picnic with Paprock's husband, you'd be willing to do another exhumation?'

'What else do we have going?'

He pushed food around his plate. 'She was a nice person – the mother. What approach would you take with her?'

'Straight and narrow. Hewitt had a friend who may be involved in other killings. Someone whose name starts with G – did Becky ever talk about him.'

He caught the waitress's eye and waved her over. She smiled and held up a finger, finished reciting the specials to a couple across the room.

'She lives near Park LaBrea,' he said. 'Near the art museum. Ramona or Rowena, something like that. I think she's in the book, though she may have unlisted it after the murder. If she did, call me at Sally's and I'll get it for you.'

He looked at our untouched plates, took a toothpick from a can on the table and poked at his incisors.

'Got your message about the Sheriff,' I said. 'When does he plan to get to the tape?'

'Next couple of days, unless some emergency comes up. Don't know what it'll accomplish, but at least we'll feel scientific.'

'Speaking of science,' I said, 'any estimates, yet, about when Katarina was killed?'

'Coroner's initial guess is anywhere from eight to twenty hours before you found her.'

'Eight's more likely. The coffee dregs were still moist. If I'd gotten there a little earlier I might have – '

'Gotten hurt yourself.' He leaned forward. 'Forget the rescue fantasies, Alex.'

My head hurt and so did my eyes. I rubbed them and drank water.

The waitress came over and looked at our uneaten meals.

'Is something wrong?'

'No,' said Milo. 'Something just came up and we've gotta run.'

'I can doggy-bag it for you.'

'No that's okay.' He handed her the cash.

She frowned. 'Oka-ay, I'll be back with your change, sir.'

'Keep it.'

Her smile was as wide as the beach. '*Thank* you, sir – we're offering a complimentary custard dessert today.'

Milo patted his gut. 'Maybe another time.'

'You're sure, sir? They're real good.' She touched his arm, briefly. '*Really.*'

'Okay,' he said, 'you twisted my arm. Pack a couple to go.'

'Right away, sir.'

She ran off and came back seconds later with a paper bag printed with the face of a happy-looking hound and the words FOR BOWSER. Milo carried it and we left the restaurant and headed for the Seville. As I got in the car, I realized he wasn't with me and I turned back to see him standing over a skinny, barechested kid of around eighteen. The kid was sitting on the breezeway in front of the motel and holding a shirt-cardboard sign that said, 'WILL WORK FOR FOOD.' His tan was intense, his cheeks were sunken, and his hair was a greasy umbrella.

Milo gave him the bag. The kid said something. Milo looked angry, but he reached into his wallet and handed the kid something green.

Then he got in the passenger seat and growled: 'Take me to work.'

23

The scene in the garage stayed with me during the drive back to L.A. Bad traffic just past Thousand Oaks had me sitting still, Katarina's mangled body filling my head. I listened to the Seville idle, thought about pain and vengeance and Robin all alone up on Benedict Canyon. Mr. Silk, whoever he was, had won a partial victory.

Things finally got moving again. I escaped the 101, made it to the 405 and had a clear-sail to Sunset. I was heading up Benedict shortly after nine-thirty when I noticed two red dots floating ahead of me.

Brake lights. A car stopped.

It seemed to be paused right in front of the narrow road that led to my adopted home, though from this distance I couldn't be sure. I put on speed, but before I got there, the lights dimmed and the car was gone, traveling too fast for me to catch up.

Probably nothing, but I was stumbling along the thin line between paranoia and caution and my heart was pounding. I waited. Everything stayed silent. I drove up to the white gate, slipped the cardkey in the slot and raced up the cypress-lined driveway.

The house was lit from within, the garage shut. I approached the front door, wet with sweat, turned the key and stepped inside, chest bursting.

Robin was stretched out on a living-room sofa reading a design magazine. The bulldog was wedged between her legs, head nestled in her lap, trapdoor mouth open and snoring.

'Beauty and the Beast,' I said, but my voice was weak.

She looked up, smiled and held out her hand. The dog opened one eye, then let the lid drop.

'Been shopping all afternoon?' I said, taking off my jacket. 'I tried calling a bunch of times.'

'Uh huh,' she said. 'Lots of errands . . . what's the matter?'

I told her what I'd found on Shoreline Drive.

'Oh no!' She propped herself on her elbows. The dog grumbled awake, but he stayed down. 'You came so close to walking in on it.'

I sat down. As she squeezed my hand, I recounted what I'd found and what I'd learned from Bert Harrison and Condon Bancroft. She listened with her fingers at her mouth.

'Whoever's behind this is relentless,' I said. 'I want you to move somewhere else temporarily.'

She sat up completely. '*What?*'

'Just for a while. I'm not safe to be around.'

'We moved so you *would* be, Alex. How could anyone know you're here?'

Thinking of the brake lights, I said, 'I'm sure no one does, but I just want to be careful. I spoke to Milo. You can move into his place. Just till things ease up.'

'It's not necessary, Alex.'

The dog was completely awake now, shifting his glance from Robin to me, his brow wrinkles deeper. The confusion and fear of a kid watching his parents fight.

'Just temporarily,' I said.

'*Temporarily?* If this person's done everything you think he has, he waits years! So what kind of temporary are we talking about, here?'

I had no answer.

She said, 'No. No way, Alex, I won't leave you. To hell with him, he can't do that to us.'

'Robin, she was pregnant. I saw what he did to her.'

'No,' she said, eyes brimming. 'Please. I don't want to hear about it.'

' Okay,' I said.

She pitched forward as if falling, and grabbed my shoulders with both hands. Pulling me closer, she held on tight, as if still off-balance. Her cheek was up against mine and her breath was in my ear, hot and quick.

'It's okay,' I said. 'We'll work it out.'

She squeezed me. 'Oh, Alex, let's just move to another planet.'

The dog jumped from the couch to the floor, sat down and stared at us. Whistling noises came from his compressed nostrils, but his eyes were clear and active, almost human.

'Hey, Spike,' I said, reaching over. 'He been good?'

'The best.'

The affection in her voice made his ears go up. He trotted up to the edge of the couch and rested his flews on her knee. She caressed his head and he lifted his chin and gave her palm a long, wet tongue-swipe.

'You could take *him* with you,' I said. 'You'd have *constant* masculine attention.'

'Put it out of your mind, Alex.' Her nails dug into my back. 'We probably won't have him much longer, anyway. I got a call this morning from a group called French Bulldog Rescue. Very sweet lady over in Burbank – you wrote to the national club and they forwarded it to her. She's putting out feelers, says these little guys are almost never intentionally abandoned so it's just a matter of time before the owners call to claim him.'

'No one's reported him missing so far?'

'No, but don't get your hopes up. She's got a pretty good communication network, seems pretty sure she'll find his owner. She offered to come by and take him off our hands but I said we'd care for him in the meantime.'

The dog was looking up at me expectantly. I rested my hand on his head and he made a low, satisfied noise.

Robin said, 'Now I know how foster parents feel.' She grabbed a handful of soft chin and kissed it. Her shorts had rolled high on her thighs and she tugged them down. 'Have you had dinner yet?'

'No.'

'I bought stuff – chile rellenos, enchiladas. Even got a six-pack of Corona, so we could pretend we were party animals. It's a little late now to start a whole feast but I can put something together if you're hungry.'

'Don't bother, I'll make a sandwich.'

'No, *let* me, Alex. I need something to do with my hands. Afterward we can get in bed with the crossword and some really bad t.v. and who knows what else.'

'Who knows,' I said, drawing her to me.

* * *

We turned off the lights around midnight. I fell away easily, but I woke up feeling as if I'd been drained of body fluids.

I endured breakfast, feeding the dog bits of scrambled egg and making conversation with Robin until the two of them went to the garage.

As soon as I was alone, I called Dr. Shirley Rosenblatt in Manhattan and got the same taped message. I repeated my pitch, told her it was more urgent than ever and asked her to get in touch as soon as possible. When no callback had come in by the time I'd finished showering, shaving, and dressing, I phoned Jean Jeffers. She was out for the day – some kind of meeting downtown – and hadn't left word with her secretary about Lyle Gritz. Remembering her eagerness to look for him, I figured she'd come up empty.

Information had no listing for a Ramona or Rowena Basille but there was a *Basille, R.* on 618 South Hauser Street. Right near Park LaBrea.

An older woman's voice answered, 'Hello.'

'Mrs. Basille?'

'This is Rolanda, who're you?' Scratchy timbre, the midwestern tones I'd grown up with.

'My name's Alex Delaware. I'm a psychologist, consulting to the Los Angeles police department – '

'Yes?' Rise in pitch.

'Sorry to be bothering you – '

'What is it? What's happened?'

'Nothing, Mrs. Basille. I was just wondering if I could ask you a few questions.'

'About Becky?'

'About someone Becky might have known.'

'Who?'

'A friend of Dorsey Hewitt's.'

The name made her groan. 'What friend? Who? I don't understand.'

'A man named Lyle Gritz – '

'What about him? What's going on?'

'Have you ever heard of him?'

'No. What's this got to do with Rebecca?'

'Nothing directly, Mrs. Basille, but Gritz may have been involved in some other crimes. He may also have used the names Silk or Merino.'

'What kind of crimes? Murders?'

'Yes.'

'I don't understand. Why's a psychologist calling – that's what you said you were, right? Psychologist, psychiatrist?'

'Psychologist – '

'If there's murders involved, why aren't the *police* calling?'

'It's not an official investigation, yet – '

Pause. 'Okay, who are you, buster? Some sleazy tabloid writer? I've already been through that and let me tell you what you can— '

'I'm not a reporter,' I said. 'I'm who I said I was, Mrs. Basille. If you'd like to verify it, you can call Detective Milo Sturgis at West L.A. detectives. He gave me your name – '

'Sturgis,' she said.

'He handled the investigation of Becky's case.'

'Which one was that – oh yeah, the big one . . . yeah, he tried to be nice. But where does he come off giving you my name? What are you doing, some kind of psychological *study*? Want to make me a guinea pig?'

'No, nothing like that – '

'What, then?'

There seemed no choice. 'My involvement's a lot more personal, Mrs. Basille. I'm a potential victim.'

'A vic— Of who, this Gritch?'

'Gritz. Lyle Edward Gritz. Or Silk or – '

'Never heard of any of those.'

'There's evidence he's been murdering psychotherapists, several of them over a five-year period.'

'Oh, no.'

'The latest occurred yesterday, in Santa Barbara. A woman named Katarina de Bosch.'

'Yester— Oh, goodness.' Her voice changed – lower, softer, still perplexed. 'And now you think he's out for *you*?'

'Yes.'

'Why?'

'He may have a thing against psychotherapists. He leaves a message at the crime scene. The words "bad love" – '

'That's the same thing that scum yelled out!'

'That's why we think there may be a connection. Last week, I received a tape with someone chanting "bad love". As well as a

247

sample of Hewitt screaming. Shortly after that, I got a crank phone call, then someone snuck onto my property and did damage.'

'What are you *saying*? That Rebecca was part of something?'

'I really don't know, Mrs. Basille.'

'But maybe that's what it *was*? Someone *else* was involved in my Becky's . . .'

A loud bang percussed in my ear. A few seconds later: 'Dropped the phone, you still there?'

'Yes.'

'So what're you saying? This Gritz could have been involved in hurting my baby?'

'I wish I could tell you, Mrs. Basille. Gritz and Hewitt were friends so it's possible Gritz had some influence on Hewitt. But there's no evidence –'

'Bad *love*,' she said. 'No one was ever able to explain to me what it meant.'

'It's a psychological term coined by Katarina de Bosch's father – Dr. Andres de Bosch.'

'Debauch?'

'De Bosch. He was a psychologist who ran a remedial school up in Santa Barbara.'

No reaction.

I said, 'Lyle Gritz may have been a patient there. For all I know, Hewitt may have been, also. Did Rebecca ever mention anything related to any of this?'

'No . . . God in heaven . . . I think I'm going to be sick.'

'I'm truly sorry, Mrs. –'

'What'd you say your name was?'

'Alex Delaware.'

'Give me your phone number.'

I did.

'Okay,' she said, 'I'm calling that Sturgis right now and checking you out.'

'He's in Santa Barbara. You can reach him at the police department there.' I fished around, retrieved Sarah Grayson's card and read off the number.

She hung up without comment.

Ten minutes later, my service put her through.

'He wasn't in,' she said, 'but I spoke to a woman cop who said you're for real. So, okay, I'm sorry for what you're going through –

once you been through it you get sorry a *lot* for other people. Okay, what can I do for you?'

'I was just wondering if Becky ever talked about her work. Said anything that might help find Gritz and clear this up.'

'Talked? Yeah, she talked. She loved her . . . hold on . . . my stomach . . . hold on, I thought I was okay but now I feel like I have to throw up again – let me go do that, and then I'll call you back – no, forget that, I hate the phone. Phone rings now, my heart starts going like it's going to explode – you want to come down and see me it's okay. Let me see what you look like, I hate the phone.'

'How about I come to your house?'

'Sure – no, forget it. The place is depressing. I never was a homemaker, now I don't do a darn thing.'

'Why don't you meet me over in Hancock Park? Not the neighborhood, the actual park – know where it is?'

'Over by the Tar Pits.'

'Yeah, meet me on the Sixth Street side, behind the museums. There's a shady area, some benches. What're you gonna wear?'

'Jeans and a white shirt.'

'Fine. I'll be wearing – no, this is wrinkled, gotta change it – I'll be wearing a . . . green blouse. Green with a white collar. Just look for an ugly old woman with a green blouse and crappy disposition.'

The blouse was grass-green. She was sitting under a thatch of mismatched trees, on a bench facing the rolling lawn that separated the County Art Museum from the dinosaur depository George Page had built with Mission Pack money. At the end of the lawn the tar pits were an oily black sump behind wrought iron pickets. Through the fence, plaster mastodons reared and glared at the traffic on Wilshire Boulevard. Tar leaked through the entire park, seeping up in random spots, and I just missed stepping in a bubbling pool as I made my way toward Rolanda Basille.

Her back was to Sixth Street but I had a three-quarter view of her body. Around sixty-five. Her collar was a snowy Peter Pan job, her slacks olive wool, much too heavy for the weather. She had hair dyed as black as the tar, cut in a flapper bob with eyebrow-length bangs. Her face was crinkled and small. Arthritic hands curled in her lap. Red tennis shoes covered her feet, over white socks, folded over once. A big, green plastic purse hung from her shoulder. If she weighed a hundred pounds, it was after Thanksgiving dinner.

The ground was covered with dry leaves and I made noise as I approached. She kept gazing out at the lawn and didn't look back. Children were playing there, mobile dots on an emerald screen, but I wasn't sure she saw them.

The random trees had been trimmed to form a canopy and the shadows they cast were absolute. Several other benches were scattered nearby, most of them empty. A black man slept on one, a paper bag next to his head. Two women of Rolanda Basille's approximate age sat on another, strumming guitars and singing.

I walked in front of her.

She barely looked up, and slapped the bench.

I sat down. Music drifted over from the two guitarists. Some sort of folksong, a foreign language.

'The Stepne sisters,' she said, sticking out her tongue. 'They're here all the time. They stink. Did you see a picture of my daughter?'

'Just in the paper.'

'That wasn't a flattering one.' She opened the big purse, searched for a while and took out a medium-sized envelope. Withdrawing three color photographs, she handed them to me.

Professional portraits, passable quality. Rebecca Basille sitting in a white wicker chair, posed three different ways in front of a mountain-stream backdrop, wearing a powder-blue dress and pearls. Big smile. Terrific teeth. Very pretty; soft, curvy build, soft arms, a trifle heavy, the dress was low-cut and showed some cleavage. Her brown hair was shiny and long and iron-curled at the ends, her eyes full of humor and just a bit of apprehension, as if she'd been sitting for a long time and had doubts about the outcome.

'Very lovely,' I said.

'She was beautiful,' said Rolanda. 'Inside and out.'

She held out her hand and I returned the photos. After she'd replaced them in the purse, she said, 'I just wanted you to see the person she was, though even these don't do it. She didn't like to have her picture taken – used to be chubby when she was little. Her face was always gorgeous.'

I nodded.

She said, 'There was a wounded bird within five miles, Becky'd find it and bring it home. Shoeboxes and cottonballs and eye-droppers. She'd tried to save anything – *bugs* – those little gray curly things?'

250

'Potato bugs?'

'Those. Moths, ladybugs, whatever, she'd save 'em. When she was *real* little she went through this stage of not wanting anyone to cut the lawn because she thought it hurt the grass.'

She tried to smile, but her lips got away from her and began trembling. She covered them with one hand.

'You see what I'm saying?' she said, finally.

'I do.'

'She never changed. In school, she went straight for the outcasts – anyone who was different, or hurting – the retarded kids, harelips, you name it. Sometimes I think she was *attracted* to hurt.'

Another forage in the purse. She found red-framed sunglasses and put them on. Given the ambient shade, they must have blacked out the world.

I said, 'I can see why she went into social work.'

'Exactly. I always figured she would do something like that, always told her nursing or social work would be perfect for her. But of course when you tell them, they do something else. So it took her a while to know what she wanted. She didn't want to go to college, did some waitressing, some file clerking, secretarial. My other kids were different. Real driven. Got a boy practicing orthopedic medicine in Reno and my older girl works in a bank in St. Louis – assistant vice president.'

'Was Becky the youngest?'

She nodded. 'Nine years between her and Kathy, eleven between her and Carl. She was – I was forty-one when I had her and her father was five years older than me. He walked out on us, right after she was born. Left me high and dry with three kids. Sugar-diabetic, and he refused to stop drinking. He started losing feeling in his feet, then the eyes started going. Finally, they began cutting pieces off of him and he decided with no toes and one arm it was time to be a swinging bachelor – crazy, huh?'

She shook her head.

'He moved to Tahoe, didn't last long after that,' she said. 'Becky was two when he died. We hadn't heard from him all that time, suddenly the government started sending me his veteran's benefits . . . you think that's what made her so vulnerable? No – what do you people call it – father role model?'

'How was Becky vulnerable?' I said.

'Too trusting.' She touched her collar, smoothed out an invisible

251

wrinkle. 'She went straight for the losers. Believed every cock and bull story.'

'What kind of losers?'

'More wounded birds. Guys she thought she could fix. She wanted to fix the world.'

Her hands began to shake and she shoved them under her purse. The Stepne sisters were singing louder. She said: 'Shut up.'

'Did the losers mistreat her?'

'Losers,' she said, as if she hadn't heard. 'The great poet with no poems to show for it, living off welfare. Bunch of musicians, so-called. Not men. Little boys. I nagged her all the time, all the dead ends she was choosing. In the end, none of that mattered a whit, did it?'

She lifted her sunglasses and wiped an eye with one finger. Putting the shades back, she said, 'You don't need to hear this, you've got your own problems.'

I saw faint reflections of myself in her black lenses, distorted and tense.

'You seem like a nice young fellow, listening to me go on like this. Ever save any bugs, yourself?'

'Maybe a couple of times.'

She smiled. 'Bet it was more than a couple. Bet you punched those holes in the top of the jars so the bugs could breathe, right? Bet your mother loved that, too, all those creepy things in the house.'

I laughed.

'I'm right, aren't I? *I* should be a psychologist.'

'It does bring back certain memories,' I said.

'Sure,' she said. 'Out to save the world, all of you. You married?'

'No.'

'A fellow like you, same attitude as my Becky, you would have been okay for her, you could have saved the world together. But to be honest, she probably wouldn't have gone for you – no offense, you're just too. . . put-together. That's a compliment, believe me.' She patted my knee. Frowned. 'I'm sorry for what you're going through. And be sure to take good care of yourself. Something happens to you, your mother's going to die, over and over. You'll be gone but she'll be left dying every *day* – understand?'

The hand on my knee clawed.

I nodded.

'Something happens to you, your mother's going to lie in bed and

252

think about you, over and over and over. Wondering how much you suffered. Wondering what you were *thinking* when it happened to you – *why* it happened to her kid and not someone else's. Do you understand what I'm saying?'

'I do.'

'So be careful.'

'That's why I'm here,' I said. 'To protect myself.'

She whipped off the sunglasses. Her eyes were so raw the whites looked brown. 'Gritz – no, she never said a word about anyone named that. Or Silk or Merino.'

Did she ever talk about Hewitt?'

'No, not really.' She seemed to be deliberating. I didn't move or speak.

The raw eyes moistened. 'She mentioned him once – maybe a week or two before. Said she was treating this really crazy person and thought she was helping him. She said it respectfully – this poor, sick fellow that she really wanted to help. Schizophrenic, whatever – hearing voices. No one else had been able to help him but she thought she could. He was starting to trust her.'

She spat on the ground.

'She mentioned him by name?'

'No. She made a point of not talking about any of them by name. Big point of following the rules.'

Remembering Becky's sketchy notes and lack of follow-through with Jean, I said, 'A real stickler, huh?'

'That was Becky. Back when she was in grade school, her teachers always said they wished they had a classroom full of Beckys. Even with her loser boyfriends, she always stayed on the straight and narrow, not using drugs, nothing. That's why they wouldn't . . .'

She shook her head. Put her glasses back on and showed me the back of her head. Between thin strands of dyed hair, her neck was liver-spotted and loose-skinned.

I said, 'Why they wouldn't what?'

No answer for a moment.

Then: 'They wouldn't stick with her – *they* always left *her*. Can you beat that? The ones who were going to get divorced, always went back to their wives. The ones who were on the wagon, always climbed back on. And left *her*. She was ten times the human being any of them were, but *they* always walked out on *her*, can you beat that?'

253

'They were the unstable ones,' I said.

'Exactly. Dead-end losers. What she needed was someone with high standards, but she wasn't attracted to that – only the broken ones.'

'Was she in a relationship at the time she died?'

'I don't know – probably. The last time I saw her couple of days before – she stopped by to give me some laundry – I asked her how her social life was and she refused to talk about it. What that usually meant was she was involved with someone she knew I'd nag her about. I got upset with her – we didn't talk much. How was I supposed to know it was the last time and I should have enjoyed every minute I had with her?'

Her shoulders bowed and quivered.

I touched one of them and she sat up suddenly.

'Enough of this – I hate this moping around. That's why I quit that survivors' group your friend Sturgis recommended. Too much self-pity. Meanwhile, I haven't done a damn thing for you.'

My head was full of assumptions and guesses. Learning of Becky's attraction to losers had firmed up the suspicions left by her notes. I smiled and said, 'It's been good talking to you.'

'Good talking to you, too. Do I get a bill?'

'No, the first hour's free.'

'Well, look at that. Handsome, a Caddy, and a sense of humor, to boot – you do pretty well, don't you?'

'I do okay.'

'Modesty – bet you do better than okay. That's what I wanted for Becky. Security. I told her, what are you wasting your time for, doing dirty work for the County? Finish up your degree, get some kind of license, open up an office in Beverly Hills and treat fat people or those women who starve themselves. Make some *money*. No crime in that, right? But she wouldn't hear of it, wanted to do important work. With people who were really *needy*.'

She shook her head.

'Saving the bugs,' she said, almost inaudibly. 'She thought she was dealing with those potato thingies but a scorpion got into the jar.'

254

24

Her description of Becky as a stickler for the rules didn't fit with Jean Jeffers's recollections. A mother's vision could be overly rosy, but she'd been frank about Becky's chronic attraction to 'losers'.

Had Becky finally been attracted to the ultimate loser? How loose had things gotten between her and Hewitt?

And what twisted dynamic bound the two of them to 'G.'?

Bad love.

Blaming the victim bothered me, but revenge seemed to be the fuel that powered the killer's engine and I had to wonder if Becky had been a target of something other than random psychosis.

I drove home straining to make sense of it. No strange vehicles within a hundred yards of the gate and last night's anxiety seemed silly. Robin was working, looking preoccupied and content, and the dog was chewing a nylon bone.

'Milo just called from Santa Barbara,' she said. 'The number's on the kitchen counter.'

I went into the house, found an 805 exchange that wasn't Sally Grayson's and punched it. A voice answered, 'Records.'

'Dr. Delaware returning Detective Sturgis's call.'

'One minute.'

I waited five.

'Sturgis.'

'Hi. Just got through talking to Becky's mother. Becky never mentioned anyone by name, but she did talk about helping a poor unfortunate psychotic who could very well have been Hewitt.'

'No mention of Gritz?'

'Nor of Silk or Merino. One thing that was interesting, though: she said Becky liked to mend broken wings and had a penchant for losers – guys who involved her in dead-end relationships. If you think of Hewitt as the ultimate loser, it supports what we suspected about things getting unprofessional between them. Having said all that, I don't know that it *leads* us anywhere.'

'Well, we're not doing much better here. No school records at Katarina's house so either she never kept them or the killer made off with them. We do have confirmation that Myra Evans was Myra Paprock, but no-go on Rodney Shipler. His tax records show him working for the L.A. Unified School District for thirty years – right after he got out of the Army. Never up here, and I verified it with the S.B. district. No connection at all to the de Bosch school.'

'What about summer vacations?' I said. 'School personnel some-times take part-time jobs during the off-season.'

'Summers he worked in L.A.'

'How long was he in the Army?'

'Fifteen years – staff sergeant, most of it over in the Philippines. Honorable discharge, no blots on his record.'

'He made somebody mad.'

'It doesn't look like it was someone at the school. In fact, we can't find any records of *anything* fishy happening out at the school. No fires or felonies or anything anybody would want to avenge, Alex. Just a few complaints about noise from Bancroft and one vehicular accident that did occur when Myra Evans was teaching there – May of seventy-three – but it was clearly an accident. One of the students stole a school truck and took a joyride. Made it up to the Riviera District and spun off a mountain road. He died, Santa Barbara PD investigated, found no foul play.'

'How old was the student?'

'Fifteen.'

'Vehicular accident off a mountain road,' I said. 'Grant Stoumen was hit by a car and Mitchell Lerner was pushed off a mountain.'

'That's a little abstract, Alex.'

'Maybe not, if matching things – achieving consistency – is part of the killer's fantasy.'

Pause. 'You'd know more about that than I would, but why focus on the school when we've got a victim with no connection to it? No obvious connection to de Bosch, period.'

'Shipler could have been connected to the symposium.'

'How? A janitor with a side-interest in psychology, or did he sweep up, afterward?'

'Maybe it's the race angle somehow. Shipler was black and de Bosch was a covert bigot.'

'Why would someone pissed off about *racism* beat a *black* man to death?'

'I don't know . . . but I'm sure de Bosch is at the core of this. The school, the conference – all of it. Merino told Harrison the conference set off something in him – maybe it was seeing de Bosch lauded publicly, when he knew the truth to be otherwise.'

'Maybe, but so far the school's got a clean record.'

'Bancroft seemed to think it was a hotbed of antisocial behavior.'

'Bancroft isn't your most reliable witness. Sally says he's been known to hit the bottle pretty hard and his world view's somewhat to the right of the Klan. Compared to his old man, he's a pussycat. The two of them had a special thing for de Bosch because de Bosch overbid Bancroft Senior for the land the school was built on. When de Bosch broke ground in sixty-two, they tried to mobilize the neighbors against it – disturbed kids running amok. But no one went along with it because the Bancrofts had alienated everyone over the years.'

'The neighbors didn't mind a school for problem kids?'

'There were some worries, but the lot being vacant bothered them more. Vagrants used to come off the highway, light fires, toss trash, make a mess. Bancroft Senior had dickered with the owner for years, making offers, withdrawing them. De Bosch's school was an improvement as far as the neighborhood was concerned. Real quiet, no problems.'

'Except for a fifteen-year-old kid in a stolen truck.'

'One incident in twenty years, Alex. Considering that de Bosch dealt with emotionally disturbed kids, wouldn't you say that's pretty good?'

'I'd say it's excellent,' I said. 'Exemplary. And one way to keep things so tidy is through firm discipline. *Very* firm discipline.'

He sighed. 'Sure, it's possible. But if de Bosch was running a torture chamber, wouldn't there be complaints?'

'Five dead people is a complaint.'

'Okay. But if you want a hostility motive, look at Bancroft. He had a *hard-on* for de Bosch for over twenty years. But that doesn't mean he ran around the country murdering everyone associated with him.'

'Maybe he *should* be looked into.'

'He will be,' he said wearily. 'He's *being* looked into. Meanwhile, you be careful and sit tight. I'm sorry, Alex, I wish the goddamn pieces had fit together neatly, but it's turning out to be messy.'

'Just like real life,' I said. 'Anything new on Katarina?'

'Coroner still can't decide if she was conscious or unconscious after those blows to the face. Her baby was, indeed, a twenty-two-week-old normal male, Caucasian. I called the sperm bank, they wouldn't even verify she was a customer. Sally and I can probably pry some information loose, eventually. Meanwhile, is Robin coming to us? Rick says no problem except for Rover – excuse me, Spike. Dog allergy. But if Robin really wants to take the pooch with her, he can put himself on antihistamines.'

'He won't need to,' I said. 'Robin insists on staying with me.'

'Must be your charm . . . well, don't sweat it, I'm sure you're safe.'

'Hope so.' I told him about the brake lights the previous night.

'Just lights, nothing funny?'

'Just lights. And then the car drove off.'

'What time was this?'

'Nine forty-five or so.'

'Any other cars around?'

'Quite a few.'

'Sounds like nothing. If you see anything funny, call Beverly Hills PD, they protect their citizenry.'

'I will. Thanks for everything . . . the kid who went off the mountain. Did he have a name?'

'Still on that, huh?' He gave a small laugh. 'His name was Delmar Parker and he originally came from New Orleans.'

'What was he being treated for at the school?'

'Don't know, there's no complete police report, because the case was closed and filed. We're working from summary cards at the coroner's office and lucky to find *them* . . . let's see . . . name, date, age, cause of death – multiple traumas and internal injuries – place of birth, N'Awleens. . . parent or guardian – here it is – the mother . . . Marie A. Parker.'

'Any address?'

'No. Why? You want to dig up *another* one?'

'No,' I said. 'I don't *want* to dig up anything, believe me. I'm just grasping, Milo.'

Silence. 'Okay, I'll try, but don't count on it. It was a long time ago. People move. People die.'

I pretended everything was normal. Robin and I ate lunch out by the pool. The sky was clear and beautiful, bracing itself for a smog cloud heading over from the east.

Lifestyles of the rich and fearful.

Terror and anger still gnawed at my spine, but I thought of the people under the freeway and knew I had it damned good.

The phone rang. My service operator said, 'There's a long-distance call for you, Dr. Delaware. From New York, a Mr. Rosenblatt.'

'Mister, not Doctor?'

'Mister's what he said.'

'Okay,' I said. 'Put him on.'

She did, but no one answered my 'Hello.' A few seconds later a young woman with an all-business voice clicked in and said, 'Schechter, Mohl and *Trimmer*, who are you holding for?'

'Mr. Rosenblatt.'

'One moment.'

A few seconds later a young voice said, 'This is Mr. Rosenblatt.'

'This is Dr. Delaware.'

Throat clear. 'Dr. Delaware, my name is Joshua Rosenblatt, I'm a practicing attorney here in New York and I'm calling to ask you to stop phoning my mother, Dr. Shirley Rosenblatt.'

'I've been phoning because I was concerned about your father – '

'Then you have nothing to be concerned about.'

'He's all right?'

Silence.

I said, 'Is he all right?'

'No. I wouldn't say that.' Pause. 'My father's deceased.'

I felt myself deflate. 'I'm sorry.'

'Be that as it may, Dr. Delaware – '

'When did it happen? Was it four years ago?'

Long silence. Throat clear. 'I really don't want to get into this, doctor.'

'Was it made to look like an accident?' I said. 'Some kind of fall? Something to do with a vehicle? Were the words "bad love" left anywhere at his death scene?'

'Doctor,' he began, but his voice broke on the second syllable and he blurted: 'We've been through enough, already. At this point, there's no need to rake it up.'

'I'm in danger,' I said. 'Maybe from the same person who killed your father.'

'What!'

'I called because I was trying to *warn* your father and I'm so sorry it is too late. I only met him once, but I liked him. He seemed like a really decent guy.'

'When did you meet him?' he said, softly.

'In nineteen seventy-nine. Here in Los Angeles. He and I co-chaired a mental health symposium called Good Love/Bad Love, Strategies in a Changing World. A tribute to a teacher of your father's named Andres de Bosch.'

No response.

'Mr. Rosenblatt?'

'None of this makes any sense.'

'You were with him on that trip,' I said. 'Don't you remember?'

'I went on lots of trips with my father.'

'I know,' I said. 'He told me. He talked about you quite a bit. Said you were his youngest. You liked hot dogs and video games – he wanted to take you to Disneyland but the park closed early in the fall so I suggested he take you to the Santa Monica Pier. Did you go?'

'Hot dogs.' His voice sounded weak. 'So what? What's the point?'

'I think that trip had something to do with his death.'

'No, no, that's crazy – no. Back in seventy-nine?'

'Some kind of long-term revenge plot,' I said. 'Something to do with Andres de Bosch. The person who murdered your father has killed other people. At least five others, maybe more.'

I gave him names, dates, places.

He said, 'I don't know any of those people. This is crazy. This is really insane.'

'Yes, it is, but it's all *true*. And I may be next. I need to talk to your mother. The killer may have presented himself to your father as a patient, lured him that way. If she's still got your father's old appointment books, it could –'

'No, she has nothing. Leave her out of this.'

'My life's at stake. Why won't your mother just talk to me? Why'd she have you call me instead of calling herself?'

'Because she can't,' he said angrily. 'Can't talk to anyone. She had a stroke a month ago and her speech was severely affected. It just came back a few weeks ago but she's still weak.'

'I'm sorry, but – '

'Listen, I'm sorry, too. For what *you're* going through. But, at this point, I just don't see what I can do for you.'

'Your mother's talking now?'

'Yes, but she's weak. Really weak. And to have her talk about my father. . . she just started rehab and she's making progress, Dr. Delaware. I can't have her interrogated.'

'You never told her I called?'

'I'm taking care of her. It calls for decisions.'

'I understand,' I said. 'But I don't want to interrogate her, I just want to talk to her. A few questions. At her pace – I can fly out to New York, if that'll help, and do it face-to-face. As many sessions as she needs. Go as slowly as she needs.'

'You'd *do* that? Fly out here?'

'What choice do I have?.'

I heard him blow out breath. 'Even so,' he said. 'Her talking about Dad – no, it's too risky. I'm sorry, but I have to hold firm.'

'I'll work with her doctors, Mr. Rosenblatt. Clear my questions with them and with you. I've done hospital work for years. I understand illness and recovery.'

'What makes you think she knows anything that could help you?'

'At this point she's my last hope, The creep who's after me is picking up his pace. He murdered someone in Santa Barbara yesterday – de Bosch's daughter. She was pregnant. He cut her up, made it a point to go after the fetus.'

'Oh, God.'

'He's stalking me,' I said. 'To tell the truth, I'd be safer in New York than here. One way or the other, I may come out.'

Another exhalation. 'I doubt she can help you, but I'll ask.'

'I really apprecia— '·

'Don't thank me yet. I'm not promising anything. And fax your credentials to me, so I can check them out. Include two verifiable references.'

'No problem,' I said. 'And if your mother won't speak to me, please ask her if she knows anything about the term "bad love". And did your father report anything unusual about the nineteen seventy-nine conference. You can also throw out some names: Lyle Gritz, Dorsey Hewitt, Silk, Merino.'

'Who're they?'

'Hewitt's a definite killer – murdered a therapist out here and was shot by the police. Gritz was his friend, may have been an accomplice. He may also be the one who killed your father. Silk and Merino are possible aliases.'

'Fake names?' he said. 'This is so bizarre.'

'One more thing,' I said. 'There's an LAPD detective working the case out here, named Milo Sturgis. I'm going to inform him of your father's murder and he'll be contacting the New York police and asking for records.'

'That won't help you,' he said. 'Believe me.'

25

Milo was no longer at Records and Sally Grayson's number was picked up by a male detective who hadn't seen her all morning and had no idea who Milo was. I left a message, and wondered why Joshua Rosenblatt had been so sure the police couldn't help?

My offer to go to New York had been impulsive – probably an escape reflex – but maybe something would come out of my talk with Shirley Rosenblatt.

I'd leave as soon as possible; Robin would *have* to move out now.

I looked out at the pool, still as a slab of turquoise. A few leaves floated on top.

Who cleaned it? How often?

I didn't know much about this place.

Didn't know when I'd be able to leave it.

I got up, ready to drive into Beverly Hills to find a fax service. Just as I put my wallet in my pants pocket, the phone rang and my service operator said, 'A Mr. Bucklear wants to talk to you, doctor.'

'Put him on.'

Click.

'Doctor? Sherman Bucklear.'

'Hello.'

'Have you received my correspondence?'

'Yes, I have.'

'I haven't received any reply, doctor.'

'Didn't know there was anything to reply to.'

'I have reason to believe you have knowledge of the whereabouts – '

'I don't.'

'Can you prove that?'

'Do I have to?'

Pause. 'Doctor, we can go about this civilly or things can get complicated.'

'Complicate away, Sherman.'

'Now, wait a sec—'

I hung up. It felt great to be petty. Before I could put down the phone, the service patched in again with a call from New York.

'Dr. Delaware? Josh Rosenblatt, again. My mother's willing to talk to you but I've got to warn you, she can't handle much – just a few minutes at a time. I haven't discussed any details with her. All she knows is you knew my father and thinks he was murdered. She may have nothing to tell you. You may end up wasting your time.'

'I'll take the chance. When would you like me there?'

'What's today – Tuesday . . . Friday's bad and she . . . weekends for total bedrest – Thursday, I guess.'

'If I can catch a flight tonight, how about tomorrow?'

'Tomorrow . . . I guess so. But it'll have to be in the afternoon. Mornings she has her therapy, then she naps. Come to my office first – Five Hundred Fifth Avenue. Schechter, Mohl, and Trimmer. The thirty-third floor. Have you faxed me your credentials, yet?'

'Just on my way out to do it.'

'Good, 'cause that'll be a prerequisite. Send me something with a picture, too. If everything checks out, I'll see you, say, twelve-thirty.'

I found a quick-print place on Canon Drive and faxed my documents to New York. Returning home, I postponed telling Robin and called an airline, booking myself a ten p.m. flight out of LAX. I asked the ticket agent about hotels.

She said, 'Midtown? I really don't know, sir, but you might try the Middleton. The executives from our company stay there, but it's expensive. 'Course, everything in New York is unless you want a real dive.'

I thanked her and phoned the hotel. A very bored-sounding man took my credit card number then grudgingly agreed to give me a single room for two hundred and twenty dollars a night. When he quoted the price, he suppressed a yawn.

I told Robin about Rosenblatt first.

She shook her head, took hold of my hand.

'Four years ago,' I said. 'Another gap filled in.'

'How'd he die?'

'The son didn't go into any details. But if the killer's being consistent, it was probably something to do with a car or a fall.'

'All those people. My God.' Pressing my hand up against her cheek, she closed her eyes. The smell of glue hung in the garage, along with coffee and dust and the sound of the dog's breathing.

I felt him nosing up against my leg. Looked down his wide, flat face. He blinked a couple of times and licked my hand.

I told Robin of my plan to fly East and offered to have her come with me.

She said, 'There'd be no point to it, would there?'

'It's not going to be a vacation, just more digging up people's misery. I'm starting to feel like a ghoul.'

She looked off, at her tools and her molds.

'Only time I've been in New York was a family trip. We went all the way up to Niagara Falls, Mom and Dad squabbling the whole time.'

'I haven't been there myself since grad school.'

She nodded, touched my bicep, rubbed it. 'You have to go – things are getting uglier and uglier. When are you leaving?'

'I was thinking tonight.'

'I'll take you to the airport – when will you be coming home, so I can pick you up?'

'Depends on what I find – probably within a day or two.'

'Do you have a place to stay?'

'I found a hotel.'

'A hotel,' she said. 'You, alone in some room . . .' She shook her head.

'Could you please stay with Milo and Rick while I'm gone? I know it's disruptive and unnecessary, but I'd have a lot more peace of mind.'

She touched my face again. 'You haven't had much of that lately, have you? Sure, why not . . .'

I tried a couple more times to reach Milo without success. Wanting to get Robin settled as soon as possible, I phoned his house. Rick was there and I told him we'd be coming over.

'We'll take good care of her, Alex. I'm really sorry for all this crap you've been going through. The big guy will get to the bottom of it.'

'I'm sure he will, too. Will the dog be a problem?'

'No, I don't think so. Milo tells me he's pretty cute.'

'Milo never expressed any affection for him in my presence.'

'Does that surprise you?'

'No,' I said.

He laughed.

'Are you badly allergic, Rick?'

'Don't know, never had a dog. But don't worry, I'll pick up some Seldane in the E.R., or write myself a scrip. Speaking of which, I have to head over to Cedars pretty soon. When were you planning on coming?'

'This evening. Any idea when Milo'll be back?'

'Your guess is as good as mine. Tell you what, I'll leave a key in back of the house. There're two sago palms growing up against the rear wall – you haven't been here since we re-landscaped, have you?'

'Just to pick up Milo.'

'Came out great, our water consumption's way down . . . the sago palms – do you know what they are?'

'Squat things with leaves that look like fan blades?'

'Exactly. I'll leave the key under the branches of the smaller one – the one on the right. Milo would kill me if he knew.' More laughter. 'We have a new alarm code, too – he changes it every couple of months.'

He rattled off five numbers. I copied them down and thanked him again.

'Pleasure,' he said. 'This should be fun, we've never had a pet.'

I packed my carry-on and Robin packed hers. We took the dog for a walk around the property and played with him, and finally he got sleepy. We left him resting and drove into town for an early dinner, taking Robin's truck. Cholesterol palace on south Beverly Drive: thick steaks and home-fried potatoes served in lumberjack portions at prices no lumberjack could afford. The food looked great and smelled great, and my taste buds told me it probably tasted great, too. But somewhere along the line the circuitry between my tongue and my brain fizzed and I found myself chewing mechanically, forcing meat down a dry, tight throat.

* * *

At seven, we cleaned the house on Benedict, picked up the dog, locked up, and drove over to West Hollywood. The key was where Rick had said it would be, placed on the ground precisely in the middle of the palm's corrugated trunk. The rest of the yard was desert-pale and composed, drought-tolerant plants spread expertly around the tiny space. The walls were higher and topped with ragged stone.

Inside, the place was different, too: whitewashed hardwood floors, big leather chairs, glass tables, gray fabric walls. The guest room was pine. An old iron bed was freshly made and turned down. A single white rose rested on the pillow and a bar of Swiss chocolate was on a dish on the nightstand.

'How sweet,' said Robin, picking up the flower and twirling it. She looked around. 'This is like a great little inn.'

Sheets of newspaper were spread on the floor next to the bed. On them were a white ceramic bowl filled with water, a plastic-wrapped hunk of cheddar cheese and a shirt-cardboard lettered in fountain-pen, in Rick's perfect, surgeon's hand:

POOCH'S CORNER

The dog went straight for the cheese – nosing it and having trouble with the concept of see-through plastic. I unwrapped it and fed it to him in bits. We let him explore, for a while, then went back inside.

'Every time I come here, they've done something else,' Robin said.

'*They*? I don't think so, Rob.'

'True. You know, sometimes I have trouble imagining Milo living here.'

'I bet he loves it. Refuge from all the ugliness, someone else to worry about the details, for a change.'

'You're probably right – we can all use a refuge, can't we?'

At eight, she drove me to LAX. The place had been rebuilt a few years ago, for the Olympics, and was a lot more manageable, but incoming arteries were still clogged and we waited to enter the Departure lanes.

The whole city had been freshened up for the games, more energy and creativity mustered during one summer than the brain-dead

267

mayor and the piss-and-moan city council had come up with in two decades. Now they were back to their old apathy-and-sleaze routine, and the city was rotting wherever the rich didn't live.

Robin pulled up to the curb. The dog couldn't enter the terminal, so we said our goodbyes right there, and, feeling lost and edgy, I entered the building.

The main hall was a painfully bright temple of transition. People looked either bone-weary or jumpy. Security clearance was slow because the western-garbed man in front of me kept setting off the metal detector. Finally, someone figured out it was due to the metal shanks in his snakeskin boots and we started moving again.

I made it to the gate by nine-fifteen. Got my boarding pass, waited a half-hour, then stood in line and finally got to my seat. The plane began taxiing at ten-ten, then stopped. We sat on the runway for a while and finally lifted off. A couple of thousand feet up, L.A. was still a giant circuit board. Then a cloud bank. Then darkness.

I slept on and off for most of the flight, woke varnished in sweat.

Kennedy was crowded and hostile. I lugged my carry-on past the hordes at the baggage carousels and picked up a cab at the curb. The car smelled of boiled cabbage and was plastered with No Smoking signs in English, Spanish, and Japanese. The driver had an unpronounceable name and he wore a blue tank top and a white ski hat. The hat was rolled triple so the edge created a brim. It resembled a soft bowler.

I said, 'The Middleton Hotel on West Fifty-Second Street.'

He grunted something and drove off, very slowly. The little I saw of Queens from the highway was low-rise and old, bricks and chrome and graffiti and . . . But when we got on the Queensboro Bridge, the water was calm and lovely and the skyline of Manhattan loomed with threat and promise.

The Middleton was twenty stories of black granite sandwiched between office buildings that dwarfed it. The doorman looked ready for retirement and the lobby was shabby, elegant and empty.

My room was on the tenth floor, small as a death row cell, filled with colonial furniture and sealed by blackout drapes. Clean and well-ordered but it smelled of mildew and roach killer. A dead quail hunt print hung over the bed. The air-conditioner was a heavy-metal instrument. Street noise made it up this far with little loss of volume.

No rose on my pillow.

Unpacking, I changed into shorts and a t-shirt, ordered a three-dollar English muffin and five-dollar eggs, then punched the operator's O and asked for a wakeup call at one. The food came surprisingly quickly and, even more amazing, was tasty.

When I finished, I put the tray on a glass-topped bureau, pulled back the covers and got into bed. The t.v. remote was bolted to the nightstand. A cardboard guide listed thirty or so cable stations. The last choice was an early morning public access show featuring a dull, pudgy nude man interviewing a dull, nude woman. He had narrow, womanish shoulders and a very hairy body.

'Okay, Velvet,' he said, leering. 'So . . . what do you do for uh . . . fun?'

A painfully thin blond with a beak nose and frizzy hair touched a nipple and said, 'Macramé.'

I switched off the set.

Lights out. The blackout drapes did their job well.

My heart was as dark as the room.

26

I beat the wake-up call by more than an hour. After showering, shaving, and dressing, I drew the drapes on a view of the red-brick building across the street. Men in white shirts and ties were framed in its windows, sitting at desks, talking into phones and stabbing the air with pens. Down below, the streets were clogged with double-parked cars. Horns blatted. Someone was using a compression drill. Even through the sealed windows I could smell the city.

I phoned Robin at just past nine, L.A. time. We told each other we were fine and chatted for a while before she put Milo on.

'Talk about bi-coastal,' he said. 'Expedition or escape?'

'Bit of both, I guess. Thanks for taking care of the lady and the tramp.'

'Pleasure. Got a little more info on Mr. Gritz. Traced him to a small town in Georgia and just got finished talking to the police chief. Seems old Lyle was a weird kid. Acted goofy, walked funny, mumbled a lot, didn't have any friends. out of school more than he was in, never learned to read properly or speak clearly. His home life was predictably bad, too. No father on the scene and he and his mother lived in a trailer on the outskirts of town. He started drinking, slid straight into trouble. Shoplifting, theft, vandalism. Once in a while he'd get into a fight with someone bigger and stronger than himself and come out the loser. Chief said he locked him up plenty, but he didn't seem to care, jail was as good as his home, or better. He used to sit in his cell and rock and talk to himself, as if he was in his own world.'

'Sounds more like the early signs of schizophrenia than a developing

270

psychopath,' I said. 'Onset during adolescence fits the schizophrenic pattern, too. What *doesn't* fit is the kind of calculated thing we're dealing with. Does this sound like a guy who could blend in at medical conferences? Delay gratification long enough to plot murders years in advance?'

'Not really. But maybe he changed when he grew up, got smoother.'

'Mr. Silk,' I said.

'Maybe he's a good faker. Always was. Faked looking nuts, even back then – psychopaths do that all the time, right?'

'They do,' I said. 'But did this police chief sound like someone easily fooled?'

'No. He said the kid was nuts but had one thing going for him. Musical talent. Taught himself to play guitar and mandolin and banjo and a bunch of other instruments.'

'The next Elvis.'

'Yeah. And for a while people thought he might actually make something of himself. Then one day, he just left town and no one heard from him again.'

'How long ago was this?'

'Nineteen seventy.'

'So he was only twelve. Any idea why he left?'

'Chief had just busted him for drunk and disorderly again, gave him the usual lecture, then added a few bucks to get some new clothes and a haircut. Figured maybe if the kid looked better he'd act better. Lyle walked out of the police station and headed straight for the train depot. Police chief later found he used the money to buy a one-way ticket to Atlanta.'

'Twelve years old,' I said. 'He could have kept traveling and ended up in Santa Barbara, been taken in by de Bosch as a charity case – de Bosch liked to put forth the humanitarian image, publicly.'

'Wish I could get a hold of school records. No one seems to have any. Not the city or the county.'

'What about Federal? If de Bosch applied for government funding for the charity cases, there might be some kind of documentation.'

'Don't know how long those agencies hold onto their records, I'll check. So far I'm drawing a blank on this bastard. First time he shows up in California is an arrest nine years ago. No NCIC record prior to that, so that's over a decade between his leaving Georgia and the beginnings of his West Coast life of crime. If he got busted for petty stuff in other small towns it might very well not have been entered into the national computer. But still, you'd expect something. He's a bad egg, where the hell was he all that time?'

'How about in a mental institution?' I said. 'Twelve years old, out on his own. God knows what could have happened to him out on the street. He might have suffered a mental breakdown and got put away. Or, if he was at the school the same time as Delmar Parker, maybe he observed Delmar's death and broke down over that.'

'Big assumption – he and Delmar knowing each other.'

'It is, but there are some factors that might point in that direction: he and Delmar were around the same age, both were Southern boys a long way from home. Maybe Gritz finally made a friend. Maybe he even had something to do with Delmar stealing the truck. If he did and escaped death but saw Delmar die, that could have pulled the rug out from under him, psychologically.'

'So now he's blaming the school and de Bosch and everyone associated with it? Sure, why not. I just wish we could push it past theory. Place Gritz in Santa Barbara, let alone the school, let alone knowing the Parker kid, etcetera, etcetera.'

'Any luck finding Parker's mother?'

'She doesn't live in New Orleans, and I haven't been able to find any other relatives. So where does this Silk–Merino thing come in? Why would a Southern boy pick himself a Latino alias?'

'Merino's a type of wool,' I said. 'Or a sheep – the flock following the shepherd, and getting misled?'

'Baaaa,' he said. 'When are you planning to see Rosenblatt's kid?'

'Couple of hours.'

'Good luck. And don't worry, everything here's cool, Ms. Castagna lends a nice touch to the place, maybe we'll keep her.'

'No, I don't think so.'

'Sure,' he said, chuckling. 'Why not? Woman's touch and all that. Hell, we can keep the beast, too. Put up a picket fence around the lawn. One big happy family.'

New York was clear as an etching, all corners and windows, vanishing rooflines, skinny strips of blue sky.

I walked to the law firm, heading south on Fifth Avenue, swept along in the midtown tide, comforted, somehow, by the forced intimacy.

Five Hundred Fifth Avenue was a six-hundred-foot limestone tower, the lobby an arena of marble and granite. I arrived with an hour to spare and walked back outside, wondering what to do with the time. I bought a hot-dog from a pushcart, ate it watching the throng. Then I spotted the main branch of the Public Library, just across Forty-Second Street, and made my way up the broad, stone stairs.

After a bit of asking and wandering, I located the periodicals room. The hour went fast as I checked four-year-old New York newspapers for obituaries on Harvey Rosenblatt. Nothing.

I thought of the psychiatrist's kind, open manner. The loving way he'd spoken about his wife and children.

A teenaged boy who'd liked hot dogs. The taste of mine was still on my lips, sour and warm.

My thoughts shifted to a twelve-year-old, leaving town on a one-way ticket to Atlanta.

Life had sneak-attacked both of them, but Josh Rosenblatt had been much more heavily armed for the ambush. I left to see how well he'd survived.

Schechter, Mohl, and Trimmer's decorator had gone for Tradition: carved, riff-oak panels with laundry-sharp creases, layers of heavy moldings, voluptuous plaster work, wool rugs over herringbone floors. The receptionist's desk was a huge, walnut antique. The receptionist was pure contemporary: mid-twenties, white-blonde, *Vogue* face, hair tied back tight enough to pucker her hairline, breasts sharp enough to turn an embrace dangerous.

She checked a ledger and said, 'Have a seat and Mr. Rosenblatt will be right with you.'

I waited twenty minutes until the door to the inner offices opened and a tall, good-looking young man stepped into the reception area.

I knew he was twenty-seven, but he looked like a college student. His face was long and grave under dark, wavy hair, nose narrow and full, his chin strong and dimpled. He wore a pinstriped charcoal suit, white tab shirt, and a red and pearl tie. Pearl pocket handkerchief, quadruple pointed, tasseled black loafers, gold Phi Beta Kappa pin in his lapel. Intense brown eyes and a golf tan. If law started to bore him, he could always pose for the Brooks Brothers catalogue.

'Dr. Delaware, Josh Rosenblatt.'

No smile. One arm out. Bone-crusher handshake.

I followed him through a quarter acre of secretaries, file-cabinets, and computers to a broad wall of doors. His was just off to the left. His name in brass, on polished oak.

His office wasn't much bigger than my hotel cubicle, but one wall was glass and it offered a falcon's-lair view of the city. On the wall were two degrees from Columbia, his Phi Beta Kappa certificate, and a lacrosse stick mounted diagonally. A gym bag sat in one corner. Documents were piled up everywhere, including on one of the straight-backed side chairs facing the desk. I took the empty chair. He removed his jacket and tossed it on the desk. Very broad shoulders, powerful chest, outsize hands.

He sat down amid the clutter, shuffled papers while studying me.

'What kind of law do you practice?' I said.

'Business.'

'Do you litigate?'

'Only when I need to get a taxi – no, I'm one of the behind the scenes guys. Mole in a suit.'

He drummed the desk with his palm a few times. Kept staring at me. Put his hands down flat.

'Same face as your picture,' he said. 'I'd expected someone older – closer to . . . Dad's age.'

'I appreciate your taking the time. Having someone you love murdered – '

'He wasn't murdered,' he said, almost barking. 'Not officially, anyway. *Officially*, he committed *suicide*, though the rabbi filed it an accident so he could be buried with his parents.'

'Suicide?'

'You met my dad – did he seem like an unhappy person?'

'On the contrary.'

'Damn *right* on the contrary.' His face reddened. 'He *loved* life – really knew how to have fun. We used to kid him that he never really grew up. That's what made him a good psychiatrist. He was such a happy guy, other psychiatrists used to make *jokes* about it. Harvey Rosenblatt, the only well-adjusted shrink in New York.'

He got up, looked down on me.

'He was *never* depressed – the least moody person I ever met. And he was a great father. Never played shrink with us at home. Just a dad. He played ball with me even though he hated sports. Couldn't

274

change a lightbulb, but no matter what he was doing, he'd put it aside to listen to you. And we knew it – all three of us. We saw what other fathers were like and we *appreciated* him. We never believed he killed himself, but they kept saying it, the goddamn police. "The evidence is clear." Over and over like a broken record.'

He cursed and slapped the desk. 'They're a bureaucracy just like everything else in this city. They went from point A to point B, found C and said, goodnight, time to punch the clock and go home. So we hired a private investigator – someone the firm had used – and all *he* did was go over the same territory the police had covered, say the same damn thing. So I guess I should be happy you're here, telling me we weren't nuts.'

'How did they say it happened?' I said. 'A car crash or some kind of fall?'

He pulled his head back as if avoiding a punch. Glared at me. Began loosening his tie, then thought better of it and tugged it up against his throat, even tighter. Picking up his jacket, he flipped it over his shoulder.

'Let's get the hell out of here.'

'You in shape?' he said, looking me up and down.

'Decent.'

'Twenty blocks do you in?'

I shook my head.

He pressed forward into the throng, heading uptown. I jogged to catch up, watching him manipulate the sidewalk like an Indy driver, swaying to fit into openings, stepping off the curb when that was the fastest way to go. Swinging his arms and looking straight ahead, sharp-eyed, watchful, self-defensive. I started to notice lots of other people with that same look. Thousands of people running the urban gauntlet.

I expected him to stop at Sixty-Fifth Street, but he kept going to Sixty-Seventh. Turning east, he led me up two blocks and stopped in front of a red-brick building, eight floors high, plain and flat, set between two ornate gray stones. On the ground floor were medical offices. The townhouse on the right housed a French restaurant with a long black awning lettered in gold at street level. A couple of limousines were parked at the curb.

He pointed upward. 'That's where it happened. An apartment on the top floor, and, yeah, they said he jumped.'

'Whose apartment was it?'

He kept staring up. Then down at the pavement. Directly in front of us, a dermatologist's window was fronted by a boxful of geraniums. Josh seemed to study the flowers. When he faced me, pain had immobilized his face. 'It's my mother's story,' he said.

Shirley and Harvey Rosenblatt had worked where they lived, in a narrow brownstone with a gated entry. Three stories, more geraniums, a maple with an iron-trunk guard surviving at the curb.

Josh produced a ring of keys and used one key to open the gate. The lobby ceiling was coffered walnut, the floor was tiny black and white hexagonal tiles backed by etched glass double doors and a brass elevator. The walls were freshly painted beige. A potted palm stood in one corner. Another was occupied by a Louis XIV chair.

Three brass mailboxes were bolted to the north wall. Number One said ROSENBLATT: Josh unlocked it and drew out a stack of envelopes before unlatching the glass doors. Behind it was a smaller vestibule, dark-paneled and gloomy. Soup and powdered-cleanser smells. Two more walnut doors, one unmarked, with a mezuzah nailed to the post, the other bearing a brass plaque that said Shirley M. Rosenblatt, Ph.D., P.C. The faint outline of where another sign had been glued, was visible just above.

Josh unlocked the plain one and held it open for me. I stepped into a narrow entry hall lined with framed Daumier prints. To my left was a bentwood hall tree from which hung a single raincoat.

A gray tabby cat came from nowhere and padded toward us on the parquet floor.

Josh stepped in front of me and said, 'Hey, Leo.'

The cat stopped, arched its tail, relaxed it and walked up to him. He dropped his hand. The cat's tongue darted. When it saw me, its yellow eyes slitted.

Josh said, 'It's okay, Leo. I guess.' He scooped up the cat, held it to his chest and told me, 'This way.'

The hall emptied into a small sitting room. To the right was a dining room furnished with mock-Chippendale, to the left a tiny kitchen, white and spotless. Though the shades were up on every window, the view was a brownstone six feet away, leaving the entire apartment dark and denlike. Simple furniture, not much of it. Some paintings, nothing flashy or expensive. Everything perfectly in place. I knew one way Josh had rebelled.

276

Beyond the sitting room was another living area, slightly larger, more casual. T.v., easy chairs, a spinet piano, three walls of bookshelves filled with hardbacks and family photos. The fourth was bisected by an arched door that Josh opened.

'Hello?' Josh said, sticking his head through. The cat fussed and he let it down. It studied me, finally disappeared behind a sofa.

The sound of another door opening. Josh stepped back as a black woman in a white nurse's uniform came out. In her forties, she had a round face, a stocky but shapely figure, and bright eyes.

'Hello, Mr. Rosenblatt.' West Indian accent.

'Selena,' he said, taking her hand. 'How is she?'

'Everything is *perfect*. She had a generous breakfast and a nice long nap. Robbie was here at ten and they did almost the full hour of exercise.'

'Good. Is she up, now?'

'Yes.' The nurse's eyes shifted to me. 'She's been waiting for you.'

'This is Dr. Delaware.'

'Hello, doctor. Selena Limberton.'

'Hello.' We shook hands. Josh said, 'Have you had your lunch break, yet?'

'No,' said the nurse.

'Now would be a good time.'

They talked a bit more, about medicines and exercises, and I studied the family portraits, settling on one that showed Harvey Rosenblatt in a dark, three-piece suit, beaming in the midst of his brood. Josh around eighteen, with long, unruly hair, a fuzzy mustache and black-rimmed eye-glasses. Next to him, a beautiful girl with a long, graceful face and sculpted cheekbones, maybe two or three years older. The same dark eyes as her brother. The oldest child was a young man in his midtwenties who resembled Josh, but thick-necked and heavier, with cruder features, curly hair, and a full, dark beard that mimicked his father's.

Shirley Rosenblatt was tiny, fair and blue-eyed, her blond hair cut very short, her smile full but frail even in health. Her shoulders weren't much wider than those of a child. It was hard to imagine her birthing the robust trio.

Mrs. Limberton said, 'All righty, then. I'll be back in an hour – where's Leo?'

Josh looked around.

I said, 'I think he's hiding behind the couch.'

The nurse went over, bent and lifted the cat. His body was limp. Nuzzling him, she said, 'I'll bring you back some chicken if you behave.' The cat blinked. She set him down on the couch and he curled up, eyes open and watchful.

Josh said, 'Did you feed the fish?'

She smiled. 'Yes. Everything's taken care of. Now you don't worry yourself about any more details, she's going to be fine. Nice meeting you, doctor. Bye bye.'

The door closed. Josh frowned.

'Don't worry?' he said. 'I went to school to learn how to worry.'

27

Another small room, this one yellow, the windows misted by lace curtains.

Shirley Rosenblatt looked better than I expected, propped up in a hospital bed and covered to the waist with a white comforter. Her hair was still blond, though dyed lighter, and she'd grown it out a little. Her delicate face had remained pretty.

A wicker bed tray was pushed into one corner. To one side of the bed was a cane chair and a pine dresser topped by perfume bottles. Opposite that a large saltwater aquarium on a teakwood base. The water bubbled silently. Gorgeous fish glided through a miniature coral reef.

Josh kissed his mother's forehead. She smiled and took hold of his hand. Her fingers barely stretched the width. The comforter dropped a couple of inches. She was wearing a flannel nightgown, buttoned to the neck and fastened with a bow. On her nightstand was a collection of pill bottles, a stack of magazines, and a coil-spring hand-grip exerciser.

Josh held onto her hand. She smiled up at him, then turned the smile on me. Gentle blue eyes. None of her children had gotten them.

Josh said, 'Here's the mail. Want me to open it?'

She shook her head and reached out. He put the stack on her lap but she left it there and continued to look at me.

'This is Dr. Delaware,' he said.

I said, 'Alex Delaware.' But I didn't hold out my hand because I didn't want to dislodge his. 'Thanks for seeing me, Dr. Rosenblatt.'

'Shirley.' Her voice was very weak and talking seemed a great effort, but the word came out clearly. She blinked a couple of times. Her right shoulder was lower than her left and her right eyelid bagged a bit.

She kissed Joshua's hand. Slowly, she said, 'You can go, hon.'

He looked at me, then back at her. 'Sure?'

Nod.

'Okay, but I'm coming back in half an hour. I already let Mrs. Limberton go to lunch and I don't want you alone for too long.'

'It's okay. She doesn't eat long.'

'I'll make sure she stays all afternoon until I get here – probably not before seven-thirty. I have paperwork. Is that okay, or do you want to eat earlier?'

'Seven-thirty is fine, honey.'

'Chinese?'

She nodded and smiled, let go of his hand.

'I can also get Thai if you want,' he said. 'That place on Fifty-Sixth.'

'Anything,' she said. 'As long as it's with you.' She reached up with both hands and he bent for a hug.

After he straightened, she said, 'Bye, Sweets.'

'Bye. Take care of yourself.'

One final look at me, and then he was gone. She pushed a button and propped herself up higher. Took a breath and said, 'I'm blessed. Working with kids. . . my own turned out great.'

'I'm sure it wasn't an accident.'

She shrugged. The higher shoulder made it all the way through the gesture. 'I don't know. . . so much is chance.'

She pointed to the cane chair.

I pulled it up close and sat down.

'You're a child therapist, too?'

I nodded.

She took a long time to touch her lip. Another while to tap her brow. 'I think I've seen your name on articles . . . anxiety?'

'Years ago.'

'Nice to meet you.' Her voice faded.

I leaned closer. 'Stroke,' she said and tried to shrug, again.

I said, 'Josh told me.'

She looked surprised. Then amused. 'He hasn't told many people. Protecting me. Sweet. All my kids are. But Josh lives here at home, we see more of each other . . .'

'Where are the others?'

280

'Sarah's in Boston. Teaches pediatrics at Tufts. David's a biologist at the National Cancer Institute in Washington.'

'Three for three,' I said.

She smiled and looked at the fish tank. 'Batting a thousand . . . Harvey liked baseball. You only met him once?'

'Yes.' I told her where and when.

'Harvey,' she said, savoring the word, 'was the nicest man I've ever known. *My* mother used to say don't marry for looks or money, both can disappear fast, so marry for nice.'

'Good advice.'

'Are you married?'

'Not yet.'

'Do you have someone?'

'Yes. And she's very nice.'

'Good.' She began laughing. Very little sound came out but her face was animated. Managing to raise one hand, she touched her chest. 'Forget the Ph.D. I'm just a Jewish mother.'

'Maybe the two aren't all that different.'

'No. They are. Therapists don't judge, right? Or at least we pretend we don't. Mothers are always judging.'

She tried to lift an envelope from the mail stack. Got hold of a corner and fumbled.

'Tell me,' she said, letting go, 'about my husband.'

I began, including the other murders but leaving out the savagery. When I reached the part about Bad Love and my revenge theory, her eyes started blinking rapidly and I was afraid I'd caused some sort of stress reaction. But when I paused, she said, 'Go on,' and as I did, she seemed to sit up straighter and taller, and a cool, analytic light sharpened her eyes.

The therapist in her driving out the patient.

I'd been there. Now I was on the couch, opening myself up to this tiny, crippled woman.

When I was finished, she looked at the dresser and said, 'Open that middle drawer and take out the file.'

I found a black and white marbled box with a snap-latch resting atop neatly folded sweaters. As I started to hand it to her, she said, 'Open it.'

I sat down beside her and unlatched the box. Inside were documents, a thick sheaf of them. On top was Harvey Rosenblatt's medical license.

'Go on,' she said.

I began leafing. Psychiatric board certification. Internship and residency papers. A certificate from the Rovert Evanston Hale Psychoanalytic Institute in Manhattan. Another from Southwick Hospital. A six-year-old letter from the Dean of NYU medical school re-affirming Rosenblatt's appointment as Associate Clinical Professor of Psychiatry. An honorable discharge from the Navy, where he'd served as a flight surgeon aboard an aircraft carrier. A couple of life insurance policies, one issued by The American Psychiatric Association. So he had been a member – the absence of obituary was probably due to shame about suicide. As I came to his Last Will and Testament, Shirley Rosenblatt looked away. Death certificate. Burial forms.

I heard her say, 'Should be next.'

Next was a stapled collection of photocopied sheets.

The face sheet was white. Handwritten on it was, 'Investig. Info.'

I removed it from the box. She sank back against the pillows and I saw that she was breathing hard. When I began to read, she closed her eyes.

Page two was a police report. The writer was one Detective Salvatore J. Giordano, Nineteenth Precinct, Borough of Manhattan, City of New York. In his opinion, and supported by subsequently entered Medical Examiner's Report, Case #1453331, Deceased Victim Rosenblatt, H. A., white male, age fifty-nine, expired as the consequence of a rapid downward descent from diagrammed window B, master bedroom, of said address on East Sixty-Seventh Street, and subsequent extreme bodily contact with pavement in front of said address.

'Descent process was most probably self-induced, as D. Victim's blood alcohol was not elevated and there is no lab evidence of drug-induced accident and no signs of coerced egress enforced on Deceased Victim on the part of another as well as no skidmarks on the carpeting of said address or defense marks on window sills, and, in summary, no evidence of the presence of any other individual at said address. Of further note is the presence of drinking glass A (see diagram) and apparatus B (see diagram) conforming to method operandus of the "Eastside Burglar".'

An aerial diagram at the bottom of the page illustrated the

locations of doors, windows, and furniture in the room where Harvey Rosenblatt had spent his last moments.

A bed, two nightstands, two dressers – one marked 'Low' the other 'High' – a television set, something marked 'antique' and a magazine rack. On one of the nightstands were written 'Glass A' and 'Apparatus B (lock-picks, files and keys).' Arrows marked the window from which the psychiatrist had leaped.

The next paragraph identified the apartment as an eighth-floor, five-room unit in a co-op building. At the time of Rosenblatt's jump, the owners and sole occupants, Mr and Mrs Malcolm Rulerad, he a banker, she an attorney, were away in Europe on a three-week vacation. Neither had ever met *'deceased victim Rosenblatt and both witnesses state unequivocally that they have no idea how d.v. gained ingress to said domicile. However, the burglary apparatus recovered from a bathroom of said domicile indicates Breaking and Entering and the fact that the day doorman, Mr. William P. O'Donnell, states he never saw D. Victim. Furthermore, Drinking Glass A, subsequently identified by Mrs. Rulerad as coming from her kitchen, was full of a dark liquid, subsequently identified as Diet Pepsi Cola, a drink favored by Mrs. M. Rulerad, and this is in conformity with the method operandus of three prior B and E burglaries within a six-block radius, previously attributed to the "East Side Burglar," in which soft drinks were displayed in a partially drunk status. Though D. Victim's wife denies a criminal history on the part of D. Victim, who she says was a psychiatrist, physical evidence indicates a "secret life" on the part of D. Victim and a possible motive: guilt over said secret life due to D. Victim being a psychiatrist and outward "solid citizen" and finally coming to grips with this unrespectable secret.'*

Next came a half-page follow-up by Detective Giordano, dated a week later:

'Case #1453331, Rosenblatt, H. Requested permission from D. Victim's wife to search home premises on E 65 St due to search for evidence related to D. Victim's death. Said search effected 4/17/85 at 3:23 p.m. to 5:17 p.m. in company of Det. B. Wildebrandt and Officer J. McGovern. Home and office premises of D. Victim searched in presence of D. Victim's wife, Shirley Rosenblatt. No contraband from previous "Eastside Burglaries" found. Permission requested to read D. Victim's psychiatric files for possible patient/fence connection, refused by S. Rosenblatt. Will consult with Chief of Dets. A.M. Talisiani.'

The following page was typed on a different machine and signed by Detective Lewis S. Jackson, Nineteenth Precinct. The date was four weeks later.

'Conf. on Det. Giordano's case, #1453331, H.A. Rosenblatt Det. Giordano on med.leave. D. Victim's wife, Shirley Rosenblatt, and son, Joshua Rosenblatt, requested meeting to review case. Wanting "progress" report. Met with them at Pcnct. Told of disposition. Very angry, said they were "deceived" as to purpose of home search. Son stated he is an attorney, knows "people." He and mother convinced hom, no sui. Stated DV not depressed, never depressed, not "criminal." Further stated "there was some sort of setup." Further stated DV had talked to wife, prior to death, about "upsetting case that could be related to what happened to my dad" but when asked for details, said he didn't know because DV was psychiatrist and kept secrets because of "ethics." When told nothing more could be done based on available evidence, son became even more irate and threatened to "go above you to get some action." Conversation reported to Chief of Dets. A. M. Talisiani.'

The final two pages consisted of a letter on heavy white bond, dated one and a half months later.

COMSAC INVESTIGATIVE SERVICES
513 Fifth Avenue
Suite 3463
New York, N.Y. 10110

June 30, 1985

Dr. Shirley Rosenblatt
c/o J. Rosenblatt, Esq.
Schechter, Mohl, & Trimmer
500 Fifth Ave.,
Ste. 3300
NY, NY 10110

Dear Dr Rosenblatt
Pursuant to your request, we have reviewed data and materials to the unfortunate death of your husband, including but not limited to detailed inspection of all case reports, forensic reports and laboratory analyses We have also interviewed police personnel involved in this

case. Personal inspection of the premises where aforesaid unfortunate death took place, was not fully accomplished because the owners of the apartment in question, Mr. and Mrs. Malcolm A. Rulerad, did not grant permission to our staff to enter and inspect. However, we do feel that we have accrued enough data with which to evaluate your case and we regret to inform you that we see no reason to doubt the conclusions of the police department in this matter. Furthermore, in view of the specific details of this case, we do not advise any further investigation into this matter.

Please feel free to get in touch if there are any questions concerning this matter.

Respectfully yours,

Robert D. Sugrue, Senior Investigator and Supervisor

INVOICE FOR SERVICES RENDERED

Twenty two (22) hours at
Sixty Five (65) Dollars per Hour: $1430.00
Minus 10% Professional Discount to
Schechter, Mohl, and Trimmer, Attys: $1287.00
Please Remit This Sum

I put down the file.

Shirley Rosenblatt's eyes were wide open and moist.

'The second death,' she said. 'Like killing him again.' Shake of head. 'Four years . . . but it's still – that's why Josh is so angry. No resolution. Now, you come . . .'

'I'm – '

'No.' She managed to place a finger over her mouth. Dropped it and smiled. 'Good. The truth outs.'

Wider smile, a different meaning behind it.

'Harvey as a burglar,' she said. 'It's almost funny. And I'm not in prolonged denial. I lived with him for thirty-one years.'

Sounding resolute, but she looked to me for confirmation, anyway.

I nodded.

She shook her head. 'So how did he get in that apartment, right? That's what they kept asking me and I didn't know what to tell them.'

'He was lured there,' I said. 'Probably under the guise of a patient call. Someone he thought he could help.'

'Harvey,' she said softly. She closed her eyes. Opened them. 'The police kept saying suicide. Over and over . . . Because Harvey was a psychiatrist, one of them – the Chief of Detectives – Talisiani – told me everyone knew psychiatrists had a high suicide rate. Then he told me to consider myself lucky that they weren't pursuing it further. That if they did, everything would come out.'

'In view of the specific details of this case,' I said.

'That's the private one, right? Comsat. At least the police were a lot more . . . direct. Talisiani told me if we made waves Harvey's name would be dragged through the slime. The whole family would be permanently coated with "slime". He seemed *offended* that we didn't want him to close the case. As if we were criminals. Everyone made us feel that way . . . and now you're coming and telling me we were right.'

She managed to press her palms together. 'Thank you.'

She slumped back on the pillow and breathed hard through dry lips. Tears filled her eyes, overflowed, and began draining down her cheeks. I wiped them with a tissue. Her lower body still hadn't moved.

'I'm so sad,' she whispered. 'Thinking about it, again . . . picturing it. But I'm glad you've come. You've . . . validated me – us. I'm only sorry you have to go through this pain. You really think it's something to do with Andres?'

'I do.'

'Harvey never said anything.'

I said, 'The upsetting case Josh told Detective Jackson about – '

'A few weeks before. . . ' Two deep breaths. 'We were lunching, Harvey and I. We had lunch almost every day. He was upset. He was rarely upset – such an even man . . . he said it was a case. A patient he'd just talked to, he'd found it very disillusioning.'

She turned toward me and her face was quaking.

'Disillusioned about Andres?' I said.

'He didn't mention Andres' name . . . didn't give me any details.'

'Nothing at all?'

'Harvey and I never talked about cases. We made that rule right at the beginning of our marriage . . . two therapists . . . it's so easy to slip. You tell yourself it's . . . okay, it's professional consultation. And then you let loose more details than you need to. And then names slip out . . . and then you're talking about patients to your therapist friends at cocktail parties.' She shook her head. 'Rules are best.'

'But Harvey must have told you something to make you suspect a connection to his death.'

'No,' she said sadly. 'We really didn't suspect . . . we were just . . . grasping. Looking for anything out of the ordinary. So the police would see Harvey didn't . . . the whole thing was so . . . psychotic. Harvey in a stranger's apartment.'

Remembered shame colored her face.

I said, 'The owners of the apartment – the Rulerads. Harvey didn't know them?'

'They were mean people. Cold. I called the wife and begged her to let the private detective in to look. I even apologized – for what I don't know. She told me I was lucky she wasn't suing me for Harvey's break-in and hung up.'

She closed her eyes for a long time and didn't move. I wondered if she'd fallen asleep.

Then she said, 'Harvey was so affected . . . by this patient. *That's* what made me suspect. Cases never got to him. To be disillusioned . . . Andres? It doesn't make sense.'

'De Bosch was his teacher, wasn't he? If Harvey learned something terrible about him, that could have disillusioned him.'

Slow, sad nod.

I said, 'How close was their relationship?'

'Teacher and student close. Harvey admired Andres, though he thought he was a little . . . authoritarian.'

'Authoritarian in what way?'

'Dogmatic – when he was convinced he was right. Harvey thought it ironic, since Andres had fought so hard against the Nazis . . . wrote so passionately for democracy . . . yet his personal style could be so . . .'

'Dictatorial?'

'At times. But Harvey still admired him. For who he was, what he'd done. Saving those French children from the Vichy government, his work on child development. And he *was* a good teacher. Once in a while I sat in on seminars. Andres holding court – like a don. He could talk for hours and keep you interested . . . lots of jokes. Tying everything in with punchlines. Sometimes he brought children in from the wards. He had a gift – they opened up to him.'

'What about Katarina?' I said. 'Harvey told me she sat in, too.'

'She did . . . just a child herself – a teenager, but she spoke up as

287

if she was a peer. And now she's . . . and those other people – how can this be!'

'Sometimes authoritarianism can go too far,' I said.

Her cheeks shook. Then her mouth turned up in a tiny, disturbing smile. 'Yes, I suppose nothing's what it seems, is it? Patients have been telling me that for thirty years and I've been nodding and saying, yes, I know . . . I really didn't know . . .'

'Did you ever go back into Harvey's files? To try to figure which patient had upset him?'

Long stare. Guilty nod.

'He kept tapes,' she said. 'He didn't like writing – arthritis – so he taped. I wouldn't let the police listen to them . . . protecting the patients. But later, I began playing them for myself. . . I gave myself an excuse. For their own good – I was responsible for them, until they found another permanent therapist. Had to call them, to notify them . . . so I needed to know them.' Downcast eyes. 'Flimsy . . . I listened anyway. Months of sessions, Harvey's voice . . . sometimes I couldn't stand it. But there was nothing on any of that would have disillusioned him. All his patients were like old friends. He hadn't taken on any new ones for two years.'

'None at all?'

She shook her head. 'Harvey was an old-fashioned analyst. The couch, free association, long-term, intensive work. The same fifteen people, three to five times a week.'

'Even an old patient might have told him something disillusioning.'

'No,' she said, 'there was nothing like that in any of the sessions. And none of his old patients brought him to harm. They all loved him.'

'What did you do with the tapes?'

Rather than answer, she said, 'He was gentle, accepting. He helped those people. They were all crushed.'

'Did you pick any of them up as patients?'

'No . . . I was in no shape to work. Not for a long time. Even my own patients . . .' She attempted another shrug. 'Things fell apart for a while. . . so many people let down. That's why I didn't pursue his death. For my kids and for his patients – his extended family. For me. I couldn't have us dragged through the slime. Do you understand?'

'Of course.' I asked her again what she'd done with the tapes.

'I destroyed them,' she said, as if hearing the question for the first time. 'Smashed the cassettes with a hammer ... one by one ... what a mess ... threw it all away.' She smiled. 'Catharsis?'

I said, 'Did Harvey attend any conventions just before his death? Any psychiatric meetings or seminars on child welfare?'

'No. Why?'

'Because professional meetings may set the killer off. Two of the other therapists were murdered at conventions. And the de Bosch symposium where I met Harvey may have triggered the killings in the first place.'

'No,' she said. 'No, he didn't attend anything. He'd sworn off conventions. Sworn off academia. Gave up his appointment at NYU so he could concentrate on his patients and his family and getting in shape – his father had died young of a heart attack. Harvey had reached that age, confronted his own mortality. He was starting to work out. Trimming the fat from his diet and his life – that's a quote ... he said he wanted to be around for me and the kids for a long, long time.'

Grimacing, she lifted her hand, with effort, and let it drop upon mine. Her palm was soft and cold. Her eyes aimed at the fish tank and stayed there.

'Is there anything else you can tell me?' I said. 'Anything at all?'

She thought for a long time. 'No ... I'm sorry, I wish there was.'

'Thanks for seeing me,' I said. Her hand weighed a ton.

'Please let me know,' she said, keeping it there. 'Whatever you find.'

'I will.'

'How long will you be in New York?'

'I think I'll try to head back this evening.'

'If you need a place to stay, you're welcome here ... if you don't mind a pull-out couch.'

'That's very kind,' I said, 'but I need to be getting back.'

'Your nice woman?'

'And my home.' Whatever that meant.

Grimacing, she exerted barely tangible pressure upon my hand. Giving *me* comfort.

We heard the door close, then footsteps. Josh came in, holding Leo, the cat. He looked at our hands and his eyebrows dipped.

'Had some time so I thought I'd stop by early,' he said to his mother. 'You okay?'

'Yes, honey . . . Dr. Delaware's been helpful. It's good you brought him.'

'Helpful how?'

'He validated us . . . about Dad.'

'Great,' said Josh, putting the cat down. 'Meanwhile you're not getting enough rest.'

Her lower lip dropped.

'Enough exertion, Mom,' he said. 'Please. You have to rest.'

'I'm okay, honey. Really.'

I felt a small tug atop my hand, not much more than a muscle twitch. Lifting her hand and placing it on the bedcovers, I stood.

Josh walked around the other side of the bed and began straightening the covers. 'You *really* need to rest, Mom. The doctor said rest is the most important thing.'

'I know . . . I'm sorry . . . I will, Josh.'

'Good.'

She made a gulping sound. Tears clouded the gentle blue eyes.

'Oh, Mom,' he cried out, sounding ten years old.

'It's okay, honey.'

'No, no, I'm being an asshole, I'm sorry, it's been a really tough day.'

'Tell me about it, baby.'

'Believe me, you don't want to hear it.'

'Yes, I do. Tell me.'

He sat down next to her. I slipped out the door and saw myself out of the apartment.

28

I reserved a seat on the next flight back to L.A., threw clothes in my bag and told Milo and Rick's message machine my arrival time. Checking out of the Middleton, I flagged a taxi to Kennedy.

A fire on Queens Boulevard slowed things down and it took an hour and three quarters to reach the airport. When I got to the check-in counter, I learned my flight had been delayed for thirty-five minutes. Pay t.v.'s were attached to some of the seats and travelers stared at their screens as if some kind of truth was being broadcast.

I found a terminal lounge that looked half-decent and downed a leathery corned beef sandwich and a club soda while eaves-dropping on a group of salesmen. Their truths were simple: the economy sucked and women didn't know what the hell they wanted.

I returned to the departure area, found a free t.v. and fed it quarters. A local station was broadcasting the news and that seemed about as good as it was going to get.

Potholes in the Bronx. Condom handouts in the public schools. The Mayor fighting with the City Council as the city accrued crushing debt. That made me feel right at home.

A few more local stories, and then the anchor woman said, 'Nationally, government statistics show a decline in consumer spending, and a Senate sub-committee is investigating charges of influence peddling by another of the President's sons. And in California, officials at Folsom Prison report that a lockdown has apparently been successful in averting riots in the wake of what

291

is believed to have been a racially motivated double murder at that maximum security facility. Early this morning, two inmates, both believed to have been associates of a white supremacist gang, were stabbed to death by unknown inmates suspected of belonging to the Nuestra Raza, a Mexican gang. The dead men, identified as Rennard Russell Haupt and Donald Dell Wallace, were both serving sentences for murder. A prison investigation into the killings continues . . .'

Nuestra Raza. NR forever. The tattoos on Roddy Rodriguez's hands . . .

I thought of Rodriguez's masonry yard, shut down, cleaned out and padlocked. The flight from the house on McVine prepared well in advance.

Evelyn had entertained me in her backyard, as her husband's homeboys honed their shanks.

Making an appointment for Wednesday, then going into the house with her husband and changing it to Thursday.

Twenty-four more hours for getaway.

Hurley Keffler's debacle at my house made sense now, as did Sherman Bucklear's nagging. Prison rumblings had probably told the Iron Priests what was brewing. Locating Rodriguez might have forestalled the hit, or, if the deed had already been done, given the Priests instant payback.

Payback.

The same old stupid cycle of violence.

Burglary tools and a quick shove out a ten-story window.

A corpse on a garage floor, a little boy baby never to be.

Two little girls on the run.

Were Chondra and Tiffani in some Mexican border town, being tutored in Fugitive-lA with more care than they'd ever been taught to read or write?

Or maybe Evelyn had taken them somewhere they could blend in. On the surface. But, suckled on violence, they'd always be different. Unable to understand why, years later, they gravitated toward cruel, violent men.

Static dripped out of the speakers – a barely comprehensible voice announcing something about boarding. I got up and took my place in line. Six thousand miles in less than twenty-four hours. My mind and my legs ached. I wondered if Shirley Rosenblatt would ever be able to walk again.

Soon, I'd be three time zones away from her problems and a lot closer to my own.

The flight got in just before midnight. The terminal was deserted and Robin was waiting outside the automatic doors.

'You look exhausted,' she said, as we walked to her truck.

'I've felt perkier.'

'Well, I've got some news that might perk you up. Milo called just before I left to pick you up. Something about the tape. I was just out the door and he was running, too, but he says he learned something important.'

'The sheriff who was working on it must have picked up something. Where's Milo now?'

'Out on some assignment. He said he'd be home when we got there.'

'Which home?'

The question threw her. 'Oh – Milo's house. He and Rick took really good care of us. And home is where the heart is, right?'

I slept in the car. We pulled up at Milo's house at twelve-forty. He was waiting in the living room, wearing a gray polo shirt and jeans. A cup of coffee was in front of him, next to a portable tape recorder. The dog snored at his feet, but woke up when we came in, giving out a few desultory licks, then collapsing again.

'Welcome home, boys and girls.'

I put my bags down. 'Did you hear about Donald Dell?'

Milo nodded.

'What?' said Robin.

I told her.

She said, 'Oh . . .'

Milo said, 'Nuestra Raza. Could be the father-in-law.'

'That's what I figured. It's probably why Evelyn postponed her appointment with me. Rodriguez told her they had to leave Wednesday. And why Hurley Keffler hassled me – where is he?'

'Still in. I found a few traffic warrants and had one of the jailers lose his paperwork – just another few days, but every little bit helps.'

Robin said, 'It never ends.'

'It's all right,' I said. 'There's no reason for the Priests to bother us.'

'True,' said Milo, too quickly. 'They and the Raza boys will be

293

concentrating on each other now. That's their main game: my turn to die, your turn to die.'

'Lovely,' said Robin.

'I had some Foothill guys drop in on them after Keffler's bust,' he said, 'but I'll see if I can arrange another visit. Don't worry about them, Rob. Really. They're the least of our problems.'

'As opposed to?'

He looked at the tape recorder.

We sat down. He punched a button.

The child's voice came on.

> 'Bad love bad love
> Don't give me the bad love.'

I looked at him. He held up a finger.

> 'Bad love bad love
> Don't give me the bad love . . .'

Same flat tones, but this time the voice was that of a man.

Ordinary, middle-pitched, male voice. Nothing remarkable about the accent or the timbre.

The child's voice transformed – some kind of electronic manipulation?

Something familiar about the voice . . . but I couldn't place it.

Someone I'd met a long time ago? In nineteen seventy-nine?

The room was silent, except for the dog's breathing.

Milo turned the recorder off and looked at me. 'Ring any bells?'

I said, 'There's something about it, but I don't know what it is.'

'The kid's voice was phony. What you just heard might be the real bad guy. No bells, huh?'

'Let me hear it again.'

Rewind. Play.

'Again,' I said.

This time, I listened with my eyes closed, squinting so hard the lids felt welded together.

Listening to someone who hated me.

Nothing registered.

Robin and Milo studied my face as if it were some great wonder. My head hurt badly.

294

'No,' I said. 'I still can't pinpoint it – I can't even be sure I've actually heard it.'

Robin touched my shoulder. Milo's face was blank but his green eyes showed disappointment.

I glanced at the recorder and nodded.

He rewound again.

This time the voice seemed even more distant – as if my memory was spiraling away from me. As if I'd missed my chance.

'Goddamn it,' I said. The dog's eyes opened. He trotted over to me and nuzzled my hand. I rubbed his head, looked at Milo. 'One more time.'

Robin said, 'You're tired. Why don't we try again in the morning?'

'Just once more,' I said.

Rewind. Play.

The voice.

Completely foreign now. Mocking me.

I buried my face in my hands. Robin's hands on my neck were an abstract comfort – I appreciated the sentiment but couldn't relax.

'What did you mean *might* be the bad guy?' I asked Milo.

'Sheriff's scientific guess. He tuned it down from the kid's voice using a preset frequency.'

'How can he be sure the kid's voice was altered in the first place?'

'Because his machines told him so. He came across it by accident – working on the screams – which, incidentally, he's ninety-nine percent positive are Hewitt's. Then he got to the kid chanting and something bothered him – the evenness of the voice.'

'The robot quality,' I said.

'Yeah. But he didn't assume brainwashing or anything else psychological. He's a techno-dude, so he analyzed the sound waves and saw something fishy with the cycle to cycle amplitude – the changes in pitch within each sound wave. Real human voices shimmer and jitter. This didn't, so he knew the tape had been messed with electronically, probably using a pitch shifter. It's a gizmo that samples a sound and changes the frequency. Tune up, you've got Alvin and the Chipmunks, tune down, you're James Earl Jones.'

'Hi-tech bad guy,' I said.

'Not really. The basic machines are pretty cheap. People attach them to phones – women living alone wanting to sound like Joe

Testosterone. They're also used for recording music – creating automatic harmonies. A singer lays down a vocal track, then creates a harmony and overdubs it, Instant Everly Brothers.'

'Sure,' said Robin. 'Shifters are used all the time. I've seen them interfaced with amps so guitarists can do multiple tracks.'

'Lyle Gritz,' I said. 'The next Elvis . . . how'd the sheriff know which frequency to tune down to?'

'He assumed we were dealing with a male bad guy using a relatively cheap shifter because, nowadays, the better machines *can* be programmed to include jitter. The cheap ones usually come with two, maybe three standard settings: tune up to kid, tune down to adult, sometimes there's an intermediate setting for adult female. By computing the pitch difference, he worked backwards, and tuned down. But if our guy's some sort of acoustics nut with fancy equipment, there may be other things he's done to his voice and what you heard may be nowhere near his real voice.'

'It may not even be his voice that he altered. He could have shifted someone else's.'

'That, too. But you think you might have heard him before.'

'That was my first impression. But I don't know. I don't trust my judgment anymore.'

'Well,' he said, 'at least we know there's no actual kid involved.'

'Thank God for that. Okay, leave the tape with me. I'll work with it tomorrow, see if anything clicks. The scream being Hewitt – what does ninety-nine percent mean?'

'It means the sheriff'll get up on the stand and testify it's highly probable to the best of his professional knowledge. Only trouble is, we need to get someone on trial first.'

'So I was right, this isn't some homeless guy. He'd need a place to keep his equipment.'

He shrugged. 'Maybe he's got a secret den somewhere and that's where he's hiding out right now. I had talks about Gritz with detectives at other substations. If the scrote's still lurking around, we'll hook him.'

'He is,' I said. 'He hasn't completed his homework.'

I told Milo what I'd learned in New York.

He said, 'Pseudo-burglary? Sounds hoky.'

'New York cops didn't think so. It matched some previous break-ins in the neighborhood: jimmied locks, people on vacation, a glass of soda left on the bedroom nightstand. Soda from the victim's kitchen. Sound familiar?'

'Were any of the other burglaries in the papers?'

'I don't know.'

'If they were, all we've probably got is a copycat. If they weren't, maybe our killer has a burglary sideline. Why don't you get a hold of some four-year-old papers, and find out. I'll phone New York and see if Gritz's name or Silk/Merino's show up on their blotters around the time of Rosenblatt's fall.'

'He's been pretty careful about keeping his nose clean, so far.'

'It doesn't have to be a major felony, Alex. Son of Sam got busted on a parking ticket. Lots of cases get solved that way, the stupid stuff.'

'Okay,' I said. 'I'll hit the library soon as it opens.'

He picked up his cup and drank. 'So what's Rosenblatt's motive for jumping supposed to have been?'

'Guilt. Coming to grips with his secret criminal identity.'

He scowled. 'What, he's standing there, about to glom jewelry, and he suddenly gets a guilt-flash? Sounds like horseshit to me.'

'The family thought so, too, but the New York police seemed convinced. They told the widow if she pressed the issue, everyone's name would be dragged through the slime. A private investigator she hired told her the same thing, more tactfully.'

I gave him names and he jotted them down.

Looking into his coffee, he said, 'You want, there's still some in the pot.'

'No, thanks.'

Robin said, 'Another fall – just like the other two.'

'Delmar Parker's run off the mountain,' I said. 'That has to be the connection. The killer was traumatized in a major way and is trying to get even. We've got to find out more about the accident.'

Milo said, 'I still haven't had any luck locating Delmar's mother. And none of the Santa Barbara papers covered the crash.'

'Out of those Corrective School alumni,' I said, 'someone's got to know.'

'Still no files, anywhere. Sally and the gang pried up Katarina's floorboards. And we can't find any records, yet, of de Bosch applying for government funds.'

Over the rim of his cup, his face was heavy and beat.

He ran his hand over it.

'It bothers me,' he said. 'Rosenblatt – an experienced psychiatrist – meeting someone in a strange apartment like that.'

'He was experienced, but he had a soft heart. The killer could have lured him there with a cry for help.'

'That's not exactly standard operating shrink procedure, is it? Was Rosenblatt some kind of avant-garde guy, believed in on-the-scene treatment?'

'His wife said he was an orthodox analyst.'

'Those guys *never* leave the office, right? Need their couches and their little notebooks.'

'True, but she also said he'd been very upset by something that happened in a session recently. Disillusioned. It's a reasonable bet it had something to do with de Bosch. Something that shook him up enough to meet the killer out of the office. He could have believed he was going to the killer's home – the killer could have given him a good rationale for meeting there. Like a disability that kept him homebound – maybe even bedridden. The window Rosenblatt went out of was in a bedroom.'

'Phony cripple,' he said, nodding. 'Then Rosenblatt goes to the window and the bad guy jumps up, shoves him out . . . very cold. And the wife had no idea what disillusioned him enough to make a house call?'

'She tried to find out. Broke her own rules and listened to his therapy tapes. But there was nothing out of the ordinary in them.'

'This disillusioning thing definitely happened during a session?'

'That's what he told her.'

'So maybe the session where he died, wasn't the first with the killer. So why wasn't the first session on tape?'

'Maybe Rosenblatt didn't take his recorder with him. Or the patient requested no taping. Rosenblatt would have complied. Or maybe the session was recorded and the tape got destroyed.'

'A stranger's bedroom – that has almost a sexual flavor to it, don't you think?'

I nodded. 'The ritual.'

'Who owned the place?'

'A couple named Rulerad. They said they'd never heard of Harvey Rosenblatt. Shirley said they were pretty hostile to her. Refused access to the private detective and threatened to sue her.'

'Can't really blame them, can you? Come home and find out

someone broke into your place and used it for a swan dive. Was Rosenblatt the type to be a soft touch for a sob story?'

'Definitely. He probably got the same kind of call Bert Harrison did and responded to it. And died because of it.'

Milo said, 'So why did the killer keep his appointment with Rosenblatt but not with Harrison? Why, now that I'm I thinking about it, was Harrison let off the hook, completely? *He* worked for de Bosch, *he* spoke at that goddamn conference, too. So how come everyone else in that boat is sunk or sinking and *he's* on shore drinking pina coladas?'

'I don't know.'

'I mean, that's funny, don't you think, Alex? That break in the pattern – maybe I should learn a little more about Harrison.'

'Maybe,' I said, feeling sick. 'Wouldn't *that* be something. There I was, sitting across the table from him trying to protect him . . . he treated Mitch Lerner. He knew where Katarina lived . . . hard to believe. He seemed like such a sweet guy.'

'Any idea where he's gone?'

I shook my head. 'But he's not exactly unobtrusive with those purple clothes.'

'Purple clothes?' said Robin.

'He says it's the only color he can see.'

'Another weird one,' said Milo. 'What is it about your profession?'

'Ask the killer,' I said. 'He's got strong opinions on the subject.'

29

We spent the night at Milo's. After he left for work, I stayed and listened to the tape another dozen times.

The chanting man sounded like an accountant tallying up a sum.

That maddening hint of familiarity, but nothing jelled.

We returned to Benedict Canyon, where Robin took the dog to the garage and I called in for messages. One from Jean Jeffers: *No record of Mr. G.* and a request to phone Judge Stephen Huff.

I reached him in his chambers.

'Hi, Alex, I assume you heard.'

'Is there anything I should know other than what's been on the news?

'They're pretty positive who did it, but can't prove it, yet. Two Mexican gang members, they're figuring some kind of drug war.'

'That's probably it,' I said.

'Well, that's one way to settle a case. Any word from the grandmother?

'Not a one.'

'Better off – the kids, I mean. Away from all of this don't you think?'

'Depends on what environment they've been placed into.'

'Oh, sure. Absolutely. Well, thanks for your help. Onward toward justice.'

Several more tries at the tape, then I left for the Beverly Hills library.

I scoured four- and five-year-old editions of New York dailies all morning, reading very slowly and carefully, but finding no record of any 'Eastside Burglar'.

No great surprise; the Nineteenth Precinct serviced a high-priced zip code and its inhabitants probably despised getting their names anywhere in the paper other than the society pages. The people who *owned* the papers and broadcast the news probably lived in the Nineteenth. The rest of the city would know exactly what they wanted it to.

Lack of coverage still didn't mean Rosenblatt's killer had committed the earlier break-ins. Local residents might be aware of the burglaries and a local could know who was on vacation and for how long. But the idea of a Nineteenth Precinct resident owning burglary tools and robbing from his neighbors seemed less than likely. So Mr. Silk probably had burgled before. Ritualistically.

The same attempt to use what was at hand, to master and dominate the victim.

Bad love.

Myra Evans Paprock.

Rodney Shipley.

Katarina.

Only at those three scenes had the words been left behind.

Three bloody, undisguised murders. No attempt made to present them as anything else.

Stoumen, Lerner and Rosenblatt, on the other hand, dispatched as phony accidents.

Two classes of victims . . . two kinds of revenge?

Butchery for the laypeople, falls for the therapists?

But *Katarina* had been a therapist.

Then I realized that at the time of Mr. Silk's trauma some time before seventy-nine, probably closer to seventy-three, the year Delmar Parker had gone off the mountain – she hadn't yet graduated. In her early twenties, still a grad student.

Two patterns . . . part of some elaborate rage-lust fantasy that a sane mind could never hope to understand?

And where did Becky Basille fit in?

Two killers . . .

I remembered the clean, bustling street where Harvey Rosenblatt had landed: French restaurants, flower boxes and limos.

How long had it taken the poor man to realize what the swift, sharp shove at the small of his back meant?

I hoped he hadn't. Hoped, against logic, that he'd felt nothing but the Icarus-pleasure of pure flight.

301

A fall, always a fall.

Delmar Parker. Had to be.

Avenging an abused child? Surely if de Bosch had been abusive, someone would remember.

Why hadn't anyone spoken out after all these years?

But no big puzzle there: without proof, who would believe them? And why rake up the dirt around a dead man's grave if it meant stirring up one's own childhood demons?

Still, *someone* had to know what happened to the boy in the stolen truck, and why it had set off a killer.

I sat there for a long time, staring at tiny, microfilmed words.

Corrective School alumni . . . how to get hold of them. Then I thought of one. Someone I'd never met, a name I'd never even learned.

A problem child whose treatment had given Katarina the leash to put around my neck.

I returned the microfilm spools and rushed to the pay phones in the library's lobby, trying to figure out who to call.

Western Pediatric, the late seventies.

The hospital had undergone a massive financial and professional overhaul during the past year. So many people gone.

But one notable one had returned.

Reuben Eagle had been Chief Resident when I'd started as a staff psychologist. He'd taken a professorship at the U.'s med school, a gifted teacher, specializing in medical education. The new Western Peds Board had just wooed him back as General Pediatrics Division Head. I'd just seen his picture in the hospital newsletter: the same tortoiseshell spectacles, the light brown hair thinner, grayer, the lean, ruddy, outdoorsman's face adorned by a trimmed, graying beard.

His secretary said he was out on the wards and I asked her to page him. He answered a few moments later, saying, 'Rube Eagle,' in a soft, pleasant voice.

'Rube, it's Alex Delaware.'

'Alex – wow, this is a surprise.'

'How're things going?'

'Not bad, how about you?'

'Hanging in. Listen, Rube, I need a small favor. I'm trying to locate one of Henry Bork's daughters and I was wondering if you had any idea how to reach her.'

'Which daughter? Henry and Mo had a bunch – three or four, I think.'

'The youngest. She had learning problems, was sent to a remedial school in Santa Barbara around seventy-six or seventy-seven. She'd be around twenty-eight or twenty-nine now.'

'That would have to be Meredith,' he said. 'I remember because one year Henry had the interns' party at his house and she was there – very good-looking, a real flirt. I thought she was older and ended up talking to her. Then someone warned me and I split fast.'

'Warned you about her age?'

'That and her problems. Supposedly a wild kid. I remember hearing something about institutionalization, apparently she really put Henry and Mo through it – did you know he died?'

'Yes,' I said.

'Ben Wardley, too. And Milt Chenier . . . how come you're looking for Meredith?'

'Long story, Rube. It has to do with the school she was sent to.'

'What about it?'

'Things may have happened there.'

'Happened? *Another* mess?' He sounded more sad than surprised.

'It's possible.'

'Anything I should know about?'

'Not unless you had something to do with the school. The Corrective School, founded by a psychologist named Andres de Bosch.'

'Nope,' he said. 'Well, I hope you clear it up. And as far as Meredith's concerned, I think she still lives in L.A. Something to do with the film business.'

'Is her name still Bork?'

'Hmm, don't know – if you'd like I can call Mo and find out. She's still pretty involved with the hospital – I can tell her I'm putting a mailing list together or something.'

'I'd really appreciate that, Rube.'

'Stay on the line, I'll see if I can get her.'

I waited for fifteen minutes with the speaker to my mouth. Pretending to look busy each time someone came by to use the phone. Finally, Rube came back on the line.

'Alex?'

'Still here.'

303

'Yes, Meredith's still here, she has her own public relations firm. I don't know if she ever married, but she still goes by Bork.'

He gave me the address and phone number and I thanked him again.

'Sure bet . . . another mess. Too bad. How'd you get involved, Alex? Through a patient?'

'No,' I said. 'Someone sent me a message.'

Bork and Roffman Public Relations, 8845 Wilshire Boulevard, Suite 304.

The eastern edge of Beverly Hills. A five-minute ride from the library.

The receptionist said, 'Ms. Bork is on another line.'

'I'll hold.'

'And what was the name again?'

'Dr. Alex Delaware. I worked with her father at Western Pediatric Hospital.'

'One moment, sir.'

A few minutes later: 'Sir? Ms. Bork will be right with you.'

Then, a smoky female voice: 'Meredith Bork.'

I introduced myself.

She said, 'I specialize in the entertainment industries, doctor – movies, theater. We write books. Have you written a book?'

'No –'

'Just want to beef up your practice, a little press exposure? Good idea in today's economy, but it's not our thing. Sorry. I'll be happy to give you the name of someone who does medical publicity, though –'

'Thanks, but I'm not looking for a publicist.'

'Oh?'

'Ms. Bork, I'm sorry to bother you but what I'm after is some information about Andres de Bosch and the Corrective School, in Santa Barbara.'

Silence.

'Ms. Bork?'

'This is for *real*?'

'Some suspicions have come up about mistreatment at the school. Things that happened during the early seventies. An accident involving a boy named Delmar Parker.'

No answer.

'May, nineteen seventy-three,' I said. 'Delmar Parker went off a mountain road and died. Do you remember hearing anything about him? Or anything about mistreatment?'

'This is too much,' she said. 'Why the fuck is this any of *your* business?'

'I work as a consultant to the police.'

'The *police* are investigating the school?'

'They're doing a preliminary investigation.'

Harsh laughter. 'You're putting me on.'

'No.' I gave her Milo as a reference.

She said, 'Okay, so? What makes you think I even went to this school?'

'I worked at Western Pediatric Hospital when your father was Chief of Staff and – '

'Word got around. Oh, I'll just bet it did. Jesus.'

'Ms. Bork, I'm really sorry – '

'I'll just bet it did . . . the Corrective School.' Another angry laugh. 'Finally.' Silence.

'After all these years. What a trip . . . the Corrective School. For bad little children in need of correction. Yeah, I was corrected, all right. I was corrected up the ying-yang.'

'Were you mistreated?'

'Mistreated?' Peals of laughter so loud I backed away from the receiver. 'How delicately put, doctor. Are you a delicate man? One of those sensitive guys really tuned in to people's feelings?'

'I try.'

'Well, goody for you – I'm sorry, this *is* serious, isn't it. My problem – always was. Not taking things seriously. Not being *mature*. Being mature's a drag, isn't it, doc? I fucking refuse. That's why I work in entertainment. Nobody in entertainment's grown up. Why do *you* do what *you* do?'

'Fame and fortune,' I said.

She laughed, harder and louder. 'Psychologists, psychiatrists, I've known a shitload of them. . . how do I know you're for real – hey, this isn't some gag, is it? Did *Ron* put you up to this?'

'Who's Ron?'

'Another sensitive guy.'

'Don't know him.'

'I'll bet.'

'I'd be happy to show you credentials.'

305

'Sure, slip them through the phone.'

'Want me to fax them?'

'Nah . . . what's the diff. So what do you really want?'

'Just to talk to you a bit about the school.'

'Good old school. School days, cruel days . . . hold on . . . ' Click. Silence. Click. 'Where are you calling from?'

'Not far from your office.'

'What – the pay phone downstairs, like in the movies?'

'Mile away. I can be there in five minutes.'

'How convenient. No, I don't want to bring my personal shit into the office. Meet me at Café Mocha in an hour, or forget it. Know where it is?'

'No.'

'Wilshire near Crescent Heights. Tacky little stripmall on the . . . southeast corner. Great coffee, people pretending to be *artistes*. I'll be in a booth near the back. If you're late, I won't wait around.'

The restaurant was a narrow storefront backed by blue gingham curtains. Pine tables and booths, half of them empty. Sacks of coffee stood on the floor near the entrance, listing like melting snowmen. A few desperate-looking types sat far from one another, poring over screenplays.

Meredith Bork was in the last booth, her back to the wall, a mug in her left hand. A big, beautiful dark-haired woman sitting high and straight. The moment I walked in, her eyes were on me and they didn't waver as I approached.

Her hair was true-black and shiny, brushed straight back from her head and worn loose around her shoulders. Her face was olive-tinted like Robin's, just a bit rounder than oval, with wide, full lips, a straight, narrow nose, and a perfect chin. Perfect cheekbones, too, below huge, gray-blue eyes. Silver-blue nail polish to match her silk blouse. Two buttons undone, freckled chest, an inch of cleavage. Strong, square shoulders, lots of bracelets around surprisingly slender wrists. Lots of gold, all over. Even in the weak light, she sparkled.

She said, 'Great. You're cute. I allow you to sit.'

She put the mug down next to a plate bearing an oversized muffin.

'Fiber,' she said. 'The religion of the nineties.'

306

A waitress came over and informed me the coffee of the day was Ethiopian. I said that was fine and received my own mug.

'Ethiopian,' said Meredith Bork. 'They're starving over there, aren't they? But they're exporting designer beans? Don't you think that's weird?'

'Someone always does okay,' I said. 'No matter how bad things get.'

'How true, how true.' She smiled. 'I like this guy. Perfect mixture of sincerity and cynicism. *Lots* of women love it, right? You probably use it to get laid, then get bored and leave them weeping, right?'

I laughed involuntarily. 'No.'

'No, you don't get *laid* or no, you don't get *bored*?'

'No, I'm not into conning women.'

'Gay?'

'No.'

'What's your problem, then?'

'Are we discussing that?'

'Why not?' Giant smile. Capped teeth. 'You want to discuss *my* problems, jocko, fair is fair.'

I raised my cup to my lips.

'How's the java?' she said. 'Those starving Ethiopians know how to grow 'em?'

'Very good.'

'I'm *so* veddy glad. Mine's Columbian. My regular fix. I keep hoping there'll be a packaging error and I'll get a little snort mixed in with the grind.'

She rubbed her nose and winked, leaned forward and showed more chest. A black lace bra cut into soft, freckled flesh. She wore a perfume I'd never smelled before. Lots of grass, lots of flowers, a bit of her own perspiration.

She giggled. 'No, I'm just joshing you, Mr. – sorry, *Doctor* No con. I know how touchy you healer types are about that. Daddy always had a *bovine* when someone called him "mister".'

'Alex is fine.'

'Alex. The Great. *Are* you great? Wanna *fuck and suck*?'

Before my mouth could close, she said, 'But seriously folks.'

Her smile was still on high beam and her breasts were still pushing forward. But she'd reddened and the muscles beneath one of the lovely cheekbones was twitching.

She said, 'What a tasteless thing to say, right? Stupid, too, in the

Virus Era. So let's forget about stripping off my *clothes* and concentrate on stripping my *psyche*, right?'

'Meredith – '

'That's the name, don't wear it out.' Her hand brushed against the mug and a few droplets of coffee spilled on the table.

'Shit,' she said, grabbing a napkin and blotting. 'Now you've *really* got me spazzing.'

'We don't need to talk about you, personally,' I said. 'Just about the school.'

'Not talk about me? That's my favorite *topic*, Alex, the sincere Shrink. I've spent Godknowshowmuch money talking to your ilk about me. They all pretended to be utterly fascinated, least you can do is fake it, too.'

I sat back and smiled.

'I don't *like* you,' she said. 'Way too agreeable. Can you get a hard-on on demand – no, scratch that, no more dirty talk. This is going to be a platonic, asexual, antiseptic discussion . . . the Corrective School. How I spent my summer vacation by Meredith Spill-the-Coffee Bork.'

'Were you there for only one summer?'

'It was enough, believe me.'

The waitress came over and asked if we wanted anything else.

'No, dear, we're in love, we don't need anything else,' said Meredith, waving her away. A wine list was propped between the salt and pepper shakers. She pulled it out and studied it. Moving her lips. Tiny droplets had formed over them. Her smooth, brown brow puckered.

She put the list down and wiped the sweat from her mouth.

'Caught me,' she said. 'Dyslexic. Not illiterate – I probably know more about what's going on than your average asshole senator. But it takes effort – little tricks so the words make sense.' Another huge smile. 'That's why I like to work with Hollywood assholes. *None* of them read.'

'Is the dyslexia why you went to the Corrective School?'

'I didn't *go*, Alex. I was sent. And no, that wasn't the official reason. The official reason was I was *acting out*. One of you guys' quaint little terms for being a naughty girl – do you want to know how?'

'If you'd like to tell me.'

'Of course I would, I'm an exhibitionist. No, scratch that. What's it your business?' She moistened her lips and smiled. 'Suffice it to say I learned about cocks when I was much too young to appreciate them.' She held out her mug to me, as if it were a microphone. 'And why was that, Contestant Number One? Why, for the washer-dryer and the trip to Hawaii, did a sweet young thing from Sierra Madre besmirch herself?'

I didn't speak.

'Buzz,' she said. 'Sorry, Number One, that's not quick enough. The correct answer is: poor self-esteem. Twentieth-century root of all evil, right? I was fourteen and could barely read, so, instead, I learned to give dynamite blowjobs.'

I looked down at my coffee.

'Oh, look, I've *embarrassed* him – don't worry, I'm okay. Damn proud of my blowjobs. You work with what you've got.'

Her grin was hard to gauge.

'One fateful morning, Mommy discovered strange, yucky stains on my junior high prom dress. Mommy consulted with learned Doctor Daddy and the two of them threw a joint shitfit. The day school ended I was shipped off to the wild and wooly hills of Santa Barbara. Little brown uniforms, ugly shoes, girls' bunks separated from the boys' bunks by a scuzzy vegetable garden. Dr. Botch stroking his little goatee and telling us this could turn out to be the best summer we ever had.'

She hid her mouth behind her mug, broke off a piece of muffin and let it crumble between her fingers.

'I couldn't read, so they sent me to Buchenwald on the Pacific. There's juvenile justice for you.'

'Did de Bosch ever diagnose your dyslexia?' I said.

'You kidding? All he did was throw this Freudian shit at me: I was frustrated because Mommy had Daddy and I wanted him. So I was trying to be a woman, rather than a girl acting *out* – in order to *displace* her.'

She laughed. 'Believe me, I *knew* what I wanted, and it wasn't *Daddy*. It was lean, young, well-hung bodies and James Dean faces. And I had the power to get it all back then. I believed in myself until Botch botched me up.'

All at once her face changed, loosening and paling. She put the mug down, hard, shook her hair like a wet puppy and rubbed her temples.

'What did he do to you?' I said.

'Tore my soul out,' she said glibly. But as she spoke she brought strands of hair forward and hid her face.

Long silence.

'Shit,' she said finally. 'This is harder than I thought it would be – how did he mess me up? Subtly. Nothing he could go to jail for, darling. So tell your police pals to go back giving parking tickets, you'll never pin him. Besides, he must be ancient, by now. Who's going to drag a poor old fart into court?'

'He's dead.'

The hair fell away. Her eyes were very still. 'Oh . . . well, that's okay by me, pal. Was it long and painful, by any chance?'

'He killed himself. He'd been sick for a while. Multiple strokes.'

'Killed himself how?'

'Pills.'

'When?'

'Nineteen-eighty.'

The eyes tightened. 'Eighty? So what's all this b.s. about an investigation?'

Her arm shot forward and she grabbed my wrist. Big, *strong* woman. 'Fess up, psych-man: Who are you and what's all this really about?'

A few heads turned. She let go of my arm.

I pulled out I.D., showed it to her and said, 'I've told you the truth and what it's about is revenge.'

I summarized the Bad Love murders, throwing out names of victims.

When I finished, she was smiling.

'Well, I'm sorry for those others, but . . .'

'But what?'

'Bad love,' she said. 'Turning his own crap against him. I like that.'

'Bad Love was something he *did*?'

'Oh, yeah,' she said through clenched jaws. 'Bad Love meant you were a worthless piece of shit who deserved to be mistreated. He used to play with our heads when we *acted out*. Bad *love* for bad little *children* – like psychological acupuncture, these tiny little needles, jabbing, twisting.'

Her wrists rotated. Jewelry flashed. 'But no scars. No, we didn't want to leave any marks on the beautiful little children.'

'What did he actually do?'

'He *bounced* us. Good Love one day, Bad Love the next. Publicly – when we were all together, in the lunch room, at an assembly – he was Joe Jolly. When visitors came, too. Joe Jolly. Laughing, telling jokes, lots of jokes. Tousling our hair, joining in our games – he was old but athletic. Used to like to play tether ball. When someone hurt their hand on the knob, he'd make a big show of cuddling them and kissing the boo-boo. Mr. Compassionate – Dr. Compassionate. Telling us we were the most beautiful children in the world, the school was the most beautiful school, the teachers the most beautiful teachers. The goddamn *vegetable* garden was beautiful, even though the stuff we planted always came out stringy and we had to eat it anyway. We were one big happy, global family, a real, sixties kind of thing – sometimes he even wore these puka shells around his neck, over his pukey tie.'

'That was Good Love,' I said.

She nodded and gave a small, ugly laugh. 'One big family – but if you got on his bad side – if you acted *out*, then he gave you a *private* session. And all of a sudden you weren't beautiful anymore, all of a sudden the world turned ugly.'

She sniffed and used her napkin to wipe her nose.

Thinking of her Columbian coffee comment, I wondered if she'd fortified herself for our appointment. She cut me off midthought: 'Don't worry, it's not nasal candy, it's plain old emotion. And the emotion I feel for that bastard, even with his being dead, is pure hatred. Isn't that amazing – after all these years? I'm surprising *myself* with how much I hate him. Because he *made* me hate *myself* – it took years to get out from under his fucking Bad Love.'

'The private sessions,' I said.

'*Real* private . . . he hit me where it counted. I didn't need anyone tearing down my self esteem, I was already fucked up enough, not able to read. Everyone blaming me, me blaming myself. . . my sisters were all A students. I got D's. I was a premature baby. Difficult labor. Must have affected my brain – the dyslexia, my other prob— '

She threw up her hands and fluttered her fingers.

'So now it's out,' she said, smiling. 'I have yet *another* problem. Want a shot at that diagnosis, Contestant Number One?'

I shook my head.

'Not a gambler? Oh well, there's no reason I should be ashamed, it's all chemistry – that was my point, wasn't it? Bipolar affective disorder. Your basic, garden variety manic-depressive maniac. You

311

tell people you're manic and they say, oh yeah, I'm feeling really manic, too. And you say, no, no, no, this is different. This is *real*, my little pretties.'

'Are you on lithium?'

Nod. 'Unless the work piles up and I need the extra push. I finally found a psychiatrist who knew what the hell he was doing. All the others were ignorant assholes like Dr. Botch. Analyzing me, blaming me. Botch nearly convinced me I *did* want to fuck Daddy. He *totally* convinced me I was *bad*.'

'With Bad Love?'

She stood suddenly and snatched up her purse. She was six feet tall, with a tiny waist, narrow hips and long legs under a charcoal-colored silk miniskirt. The skirt had ridden up, revealing sleek thigh. If she realized it, she didn't choose to fix it.

'He's worried I'm leaving.' She laughed. 'Mellow out, son. Just going to pee.'

She made an abrupt about-face and sashayed toward the rear of the restaurant. A few moments later, I got up and verified that the restrooms were back there, and the only exit a grimy gray door with a bar across it marked EMERGENCY.

She returned a few minutes later, hair fluffed, eyes puffy but freshly shadowed. Sitting down, she nudged my shin with a toe and gave a weak smile. Waving for the waitress, she got a refill and drank half the cup, taking long, silent swallows.

Looking ready to choke. My therapeutic impulse was to pat her hand. I resisted it.

'Bad Love,' she said, softly. 'Little rooms. Little locked cells. Bare bulbs – or sometimes he'd just light a candle. Candles *we* made in Crafts. *Beautiful* candles – actually they were ugly pieces of shit, with this really disgusting scent. Nothing in the cell but two chairs. He'd sit opposite you, your knees almost touching. Nothing between you. Then he'd stare at you for a long time. A *long* time. Then he'd start talking in this low, relaxed voice like it was just a chat, like it was just two people having a nice, civil conversation. And at first you'd think you were getting away easy, he'd sound so pleasant. Smiling, playing with that stupid little beard or his puka shells.'

She said, 'Shit,' and drank coffee.

'What did he talk about?'

'He'd start off lecturing about human nature. How everyone had good parts of their character and bad parts and the difference between the successful people and the unsuccessful people was which part you used. And that we kids were there because we were using too much bad part and not enough good part. Because we'd gotten warped, somehow *damaged* was the way he put it – from wanting to sleep with our mommies and our daddies. But how everyone else at the school was now doing great. *Everyone except you, young lady, is controlling their impulses and learning to use the good part. They are going to be okay. They deserve Good Love and are going to have happy lives.*'

She closed her eyes. Took a deep breath. Funneled her lips into a pinhole and blew air out through it.

'Then he'd stop. To let it all sink in. And stare some more. And get even closer. His breath always stank of cabbage . . . the room was so small the smell filled it – *he* filled it. He wasn't a big man, but in there he was *huge*. You felt like an ant, about to be crushed – like the room was running out of air and you were going to strangle . . . the way his eyes were like drills. And the look – when you got the Bad Love. After the soft talk was through. This hatred – letting you know you were scum.

' "You," he'd say. And then he'd repeat it. "You, you, you." And then it would start – *you* were the only one who wasn't doing good. *You* couldn't control your impulses, *you* weren't trying – *you* were acting just like an animal. A dirty, filthy animal – a *vermin* animal. That was a favorite of his. Vermin animals – in his creepy Inspector Clouseau accent. *Verrmen aneemals.* Then he'd start calling you other names. Fool, idiot, weakling, moron, savage, excrement. No curse words, just one insult after another, sometimes in French. Saying them so quietly you could barely hear them. But you had to hear them because there was nothing else to hear in that room. Just the wax dripping, sometimes a plumbing pipe would rumble, but mostly it was silent. You *had* to listen.'

A lost look came into her eyes. She shifted as far from me as the booth would allow. When she spoke again, her voice was even softer, but deeper, almost masculine.

'*You are* acting *like vermin animal, young lady. You are going to* live *like vermin animal and you will end up* dying *like vermin animal.* And then he'd go into these detailed descriptions of how vermin lived and died and how no one loved them and gave them Good Love because they didn't deserve it and how the only thing they deserved was Bad Love and filth and humiliation.'

She reached for her mug. Her hand shook and she braced it with the other one before raising the coffee to her lips.

'He'd keep going like that. Don't ask me how long because I don't know – it felt like years. *Chanting*. Over and over and over. You *will* get the Bad Love, you *will* get the Bad Love . . . pain, and suffering and loneliness that would never end – prison, where people will rape you and cut you and tie you up so you can't move. Horrible diseases you will get – he'd go into the symptoms. Talk about the loneliness, how you'd always be alone. Like a corpse left out in the desert to dry. Like a piece of dirt on some cold, distant planet – he was full of analogies, Dr. B. was, *playing* loneliness like an instrument. *Your life will be as empty and dark as this room we are sitting in, young lady. Your entire future will be desolate. No good love from anyone, no good love, just bad love, filth and degradation. Because that is what bad children deserve. A cold, lonely world for children who act like vermin animals.* Then he'd show photos. Dead bodies, concentration camp stuff. *This is how you will end up!*

She shifted closer.

'He'd just *chant* it,' she said, touching my cuff. 'Like some priest . . . throwing out these images. Not giving you a chance to speak. He made you feel you were the only bad person in a beautiful world – a shit smear on silk. And you believed him. You believed everyone was changing for the better, learning to control themselves. Everyone was on his side, you were the *only* piece of shit.'

'Cutting you off,' I said, 'so you wouldn't confide in the other kids.'

'It worked; I never confided in anyone. Later, when I was out of there – *years* later – I realized it was stupid, I couldn't have been the only one. I'd seen other kids go into the rooms, it seems so ridiculously logical, now. But back then, I couldn't – he kept focusing me in on *myself*. On the bad parts of me. The *vermin animal* parts.'

'You were isolated right from the beginning. New environment, new routine.'

'Exactly!' she said, squeezing my arm. 'I was scared shitless. My parents never told me where we were going, just shoved me in the car and tossed in a suitcase. The whole ride up there, they wouldn't speak to me. When we got there, they drove through the gates, dumped me in the office, left me there and drove away. Later I found out that's what he instructed them to do. Have a happy summer, Meredith . . .

314

Her eyes got wet. 'I'd just repeated seventh grade. Finally faked enough to barely pass and was looking to a vacation. I thought summer would be the beach and Lake Arrowhead – we had a cabin, always went there as a family. They dumped me and went without me . . . no apologies, no explanation. I thought I'd died and gone to hell – sitting in that office, all those brown uniforms, no one talking to me. Then *he* came out, smiling like a clown, saying what a pretty girl you are, telling me to come with him, *he'd* be taking care of me. I thought what a jerk, no problem putting it over on him. The first time I stepped out of line, he let it pass. The second time, he pulled me into a room and Bad-Loved me. I walked out of there in a semicoma . . . blitzed, wasted – it's hard to explain, but it was almost like dying. Like bad dope – I felt I was on a rocky island in the middle of a storm. This crazy, black, roaring sea, with sharks all around . . . no escape, him working on my bad parts chewing me *up*!'

'What a nightmare,' I said.

'The first week I hardly slept or ate. Lost ten pounds. The worst part was that you believed him. He had a way of taking over your head – like he was sitting in your skull, scraping away at your brain. You really felt you were shit and belonged in hell.'

'None of the kids *ever* talked to each other?'

'Maybe some did, I didn't. Maybe I could've, I don't know – I sure didn't *feel* I could. Everyone walking around smiling, saying how great Dr. B. was. Such a *beautiful* guy. You found yourself saying it, too, mouthing along without thinking, like one of those dumb camp songs. There was this – this *feverish* atmosphere to the place. Grinning idiots. Like a cult. You felt if you spoke out against him, someone would pour poison Kool-Aid down your throat.'

'Was physical punishment ever part of Bad Love?'

'Once in a while – usually a slap, a pinch, nothing that hurt too much. It was mostly the humiliation – the surprise. When he *wanted* to hurt you, he'd poke you in the elbow or the shoulder. Flick his finger on the bone. He knew all the spots . . . nothing that would leave a scar, not that anyone would have believed us, anyway. Who were we? Truants, fuckups, rejects. Even *now*, would I be credible? Four abortions, Valium, Librium, Thorazine, Elavil, lithium? All the other things I've done? Wouldn't some lawyer dig that up and put *me* on trial? Wouldn't I be a piece of *shit* all over again?'

'Probably.'

Her smile was rich with disgust. 'I'm *jazzed* that he's dead – doubly jazzed he did it to himself – his turn for humiliation.'

She looked up at the ceiling.

'What is it?' I said.

'Killing himself – do you think he could have felt some guilt?'

'With what you've told me, it's hard to imagine.'

'Yeah. You're probably right . . . yeah, he slapped me plenty of times, but the pain was *welcome*. 'Cause when he was getting *physical*, he wasn't *talking*. His voice. His *words*. He could reach into your center and squeeze the life out of you . . . did you know he used to write columns in magazines – humane child-rearing? People sent in problems and he'd offer fucking *solutions*?'

I sighed.

'Yes,' she said. 'My sad, sad story – such pathos.' Looking around the restaurant, she cupped one ear. 'Any daytime serial people listening? Got a bitchin' script for you.'

'You never told anyone?'

'Not until you, dear.' Smile. 'Aren't you flattered? All those shrinks and you're the *very* first – why, you've deflowered me – busted my psychological *cherry*!'

'Interesting way to put it.'

'But fitting, right? Therapy's just like fucking – you open yourself up to a stranger and hope for the best.'

I said, 'You said you saw other kids going into the rooms. Were they taken by other people, or just de Bosch?'

'Mostly by him, sometimes by that creepy daughter of his. I always got personal attention from the Big Cheese Daddy's social position and all that.'

'Katarina was involved in treatment? When exactly were you there?'

'Seventy-six.'

'She was only twenty-three. Still a student.'

Shrug. 'Everyone treated her as if she was a shrink. What she was was a real *bitch*. Walking around with this smug look on her face – Daddy was the king and she was the princess. Now there's one dutiful daughter who really *did* want to fuck Papa.'

'Did you have any direct dealings with her?'

'Other than a sneer in the hall? No.'

'What about other staffers? Did you see any of them doing private sessions?'

'No.'

'None of those names I mentioned rang a bell?'

She gave a pained look. 'It all blurs – I've been through changes, my whole *life* until a few years ago is a blur.'

'Can I go over those names again?'

'Sure, why not.' She picked up her cup and drank.

'Grant Stoumen.'

Headshake.

'Mitchell Lerner.'

'Maybe . . . that one's a little familiar, but I have no face to go with it.'

I gave her some time to think.

She said, 'Nope.'

'Harvey Rosenblatt.'

'Uh uh.'

'Wilbert Harrison.'

'No.'

'He's a little man who wears purple all the time.'

'Does he ride a pink elephant?' Grin.

'Myra Evans.'

Eyeblink. Frown.

I repeated the name.

'You used another name before,' she said. 'Myra something hyphenated.'

'Evans-Paprock – Paprock was her married name.'

'Evans.' Another smile, not at all happy. 'Myra Evans – Myra the Bitch. She was a teacher, right? A little blond with a tight butt and an attitude – am I right?'

I nodded.

'Yeah,' she said. 'Myra the Bitch. She was assigned to tread where others had failed. Like teaching *moi* how to read. She kept drilling me, harassing me, forcing me to do stupid exercises that didn't do a fucking bit of good because the words stayed all scrambled. When I got something wrong, she'd clap her hands together and say "No" in this loud voice. Like training a dog. Telling me I was stupid, a moron, not paying attention – she used to clamp her hands on my face and force me to look into her eyes.'

She placed her hands on my cheeks and pressed them together, hard. Her palms were wet and her mouth was parted. She brought

317

me forward and I thought she might kiss me. Instead she said, 'Pay attention! Listen, you moron!' in a grating voice.

I suppressed the impulse to twist free. That instant of confinement drove my empathy up another notch.

'Pay *attention*! Stop *wandering*, stupid! This is *important*! You need to *learn* this! If you don't pay *attention*, you can't *learn*!'

She squeezed harder. Let go. Smiled again. 'Breath mints – that was her smell. Isn't it funny how you remember the smells? Mints, but her breath was still shitty. She thought she was hot. Kinda young, little miniskirts, big boobs . . . maybe she was letting Dr. B slip it to her.'

'Why do you say that?'

'Because of the way she acted around him. Looks. Following him around. She reported directly to him. One thing you could count on, after a difficult session with Miss Bitch, you'd soon be seeing Dr. Botch for candles and needle-twisting. So she got murdered, huh?'

'Very nastily.'

'Too bad.' She pouted, then smiled. 'See, hypocrite, too. It's called acting, I work with people who do it for a living – we all do, actually, don't we?'

'What about Rodney Shipler? Does that name mean anything to you?'

'Nope.'

'Delmar Parker – the boy I told you about over the phone.'

'Yeah, the truck. That's how I knew you were for real. He was before my time.'

'May, seventy-three. You heard about it?'

'I heard about it from *Botch*. Boy, did I.'

'During a Bad Love session?'

Nod. 'The wages of sin. I'd committed some major felony – I think it was not wearing underwear, or something. Or maybe he caught me with a boy – I don't remember. He said I was a *vermeen aneemal* and stupid, then gave me this whole spiel about a *vermeen aneemal* boy who'd received the ultimate punishment for *his* stupidity. "Death, young lady. Death."'

'What did he say happened?'

'The kid stole a truck, ran it off the road and got killed. Proof positive of what happened to *verrmeen aneemal* moron children. Botch had a good time with it – making fun of the kid, laughing a lot, as if it were just a big joke. "*Do you comprehend, you bad, styupid girl? A boy so styupid. He steals a truck even though he doesn't know how to drive? Ha ha ha. A boy so* styupid, *he virtually choreographs his own death? Ha ha ha.*"'

'He used that word? Choreograph?'

'Yes,' she said, looking surprised. 'I believe he actually did.'

'What else did he say about the accident?'

'Disgusting details – that was part of Bad Love. Grossing you out. He had a ball with this one. How they didn't find the boy right away and when they did there were maggots in his mouth and crawling in and out of his eyes – "*he is being eaten by maggots, my dear Meredith. Feasted upon. Consumed. And the animals have feasted upon him, too. Chewed away most of his face – it is a real mess – just like your character, styupid Meredith. You are not listening, you are not concentrating. You bad, styupid girl. We are trying to mold you into something decent but you refuse to cooperate. Think, Meredith. Think of that styupid boy. The Bad Love he received from the maggots. That is what happens when* verrmeen aneemals *don't change their ways.*"'

She gave a hard, dry laugh and dabbed her nose again.

'That might not be an exact quote, but it's pretty damn close. He also got into this whole racist rap – said the kid in the truck was black. "A *savage*, Meredith. A jungle *native*. Why would you want to imitate the savages when there's a world of *civilization* out there?" On top of everything else, he's a racist, too. Even without the rap, you could tell. The looks he gave to minority kids.'

'Were there a lot of minority kids?'

She shook her head. 'Just a few. Tokens, probably part of the public image. In public he was Mr. Liberal – pictures of Martin Luther King and Gandhi and the Kennedys all over the place. Like I said, it's all acting – the world is a fucking stage.'

She placed her hands flat on the table, looking ready to get up again.

'A couple more names,' I said. 'Silk.'

Headshake.

'Merino.'

'What is this, a fabric show? Uh uh.'

'Lyle Gritz?'

'Grits and toast,' she said. 'Nope. How many people have gotten bumped off, anyway?'

'Lots. I'm on the list, too.'

Her eyes rounded. 'You? Why?'

'I co-chaired a symposium on de Bosch's work. At Western Peds.'

'Why?' she said coldly. 'Were you a fan?'

'No. Actually, your father requested it of me.'

'Requested it, huh? What approach did he take? Squeezing your balls or kissing your ass?'

'Squeezing. He did it as a favor to Katarina.'

'Symposium, huh? Gee thanks, Dad. The man tortures me so you throw him a party – when did this take place?'

'Seventy-nine.'

She thought. 'Seventy-nine – I was in Boston in seventy-nine. Catholic girls' school even though we weren't Catholic.'

'You never told your parents anything that happened at the Corrective School?'

'Nothing – I was too numb and they wouldn't have listened, anyway. After that summer, I didn't talk to anyone, just went along, like some robot. They handed Botch a naughty *acting-out* girl and got back this compliant little zombie. They thought it was a miracle *cure*. Years later, they were still saying it was the best decision they ever made. I'd just stare at them, want to kill them, keep my feelings all inside.'

The pale eyes were wet.

'How long did you stay that way?' I said, softly.

'I don't know – months, years, like I said, it blurs. All I know is it took a real long time to get back to my true self, get smart enough to mess around and cover my tracks. No sticky stains on the clothes.'

She licked her lips and grinned. A tear dripped down one cheek. She wiped it away angrily.

'When I was eighteen, I told them fuck you and left – ran away with a guy who came to unclog the toilet.'

'Sounds like you've done pretty well, since.'

'How kind of you to say so, dear – oh yeah, it's been a blast. P.R.'s a bullshit business, so I'm perfect for it. Throwing parties, setting up promos. Feeding rumors to the idiot press. Well, the show must go on. Ciao. It was real, stud.'

She stood and nearly ran out of the restaurant.

I put money on the table and followed her, caught up as she was getting into a red Mustang convertible. The car looked new but there were dings and dents all along the driver's side.

'Uh uh, no more,' she said, starting the engine. 'You get a quicky mind-fuck for your ten bucks, and that's it.'

'Just wanted to thank you,' I said.

'Polite, too,' she said. 'I *really* don't like you.'

30

R obin said, 'Bad love. The hypocrisy.'
'The bastard coins a phrase to describe poor child-rearing, but has his own private meaning for it.'

'Victimizing little kids.' Her hands tightened around the handle of a wood rasp. The blade caught on a piece of rosewood, and she pulled it free and put it down.

'And,' I said, 'if this woman's typical, the victimization was perfectly legal. De Bosch didn't sexually molest anyone, and none of the physical things he did would fall under any child abuse statutes but Sweden's.'

'Not the poking and slapping?'

'No bruises, no case, and usually you need deep wounds and broken bones to get anywhere legally. Corporal punishment's still allowed in many schools. Back then, it was accepted procedure. And there's never been any law against mind control or psychological abuse – how can you pin down the criteria? Basically, de Bosch behaved like a really rotten parent and that's no crime.'

She shook her head. 'And no one ever said anything.'

'Maybe some of the children did, but I doubt anyone believed them. These were problem kids. Their credibility was low and their parents were angry. In some cases de Bosch was probably the court of last resort. This woman came back to her family traumatized but perfectly compliant. They never suspected the summer at the school was anything but successful.'

'Some success.'

'We're talking ultra-high levels of parental frustration, Rob. Even if what de Bosch did had come to light and some parents had pulled their kids out, I'll bet you others would have rushed to enroll theirs. De Bosch's victims never had any legal recourse. One of them's evening the score his own way.'

'The same old chain,' she said. 'Victims and victimizers.'

'The thing that bothers me, though, is why the killer didn't strike out against de Bosch, only the disciples. Unless de Bosch died before the killer was old enough – or assertive enough – to put together a revenge plot.'

'Or crazy enough.'

'That, too. If I'm right about the killer being directly traumatized by Delmar Parker's accident, we're talking about someone who was a student at the school in nineteen seventy-three. De Bosch died seven years later, so the killer may still have been a kid. Felons that young rarely commit carefully planned crimes. They're more into impulsive stuff. Another thing that could have stopped him from getting de Bosch was being locked up. Jail or a mental institution. That fits with our Mr. Gritz – the ten years unaccounted for between his leaving Georgia and getting arrested here.'

'More frustration,' she said.

'Exactly. Not being able to punish de Bosch directly could have heated him up even further. The first murder occurred five years ago. Myra Paprock. Maybe that was the year he was released. Myra would have been a good target for him. A trusted disciple, dictatorial.'

'Makes sense,' she said, looking down at her workbench and arranging some files, 'if de Bosch really killed himself. But what if he was murdered and made to look like a suicide?'

'I don't think so,' I said. 'His death was too peaceful – overdose of medication. Why would the killer butcher subordinates and allow the boss to get off so easy? And a ritual approach – one that fulfilled a psychological need – would have meant leaving the best for last, not starting with de Bosch first and working backwards.'

'Best for last,' she said, in a tremulous voice. 'So where do you fit in?'

'The only thing I can think of is that damned symposium.'

She started to switch off her tools. The dog tagged after her, stopping each time she did, looking up, as if seeking approval.

'Alex,' she said, removing her apron, 'if de Bosch did commit suicide, do you think it could have been due to remorse? It doesn't mean much, but it would be nice to think of him having some self-doubts.'

'The woman asked me the same thing. I'd have liked to say yes – *she'd* have loved to hear it but she wouldn't have bought it. The man she described didn't sound very conscience-laden. My guess is his motivation was just what the papers printed: despondency over ill health. The slides his daughter flashed at the symposium showed a physical wreck.'

'A wrecker,' she said.

'Yeah. Who knows how many kids he messed up over the years.' The dog heard the tension in my voice and cocked his head. I petted him and said, 'So who's the higher life form, anyway, bub?'

Robin picked up a broom and began to sweep wood shavings.

'Any other calls?' I said, holding the dustpan for her.

'Uh-uh.' She finished and wiped her hands. We stepped out of the garage and she pulled down the door. The mountains across the canyon were clear and greening. Drought-starved shoots, trying for another season.

All at once the big, low house seemed more foreign than ever. We went inside. The furniture looked strange.

In the bedroom, Robin unbuttoned her work shirt and unsnapped her bra and cupped her breasts. They were warm and heavy in my palms and as I touched her, she arched her back. Then she stepped away from me and crossed her arms over her chest.

'Let's get out of here, Alex – out of the city.'

'Sure,' I said, looking over at the dog head-butting the bedcovers. 'Do we take him with us?'

'I'm not talking summer vacation, just dinner. Somewhere far enough to feel *different*. He'll be fine. We'll leave food and water, the air-conditioning on, give him a couple of chew-bones.'

'Okay, where would you like to go?'

Her smile was barren. 'Normally I'd say Santa Barbara.'

I forced myself to laugh. 'How about the other direction – Laguna Beach?'

'Laguna would be peachy.' She came over and placed my hands on her hips. 'Remember that place with the ocean view? "

'Yeah,' I said. 'Calamari and pictures of weeping clowns – wonder if it's still in business.'

'If it isn't, there'll be someplace else. The main thing is we get away.'

* * *

We left at seven-thirty, to avoid the freeway jam, taking the truck because the gas tank was fuller. I drove, enjoying the height and the heft and the power. A tape Robin had picked up at McCabes was in the deck: a teenager named Allison Krause, singing bluegrass in a voice sweet and clear as first love and running off fiddle solos that had the wondrous ease of the prodigy.

I hadn't called Milo to tell him about Meredith.

Another scumbag, he'd say, world-weary. Then he'd rub his face . . .

I thought of the man on the tape, chanting like a child, reliving his past . . .

Bad thoughts intruding.

I felt Robin tighten up. Her fingers had been tapping my thigh in time with the music, now they stopped. I squeezed them. Strummed the fingertips, let my hand wander to her small, hard waist as the truck roared in the fast lane.

She had on black leotards under a short denim skirt. Her hair was tied up, showing off her neck, smooth as cream. A man with a functioning brain would have thanked God for sitting next to her.

I pressed my cheek against hers. Let my shoulders drop and bobbed my head to the music. Not fooling her, but she knew I was trying and she put her hand high on my thigh.

A babe and a truck and the open road.

By the time I reached Long Beach, it started to feel real.

Laguna was quieter and darker than I remembered, the art fair over, nearly all the tourist traps and galleries closed.

The place with the squid and clowns was no longer in business; a karaoke bar had taken its place – people getting slogged on margaritas, and pretending to be a Righteous Brother. The painful sounds made their way to the sidewalk.

We found a pleasant-looking café further up the street, ate huge, cold salads, decent swordfish and excellent Chilean sea bass with french fries and cole slaw, and drank a bit of wine, then strong, black coffee.

Walking it off, we went far enough past the commercial zone to get an ocean glimpse of our own. The water was a thousand miles of black beyond a white thread of sand. The waves rolled drunkenly, sending up ice-chips of spray and an occasional roar that sounded like applause. We held hands so tightly our fingers ached, grabbed at each other and kissed until our tongues throbbed.

Barely enough light to see Robin's dark eyes, narrowing.

She bit my lower lip and I knew some of it was passion, the rest, anger. I kissed her behind her ear and we embraced for a long time, then we returned to the truck and drove north, out of town.

'Don't get on the freeway,' she said. 'Drive awhile.'

I got onto Laguna Canyon Road, went for several miles and made a random turn onto an unmarked strip that corkscrewed up into the mountains.

No talk or music. Her hands on me as she cried out her tension. We passed a pottery studio, its wooden sign barely lit by a dusty bulb. A glimpse of chicken-wire fencing. A couple of horse ranches, an unmarked shack. Then nothing for a long time and the road dead-ended at brush.

Crickets and shadows, the ocean nowhere in sight.

I put the truck in reverse. Robin stopped me and turned off the engine.

We locked eyes and kissed, fumbling with each other's clothing.

Stripped completely naked, we held each other, shivering, knitting our limbs. Breathing into one another, fighting for oblivion.

The ride back was slow and silent and I managed to keep reality at bay till we got off the freeway. Robin slept, as she had since we'd crossed the L.A. county line, low in the seat, half-smiling.

It was one forty-two in the morning and Sunset was nearly bare of cars. The familiar eastward cruise was solitary and peaceful. As I approached the Beverly Glen intersection, I prepared to shoot through the green light. Then wailing sirens sounded from somewhere I couldn't pinpoint, surrounding me, growing louder.

I slowed and stopped. Robin startled, sitting up just as flashing red lights popped out from around the bend and the sirens became unbearable. A hook-and-ladder came at us from the east, bearing down; for an instant I felt trapped. Then the engine made a sharp right turn, northward, onto the Glen, followed closely by another fire truck, then another smaller unit. A cherry-topped sedan brought up the rear as the sirens tapered off to a distant whistle.

Robin was clutching the armrest. Her eyes were gigantic, as if the lids had been stapled back.

We looked at each other.

I turned left and followed the shrieking caravan.

A hundred yards in I could smell it. A pot left too long on the stove, overlaid with gasoline.

I put on speed, just able to see the fire car's tail-lights. Hoping the company would continue on up, toward Mulholland and beyond. But they hooked west.

Up an old bridle path that led to a solitary property.

Robin held her head and moaned as I floored the truck. Coming to my street, I sped up the slope. The road was blocked by the newly arrived fire trucks and I had to pull over and park.

Work lights were scattered about, highlighting the firefighters' yellow hats. Lots of movement, but the night blocked out the details.

Robin and I jumped out and began running up the hill. The burnt stench was stronger now, the sky a black, camouflaging host for the plumes of dark smoke that shot upward in greasy gray spirals. I could feel the fire – the caustic heat – better than I could see it. My body was drenched with sweat. I felt cold to the marrow.

The firefighters were uncoiling hoses and shouting, too busy to notice us.

What had once been my pond gate was charcoal. The carport had collapsed and the entire right side of my house was smoldering. The back of the building was haloed in orange. Tongues of fire licked the sky. Sparks jumped and died, wood crackled and crashed.

A tall firefighter handed a hose to another man and pulled off his gloves. He saw us and came forward, gesturing us back.

We walked toward him.

'It's our house,' I said.

The look of pity on his face cut me deeply. He was black, with a big jaw and wide, dark mustache. 'Sorry, folks – we're working hard on it, got here as quick as we could from the Mullholland substation. Reinforcements just came in from Beverly Hills.'

Robin said, 'Is it all gone?'

He removed his hat and wiped his forehead, exhaling. 'It wasn't as of a few minutes ago, ma'am, and we've controlled it – you should start to see that smoke turn white real soon.'

'How bad is it?'

He hesitated. 'To be frank, ma'am, you've suffered some serious structural damage all along the rear. What with the drought and all

327

that wood siding – your roof's half-gone, must have been pretty dry up there. What was it, ceramic tile?'

'Some sort of tile,' I said. 'It came with the house, I don't know.'

'Those old roofs . . . give thanks it wasn't wood shingle, that would have been like a pile of kindling.'

Robin was looking at him but she wasn't listening to him. He bit his lip, started to place a hand on her shoulder, but stopped himself. Putting his glove back on, he turned to me.

'If the wind doesn't do squirrely things, we should be able to save.some of it. Get you in there as soon as possible to start taking a look.'

Robin started to cry.

The fireman said, 'I'm real sorry, ma'am – if you need a blanket, we've got some in the truck.'

'No,' she said. 'What happened?'

'Don't know exactly, yet – why don't you talk to the captain – that gentleman over there? Captain Gillespie. He should be able to help you.'

After pointing to a medium-sized man up near the carport, he ran off. We made our way to the captain. His back was to us and I tapped him on the shoulder. He turned quickly, looking ready to snap. One look at us shut his mouth. He was in his fifties and had a deeply scored face that was almost a perfect square.

Tugging at his chin-strap: 'Owners?'

Two nods.

'Sorry, folks – out for the night?'

More nods. I felt encased in sand. Movement was an ordeal.

'Well, we've been at it for about half an hour, and I think we got to it relatively fast after ignition. Luckily, someone driving up the Glen smelled it and phoned it in on cellular. We've got most of the really hot spots out. Look for white smoke soon, Mr. – ?'

'Alex Delaware. This is Robin Castagna.'

'Ron Gillespie, Mr. Delaware. Are you the legal owners or tenants?'

'Owners.'

Another pitying look. A whooshing sound came from the house. He glanced over his shoulder, then looked back.

'We should be able to save at least half of it, but our water does some damage, too.' He looked back again. Something creased his brow. 'One minute.' Jogging over to a group of new arrivals, he pointed at my flaming roof and spread his arms like a preacher.

When he came back, he said, 'You folks want something to drink? C'mon, let's get away from the heat.'

We followed him down the road a bit. The house was still in sight. Some of the smoke had started to lighten, pluming upward like an earthborn cloud.

He pulled a canteen out of his jacket and held it out to us.

Robin shook her head.

I said, 'No thanks.'

Gillespie opened the bottle and drank. Screwing the cap back on, he said, 'Do you know of anyone who'd want to do this to you?'

'Why?'

He stared at me. 'Usually, people say no.'

'There is someone,' I said. 'I don't know who – it's a long story – there's a police detective you can talk to.' I gave him Milo's name and he wrote it down.

'I'd better call him now,' he said. 'Our arson investigators will be in on it, too. This is an obvious intentional, we've got three discrete points of origin and we found a gasoline can out back that's probably the accelerant – looks like the bastard didn't even try to hide it.'

'No,' I said. 'He wouldn't want to do that.'

He stared at me again. I looked back without focusing.

Gillespie said, 'I'll go call that detective now.'

31

Milo spent a few seconds of silent comfort with us, then he huddled with Gillespie.

The fire went out, sending off columns of white smoke. Some time after – I still don't know how long – Robin and I were able to tour the damage, accompanied by a fireman with a flashlight who looked out for our safety but hung back, diplomatically, as we stumbled and cursed in the dark.

The garden and the rear half of the house were a total loss, the air still hot and bitter. The front rooms were sodden and putrid, ash-filled, already moldering. I ran my hand along scorched furniture, fingered hot dust, looked at ruined art and decimated keepsakes, t.v. and stereo equipment that had blistered and burst. After a while it got too difficult. I pulled the paintings and prints that looked intact off the wall and made a neat stack. Short stack. My Bellows boxing print seemed to have come out okay, but the frame was blackened around the edges.

Robin was across the living room when I said, 'I've got to get out of here.'

She gave a dull nod – more of a bow. We carried the art out and took it to the truck.

Beyond the vehicles, Milo and Gillespie were still conferring and a third man had joined them – young, chubby, balding, with bristly red hair. He held a pad and his writing hand was busy.

'Drew Seaver,' he said, holding out the other one. 'Fire Department. Arson Investigator. Detective Sturgis has been filling me in, sounds like you've really been through it. I'll have some questions for you, but they can wait a couple of days.'

330

Milo told him, 'I'll get you whatever you need.'

'Fine,' said Seaver. 'What's your insurance situation, doctor?'

As if cued, Captain Gillespie said, 'Better be getting back – good luck, folks.'

When he was gone, Seaver repeated his insurance question.

I said, 'I never really checked the details. I'm up to date on my premiums.'

'Well, that's good. Those insurance guys are real sonofa's, believe me. Dot your t wrong and they'll find a way not to pay you. You need any help with justification,

He handed me his card. 'That and a statement from Detective Sturgis should handle it.'

'What needs to be handled?' said Robin. 'What do we need to justify?'

Seaver picked at his chin. His lips were thick, pink, and soft-looking, with a natural turn-down that made him look sad.

'Arson fires tend to be self-generated, Mrs. Delaware. In lots of cases, anyway. Like I said, insurance companies'll do anything not to divvy up. First thing they're going to be assuming is you're behind this.'

'Then fuck 'em,' said Milo. To us: 'Don't sweat it, I'll handle it.'

Seaver said, 'Okay . . . well, better be looking around some more.' Cracking a brief smile, he left.

Milo's hair was ragged, his eyes electric. He had on a shirt and tie but the tie was crooked and his collar was loosened. In the darkness his acne-scarred face looked like moonscape. His hand moved over it rapidly and repeatedly – almost tic-like.

'It's okay,' said Robin.

'No, no,' he said, 'uh uh, don't comfort me – you're the victims – goddamn protect and serve – some protection – I know it sounds like a crock but we *are* gonna get him – one fucking way or the other, he's history, we'll get free of this.'

The three of us walked back to the truck. Milo's unmarked was parked behind it. None of us looked back.

The firefighter's lights were going out, one by one as some of the trucks pulled away. Sunrise was several hours away. Without the bulbs and the flames, the night seemed hollow, just a thin membrane holding back the void.

'Wanna go back with me?' said Milo.

'No,' I said. 'I can handle it.'

331

Robin stood on tiptoes and kissed his cheek.

'I found out what de Bosch's sin was,' I said. I told him of Meredith Bork's experience.

'You stab me, I'll stab you,' he said. 'No fucking excuse.'

'Can we be sure this wasn't the Iron Priests?'

'We can't be sure of anything,' he said furiously. 'But it's not them. No offense, but you're just not important enough to them, they want Raza blood. No, this was our Bad Love Buddy – remember Bancroft's comment about firesetters at the school?'

'You told me there was no record of any fires there.'

'Yeah . . . the kids behaved themselves there. It's when they graduated that the problems started.'

I drove but I felt as if I was being towed. Each segment of white line diminished me. Across the truck, Robin wept, unable to stop, finally surrendering to deep, wracking sobs.

I was beyond tears.

Just as I crossed into Beverly Hills, she took a sucking breath and pressed fisted hands together.

'Oh well,' she said, ' I always wanted to redecorate.'

I must have laughed, because my throat hurt and I heard two voices chuckling hysterically.

'What style should we choose?' I said. 'Phoenix Rococo?'

Benedict Canyon appeared. Red light. I stopped. My eyes felt acid-washed.

'It was a crummy little place anyway,' she said. 'No, it *wasn't*, it was a *beautiful* little place – oh, Alex!'

I pulled her to me. Her body felt heavy but boneless.

Green light. My brain said Go but my foot was slow to follow. Trying not to think of everything I'd lost – and everything yet to lose – I managed to complete the left turn and began a solitary crawl up Benedict.

Home temporary home.

The dog would run out to greet us. I felt inadequate for the role of animal-buddy. For anything.

I drove up to the white gate. It took a long time to find the card-key, even longer to slip in the slot. Moving the truck up the drive, I counted cypress trees in an effort to settle my mind on something.

I parked next to the Seville and we got out.

The dog didn't rush out to greet us.

I fumbled with the key to the front door. Turned it. As I walked through the door, something cold and hard pressed against my left temple and a hand reached around and clapped me hard on the right side of my head.

Immobilizing my skull.

'Hello, doctor,' said a voice from a chant. 'Welcome to Bad Love.'

32

He said, 'Don't move or speak, pardon the cliché.'

The pressure on my temple was intense. Strong fingers dug into my cheek.

'Good,' he said. 'Obedient. You must have been a good student.'

Dig.

'*Were* you?'

'I was okay.'

'Such modesty – you were a lot *better* than okay. Your fourth grade teacher, Mrs. Lyndon, said you were one of the best students she ever had – do you remember Mrs. Lyndon?'

Squeeze and shake.

'Yes.'

'She remembers you . . . such a *good* little boy . . . keep being good: hands on head.'

As my fingers touched my hair, the lights went on.

One of the couches was out of place, pushed closer to the coffee table. There were drinks and plates on the coffee table. A glass of something brown. The bag of taco chips Robin had bought a couple of days ago, open, crumbs scattered on the table.

Making himself comfortable.

Knowing we'd be gone for a while but would come back, nowhere else to go.

Because he'd used the fire to flush me out. Used the time to prepare the scene.

The ritual.

Choreographing death.

Firesetters and felons . . .

334

I considered how to get at him. Felt the pressure, saw only dark sleeve. Where was Robin?

'Forward march,' he said, but he continued to hold me still.

Footsteps on marble. Someone walked into my line of sight, holding Robin the same way.

Tall. Bulky black sweater. Baggy black slacks. Black ski mask with eye holes. Shiny eyes, the color indeterminate at this distance. He towered over Robin, gripping her face and forcing her eyes up at the ceiling. Her neck was stretched, exposed.

I gave an involuntary start and the hand gripped my head harder.

Imprisoning it.

I knew where they'd learned that.

Bumping and scratching from the back of the house. The dog tied out there, behind drapes that had been drawn over the French doors.

Something else at Robin's head besides a hand. Automatic pistol, small, chrome-plated. Bump, scratch.

The voice behind me laughed.

'Great attack dog . . . some tight security you've got here. Alarm system with an obvious home-run, one snip and bye bye. Fancy electric gate a dwarf could climb over, and a cute little closed circuit t.v. to announce your arrival.'

More laughter. The tall man with Robin didn't move or make a sound.

Two types of killing. Two killers . . .

My captor said, 'Okay, campers.'

The tall man shifted his free hand from Robin's face to the small of her back and began propelling her down the hallway toward the bedrooms.

Swinging his hips. Effeminate.

Walking the way Robin walked.

A woman? A tall woman with strong shoulders . . .

I'd talked to a tall, angry woman this afternoon.

A Corrective School alumna with plenty of reason to hate.

I really don't like you.

I'd called Meredith out of the blue, yet she'd been willing to talk to me – too eager.

And she had a special reason to feel rage over the Western Peds symposium.

Thanks, Dad.

I'd just stare at them, wanted to kill them, kept my feelings inside.

Alone with Robin, now. Her appetites and anger . . .

'Forward march, fool.' The gun stayed in place as the hand moved from my face. No more pressure but his touch lingered like phantom pain.

A sharp prod to my kidneys as he shoved me further into the room. Onto a couch. As I bounced – my hands left my head.

His foot met my shin and pain burned through my leg.

'Back up – up, up, up!'

I complied, waiting to be tied or restrained.

But he let me stay there, hands on head, and sat down facing me, just out of reach.

I saw the gun first. Another automatic – bigger than Meredith's. Dull-black, a dark wooden grip. Freshly oiled; I could smell it.

He looked tall too. Long waist, and long legs that he planted firmly on the marble. A little narrow in the shoulders. Arms a bit short. Navy blue sweatshirt with a designer logo. Black jeans, black leather, high-top athletic shoes that looked spanking new.

The chic thing to wear for homicide; the avenger reads GQ.

His mask had a mouth cutout. A sharklike smile filled the hole.

The dog scratched some more.

Under the mask, his forehead moved. Consternation?

He crossed his legs, keeping the big black gun a couple of feet from the center of my chest. Breathing fast but his arm was stable.

Using his free hand, he reached up and began rolling his mask up, doing it deftly, so that his eyes never moved from mine and his gun arm never faltered.

Doing it slowly.

The wool peeled away like a snake's molt, exposing a soft, unremarkable face with fine features.

Rosy cheeks. The hair brass colored, thinning, worn thicker at the sides, now matted by the mask.

Andrew Coburg.

The storefront lawyer's smile was wide, wet – impish.

A surprise-party smile.

He twirled the mask and tossed it over his shoulder. '*Voilà.*'

I struggled to make sense of it – Coburg directing me to Gritz. Misdirecting me. Careful researcher . . . Mrs. Lyndon . . .

'I really *like* this place,' he said. 'Despite all the queer art. Nice,

336

crisp, cruel, L.A. ambience. Much better than that little yuppie log cabin of yours. And cliffside – talk about perfect. Not to mention your little friend's *truck* – unbelievable. Couldn't have set it up better myself.'

He winked. 'Makes you almost believe in God, doesn't it? Fate, karma, predestination, collective unconscious – choose your dogma . . . do you have any idea what I'm talking about?'

'Delmar Parker,' I said.

The dead boy's name blotted out his smile.

'I'm talking about consonance,' he said. 'Making it *right*.'

'But Delmar has something to do with it, doesn't he? Something beyond Bad Love.'

He uncrossed his legs. The gun made a small arc. 'What do you know about Bad Love, you pretentious yuppie prick?'

The gun arm was board-rigid. Then it began vibrating. He looked at it for just a second. Laughed, as if trying to erase his outburst.

Scratch, bump. The dog was throwing himself hard against the glass.

Coburg snickered. 'Little *pit* puppy. Maybe after it's over I'll take him home with me.'

Smiling but sweating. The rosy cheeks deep with color.

Trying to keep my face neutral, I strained to hear sounds from the bedrooms. Nothing.

'So you think you know about Bad Love,' said Coburg.

'Meredith told me about it,' I said.

His brow tightened and mottled.

The dog kept scraping. The old-man whining sound filtered through the glass. Coburg gave a disgusted look.

'You don't know anything,' he said.

'So tell me.'

'Shut your mouth.' The gun arm shot forward again.

I didn't move.

He said, 'You don't know a *tenth* of it. Don't flatter yourself with empathy, *fuck* your empathy.'

The dog bumped some more. Coburg's eyes flattened.

'Maybe I'll just shoot it . . . skin it and gut it . . . how good can a shrink's dog be, anyway – how many shrinks does it take to change a lightbulb? None. They're all dead.'

He laughed a bit more. Wiped sweat from his nose. I concentrated

337

on the gun arm. It remained firmly in place, as if cut off from the rest of him.

'Do you know what *my* sin was?' he said. 'The great transgression that bought me a ticket to hell?'

Ticket to hell. Meredith had called the school the same thing.

I shook my head. My armpits were aching, my fingers turning numb.

He said, 'Enuresis. When I was a kid I used to piss my bed.' He laughed. 'They treated me as if I *liked* it,' he said. 'Mumsy and Evil Step Daddy. As if I liked clammy sheets and that litter-box smell. They were *convinced* I was doing it on purpose so they beat me. So I got more nervous and pissed gallons. So then what did they do?'

Looking at me, waiting.

'They beat you some more.'

'Bingo. *And* washed my dick with lye soap and all sorts of other wonderful stuff.'

Still smiling but his cheeks were scarlet. His hair was plastered to his forehead, his shoulders hunched under the designer sweatshirt.

My first thought, seeing those rosy cheeks had been, *a beautiful baby.*

'So I started to do other things,' he said. 'Really naughty things. Could anyone blame me? Being tortured for something that I had no control over?'

I shook my head again. For a split second I felt my agreement meant something to him. Then a distracted look came into his eyes. The gun arm pushed forward and the black-metal barrel edged closer to my heart.

'What's the current lowdown on enuresis, anyway?' he said. 'Do you pricks still tell parents it's a mental disease?'

'It's genetic,' I said. 'Related to sleep patterns. Generally it goes away by itself.'

'You don't treat it anymore?'

'Sometimes behavior therapy.'

'*You* ever treat kids for it?'

'When they want to be treated.'

'Sure,' he grinned. 'You're a real humanitarian.' The grin died. 'So what were you doing making speeches – paying homage to *Hitler*?'

'I –'

'Shut up.' The gun jabbed my chest. 'That was rhetorical, don't speak unless you're spoken to . . . sleep patterns, huh? You quacks weren't saying that back when I was getting beaten with a strap. You had all sorts of other voodoo theories back then – one of your fellow quacks told Mumsy and Evil that I was screwed up sexually. Another said I was seriously depressed and needed to be hospitalized. And one genius told them I was doing it because I was angry about their marriage. Which was true. But I wasn't *pissing* because of it. *That* one they bought. Evil really got into expressing *his* anger. Big financial man. Spiffy dresser – he had a whole collection of fancy belts. Lizard, alligator, calfskin, all with nice sharp buckles. One day I went to school with an especially nice collection of *welts* on my arm. A teacher started asking questions and the next thing I knew I was on a plane with dear old Mumsy to sunny California. Go West, little bad boy.'

He let his free hand drop to his lap. His eyes looked tired and his shoulders rounded.

The dog was still throwing himself against the glass.

Coburg stared straight at me.

I said, 'How old were you when they put you in the school?'

The gun jabbed again, forcing me backward against the couch. All at once his face was up against mine, breathing licorice. I could see dried mucus in his nostrils. He spat. His saliva was cold and thick as it oozed down the side of my face.

'I'm not *there*, yet,' he said, between barely moving lips. 'Why don't you shut up and let me *tell* it?'

Breathing hard and fast. I made myself look into his eyes, feeling the gun without seeing it. My pulse thundered in my ears. The spit continued its downward trail. Reaching my chin. Dripping onto my shirt.

He looked repulsed, struck out, slapping me and wiping me simultaneously. Wiped his hand on the seat cushion.

'They didn't *put* me there, right away. They put me in another dungeon first. Right across the street – can you believe that, two hellholes on the same street – what was it, zoned H1 for hell? A real shithole run by a nincompoop alkie, but expensive as hell, so, of course Mumsy thought it was good, the woman was always such an *arriviste*.'

I tried to look like a fascinated student . . . still no sounds from the bedroom.

Coburg said, 'A nincompoop. Not even a challenge. A book of matches and some notebook paper.' Smile.

Firesetters and truants . . . Bancroft hadn't said the fire was at his school.

'Poor Mumsy was *stymied*, out on the next plane, the poor thing. This wonderful look of *hopelessness* on her face – and she being such an educated woman. Crying as we waited for our taxi, I thought I'd finally scored a point. Then he walked over. From across the street. This *goatish* thing in a black suit and cheap shoes. Taking Mummy's hand, telling her he'd heard what had happened, tsk-tsking and letting her cry some more about her bad little boy. Then telling her *his* school could handle those kinds of things. Guaranteed. All the while tussling my hair – twelve years old and he was tussling my fucking hair. His hand stank of cabbage and bay rum.'

The gun hand wavered a bit . . . not enough.

Scratch, bump.

'Mummy was *thrilled* – she knew him from his magazine articles. A famous man willing to tame her wild child.' His free hand fluttered. 'The cab came and she sent it off empty.'

The gun withdrew far enough for me to see its black snout, dark against his white knuckles.

Two hellholes *on* the same street. De Bosch exploiting Bancroft's failures. An alumnus of both schools, coming back years later, a tramp . . . the clean-cut face in front of me bore no street-scars. But sometimes the wounds that healed weren't the important ones.

'Across the street I went. Mummy signed some papers and left me alone with Hitler. He smiled at me and said, "Andrew, little Andrew. We have the same name, let's be friends." Me saying "Fuck you, old goat." He smiled again and patted my head. Took me down a long dark hall, shoved me into a cell and locked it. I cried all night. When they let me out for lunch, I snuck into the kitchen and found matches.'

A wistful look came into his eyes.

'How thorough was I tonight? Did I leave anything standing at Casa del Shrinko?'

I remained silent.

The gun poked me. '*Did* I?'

'Not much.'

'Good. It's a shoddy world, thoroughness is so rare a quality. You personify shoddiness. You were as easy to get to as a sardine in a can.

All of you were – tell me, why are psychotherapists such a passive, *helpless* bunch? Why are you all such absolute *wimps* – *talking* about life rather than *doing* anything?'

I didn't answer.

He said, 'You really are, you know, such an *unimpressive* group. Stripped of your jargon, you're noth— if that dog of yours doesn't shut up, I'm going to kill him – better yet, I'll make you kill him. Make you *eat* him – we can grill him on that barbecue you've got out back. A nice little hot-dog – that would be justice, wouldn't it – making you confront your own cruelty? Give you a taste of *empathy*?'

'Why don't we just let him go,' I said. 'He's not mine, just a stray I took in.'

'How kind of you.' Jab. My breastbone felt inflamed.

I said, 'Why don't we let my friend go, too. She hasn't seen your faces.'

He smiled and settled back a bit.

'Shoddiness,' he said. 'That's the big problem. Phony science, false premises, false promises. You pretend to help people but you just mind-fuck them.'

He leaned forward. 'How do you manage to live with yourself, knowing you're a fake?'

Jab. 'Answer me.'

'I've helped people.'

'How? With voodoo? With Bad Love?'

Trying to keep the whine out of *my* voice, I said, 'I had nothing to do with de Bosch except for that symposium.'

'*Except* for? *Except* for! That's like Eichmann saying he had nothing to do with Hitler *except* for getting those trains to the camps. That symposium was a public *love,* you hypocrite! You stood up there and canonized him! He tortured children and you *canonized* him!'

'I didn't know.'

'Yeah, you and all the other good Germans.'

He spat at me again. The knuckles of his gun hand were tiny cauliflowers. Sweat popped at his hairline.

'That's *it*?' he said. 'That's your excuse – I didn't *know*? *Pathetic*. Just like all the others. For a bunch of supposedly educated people, you can't even *plead* for yourselves effectively. No class. Delmar had more class in his little finger than the lot of you put together, and he was *retarded*. Not that it stopped them from Bad Loving him day in and day out.'

He shook his head and flung sweat. I saw his index finger move up and down the trigger. The painful, hungry look on his face made my bowels churn. But then it was gone and he was smiling again.

'Retarded,' he said, as if enjoying the word. 'Fourteen, but he was more like a seven-year-old. I was twelve but I ended up being his big brother. He was the only one in the place who'd talk to me – beware the dangerous pyromaniac – Hitler warned them all against having anything to do with me I was completely shunned except by Delmar. He couldn't think clearly, but he had a heart of gold. Hitler took him in for the publicity – poor little Negro retardo helped by The Great White Doctor. When visitors came, he always had his hand on Delmar's wooly little head. But Delmar was no great success. Delmar couldn't remember rules, or learn how to read and write. So when there were no visitors around, he kept Bad Loving him, over and over. And when that didn't work, they sent in The She-Beast.'

'Myra Evans?'

'No, not her, you idiot. She was the *Bitch*, I'm talking about the *Beast* – Dr. *Daughter*. Kill Me *Kate* – thank you, I already have.'

High-pitched laughter. The gun moved back some more and I stared into its single, black eye.

The dog began scratching again, but Coburg didn't notice.

'When the *Beast* finished with Delmar, he was drooling and crapping his pants and banging his head against the wall.'

'What did she do to him?'

'What did she *do*? She did a number on his *head*. And other parts of his body.'

'She molested him?'

His free hand touched his cheek and he arched his eyebrows.

'Such *shock*, the poor man is *shocked*! Yeah, she *molested* him, you idiot. In ways that *hurt*. He'd come back from sessions with her, crying and *holding* himself. Crawl into bed, weeping. I had the room next door. I'd pick the lock and sneak him something to drink. When I asked him what the matter was, he wouldn't tell me. Not for weeks. Then he finally did. I didn't know much about sex, period, let alone ugly things. He pulled down his pants and showed me the marks. Dried blood all over his shorts. *That* was my introduction to the birds and the bees. It *altered* me, it altered me.'

His lips vibrated and he swallowed hard a couple of times. The gun arm like steel.

The glass door vibrated.

'So he took the truck,' I said. 'To escape what she was doing to him.'

'*We* took it. I knew how to drive because Evil had a farm in Connecti— a summer place, lots of trucks and tractors. One of the farmhands taught me. Planning the break was hard because Delmar had trouble remembering details. We had a bunch of false starts. Finally we made it out, late at night, everyone asleep. Delmar was scared. I had to drag him.'

The gun barrel made tiny arcs.

'I had no idea which way to go so I just drove. The roads kept getting curvier.

'Delmar was scared out of his mind, crying for his mama. I'm telling him everything's okay – but some idiot left sawhorses in the middle of the road – a ditch, no warning lights. We skidded . . . off the road . . . I yelled for Delmar to jump free, tried to *pull* him out but he was too heavy – then my door flipped open and I was thrown out. Delmar . . .'

He licked his lips and breathed with forced deliberation. His finger tapped the trigger.

'Boom. Kaboom,' he said. 'Life is so tenous, isn't it?'

He looked winded, dripping perspiration. The big smile on his face was forced.

'He . . . it took me two hours to walk back to hell. My clothes were torn and I'd twisted my ankle. It was a miracle – I was alive. Meant for something. I managed to crawl into bed . . . my teeth were chattering so loud I was sure everyone would wake up. It took a while till the commotion began. Talking, footsteps, lights going on. Then Hitler came stomping into my room, tore the covers off me and stared at me – foaming at the mouth. I looked right back at him. This crazy look came into his eyes and he lifted his hands – like he was ready to claw me. I stared right back at him and pulled my pud. And he just let his arms drop. Walked out. Never spoke to me again. I was locked in my room for three days. On the fourth day, Mummy came and picked me up. Go east young victor.'

'So you won,' I said.

'Oh, yeah,' he said. 'I was the conquering hero.' Jab. 'My victory bought me more dungeons. More sadists, pills and needles. That's what your places are about whether you call them hospitals or jails or *schools*. Killing the *spirit*.'

I remembered the flash of anger he'd shown in his office, when we'd talked about Dorsey Hewitt.

He should have been taken care of.

Institutionalized?

Taken care of. Not jailed – oh, hell, even jail wouldn't have been bad if that would have meant treatment. But it never does.

'But you got past that,' I said. 'You made it through law school, you're helping other people.'

He laughed and the gun retreated an inch or two.

'Don't patronize me, you fuck. Yeah, let's hear it for higher education. You know where I learned my torts and jurisprudence? The library at Rahway State Prison. Filing *appeals* for myself and the other wretches. *That's* where I learned the law was written by the oppressors to benefit the oppressors. But I like fire, you could learn to use it. Make it *work* for you.'

He laughed again and wiped his forehead. 'The only bars I ever passed were the ones on my *cell*. For five years, I've been going up against yuppie careerist assholes from Harvard and Stanford and kicking their asses in court. I've had judges compliment my work.'

'Five years,' I said. 'Right after Myra.'

'Right *before*.' He grinned. 'The Bitch was a gift to myself. I'd just gotten the gig at the center. Gave myself two gifts. The Bitch and a new guitar – black Les Paul Special. You remember my guitar, don't you? All that rapport-building crap you slung at me in my office?'

The guitar-pick tie-pin . . .

What do you do mostly, electric or acoustic?

Lately I've been getting into electric.

Special effects, too. Phase shifters . . .

He grinned and raised his free hand as if for a high-five. 'Hey, bro, let's jam and cut a record.'

'Is that the offer you gave Lyle Gritz?'

The grin shrank.

'A human decoy,' I said, 'to throw me off-track?'

He jabbed me hard with the gun and slapped my face with his free hand. 'Shut up and stop *controlling* or I'll do you right here and make your little friend in there clean it up. Keep those fucking hands up – up!'

I felt more spit hit my cheek again and roll over my lips.

Silence from the bedroom. The dog's struggles had become background noise.

'Say you're sorry,' he said, 'for trying to control.'

'I'm sorry.'

He reached over and patted my cheek. Almost tenderly.

'The Bitch,' he said wistfully. 'She was *given* to me. Served on a plate with parsley and new potatoes.'

The gun wavered, then straightened. He crossed his legs. The soles of his shoes were unmarked except for a few bits of gravel stuck in the treads.

'Karma,' he said. 'I was living out in the Valley, nice little bachelor pad in Van Nuys. Driving home on a Sunday. These flags out at the curb. Open house for sale. When I was a kid, I liked other people's houses – anything better than my own. I got good at getting *into* other people's houses. This one looked like it might have a few souvenirs, so I stopped to check it out. I ring the bell. The real estate agent comes to the door and right away she's giving me her pitch. Da *da*, da *da*, da *da*, da *da*.

'But I'm not hearing a word she's saying. I'm looking at her face and it's *the Bitch*. Some wrinkles, her boobs are sagging, but there's no doubt about it. She's shaking my hand, talking about pride of ownership, owner will carry. And it hits me: This is no accident. This is *karma*. All these years I'd been thinking about justice. All those nights I lay in bed thinking about getting Hitler, but the fuck beat me to it.'

He grimaced, as if stung. 'I thought I'd put *that* behind me, then I looked into the Bitch's eyes and realized I hadn't. And she made it so easy – playing *her* part. Turning her back and walking right in front of me. Open invitation.'

He coughed. Cleared his throat. The gun bumped against my sternum.

'Everything was perfect – no one around. I locked all the doors without her noticing, she's too busy giving me her spiel. When we reached an inner bathroom with no windows, I hit her. And did her. She fell apart as if she was made of nothing. At first it was mess. Then it got easier. Like a good riff, the rhythm.'

He talked on for a long while, slipping into a drone, like a surgeon dictating operating room notes. Giving me details I didn't want to hear. I tuned out, listening to the dog thump and bark, listening for sounds from the bedroom that never came.

Silence. Sighing. He said, 'I found my life's work.'

'Rodney Shipler,' I said. 'He didn't work at the school, did he? Was he a relative of Delmar's?'

'Father. In name only.'

'What was his crime?'

'Complicity. Delmar's mom was dead, Shipler was the only member of Delmar's family I could find. Delmar told me his dad was named Rodney and he worked for the L.A. schools – I thought he was a teacher. Finally I located him over in South Central. A janitor. This tired old asshole, big and fat, living by himself, drinking whiskey out of a Dixie cup. I told him I was a lawyer and I knew what really happened to his son. Said we could sue, class action – even after the Bitch, I was still trying to work within the system. He sat there drinking and listening, then asked me could I guarantee him a lot of money in his pocket. I told him no, money wasn't the issue. The publicity would expose Hitler for what he'd really been. Delmar would be a hero.'

Jab. 'Shipler poured himself another cup and told me he didn't give a shit about that. Said Delmar's mom had been some whore he'd met in Manila who wasn't worth the time of day. Said Delmar had been a fool and a troublemaker from day one. I tried to reason with him – show him the importance of exposing Hitler. He told me to get the hell out. Tried to push me out.'

Coburg's eyes flared. The gun seemed fused to his hand.

'Another good German. He tried to push me out – real bully, but I taught him about justice. After that I knew the only way was swift punishment, the system wasn't set up to do the job.'

I said, 'One form of punishment for the underlings, another for the high command.'

'Exactly. Fair is fair.' He smiled. 'Finally *someone* catches on. Mrs. Lyndon was *right*, you *are* a clever piece of work. I told her I was a reporter, doing a story on you. She was so happy to help. . . her little A student.' The gun tickled my ribs. 'You deserve something for paying attention – maybe I'll knock you unconscious before I roll you over the cliff outside. Such a perfect setup . . . ' Head cock toward the front door. 'Would you like that?'

Before I could answer: 'Just *kidding*! Your eyes will be taped *open*, you'll experience every *second* of hell, just like I did.'

He laughed. Droned some more, describing how he'd beaten Rodney Shipler to death, blow by blow.

When he was through, I said, 'Katarina was high command, also. Why'd you wait so long for her?'

Trying to buy time with questions – but to what end? A longer ordeal for Robin – why was it so quiet in there?

My eyes shifted downward. The damn gun arm wasn't moving.

He said, 'Why do you think, clever boy? Saving the best for last – and you messed me up royal. *You* were supposed to go before *her* but then you started snooping around, sending your queer police buddy snooping, so I had to do her out of sequence . . . I'm pissed at you for that. Maybe I'll put your girlfriend on the *barbecue*. Make you watch that with your eyelids taped open.'

Smiling. Sighing. 'Still, She-Beast got done, and what's done is done . . . do you know how she handled her fate? Total *passivity*. Just like the *rest* of you.' Jab. 'What kind of person would want to spend his life just sitting there listening – not *doing* anything?'

He laughed.

'She got down on her knees and begged. Her She-Beast throat got all clogged up like a toilet full of shit . . . she was eating breakfast, I just strolled in, put this gun to her head, said "Bad Love, She Beast." And she just fell apart.'

Shaking his head, as if still not believing. Slight shift of the gun.

'Not an ounce of fight. No fun. I had to stand her up and order her to make a run for it. Kicked her *butt* to get her to move. Even with that, all she could do was stumble into the garage and get down on her knees again. *Then* she snapped out of her trance. *Then*, she started begging. Crying, pointing to her stomach, telling me she's pregnant, please have pity on my baby. Like *she* had pity . . . then she pulled a card out of her pocket, trying to prove it to me. A sperm bank. Which makes sense, who would have *done* her?' Laughter. 'Like that was a reason. Saving her beastly fetus. Au contraire, that was the best reason of *all* to *do* her. Put an end to Hitler's seed.'

Another shake of the head. 'Unbelievable. She bloodies Delmar's shorts and thinks that's a good reason . . . She started to tell me she was on my side, she'd helped me, killing *him*.'

'She killed her father?'

'She claimed she O.D'd him on pills. Like she'd gotten some insight. But I knew she did it as a favor to *him*. Putting him out of his misery. Making sure *I'd* never get to him. Giving me *another* reason to do her hard and long, she's blabbing and just digging herself deeper.' Smile. 'I made sure to do the baby first.

Pulled it out, still attached to her, showed it to her and put it back in her.'

The dog's struggles seemed to be weakening; I thought I heard him whimper.

Coburg said, 'You messed up my order, but that's okay, I'll get creative. You and your little friend will be an adequate final act.'

'What about the others?' I said, fighting to keep my voice even. Fighting to focus my own rage. 'Why'd you choose the order you did?'

'I keep telling you, I didn't choose *anything*. The pattern constructed itself. I put your names into a hat and drew them out, eeny meeny – all the meanies.'

'The names of the people who spoke at the symposium.'

Nod. 'All you good Germans. I'd been thinking about all of you for years – even before doing the Bitch.'

'You were there,' I said. 'Listening to us.'

'Sitting in a back row, taking it all in.'

'You were a kid. How'd you come to be there?'

'More karma. I was nineteen, living in Hollywood and crashing at a halfway-house on Serrano.'

Just a few blocks from Western Peds.

' . . . taking a walk on Sunset and I saw this program board out in front. Psychiatric symposium, tomorrow morning.'

Tensing up, he waved the gun, arm dipping for just one second, then snapping back into place, the barrel touching my shirt.

'*His* name . . . I went in and picked up a brochure at the information desk. Shaved and showered and put on my best clothes and just walked in. And watched all you hypocritical bastards get up there and say what a *pioneer* he'd been. Child *advocate*. Gifted *teacher*. The She-Beast and her home movies. Everyone smiling and applauding – I could barely sit there without screaming – I should have screamed. Should have gotten up and told all of you what you really were. But I was young, no confidence. So instead, I went out that night and hurt *myself*. Which bought me another dungeon. *Lots* of time to think and get my focus. I'd cut out your pictures. Pasted them on a piece of paper. Kept the paper in a box. Along with other important things. I've lived with you assholes longer than most people stay married.'

'Why was Dr. Harrison spared?

He stared at me, as if I'd said something stupid. 'Because he *listened*. Right after the Hitler canonization, I called him and told him it had bothered me. And he *listened*. I could tell he was taking me seriously. He made an appointment to speak to me. I was going to show up, but something came up – another dungeon.'

'Why'd you tell him your name was Merino? Why'd you tell *me* you were Mr. Silk?'

Wrinkled forehead. 'You spoke to Harrison? Maybe I'll visit him after all.'

A sick feeling flooded me. 'He doesn't know anyth— '

'Don't fret, fool, I'm fair, always have been. I gave all of you the same chance I gave Harrison. But the rest of you flunked.'

'You never called me,' I said.

Smile. 'I tried. November thirtieth, nineteen seventy-nine. Two p.m. I have a written record of it. Your snotty secretary insisted you only treated children and couldn't see me.'

'She wasn't supposed to screen – I never knew.'

'That's an *excuse*? When the troops fuck up, the general's culpable. And it was a chance you didn't even deserve – a lot more than I got, or Delmar, or any of the other *loved* ones. You muffed it, bro.'

'But Rosenblatt,' I said. 'He *did* see you.'

'He was the *biggest* hypocrite. Pretending to understand – the soft voice, the phony *empathy*. Then he revealed his true colors. Quizzing me, trying to get into *my* head.' Coburg put on an unctuous look: ' "I'm hearing a lot of pain . . . one thing you might consider is talking about this more." ' Fury compressed the light brown eyes. 'The phony bastard wanted to give me *psychoanalysis* to deal with my *conflicts*. Hundred buck an hour *couchwork* as a cure for political oppression because he couldn't accept the fact that he'd worshipped Hitler. He sat there and *pretended* to hear, but he didn't believe me. Just wanted to mess with my head – the worst one of all, bye bye birdy.'

He made a shoving motion with his free hand and smiled.

I said, 'How'd you get him to see you outside his office?'

'I told him I was bedridden. Crippled by something Hitler had done. *That* piqued his interest, he came right over that evening, with his kind looks and his beard and his bad, tweed suit – it was hot but he needed his little shrink costume. The whole time he was there, I stayed in bed. The second time also. I had him bring me a drink ... serving *me*. It was a really muggy day, the window was *wide* open for air. Tissue box on the ledge – karma. I pretended to sneeze and asked him to get me a tissue.' Shove. 'Fly away, hypocrite bird.'

Other people's houses. A financial man ... A farm in Connecticut. Did that mean an apartment in New York city? *And her such an educated woman.*

She a lawyer, he a banker.

I said, 'The apartment belonged to your mother and stepfather.'

He shook his head joyfully. 'Clever little Alex. Mrs. Lyndon would be so proud ... Mummy and Evil were in Europe so I decided to crash at the old homestead. Rosenblatt's office two blocks away ... karma. Eight floors up, have a nice flight.

'Mr. and Mrs. Malcolm A. Rulerad. Cold people, Shirley Rosenblatt had said. Unwilling to let a private investigator search their place. Guarding more than privacy? How much had they known?

'You left burglar tools behind,' I said. 'Did you need them to get in or were you just setting it up as another Eastside burglary?'

He tried to mask his surprise with a slow, languid smile. 'My, my, we *have* been busy. No, I had a key. One keeps looking for Home Sweet Home. The Big Brady Bunch in the sky.'

'Stoumen and Lerner,' I said. 'Did they meet with you?'

'No,' he said, suddenly angry again. 'Stoumen's excuse was that he was retired. Another flunkie shutting me out, did I want to speak to the doctor on call – you people really don't know how to delegate authority properly. And Lerner made an appointment but didn't show up, the rude bastard.'

The unreliability Harrison had spoken of: *it had affected his work – missed appointments.*

'So you tracked them down at conferences – how'd you get hold of the membership lists?'

'Some of us are thorough – Mrs. Lyndon would have liked me, too – what a kindly old bag, all that midwestern salt-of-the-earth friendliness. Research is *such* fun, maybe I'll visit *her* in person some day.'

'Did Meredith help you get the lists?' I said. 'Was she doing publicity for the conventions?'

Pursed lips. Tense brow. The hand wavered. 'Meredith ... ah,

350

yes, dear *Meredith*. She's been a great help – now, stop asking stupid questions and get down on your knees – keep those hands up – keep them up!'

Moving as slowly as I could, I got off the couch and kneeled, trying to keep a fix on the gun.

Silence, then another impact that shook the glass.

'The dog's definitely chops and steaks,' he said.

The gun touched the crown of my head. He ruffled my hair with the barrel and I knew he was remembering.

The weapon pressed down on me, harder, as if boring into my skull. All I could see were his shoes, the bottoms of his jeans. A grout seam between two marble tiles.

'Say you're sorry,' he said.

'Sorry.'

'Louder.'

'Sorry.'

'Personalize it – "I'm sorry, Andrew."'

'I'm sorry, Andrew.'

'More sincerity.'

'I'm sorry, Andrew.'

He made me repeat it six times, then he sighed. 'I guess that's as good as it's going to get. How are you feeling, right now?'

'I've been better.'

Chuckle. 'I'll bet you have – stand up slowly – *slowly*. Slo-o-o-wly. Keep those hands up – hands on head – Simon says.'

He stepped back, the gun trained on my head. Behind me was the couch. Chairs all around. An upholstered prison, nowhere to go . . . a run for it would be suicide, leaving Robin to deal with his frustration . . .

The dog throwing himself, harder . . .

I was upright now. He stepped closer. We came face to face. Licorice and rage, lowering the gun and pushing it against my navel. Then up at my throat. Then down again.

Playing.

Choreography.

'I see it,' he said. 'Behind your eyes – the fear – you *know* where you're going, don't you?'

I said nothing.

'*Don't you?*'

'Where am I going?'

'Straight to hell. One-way ticket.'

The gun nudged my groin. Moved up to my throat again. Pressed against my heart. Back down to my crotch.

Taking on a rhythm – the musician in him . . . moving his hips.

I was altered.

Groin. Heart. Groin.

He poked my crotch and laughed. When he raised the gun again, I exploded. Chopping the gun wrist with my right hand as I stabbed at his eye with the stiffened fingertips of my left.

The gun fired as he lost balance.

He landed on his side, the gun still laced between his fingers. I stomped on his wrist. His free hand was clamped over his face. When he pulled it free and grabbed at my leg, his eye was shut, bleeding.

I stomped again and again. He roared with pain. The gun hand was limp but the weapon remained entangled. He struggled to lift it and aim. I dropped my knee full-force on his arm, got hold of the hand, tugging, twisting, finally freeing the automatic.

My turn to aim. My hands were numb. I had trouble bending my fingers around the trigger. He slid across the carpet on his back, kicking out randomly, holding his eye. Blood ran over his hand. His escape was blocked by a sofa. Flailing and kicking – he looked at me.

No – behind me.

He screamed, 'Do it!' as I ducked and wheeled, facing the hallway.

The smaller gun in my face. A woman's hand behind it. Red nails. Coburg shouting, 'Do it! Do it! Do it!' Starting to get up.

I dropped to the floor just as the little gun went off.

More gunshots. Hollow pops, softer than the black pistol's thunder.

Coburg on me. We rolled. I struck out with the black gun and caught the side of his head. He fell back, soundlessly, landed on his back. Not moving.

Where was the silver gun? Arcing toward me again from across the room. Two red-nailed hands starting to squeeze.

I dove behind the couch.

Pop! The fabric puckered and gobbets of stuffing flew inches from my face.

I pressed myself flush to the marble.

352

Pop! Pop, pop!

Heavy breathing – gasping – but whose I couldn't tell.

Pop!

A dull noise from my back then the windchime song of shattered glass. Scampering feet.

A small, black blur raced past me toward Meredith.

Hooking my arm around the couch, I fired the big black automatic blindly, trying to aim well above dog-level. The recoil drove me backward. Something crashed.

Barks and growls and female screams.

I scuttled to the opposite side of the couch, squeezed the trigger, waited for return fire.

More screams. Footsteps. Human. Getting distant.

I hazarded a look around the couch, saw her heading for the front door, silver gun dangling like a purse. Coburg still down.

Where was the dog?

Meredith was almost at the door now. The bolt was thrown – she was having trouble with it.

I rushed her, pointing the black gun, feeling the trigger's heavy action start to give.

Swift justice.

Screaming 'Stop!' I fired into a wall.

She obeyed. Held onto the silver gun.

'Drop it, drop it!'

The gun fell to the floor and skidded away.

She said, 'I'm sorry, I didn't want to – he made me.'

'Turn around.'

She did. I yanked off her mask.

Her face was trembling but she tossed her hair in a gesture more suited for a teenager.

Blond hair.

My hand was still compressing the trigger. I forced myself not to move.

Jean Jeffers said, 'He made me,' and glanced at Coburg. He remained open-mouthed and inert and her eyes died. She tried tears.

'You rescued me,' she said. 'Thanks.'

'What'd you do with Robin?'

'She's fine – I promise. She's in there – go see.'

'Step out in front of me.'

353

'Sure, but this is silly. Alex. He made me – he's crazy – we're on the same side, Alex.'

Another look at Coburg.

His chest wasn't moving.

Keeping the black gun on Jeffers, I stooped and pocketed the silver one. Maintaining a clear view of her, I managed to pull a large, upholstered chair over the bottom half of Coburg's body. Not worth much, but it would have to do for the moment.

I walked Jeffers back to the bedroom. The door was closed. The dog stood on his hind legs, scratching at it, gouging the paint. An acetone stink came from the other side.

'Open it,' I said.

She did.

Robin was spread-eagled on the bed, hands and feet tied to the posts with nylon fishing line, duct tape over her mouth, a bandana over her eyes. On the nightstand were the spool of line, scissors, nail polish, a box of tissues and manicure set.

Nail polish remover – the acetone.

A used emery board. Jeffers had passed the time by doing her nails.

She said, 'Let me free her, right now.'

I pocketed the scissors and let her, using her hands. She worked clumsily, the dog up on the bed, growling at her, circling Robin, licking Robin's face. Specks of blood dappled his fur. Diamond glints of broken glass . . . Robin sat up and rubbed her wrists and looked at me, stunned.

I motioned her off the bed and gave her the silver gun. Shoved Jeffers down on it, belly down, hands behind her back.

'Did she hurt you?' I said.

Jeffers said, 'Of course I didn't.'

Robin shook her head.

Jeffers' red nails were so fresh they still looked wet.

She said, 'Can we please – '

Robin tied her up quickly. Then we returned to the living room. Coburg's head where I'd hit him was huge, soft, eggplant-purple. He was starting to move a bit but hadn't regained consciousness.

Robin trussed him expertly, those good, strong hands.

The dog was at my feet, panting. I got down and inspected him. He licked my hands. Licked the gun.

Superficial cuts, no sign he was suffering. Robin picked the glass out of his fur and lifted him, kissing him, cradling him like a baby.

I picked up the phone.

33

Three days later, I waited for Milo at a place named Angela's, across the street from the West L.A. stationhouse. The front was a coffee shop. In the back was a cocktail lounge where detectives, lawyers, bailbondsmen and felons drank and worked on their lung tumors.

I took a booth at the rear of the lounge, drinking coffee and trying to concentrate on the morning paper. Nothing yet on the Bad Love murders, orders of the brass it got sorted out. Coburg was in the hospital and Milo had been virtually sequestered with Jean Jeffers at County Jail.

When he showed up, fifteen minutes late, a woman was with him, thirties, black. The two of them stood in the doorway of the lounge, outlined by hazy, gray light.

Adeline Potthurst, the social worker I'd seen on film, Dorsey Hewitt's knife up against her throat.

She looked older and heavier. A big white purse was clutched in front of her, like a fig leaf.

Milo said something to her. She glanced over at me and replied. A bit more conversation, then they shook hands and she left.

He came over and slid into the booth. 'Remember her? She's talking to me.'

'She have anything interesting to say?'

He smiled, lit up a cigar and added to the pollution. 'Oh, yeah.'

Before he could elaborate, a waitress arrived and took his Diet Coke order.

When she left, he said, 'Lots happening. I've got New York records placing Coburg in Manhattan during all the Eastside break-ins

356

up till the day after Rosenblatt's death: bust for shoplifting, he was arrested in Times Square two days before the first burglary, went to court the day he shoved Rosenblatt out the window, but his attorney got a continuance. Records listed his address as some dive near Times Square.'

'So he celebrated with murder.'

He nodded, grimly. 'Jivin' Jean finally opened up, her attorney convinced her to sell out Coburg for a reduced plea to accessory. Names, dates, places, she's puttin' on a good show.'

'What's her connection to de Bosch?'

'She says none,' he said. 'Claims the revenge thing was all Coburg's game, she didn't really know what he was up to. She says she met him at a mental health convention advocacy for the homeless. Struck up a conversation at the bar and found they had lots in common.'

'Social worker encounters public interest lawyer,' I said. 'A couple of idealists, huh?'

'God help us.' He loosened his tie.

'Coburg probably went to lots of conventions. With his phony law degree and his public-interest persona, he would have fit right in. Meanwhile, he's looking for de Bosch disciples. *And* trying to undo his past. Symbolically. All those years he spent in institutions. Now he's in the power role, hobnobbing with therapists. He was like a little kid, thinking magically. Pretending he could make it all go away.'

'We're still trying to unravel his travel schedule, place him and Jeffers together at least once: Acapulco, the week Mitchell Lerner was killed. Jeffers admits going along for the weekend – she presented a paper – but claims to know nothing about Lerner. She also admits using her position to get Coburg shrink mailing lists but says she thought he just wanted to use them in order to advertise the law center.'

'How does she explain trussing up Robin and taking potshots at me?'

He grinned. 'What do you think?'

'The Devil made her do it.'

'You bet. As their relationship developed, Coburg began to domi-nate her psychologically and physically. She'd started to have some suspicions about him, but was too afraid to back away from him.'

'Does physically mean sexually?'

'She says there was some of that, but mostly she claims he used

357

mind-control, threats, and intimidation to get into her head. Kind of a mini-Manson thing: poor, vulnerable woman taken in by psychopathic Svengali. She says the night he announced he was going to get you, she didn't want any part of it. But Coburg threatened to tell her husband the two of them had been screwing for five years and when that didn't work, he flat-out said he'd kill her.'

'How does she explain being so vulnerable?'

'Because she'd been abused as a kid. She says that was what drew her to Coburg – their mutual experiences. At first, their relationship was platonic. Lunch, talking about work, Coburg helping some of her clients out of legal jams, she helping *him* get social services for his. Eventually, it got more personal, but still no sex. Then one day, Coburg took her to his apartment, cooked lunch, had a heart to heart and told her all the shit he'd been through as a kid. She told him she had, too, and they ended up having this big emotional scene – cathartic, she called it. *Then* they went to bed and the whole relationship started taking another turn.'

'Five years,' I said. 'When the murders began . . . who does she say abused her?'

'Daddy. She's free and easy with the ugly details but it'll be impossible to verify – both parents and her only sibling – a brother – are dead.'

'Natural causes?'

'We're looking into it.'

'Convenient,' I said. 'Everyone's a victim. I guess she could be telling the truth about being abused. First time I met her she told me violating a child's trust was the lowest, she could never work with abuse cases. Then again, she could have been toying with me – she and Coburg got off on playing games.'

'Even if it's true, it doesn't change the fact that she's a psychopathic witch. *Couple* of goddamn psychopaths – there's your two pathologies scenario.'

'The bond between them couldn't be that deep. It didn't take long for her to sell him out.'

'Honor among scumbags.' His drink came and he cooled his hands on the glass.

I said, 'So what about Becky? What does Jean say the link was between her and Coburg?'

'She claims to have no idea what his motive was, there.'

Smile. 'And guess what? He didn't have one, other than making Jean happy.'

'Becky was *Jean's* thing?'

'You bet. And that's what I'm gonna get her on. All her cooperation on the other murders isn't going to help her there, because I've got independent info on a motive: Becky and Dick Jeffers were having an affair. For six months.'

'How'd you find that out?'

'From the newly talkative Ms. Adeline Potthurst. Adeline saw Becky and Dick Jeffers together, sneaking off during a Christmas party at the center. Kissing passionately, his hand up her skirt.'

'Not very discreet.'

'Apparently Becky and Dick weren't, he used to come by to pick up Jean and end up talking to Becky, body language all over the place. The affair was semipublic knowledge at the center – I checked it out with some of the other workers and they confirm it.'

'Meaning Jean knew.'

'Jean knew because Dickie told her. I had a chat with him this morning – guy's a basket case – and he admitted everything. Six months of illicit passion. Said he was planning to leave Jean for Becky and he let Jean know it.'

'How'd she react?'

'Calmly. They had a nice chat and she told him she loved him, was committed to him, please give it some thought, let's get some counseling, etcetera.'

'Did they?'

'No. A month later, Becky's dead. And there's no reason for anyone to make a connection – a nut hacking her up. The way I see it, it's just like you said: Jean and Coburg searched for a nut who could be *manipulated* to hack her up and came up with Hewitt – both of them had ties to him.'

'What was Jeffers' tie?'

'She was his therapist before transferring him to Becky – supposedly because of a heavy workload.'

'She told me Becky was the only therapist he had.'

'Adeline says no, Jeffers definitely treated him. And Mary Chin, Jeffers' secretary, confirms it. Twice-a-week sessions, sometimes more, for at least three or four months before Becky took over. We can't find any therapy notes – no doubt Jeffers destroyed them – but that only makes it look worse for her.'

I said, 'She made a point of telling me she didn't do therapy any more – another mindgame . . . why didn't the fact that she was working with Hewitt ever come out after Becky's murder?'

The hand went over his face. 'We didn't ask and no one volunteered. Why would they? Everyone saw it as psycho kills girl. And we killed the psycho. No one suspected a damn thing – none of the staffers at the center or Dick Jeffers. He's pretty freaked out, now. Coming to grips with the monster he's been living with. Says he's willing to testify against her – whether or not he sticks with that remains to be seen.'

'An affair,' I said. 'So goddamned mundane. Jean sleeps with Coburg for five years, but Becky gets the death penalty . . . typical psychopathic thinking, the ego out of control: you hurt me, I kill you.'

'Yeah,' he said, drinking and licking his lips. 'So tell me specifically, how would you get a nut like Hewitt to kill?'

'I'd pick someone with strong paranoid tendencies whose fantasies got violent when he was off his medicine. Then I'd *get* him off his medicine, either by convincing him to stop taking it or by substituting a placebo, and try to get as much control as I could over his psyche as he deteriorated. Maybe use some age-regression techniques – hypnosis or free association, bring him back to his childhood – get him to confront the helplessness of childhood. To *feel* it. The pain, the rage.'

'The screams,' he said.

I nodded. 'That's probably why they taped him. They got him to scream out his pain, played it back for him – you remember how hard it was to listen to. Can you imagine a schizophrenic dealing with that? Meanwhile, they're also teaching him about bad love, evil shrinks – indoctrinating him, telling him he's been a victim. And insinuating Becky into the delusion as a major-league evil shrink – the purveyor of bad love. They continue to increase his paranoia by praising him for it. Convincing him he's some kind of soldier on a mission: get Becky. Then they transfer him to her. But I'll bet Jean continued to see him on the side. Prepping him, directing him. Backed up by Coburg – another authority figure for Hewitt. And the beauty of it is even if Hewitt hadn't been killed at the scene and had talked, who would have believed him? He was crazy.'

'That's about the way I had it,' he said. 'But hearing you organize it that way helps.'

'It's not hard evidence.'

'I know, but the circumstantial case is building up, bit by bit. The D.A.'s going to let Coburg's attorney know how extensively Jeffers is ratting him out, then offer a deal: no death penalty in return for Coburg ratting on Jeffers over Becky. My bet is Coburg takes it. We'll get both of them.'

'Poor Becky.'

'Yeah. Guess how she and Dick got started? Jean had Becky over for dinner, supervisor–student rapport and all that. Eyes across the fried chicken, a couple of knee-nudges. Next day Becky and Dick are at a motel.'

'Mrs. Basille said she thought Becky had a new beau. Becky wouldn't talk about it which led Mrs. Basille to suspect it was someone she wouldn't have approved of – what she called a loser. Becky'd gone with married men before – guys who promised to get divorced but never did. Dick was *exactly* her type – married *and* disabled.'

'What does disabled have to do with it?'

'Becky had a thing for guys with problems. Wounded birds. Jeffers' missing leg meshed nicely with that.'

'He's missing a leg? That's what the limp is?'

'He wears a prosthesis. Becky's dad was diabetic. Lost some of *his* limbs.'

'Jesus.' He smoked. 'So maybe there is something to this psychology stuff, huh?'

I thought about Becky Basille, trapped in a locked room with a madman. 'Everything Jean and Coburg *did* was part of the ritual. Like forging Becky's therapy notes and scripting them to make it seem Becky was having an affair with *Hewitt*. In addition to diverting us, once more, to Gritz, it added insult to injury by humiliating Becky. As if that could undo the humiliation Becky'd caused Jean.'

He stubbed out his cigar. 'Speaking of Gritz, I think I found him. Once I realized Coburg and Jeffers were probably using him as a distraction, I figured the poor sucker's life expectancy wasn't too great and started to call around at morgues. Long Beach has someone who fits his description perfectly. Multiple stab wounds and ligature around the neck – a guitar string.'

'The next Elvis. I'd check Coburg's guitar case.'

'Del Hardy already did. Coburg's got a bunch of guitars. And a phase shifter and other recording stuff. In one of the cases was a set of brand new strings. Missing the low E. The other interesting things that came up were a man's shirt too small to be Coburg's, torn up and used for a rag, still stinking of booze. And an old Corrective School attendance roster with nineteen seventy-three ripped out.'

'Small shirt,' I said. 'Gritz was a little man.'

He nodded. 'And a client of the law center. Coburg had gotten *him* off a theft thing, too, couple of months ago.'

'Any indication he ever knew Hewitt?'

'No.'

'Poor guy,' I said. 'They probably lured him with notions of being a recording star – let him play with the guitars and the gizmos. That's why he talked about getting rich. Then they killed him and used him as a red herring. No family connections, the perfect victim. Where was the body found?'

'Near the harbor. Naked, no I.D., quite a bit the worse for wear. He'd been in one of their coolers with a John Doe toe tag. They figure he's been dead anywhere from four days to a week.'

'Right around the time you called Jeffers and asked her to speak to me. You said she thought she recognized my name. When I got there she pretended it was because of the Casa de los Ninos case. But she knew it from Coburg's hit list – it must have shocked them, their next victim in their face, like that. Your making the connection between the bad love tape and what happened to Becky. Someone else might have backed off, but clearing the list just meant too much to Coburg – he couldn't let go of it. So he and Jean decided to stay on track and use Gritz as extra insurance. Jeffers sends me to Coburg, Coburg just happens to remember Gritz was Hewitt's friend and directs me to Little Calcutta. Then, just in case we still weren't biting, Jeffers produces the therapy notes with all those references to "G." Maybe I should have wondered Jeffers made such a big deal about Becky being a lousy notetaker, then magically these appear. Mrs. Basille said Becky was a real stickler for the rules but I figured she was just out of touch.'

'There was no way to know,' he said. 'These people are from another planet.'

'That lunch with Jeffers,' I said, feeling suddenly chilled. 'She sat across from me – touching my hand, letting loose the tears. Bringing Dick along was another ritual: Becky vanquished, Jean showing off her spoils. After we were finished eating, she insisted on walking me to my car. Stood on the sidewalk, misbuttoned her sweater and had to redo it. Probably a signal to Coburg, waiting somewhere across the street. She stayed with me all the way to the Seville – tagging the car for Coburg. He followed me up to Benedict and learned where I was hiding out.'

He shook his head. 'We hadnta caught them, they'd probably run for office.'

'At lunch, I told Jeffers that I was going to Santa Barbara the next day to talk to Katarina. That got them worried I'd learn something – maybe bring back the school roster. So they were forced to break sequence – Coburg beat me up there and killed Katarina before me. And tossed in the house.'

'Interesting thing about the house,' he said. 'Sally Grayson said the outer rooms were trashed but the office was left intact except for "bad love" written in blood on a wall.

'And it looked to have been de Bosch's office, not Katarina's. His books and pipe and sweater all laid out. Katarina'd made some kind of shrine out of it – everyone's got their little game.'

'Any idea why Coburg called himself Silk and Merino?'

'I asked the asshole. He didn't answer, just smiled that creepy smile. I started to walk out and then he said, "Look it up." So I did. In the dictionary. Coburg is an old English word for imitation silk or wool.'

'Imitation,' I said. 'He doesn't know what part of him's real and what isn't.'

'Yeah. Enough of this, my head's splitting . . . how are you and Robin doing?'

'We've been able to go back to the house.'

'Anything left?'

'Mostly ashes.'

He shook his head. 'I'm sorry, Alex.'

I said, 'We'll survive – we're surviving. And living in the shop's not bad – the smallness is actually kind of comforting.'

'Insurance company jerking you around?'

'As predicted.'

'Let me know if I can do anything.'

'I will.'

'And when you're ready for a contractor, I've got a possible for you – ex-cop, does nice work relatively cheap.'

'Thanks,' I said. 'Thanks for everything – and sorry about the rental house. I'm sure your banker didn't expect bullet holes in his walls. Tell him to send me the bill.'

'Don't worry about it. It's the most exciting thing's ever happened to him.'

I smiled. He looked away.

'Shootout at the Beverly Hills corral,' he said. 'I should have been there.'

'How could you have known?'

'Knowing's my job.'

'You offered to drive us home, I turned you down.'

'I shouldn't have listened to you.'

'Come on, Milo. You did everything you could. To paraphrase a friend of mine: "Don't flog yourself."'

He frowned, tilted his glass, poured ice down his gullet and crunched. 'How's Rove – Spike?'

'A few surface cuts. The vet said bulldogs have high pain thresholds. A throwback to when they were used for baiting.'

'Right through the glass.' He shook his head. 'Little maniac must have taken a running start and gone ballistic. Talk about devotion.'

'You see it from time to time,' I said. Then I ordered him another Coke.

34

I drove back to Venice. The shop was empty and Robin had left a note on her workbench:

> *11:45p.m. Had to run to the lumber yard.*
> *Back at 2. Pls. call Mrs. Braithwaite.*
> *Says she's Spike's owner.*

Pacific Palisades exchange. I phoned it before the disappointment could sink in.

A middle-aged female voice said, 'Hello?'

'Mrs. Braithwaite? Dr. Delaware returning your call.'

'Oh, doctor! Thank you for calling and thank you for caring for our little Barry! Is he all right?'

'Perfect. He's a great dog,' I said.

'Yes, he is. We were so worried, starting to give up hope.'

'Well, he's in the pink.'

'That's wonderful!'

'I guess you'd like to come by to get him. He should be back by two.'

Hesitation. 'Oh, certainly. Two it is.'

I busied myself with the phone. Calling Shirley Rosenblatt and having a half-hour talk with her. Calling Bert Harrison, then the insurance company where I dealt with some truly vile individuals.

I thought about the Wallace girls for a while, then remembered another little girl, the one who'd lost her boxer – Karen Alnord. I

365

had no record of her number. All my papers were gone. Where had she lived – Reseda. On Cohasset.

I got the number from Information. A woman answered and I asked for Karen.

'She's at school.' Brilliant, Delaware. 'Who's this?'

I gave her my name. 'She called me about her boxer. I was just wondering if you found him.'

'Yes, we have,' she said edgily.

'Great. Thanks.'

'For what?'

'Good news.'

Mrs. Braithwaite showed up at one forty-five. She was short, thin, and sixtyish, with an upswept, tightly-waved, tapioca-colored hairdo, sun wrinkles and narrow brown eyes behind pearloid-framed glasses. Her maroon I. Magnin suit would have fetched top dollar at a vintage boutique and her pearls were real. She carried a bag that matched the suit and wore a bejeweled American flag lapel pin.

She looked around the shop, confused.

'Robin's place of business,' I said. 'We're in between houses – planning some construction.'

'Well, good luck on that. I've been through it, and one meets such an unsavory element.'

'Can I offer you something to drink?'

'No, thank you.'

I pulled up a chair for her. She remained standing and opened her handbag. Taking out a check, she tried to give it to me.

Ten dollars.

'No, no,' I said.

'Oh, doctor, I insist.'

'It's not necessary.'

'But the expenses – I know how Barry eats.'

'He's earned his way.' I smiled. 'Charming fellow.'

'Yes, isn't he?' she said, but with a curious lack of passion. 'Are you sure I can't reimburse you?'

'Give it to charity.'

She thought. 'All right, that's a good idea – Planned Parenthood always needs help.'

She sat down. I repeated my drink offer and she said, 'It's really not necessary, but iced tea would be fine if you have it.'

As I fixed the drink, she inspected the shop some more.

When I gave her the glass, she thanked me again and sipped daintily.

'Does your wife fix violins?'

'A few. Mostly guitars and mandolins. She fixes and makes them.'

'My father played the violin – quite well, actually. We went to the Bowl every summer to hear Jascha Heifetz play. Back when you could still enjoy a civilized drive through Hollywood. He taught at USC – Heifetz did, not Father. Though Father was an alumnus. So is my son. He's in marketing.'

I smiled.

'May I ask what kind of doctor you are?'

'Psychologist.'

Sip. 'And where did you find Barry?'

'He showed up at my house.'

'Where's that, doctor?'

'Just off Beverly Glen.'

'South of Sunset, or north?'

'A mile and a half north.'

'How odd . . . well thank heavens for Good Samaritans. It's so nice to have one's faith in human nature restored.'

'How did you find me, Mrs. Braithwaite?'

'From Mae Josephs at Frenchie Rescue – we were in Palm Desert and didn't get her message until today.'

The door opened and Robin came in, carrying a bag and holding the dog by the leash.

'Barry!' said Mrs. Braithwaite. She got off the chair. The dog trotted straight to her and licked her hand.

'Barry, Barry, little Barry. You've had quite an adventure, haven't you!' She petted him.

He licked her some more, then turned around, stared at me and cocked his head.

'You look wonderful, Barry,' said Mrs. Braithwaite. To us: 'He looks *wonderful*, thank you so much.'

'Our pleasure,' said Robin. 'He's a great little guy.'

'Yes, he is – *aren't* you, Barrymore? Such a *sweet* boy, even with your snoring – did he snore?'

'Loud and clear,' said Robin. Smiling, but her eyes had that pre-tears look I knew so well. I took her hand. She squeezed it and began emptying the bag. Ebony bridge blanks.

The dog padded back over to us and propped his forelegs on Robin's thigh. She rubbed him under the chin. He pressed his little head to her leg.

'Mother loved that. The snoring. Barry was actually Mother's – she kept English bulldogs and Frenchies for over fifty years. Did quite a bit of breeding and showing in her day. And obedience training.'

'Did she perimeter train him?' I said. 'To avoid water?'

'Oh, of course. She trained all her dogs. She had lily ponds and a big pool and the poor things sink like stones. Then her back started to go and the English were too heavy for her to carry so she kept only Frenchies. Then she got too weak even for the Frenchies. Barry was her last little boy. She imported him three years ago. Flew him all the way from Holland.'

A linen hankie came out of the handbag. She took off her glasses and dabbed at her eyes.

'Mother passed away three weeks ago. She'd been ill for a while and Barry was her faithful companion – weren't you, sweetie?'

She reached out her hand. The dog settled on all fours but remained next to Robin.

Mrs. Braithwaite dabbed some more. 'He stayed in bed with her, barked for the nurse when she started to – I do believe he was the reason she kept going as long as she did. But of course, in – when she – the last time we had to call the paramedics, such terror and commotion. Barry must have slipped out. I didn't realize it until later . . .'

'Where did your mother live?' I said.

'Little Holmby. Just off Comstock, south of the boulevard.'

Two miles from my house.

She said, 'He managed to cross Sunset – all that traffic.' Dab. 'Poor little *boy*, if anything had *happened* to you!'

'Well,' said Robin, 'thank God he made it.'

'Yes, yes, I can see that – you've made a nice little home for him, haven't you?'

'We tried.'

'Yes, yes, I can see that . . . yes . . . would you like to have him?'

Robin's mouth dropped open. She looked at me.

I said, 'You don't want him?'

'It's not a matter of that, doctor. I *adore* animals, but my husband doesn't. Or, rather, *they* don't like *him*. Allergies. Severe ones. Dogs, cats, horses, hamsters – anything with fur sets him off and he swells up like a balloon. As is, I'm going to have to take a bubble bath the moment I get home, or Monty will be wheezing the moment he sees me.'

She pulled something else out of the purse and gave it to me.

An AKC pedigree sheet for *Van Der Legyh's Lionel Barrymore On Stage*. A family tree that put mine to shame.

Mrs. Braithwaite said, 'Isn't that noble?'

'Very.'

Robin said, 'We'd love to take him.'

'Good. I was hoping you were nice people.'

Smiling, but she took another dubious look around the shop. 'He likes his liver snaps and his sausage sticks. Cheese as well, of course. Though he doesn't seem to have any affection for Edam – isn't that odd, his being Dutch?'

Robin said, 'We'll support him in the lifestyle to which he's become accustomed.'

'Ye-ess . . . ' She glanced furtively around the shop. 'I'm sure he'll love your *new* home – will it be in the same location?'

'Absolutely,' I said, scooping up the dog and rubbing his tummy. 'We've been happy there.'

35

I t came in a plain white envelope.
  Pressed into my hand as I walked out the shop's side door
with Spike.

I looked up to see Ruthanne Wallace's kid sister, Bonnie. Tight
jeans tucked into cowboy boots, white blouse, no bra, nipples
assertive.

She winked at me, tickled my palm with her finger and ran to
the curb. A dark blue Chevy Caprice with chrome wheels and black
windows was idling there, blowing smoke. She jumped in, slammed
the door and the car sped off.

No postmark on the envelope, no lettering. Too thin to have
anything in it but paper.

I slit it open with my fingernail.

A piece of notebook paper, torn evenly in half.

A note on the first:

> Dear doctor.
> I am fine. I am happy. Thank you for try to help us. Jesus loves you.
> Tiffani.

A drawing on the second. Blue skies, golden sun, green grass, red
flowers.

A girl sitting in what looked like an above-ground swimming
pool. Fat droplets of water scattering, the girl's face a perfect circle
bisected by a crescent-shaped smile.

A signature in the lower right corner:

> Chondra W.

A title next to the sun:

HAVING FUN.

'Sounds like a good idea,' I said to Spike.
Snort, snort.